ANNE
of Green Gables

& ANNE
of Avonlea

LUCY MAUD MONTGOMERY

NIMBUS
PUBLISHING
— NIMBUS.CA —

Nimbus Publishing, 2023
First published 1908

Nimbus Publishing Limited
3660 Strawberry Hill St, Halifax, NS B3K 5A9
(902) 455-4286 nimbus.ca

Cover artwork by Briana Corr Scott
Printed and bound in China
NB1751

*Nimbus Publishing is based in Kjipuktuk, Mi'kma'ki, the traditional
territory of the Mi'kmaq People.*

Library and Archives Canada Cataloguing in Publication

Title: Anne of Green Gables ; & Anne of Avonlea / Lucy Maud
Montgomery.
Other titles: Novels. Selections (Nimbus Publishing) | Anne of
Avonlea
Names: Montgomery, L. M. (Lucy Maud), 1874-1942, author. |
Container of (work): Montgomery, L. M.
   (Lucy Maud), 1874-1942. Anne of Green Gables. | Container of
(work): Montgomery, L. M. (Lucy
   Maud), 1874-1942. Anne of Avonlea.
Identifiers: Canadiana 20230587933 |
ISBN 9781774712627 (softcover)
Subjects: LCGFT: Novels.
Classification: LCC PS8526.O55 A6 2024 | DDC C813/.52—dc23

Canada NOVA SCOTIA   Canada Council   Conseil des arts
                     for the Arts   du Canada

Nimbus Publishing acknowledges the financial support for
its publishing activities from the Government of Canada, the
Canada Council for the Arts, and from the Province of Nova
Scotia. We are pleased to work in partnership with the Province
of Nova Scotia to develop and promote our creative industries
for the benefit of all Nova Scotians.

ANNE
of Green Gables

LUCY MAUD MONTGOMERY

NIMBUS
PUBLISHING LTD.
— NIMBUS.CA —

TO
THE MEMORY OF
MY FATHER AND MOTHER

Anne
of Green Gables

Contents

Chapter		Page

Anne of Avonlea

Contents

ANNE OF GREEN GABLES

CHAPTER I

MRS RACHEL LYNDE IS SURPRISED

MRS RACHEL LYNDE lived just where the Avonlea main road dipped down into a little hollow, fringed with alders and ladies' ear-drops, and traversed by a brook that had its source away back in the woods of the old Cuthbert place; it was reputed to be an intricate, headlong brook in its earlier course through those woods, with dark secrets of pool and cascade; but by the time it reached Lynde's Hollow it was a quiet, well-conducted little stream, for not even a brook could run past Mrs Rachel Lynde's door without due regard for decency and decorum; it probably was conscious that Mrs Rachel was sitting at her window, keeping a sharp eye on everything that passed, from brooks and children up, and that if she noticed anything odd or out of place she would never rest until she had ferreted out the whys and wherefores thereof.

There are plenty of people, in Avonlea and out of it, who can attend closely to their neighbours' business by dint of neglecting their own; but Mrs Rachel Lynde was one of those capable creatures who can manage their own concerns and those of other folks into the bargain. She was a notable housewife; her work was always done and well done; she 'ran' the Sewing Circle, helped run the Sunday School, and was the strongest prop of the Church Aid Society and Foreign Missions Auxiliary. Yet with all this Mrs Rachel found abundant time to sit for hours at her kitchen window, knitting ' cotton warp ' quilts —she had knitted sixteen of them, as Avonlea house-keepers were wont to tell in awed voices—and keeping a sharp eye on the main road that crossed the hollow and wound up the steep red hill beyond. Since Avon-lea occupied a little triangular peninsula jutting out into the Gulf of St Lawrence, with water on two sides of it, anybody who went out of it or into it had to pass over that hill road and so run the unseen gauntlet of Mrs Rachel's all-seeing eye.

She was sitting there one afternoon in early June. The sun was coming in at the window warm and bright ; the orchard on the slope below the house was in a bridal flush of pinky-white bloom, hummed over by a myriad of bees. Thomas Lynde—a meek little man whom Avonlea people called " Rachel Lynde's husband "—was sowing his late turnip seed on the hill field beyond the barn ; and Matthew Cuthbert ought to have been sowing his on the big red brook field away over by Green Gables. Mrs Rachel knew that he ought because she had heard him tell Peter Morrison the evening before in William J. Blair's store over at Carmody that he meant to sow his turnip seed the next afternoon. Peter had asked him, of course, for Matthew Cuthbert had never been known to volunteer information about anything in his whole life.

And yet here was Matthew Cuthbert, at half-past three on the afternoon of a busy day, placidly driving over the hollow and up the hill ; moreover, he wore a white collar and his best suit of clothes, which was plain proof that he was going out of Avonlea ; and he had the buggy and the sorrel mare, which be-tokened that he was going a considerable distance.

Now where was Matthew Cuthbert going, and why was he going there ?

Had it been any other man in Avonlea Mrs Rachel, deftly putting this and that together, might have given a pretty good guess as to both questions. But Matthew so rarely went from home that it must be something pressing and unusual which was taking him ; he was the shyest man alive and hated to have to go among strangers or to any place where he might have to talk. Matthew, dressed up with a white collar and driving in a buggy, was something that didn't happen often. Mrs Rachel, ponder as she might, could make nothing of it, and her afternoon's enjoyment was spoiled.

" I'll just step over to Green Gables after tea and find out from Marilla where he's gone and why," the worthy woman finally concluded. " He doesn't generally go to town this time of year and he *never* visits ; if he'd run out of turnip seed he wouldn't dress up and take the buggy to go for more ; he wasn't driving fast enough to be going for a doctor. Yet something must have happened since last night to start him off. I'm clean puzzled, that's what, and I won't know a minute's peace of mind or conscience until I know what has taken Matthew Cuthbert out of Avonlea to-day."

Accordingly after tea Mrs Rachel set out ; she had not far to go ; the big, rambling, orchard-embowered house where the Cuthberts lived was a scant quarter of a mile up the road from Lynde's Hollow. To be sure, the long lane made it a good deal farther. Matthew Cuthbert's father, as shy and silent as his son after him, had got as far away as he possibly could from his fellow men without actually retreating into the woods when he founded his homestead. Green Gables was built at the farthest edge of his cleared land, and there it was to this day, barely visible from the main road along which all the other Avonlea houses were so sociably situated. Mrs Rachael Lynde did not call living in such a place *living* at all.

" It's just *staying*, that's what," she said, as she stepped along the deep-rutted, grassy lane bordered with wild rose bushes. " It's no wonder Matthew and Marilla are both a little odd, living away back here by themselves. Trees aren't much company, though dear knows if they were there'd be enough of them. I'd rather look at people. To be sure, they seem contented enough ; but then, I suppose, they're used to it. A body can get used to anything, even to being hanged, as the Irishman said."

With this Mrs Rachel stepped out of the lane into the backyard of Green Gables. Very green and neat and precise was that yard, set about on one side with great patriarchal willows and on the other with prim Lombardies. Not a stray stick nor stone was to be seen, for Mrs Rachel would have seen it if there had been. Privately she was of the opinion that Marilla Cuthbert swept that yard as often as she swept her house. One could have eaten a meal off the ground without overbrimming the proverbial peck of dirt.

Mrs Rachel rapped smartly at the kitchen door and stepped in when bidden to do so. The kitchen at Green Gables was a cheerful apartment—or would have been cheerful if it had not been so painfully clean as to give it something of the appearance of an unused parlour. Its windows looked east and west ; through the west one, looking out on the back yard, came a flood of mellow June sunlight ; but the east one, whence you got a glimpse of the bloom-white cherry-trees in the left orchard and nodding, slender birches down in the hollow by the brook, was greened over by a tangle of vines. Here sat Marilla Cuthbert, when she sat at all, always slightly distrustful of sunshine, which seemed to her too dancing and irresponsible a thing for a world which was meant to be taken seriously ; and here she sat now, knitting, and the table behind her was laid for supper.

Mrs Rachel, before she had fairly closed the door, had taken mental note of everything that was on that table. There were three plates laid, so that Marilla must be expecting some one home with Matthew to tea ; but the dishes were everyday dishes and there was only crab-apple preserves and one kind of cake, so that the expected company could not be any particular company. Yet what of Matthew's white collar and the sorrel mare ? Mrs Rachel was getting fairly dizzy with this unusual mystery about quiet, unmysterious Green Gables.

" Good evening, Rachel," Marilla said briskly. " This is a real fine evening, isn't it ? Won't you sit down ? How are all your folks ? "

Something that for lack of any other name might be called friendship existed and always had existed between Marilla Cuthbert and Mrs Rachel, in spite of—or perhaps because of—their dissimilarity.

Marilla was a tall, thin woman, with angles and without curves ; her dark hair showed some grey streaks and was always twisted up in a hard little knot behind with two wire hairpins stuck aggressively through it. She looked like a woman of narrow experience and rigid conscience, which she was ; but there was a saving something about her mouth which, if it had been ever so slightly developed, might have been considered indicative of a sense of humour.

" We're all pretty well," said Mrs Rachel. " I was kind of afraid *you* weren't, though, when I saw Matthew starting off to-day. I thought maybe he was going to the doctor's."

Marilla's lips twitched understandingly. She had

expected Mrs Rachel up ; she had known that the sight of Matthew jaunting off so unaccountably would be too much for her neighbour's curiosity.

" Oh, no, I'm quite well, although I had a bad headache yesterday," she said. " Matthew went to Bright River. We're getting a little boy from an orphan asylum in Nova Scotia, and he's coming on the train to-night."

If Marilla had said that Matthew had gone to Bright River to meet a kangaroo from Australia Mrs Rachel could not have been more astonished. She was actually stricken dumb for five seconds. It was unsupposable that Marilla was making fun of her, but Mrs Rachel was almost forced to suppose it.

" Are you in earnest, Marilla ? " she demanded when voice returned to her.

" Yes, of course," said Marilla, as if getting boys from orphan asylums in Nova Scotia were part of the usual spring work on any well-regulated Avonlea farm instead of being an unheard-of innovation.

Mrs Rachel felt that she had received a severe mental jolt. She thought in exclamation points. A boy ! Marilla and Matthew Cuthbert of all people adopting a boy ! From an orphan asylum ! Well, the world was certainly turning upside down ! She would be surprised at nothing after this ! Nothing !

" What on earth put such a notion into your head ? " she demanded disapprovingly.

This had been done without her advice being asked, and must perforce be disapproved.

" Well, we've been thinking about it for some time —all winter in fact," returned Marilla. " Mrs Alexander Spencer was up here one day before Christmas and she said she was going to get a little girl from the asylum over in Hopetown in the spring. Her cousin lives there and Mrs Spencer has visited her and knows all about it. So Matthew and I have talked it over off and on ever since. We thought we'd get a boy. Matthew is getting up in years, you know—he's sixty —and he isn't so spry as he once was. His heart troubles him a good deal. And you know how desperate hard it's got to be to get hired help. There's never anybody to be had but those stupid, half-grown little French boys ; and as soon as you do get one broke into your ways and taught something he's up and off to the lobster canneries or the States. At first Matthew suggested getting a 'Home' boy. But I said 'no' flat to that. 'They may be all right— I'm not saying they're not—but no London street arabs for me,' I said. 'Give me a native born at least. There'll be a risk, no matter who we get. But I'll feel easier in my mind and sleep sounder at nights if we get a born Canadian.' So in the end we decided to ask Mrs Spencer to pick us out one when she went over to get her little girl. We heard last week she was going, so we sent her word by Richard Spencer's folks at Carmody to bring us a smart, likely boy of about ten or eleven. We decided that would be the best age—old enough to be of some use in doing chores right off and young enough to be trained up proper. We mean to give him a good home and schooling. We had a telegram from Mrs Alexander Spencer to-day—the mail-man brought it from the station— saying they were coming on the five-thirty train to-night. So Matthew went to Bright River to meet him. Mrs Spencer will drop him off there. Of course she goes on to White Sands station herself."

Mrs Rachel prided herself on always speaking her mind ; she proceeded to speak it now, having adjusted her mental attitude to this amazing piece of news.

"Well, Marilla, I'll just tell you plain that I think you're doing a mighty foolish thing—a risky thing, that's what. You don't know what you're getting. You're bringing a strange child into your house and home, and you don't know a single thing about him nor what his disposition is like nor what sort of parents he had nor how he's likely to turn out. Why, it was only last week I read in the paper how a man and his wife up west of the Island took a boy out of an orphan asylum and he set fire to the house at night—set it *on purpose*, Marilla—and nearly burnt them to a crisp in their beds. And I know another case where an adopted boy used to suck the eggs—they couldn't break him of it. If you had asked my advice in the matter—which you didn't do, Marilla—I'd have said for mercy's sake not to think of such a thing, that's what."

This Job's comforting seemed neither to offend nor alarm Marilla. She knitted steadily on.

" I don't deny there's something in what you say, Rachel. I've had some qualms myself. But Matthew was terrible set on it. I could see that, so I gave in. It's so seldom Matthew sets his mind on anything that when he does I always feel it's my duty to give in. And as for the risk, there's risks in pretty near everything a body does in this world. There's risks in people's having children of their own if it comes to that—they don't always turn out well. And then Nova Scotia is right close to the Island. It isn't as if we were getting him from England or the States. He can't be much different from ourselves."

" Well, I hope it will turn out all right," said Mrs Rachel in a tone that plainly indicated her painful doubts. " Only don't say I didn't warn you if he burns Green Gables down or puts strychnine in the well—I heard of a case over in New Brunswick where an orphan asylum child did that, and the whole family died in fearful agonies. Only, it was a girl in that instance."

" Well, we're not getting a girl," said Marilla, as if poisoning wells were a purely feminine accomplishment and not to be dreaded in the case of a boy.   " I'd never dream of taking a girl to bring up. I wonder at Mrs Alexander Spencer for doing it. But there, *she* wouldn't shrink from adopting a whole orphan asylum if she took it into her head."

Mrs Rachel would have liked to stay until Matthew came home with his imported orphan. But reflecting that it would be a good two hours at least before his arrival she concluded to go up the road to Robert Bell's and tell them the news.   It would certainly make a sensation second to none, and Mrs Rachel dearly loved to make a sensation. So she took herself away, somewhat to Marilla's relief, for the latter felt her doubts and fears reviving under the influence of Mrs Rachel's pessimism.

" Well, of all things that ever were or will be ! " ejaculated Mrs Rachel when she was safely out in the lane.   " It does really seem as if I must be dreaming. Well, I'm sorry for that poor young one and no mistake. Matthew and Marilla don't know anything about children and they'll expect him to be wiser and steadier than his own grandfather, if so be's he ever had a grandfather, which is doubtful. It seems uncanny to think of a child at Green Gables somehow ; there's never been one there, for Matthew and Marilla were grown up when the new house was built—if they ever *were* children, which is hard to believe when one looks at them. I wouldn't be in that orphan's shoes for anything. My, but I pity him, that's what."

So said Mrs Rachel to the wild rose bushes out of the fullness of her heart ; but if she could have seen the child who was waiting patiently at the Bright River station at that very moment her pity would have been still deeper and more profound.

CHAPTER II

MATTHEW CUTHBERT IS SURPRISED

MATTHEW CUTHBERT and the sorrel mare jogged comfortably over the eight miles to Bright River. It was a pretty road, running along between snug farmsteads, with now and again a bit of balsamy fir wood to drive through, or a hollow where wild plums hung out their filmy bloom. The air was sweet with the breath of many apple orchards, and the meadows sloped away in the distance to horizon mists of pearl and purple; while

> The little birds sang as if it were
> The one day of summer in all the year.

Matthew enjoyed the drive after his own fashion, except during the moments when he met women and had to nod to them—for in Prince Edward Island you are supposed to nod to all and sundry you meet on the road whether you know them or not.

Matthew dreaded all women except Marilla and Mrs Rachel; he had an uncomfortable feeling that the mysterious creatures were secretly laughing at him. He may have been quite right in thinking so, for he was an odd-looking personage, with an ungainly figure and long iron-grey hair that touched his stooping shoulders, and a full, soft brown beard which he had worn ever since he was twenty. In fact, he had looked at twenty very much as he looked at sixty, lacking a little of the greyness.

When he reached Bright River there was no sign of any train; he thought he was too early, so he tied his

horse in the yard of the small Bright River hotel and
went over to the station-house.   The long platform was
almost deserted ; the only living creature in sight being
a girl who was sitting on a pile of shingles at the extreme
end.   Matthew, barely noting that it *was* a girl, sidled
past her as quickly as possible without looking at her.
Had he looked he could hardly have failed to notice
the tense rigidity and expectation of her attitude and
expression.   She was sitting there waiting for something or somebody, and, since sitting and waiting was
the only thing to do just then, she sat and waited with
all her might and main.

Matthew encountered the station-master locking up
the ticket-office preparatory to going home for supper,
and asked him if the five-thirty train would soon be
along.

" The five-thirty train has been in and gone half
an hour ago," answered that brisk official.   " But there
was a passenger dropped off for you—a little girl.
She's sitting out there on the shingles.   I asked her
to go into the ladies' waiting-room, but she informed
me gravely that she preferred to stay outside.   ' There
was more scope for imagination,' she said.   She's a
case, I should say."

" I'm not expecting a girl," said Matthew blankly.
" It's a boy I've come for.   He should be here.   Mrs
Alexander Spencer was to bring him over from Nova
Scotia for me."

The station-master whistled.   " Guess there's some
mistake," he said.   " Mrs Spencer came off the train
with that girl and gave her into my charge.   Said you
and your sister were adopting her from an orphan
asylum and that you would be along for her presently.
That's all *I* know about it—and I haven't got any
more orphans concealed hereabouts."

" I don't understand," said Matthew helplessly,

wishing that Marilla was at hand to cope with the situation.

"Well, you'd better question the girl," said the station-master carelessly. "I dare say she'll be able to explain—she's got a tongue of her own, that's certain. Maybe they were out of boys of the brand you wanted."

He walked jauntily away, being hungry, and the unfortunate Matthew was left to do that which was harder for him than bearding a lion in its den—walk up to a girl—a strange girl—an orphan girl—and demand of her why she wasn't a boy. Matthew groaned in spirit as he turned about and shuffled gently down the platform towards her.

She had been watching him ever since he had passed her and she had her eyes on him now. Matthew was not looking at her and would not have seen what she was really like if he had been, but an ordinary observer would have seen this :

A child of about eleven, garbed in a very short, very tight, very ugly dress of yellowish white wincey. She wore a faded brown sailor hat and beneath the hat, extending down her back, were two braids of very thick, decidedly red hair. Her face was small, white and thin, also much freckled ; her mouth was large and so were her eyes, that looked green in some lights and moods and grey in others.

So far, the ordinary observer; an extraordinary observer might have seen that the chin was very pointed and pronounced ; that the big eyes were full of spirit and vivacity ; that the mouth was sweet-lipped and expressive; that the forehead was broad and full ; in short, our discerning extraordinary observer might have concluded that no commonplace soul inhabited the body of this stray woman-child of whom shy Matthew Cuthbert was so ludicrously afraid.

Matthew, however, was spared the ordeal of speaking first, for as soon as she concluded that he was coming to her she stood up, grasping with one thin brown hand the handle of a shabby, old-fashioned carpet-bag ; the other she held out to him.

" I suppose you are Mr Matthew Cuthbert of Green Gables ? " she said in a peculiarly clear, sweet voice. " I'm very glad to see you. I was beginning to be afraid you weren't coming for me and I was imagining all the things that might have happened to prevent you. I had made up my mind that if you didn't come for me to-night I'd go down the track to that big wild cherry-tree at the bend, and climb up into it to stay all night. I wouldn't be a bit afraid, and it would be lovely to sleep in a wild cherry-tree all white with bloom in the moonshine, don't you think ? You could imagine you were dwelling in marble halls, couldn't you ? And I was quite sure you would come for me in the morning, if you didn't to-night."

Matthew had taken the scrawny little hand awkwardly in his ; then and there he decided what to do. He could not tell this child with the glowing eyes that there had been a mistake ; he would take her home and let Marilla do that. She couldn't be left at Bright River anyhow, no matter what mistake had been made, so all questions and explanations might as well be deferred until he was safely back at Green Gables.

" I'm sorry I was late," he said shyly. " Come along. The horse is over in the yard. Give me your bag."

" Oh, I can carry it," the child responded cheerfully. " It isn't heavy. I've got all my worldly goods in it, but it isn't heavy. And if it isn't carried in just a certain way the handle pulls out—so I'd better keep it because I know the exact knack of it. It's an extremely old carpet-bag. Oh, I'm very glad you've come, even if it would have been nice to sleep in a wild cherry-tree. We've got to drive a long piece, haven't we? Mrs Spencer said it was eight miles. I'm glad, because I love driving. Oh, it seems so wonderful that I'm going to live with you and belong to you. I've never belonged to anybody—not really. But the asylum was the worst. I've only been in it four months, but that was enough. I don't suppose you ever were an orphan in an asylum, so you can't possibly understand what it is like. It's worse than anything you could imagine. Mrs Spencer said it was wicked of me to talk like that, but I didn't mean to be wicked. It's so easy to be wicked without knowing it, isn't it? They were good, you know—the asylum people. But there is so little scope for the imagination in an asylum —only just in the other orphans. It *was* pretty interesting to imagine things about them—to imagine that perhaps the girl who sat next to you was really the daughter of a belted earl, who had been stolen away from her parents in her infancy by a cruel nurse who died before she could confess. I used to lie awake at nights and imagine things like that, because I didn't have time in the day. I guess that's why I'm so thin —I *am* dreadfully thin, ain't I? There isn't a pick on my bones. I do love to imagine I'm nice and plump, with dimples in my elbows."

With this Matthew's companion stopped talking, partly because she was out of breath and partly because they had reached the buggy. Not another word did she say until they had left the village and were driving down a steep little hill, the road part of which had been cut so deeply into the soft soil that the banks, fringed with blooming wild cherry-trees and slim white birches, were several feet above their heads.

The child put out her hand and broke off a branch of wild plum that brushed against the side of the buggy.

" Isn't that beautiful ?   What did that tree, leaning
out from the bank, all white and lacy, make you think
of ? " she asked.

" Well now, I dunno," said Matthew.

" Why, a bride, of course—a bride all in white with
a lovely misty veil. I've never seen one, but I can
imagine what she would look like. I don't ever expect to be a bride myself. I'm so homely nobody will
ever want to marry me—unless it might be a foreign
missionary. I suppose a foreign missionary mightn't
be very particular. But I do hope that some day I
shall have a white dress. That is my highest ideal
of earthly bliss. I just love pretty clothes. And I've
never had a pretty dress in my life that I can remember
—but of course it's all the more to look forward to,
isn't it ?   And then I can imagine that I'm dressed
gorgeously. This morning when I left the asylum I
felt so ashamed because I had to wear this horrid old
wincey dress. All the orphans had to wear them, you
know. A merchant in Hopetown last winter donated
three hundred yards of wincey to the asylum. Some
people said it was because he couldn't sell it, but I'd
rather believe that it was out of the kindness of his
heart, wouldn't you ?   When we got on the train I
felt as if everybody must be looking at me and pitying
me. But I just went to work and imagined that I
had on the most beautiful pale blue silk dress—because
when you *are* imagining you might as well imagine
something worth while—and a big hat all flowers and
nodding plumes, and a gold watch, and kid gloves and
boots. I felt cheered up right away and I enjoyed
my trip to the Island with all my might. I wasn't a
bit sick coming over in the boat. Neither was Mrs
Spencer, although she generally is. She said she hadn't
time to get sick, watching to see that I didn't fall overboard. She said she never saw the beat of me for

prowling about. But if it kept her from being seasick it's a mercy I did prowl, isn't it ? And I wanted to see everything that was to be seen on that boat, because I didn't know whether I'd ever have another opportunity. Oh, there are a lot more cherry-trees all in bloom ! This Island is the bloomiest place. I just love it already, and I'm so glad I'm going to live here. I've always heard that Prince Edward Island was the prettiest place in the world, and I used to imagine I was living here, but I never really expected I would. It's delightful when your imaginations come true, isn't it ? But those red roads are so funny. When we got into the train at Charlottetown and the red roads began to flash past I asked Mrs Spencer what made them red and she said she didn't know, and for pity's sake not to ask her any more questions. She said I must have asked her a thousand already. I suppose I had, too, but how are you going to find out about things if you don't ask questions ? And what *does* make the roads red ? "

" Well, now, I dunno," said Matthew.

" Well, that is one of the things to find out sometime. Isn't it splendid to think of all the things there are to find out about ? It just makes me feel glad to be alive—it's such an interesting world. It wouldn't be half so interesting if we knew all about everything, would it ? There'd be no scope for imagination then, would there ? But am I talking too much ? People are always telling me I do. Would you rather I didn't talk ? If you say so I'll stop. I *can* stop when I make up my mind to it, although it's difficult."

Matthew, much to his own surprise, was enjoying himself. Like most quiet folks he liked talkative people when they were willing to do the talking themselves and did not expect him to keep up his end of it. But he had never expected to enjoy the society of a little girl. Women were bad enough in all conscience, but little girls were worse. He detested the way they had of sidling past him timidly, with sidewise glances, as if they expected him to gobble them up at a mouthful if they ventured to say a word. This was the Avonlea type of well-bred little girl. But this freckled witch was very different, and although he found it rather difficult for his slower intelligence to keep up with her brisk mental processes he thought that he " kind of liked her chatter." So he said as shyly as usual :

" Oh, you can talk as much as you like. I don't mind."

" Oh, I'm so glad. I know you and I are going to get along together fine. It's such a relief to talk when one wants to, and not be told that children should be seen and not heard. I've had that said to me a million times if I have once. And people laugh at me because I use big words. But if you have big ideas you have to use big words to express them, haven't you ? "

" Well, now, that seems reasonable," said Matthew.

" Mrs Spencer said that my tongue must be hung in the middle. But it isn't—it's firmly fastened at one end. Mrs Spencer said your place was named Green Gables. I asked her all about it. And she said there were trees all around it. I was gladder than ever. I just love trees. And there weren't any at all about the asylum, only a few poor weeny-teeny things out in front with little whitewashed cagey things about them. They just looked like orphans themselves, those trees did. It used to make me want to cry to look at them. I used to say to them, ' Oh, you *poor* little things ! If you were out in a great big woods with other trees all around you and little mosses and Junebells growing over your roots and a brook not far away and birds singing in your branches, you could grow, couldn't you ? But you can't where you are. I know just exactly how you feel, little trees.' I felt sorry to leave them behind this morning. You do get so attached to things like that, don't you ? Is there a brook anywhere near Green Gables ? I forgot to ask Mrs Spencer that."

" Well now, yes, there's one right below the house."

" Fancy ! It's always been one of my dreams to live near a brook. I never expected I would, though. Dreams don't often come true, do they ? Wouldn't it be nice if they did ? But just now I feel pretty nearly perfectly happy. I can't feel exactly perfectly happy because—well, what colour would you call this ? "

She twitched one of her long glossy braids over her thin shoulder and held it up before Matthew's eyes. Matthew was not used to deciding on the tints of ladies' tresses, but in this case there couldn't be much doubt.

" It's red, ain't it ? " he said.

The girl let the braid drop back with a sigh that seemed to come from her very toes and to exhale forth all the sorrows of the ages.

" Yes, it's red," she said resignedly. " Now you see why I can't be perfectly happy. Nobody could who had red hair. I don't mind the other things so much—the freckles and the green eyes and my skinniness. I can imagine them away. I can imagine that I have a beautiful rose-leaf complexion and lovely starry violet eyes. But I *cannot* imagine that red hair away. I do my best. I think to myself, ' Now my hair is a glorious black, black as the raven's wing.' But all the time I *know* it is just plain red, and it breaks my heart. It will be my lifelong sorrow. I read of a girl once in a novel who had a lifelong sorrow,

but it wasn't red hair.   Her hair was pure gold, rippling
back from her alabaster brow.   What is an alabaster
brow ?   I never could find out.   Can you tell me ? "

" Well now, I'm afraid I can't," said Matthew, who
was getting a little dizzy.   He felt as he had once felt
in his rash youth when another boy had enticed him
on the merry-go-round at a picnic.

" Well, whatever it was it must have been something
nice because she was divinely beautiful.   Have you
ever imagined what it must feel like to be divinely
beautiful ? "

" Well now, no, I haven't," confessed Matthew in-
genuously.

" I have, often.   Which would you rather be if you
had the choice—divinely beautiful or dazzlingly clever
or angelically good ? "

" Well now, I—I don't know exactly."

" Neither do I.   I can never decide.   But it doesn't
make much real difference, for it isn't likely I'll ever
be either.   It's certain I'll never be angelically good.
Mrs Spencer says—oh, Mr Cuthbert !   Oh, Mr Cuthbert ! !   Oh, Mr Cuthbert ! ! ! "

That was not what Mrs Spencer had said ;   neither
had the child tumbled out of the buggy, nor had Matthew done anything astonishing.   They had simply
rounded a curve in the road and found themselves in
the " Avenue."

The " Avenue," so called by the Newbridge people,
was a stretch of road four or five hundred yards
long, completely arched over with huge, wide-spreading
apple-trees, planted years ago by an eccentric old
farmer.   Overhead was one long canopy of snowy,
fragrant bloom.   Below the boughs the air was full
of a purple twilight and far ahead a glimpse of painted
sunset sky shone like a great rose window at the end
of a cathedral aisle.

Its beauty seemed to strike the child dumb. She leaned back in the buggy, her thin hands clasped before her, her face lifted rapturously to the white splendour above. Even when they had passed out and were driving down the long slope to Newbridge, she never moved or spoke. Still with rapt face she gazed afar into the sunset west, with eyes that saw visions trooping splendidly across that glowing background. Through Newbridge, a bustling little village where dogs barked at them and small boys hooted and curious faces peered from the windows, they drove, still in silence. When three more miles had dropped away behind them the child had not spoken. She could keep silence, it was evident, as energetically as she could talk.

" I guess you're feeling pretty tired and hungry," Matthew ventured at last, accounting for her long visitation of dumbness with the only reason he could think of. " But we haven't very far to go now—only another mile."

She came out of her reverie with a deep sigh and looked at him with the dreamy gaze of a soul that had been wandering afar, star-led.

" Oh, Mr Cuthbert," she whispered, " that place we came through—that white place—what was it ? "

" Well now, you must mean the Avenue," said Matthew after a few moments' profound reflection. " It is a kind of pretty place."

" Pretty ? Oh, *pretty* doesn't seem the right word to use. Nor beautiful, either. They don't go far enough. Oh, it was wonderful—wonderful. It's the first thing I ever saw that couldn't be improved upon by imagination. It just satisfied me here "—she put one hand on her breast—" it made a queer funny ache and yet it was a pleasant ache. Did you ever have an ache like that, Mr Cuthbert ? "

" Well now, I just can't recollect that I ever had."

" I have it lots of times—whenever I see anything royally beautiful.   But they shouldn't call that lovely place the Avenue.   There is no meaning in a name like that.   They should call it—let me see—the White Way of Delight.   Isn't that a nice imaginative name ? When I don't like the name of a place or a person I always imagine a new one and always think of them so. There was a girl at the asylum whose name was Hepzibah Jenkins, but I always imagined her as Rosalia De Vere.   Other people may call that place the Avenue, but I shall always call it the White Way of Delight. Have we really only another mile to go before we get home ?   I'm glad and I'm sorry.   I'm sorry because this drive has been so pleasant and I'm always sorry when pleasant things end.   Something still pleasanter may come after, but you can never be sure.   And it's so often the case that it isn't pleasanter.   That has been my experience anyhow.   But I'm glad to think of getting home.   You see, I've never had a real home since I can remember.   It gives me that pleasant ache again just to think of coming to a really truly home. Oh, isn't that pretty ! "

They had driven over the crest of a hill.   Below them was a pond, looking almost like a river so long and winding was it.   A bridge spanned it midway, and from there to its lower end, where an amber-hued belt of sand-hills shut it in from the dark blue gulf beyond, the water was a glory of many shifting hues —the most spiritual shadings of crocus and rose and ethereal green, with other elusive tintings for which no name has ever been found.   Above the bridge the pond ran up into fringing groves of fir and maple and lay all darkly translucent in their wavering shadows. Here and there a wild plum leaned out from the bank like a white-clad girl tip-toeing to her own reflection. From the marsh at the head of the pond came the clear, mournfully sweet chorus of the frogs. There was a little grey house peering around a white apple orchard on a slope beyond, and, although it was not yet quite dark, a light was shining from one of its windows.

" That's Barry's pond," said Matthew.

" Oh, I don't like that name, either. I shall call it—let me see—the Lake of Shining Waters. Yes, that is the right name for it. I know because of the thrill. When I hit on a name that suits exactly it gives me a thrill. Do things ever give you a thrill ? "

Matthew ruminated.

" Well now, yes. It always kind of gives me a thrill to see them ugly white grubs that spade up in the cucumber beds. I hate the look of them."

" Oh, I don't think that can be exactly the same kind of a thrill. Do you think it can ? There doesn't seem to be much connection between grubs and lakes of shining waters, does there ? But why do other people call it Barry's pond ? "

" I reckon because Mr Barry lives up there in that house. Orchard Slope's the name of his place. If it wasn't for that big bush behind it you could see Green Gables from here. But we have to go over the bridge and round by the road, so it's near half a mile further."

" Has Mr Barry any little girls ? Well, not so very little either—about my size."

" He's got one about eleven. Her name is Diana."

" Oh ! " with a long indrawing of breath. " What a perfectly lovely name ! "

" Well now, I dunno. There's something dreadful heathenish about it, seems to me. I'd ruther Jane or Mary or some sensible name like that. But when Diana was born there was a schoolmaster boarding there and they gave him the naming of her and he called her Diana."

" I wish there had been a schoolmaster like that around when *I* was born, then. Oh, here we are at the bridge. I'm going to shut my eyes tight. I'm always afraid going over bridges. I can't help imagining that perhaps, just as we get to the middle, they'll crumple up like a jack-knife and nip us. So I shut my eyes. But I always have to open them for all when I think we're getting near the middle. Because, you see, if the bridge *did* crumple up I'd want to *see* it crumple. What a jolly rumble it makes ! I always like the rumble part of it. Isn't it splendid there are so many things to like in this world ? There, we're over. Now I'll look back. Good night, dear Lake of Shining Waters. I always say good-night to the things I love, just as I would to people. I think they like it. That water looks as if it was smiling at me."

When they had driven up the further hill and around a corner Matthew said :

" We're pretty near home now. That's Green Gables over——"

" Oh, don't tell me," she interrupted breathlessly, catching at his partially raised arm and shutting her eyes that she might not see his gesture. " Let me guess. I'm sure I'll guess right."

She opened her eyes and looked about her. They were on the crest of a hill. The sun had set some time since, but the landscape was still clear in the mellow afterlight. To the west a dark church spire rose up against a marigold sky. Below was a little valley, and beyond a long, gently-rising slope with snug farmsteads scattered along it. From one to another the child's eyes darted, eager and wistful. At last they lingered on one away to the left, far back from the road, dimly white with blossoming trees in the twilight of the surrounding woods. Over it, in the stainless south-west sky, a great crystal-white star was shining like a lamp of guidance and promise.

" That's it, isn't it ? " she said, pointing.

Matthew slapped the reins on the sorrel's back delightedly.

" Well now, you've guessed it ! But I reckon Mrs Spencer described it so's you could tell."

" No, she didn't—really she didn't. All she said might just as well have been about most of those other places. I hadn't any real idea what it looked like. But just as soon as I saw it I felt it was home. Oh, it seems as if I must be in a dream. Do you know, my arm must be black and blue from the elbow up, for I've pinched myself so many times to-day. Every little while a horrible sickening feeling would come over me and I'd be so afraid it was all a dream. Then I'd pinch myself to see if it was real—until suddenly I remembered that even supposing it was only a dream I'd better go on dreaming as long as I could ; so I stopped pinching. But it *is* real and we're nearly home."

With a sigh of rapture she relapsed into silence. Matthew stirred uneasily. He felt glad that it would be Marilla and not he who would have to tell this waif of the world that the home she longed for was not to be hers after all. They drove over Lynde's Hollow, where it was already quite dark, but not so dark that Mrs Rachel could not see them from her window vantage, and up the hill and into the long lane of Green Gables. By the time they arrived at the house Matthew was shrinking from the approaching revelation with an energy he did not understand. It was not of Marilla or himself he was thinking or of the trouble this mistake was probably going to make for them, but of the child's disappointment. When he thought of that rapt light being quenched in her eyes he had

an uncomfortable feeling that he was going to assist
at murdering something—much the same feeling that
came over him when he had to kill a lamb or calf or
any other innocent little creature.

The yard was quite dark as they turned into it, and
the poplar leaves were rustling silkily all round it.

" Listen to the trees talking in their sleep," she
whispered, as he lifted her to the ground. " What
nice dreams they must have ! "

Then, holding tightly to the carpet bag which contained " all her worldly goods." she followed him into
the house.

CHAPTER III

MARILLA CUTHBERT IS SURPRISED

MARILLA came briskly forward as Matthew opened the door. But when her eyes fell on the odd little figure in the stiff, ugly dress, with the long braids of red hair and the eager, luminous eyes, she stopped short in amazement.

" Matthew Cuthbert, who's that ? " she ejaculated. " Where is the boy ? "

" There wasn't any boy," said Matthew wretchedly. " There was only *her*."

He nodded at the child, remembering that he had never even asked her name.

" No boy ! But there *must* have been a boy," insisted Marilla. " We sent word to Mrs Spencer to bring a boy."

" Well, she didn't. She brought *her*. I asked the station-master. And I had to bring her home. She couldn't be left there, no matter where the mistake had come in."

" Well, this is a pretty piece of business ! " ejaculated Marilla.

During this dialogue the child had remained silent, her eyes roving from one to the other, all the animation fading out of her face. Suddenly she seemed to grasp the full meaning of what had been said. Dropping her precious carpet-bag she sprang forward a step and clasped her hands.

" You don't want me ! " she cried. " You don't want me because I'm not a boy ! I might have expected it. Nobody ever did want me. I might have known it was all too beautiful to last. I might have known nobody really did want me. Oh, what shall I do ? I'm going to burst into tears ! "

Burst into tears she did. Sitting down on a chair by the table, flinging her arms out upon it, and burying her face in them, she proceeded to cry stormily. Marilla and Matthew looked at each other deprecatingly across the stove. Neither of them knew what to say or do. Finally Marilla stepped lamely into the breach.

" Well, well, there's no need to cry so about it."

" Yes, there *is* need ! " The child raised her head quickly, revealing a tear-stained face and trembling lips. " *You* would cry, too, if you were an orphan and had come to a place you thought was going to be home and found that they didn't want you because you weren't a boy. Oh, this is the most *tragical* thing that ever happened to me ! "

Something like a reluctant smile, rather rusty from long disuse, mellowed Marilla's grim expression.

" Well, don't cry any more. We're not going to turn you out-of-doors to-night. You'll have to stay here until we investigate this affair. What's your name ? "

The child hesitated for a moment.

" Will you please call me Cordelia ? " she said eagerly.

" *Call* you Cordelia ! Is that your name ? "

" No-o-o, it's not exactly my name, but I would love to be called Cordelia. It's such a perfectly elegant name."

" I don't know what on earth you mean. If Cordelia isn't your name, what is ? "

" Anne Shirley," reluctantly faltered forth the owner of that name, " but oh, please do call me Cordelia. It can't matter much to you what you call me if I'm only going to be here a little while, can it ?   And Anne is such an unromantic name."

" Unromantic fiddlesticks ! " said the unsympathetic Marilla. " Anne is a real good plain sensible name. You've no need to be ashamed of it."

" Oh, I'm not ashamed of it," explained Anne, " only I like Cordelia better. I've always imagined that my name was Cordelia—at least, I always have of late years. When I was young I used to imagine it was Geraldine, but I like Cordelia better now. But if you call me Anne, please call me Anne spelled with an *e*."

" What difference does it make how it's spelled ? " asked Marilla with another rusty smile as she picked up the teapot.

" Oh, it makes *such* a difference. It *looks* so much nicer. When you hear a name pronounced can't you always see it in your mind, just as if it was printed out ? I can ; and A-n-n looks dreadful, but A-n-n-e looks so much more distinguished. If you'll only call me Anne spelled with an *e* I shall try to reconcile myself to not being called Cordelia."

" Very well, then, Anne spelled with an *e*, can you tell us how this mistake came to be made ? We sent word to Mrs Spencer to bring us a boy. Were there no boys at the asylum ? "

" Oh, yes, there was an abundance of them. But Mrs Spencer said *distinctly* that you wanted a girl about eleven years old. And the matron said she thought I would do. You don't know how delighted I was. I couldn't sleep all last night for joy. Oh," she added reproachfully, turning to Matthew, " why didn't you tell me at the station that you didn't want me and leave me there ? If I hadn't seen the White Way of Delight and the Lake of Shining Waters it wouldn't be so hard."

" What on earth does she mean ? " demanded Marilla staring at Matthew.

" She—she's just referring to some conversation we had on the road," said Matthew hastily. " I'm going out to put the mare in, Marilla. Have tea ready when I come back."

" Did Mrs Spencer bring anybody over besides you ?" continued Marilla when Matthew had gone out.

" She brought Lily Jones for herself. Lily is only five years old and she is very beautiful. She has nut-brown hair. If I was very beautiful and had nut-brown hair would you keep me ? "

" No. We want a boy to help Matthew on the farm. A girl would be of no use to us. Take off your hat. I'll lay it and your bag on the hall table."

Anne took off her hat meekly. Matthew came back presently and they sat down to supper. But Anne could not eat. In vain she nibbled at the bread and butter and pecked at the crab-apple preserve out of the little scalloped glass dish by her plate. She did not really make any headway at all.

" You're not eating anything," said Marilla sharply, eyeing her as if it were a serious shortcoming.

Anne sighed.

" I can't. I'm in the depths of despair. Can you eat when you are in the depths of despair ? "

" I've never been in the depths of despair, so I can't say," responded Marilla.

" Weren't you ? Well, did you ever try to *imagine* you were in the depths of despair ? "

" No, I didn't."

" Then I don't think you can understand what it's like. It's a very uncomfortable feeling indeed. When you try to eat a lump comes right up in your throat and you can't swallow anything, not even if it was a chocolate caramel. I had one chocolate caramel once two years ago and it was simply delicious. I've often dreamed since then that I had a lot of chocolate caramels, but I always wake up just when I'm going to eat them. I do hope you won't be offended because I can't eat. Everything is extremely nice, but still I cannot eat."

"I guess she's tired," said Matthew, who hadn't spoken since his return from the barn. "Best put her to bed, Marilla."

Marilla had been wondering where Anne should be put to bed. She had prepared a couch in the kitchen chamber for the desired and expected boy. But, although it was neat and clean, it did not seem quite the thing to put a girl there somehow. But the spare room was out of the question for such a stray waif, so there remained only the east gable room. Marilla lighted a candle and told Anne to follow her, which Anne spiritlessly did, taking her hat and carpet-bag from the hall table as she passed. The hall was fearsomely clean ; the little gable chamber in which she presently found herself seemed still cleaner.

Marilla set the candle on a three-legged, three-cornered table and turned down the bedclothes.

"I suppose you have a nightgown ? " she questioned.

Anne nodded.

"Yes, I have two. The matron of the asylum made them for me. They're fearfully skimpy. There is never enough to go around in an asylum, so things are always skimpy—at least in a poor asylum like ours. I hate skimpy night-dresses. But one can dream just as well in them as in lovely trailing ones, with frills around the neck, that's one consolation."

"Well, undress as quick as you can and go to bed. I'll come back in a few minutes for the candle. I daren't trust you to put it out yourself. You'd likely set the place on fire."

When Marilla had gone Anne looked around her wistfully. The whitewashed walls were so painfully bare and staring that she thought they must ache over their own bareness. The floor was bare, too, except for a round braided mat in the middle such as Anne had never seen before. In one corner was the bed, a high, old-fashioned one, with four dark, low-turned posts. In the other corner was the aforesaid three-cornered table adorned with a fat, red velvet pincushion hard enough to turn the point of the most adventurous pin. Above it hung a little six-by-eight mirror. Midway between table and bed was the window, with an icy white muslin frill over it, and opposite it was the wash-stand. The whole apartment was of a rigidity not to be described in words, but which sent a shiver to the very marrow of Anne's bones. With a sob she hastily discarded her garments, put on the skimpy nightgown and sprang into bed, where she burrowed face downward into the pillow and pulled the clothes over her head. When Marilla came up for the light, various skimpy articles of raiment scattered most untidily over the floor and a certain tempestuous appearance of the bed were the only indications of any presence save her own.

She deliberately picked up Anne's clothes, placed them neatly on a prim yellow chair, and then, taking up the candle, went over to the bed.

" Good-night," she said, a little awkwardly, but not unkindly.

Anne's white face and big eyes appeared over the bedclothes with a startling suddenness.

" How can you call it a *good* night when you know it must be the very worst night I've ever had ? " she said reproachfully.

Then she dived down into invisibility again.

Marilla went slowly down to the kitchen and

proceeded to wash the supper dishes. Matthew was smoking—a sure sign of perturbation of mind. He seldom smoked, for Marilla set her face against it as a filthy habit ; but at certain times and seasons he felt driven to it and then Marilla winked at the practice, realizing that a mere man must have some vent for his emotions.

" Well, this is a pretty kettle of fish," she said wrathfully. " This is what comes of sending word instead of going ourselves. Robert Spencer's folks have twisted that message somehow. One of us will have to drive over and see Mrs Spencer to-morrow, that's certain. This girl will have to be sent back to the asylum."

" Yes, I suppose so," said Matthew reluctantly.

" You *suppose* so ! Don't you know it ? "

" Well now, she's a real nice little thing, Marilla. It's kind of a pity to send her back when she's so set on staying here."

" Matthew Cuthbert, you don't mean to say you think we ought to keep her ! "

Marilla's astonishment could not have been greater if Matthew had expressed a predilection for standing on his head.

" Well now, no, I suppose not—not exactly," stammered Matthew, uncomfortably driven into a corner for his precise meaning. " I suppose—we could hardly be expected to keep her."

" I should say not. What good would she be to us ? "

" We might be some good to her," said Matthew suddenly and unexpectedly.

" Matthew Cuthbert, I believe that child has bewitched you ! I can see as plain as plain that you want to keep her."

" Well now, she's a real interesting little thing,"

persisted Matthew. " You should have heard her talk coming from the station."

" Oh, she can talk fast enough. I saw that at once. It's nothing in her favour, either. I don't like children who have so much to say. I don't want an orphan girl and if I did she isn't the style I'd pick out. There's something I don't understand about her. No, she's got to be despatched straightway back to where she came from."

" I could hire a French boy to help me," said Matthew, " and she'd be company for you."

" I'm not suffering for company," said Marilla shortly. " And I'm not going to keep her."

" Well now, it's just as you say, of course, Marilla," said Matthew, rising and putting his pipe away. " I'm going to bed."

To bed went Matthew. And to bed, when she had put her dishes away, went Marilla, frowning most resolutely. And upstairs, in the east gable, a lonely, heart-hungry, friendless child cried herself to sleep.

CHAPTER IV

MORNING AT GREEN GABLES

IT was broad daylight when Anne awoke and sat up in bed staring confusedly at the window through which a flood of cheery sunshine was pouring and outside of which something white and feathery waved across glimpses of blue sky.

For a moment she could not remember where she was. First came a delightful thrill, as of something very pleasant; then a horrible remembrance. This was Green Gables and they didn't want her because she wasn't a boy!

But it was morning and, yes, it was a cherry-tree in full bloom outside of her window. With a bound she was out of bed and across the floor. She pushed up the sash—it went up stiffly and creakily, as if it hadn't been opened for a long time, which was the case; and it stuck so tight that nothing was needed to hold it up.

Anne dropped on her knees and gazed out into the June morning, her eyes glistening with delight. Oh, wasn't it beautiful? Wasn't it a lovely place? Suppose she wasn't really going to stay here! She would imagine she was. There was scope for imagination here.

A huge cherry-tree grew outside, so close that its boughs tapped against the house, and it was so thick-set with blossoms that hardly a leaf was to be seen. On both sides of the house was a big orchard, one of apple-trees and one of cherry-trees, also showered over with blossoms; and their grass was all sprinkled with dandelions. In the garden below were lilac-trees purple with flowers, and their dizzily sweet fragrance drifted up to the window on the morning wind.

Below the garden a green field lush with clover sloped down to the hollow where the brook ran and where scores of white birches grew, upspringing airily out of an undergrowth suggestive of delightful possibilities in ferns and mosses and woodsy things generally. Beyond it was a hill, green and feathery with spruce and fir ; there was a gap in it where the grey gable end of the little house she had seen from the other side of the Lake of Shining Waters was visible.

Off to the left were the big barns and beyond them, away down over green, low-sloping fields, was a sparkling blue glimpse of sea.

Anne's beauty-loving eyes lingered on it all, taking everything greedily in ; she had looked on so many unlovely places in her life, poor child ; but this was as lovely as anything she had ever dreamed.

She knelt there, lost to everything but the loveliness around her, until she was startled by a hand on her shoulder. Marilla had come in unheard by the small dreamer.

" It's time you were dressed," she said curtly.

Marilla really did not know how to talk to the child, and her uncomfortable ignorance made her crisp and curt when she did not mean to be.

Anne stood up and drew a long breath.

" Oh, isn't it wonderful ? " she said, waving her hand comprehensively at the good world outside.

" It's a big tree," said Marilla, " and it blooms great, but the fruit don't amount to much never—small and wormy."

" Oh, I don't mean just the tree ; of course it's lovely—yes, it's *radiantly* lovely—it blooms as if it meant it—but I meant everything, the garden and the orchard and the brook and the woods, the whole big dear world. Don't you feel as if you just loved the world on a morning like this ? And I can hear the brook laughing all the way up here. Have you ever noticed what cheerful things brooks are ? They're always laughing. Even in winter-time I've heard them under the ice. I'm so glad there's a brook near Green Gables. Perhaps you think it doesn't make any difference to me when you're not going to keep me, but it does. I shall always like to remember that there is a brook at Green Gables even if I never see it again. If there wasn't a brook I'd be *haunted* by the uncomfortable feeling that there ought to be one. I'm not in the depths of despair this morning. I never can be in the morning. Isn't it a splendid thing that there are mornings ? But I feel very sad. I've just been imagining that it was really me you wanted after all and that I was to stay here for ever and ever. It was a great comfort while it lasted. But the worst of imagining things is that the time comes when you have to stop, and that hurts."

" You'd better get dressed and come downstairs and never mind your imaginings," said Marilla as soon as she could get a word in edgewise. " Breakfast is waiting. Wash your face and comb your hair. Leave the window up and turn your bedclothes back over the foot of the bed. Be as smart as you can."

Anne could evidently be smart to some purpose, for she was downstairs in ten minutes' time, with her clothes neatly on, her hair brushed and braided, her face washed, and a comfortable consciousness pervading her soul that she had fulfilled all Marilla's requirements. As a matter of fact, however, she had forgotten to turn back the bedclothes.

" I'm pretty hungry this morning," she announced, as she slipped into the chair Marilla placed for her. " The world doesn't seem such a howling wilderness as

it did last night.   I'm so glad it's a sunshiny morning.
But I like rainy mornings real well, too.   All sorts of
mornings are interesting, don't you think ?   You don't
know what's going to happen through the day, and
there's so much scope for imagination.   But I'm glad
it's not rainy to-day because it's easier to be cheerful
and bear up under affliction on a sunshiny day.   I feel
that I have a good deal to bear up under.   It's all very
well to read about sorrows and imagine yourself living
through them heroically, but it's not so nice when you
really come to have them, is it ? "

" For pity's sake hold your tongue," said Marilla.
" You talk entirely too much for a little girl."

Thereupon Anne held her tongue so obediently and
thoroughly that her continued silence made Marilla
rather nervous, as if in the presence of something not
exactly natural.   Matthew also held his tongue—but
this at least was natural—so that the meal was a very
silent one.

As it progressed Anne became more and more ab-
stracted, eating mechanically, with her big eyes fixed
unswervingly and unseeingly on the sky outside the
window.   This made Marilla more nervous than ever ;
she had an uncomfortable feeling that while this odd
child's body might be there at the table, her spirit was
far away in some remote airy cloudland, borne aloft
on the wings of imagination.   Who would want such
a child about the place ?

Yet Matthew wished to keep her, of all unaccountable things !   Marilla felt that he wanted it just as
much this morning as he had the night before, and that
he would go on wanting it.   That was Matthew's way
—take a whim into his head and cling to it with the
most amazing silent persistency—a persistency ten
times more potent and effectual in its very silence than
if he had talked it out.

When the meal was ended, Anne came out of her reverie and offered to wash the dishes.

" Can you wash dishes right ? " asked Marilla distrustfully.

" Pretty well. I'm better at looking after children, though. I've had so much experience at that. It's such a pity you haven't any here for me to look after."

" I don't feel as if I wanted any more children to look after than I've got at present. *You're* problem enough in all conscience. What's to be done with you I don't know. Matthew is a most ridiculous man."

" I think he's lovely," said Anne reproachfully. " He is so very sympathetic. He didn't mind how much I talked—he seemed to like it. I felt that he was a kindred spirit as soon as ever I saw him."

" You're both queer enough, if that's what you mean by kindred spirits," said Marilla with a sniff. " Yes, you may wash the dishes. Take plenty of hot water, and be sure you dry them well. I've got enough to attend to this morning for I'll have to drive over to White Sands in the afternoon and see Mrs Spencer. You'll come with me and we'll settle what's to be done with you. After you've finished the dishes go upstairs and make your bed."

Anne washed the dishes deftly enough, as Marilla, who kept a sharp eye on the process, discerned. Later on she made her bed less successfully, for she had never learned the art of wrestling with a feather tick. But it was done somehow and smoothed down ; and then Marilla, to get rid of her, told her she might go out-of-doors and amuse herself until dinner-time.

Anne flew to the door, face alight, eyes glowing. On the very threshold she stopped short, wheeled about, came back and sat down by the table, light and glow as effectually blotted out as if someone had clapped an extinguisher on her.

" What's the matter now ? " demanded Marilla.

" I don't dare go out," said Anne, in the tone of a martyr relinquishing all earthly joys. " If I can't stay here there is no use in my loving Green Gables. And if I go out there and get acquainted with all those trees and flowers and the orchard and the brook I'll not be able to help loving it. It's hard enough now, so I won't make it any harder. I want to go out so much—everything seems to be calling to me, ' Anne, Anne, come out to us. Anne, Anne, we want a play-mate '—but it's better not. There is no use in loving things if you have to be torn from them, is there ? And it's *so* hard to keep from loving things, isn't it ? That was why I was so glad when I thought I was going to live here. I thought I'd have so many things to love and nothing to hinder me. But that brief dream is over. I am resigned to my fate now, so I don't think I'll go out for fear I'll get unresigned again. What is the name of that geranium on the window-sill, please ?"

" That's the apple-scented geranium."

" Oh, I don't mean that sort of a name. I mean just a name you gave it yourself. Didn't you give it a name ? May I give it one then ? May I call it— let me see—Bonny would do—may I call it Bonny while I'm here ? Oh, do let me ! "

" Goodness, I don't care. But where on earth is the sense of naming a geranium ? "

" Oh, I like things to have handles even if they are only geraniums. It makes them seem more like people. How do you know but that it hurts a geranium's feel-ings just to be called a geranium and nothing else ? You wouldn't like to be called nothing but a woman all the time. Yes, I shall call it Bonny. I named that cherry-tree outside my bedroom window this morning. I called it Snow Queen because it was so white. Of course, it won't always be in blossom, but one can imagine that it is, can't one ? "

" I never in all my life saw or heard anything to equal her," muttered Marilla, beating a retreat down cellar after potatoes. " She *is* kind of interesting, as Matthew says. I can feel already that I'm wondering what on earth she'll say next. She'll be casting a spell over me, too. She's cast it over Matthew. That look he gave me when he went out said everything he said or hinted last night over again. I wish he was like other men and would talk things out. A body could answer back then and argue him into reason. But what's to be done with a man who just *looks* ? "

Anne had relapsed into reverie, with her chin in her hands and her eyes on the sky, when Marilla returned from her cellar pilgrimage. There Marilla left her until the early dinner was on the table.

" I suppose I can have the mare and buggy this afternoon, Matthew ? " said Marilla.

Matthew nodded and looked wistfully at Anne. Marilla intercepted the look and said grimly :

" I'm going to drive over to White Sands and settle this thing. I'll take Anne with me and Mrs Spencer will probably make arrangements to send her back to Nova Scotia at once. I'll set your tea out for you and I'll be home in time to milk the cows."

Still Matthew said nothing and Marilla had a sense of having wasted words and breath. There is nothing more aggravating than a man who won't talk back— unless it is a woman who won't.

Matthew hitched the sorrel into the buggy in due time and Marilla and Anne set off. Matthew opened the yard gate for them, and as they drove slowly through, he said, to nobody in particular as it seemed :

" Little Jerry Buote from the Creek was here this

morning, and I told him I guessed I'd hire him for the summer."

Marilla made no reply, but she hit the unlucky sorrel such a vicious clip with the whip that the fat mare, unused to such treatment, whizzed indignantly down the lane at an alarming pace. Marilla looked back once as the buggy bounced along and saw that aggravating Matthew leaning over the gate, looking wistfully after them.

CHAPTER V

ANNE'S HISTORY

"DO you know," said Anne confidentially, "I've made up my mind to enjoy this drive. It's been my experience that you can nearly always enjoy things if you make up your mind firmly that you will. Of course, you must make it up *firmly*. I am not going to think about going back to the asylum while we're having our drive. I'm just going to think about the drive. Oh, look, there's one little early wild rose out! Isn't it lovely? Don't you think it must be glad to be a rose? Wouldn't it be nice if roses could talk? I'm sure they could tell us such lovely things. And isn't pink the most bewitching colour in the world? I love it, but I can't wear it. Redheaded people can't wear pink, not even in imagination. Did you ever know of anybody whose hair was red when she was young, but got to be another colour when she grew up?"

"No, I don't know as I ever did," said Marilla mercilessly, "and I shouldn't think it likely to happen in your case, either."

Anne sighed.

"Well, that is another hope gone. My life is a perfect graveyard of buried hopes. That's a sentence I read in a book once, and I say it over to comfort myself whenever I'm disappointed in anything."

"I don't see where the comforting comes in myself," said Marilla.

"Why, because it sounds so nice and romantic, just as if I were a heroine in a book, you know. I am so fond of romantic things, and a graveyard full of buried hopes is about as romantic a thing as one can imagine, isn't it ? I'm rather glad I have one. Are we going across the Lake of Shining Waters to-day ? "

" We're not going over Barry's pond, if that's what you mean by your Lake of Shining Waters. We're going by the shore road."

" Shore road sounds nice," said Anne dreamily. " Is it as nice as it sounds ? Just when you said ' shore road ' I saw it in a picture in my mind, as quick as that ! And White Sands is a pretty name, too ; but I don't like it as well as Avonlea. Avonlea is a lovely name. It just sounds like music. How far is it to White Sands ? "

" It's five miles ; and as you're evidently bent on talking you might as well talk to some purpose by telling me what you know about yourself."

" Oh, what I *know* about myself isn't really worth telling," said Anne eagerly. " If you'll only let me tell you what I *imagine* about myself you'll think it ever so much more interesting."

" No, I don't want any of your imaginings. Just you stick to bald facts. Begin at the beginning. Where were you born and how old are you ? "

" I was eleven last March," said Anne, resigning herself to bald facts with a little sigh. " And I was born in Bolingbroke, Nova Scotia. My father's name was Walter Shirley, and he was a teacher in the Bolingbroke High School. My mother's name was Bertha Shirley. Aren't Walter and Bertha lovely names ? I'm so glad my parents had nice names. It would be a real disgrace to have a father named—well, say Jedediah, wouldn't it ? "

" I guess it doesn't matter what a person's name is as long as he behaves himself," said Marilla, feeling herself called upon to inculcate a good and useful moral.

" Well, I don't know." Anne looked thoughtful.
" I read in a book once that a rose by any other name
would smell as sweet, but I've never been able to
believe it. I don't believe a rose *would* be as nice if
it was called a thistle or a skunk-cabbage. I suppose
my father could have been a good man even if he had
been called Jedediah ; but I'm sure it would have been
a cross. Well, my mother was a teacher in the High
School, too, but when she married father she gave up
teaching, of course. A husband was enough responsibility. Mrs Thomas said that they were a pair of
babies and as poor as church mice. They went to
live in a weeny-teeny little yellow house in Bolingbroke.
I've never seen that house, but I've imagined it thousands of times. I think it must have had honeysuckle
over the parlour window and lilacs in the front yard
and lilies of the valley just inside the gate. Yes, and
muslin curtains in all the windows. Muslin curtains
give a house such an air. I was born in that house.
Mrs Thomas said I was the homeliest baby she ever
saw, I was so scrawny and tiny and nothing but eyes,
but that mother thought I was perfectly beautiful.
I should think a mother would be a better judge than
a poor woman who came in to scrub, wouldn't you ?
I'm glad she was satisfied with me anyhow ; I would
feel so sad if I thought I was a disappointment to her
—because she didn't live very long after that, you see.
She died of fever when I was just three months old.
I do wish she'd lived long enough for me to remember
calling her mother. I think it would be so sweet to
say ' mother,' don't you ? And father died four days
afterwards from fever, too. That left me an orphan
and folks were at their wits' end, so Mrs Thomas said,
what to do with me. You see, nobody wanted me
even then. It seems to be my fate. Father and
mother had both come from places far away and it was

well known they hadn't any relatives living. Finally
Mrs Thomas said she'd take me, though she was poor
and had a drunken husband. She brought me up by
hand. Do you know if there is anything in being
brought up by hand that ought to make people who
are brought up that way better than other people?
Because whenever I was naughty Mrs Thomas would
ask me how I could be such a bad girl when she had
brought me up by hand—reproachful-like.

" Mr and Mrs Thomas moved away from Bolingbroke
to Marysville, and I lived with them until I was eight
years old. I helped look after the Thomas children—
there were four of them younger than me—and I can
tell you they took a lot of looking after. Then Mr
Thomas was killed falling under a train, and his mother
offered to take Mrs Thomas and the children, but she
didn't want me. Mrs Thomas was at *her* wits' end,
so she said, what to do with me. Then Mrs Hammond
from up the river came down and said she'd take me,
seeing I was handy with children, and I went up the
river to live with her in a little clearing among the
stumps. It was a very lonesome place. I'm sure I
could never have lived there if I hadn't an imagination.
Mr Hammond worked a little saw-mill up there, and
Mrs Hammond had eight children. She had twins
three times. I like babies in moderation, but twins
three times in succession is *too much*. I told Mrs Hammond so firmly, when the last pair came. I used to
get so dreadfully tired carrying them about.

" I lived up river with Mrs Hammond over two
years, and then Mr Hammond died and Mrs Hammond
broke up housekeeping. She divided her children
among her relatives and went to the States. I had to
go to the asylum at Hopeton, because nobody would
take me. They didn't want me at the asylum, either;
they said they were overcrowded as it was. But they

had to take me and I was there four months until Mrs Spencer came."

Anne finished up with another sigh, of relief this time. Evidently she did not like talking about her experiences in a world that had not wanted her.

" Did you ever go to school ? " demanded Marilla, turning the sorrel mare down the shore road.

" Not a great deal. I went a little the last year I stayed with Mrs Thomas. When I went up river we were so far from a school that I couldn't walk it in winter and there was vacation in summer, so I could only go in the spring and fall. But of course I went while I was at the asylum. I can read pretty well and I know ever so many pieces of poetry off by heart—' The Battle of Hohenlinden ' and ' Edinburgh after Flodden,' and ' Bingen on the Rhine,' and lots of the ' Lady of the Lake ' and most of ' The Seasons,' by James Thomson. Don't you just love poetry that gives you a crinkly feeling up and down your back ? There is a piece in the Fifth Reader—' The Downfall of Poland '—that is just full of thrills. Of course, I wasn't in the Fifth Reader—I was only in the Fourth—but the big girls used to lend me theirs to read."

" Were those women—Mrs Thomas and Mrs Hammond—good to you ? " asked Marilla, looking at Anne out of the corner of her eye.

" O-o-o-h," faltered Anne. Her sensitive little face suddenly flushed scarlet and embarrassment sat on her brow. " Oh, they *meant* to be—I know they meant to be just as good and kind as possible. And when people mean to be good to you, you don't mind very much when they're not quite—always. They had a good deal to worry them, you know. It's very trying to have a drunken husband, you see ; and it must be very trying to have twins three times in suc-

cession, don't you think ?   But I feel sure they meant
to be good to me."

Marilla asked no more questions.   Anne gave herself
up to a silent rapture over the shore road and Marilla
guided the sorrel abstractedly while she pondered
deeply.   Pity was suddenly stirring in her heart for
the child.   What a starved, unloved life she had had
—a life of drudgery and poverty and neglect ;   for
Marilla was shrewd enough to read between the lines
of Anne's history and divine the truth.   No wonder
she had been so delighted at the prospect of a real
home.   It was a pity she had to be sent back.   What
if she, Marilla, should indulge Matthew's unaccountable
whim and let her stay ?   He was set on it ;   and the
child seemed a nice, teachable little thing.

" She's got too much to say," thought Marilla, " but
she might be trained out of that.   And there's nothing
rude or slangy in what she does say.   She's ladylike.
It's likely her people were nice folks."

The shore road was " woodsy and wild and lonesome."   On the right hand, scrub firs, their spirits
quite unbroken by long years of tussle with the gulf
winds, grew thickly.   On the left were the steep red
sandstone cliffs, so near the track in places that a
mare of less steadiness than the sorrel might have tried
the nerves of the people behind her.   Down at the
base of the cliffs were heaps of surf-worn rocks or little
sandy coves inlaid with pebbles as with ocean jewels ;
beyond lay the sea, shimmering and blue, and over it
soared the gulls, their pinions flashing silvery in the
sunlight.

" Isn't the sea wonderful ? " said Anne, rousing from
a long, wide-eyed silence.   " Once, when I lived in
Marysville, Mr Thomas hired an express-wagon and
took us all to spend the day at the shore ten miles
away.   I enjoyed every moment of that day, even if

I had to look after the children all the time. I lived it over in happy dreams for years. But this shore is nicer than the Marysville shore. Aren't those gulls splendid ? Would you like to be a gull ? I think I would—that is, if I couldn't be a human girl. Don't you think it would be nice to wake up at sunrise and swoop down over the water and away out over that lovely blue all day ; and then at night to fly back to one's nest ? Oh, I can just imagine myself doing it. What big house is that just ahead, please ? "

" That's the White Sands Hotel. Mr Kirke runs it, but the season hasn't begun yet. There are heaps of Americans come there for the summer. They think this shore is just about right."

" I was afraid it might be Mrs Spencer's place," said Anne mournfully. " I don't want to get there. Somehow, it will seem like the end of everything."

CHAPTER VI

MARILLA MAKES UP HER MIND

GET there they did, however, in due season. Mrs Spencer lived in a big yellow house at White Sands Cove, and she came to the door with surprise and welcome mingled on her benevolent face.

" Dear, dear," she exclaimed, " you're the last folks I was looking for to-day, but I'm real glad to see you. You'll put your horse in ? And how are you, Anne ? "

" I'm as well as can be expected, thank you," said Anne smilelessly. A blight seemed to have descended on her.

" I suppose we'll stay a little while to rest the mare," said Marilla, " but I promised Matthew I'd be home early. The fact is, Mrs Spencer, there's been a queer mistake somewhere, and I've come over to see where it is. We sent word, Matthew and I, for you to bring us a boy from the asylum. We told your brother Robert to tell you we wanted a boy ten or eleven years old."

" Marilla Cuthbert, you don't say so ! " said Mrs Spencer in distress. " Why, Robert sent the word down by his daughter Nancy and she said you wanted a girl—didn't she, Flora Jane ? " appealing to her daughter who had come out to the steps.

" She certainly did, Miss Cuthbert," corroborated Flora Jane earnestly.

" I'm dreadfully sorry," said Mrs Spencer. " It is too bad ; but it certainly wasn't my fault, you see, Miss

Cuthbert. I did the best I could and I thought I was following your instructions. Nancy is a terrible flighty thing. I've often had to scold her well for her heedlessness."

" It was our own fault," said Marilla resignedly. " We should have come to you ourselves and not left an important message to be passed along by word of mouth in that fashion. Anyhow, the mistake has been made and the only thing to do now is to set it right. Can we send the child back to the asylum ? I suppose they'll take her back, won't they ? "

" I suppose so," said Mrs Spencer thoughtfully, " but I don't think it will be necessary to send her back. Mrs Peter Blewett was up here yesterday, and she was saying to me how much she wished she'd sent by me for a little girl to help her. Mrs Peter has a large family, you know, and she finds it hard to get help. Anne will be the very girl for her. I call it positively providential."

Marilla did not look as if she thought Providence had much to do with the matter. Here was an unexpectedly good chance to get this unwelcome orphan off her hands, and she did not even feel grateful for it.

She knew Mrs Peter Blewett only by sight as a small, shrewish-faced woman without an ounce of superfluous flesh on her bones. But she had heard of her. " A terrible worker and driver," Mrs Peter was said to be ; and discharged servant girls told fearsome tales of her temper and stinginess, and her family of pert, quarrelsome children. Marilla felt a qualm of conscience at the thought of handing Anne over to her tender mercies.

" Well, I'll go in and we'll talk the matter over," she said.

" And if there isn't Mrs Peter coming up the lane this blessed minute ! " exclaimed Mrs Spencer, bustling her guests through the hall into the parlour, where a deadly chill struck on them as if the air had been strained so long through dark green, closely drawn blinds that it had lost every particle of warmth it had ever possessed. "That is real lucky, for we can settle the matter right away. Take the armchair, Miss Cuthbert. Anne, you sit here on the ottoman and don't wriggle. Let me take your hats. Flora Jane, go out and put the kettle on. Good afternoon, Mrs Blewett. We were just saying how fortunate it was you happened along. Let me introduce you two ladies. Mrs Blewett, Miss Cuthbert. Please excuse me for just a moment. I forgot to tell Flora Jane to take the buns out of the oven."

Mrs Spencer whisked away, after pulling up the blinds. Anne, sitting mutely on the ottoman, with her hands clasped tightly in her lap, stared at Mrs Blewett as one fascinated. Was she to be given into the keeping of this sharp-faced, sharp-eyed woman? She felt a lump coming up in her throat and her eyes smarted painfully. She was beginning to be afraid she couldn't keep the tears back when Mrs Spencer returned, flushed and beaming, quite capable of taking any and every difficulty, physical, mental or spiritual, into consideration and settling it out of hand.

"It seems there's been a mistake about this little girl, Mrs Blewett," she said. "I was under the impression that Mr and Miss Cuthbert wanted a little girl to adopt. I was certainly told so. But it seems it was a boy they wanted. So if you're still of the same mind you were yesterday, I think she'll be just the thing for you."

Mrs Blewett darted her eyes over Anne from head to foot.

"How old are you and what's your name?" she demanded.

" Anne Shirley," faltered the shrinking child, not daring to make any stipulations regarding the spelling thereof, " and I'm eleven years old."

" Humph ! You don't look as if there was much to you. But you're wiry. I don't know but the wiry ones are the best after all. Well, if I take you you'll have to be a good girl, you know—good and smart and respectful. I'll expect you to earn your keep, and no mistake about that. Yes, I suppose I might as well take her off your hands, Miss Cuthbert. The baby's awful fractious, and I'm clean worn out attending to him. If you like I can take her right home now."

Marilla looked at Anne and softened at sight of the child's pale face with its look of mute misery—the misery of a helpless little creature who finds itself once more caught in the trap from which it had escaped. Marilla felt an uncomfortable conviction that, if she denied the appeal of that look, it would haunt her to her dying day. Moreover, she did not fancy Mrs Blewett. To hand a sensitive, " high-strung " child over to such a woman ! No, she could not take the responsibility of doing that !

" Well, I don't know," she said slowly. " I didn't say that Matthew and I had absolutely decided that we wouldn't keep her. In fact, I may say that Matthew is disposed to keep her. I just came over to find out how the mistake had occurred. I think I'd better take her home again and talk it over with Matthew. I feel that I oughtn't to decide on anything without consulting him. If we make up our mind not to keep her we'll bring or send her over to you to-morrow night. If we don't you may know that she is going to stay with us. Will that suit you, Mrs Blewett ? "

" I suppose it'll have to," said Mrs Blewett ungraciously.

During Marilla's speech a sunrise had been dawning on Anne's face. First the look of despair faded out ; then came a faint flush of hope ; her eyes grew deep and bright as morning stars. The child was quite transfigured ; and, a moment later, when Mrs Spencer and Mrs Blewett went out in quest of a recipe the latter had come to borrow, she sprang up and flew across the room to Marilla.

" Oh, Miss Cuthbert, did you really say that perhaps you would let me stay at Green Gables ? " she said, in a breathless whisper, as if speaking aloud might shatter the glorious possibility. " Did you really say it ? Or did I only imagine that you did ? "

" I think you'd better learn to control that imagination of yours, Anne, if you can't distinguish between what is real and what isn't," said Marilla crossly. " Yes, you did hear me say just that and no more. It isn't decided yet and perhaps we will conclude to let Mrs Blewett take you after all. She certainly needs you much more than I do."

" I'd rather go back to the asylum than go to live with her," said Anne passionately. " She looks exactly like a—like a gimlet."

Marilla smothered a smile under the conviction that Anne must be reproved for such a speech.

" A little girl like you should be ashamed of talking so about a lady and a stranger," she said severely. " Go back and sit down quietly and hold your tongue, and behave as a good girl should."

" I'll try to do and be anything you want me, if you'll only keep me," said Anne, returning meekly to her ottoman.

When they arrived back at Green Gables that evening Matthew met them in the lane. Marilla from afar had noted him prowling along it, and guessed his motive. She was prepared for the relief she read in his face when he saw that she had at least brought Anne back with her. But she said nothing to him, relative to the affair, until they were both out in the yard behind the barn milking the cows. Then she briefly told him Anne's history and the result of the interview with Mrs Spencer.

" I wouldn't give a dog I liked to that Blewett woman," said Matthew with unusual vim.

" I don't fancy her style myself," admitted Marilla, " but it's that or keeping her ourselves, Matthew. And, since you seem to want her, I suppose I'm willing —or have to be. I've been thinking over the idea until I've got kind of used to it. It seems a sort of duty. I've never brought up a child, especially a girl, and I dare say I'll make a terrible mess of it. But I'll do my best. So far as I'm concerned, Matthew, she may stay."

Matthew's shy face was a glow of delight.

" Well now, I reckoned you'd come to see it in that light, Marilla," he said. " She's such an interesting little thing."

" It'd be more to the point if you could say she was a useful little thing," retorted Marilla, " but I'll make it my business to see she's trained to be that. And mind, Matthew, you're not to go interfering with my methods. Perhaps an old maid doesn't know much about bringing up a child, but I guess she knows more than an old bachelor. So you just leave me to manage her. When I fail it'll be time enough to put your oar in."

" There, there, Marilla, you can have your own way," said Matthew reassuringly. " Only be as good and kind to her as you can be without spoiling her. I kind of think she's one of the sort you can do anything with if you only get her to love you."

Marilla sniffed, to express her contempt for Matthew's opinions concerning anything feminine, and walked off to the dairy with the pails.

" I won't tell her to-night that she can stay," she reflected, as she strained the milk into the creamers. " She'd be so excited that she wouldn't sleep a wink. Marilla Cuthbert, you're fairly in for it.   Did you ever suppose you'd see the day when you'd be adopting an orphan girl ?   It's surprising enough ; but not so surprising as that Matthew should be at the bottom of it, him that always seemed to have such a mortal dread of little girls.   Anyhow, we've decided on the experiment and goodness only knows what will come of it."

CHAPTER VII

ANNE SAYS HER PRAYERS

WHEN Marilla took Anne up to bed that night she said stiffly :

" Now, Anne, I noticed last night that you threw your clothes all about the floor when you took them off. That is a very untidy habit, and I can't allow it at all. As soon as you take off any article of clothing fold it neatly and place it on the chair. I haven't any use at all for little girls who aren't neat."

" I was so harrowed up in my mind last night that I didn't think about my clothes at all," said Anne. " I'll fold them nicely to-night. They always made us do that at the asylum. Half the time, though, I'd forget, I'd be in such a hurry to get into bed, nice and quiet, and imagine things."

" You'll have to remember a little better if you stay here," admonished Marilla. " There, that looks something like. Say your prayers now and get into bed."

" I never say any prayers," announced Anne.

Marilla looked horrified astonishment.

" Why, Anne, what do you mean ? Were you never taught to say your prayers ? God always wants little girls to say their prayers. Don't you know who God is, Anne ? "

" ' God is a spirit, infinite, eternal and unchangeable, in His being, wisdom, power, holiness, justice, goodness and truth,' " responded Anne promptly and glibly.

Marilla looked rather relieved.

" So you do know something then, thank goodness ! You're not quite a heathen. Where did you learn that ? "

" Oh, at the asylum Sunday school. They made us learn the whole catechism. I liked it pretty well. There's something splendid about some of the words. ' Infinite, eternal and unchangeable.' Isn't that grand? It has such a roll to it—just like a big organ playing. You couldn't quite call it poetry, I suppose, but it sounds a lot like it, doesn't it ? "

" We're not talking about poetry, Anne—we are talking about saying your prayers. Don't you know it's a terrible wicked thing not to say your prayers every night ? I'm afraid you are a very bad little girl."

" You'd find it easier to be bad than good if you had red hair," said Anne reproachfully. " People who haven't red hair don't know what trouble is. Mrs Thomas told me that God made my hair red *on purpose*, and I've never cared about Him since. And anyhow, I'd always be too tired at night to bother saying prayers. People who have to look after twins can't be expected to say their prayers. Now, do you honestly think they can ? "

Marilla decided that Anne's religious training must be begun at once. Plainly there was no time to be lost.

" You must say your prayers while you are under my roof, Anne."

" Why, of course, if you want me to," assented Anne cheerfully. " I'd do anything to oblige you. But you'll have to tell me what to say for this once. After I get into bed I'll imagine out a real nice prayer to say always. I believe that it will be quite interesting, now that I come to think of it."

" You must kneel down," said Marilla in embarrassment.

Anne knelt at Marilla's knee and looked up gravely.

" Why must people kneel down to pray ? If I really wanted to pray I'll tell you what I'd do. I'd go out into a great big field all alone or into the deep, deep woods, and I'd look up into the sky—up—up—up—into that lovely blue sky that looks as if there was no end to its blueness. And then I'd just *feel* a prayer. Well, I'm ready. What am I to say ? "

Marilla felt more embarrassed than ever. She had intended to teach Anne the childish classic, " Now I lay me down to sleep." But she had, as I have told you, the glimmerings of a sense of humour—which is simply another name for a sense of the fitness of things ; and it suddenly occurred to her that that simple little prayer, sacred to white-robed childhood lisping at motherly knees, was entirely unsuited to this freckled witch of a girl who knew and cared nothing about God's love, since she had never had it translated to her through the medium of human love.

" You're old enough to pray for yourself, Anne," she said finally. " Just thank God for your blessings and ask Him humbly for the things you want."

" Well, I'll do my best," promised Anne, burying her face in Marilla's lap. " Gracious heavenly Father —that's the way the ministers say it in church, so I suppose it's all right in a private prayer, isn't it ? " she interjected, lifting her head for a moment. " Gracious heavenly Father, I thank Thee for the White Way of Delight and the Lake of Shining Waters and Bonny and the Snow Queen. I'm really extremely grateful for them. And that's all the blessings I can think of just now to thank Thee for. As for the things I want, they're so numerous that it would take a great deal of time to name them all, so I will only mention the two most important. Please let me stay at Green Gables ; and please let me be good-looking when I grow up. I remain,

" Yours respectfully,

" ANNE SHIRLEY."

" There, did I do it all right ? " she asked eagerly, getting up. " I could have made it much more flowery if I'd had a little more time to think it over."

Poor Marilla was only preserved from complete collapse by remembering that it was not irreverence, but simply spiritual ignorance on the part of Anne that was responsible for this extraordinary petition. She tucked the child up in bed, mentally vowing that she should be taught a prayer the very next day, and was leaving the room with the light when Anne called her back.

" I've just thought of it now. I should have said ' Amen ' in place of ' yours respectfully,' shouldn't I ?—the way the ministers do. I'd forgotten it, but I felt a prayer should be finished off in some way, so I put in the other. Do you suppose it will make any difference ? "

" I—I don't suppose it will," said Marilla. " Go to sleep now like a good child. Good night."

" I can say good night to-night with a clear conscience," said Anne, cuddling luxuriously down among her pillows.

Marilla retreated to the kitchen, set the candle firmly on the table, and glared at Matthew.

" Matthew Cuthbert, it's about time somebody adopted that child and taught her something. She's next door to a perfect heathen. Will you believe that she never said a prayer in her life till to-night ? I'll send to the manse to-morrow and borrow the Peep of Day series, that's what I'll do. And she shall go to Sunday school just as soon as I can get some suitable clothes made for her. I foresee that I shall have my hands full. Well, well, we can't get through this world without our share of trouble. I've had a pretty easy life of it so far, but my time has come at last and I suppose I'll just have to make the best of it."

CHAPTER VIII

ANNE'S BRINGING-UP IS BEGUN

FOR reasons best known to herself, Marilla did not tell Anne that she was to stay at Green Gables until the next afternoon. During the forenoon she kept the child busy with various tasks and watched over her with a keen eye while she did them. By noon she had concluded that Anne was smart and obedient, willing to work and quick to learn ; her most serious shortcoming seemed to be a tendency to fall into daydreams in the middle of a task and forget all about it until such time as she was sharply recalled to earth by a reprimand or a catastrophe.

When Anne had finished washing the dinner dishes she suddenly confronted Marilla with the air and expression of one desperately determined to learn the worst. Her thin little body trembled from head to foot ; her face flushed and her eyes dilated until they were almost black ; she clasped her hands tightly and said in an imploring voice :

" Oh, please, Miss Cuthbert, won't you tell me if you are going to send me away or not ? I've tried to be patient all the morning, but I really feel that I cannot bear not knowing any longer. It's a dreadful feeling. Please tell me."

" You haven't scalded the dish-cloth in clean hot water as I told you to do," said Marilla immovably. " Just go and do it before you ask any more questions, Anne."

Anne went and attended to the dish-cloth. Then she returned to Marilla and fastened imploring eyes on the latter's face.

" Well," said Marilla, unable to find any excuse for deferring her explanation longer, " I suppose I might as well tell you.   Matthew and I have decided to keep you—that is, if you will try to be a good little girl and show yourself grateful.   Why, child, whatever is the matter ? "

" I'm crying," said Anne in a tone of bewilderment. " I can't think why.   I'm glad as glad can be.   Oh, *glad* doesn't seem the right word at all.   I was glad about the White Way and the cherry blossoms—but this !   Oh, it's something more than glad.   I'm so happy.   I'll try to be so good.   It will be uphill work, I expect, for Mrs Thomas often told me I was desperately wicked.   However, I'll do my very best. But can you tell me why I'm crying ? "

" I suppose it's because you're all excited and worked up," said Marilla disapprovingly.   " Sit down on that chair and try to calm yourself.   I'm afraid you both cry and laugh far too easily.   Yes, you can stay here and we will try to do right by you.   You must go to school ; but it's only a fortnight till vacation, so it isn't worth while for you to start before it opens again in September."

" What am I to call you ? " asked Anne.   " Shall I always say Miss Cuthbert ?   Can I call you Aunt Marilla ? "

" No ; you'll call me just plain Marilla.   I'm not used to being called Miss Cuthbert and it would make me nervous."

" It sounds awfully disrespectful to say just Marilla," protested Anne.

" I guess there'll be nothing disrespectful in it if you're careful to speak respectfully.   Everybody, young and old, in Avonlea calls me Marilla except the minister.   He says Miss Cuthbert—when he thinks of it."

" I'd love to call you Aunt Marilla," said Anne
wistfully. " I've never had an aunt or any relation
at all—not even a grandmother. It would make me
feel as if I really belonged to you. Can't I call you
Aunt Marilla ? "

" No. I'm not your aunt and I don't believe in
calling people names that don't belong to them."

" But we could imagine you were my aunt."

" I couldn't," said Marilla grimly.

" Do you never imagine things different from what
they really are ? " asked Anne wide-eyed.

" No."

" Oh ! " Anne drew a long breath. " Oh, Miss—
Marilla, how much you miss ! "

" I don't believe in imagining things different from
what they really are," retorted Marilla. " When the
Lord puts us in certain circumstances He doesn't mean
for us to imagine them away. And that reminds me.
Go into the sitting-room, Anne—be sure your feet are
clean and don't let any flies in—and bring me out the
illustrated card that's on the mantelpiece. The Lord's
Prayer is on it and you'll devote your spare time this
afternoon to learning it off by heart. There's to be
no more of such praying as I heard last night."

" I suppose I was very awkward," said Anne apologetically, " but then, you see, I'd never had any practice. You couldn't really expect a person to pray very
well the first time she tried, could you ? I thought
out a splendid prayer after I went to bed, just as I
promised you I would. It was nearly as long as a
minister's and so poetical. But would you believe it ?
I couldn't remember one word when I woke up this
morning. And I'm afraid I'll never be able to think
out another one as good. Somehow, things never are
so good when they're thought out a second time. Have
you ever noticed that ? "

" Here is something for you to notice, Anne.   When
I tell you to do a thing I want you to obey me at once
and not stand stock-still and discourse about it.   Just
you go and do as I bid you."

Anne promptly departed for the sitting-room across
the hall ; she failed to return ; after waiting ten
minutes Marilla laid down her knitting and marched
after her with a grim expression.   She found Anne
standing motionless before a picture hanging on the
wall between the two windows, with her hands clasped
behind her, her face uplifted, and her eyes astar with
dreams.   The white and green light strained through
apple-trees and clustering vines outside fell over the
rapt little figure with a half-unearthly radiance.

" Anne, whatever are you thinking of ? " demanded
Marilla sharply.

Anne came back to earth with a start.

" That," she said, pointing to the picture—a rather
vivid chromo entitled, " Christ Blessing Little Children "—" and I was just imagining I was one of them—
that I was the little girl in the blue dress, standing off
by herself in the corner as if she didn't belong to anybody, like me.   She looks lonely and sad, don't you
think ?   I guess she hadn't any father or mother of
her own.   But she wanted to be blessed, too, so she
just crept shyly up on the outside of the crowd, hoping
nobody would notice her—except Him.   I'm sure I
know just how she felt.   Her heart must have beat and
her hands must have got cold, like mine did when I
asked you if I could stay.   She was afraid He mightn't
notice her.   But it's likely He did, don't you think ?
I've been trying to imagine it all out—her edging a
little nearer all the time until she was quite close to
Him ; and then He would look at her and put His
hand on her hair and oh, such a thrill of joy would
run over her !   But I wish the artist hadn't painted

Him so sorrowful-looking. All His pictures are like that, if you've noticed. But I don't believe He could really have looked so sad or the children would have been afraid of Him."

" Anne," said Marilla, wondering why she had not broken into this speech long before, " you shouldn't talk that way. It's irreverent—positively irreverent."

Anne's eyes marvelled.

" Why, I felt just as reverent as could be. I'm sure I didn't mean to be irreverent."

" Well, I don't suppose you did—but it doesn't sound right to talk so familiarly about such things. And another thing, Anne, when I send you after something you're to bring it at once and not fall into mooning and imagining before pictures. Remember that. Take that card and come right to the kitchen. Now, sit down in the corner and learn that prayer off by heart."

Anne set the card up against the jugful of apple blossoms she had brought in to decorate the dinner-table—Marilla had eyed that decoration askance, but had said nothing—propped her chin on her hands, and fell to studying it intently for several silent minutes.

" I like this," she announced at length. " It's beautiful. I've heard it before—I heard the superintendent of the asylum Sunday school say it over once. But I didn't like it then. He had such a cracked voice and he prayed it so mournfully. I really felt sure he thought praying was a disagreeable duty. This isn't poetry, but it makes me feel just the same way poetry does. ' Our Father which art in heaven, hallowed be Thy name.' That is just like a line of music. Oh, I'm so glad you thought of making me learn this, Miss —Marilla."

" Well, learn it, and hold your tongue," said Marilla shortly.

Anne tipped the vase of apple blossoms near enough to bestow a soft kiss on a pink-cupped bud, and then studied diligently for some moments longer.

" Marilla," she demanded presently, " do you think that I shall ever have a bosom friend in Avonlea ? "

" A—a what kind of a friend ? "

" A bosom friend—an intimate friend, you know—a really kindred spirit to whom I can confide my inmost soul. I've dreamed of meeting her all my life. I never really supposed I would, but so many of my loveliest dreams have come true all at once that perhaps this one will, too. Do you think it's possible ? "

" Diana Barry lives over at Orchard Slope, and she's about your age. She's a very nice little girl, and perhaps she will be a playmate for you when she comes home. She's visiting her aunt over at Carmody just now. You'll have to be careful how you behave yourself, though. Mrs Barry is a very particular woman. She won't let Diana play with any little girl who isn't nice and good."

Anne looked at Marilla through the apple blossoms, her eyes aglow with interest.

" What is Diana like ? Her hair isn't red, is it ? Oh, I hope not. It's bad enough to have red hair myself, but I positively couldn't endure it in a bosom friend."

" Diana is a very pretty little girl. She has black eyes and hair and rosy cheeks. And she is good and smart, which is better than being pretty."

Marilla was as fond of morals as the Duchess in Wonderland, and was firmly convinced that one should be tacked on to every remark made to a child who was being brought up.

But Anne waved the moral inconsequently aside and seized only on the delightful possibilities before it.

" Oh, I'm so glad she's pretty. Next to being beautiful oneself—and that's impossible in my case—it would be best to have a beautiful bosom friend. When I lived with Mrs Thomas she had a bookcase in her sitting-room with glass doors. There weren't any books in it ; Mrs Thomas kept her best china and her preserves there—when she had any preserves to keep. One of the doors was broken. Mr Thomas smashed it one night when he was slightly intoxicated. But the other was whole and I used to pretend that my reflection in it was another little girl who lived in it. I called her Katie Maurice, and we were very intimate. I used to talk to her by the hour, especially on Sunday, and tell her everything. Katie was the comfort and consolation of my life. We used to pretend that the bookcase was enchanted and that if I only knew the spell I could open the door and step right into the room where Katie Maurice lived, instead of into Mrs Thomas' shelves of preserves and china. And then Katie Maurice would have taken me by the hand and led me out into a wonderful place, all flowers and sunshine and fairies, and we would have lived there happy for ever after. When I went to live with Mrs Hammond it just broke my heart to leave Katie Maurice. She felt it dreadfully, too, I know she did, for she was crying when she kissed me good-bye through the bookcase door. There was no bookcase at Mrs Hammond's. But just up the river a little way from the house there was a long green little valley, and the loveliest echo lived there. It echoed back every word you said, even if you didn't talk a bit loud. So I imagined that it was a little girl called Violetta and we were great friends and I loved her almost as well as I loved Katie Maurice—not quite, but almost, you know. The night before I went to the asylum I said good-bye to Violetta, and oh, her good-bye came back to me in such sad,

sad tones. I had become so attached to her that I hadn't the heart to imagine a bosom friend at the asylum, even if there had been any scope for imagination there."

" I think it's just as well there wasn't," said Marilla drily. " I don't approve of such goings-on. You seem to half believe your own imaginations. It will be well for you to have a real live friend to put such nonsense out of your head. But don't let Mrs Barry hear you talking about your Katie Maurices and your Violettas or she'll think you tell stories."

" Oh, I won't. I couldn't talk of them to everybody —their memories are too sacred for that. But I thought I'd like to have you know about them. Oh, look, here's a big bee just tumbled out of an apple blossom. Just think what a lovely place to live— in an apple blossom ! Fancy going to sleep in it when the wind was rocking it. If I wasn't a human girl I think I'd like to be a bee and live among the flowers."

" Yesterday you wanted to be a seagull," sniffed Marilla. " I think you are very fickle-minded. I told you to learn that prayer and not talk. But it seems impossible for you to stop talking if you've got anybody that will listen to you. So go up to your room and learn it."

" Oh, I know it pretty nearly all now—all but just the last line."

" Well, never mind, do as I tell you. Go to your room and finish learning it well, and stay there until I call you down to help me get tea."

" Can I take the apple blossoms with me for company ? " pleaded Anne.

" No ; you don't want your room cluttered up with flowers. You should have left them on the tree in the first place."

" I did feel a little that way, too," said Anne. " I kind of felt I shouldn't shorten their lovely lives by picking them—I wouldn't want to be picked if I were an apple blossom. But the temptation was *irresistible*. What do you do when you meet with an irresistible temptation ? "

" Anne, did you hear me tell you to go to your room ? "

Anne sighed, retreated to the east gable, and sat down in a chair by the window.

" There—I know this prayer. I learned that last sentence coming upstairs. Now I'm going to imagine things into this room so that they'll always stay imagined. The floor is covered with a white velvet carpet with pink roses all over it and there are pink silk curtains at the windows. The walls are hung with gold and silver brocade tapestry. The furniture is mahogany I never saw any mahogany, but it does sound *so* luxurious. This is a couch all heaped with gorgeous silken cushions, pink and blue and crimson and gold, and I am reclining gracefully on it. I can see my reflection in that splendid big mirror hanging on the wall. I am tall and regal, clad in a gown of trailing white lace, with a pearl cross on my breast and pearls in my hair. My hair is of midnight darkness, and my skin is a clear ivory pallor. My name is the Lady Cordelia Fitzgerald. No, it isn't—I can't make *that* seem real."

She danced up to the little looking-glass and peered into it. Her pointed freckled face and solemn grey eyes peered back at her.

" You're only Anne of Green Gables," she said earnestly, " and I see you, just as you are looking now, whenever I try to imagine I'm the Lady Cordelia. But it's a million times nicer to be Anne of Green Gables than Anne of nowhere in particular, isn't it ? "

She bent forward, kissed her reflection affectionately, and betook herself to the open window.

" Dear Snow Queen, good afternoon. And good afternoon, dear birches down in the hollow. And good afternoon, dear grey house up on the hill. I wonder if Diana is to be my bosom friend. I hope she will, and I shall love her very much. But I must never quite forget Katie Maurice and Violetta. They would feel so hurt if I did and I'd hate to hurt anybody's feelings, even a little bookcase-girl's or a little echo-girl's. I must be careful to remember them and send them a kiss every day."

Anne blew a couple of airy kisses from her finger-tips past the cherry blossoms and then, with her chin in her hands, drifted luxuriously out on a sea of day-dreams.

CHAPTER IX

ANNE had been a fortnight at Green Gables before Mrs Lynde arrived to inspect her. Mrs Rachel, to do her justice, was not to blame for this. A severe and unseasonable attack of grippe had confined that good lady to her house ever since the occasion of her last visit to Green Gables. Mrs Rachel was not often sick and had a well-defined contempt for people who were; but grippe, she asserted, was like no other illness on earth and could only be interpreted as one of the special visitations of Providence. As soon as her doctor allowed her to put her foot out of doors she hurried up to Green Gables, bursting with curiosity to see Matthew's and Marilla's orphan, concerning whom all sorts of stories and suppositions had gone abroad in Avonlea.

Anne had made good use of every waking moment of that fortnight. Already she was acquainted with every tree and shrub about the place. She had discovered that a lane opened out below the apple orchard and ran up through a belt of woodland; and she had explored it to its farthest end in all its delicious vagaries of brook and bridge, fir coppice and wild cherry arch, corners thick with fern, and branching byways of maple and mountain ash.

She had made friends with the spring down in the hollow—that wonderful deep, clear, icy-cold spring; it was set about with smooth red sandstones and rimmed in by great palm-like clumps of water fern; and beyond it was a log bridge over the brook.

That bridge led Anne's dancing feet up over a wooded hill beyond, where perpetual twilight reigned under the straight, thick-growing firs and spruces; the only flowers there were myriads of delicate ' June bells,' those shyest and sweetest of woodland blooms, and a few pale, aerial starflowers, like the spirits of last year's blossoms. Gossamers glimmered like threads of silver among the trees and the fir boughs and tassels seemed to utter friendly speech.

All these raptured voyages of exploration were made in the odd half-hours which she was allowed for play, and Anne talked Matthew and Marilla half-deaf over her discoveries. Not that Matthew complained, to be sure; he listened to it all with a wordless smile of enjoyment on his face; Marilla permitted the " chatter " until she found herself becoming too interested in it, whereupon she always promptly quenched Anne by a curt command to hold her tongue.

Anne was out in the orchard when Mrs Rachel came, wandering at her own sweet will through the lush, tremulous grasses splashed with ruddy evening sunshine; so that good lady had an excellent chance to talk her illness fully over, describing every ache and pulse-beat with such evident enjoyment that Marilla thought even grippe must bring its compensations. When details were exhausted, Mrs Rachel introduced the real reason of her call.

" I've been hearing some surprising things about you and Matthew."

" I don't suppose you are any more surprised than I am myself," said Marilla. " I'm getting over my surprise now."

" It was too bad there was such a mistake," said Mrs Rachel sympathetically. " Couldn't you have sent her back ? "

" I suppose we could, but we decided not to. Matthew took a fancy to her. And I must say I like her myself—although I admit she has her faults. The house seems a different place already. She's a real bright little thing."

Marilla said more than she had intended to say when she began, for she read disapproval in Mrs Rachel's expression.

" It's a great responsibility you've taken on your-self," said that lady gloomily, " especially when you've never had any experience with children. You don't know much about her or her real disposition, I suppose, and there's no guessing how a child like that will turn out. But I don't want to discourage you I'm sure, Marilla."

" I'm not feeling discouraged," was Marilla's dry response. " When I make up my mind to do a thing it stays made up. I suppose you'd like to see Anne. I'll call her in."

Anne came running in presently, her face sparkling with the delight of her orchard rovings ; but, abashed at finding herself in the unexpected presence of a stranger, she halted confusedly inside the door. She certainly was an odd-looking little creature in the short, tight wincey dress she had worn from the asylum, below which her thin legs seemed ungracefully long. Her freckles were more numerous and obtrusive than ever ; the wind had ruffled her hatless hair into over-brilliant disorder ; it had never looked redder than at that moment.

" Well, they didn't pick you for your looks, that's sure and certain," was Mrs Rachel Lynde's emphatic comment. Mrs Rachel was one of those delightful and popular people who pride themselves on speaking their mind without fear or favour. " She's terrible skinny and homely, Marilla. Come here, child, and let me have a look at you. Lawful heart, did any one ever see such freckles ? And hair as red as carrots ! Come here, child, I say."

Anne " came there," but not exactly as Mrs Rachel expected. With one bound she crossed the kitchen floor and stood before Mrs Rachel, her face scarlet with anger, her lips quivering, and her whole slender form trembling from head to foot.

" I hate you," she cried in a choked voice, stamping her foot on the floor. " I hate you—I hate you—I hate you—" a louder stamp with each assertion of hatred. " How dare you call me skinny and ugly ? How dare you say I'm freckled and red-headed ? You are a rude, impolite, unfeeling woman ! "

" Anne ! " exclaimed Marilla in consternation.

But Anne continued to face Mrs Rachel undauntedly, head up, eyes blazing, hands clenched, passionate indignation exhaling from her like an atmosphere.

" How dare you say such things about me ? " she repeated vehemently. " How would you like to have such things said about you ? How would you like to be told that you are fat and clumsy and probably hadn't a spark of imagination in you ? I don't care if I do hurt your feelings by saying so ! I hope I hurt them. You have hurt mine worse than they were ever hurt before even by Mrs Thomas' intoxicated husband. And I'll *never* forgive you for it, never, never ! "

Stamp ! Stamp !

" Did anybody ever see such a temper ! " exclaimed the horrified Mrs Rachel.

" Anne, go to your room and stay there until I come up," said Marilla, recovering her powers of speech with difficulty.

Anne, bursting into tears, rushed to the hall door, slammed it until the tins on the porch wall outside rattled in sympathy, and fled through the hall and up the stairs like a whirlwind. A subdued slam above told that the door of the east gable had been shut with equal vehemence.

" Well, I don't envy you your job bringing *that* up, Marilla," said Mrs Rachel with unspeakable solemnity.

Marilla opened her lips to say she knew not what of apology or deprecation. What she did say was a surprise to herself then and ever afterwards.

" You shouldn't have twitted her about her looks, Rachel."

" Marilla Cuthbert, you don't mean to say that you are upholding her in such a terrible display of temper as we've just seen ? " demanded Mrs Rachel indignantly

" No," said Marilla slowly, " I'm not trying to excuse her. She's been very naughty and I'll have to give her a talking to about it. But we must make allowances for her. She's never been taught what is right. And you *were* too hard on her, Rachel."

Marilla could not help tacking on that last sentence, although she was again surprised at herself for doing it. Mrs Rachel got up with an air of offended dignity.

" Well, I see that I'll have to be very careful what I say after this, Marilla, since the fine feelings of orphans, brought from goodness knows where, have to be considered before anything else. Oh, no, I'm not vexed—don't worry yourself. I'm too sorry for you to leave any room for anger in my mind. You'll have your own troubles with that child. But if you'll take my advice—which I suppose you won't do, although I've brought up ten children and buried two —you'll do that ' talking to ' you mention with a fair-sized birch switch. I should think *that* would be the most effective language for that kind of a child. Her temper matches her hair I guess. Well, good evening, Marilla. I hope you'll come down to see me often as usual. But you can't expect me to visit here again in a hurry, if I'm liable to be flown at and insulted in such a fashion. It's something new in *my* experience."

Whereat Mrs Rachel swept out and away—if a fat woman who always waddled *could* be said to sweep away—and Marilla with a very solemn face betook herself to the east gable.

On the way upstairs she pondered uneasily as to what she ought to do. She felt no little dismay over the scene that had just been enacted. How unfortunate that Anne should have displayed such temper before Mrs Rachel Lynde, of all people ! Then Marilla suddenly became aware of an uncomfortable and rebuking consciousness that she felt more humiliation over this than sorrow over the discovery of such a serious defect in Anne's disposition. And how was she to punish her ? The amiable suggestion of the birch switch—to the efficiency of which all of Mrs Rachel's own children could have borne smarting testimony— did not appeal to Marilla. She did not believe she could whip a child. No, some other method of punishment must be found to bring Anne to a proper realization of the enormity of her offence.

Marilla found Anne face downward on her bed, crying bitterly, quite oblivious of muddy boots on a clean counterpane.

" Anne," she said, not ungently.

No answer.

" Anne," with greater severity, " get off that bed this minute and listen to what I have to say to you."

Anne squirmed off the bed and sat rigidly on a chair beside it, her face swollen and tear-stained and her eyes fixed stubbornly on the floor.

" This is a nice way for you to behave, Anne ! Aren't you ashamed of yourself ? "

" She hadn't any right to call me ugly and red-headed," retorted Anne, evasive and defiant.

" You hadn't any right to fly into such a fury and talk the way you did to her, Anne. I was ashamed of you—thoroughly ashamed of you. I wanted you to behave nicely to Mrs Lynde, and instead of that you have disgraced me. I'm sure I don't know why you should lose your temper like that just because Mrs Lynde said you were red-haired and homely. You say it yourself often enough."

" Oh, but there's such a difference between saying a thing yourself and hearing other people say it," wailed Anne. " You may know a thing is so, but you can't help hoping other people don't quite think it is. I suppose you think I have an awful temper, but I couldn't help it. When she said those things something just rose right up in me and choked me. I *had* to fly out at her."

" Well, you made a fine exhibition of yourself I must say. Mrs Lynde will have a nice story to tell about you everywhere—and she'll tell it, too. It was a dreadful thing for you to lose your temper like that, Anne."

" Just imagine how you would feel if somebody told you to your face that you were skinny and ugly," pleaded Anne tearfully.

An old remembrance suddenly rose up before Marilla. She had been a very small child when she had heard one aunt say of her to another, " What a pity she is such a dark, homely little thing." Marilla was every day of fifty before the sting had gone out of that memory.

" I don't say that I think Mrs Lynde was exactly right in saying what she did to you, Anne," she admitted in a softer tone. " Rachel is too outspoken. But that is no excuse for such behaviour on your part. She was a stranger and an elderly person and my visitor—all three very good reasons why you should have been respectful to her. You were rude and saucy and "—Marilla had a saving inspiration of punishment —" you must go to her and tell her you are very sorry for your bad temper and ask her to forgive you."

" I can never do that," said Anne determinedly and darkly. " You can punish me in any way you like, Marilla. You can shut me up in a dark, damp dungeon inhabited by snakes and toads and feed me only on bread and water and I shall not complain. But I cannot ask Mrs Lynde to forgive me."

" We're not in the habit of shutting people up in dark, damp dungeons," said Marilla drily, " especially as they're rather scarce in Avonlea. But apologize to Mrs Lynde you must and shall, and you'll stay here in your room until you can tell me you're willing to do it."

" I shall have to stay here for ever then," said Anne mournfully, " because I can't tell Mrs Lynde I'm sorry I said those things to her. How can I ? I'm *not* sorry. I'm sorry I've vexed you ; but I'm *glad* I told her just what I did. It was a great satisfaction. I can't say I'm sorry when I'm not, can I ? I can't even *imagine* I'm sorry."

" Perhaps your imagination will be in better working order by the morning," said Marilla, rising to depart. " You'll have the night to think over your conduct in and come to a better frame of mind. You said you would try to be a very good girl if we kept you at Green Gables, but I must say it hasn't seemed very much like it this evening."

Leaving this Parthian shaft to rankle in Anne's stormy bosom, Marilla descended to the kitchen, grievously troubled in mind and vexed in soul. She was as angry with herself as with Anne, because, whenever she recalled Mrs Rachel's dumbfounded countenance her lips twitched with amusement and she felt a most reprehensible desire to laugh.

CHAPTER X

ANNE'S APOLOGY

MARILLA said nothing to Matthew about the affair that evening ; but when Anne proved still refractory the next morning an explanation had to be made to account for her absence from the breakfast-table. Marilla told Matthew the whole story, taking pains to impress him with a due sense of the enormity of Anne's behaviour.

" It's a good thing Rachel Lynde got a calling down ; she's a meddlesome old gossip," was Matthew's consolatory rejoinder.

" Matthew Cuthbert, I'm astonished at you. You know that Anne's behaviour was dreadful, and yet you take her part ! I suppose you'll be saying next thing that she oughtn't to be punished at all."

" Well now—no—not exactly," said Matthew uneasily. " I reckon she ought to be punished a little. But don't be too hard on her, Marilla. Recollect she hasn't ever had anyone to teach her right. You're —you're going to give her something to eat, aren't you ? "

" When did you ever hear of me starving people into good behaviour ? " demanded Marilla indignantly. " She'll have her meals regular, and I'll carry them up to her myself. But she'll stay up there until she's willing to apologize to Mrs Lynde, and that's final, Matthew."

Breakfast, dinner, and supper were very silent meals —for Anne still remained obdurate. After each meal Marilla carried a well-filled tray to the east gable and brought it down later on not noticeably depleted.

Matthew eyed its last descent with a troubled eye. Had Anne eaten anything at all ?

When Marilla went out that evening to bring the cows from the back pasture, Matthew, who had been hanging about the barns and watching, slipped into the house with the air of a burglar and crept upstairs. As a general thing Matthew gravitated between the kitchen and the little bedroom off the hall where he slept ; once in a while he ventured uncomfortably into the parlour or sitting-room when the minister came to tea. But he had never been upstairs in his own house since the spring he helped Marilla paper the spare bedroom, and that was four years ago.

He tiptoed along the hall and stood for several minutes outside the door of the east gable before he summoned courage to tap on it with his fingers and then open the door to peep in.

Anne was sitting on the yellow chair by the window, gazing mournfully out into the garden. Very small and unhappy she looked, and Matthew's heart smote him. He softly closed the door and tiptoed over to her.

" Anne," he whispered, as if afraid of being overheard, " how are you making it, Anne ? "

Anne smiled wanly.

" Pretty well. I imagine a good deal, and that helps to pass the time. Of course, it's rather lonesome. But, then, I may as well get used to that."

Anne smiled again, bravely facing the long years of solitary imprisonment before her.

Matthew recollected that he must say what he had come to say without loss of time, lest Marilla return prematurely.

" Well now, Anne, don't you think you'd better do it and have it over with ? " he whispered. " It'll have to be done sooner or later, you know, for Marilla's a dreadful determined woman—dreadful determined, Anne. Do it right off, I say, and have it over."

" Do you mean apologize to Mrs Lynde ? "

" Yes—apologize—that's the very word," said Matthew eagerly. " Just smooth it over so to speak. That's what I was trying to get at."

" I suppose I could do it to oblige you," said Anne thoughtfully. " It would be true enough to say I am sorry, because I *am* sorry now. I wasn't a bit sorry last night. I was mad clear through, and I stayed mad all night. I know I did because I woke up three times and I was just furious every time. But this morning it was all over. I wasn't in a temper any more—and it left a dreadful sort of goneness, too. I felt so ashamed of myself. But I just couldn't think of going and telling Mrs Lynde so. It would be so humiliating. I made up my mind I'd stay shut up here for ever rather than do that. But still— I'd do anything for you—if you really want me to——"

" Well now, of course I do. It's terrible lonesome downstairs without you. Just go and smooth it over —that's a good girl."

" Very well," said Anne resignedly. " I'll tell Marilla as soon as she comes in that I've repented."

" That's right—that's right, Anne. But don't tell Marilla I said anything about it. She might think I was putting my oar in and I promised not to do that."

" Wild horses won't drag the secret from me," promised Anne solemnly. " How would wild horses drag a secret from a person anyhow ? "

But Matthew was gone, scared at his own success. He fled hastily to the remotest corner of the horse pasture lest Marilla should suspect what he had been up to. Marilla herself, upon her return to the house, was agreeably surprised to hear a plaintive voice calling, " Marilla," over the banisters.

" Well ? " she said, going into the hall.

" I'm sorry I lost my temper and said rude things, and I'm willing to go and tell Mrs Lynde so."

" Very well." Marilla's crispness gave no sign of her relief. She had been wondering what under the canopy she should do if Anne did not give in. " I'll take you down after milking."

Accordingly, after milking, behold Marilla and Anne walking down the lane, the former erect and triumphant, the latter drooping and dejected. But half-way down, Anne's dejection vanished as if by enchantment. She lifted her head and stepped lightly along, her eyes fixed on the sunset sky and an air of subdued exhilaration about her. Marilla beheld the change disapprovingly. This was no meek penitent such as it behoved her to take into the presence of the offended Mrs Lynde.

" What are you thinking of, Anne ? " she asked sharply.

" I'm imagining out what I must say to Mrs Lynde," answered Anne dreamily.

This was satisfactory—or should have been so. But Marilla could not rid herself of the notion that something in her scheme of punishment was going askew. Anne had no business to look so rapt and radiant.

Rapt and radiant Anne continued until they were in the very presence of Mrs Lynde, who was sitting knitting by her kitchen window. Then the radiance vanished. Mournful penitence appeared on every feature. Before a word was spoken Anne suddenly went down on her knees before the astonished Mrs Rachel and held out her hands beseechingly.

" Oh, Mrs Lynde, I am so extremely sorry," she said with a quiver in her voice. " I could never express all my sorrow, no, not if I used up a whole dictionary. You must just imagine it. I behaved terribly to you —and I've disgraced the dear friends, Matthew and Marilla, who have let me stay at Green Gables although I'm not a boy. I'm a dreadfully wicked and ungrateful girl, and I deserve to be punished and cast out by respectable people for ever. It was very wicked of me to fly into a temper because you told me the truth. It *was* the truth ; every word you said was true. My hair is red and I'm freckled and skinny and ugly. What I said to you was true, too, but I shouldn't have said it. Oh, Mrs Lynde, please, please, forgive me. If you refuse it will be a lifelong sorrow to me. You wouldn't like to inflict a lifelong sorrow on a poor little orphan girl, would you, even if she had a dreadful temper ? Oh, I am sure you wouldn't. Please say you forgive me, Mrs Lynde."

Anne clasped her hands together, bowed her head, and waited for the word of judgment.

There was no mistaking her sincerity—it breathed in every tone of her voice. Both Marilla and Mrs Lynde recognized its unmistakable ring. But the former understood in dismay that Anne was actually enjoying her valley of humiliation—was revelling in the thoroughness of her abasement. Where was the wholesome punishment upon which she, Marilla, had plumed herself ? Anne had turned it into a species of positive pleasure.

Good Mrs Lynde, not being overburdened with perception, did not see this. She only perceived that Anne had made a very thorough apology and all resentment vanished from her kindly, if somewhat officious, heart.

" There, there, get up, child," she said heartily. " Of course I forgive you. I guess I was a little too hard on you, anyway. But I'm such an outspoken person. You just mustn't mind me, that's what. It can't be denied your hair is terrible red ; but I knew a girl once—went to school with her, in fact—whose hair was every mite as red as yours when she was young, but when she grew up it darkened to a real handsome auburn. I wouldn't be a mite surprised if yours did, too—not a mite."

"Oh, Mrs Lynde!" Anne drew a long breath as she rose to her feet. "You have given me a hope. I shall always feel that you are a benefactor. Oh, I could endure anything if I only thought my hair would be a handsome auburn when I grew up. It would be so much easier to be good if one's hair was a handsome auburn, don't you think? And now may I go out into your garden and sit on that bench under the apple-trees while you and Marilla are talking? There is so much more scope for imagination out there."

"Laws, yes, run along, child. And you can pick a bouquet of them white June lilies over in the corner if you like."

As the door closed behind Anne, Mrs Lynde got briskly up to light a lamp.

"She's a real odd little thing. Take this chair, Marilla; it's easier than the one you've got; I just keep that for the hired boy to sit on. Yes, she certainly is an odd child, but there is something kind of taking about her after all. I don't feel so surprised at you and Matthew keeping her as I did—nor so sorry for you, either. She may turn out all right. Of course, she has a queer way of expressing herself—a little too—well, too kind of forcible, you know; but she'll likely get over that now that she's come to live among civilized folks. And then, her temper's pretty quick, I guess; but there's one comfort, a child that has a quick temper, just blaze up and cool down, ain't never likely to be sly or deceitful. Preserve me from a sly child, that's what. On the whole, Marilla, I kind of like her."

When Marilla went home, Anne came out of the fragrant twilight of the orchard with a sheaf of white narcissi in her hands.

"I apologized pretty well, didn't I?" she said proudly as they went down the lane. "I thought since I had to do it I might as well do it thoroughly."

" You did it thoroughly, all right enough," was Marilla's comment. Marilla was dismayed at finding herself inclined to laugh over the recollection. She had also an uneasy feeling that she ought to scold Anne for apologizing so well ; but then, that was ridiculous ! She compromised with her conscience by saying severely :

" I hope you won't have occasion to make many more such apologies. I hope you'll try to control your temper now, Anne."

" That wouldn't be so hard if people wouldn't twit me about my looks," said Anne with a sigh. " I don't get cross about other things ; but I'm *so* tired of being twitted about my hair and it just makes me boil right over. Do you suppose my hair will really be a handsome auburn when I grow up ? "

" You shouldn't think so much about your looks, Anne. I'm afraid you are a very vain little girl."

" How can I be vain when I know I'm homely ? " protested Anne. " I love pretty things ; and I hate to look in the glass and see something that isn't pretty. It makes me feel so sorrowful—just as I feel when I look at any ugly thing. I pity it because it isn't beautiful."

" Handsome is as handsome does," quoted Marilla.

" I've had that said to me before, but I have my doubts about it," remarked sceptical Anne, sniffing at her narcissi. " Oh, aren't these flowers sweet ! It was lovely of Mrs Lynde to give them to me. I have no hard feelings against Mrs Lynde now. It gives you a lovely, confortable feeling to apologize and be forgiven, doesn't it ? Aren't the stars bright to-night ? If you could live in a star, which one would you pick ? I'd like that lovely clear big one away over there above that dark hill."

" Anne, do hold your tongue," said Marilla, thoroughly worn out trying to follow the gyrations of Anne's thoughts.

Anne said no more until they turned into their own lane.   A little gipsy wind came down it to meet them, laden with the spicy perfume of young dew-wet ferns. Far up in the shadows a cheerful light gleamed out through the trees from the kitchen at Green Gables. Anne suddenly came close to Marilla and slipped her hand into the older woman's hard palm.

" It's lovely to be going home and know it's home," she said.   " I love Green Gables already, and I never loved any place before.   No place ever seemed like home.   Oh, Marilla, I'm so happy.   I could pray right now and not find it a bit hard."

Something warm and pleasant welled up in Marilla's heart at touch of that thin little hand in her own—a throb of the maternity she had missed, perhaps.   Its very unaccustomedness and sweetness disturbed her. She hastened to restore her sensations to their normal calm by inculcating a moral.

" If you'll be a good girl you'll always be happy, Anne.   And you should never find it hard to say your prayers."

" Saying one's prayers isn't exactly the same thing as praying," said Anne meditatively.   " But I'm going to imagine that I'm the wind that is blowing up there in those tree-tops.   When I get tired of the trees I'll imagine I'm gently waving down here in the ferns— and then I'll fly over to Mrs Lynde's garden and set the flowers dancing—and then I'll go with one great swoop over the clover field—and then I'll blow over the Lake of Shining Waters and ripple it all up into little sparkling waves.   Oh, there's so much scope for imagination in a wind !   So I'll not talk any more just now, Marilla."

" Thanks be to goodness for that," breathed Marilla in devout relief.

CHAPTER XI

WELL, how do you like them ? " said Marilla. Anne was standing in the gable-room, looking solemnly at three new dresses spread out on the bed. One was of snuffy-coloured gingham which Marilla had been tempted to buy from a peddler the preceding summer because it looked so serviceable ; one was of black-and-white checked sateen which she had picked up at a bargain counter in the winter ; and one was a stiff print of an ugly blue shade which she had purchased that week at a Carmody store.

She had made them up herself, and they were all made alike—plain skirts fulled tightly to plain waists, with sleeves as plain as waist and skirt and tight as sleeves could be.

" I'll imagine that I like them," said Anne soberly.

" I don't want you to imagine it," said Marilla, offended. " Oh, I can see you don't like the dresses ! What is the matter with them ? Aren't they neat and clean and new ? "

" Yes."

" Then why don't you like them ? "

" They're—they're not—pretty," said Anne reluctantly.

" Pretty ! " Marilla sniffed. " I didn't trouble my head about getting pretty dresses for you. I don't believe in pampering vanity, Anne, I'll tell you that right off. Those dresses are good, sensible, serviceable dresses, without any frills or furbelows about them, and they're all you'll get this summer. The brown

gingham and the blue print will do you for school when
you begin to go.   The sateen is for church and Sunday
school.   I'll expect you to keep them neat and clean
and not to tear them.   I should think you'd be grateful
to get most anything after those skimpy wincey things
you've been wearing."

" Oh, I *am* grateful," protested Anne.   " But I'd
be ever so much gratefuller if—if you'd made just one
of them with puffed sleeves.   Puffed sleeves are so
fashionable now.   It would give me such a thrill,
Marilla, just to wear a dress with puffed sleeves."

" Well, you'll have to do without your thrill.   I
hadn't any material to waste on puffed sleeves.   I think
they are ridiculous-looking things anyhow.   I prefer the
plain, sensible ones."

" But I'd rather look ridiculous when everybody else
does than plain and sensible all by myself," persisted
Anne mournfully.

" Trust you for that !   Well, hang those dresses
carefully up in your closet, and then sit down and learn
the Sunday school lesson.   I got a quarterly from Mr
Bell for you, and you'll go to Sunday school to-morrow,"
said Marilla, disappearing downstairs in high dudgeon.

Anne clasped her hands and looked at the dresses.

" I did hope there would be a white one with puffed
sleeves," she whispered disconsolately.   " I prayed for
one, but I didn't much expect it on that account.   I
didn't suppose God would have time to bother about
a little orphan girl's dress.   I knew I'd just have to
depend on Marilla for it.   Well, fortunately I can
imagine that one of them is of snow-white muslin with
lovely lace frills and three-puffed sleeves."

The next morning warnings of a sick headache pre-
vented Marilla from going to Sunday school with
Anne.

" You'll have to go down and call for Mrs Lynde

Anne," she said. "She'll see that you get into the right class. Now, mind you behave yourself properly. Stay to preaching afterwards and ask Mrs Lynde to show you our pew. Here's a cent for collection. Don't stare at people and don't fidget. I shall expect you to tell me the text when you come home."

Anne started off irreproachably, arrayed in the stiff black-and-white sateen, which, while decent as regards length and certainly not open to the charge of skimpiness, contrived to emphasize every corner and angle of her thin figure. Her hat was a little, flat, glossy, new sailor, the extreme plainness of which had likewise much disappointed Anne, who had permitted herself secret visions of ribbon and flowers. The latter, however, were supplied before Anne reached the main road; for, being confronted half-way down the lane with a golden frenzy of wind-stirred buttercups and a glory of wild roses, Anne promptly and liberally garlanded her hat with a heavy wreath of them. Whatever other people might have thought of the result it satisfied Anne, and she tripped gaily down the road, holding her ruddy head with its decoration of pink and yellow very proudly.

When she reached Mrs Lynde's house she found that lady gone. Nothing daunted, Anne proceeded onward to the church alone. In the porch she found a crowd of little girls, all more or less gaily attired in whites and blues and pinks, and all staring with curious eyes at this stranger in their midst, with her extraordinary head adornment. Avonlea little girls had already heard queer stories about Anne ; Mrs Lynde said she had an awful temper ; Jerry Buote, the hired boy at Green Gables, said she talked all the time to herself or to the trees and flowers like a crazy girl. They looked at her and whispered to each other behind their quarterlies. Nobody made any friendly advances, then or later on when the opening exercises were over and Anne found herself in Miss Rogerson's class.

Miss Rogerson was a middle-aged lady who had taught a Sunday school class for twenty years. Her method of teaching was to ask the printed questions from the quarterly and look sternly over its edge at the particular little girl she thought ought to answer the question. She looked very often at Anne, and Anne, thanks to Marilla's drilling, answered promptly ; but it may be questioned if she understood very much about either question or answer.

She did not think she liked Miss Rogerson, and she felt very miserable ; every other little girl in the class had puffed sleeves. Anne felt that life was really not worth living without puffed sleeves.

" Well, how did you like Sunday school ? " Marilla wanted to know when Anne came home. Her wreath having faded, Anne had discarded it in the lane, so Marilla was spared the knowledge of that for a time.

" I didn't like it a bit. It was horrid."

" Anne Shirley ! " said Marilla rebukingly.

Anne sat down on the rocker with a long sigh, kissed one of Bonny's leaves, and waved her hand to a blossoming fuchsia.

" They might have been lonesome while I was away," she explained. " And now about the Sunday school. I behaved well, just as you told me. Mrs Lynde was gone, but I went right on myself. I went into the church, with a lot of other little girls, and I sat in the corner of a pew by the window while the opening exercises went on. Mr Bell made an awfully long prayer. I would have been dreadfully tired before he got through if I hadn't been sitting by that window. But it looked right out on the Lake of Shining Waters, so I just gazed at that and imagined all sorts of splendid things."

" You shouldn't have done anything of the sort. You should have listened to Mr Bell."

" But he wasn't talking to me," protested Anne. " He was talking to God and he didn't seem to be very much interested in it, either. I think he thought God was too far off to make it worth while. I said a little prayer myself, though. There was a long row of white birches hanging over the lake and the sunshine fell down through them, 'way, 'way down, deep into the water. Oh, Marilla, it was like a beautiful dream ! It gave me a thrill and I just said, ' Thank you for it, God,' two or three times."

" Not out loud, I hope," said Marilla anxiously.

" Oh, no, just under my breath. Well, Mr Bell did get through at last and they told me to go into the class-room with Miss Rogerson's class. There were nine other girls in it. They all had puffed sleeves. I tried to imagine mine were puffed, too, but I couldn't. Why couldn't I ? It was as easy as could be to imagine they were puffed when I was alone in the east gable, but it was awfully hard there among the others who had really truly puffs."

" You shouldn't have been thinking about your sleeves in Sunday school. You should have been attending to the lesson. I hope you knew it."

" Oh, yes ; and I answered a lot of questions. Miss Rogerson asked ever so many. I don't think it was fair for her to do all the asking. There were lots I wanted to ask her, but I didn't like to because I didn't think she was a kindred spirit. Then all the other little girls recited a paraphrase. She asked me if I knew any. I told her I didn't, but I could recite, ' The Dog at His Master's Grave,' if she liked. That's in the *Third Royal Reader*. It isn't a really truly religious piece of poetry, but it's so sad and melancholy that it might as well be. She said it wouldn't do and she told

me to learn the nineteenth paraphrase for next Sunday.
I read it over in church afterwards and it's splendid.
There are two lines in particular that just thrill me.

> Quick as the slaughtered squadrons fell
> In Midian's evil day.

I don't know what ' squadrons ' means nor ' Midian,'
either, but it sounds *so* tragical. I can hardly wait
until next Sunday to recite it. I'll practice it all the
week. After Sunday school I asked Miss Rogerson—
because Mrs Lynde was too far away—to show me
your pew. I sat just as still as I could and the text
was Revelations, third chapter, second and third verses.
It was a very long text. If I was a minister I'd pick
the short, snappy ones. The sermon was awfully long,
too. I suppose the minister had to match it to the
text. I didn't think he was a bit interesting. The
trouble with him seems to be that he hasn't enough
imagination. I didn't listen to him very much. I
just let my thoughts run and I thought of the most
surprising things."

Marilla felt helplessly that all this should be sternly
reproved, but she was hampered by the undeniable
fact that some of the things Anne had said, especially
about the minister's sermons and Mr Bell's prayers,
were what she herself had really thought deep down
in her heart for years, but had never given expression
to. It almost seemed to her that those secret, un-
uttered, critical thoughts had suddenly taken visible
and accusing shape and form in the person of this
outspoken morsel of neglected humanity.

CHAPTER XII

A SOLEMN VOW AND PROMISE

IT was not until the next Friday that Marilla heard the story of the flower-wreathed hat. She came home from Mrs Lynde's and called Anne to account.

" Anne, Mrs Rachel says you went to church last Sunday with your hat rigged out ridiculous with roses and buttercups. What on earth put you up to such a caper ? A pretty-looking object you must have been ! "

" Oh, I know pink and yellow aren't becoming to me," began Anne.

" Becoming fiddlesticks ! It was putting flowers on your hat at all, no matter what colour they were, that was ridiculous. You are the most aggravating child ! "

" I don't see why it's any more ridiculous to wear flowers on your hat than on your dress," protested Anne. " Lots of little girls there had bouquets pinned on their dresses. What was the difference ? '

Marilla was not to be drawn from the safe concrete into dubious paths of the abstract.

" Don't answer me back like that, Anne. It was very silly of you to do such a thing. Never let me catch you at such a trick again. Mrs Rachel says she thought she would sink through the floor when she saw you come in all rigged out like that. She couldn't get near enough to tell you to take them off till it was too late. She says people talked about it something dreadful. Of course they would think I had no better sense than to let you go decked out like that."

" Oh, I'm so sorry," said Anne, tears welling into her eyes. " I never thought you'd mind. The roses and buttercups were so sweet and pretty I thought they'd look lovely on my hat. Lots of the little girls had artificial flowers on their hats. I'm afraid I'm going to be a dreadful trial to you. Maybe you'd better send me back to the asylum. That would be terrible ; I don't think I could endure it ; most likely I would go into consumption ; I'm so thin as it is, you see. But that would be better than being a trial to you."

" Nonsense," said Marilla, vexed at herself for having made the child cry. " I don't want to send you back to the asylum, I'm sure. All I want is that you should behave like other little girls and not make yourself ridiculous. Don't cry any more. I've got some news for you. Diana Barry came home this afternoon. I'm going up to see if I can borrow a skirt pattern from Mrs Barry, and if you like you can come with me and get acquainted with Diana."

Anne rose to her feet, with clasped hands, the tears still glistening on her cheeks ; the dish-towel she had been hemming slipped unheeded to the floor.

" Oh, Marilla, I'm frightened—now that it has come I'm actually frightened. What if she shouldn't like me ! It would be the most tragical disappointment of my life."

" Now, don't get into a fluster. And I do wish you wouldn't use such long words. It sounds so funny in a little girl. I guess Diana'll like you well enough. It's her mother you've got to reckon with. If she doesn't like you it won't matter how much Diana does. If she has heard about your outburst to Mrs Lynde and going to church with buttercups round your hat I don't know what she'll think of you. You must be polite and well-behaved, and don't make any of your startling speeches. For pity's sake, if the child isn't actually trembling ! "

Anne *was* trembling. Her face was pale and tense.

" Oh, Marilla, you'd be excited, too, if you were going to meet a little girl you hoped to be your bosom friend and whose mother mightn't like you," she said as she hastened to get her hat.

They went over to Orchard Slope by the short cut across the brook and up the firry hill grove. Mrs Barry came to the kitchen door in answer to Marilla's knock. She was a tall, black-eyed, black-haired woman, with a very resolute mouth. She had the reputation of being very strict with her children.

" How do you do, Marilla ? " she said cordially. " Come in. And this is the little girl you have adopted, I suppose ? "

" Yes, this is Anne Shirley," said Marilla.

" Spelled with an *e*," gasped Anne, who, tremulous and excited as she was, was determined there should be no misunderstanding on that important point.

Mrs Barry, not hearing or not comprehending, merely shook hands and said kindly :

" How are you ? "

" I am well in body although considerably rumpled up in spirit, thank you, ma'am," said Anne gravely. Then aside to Marilla in an audible whisper, " There wasn't anything startling in that, was there, Marilla ? "

Diana was sitting on the sofa, reading a book which she dropped when the callers entered. She was a very pretty little girl, with her mother's black eyes and hair, and rosy cheeks, and the merry expression which was her inheritance from her father.

" This is my little girl, Diana," said Mrs Barry. " Diana, you might take Anne out into the garden and show her your flowers. It will be better for you than straining your eyes over that book. She reads entirely

too much—" this to Marilla as the little girls went out
—" and I can't prevent her, for her father aids and
abets her. She's always poring over a book. I'm
glad she has the prospect of a playmate—perhaps it
will take her more out-of-doors."

Outside in the garden, which was full of mellow
sunset light streaming through the dark old firs to
the west of it, stood Anne and Diana, gazing bashfully
at one another over a clump of gorgeous tiger lilies.

The Barry garden was a bowery wilderness of flowers
which would have delighted Anne's heart at any time
less fraught with destiny. It was encircled by huge
old willows and tall firs, beneath which flourished
flowers that loved the shade. Prim, right-angled paths,
neatly bordered with clam-shells, intersected it like
moist red ribbons, and in the beds between old-
fashioned flowers ran riot. There were rosy bleeding-
hearts and great splendid crimson peonies ; white,
fragrant narcissi and thorny, sweet Scotch roses ; pink
and blue and white columbines and lilac-tinted Bounc-
ing Bets ; clumps of southernwood and ribbon grass
and mint ; purple Adam-and-Eve, daffodils, and masses
of sweet clover white with its delicate, fragrant, feathery
sprays ; scarlet lightning that shot its fiery lances
over prim white musk-flowers ; a garden it was where
sunshine lingered and bees hummed, and winds,
beguiled into loitering, purred and rustled.

" Oh, Diana," said Anne at last, clasping her hands
and speaking almost in a whisper, " do you think—oh,
do you think you can like me a little—enough to be
my bosom friend ? "

Diana laughed. Diana always laughed before she
spoke.

" Why, I guess so," she said frankly. " I'm awfully
glad you've come to live at Green Gables. It will be
jolly to have somebody to play with. There isn't any

other girl who lives near enough to play with, and I've no sisters big enough."

" Will you swear to be my friend for ever and ever ? " demanded Anne eagerly.

Diana looked shocked.

" Why, it's dreadfully wicked to swear," she said rebukingly.

" Oh no, not my kind of swearing. There are two kinds, you know."

" I never heard of but one kind," said Diana doubtfully.

" There really is another. Oh, it isn't wicked at all. It just means vowing and promising solemnly."

" Well, I don't mind doing that," agreed Diana, relieved. " How do you do it ? "

" We must join hands—so," said Anne gravely. " It ought to be over running water. We'll just imagine this path is running water. I'll repeat the oath first. I solemnly swear to be faithful to my bosom friend, Diana Barry, as long as the sun and moon shall endure. Now you say it and put my name in."

Diana repeated the ' oath ' with a laugh fore and aft. Then she said :

" You're a queer girl, Anne. I heard before that you were queer. But I believe I'm going to like you real well."

When Marilla and Anne went home, Diana went with them as far as the log bridge. The two little girls walked with their arms about each other. At the brook they parted with many promises to spend the next afternoon together.

" Well, did you find Diana a kindred spirit ? " asked Marilla as they went up through the garden of Green Gables.

" Oh, yes," sighed Anne, blissfully unconscious of any sarcasm on Marilla's part. " Oh, Marilla, I'm

the happiest girl on Prince Edward Island this very
moment. I assure you I'll say my prayers with a right
good will to-night. Diana and I are going to build
a playhouse in Mr William Bell's birch grove to-morrow.
Can I have those broken pieces of china that are out
in the wood-shed ? Diana's birthday is in February
and mine is in March. Don't you think that is a very
strange coincidence ? Diana is going to lend me a book
to read. She says it's perfectly splendid and tremenjusly exciting. She's going to show me a place back
in the woods where rice lilies grow. Don't you think
Diana has got very soulful eyes ? I wish I had soulful
eyes. Diana is going to teach me to sing a song called
' Nelly in the Hazel Dell.' She's going to give me a
picture to put up in my room ; it's a perfectly beautiful
picture, she says—a lovely lady in a pale blue silk
dress. A sewing-machine agent gave it to her. I wish
I had something to give Diana. I'm an inch taller than
Diana, but she is ever so much fatter ; she says she'd
like to be thin because it's so much more graceful,
but I'm afraid she only said it to soothe my feelings.
We're going to the shore some day to gather shells.
We have agreed to call the spring down by the log
bridge the Dryad's Bubble. Isn't that a perfectly elegant name ? I read a story once about a spring called
that. A dryad is a sort of grown-up fairy, I think."

" Well, all I hope is you won't talk Diana to death,"
said Marilla. " But remember this in all your planning, Anne. You're not going to play all the time nor
most of it. You'll have your work to do and it'll have
to be done first."

Anne's cup of happiness was full, and Matthew caused
it to overflo . He had just got home from a trip to
the store at Carmody, and he sheepishly produced a
small parcel from his pocket and handed it to Anne,
with a deprecatory look at Marilla.

" I heard you say you liked chocolate sweeties, so I got you some," he said.

" Humph," sniffed Marilla. " It'll ruin her teeth and stomach. There, there, child, don't look so dismal. You can eat those, since Matthew has gone and got them. He'd better have brought you peppermints. They're wholesomer. Don't sicken yourself eating them all at once now."

" Oh, no, indeed, I won't," said Anne eagerly. " I'll just eat one to-night, Marilla. And I can give Diana half of them, can't I ? The other half will taste twice as sweet to me if I give some to her. It's delightful to think I have something to give her."

" I will say it for the child," said Marilla when Anne had gone to her gable, " she isn't stingy. I'm glad, for of all faults I detest stinginess in a child. Dear me, it's only three weeks since she came, and it seems as if she's been here always. I can't imagine the place without her. Now, don't be looking I-told-you-so, Matthew. That's bad enough in a woman, but it isn't to be endured in a man. I'm perfectly willing to own up that I'm glad I consented to keep the child and that I'm getting fond of her, but don't you rub it in, Matthew Cuthbert."

CHAPTER XIII

THE DELIGHTS OF ANTICIPATION

"IT'S time Anne was in to do her sewing," said Marilla, glancing at the clock and then out into the yellow August afternoon where everything drowsed in the heat. "She stayed playing with Diana more than half an hour more'n I gave her leave to; and now she's perched out there on the woodpile talking to Matthew, nineteen to the dozen, when she knows perfectly well that she ought to be at her work. And of course he's listening to her like a perfect ninny. I never saw such an infatuated man. The more she talks and the odder the things she says, the more he's delighted evidently. Anne Shirley, you come right in here this minute, do you hear me!"

A series of staccato taps on the west window brought Anne flying in from the yard, eyes shining, cheeks faintly flushed with pink, unbraided hair streaming behind her in a torrent of brightness.

"Oh, Marilla," she exclaimed breathlessly, "there's going to be a Sunday school picnic next week—in Mr Harmon Andrews' field, right near the Lake of Shining Waters. And Mrs Superintendent Bell and Mrs Rachel Lynde are going to make ice-cream—think of it, Marilla—*ice-cream!* And oh, Marilla, can I go to it?"

"Just look at the clock, if you please, Anne. What time did I tell you to come in?"

"Two o'clock—but isn't it splendid about the picnic, Marilla? Please can I go? Oh, I've never been to a picnic—I've dreamed of picnics, but I've never——"

"Yes, I told you to come at two o'clock. And it's

a quarter to three. I'd like to know why you didn't obey me, Anne."

" Why, I meant to, Marilla, as much as could be. But you have no idea how fascinating Idlewild is. And then, of course, I had to tell Matthew about the picnic. Matthew is such a sympathetic listener. Please can I go ? "

" You'll have to learn to resist the fascination of Idle-whatever-you-call-it. When I tell you to come in at a certain time I mean that time and not half an hour later. And you needn't stop to discourse with sympathetic listeners on your way, either. As for the picnic, of course you can go. You're a Sunday school scholar, and it's not likely I'd refuse to let you go when all the other little girls are going."

" But—but," faltered Anne, " Diana says that everybody must take a basket of things to eat. I can't cook, as you know, Marilla, and—and—I don't mind going to a picnic without puffed sleeves so much, but I'd feel terribly humiliated if I had to go without a basket. It's been preying on my mind ever since Diana told me."

" Well, it needn't prey any longer. I'll bake you a basket."

" Oh, you dear good Marilla. Oh, you are so kind to me. Oh, I'm so much obliged to you."

Getting through with her ' ohs ' Anne cast herself into Marilla's arms and rapturously kissed her sallow cheek. It was the first time in her whole life that childish lips had voluntarily touched Marilla's face. Again that sudden sensation of startling sweetness thrilled her. She was secretly vastly pleased at Anne's impulsive caress, which was probably the reason why she said brusquely :

" There, there, never mind your kissing nonsense. I'd sooner see you doing strictly as you're told. As for cooking, I mean to begin giving you lessons in that some of these days. But you're so feather-brained, Anne, I've been waiting to see if you'd sober down a little and learn to be steady before I begin. You've got to keep your wits about you in cooking and not stop in the middle of things to let your thoughts rove over all creation. Now, get out your patchwork and have your square done before tea-time."

" I do *not* like patchwork," said Anne dolefully, hunting out her workbasket and sitting down before a little heap of red and white diamonds with a sigh. " I think some kinds of sewing would be nice ; but there's no scope for imagination in patchwork. It's just one little seam after another and you never seem to be getting anywhere. But of course I'd rather be Anne of Green Gables sewing patchwork than Anne of any other place with nothing to do but play. I wish time went as quick sewing patches as it does when I'm playing with Diana, though. Oh, we do have such elegant times, Marilla. I have to furnish most of the imagination, but I'm well able to do that. Diana is simply perfect in every other way. You know that little piece of land across the brook that runs up between our farm and Mr Barry's. It belongs to Mr William Bell, and right in the corner there is a little ring of white birch-trees—the most romantic spot, Marilla. Diana and I have our playhouse there. We call it Idlewild. Isn't that a poetical name ? I assure you it took me some time to think it out. I stayed awake nearly a whole night before I invented it. Then, just as I was dropping off to sleep, it came like an inspiration. Diana was *enraptured* when she heard it. We have got our house fixed up elegantly. You must come and see it, Marilla—won't you ? We have great big stones, all covered with moss, for seats, and boards from tree to tree for shelves. And we have all our dishes on them. Of course, they're all broken but it's the easiest thing in the world to imagine that they are whole. There's a piece of a plate with a spray of red and yellow ivy on it that is especially beautiful. We keep it in the parlour and we have the fairy glass there, too. The fairy glass is as lovely as a dream. Diana found it out in the woods behind their chicken house. It's all full of rainbows—just little young rainbows that haven't grown big yet—and Diana's mother told her it was broken off a hanging lamp they once had. But it's nicer to imagine the fairies lost it one night when they had a ball, so we call it the fairy glass. Matthew is going to make us a table. Oh, we have named that little round pool over in Mr Barry's field Willowmere. I got that name out of the book Diana lent me. That was a thrilling book, Marilla. The heroine had five lovers. I'd be satisfied with one, wouldn't you ? She was very handsome and she went through great tribulations. She could faint as easy as anything. I'd love to be able to faint, wouldn't you, Marilla ? It's so romantic. But I'm really very healthy for all I'm so thin. I believe I'm getting fatter, though. Don't you think I am ? I look at my elbows every morning when I get up to see if any dimples are coming. Diana is having a new dress made with elbow sleeves. She is going to wear it to the picnic. Oh, I do hope it will be fine next Wednesday. I don't feel that I could endure the disappointment if anything happened to prevent me from getting to the picnic. I suppose I'd live through it, but I'm certain it would be a lifelong sorrow. It wouldn't matter if I got to a hundred picnics in after years ; they wouldn't make up for missing this one. They're going to have boats on the Lake of Shining Waters—and ice-cream as I told you. I have never tasted ice-cream. Diana tried to explain what it was like, but I guess ice-cream is one of those things that are beyond imagination."

" Anne, you have talked even on for ten minutes by the clock," said Marilla. " Now, just for curiosity's sake, see if you can hold your tongue for the same length of time."

Anne held her tongue as desired. But for the rest of the week she talked picnic and thought picnic and dreamed picnic. On Saturday it rained and she worked herself up into such a frantic state lest it should keep on raining until and over Wednesday, that Marilla made her sew an extra patchwork square by way of steadying her nerves.

On Sunday Anne confided to Marilla on the way home from church that she grew actually cold all over with excitement when the minister announced the picnic from the pulpit.

" Such a thrill as went up and down my back, Marilla ! I don't think I'd ever really believed until then that there was honestly going to be a picnic. I couldn't help fearing I'd only imagined it. But when a minister says a thing in the pulpit you just have to believe it."

" You set your heart too much on things, Anne," said Marilla with a sigh. " I'm afraid there'll be a great many disappointments in store for you through life."

" Oh, Marilla, looking forward to things is half the pleasure of them," exclaimed Anne. " You mayn't get the things themselves ; but nothing can prevent you from having the fun of looking forward to them. Mrs Lynde says, ' Blessed are they who expect nothing for they shall not be disappointed.' But I think it would be worse to expect nothing than to be disappointed."

Marilla wore her amethyst brooch to church that day

as usual. Marilla always wore her amethyst brooch to church. She would have thought it rather sacrilegious to leave it off—as bad as forgetting her Bible or her collection dime. That amethyst brooch was Marilla's most treasured possession. A sea-faring uncle had given it to her mother who in turn had bequeathed it to Marilla. It was an old-fashioned oval, containing a braid of her mother's hair, surrounded by a border of very fine amethysts. Marilla knew too little about precious stones to realize how fine the amethysts actually were ; but she thought them very beautiful and was always pleasantly conscious of their violet shimmer at her throat, above her good brown satin dress, even although she could not see it.

Anne had been smitten with delighted admiration when she first saw that brooch.

" Oh, Marilla, it's a perfectly elegant brooch. I don't know how you can pay attention to the sermon or the prayers when you have it on. *I* couldn't, I know. I think amethysts are just sweet. They are what I used to think diamonds were like. Long ago, before I had ever seen a diamond, I read about them, and I tried to imagine what they would be like. I thought they would be lovely glimmering purple stones. When I saw a real diamond in a lady's ring one day I was so disappointed I cried. Of course, it was very lovely, but it wasn't my idea of a diamond. Will you let me hold the brooch for one minute, Marilla ? Do you think amethysts can be the souls of good violets ? "

CHAPTER XIV

ANNE'S CONFESSION

ON the Monday evening before the picnic Marilla came down from her room with a troubled face. "Anne," she said to that small personage, who was shelling peas by the spotless table and singing " Nelly of the Hazel Dell " with a vigour and expression that did credit to Diana's teaching, " did you see anything of my amethyst brooch ? I thought I stuck it in my pincushion when I came home from church yesterday evening, but I can't find it anywhere."

" I—I saw it this afternoon when you were away at the Aid Society," said Anne, a little slowly. " I was passing your door when I saw it on the cushion so I went in to look at it."

" Did you touch it ? " said Marilla sternly.

" Y-e-e-s," admitted Anne. " I took it up and I pinned it on my breast just to see how it would look."

" You had no business to do anything of the sort. It's very wrong in a little girl to meddle. You shouldn't have gone into my room in the first place and you shouldn't have touched a brooch that didn't belong to you in the second. Where did you put it ? "

" Oh, I put it back on the bureau. I hadn't it on a minute. Truly, I didn't mean to meddle, Marilla. I didn't think about its being wrong to go in and try on the brooch ; but I see now that it was, and I'll never do it again. That's one good thing about me. I never do the same naughty thing twice."

" You didn't put it back," said Marilla. " That

brooch isn't anywhere on the bureau. You've taken it out or something, Anne."

" I *did* put it back," said Anne quickly—pertly, Marilla thought. " I don't just remember whether I stuck it on the pincushion or laid it in the china tray. But I'm perfectly certain I put it back."

" I'll go and have another look," said Marilla, determining to be just. " If you put that brooch back it's there still. If it isn't I'll know you didn't, that's all ! "

Marilla went to her room and made a thorough search, not only over the bureau but in every other place she thought the brooch might possibly be. It was not to be found and she returned to the kitchen.

" Anne, the brooch is gone. By your own admission you were the last person to handle it. Now, what have you done with it ? Tell me the truth at once. Did you take it out and lose it ? "

" No, I didn't," said Anne solemnly, meeting Marilla's angry gaze squarely. " I never took the brooch out of your room and that is the truth, if I was to be led to the block for it—although I'm not very certain what a block is. So there, Marilla."

Anne's " so there " was only intended to emphasize her assertion, but Marilla took it as a display of defiance.

" I believe you are telling me a falsehood, Anne," she said sharply. " I know you are. There, now, don't say anything more unless you are prepared to tell the whole truth. Go to your room and stay there until you are ready to confess."

" Will I take the peas with me ? " said Anne meekly.

" No, I'll finish shelling them myself. Do as I bid you."

When Anne had gone, Marilla went about her evening tasks in a very disturbed state of mind. She was worried about her valuable brooch. What if Anne had lost it ? And how wicked of the child to deny having taken it, when anybody could see she must have! With such an innocent face, too !

" I don't know what I wouldn't sooner have had happen," thought Marilla, as she nervously shelled the peas. " Of course, I don't suppose she meant to steal it or anything like that. She's just taken it to play with or help along that imagination of hers. She must have taken it, that's clear, for there hasn't been a soul in that room since she was in it, by her own story, until I went up to-night. And the brooch is gone, there's nothing surer. I suppose she has lost it and is afraid to own up for fear she'll be punished. It's a dreadful thing to think she tells falsehoods. It's a far worse thing than her fit of temper. It's a fearful responsibility to have a child in your house you can't trust. Slyness and untruthfulness—that's what she has displayed. I declare I feel worse about that than about the brooch. If she'd only have told the truth about it I wouldn't mind so much."

Marilla went to her room at intervals all through the evening and searched for the brooch, without finding it. A bed-time visit to the east gable produced no result. Anne persisted in denying that she knew anything about the brooch but Marilla was only the more firmly convinced that she did.

She told Matthew the story the next morning. Matthew was confounded and puzzled ; he could not so quickly lose faith in Anne but he had to admit that circumstances were against her.

" You're sure it hasn't fell down behind the bureau ?" was the only suggestion he could offer.

" I've moved the bureau and I've taken out the drawers and I've looked in every crack and cranny," was Marilla's positive answer. " The brooch is gone and that child has taken it and lied about it. That's the plain, ugly truth, Matthew Cuthbert, and we might as well look it in the face."

" Well, now, what are you going to do about it ? " Matthew asked forlornly, feeling secretly thankful that Marilla and not he had to deal with the situation. He felt no desire to put his oar in this time.

" She'll stay in her room until she confesses," said Marilla grimly, remembering the success of this method in the former case. " Then we'll see. Perhaps we'll be able to find the brooch if she'll only tell where she took it ; but in any case she'll have to be severely punished, Matthew."

" Well now, you'll have to punish her," said Matthew, reaching for his hat. " I've nothing to do with it, remember. You warned me off yourself."

Marilla felt deserted by everyone. She could not even go to Mrs Lynde for advice. She went up to the east gable with a very serious face and left it with a face more serious still. Anne steadfastly refused to confess. She persisted in asserting that she had not taken the brooch. The child had evidently been crying and Marilla felt a pang of pity which she sternly repressed. By night she was, as she expressed it, " beat out."

" You'll stay in this room until you confess, Anne. You can make up your mind to that," she said firmly.

" But the picnic is to-morrow, Marilla," cried Anne. " You won't keep me from going to that, will you ? You'll just let me out for the afternoon, won't you ? Then I'll stay here as long as you like afterwards *cheerfully*. But I *must* go to the picnic."

" You'll not go to picnics nor anywhere else until you've confessed, Anne."

" Oh, Marilla," gasped Anne.

But Marilla had gone out and shut the door.

Wednesday morning dawned as bright and fair as

if expressly made to order for the picnic. Birds sang around Green Gables ; the Madonna lilies in the garden sent out whiffs of perfume that entered in on viewless winds at every door and window, and wandered through halls and rooms like spirits of benediction. The birches in the hollow waved joyful hands as if watching for Anne's usual morning greeting from the east gable. But Anne was not at her window. When Marilla took her breakfast up to her she found the child sitting primly on her bed, pale and resolute, with tight-shut lips and gleaming eyes.

" Marilla, I'm ready to confess."

" Ah ! " Marilla laid down her tray. Once again her method had succeeded ; but her success was very bitter to her. " Let me hear what you have to say then, Anne."

" I took the amethyst brooch," said Anne, as if repeating a lesson she had learned. " I took it just as you said. I didn't mean to take it when I went in. But it did look so beautiful, Marilla, when I pinned it on my breast that I was overcome by an irresistible temptation. I imagined how perfectly thrilling it would be to take it to Idlewild and play I was the Lady Cordelia Fitzgerald. It would be so much easier to imagine I was the Lady Cordelia if I had a real amethyst brooch on. Diana and I made necklaces of roseberries, but what are roseberries compared to amethysts ? So I took the brooch. I thought I could put it back before you came home. I went all the way around by the road to lengthen out the time. When I was going over the bridge across the Lake of Shining Waters I took the brooch off to have another look at it. Oh, how it did shine in the sunlight ! And then, when I was leaning over the bridge, it just slipped through my fingers—so—and went down—down— down, all purply-sparkling, and sank forevermore beneath the Lake of Shining Waters. And that's the best I can do at confessing, Marilla."

Marilla felt hot anger surge up into her heart again. This child had taken and lost her treasured amethyst brooch and now sat there calmly reciting the details thereof without the least apparent compunction or repentance.

"Anne, this is terrible," she said, trying to speak calmly. "You are the very wickedest girl I ever heard of."

"Yes, I suppose I am," agreed Anne tranquilly. "And I know I'll have to be punished. It'll be your duty to punish me, Marilla. Won't you please get it over right off because I'd like to go to the picnic with nothing on my mind."

"Picnic, indeed! You'll go to no picnic to-day, Anne Shirley. That shall be your punishment. And it isn't half severe enough either for what you've done!"

"Not go to the picnic!" Anne sprang to her feet and clutched Marilla's hand. "But you *promised* me I might! Oh, Marilla, I must go to the picnic. That was why I confessed. Punish me any way you like but that. Oh, Marilla, please, please, let me go to the picnic. Think of the ice-cream! For anything you know I may never have a chance to taste ice-cream again."

Marilla disengaged Anne's clinging hands stonily.

"You needn't plead, Anne. You are not going to the picnic and that's final. No, not a word."

Anne realized that Marilla was not to be moved. She clasped her hands together, gave a piercing shriek, and then flung herself face downwards on the bed, crying and writhing in an utter abandonment of disappointment and despair.

"For the land's sake!" gasped Marilla, hastening from the room. "I believe the child is crazy. No child in her senses would behave as she does. If she isn't she's utterly bad. Oh dear, I'm afraid Rachel was right from the first. But I've put my hand to the plough, and I won't look back."

That was a dismal morning. Marilla worked fiercely and scrubbed the porch floor and the dairy shelves when she could find nothing else to do. Neither the shelves nor the porch needed it—but Marilla did. Then she went out and raked the yard.

When dinner was ready she went to the stairs and called Anne. A tear-stained face appeared, looking tragically over the banisters.

" Come down to your dinner, Anne."

" I don't want any dinner, Marilla," said Anne sobbingly. " I couldn't eat anything. My heart is broken. You'll feel remorse of conscience some day, I expect, for breaking it, Marilla, but I forgive you. Remember when the time comes that I forgive you. But please don't ask me to eat anything, especially boiled pork and greens. Boiled pork and greens are so unromantic when one is in affliction."

Exasperated Marilla returned to the kitchen and poured out her tale of woe to Matthew, who, between his sense of justice and his unlawful sympathy with Anne, was a miserable man.

" Well now, she shouldn't have taken the brooch, Marilla, or told stories about it," he admitted, mournfully surveying his plateful of unromantic pork and greens as if he, like Anne, thought it a food unsuited to crises of feeling, " but she's such a little thing—such an interesting little thing. Don't you think it's pretty rough not to let her go to the picnic when she's so set on it ? "

" Matthew Cuthbert, I'm amazed at you. I think I've let her off entirely too easy. And she doesn't appear to realize how wicked she's been at all—that's what worries me most. If she'd really felt sorry it wouldn't be so bad. And you don't seem to realize it neither ; you're making excuses for her all the time to yourself—I can see that."

" Well now, she's such a little thing," feebly reiterated Matthew. " And there should be allowances made, Marilla. You know she's never had any bringing up."

" Well, she's having it now," retorted Marilla.

The retort silenced Matthew if it did not convince him. That dinner was a very dismal meal. The only cheerful thing about it was Jerry Buote, the hired boy, and Marilla resented his cheerfulness as a personal insult.

When her dishes were washed and her bread sponge set and her hens fed Marilla remembered that she had noticed a small rent in her best black lace shawl when she had taken it off on Monday afternoon on returning from the Ladies' Aid. She would go and mend it.

The shawl was in a box in her trunk. As Marilla lifted it out, the sunlight, falling through the vines that clustered thickly about the window, struck upon something caught in the shawl—something that glittered and sparkled in facets of violet light. Marilla snatched at it with a gasp. It was the amethyst brooch, hanging to a thread of the lace by its catch !

" Dear life and heart," said Marilla blankly, " what does this mean ? Here's my brooch safe and sound that I thought was at the bottom of Barry's pond. Whatever did that girl mean by saying she took it and lost it ? I declare I believe Green Gables is bewitched. I remember now that when I took off my shawl Monday afternoon I laid it on the bureau for a minute. I suppose the brooch got caught in it somehow. Well ! "

Marilla betook herself to the east gable, brooch in hand. Anne had cried herself out and was sitting dejectedly by the window.

" Anne Shirley," said Marilla solemnly, " I've just found my brooch hanging to my black lace shawl.   Now I want to know what that rigmarole you told me this morning meant."

" Why, you said you'd keep me here until I confessed," returned Anne wearily, " and so I decided to confess because I was bound to get to the picnic.   I thought out a confession last night after I went to bed and made it as interesting as I could.   And I said it over and over so that I wouldn't forget it.   But you wouldn't let me go to the picnic after all, so all my trouble was wasted."

Marilla had to laugh in spite of herself.   But her conscience pricked her.

" Anne, you do beat all !   But I was wrong—I see that now.   I shouldn't have doubted your word when I'd never known you to tell a story.   Of course, it wasn't right for you to confess to a thing you hadn't done—it was very wrong to do so.   But I drove you to it.   So if you'll forgive me, Anne, I'll forgive you and we'll start square again.   And now get yourself ready for the picnic."

Anne flew up like a rocket.

" Oh, Marilla, isn't it too late ? "

" No, it's only two o'clock.   They won't be more than well gathered yet and it'll be an hour before they have tea.   Wash your face and comb your hair and put on your gingham.   I'll fill a basket for you. There's plenty of stuff baked in the house.   And I'll get Jerry to hitch up the sorrel and drive you down to the picnic ground."

" O, Marilla," exclaimed Anne, flying to the washstand.   " Five minutes ago I was so miserable I was wishing I'd never been born and now I wouldn't change places with an angel ! "

That night a thoroughly happy, completely tired-out

Anne returned to Green Gables in a state of beatification impossible to describe.

" Oh, Marilla, I've had a perfectly scrumptious time. Scrumptious is a new word I learned to-day. I heard Mary Alice Bell use it. Isn't it very expressive? Everything was lovely. We had a splendid tea and then Mr Harmon Andrews took us all for a row on the Lake of Shining Waters—six of us at a time. And Jane Andrews nearly fell overboard. She was leaning out to pick water lilies and if Mr Andrews hadn't caught her by her sash just in the nick of time she'd have fallen in and prob'ly been drowned. I wish it had been me. It would have been such a romantic experience to have been nearly drowned. It would be such a thrilling tale to tell. And we had the ice-cream. Words fail me to describe that ice-cream. Marilla, I assure you it was sublime."

That evening Marilla told the whole story to Matthew over her stocking basket.

" I'm willing to own up that I made a mistake," she concluded candidly, " but I've learned a lesson. I have to laugh when I think of Anne's ' confession,' although I suppose I shouldn't for it really was a falsehood. But it doesn't seem as bad as the other would have been, somehow, and anyhow I'm responsible for it. That child is hard to understand in some respects. But I believe she'll turn out all right yet. And there's one thing certain, no house will ever be dull that she's in."

CHAPTER XV

A TEMPEST IN THE SCHOOL TEAPOT

WHAT a splendid day ! " said Anne, drawing a long breath. " Isn't it good just to be alive on a day like this ? I pity the people who aren't born yet for missing it. They may have good days, of course, but they can never have this one. And it's splendider still to have such a lovely way to go to school by isn't it ? "

" It's a lot nicer than going round by the road ; that is so dusty and hot," said Diana practically, peeping into her dinner basket and mentally calculating if the three juicy, toothsome, raspberry tarts reposing there were divided among ten girls how many bites each girl would have.

The little girls of Avonlea school always pooled their lunches, and to eat three raspberry tarts all alone or even to share them only with one's best chum would have for ever and ever branded as " awful mean " the girl who did it. And yet, when the tarts were divided among ten girls you just got enough to tantalize you.

The way Anne and Diana went to school *was* a pretty one. Anne thought those walks to and from school with Diana couldn't be improved upon even by imagination. Going around by the main road would have been so unromantic ; but to go by Lovers' Lane and Willowmere and Violet Vale and the Birch Path was romantic, if ever anything was.

Lover's Lane opened out below the orchard at Green Gables and stretched far up into the woods to the end of the Cuthbert Farm. It was the way by which the cows were taken to the back pasture and the wood hauled home in winter. Anne had named it Lovers' Lane before she had been a month at Green Gables.

" Not that lovers ever really walk there," she explained to Marilla, " but Diana and I are reading a perfectly magnificent book and there's a Lovers' Lane in it. So we want to have one, too. And it's a very pretty name, don't you think ? So romantic ! We can imagine the lovers into it, you know. I like that lane because you can think out loud there without people calling you crazy."

Anne, starting out alone in the morning, went down Lovers' Lane as far as the brook. Here Diana met her, and the two little girls went on up the lane under the leafy arch of maples—" maples are such sociable trees," said Anne ; " they're always rustling and whispering to you,"—until they came to a rustic bridge. Then they left the lane and walked through Mr Barry's back field and past Willowmere. Beyond Willowmere came Violet Vale—a little green dimple in the shadow of Mr Andrew Bell's big woods. " Of course there are no violets there now," Anne told Marilla, " but Diana says there are millions of them in spring. Oh, Marilla, can't you just imagine you see them ? It actually takes away my breath. I named it Violet Vale. Diana says she never saw the beat of me for hitting on fancy names for places. It's nice to be clever at something, isn't it ? But Diana named the Birch Path. She wanted to, so I let her ; but I'm sure I could have found something more poetical than plain Birch Path. Anybody can think of a name like that. But the Birch Path is one of the prettiest places in the world, Marilla."

It was. Other people besides Anne thought so when they stumbled on it. It was a little narrow, twisting path, winding down over a long hill straight through

Mr Bell's woods, where the light came down sifted
through so many emerald screens that it was as flawless
as the heart of a diamond.   It was fringed in all its
length with slim young birches, white-stemmed and
lissom-boughed ; ferns and starflowers and wild lilies-
of-the-valley and scarlet tufts of pigeon berries grew
thickly along it ; and always there was a delightful
spiciness in the air and music of bird calls and the
murmur and laugh of wood winds in the trees overhead.
Now and then you might see a rabbit skipping across
the road if you were quiet—which, with Anne and
Diana, happened about once in a blue moon.   Down
in the valley the path came out to the main road and
then it was just up the spruce hill to the school.

The Avonlea school was a whitewashed building
low in the eaves and wide in the windows, furnished
inside with comfortable substantial old-fashioned desks
that opened and shut, and were carved all over their
lids with the initials and hieroglyphics of three genera-
tions of school-children.   The schoolhouse was set
back from the road and behind it was a dusky fir wood
and a brook where all the children put their bottles of
milk in the morning to keep cool and sweet until
dinner hour.

Marilla had seen Anne start off to school on the first
day of September with many secret misgivings.   Anne
was such an odd girl.   How would she get on with the
other children ?   And how on earth would she ever
manage to hold her tongue during school hours ?

Things went better than Marilla feared, however.
Anne came home that evening in high spirits.

" I think I'm going to like school here," she announced.   " I don't think much of the master, though.
He's all the time curling his moustache and making
eyes at Prissy Andrews.   Prissy is grown-up, you
know.   She's sixteen and she's studying for the en-

trance examination into Queen's Academy at Charlotte-town next year. Tillie Boulter says the master is *dead gone* on her. She's got a beautiful complexion and curly brown hair and she does it up so elegantly. She sits in the long seat at the back and he sits there, too, most of the time—to explain her lessons, he says. But Ruby Gillis says she saw him writing something on her slate and when Prissy read it she blushed as red as a beet and giggled ; and Ruby Gillis says she doesn't believe it had anything to do with the lesson."

" Anne Shirley, don't let me hear you talking about your teacher in that way again," said Marilla sharply. " You don't go to school to criticize the master. I guess he can teach *you* something and it's your business to learn. And I want you to understand right off that you are not to come home telling tales about him. That is something I won't encourage. I hope you were a good girl."

" Indeed I was," said Anne comfortably. " It wasn't so hard as you might imagine, either. I sit with Diana. Our seat is right by the window and we can look down to the Lake of Shining Waters. There are a lot of nice girls in school and we had scrumptious fun playing at dinner time. It's so nice to have a lot of little girls to play with. But of course I like Diana best and always will. I *adore* Diana. I'm dreadfully far behind the others. They're all in the fifth book and I'm only in the fourth. I feel that it's a kind of a disgrace. But there's not one of them has such an imagination as I have, and I soon found that out. We had reading and geography and Canadian History and dictation to-day. Mr Phillips said my spelling was disgraceful and he held up my slate so that every-body could see it, all marked over. I felt so mortified, Marilla ; he might have been politer to a stranger, I think. Ruby Gillis gave me an apple and Sophia

Sloane lent me a lovely pink card with 'May I see you home?' on it. I'm to give it back to her to-morrow. And Tillie Boulter let me wear her bead ring all the afternoon. Can I have some of those pearl beads off the old pincushion in the garret to make myself a ring? And oh, Marilla, Jane Andrews told me that Minnie MacPherson told her that she heard Prissy Andrews tell Sara Gillis that I had a very pretty nose. Marilla, that is the first compliment I have ever had in my life and you can't imagine what a strange feeling it gave me. Marilla, have I really a pretty nose? I know you'll tell me the truth."

"Your nose is well enough," said Marilla shortly. Secretly she thought Anne's nose was a remarkably pretty one; but she had no intention of telling her so.

That was three weeks ago and all had gone smoothly so far. And now, this crisp September morning, Anne and Diana were tripping blithely down the Birch Path, two of the happiest little girls in Avonlea.

"I guess Gilbert Blythe will be in school to-day," said Diana. "He's been visiting his cousins over in New Brunswick all summer and he only came home Saturday night. He's *aw'fly* handsome, Anne. And he teases the girls something terrible. He just tor-ments our lives out."

Diana's voice indicated that she rather liked having her life tormented out than not.

"Gilbert Blythe?" said Anne. "Isn't it his name that's written up on the porch wall with Julia Bell's and a big 'Take Notice' over them?"

"Yes," said Diana, tossing her head, "but I'm sure he doesn't like Julia Bell so very much. I've heard him say he studied the multiplication table by her freckles."

"Oh, don't speak about freckles to me," implored Anne. "It isn't delicate when I've got so many. But

I do think that writing take-notices up on the wall about the boys and girls is the silliest ever. I should just like to see anybody dare to write my name up with a boy's. Not, of course," she hastened to add, " that anybody would."

Anne sighed. She didn't want her name written up. But it was a little humiliating to know that there was no danger of it.

" Nonsense," said Diana, whose black eyes and glossy tresses had played such havoc with the hearts of Avonlea schoolboys that her name figured on the porch walls in half a dozen take-notices. " It's only meant as a joke. And don't you be too sure your name won't ever be written up. Charlie Sloane is *dead gone* on you. He told his mother—his *mother*, mind you— that you were the smartest girl in school. That's better than being good-looking."

" No, it isn't," said Anne, feminine to the core. " I'd rather be pretty than clever. And I hate Charlie Sloane. I can't bear a boy with goggle eyes. If any one wrote my name up with his I'd *never* get over it, Diana Barry. But it *is* nice to keep head of your class."

" You'll have Gilbert in your class after this," said Diana, " and he's used to being head of his class, I can tell you. He's only in the fourth book although he's nearly fourteen. Four years ago his father was sick and had to go out to Alberta for his health and Gilbert went with him. They were there three years and Gil didn't go to school hardly any until they came back. You won't find it so easy to keep head after this, Anne."

" I'm glad," said Anne quickly. " I couldn't really feel proud of keeping head of little boys and girls of just nine or ten. I got up yesterday spelling ' ebullition.' Josie Pye was head and, mind you, she peeped in her book. Mr Phillips didn't see her—he was looking at Prissy Andrews—but I did. I just swept her a look of freezing scorn and she got as red as a beet and spelled it wrong after all."

" Those Pye girls are cheats all round," said Diana indignantly, as they climbed the fence of the main road. " Gertie Pye actually went and put her milk bottle in my place in the brook yesterday. Did you ever ? I don't speak to her now."

When Mr Phillips was in the back of the room hearing Prissy Andrews' Latin, Diana whispered to Anne :

" That's Gilbert Blythe sitting right across the aisle from you, Anne. Just look at him and see if you don't think he's handsome."

Anne looked accordingly. She had a good chance to do so, for the said Gilbert Blythe was absorbed in stealthily pinning the long yellow braid of Ruby Gillis, who sat in front of him, to the back of her seat. He was a tall boy, with curly brown hair, roguish hazel eyes and a mouth twisted into a teasing smile. Presently Ruby Gillis started up to take a sum to the master ; she fell back into her seat with a little shriek, believing that her hair was pulled out by the roots. Everybody looked at her and Mr Phillips glared so sternly that Ruby began to cry. Gilbert had whisked the pin out of sight and was studying his history with the soberest face in the world ; but when the commotion subsided he looked at Anne and winked with inexpressible drollery.

" I think your Gilbert Blythe *is* handsome," confided Anne to Diana, " but I think he's very bold. It isn't good manners to wink at a strange girl."

But it was not until the afternoon that things really began to happen.

Mr Phillips was back in the corner explaining a problem in algebra to Prissy Andrews and the rest of the scholars were doing pretty much as they pleased, eating green apples, whispering, drawing pictures on their slates, and driving crickets, harnessed to strings, up and down the aisle. Gilbert Blythe was trying to make Anne Shirley look at him and failing utterly, because Anne was at that moment totally oblivious, not only of the very existence of Gilbert Blythe, but of every other scholar in Avonlea school and of Avonlea school itself. With her chin propped on her hands and her eyes fixed on the blue glimpse of the Lake of Shining Waters that the west window afforded, she was far away in a gorgeous dreamland, hearing and seeing nothing save her own wonderful visions.

Gilbert Blythe wasn't used to putting himself out to make a girl look at him and meeting with failure. She *should* look at him, that red-haired Shirley girl with the little pointed chin and the big eyes that weren't like the eyes of any other girl in Avonlea school.

Gilbert reached across the aisle, picked up the end of Anne's long red braid, held it out at arm's length and said in a piercing whisper:

" Carrots ! Carrots ! "

Then Anne looked at him with a vengeance !

She did more than look. She sprang to her feet, her bright fancies fallen into cureless ruin. She flashed one indignant glance at Gilbert from eyes whose angry sparkle was swiftly quenched in equally angry tears.

" You mean, hateful boy ! " she exclaimed passionately. " How dare you ! "

And then—Thwack ! Anne had brought her slate down on Gilbert's head and cracked it—slate, not head—clear across.

Avonlea school always enjoyed a scene. This was an especially enjoyable one. Everybody said, " Oh," in horrified delight. Diana gasped. Ruby Gillis, who was inclined to be hysterical, began to cry. Tommy Sloane let his team of crickets escape him altogether while he stared open-mouthed at the tableau.

Mr Phillips stalked down the aisle and laid his hand heavily on Anne's shoulder.

" Anne Shirley, what does this mean ? " he said angrily.

Anne returned no answer. It was asking too much of flesh and blood to expect her to tell before the whole school that she had been called " carrots." Gilbert it was who spoke up stoutly.

" It was my fault, Mr Phillips. I teased her."

Mr Phillips paid no heed to Gilbert.

" I am sorry to see a pupil of mine displaying such a temper and such a vindictive spirit," he said in a solemn tone, as if the mere fact of being a pupil of his ought to root out all evil passions from the hearts of small imperfect mortals. " Anne, go and stand on the platform in front of the blackboard for the rest of the afternoon."

Anne would have infinitely preferred a whipping to this punishment, under which her sensitive spirit quivered as from a whiplash. With a white, set face she obeyed. Mr Phillips took a chalk crayon and wrote on the blackboard above her head :

" Ann Shirley has a very bad temper. Ann Shirley must learn to control her temper," and then read it out loud so that even the primer class, who couldn't read writing, should understand it.

Anne stood there the rest of the afternoon with that legend above her. She did not cry or hang her head. Anger was still too hot in her heart for that and it sustained her amid all her agony of humiliation. With resentful eyes and passion-red cheeks she confronted alike Diana's sympathetic gaze and Charlie Sloane's indignant nods and Josie Pye's malicious smiles. As

for Gilbert Blythe, she would not even look at him.
She would *never* look at him again ! She would never
speak to him ! !

When school was dismissed Anne marched out with
her red head held high. Gilbert Blythe tried to inter-
cept her at the porch door.

" I'm awfully sorry I made fun of your hair, Anne,"
he whispered contritely. " Honest I am. Don't be
mad for keeps, now."

Anne swept by disdainfully, without look or sign of
hearing. " Oh, how could you, Anne ? " breathed
Diana as they went down the road, half reproachfully,
half admiringly. Diana felt that *she* could never have
resisted Gilbert's plea.

" I shall never forgive Gilbert Blythe," said Anne
firmly. " And Mr Phillips spelled my name without
an *e*, too. The iron has entered into my soul, Diana."

Diana hadn't the least idea what Anne meant, but
she understood it was something terrible.

" You mustn't mind Gilbert making fun of your
hair," she said soothingly. " Why, he makes fun of
all the girls. He laughs at mine because it's so black.
He's called me a crow a dozen times ; and I never
heard him apologize for anything before, either."

" There's a great deal of difference between being
called a crow and being called carrots," said Anne
with dignity. " Gilbert Blythe has hurt my feelings
excruciatingly, Diana."

It is possible the matter might have blown over
without more excruciation if nothing else had happened. But when things begin to happen they are apt
to keep on.

Avonlea scholars often spent noon hour picking gum
in Mr Bell's spruce grove over the hill and across his
big pasture field. From there they could keep an eye
on Eben Wright's house, where the master boarded.

When they saw Mr Phillips emerging therefrom they ran for the schoolhouse ; but the distance being about three times longer than Mr Wright's lane they were very apt to arrive there, breathless and gasping, some three minutes too late.

On the following day Mr Phillips was seized with one of his spasmodic fits of reform and announced, before going home to dinner, that he should expect to find all the scholars in their seats when he returned. Anyone who came in late would be punished.

All the boys and some of the girls went to Mr Bell's spruce grove as usual, fully intending to stay only long enough to " pick a chew." But spruce groves are seductive and yellow nuts of gum beguiling ; they picked and loitered and strayed ; and as usual the first thing that recalled them to a sense of the flight of time was Jimmy Glover shouting from the top of a patriarchial old spruce, " Master's coming."

The girls, who were on the ground, started first and managed to reach the schoolhouse in time, but without a second to spare. The boys, who had to wriggle hastily down from the trees, were later ; and Anne, who had not been picking gum at all but was wandering happily in the far end of the grove, waist deep among the bracken, singing softly to herself, with a wreath of rice lilies on her hair as if she were some wild divinity of the shadowy places, was latest of all. Anne could run like a deer, however ; run she did with the impish result that she overtook the boys at the door and was swept into the schoolhouse among them just as Mr Phillips was in the act of hanging up his hat.

Mr Phillips' brief reforming energy was over ; he didn't want the bother of punishing a dozen pupils ; but it was necessary to do something to save his word, so he looked about for a scapegoat and found it in Anne, who had dropped into her seat, gasping for breath, with her forgotten lily wreath hanging askew over one ear and giving her a particularly rakish and dishevelled appearance.

" Anne Shirley, since you seem to be so fond of the boys' company we shall indulge your taste for it this afternoon," he said sarcastically. " Take those flowers out of your hair and sit with Gilbert Blythe."

The other boys snickered. Diana, turning pale with pity, plucked the wreath from Anne's hair and squeezed her hand. Anne stared at the master as if turned to stone.

" Did you hear what I said, Anne ? " queried Mr Phillips sternly.

" Yes, sir," said Anne slowly, " but I didn't suppose you really meant it."

" I assure you I did "—still with the sarcastic inflection which all the children, and Anne especially, hated. It flicked on the raw. " Obey me at once."

For a moment Anne looked as if she meant to disobey. Then, realizing that there was no help for it, she rose haughtily, stepped across the aisle, sat down beside Gilbert Blythe, and buried her face in her arms on the desk. Ruby Gillis, who got a glimpse of it as it went down, told the others going home from school that she'd " acksually never seen anything like it—it was so white, with awful little red spots in it."

To Anne, this was as the end of all things. It was bad enough to be singled out for punishment from among a dozen equally guilty ones ; it was worse still to be sent to sit with a boy ; but that that boy should be Gilbert Blythe was heaping insult on injury to a degree utterly unbearable. Anne felt that she could *not* bear it and it would be of no use to try. Her whole being seethed with shame and anger and humiliation.

At first the other scholars looked and whispered and giggled and nudged. But as Anne never lifted her

head and as Gilbert worked fractions as if his whole
soul was absorbed in them and them only, they soon
returned to their own tasks and Anne was forgotten.
When Mr Phillips called the history class out Anne
should have gone ; but Anne did not move, and Mr
Phillips, who had been writing some verses " To
Priscilla " before he called the class, was thinking about
an obstinate rhyme still and never missed her.   Once,
when nobody was looking, Gilbert took from his desk
a little pink candy heart with a gold motto on it,
" You are sweet," and slipped it under the curve of
Anne's arm.   Whereupon Anne arose, took the pink
heart gingerly between the tips of her fingers, dropped
it on the floor, ground it to powder beneath her heel,
and resumed her position without deigning to bestow
a glance on Gilbert.

When school went out Anne marched to her desk,
ostentatiously took out everything therein, books and
writing tablet, pen and ink, testament and arithmetic,
and piled them neatly on her cracked slate.

" What are you taking all those things home for,
Anne ? " Diana wanted to know, as soon as they were
out on the road.   She had not dared to ask the question before.

" I am not coming back to school any more," said
Anne.

Diana gasped and stared at Anne to see if she meant it.

" Will Marilla let you stay home ? " she asked.

" She'll have to," said Anne.   " I'll *never* go to
school to that man again."

" Oh, Anne ! "   Diana looked as if she were ready
to cry.   " I do think you're mean.   What shall I do ?
Mr Phillips will make me sit with that horrid Gertie
Pye—I know he will, because she is sitting alone.   Do
come back, Anne."

" I'd do almost anything in the world for you,

Diana," said Anne sadly. " I'd let myself be torn limb from limb if it would do you any good. But I can't do this, so please don't ask it. You harrow up my very soul."

" Just think of all the fun you will miss," mourned Diana. " We are going to build the loveliest new house down by the brook ; and we'll be playing ball next week and you've never played ball, Anne. It's tremenjusly exciting. And we're going to learn a new song—Jane Andrews is practising it up now ; and Alice Andrews is going to bring a new Pansy book next week and we're all going to read it out loud, chapter about, down by the brook. And you know you are so fond of reading out loud, Anne."

Nothing moved Anne in the least. Her mind was made up. She would not go to school to Mr Phillips again ; she told Marilla so when she got home.

" Nonsense," said Marilla.

" It isn't nonsense at all," said Anne, gazing at Marilla with solemn, reproachful eyes. " Don't you understand, Marilla ? I've been insulted."

" Insulted fiddlesticks ! You'll go to school to-morrow as usual."

" Oh, no." Anne shook her head gently. " I'm not going back, Marilla. I'll learn my lessons at home and I'll be as good as I can be and hold my tongue all the time if it's possible at all. But I will not go back to school I assure you."

Marilla saw something remarkably like unyielding stubbornness looking out of Anne's small face. She understood that she would have trouble in overcoming it ; but she resolved wisely to say nothing more just then.

" I'll run down and see Rachel about it this evening," she thought. " There's no use reasoning with Anne now. She's too worked up and I've an idea she can be awful stubborn if she takes the notion. Far as I can make out from her story, Mr Phillips has been carrying matters with a rather high hand. But it would never do to say so to her. I'll just talk it over with Rachel. She's sent ten children to school and she ought to know something about it. She'll have heard the whole story, too, by this time."

Marilla found Mrs Lynde knitting quilts as industriously and cheerfully as usual.

" I suppose you know what I've come about," she said, a little shamefacedly.

Mrs Rachel nodded.

" About Anne's fuss in school, I reckon," she said. " Tillie Boulter was in on her way home from school and told me about it."

" I don't know what to do with her," said Marilla. " She declares she won't go back to school. I never saw a child so worked up. I've been expecting trouble ever since she started to school. I knew things were going too smooth to last. She's so high-strung. What would you advise, Rachel ? "

" Well, since you've asked my advice, Marilla," said Mrs Lynde amiably—Mrs Lynde dearly loved to be asked for advice—" I'd just humour her a little at first, that's what I'd do. It's my belief that Mr Phillips was in the wrong. Of course, it doesn't do to say so to the children, you know. And of course he did right to punish her yesterday for giving way to temper. But to-day it was different. The others who were late should have been punished as well as Anne, that's what. And I don't believe in making the girls sit with the boys for punishment. It isn't modest. Tillie Boulter was real indignant. She took Anne's part right through and said all the scholars did, too. Anne seems real popular among them, somehow. I never thought she'd take with them so well."

" Then you really think I'd better let her stay home,"
said Marilla in amazement.

" Yes. That is, I wouldn't say school to her again
until she said it herself. Depend upon it, Marilla,
she'll cool off in a week or so and be ready enough to
go back of her own accord, that's what, while, if you
were to make her go back right off, dear knows what
freak or tantrum she'd take next and make more
trouble than ever. The less fuss made the better, in
my opinion. She won't miss much by not going to
school, as far as *that* goes. Mr Phillips isn't any good
at all as a teacher. The order he keeps is scandalous,
that's what, and he neglects the young fry and puts
all his time on those big scholars he's getting ready for
Queen's. He'd never have got the school for another
year if his uncle hadn't been a trustee—*the* trustee,
for he just leads the other two around by the nose,
that's what. I declare, I don't know what education
in this Island is coming to."

Mrs Rachel shook her head, as much as to say if
she were only at the head of the educational system
of the Province things would be much better managed.

Marilla took Mrs Rachel's advice and not another
word was said to Anne about going back to school.
She learned her lessons at home, did her chores, and
played with Diana in the chilly purple autumn twilights ; but when she met Gilbert Blythe on the road
or encountered him in Sunday school she passed him
by with an icy contempt that was no whit thawed by
his evident desire to appease her. Even Diana's efforts
as a peacemaker were of no avail. Anne had evidently
made up her mind to hate Gilbert Blythe to the end
of life.

As much as she hated Gilbert, however, did she love
Diana, with all the love of her passionate little heart,
equally intense in its likes and dislikes. One evening

Marilla, coming in from the orchard with a basket of apples, found Anne sitting alone by the east window in the twilight, crying bitterly.

" Whatever's the matter now, Anne ? " she asked.

" It's about Diana," sobbed Anne luxuriously. " I love Diana so, Marilla. I cannot ever live without her. But I know very well when we grow up that Diana will get married and go away and leave me. And oh, what shall I do ? I hate her husband—I just hate him furiously. I've been imagining it all out—the wedding and everything—Diana dressed in snowy garments, with a veil, and looking as beautiful and regal as a queen ; and me the bridesmaid, with a lovely dress, too, and puffed sleeves, but with a breaking heart hid beneath my smiling face. And then bidding Diana good-bye-e-e——" Here Anne broke down entirely and wept with increasing bitterness.

Marilla turned quickly away to hide her twitching face ; but it was no use ; she collapsed on the nearest chair and burst into such a hearty and unusual peal of laughter that Matthew, crossing the yard outside, halted in amazement. When had he heard Marilla laugh like that before ?

" Well, Anne Shirley," said Marilla as soon as she could speak, " if you must borrow trouble, for pity's sake borrow it handier home. I should think you had an imagination, sure enough."

CHAPTER XVI

DIANA IS INVITED TO TEA, WITH TRAGIC RESULTS

OCTOBER was a beautiful month at Green Gables, when the birches in the hollow turned as golden as sunshine and the maples behind the orchard were royal crimson and the wild cherry-trees along the lane put on the loveliest shades of dark red and bronzy green, while the fields sunned themselves in aftermaths.

Anne revelled in the world of colour about her.

" Oh, Marilla," she exclaimed one Saturday morning, coming dancing in with her arms full of gorgeous boughs, " I'm so glad I live in a world where there are Octobers. It would be terrible if we just skipped from September to November, wouldn't it ? Look at these maple branches. Don't they give you a thrill—several thrills ? I'm going to decorate my room with them."

" Messy things," said Marilla, whose aesthetic sense was not noticeably developed. " You clutter up your room entirely too much with out-of-doors stuff, Anne. Bedrooms were made to sleep in."

" Oh, and dream in, too, Marilla. And you know one can dream so much better in a room where there are pretty things. I'm going to put these boughs in the old blue jug and set them on my table."

" Mind you don't drop leaves all over the stairs then. I'm going to a meeting of the Aid Society at Carmody this afternoon, Anne, and I won't likely be home before dark. You'll have to get Matthew and Jerry their supper, so mind you don't forget to put the tea to draw until you sit down at the table as you did last time."

" It was dreadful of me to forget," said Anne apologetically, " but that was the afternoon I was trying to think of a name for Violet Vale and it crowded other things out. Matthew was so good. He never scolded a bit. He put the tea down himself and said we could wait awhile as well as not. And I told him a lovely fairy story while we were waiting, so he didn't find the time long at all. It was a beautiful fairy story, Marilla. I forgot the end of it, so I made up an end for it myself and Matthew said he couldn't tell where the join came in."

" Matthew would think it all right, Anne, if you took a notion to get up and have dinner in the middle of the night. But you keep your wits about you this time. And—I don't really know if I'm doing right—it may make you more addle-pated than ever—but you can ask Diana to come over and spend the afternoon with you and have tea here."

" Oh, Marilla ! " Anne clasped her hands. " How perfectly lovely ! You *are* able to imagine things after all or else you'd never have understood how I've longed for that very thing. It will seem so nice and grown-uppish. No fear of my forgetting to put the tea to draw when I have company. Oh, Marilla, can I use the rosebud spray tea-set ? "

" No, indeed ! The rosebud tea-set ! Well, what next ? You know I never use that except for the minister or the Aids. You'll put down the old brown tea-set. But you can open the little yellow crock of cherry preserves. It's time it was being used anyhow —I believe it's beginning to go. And you can cut some fruit-cake and have some of the cookies and snaps."

" I can just imagine myself sitting down at the head

of the table and pouring out the tea," said Anne, shutting her eyes ecstatically. " And asking Diana if she takes sugar ! I know she doesn't, but of course I'll ask her just as if I didn't know. And then pressing her to take another piece of fruit-cake and another helping of preserves. Oh, Marilla, it's a wonderful sensation just to think of it. Can I take her into the spare room to lay off her hat when she comes ? And then into the parlour to sit ? "

" No. The sitting-room will do for you and your company. But there's a bottle half full of raspberry cordial that was left over from the church social the other night. It's on the second shelf of the sitting-room closet and you and Diana can have it if you like, and a cooky to eat with it along in the afternoon, for I daresay Matthew'll be late coming in to tea since he's hauling potatoes to the vessel."

Anne flew down to the hollow, past the Dryad's Bubble and up the spruce path to Orchard Slope, to ask Diana to tea. As a result, just after Marilla had driven off to Carmody, Diana came over, dressed in her second best dress and looking exactly as it is proper to look when asked out to tea. At other times she was wont to run into the kitchen without knocking ; but now she knocked primly at the front door. And when Anne, dressed in *her* second best, as primly opened it, both little girls shook hands as gravely as if they had never met before. This unnatural solemnity lasted until after Diana had been taken to the east gable to lay off her hat and then had sat for ten minutes in the sitting-room, toes in position.

" How is your mother ? " inquired Anne politely just as if she had not seen Mrs Barry picking apples that morning in excellent health and spirits.

" She is very well, thank you. I suppose Mr Cuthbert is hauling potatoes to the *Lily Sands* this afternoon, is he ? " said Diana, who had ridden down to Mr Harmon Andrews' that morning in Matthew's cart.

" Yes. Our potato crop is very good this year. I hope your father's potato crop is good, too."

" It is fairly good, thank you. Have you picked many of your apples yet ? "

" Oh, ever so many," said Anne, forgetting to be dignified and jumping up quickly. " Let's go out to the orchard and get some of the Red Sweetings, Diana. Marilla says we can have all that are left on the tree. Marilla is a very generous woman. She said we could have fruit-cake and cherry preserves for tea. But it isn't good manners to tell your company what you are going to give them to eat, so I won't tell you what she said we could have to drink. Only it begins with an *r* and a *c* and it's a bright red colour. I love bright red drinks, don't you ? They taste twice as good as any other colour."

The orchard, with its great sweeping boughs that bent to the ground with fruit, proved so delightful that the little girls spent most of the afternoon in it, sitting in a grassy corner where the frost had spared the green and the mellow autumn sunshine lingered warmly, eating apples and talking as hard as they could. Diana had much to tell Anne of what went on in school. She had to sit with Gertie Pye and she hated it ; Gertie squeaked her pencil all the time and it just made her— Diana's—blood run cold ; Ruby Gillis had charmed all her warts away, true's you live, with a magic pebble that old Mary Joe from the Creek gave her. You had to rub the warts with the pebble and then throw it away over your left shoulder at the time of the new moon and the warts would all go. Charlie Sloane's name was written up with Em White's on the porch wall and Em White was *awful mad* about it ; Sam Boulter had 'sassed' Mr Phillips in class and Mr Phillips whipped him and

Sam's father came down to the school and dared Mr Phillips to lay a hand on one of his children again ; and Mattie Andrews had a new red hood and a blue crossover with tassels on it, and the airs she put on about it were perfectly sickening ; and Lizzie Wright didn't speak to Mamie Wilson because Mamie Wilson's grown-up sister had cut out Lizzie Wright's grown-up sister with her beau ; and everybody missed Anne so and wished she'd come to school again ; and Gilbert Blythe——

But Anne didn't want to hear about Gilbert Blythe. She jumped up hurriedly and said suppose they go in and have some raspberry cordial.

Anne looked on the second shelf of the room pantry, but there was no bottle of raspberry cordial there. Search revealed it away back on the top shelf. Anne put it on a tray and set it on the table with a tumbler.

" Now, please help yourself, Diana," she said politely. " I don't believe I'll have any just now. I don't feel as if I wanted any after all those apples."

Diana poured herself out a tumblerful, looked at its bright red hue admiringly, and then sipped it daintily.

" That's awfully nice raspberry cordial, Anne," she said. " I didn't know raspberry cordial was so nice."

" I'm real glad you like it. Take as much as you want. I'm going to run out and stir the fire up. There are so many responsibilities on a person's mind when they're keeping house, isn't there ? "

When Anne came back from the kitchen Diana was drinking her second glassful of cordial ; and, being entreated thereto by Anne, she offered no particular objection to the drinking of a third. The tumblerfuls were generous ones and the raspberry cordial was certainly very nice.

" The nicest I ever drank," said Diana. " It's

ever so much nicer than Mrs Lynde's although she brags of hers so much. It doesn't taste a bit like hers."

" I should think Marilla's raspberry cordial would prob'ly be much nicer than Mrs Lynde's," said Anne loyally. " Marilla is a famous cook. She is trying to teach me to cook but I assure you, Diana, it is uphill work. There's so little scope for imagination in cookery. You just have to go by rules. The last time I made a cake I forgot to put the flour in. I was thinking the loveliest story about you and me, Diana. I thought you were desperately ill with smallpox and everybody deserted you, but I went boldly to your bedside and nursed you back to life ; and then I took the smallpox and died and I was buried under those poplar-trees in the graveyard and you planted a rose-bush by my grave and watered it with your tears ; and you never, never forgot the friend of your youth who sacrificed her life for you. Oh, it was such a pathetic little tale, Diana. The tears just rained down over my cheeks while I mixed the cake. But I forgot the flour and the cake was a dismal failure. Flour is so essential to cakes, you know. Marilla was very cross and I don't wonder. I'm a great trial to her. She was terribly mortified about the pudding sauce last week. We had a plum pudding for dinner on Tuesday and there was half the pudding and a pitcherful of sauce left over. Marilla said there was enough for another dinner and told me to set it on the pantry shelf and cover it. I meant to cover it just as much as could be, Diana, but when I carried it in I was imagining I was a nun—of course I'm a Protestant, but I imagined I was a Catholic— taking the veil to bury a broken heart in cloistered seclusion ; and I forgot all about covering the pudding sauce. I thought of it next morning and ran to the pantry. Diana, fancy if you can my extreme horror

at finding a mouse drowned in that pudding sauce !
I lifted the mouse out with a spoon and threw it out
in the yard and then I washed the spoon in three waters.
Marilla was out milking and I fully intended to ask
her when she came in if I'd give the sauce to the pigs ;
but when she did come in I was imagining that I was
a frost-fairy going through the woods turning the trees
red and yellow, whichever they wanted to be, so I never
thought about the pudding sauce again and Marilla
sent me out to pick apples.   Well, Mr and Mrs Chester
Ross from Spencervale came here that morning.   You
know they are very stylish people, especially Mrs
Chester Ross.   When Marilla called me in, dinner was
all ready and everybody was at the table.   I tried to
be as polite and dignified as I could be, for I wanted
Mrs Chester Ross to think I was a ladylike little girl
even if I wasn't pretty.   Everything went right until
I saw Marilla coming with the plum pudding in one
hand and the pitcher of pudding sauce, *warmed up*,
in the other.   Diana, that was a terrible moment.   I
remembered everything and I just stood up in my place
and shrieked out, ' Marilla, you mustn't use that pudding sauce.   There was a mouse drowned in it.   I
forgot to tell you before.'   Oh, Diana, I shall never
forget that awful moment if I live to be a hundred.
Mrs Chester Ross just *looked* at me and I thought I
would sink through the floor with mortification.   She
is such a perfect housekeeper and fancy what she must
have thought of us.   Marilla turned red as fire but she
never said a word—then.   She just carried that sauce
and pudding out and brought in some strawberry
preserves.   She even offered me some, but I couldn't
swallow a mouthful.   It was like heaping coals of fire
on my head.   After Mrs Chester Ross went away
Marilla gave me a dreadful scolding.   Why, Diana,
what is the matter ? "

Diana had stood up very unsteadily ; then she sat down again, putting her hands to her head.

" I'm—I'm awful sick," she said, a little thickly. " I—I—must go right home."

" Oh, you mustn't dream of going home without your tea," cried Anne in distress. " I'll get it right off—I'll go and put the tea down this very minute."

" I must go home," repeated Diana, stupidly but determinedly.

" Let me get you a lunch anyhow," implored Anne. " Let me give you a bit of fruit-cake and some of the cherry preserves. Lie down on the sofa for a little while and you'll be better. Where do you feel bad ? "

" I must go home," said Diana, and that was all she would say. In vain Anne pleaded.

" I never heard of company going home without tea," she mourned. " Oh, Diana, do you suppose that it's possible you're really taking the smallpox ? If you are I'll go and nurse you, you can depend on that. I'll never forsake you. But I do wish you'd stay till after tea. Where do you feel bad ? "

" I'm awful dizzy," said Diana.

And indeed, she walked very dizzily. Anne, with tears of disappointment in her eyes, got Diana's hat and went with her as far as the Barry yard fence. Then she wept all the way back to Green Gables, where she sorrowfully put the remainder of the raspberry cordial back into the pantry and got tea ready for Matthew and Jerry, with all the zest gone out of the performance.

The next day was Sunday and as the rain poured down in torrents from dawn till dusk, Anne did not stir abroad from Green Gables. Monday afternoon Marilla sent her down to Mrs Lynde's on an errand. In a very short space of time Anne came flying back up the lane, with tears rolling down her cheeks. Into the kitchen she dashed and flung herself face downwards on the sofa in an agony.

" Whatever has gone wrong now, Anne ? " queried Marilla in doubt and dismay. " I do hope you haven't gone and been saucy to Mrs Lynde again."

No answer from Anne save more tears and stormier sobs !

" Anne Shirley, when I ask you a question I want to be answered. Sit right up this very minute and tell me what you are crying about."

Anne sat up, tragedy personified.

" Mrs Lynde was up to see Mrs Barry to-day and Mrs Barry was in an awful state," she wailed. " She says that I set Diana *drunk* Saturday and sent her home in a disgraceful condition. And she says I must be a thoroughly bad, wicked little girl and she's never, never going to let Diana play with me again. Oh, Marilla, I'm just overcome with woe."

Marilla stared in blank amazement.

" Set Diana drunk ! " she said when she found her voice. " Anne, are you or Mrs Barry crazy ? What on earth did you give her ? "

" Not a thing but raspberry cordial," sobbed Anne. " I never thought raspberry cordial would set people drunk, Marilla—not even if they drank three big tumblerfuls as Diana did. Oh, it sounds so—so—like Mrs Thomas' husband ! But I didn't mean to set her drunk."

" Drunk fiddlesticks ! " said Marilla, marching to the sitting-room pantry. There on the shelf was a bottle which she at once recognized as one containing some of her three year old home-made currant wine, for which she was celebrated in Avonlea, although certain of the stricter sort, Mrs Barry among them, disapproved strongly of it. And at the same time Marilla recollected that she had put the bottle of raspberry cordial down in the cellar instead of in the pantry as she had told Anne.

She went back to the kitchen with the wine bottle in her hand. Her face was twitching in spite of herself.

" Anne, you certainly have a genius for getting into trouble. You went and gave Diana currant wine instead of raspberry cordial. Didn't you know the difference yourself ? "

" I never tasted it," said Anne. " I thought it was the cordial. I meant to be so—so—hospitable. Diana got awfully sick and had to go home. Mrs Barry told Mrs Lynde she was simply dead drunk. She just laughed silly-like when her mother asked her what was the matter and went to sleep and slept for hours. Her mother smelled her breath and knew she was drunk. She had a fearful headache all day yesterday. Mrs Barry is so indignant. She will never believe but what I did it on purpose."

" I should think she would better punish Diana for being so greedy as to drink three glassfuls of anything," said Marilla shortly. " Why, three of those big glasses would have made her sick even if it had only been cordial. Well, this story will be a nice handle for those folks who are so down on me for making currant wine, although I haven't made any for three years ever since I found out that the minister didn't approve. I just kept that bottle for sickness. There, there, child, don't cry. I can't see as you were to blame although I'm sorry it happened so."

" I must cry," said Anne. " My heart is broken. The stars in their courses fight against me, Marilla. Diana and I are parted forever. Oh, Marilla, I little dreamed of this when first we swore our vows of friendship."

" Don't be foolish, Anne. Mrs Barry will think better of it when she finds you're not really to blame. I suppose she thinks you've done it for a silly joke or something of that sort. You'd best go up this evening and tell her how it was."

" My courage fails me at the thought of facing Diana's injured mother," sighed Anne. " I wish you'd go, Marilla. You're so much more dignified than I am. Likely she'd listen to you quicker than to me."

" Well, I will," said Marilla, reflecting that it would probably be the wiser course. " Don't cry any more, Anne. It will be all right."

Marilla had changed her mind about its being all right by the time she got back from Orchard Slope. Anne was watching for her coming and flew to the porch door to meet her.

" Oh, Marilla, I know by your face that it's been no use," she said sorrowfully. " Mrs Barry won't forgive me ? "

" Mrs Barry, indeed ! " snapped Marilla. " Of all the unreasonable women I ever saw she's the worst. I told her it was all a mistake and you weren't to blame, but she just simply didn't believe me. And she rubbed it well in about my currant wine and how I'd always said it couldn't have the least effect on anybody. I just told her plainly that currant wine wasn't meant to be drunk three tumblerfuls at a time and that if a child I had to do with was so greedy I'd sober her up with a right good spanking."

Marilla whisked into the kitchen, grievously disturbed, leaving a very much distracted little soul in the porch behind her. Presently Anne stepped out bare-headed into the chill autumn dusk ; very determinedly and steadily she took her way down through the sere clover field over the log bridge and up through the spruce grove, lighted by a pale little moon hanging low over the western woods. Mrs Barry, coming to the door in answer to a timid knock, found a white-lipped, eager-eyed suppliant on the doorstep.

Her face hardened. Mrs Barry was a woman of strong prejudices and dislikes, and her anger was of the cold, sullen sort which is always hardest to overcome. To do her justice, she really believed Anne had made Diana drunk out of sheer malice prepense, and she was honestly anxious to preserve her little daughter from the contamination of further intimacy with such a child.

" What do you want ? " she said stiffly.

Anne clasped her hands.

" Oh, Mrs Barry, please forgive me. I did not mean to—to—intoxicate Diana. How could I ? Just imagine if you were a poor little orphan girl that kind people had adopted and you had just one bosom friend in all the world. Do you think you would intoxicate her on purpose ? I thought it was only raspberry cordial. I was firmly convinced it was raspberry cordial. Oh, please don't say that you won't let Diana play with me any more. If you do you will cover my life with a dark cloud of woe."

This speech, which would have softened good Mrs Lynde's heart in a twinkling, had no effect on Mrs Barry except to irritate her still more. She was suspicious of Anne's big words and dramatic gestures and imagined that the child was making fun of her. So she said, coldly and cruelly :

" I don't think you are a fit little girl for Diana to associate with. You'd better go home and behave yourself."

Anne's lip quivered.

" Won't you let me see Diana just once to say fare-well ? " she implored.

" Diana has gone over to Carmody with her father,' said Mrs Barry, going in and shutting the door.

Anne went back to Green Gables calm with despair.

" My last hope is gone," she told Marilla. " I went

up and saw Mrs Barry myself and she treated me very insultingly. Marilla, I do *not* think she is a well-bred woman. There is nothing more to do except to pray and I haven't much hope that that'll do much good because, Marilla, I do not believe that God Himself can do very much with such an obstinate person as Mrs Barry."

" Anne, you shouldn't say such things," rebuked Marilla, striving to overcome that unholy tendency to laughter which she was dismayed to find growing upon her. And indeed, when she told the whole story to Matthew that night, she did laugh heartily over Anne's tribulations.

But when she slipped into the east gable before going to bed and found that Anne had cried herself to sleep an unaccustomed softness crept into her face.

" Poor little soul," she murmured, lifting a loose curl of hair from the child's tear-stained face. Then she bent down and kissed the flushed cheek on the pillow.

CHAPTER XVII

A NEW INTEREST IN LIFE

THE next afternoon Anne, bending over her patchwork at the kitchen window, happened to glance out and beheld Diana down by the Dryad's Bubble beckoning mysteriously. In a trice Anne was out of the house and flying down to the hollow astonishment and hope struggling in her expressive eyes. But the hope faded when she saw Diana's dejected countenance.

" Your mother hasn't relented ? " she gasped.

Diana shook her head mournfully.

" No ; and oh, Anne, she says I'm never to play with you again. I've cried and cried and I told her it wasn't your fault, but it wasn't any use. I had ever such a time coaxing her to let me come down and say good-bye to you. She said I was only to stay ten minutes and she's timing me by the clock."

" Ten minutes isn't very long to say an eternal farewell in," said Anne tearfully. " Oh, Diana, will you promise faithfully never to forget me, the friend of your youth, no matter what dearer friends may caress thee ?"

" Indeed I will," sobbed Diana, " and I'll never have another bosom friend—I don't want to have. I couldn't love anybody as I love you."

" Oh, Diana," cried Anne, clasping her hands, " do you *love* me ? "

" Why, of course I do. Didn't you know that ? "

" No." Anne drew a long breath. " I thought you *liked* me of course, but I never hoped you *loved* me. Why, Diana, I didn't think anybody could love me.

Nobody ever has loved me since I can remember. Oh, this is wonderful ! It's a ray of light which will forever shine on the darkness of a path severed from thee, Diana. Oh, just say it once again."

" I love you devotedly, Anne," said Diana stanchly, " and I always will, you may be sure of that."

" And I will always love thee, Diana," said Anne, solemnly extending her hand. " In the years to come thy memory will shine like a star over my lonely life, as that last story we read together says. Diana, wilt thou give me a lock of thy jet-black tresses in parting to treasure for evermore ? "

" Have you got anything to cut it with ? " queried Diana, wiping away the tears which Anne's affecting accents had caused to flow afresh, and returning to practicalities.

" Yes. I've got my patchwork scissors in my apron pocket fortunately," said Anne. She solemnly clipped one of Diana's curls. " Fare thee well, my beloved friend. Henceforth we must be as strangers though living side by side. But my heart will ever be faithful to thee."

Anne stood and watched Diana out of sight, mournfully waving her hand to the latter whenever she turned to look back. Then she returned to the house, not a little consoled for the time being by this romantic parting.

" It is all over," she informed Marilla. " I shall never have another friend. I'm really worse off than ever before, for I haven't Katie Maurice and Violetta now. And even if I had it wouldn't be the same. Somehow, little dream girls are not satisfying after a real friend. Diana and I had such an affecting farewell down by the spring. It will be sacred in my memory forever. I used the most pathetic language I could think of and said ' thou ' and ' thee.' ' Thou '

and ' thee ' seem so much more romantic than ' you.'
Diana gave me a lock of her hair and I'm going to sew
it up in a little bag and wear it around my neck all my
life.   Please see that it is buried with me, for I don't
believe I'll live very long.   Perhaps when she sees me
lying cold and dead before her Mrs Barry may feel
remorse for what she has done and will let Diana come
to my funeral."

" I don't think there is much fear of your dying of
grief as long as you can talk, Anne," said Marilla
unsympathetically.

The following Monday Anne surprised Marilla by
coming down from her room with her basket of books
on her arm and her lips primmed up into a line of
determination.

" I'm going back to school," she announced.   " That
is all there is left in life for me, now that my friend
has been ruthlessly torn from me.   In school I can
look at her and muse over days departed."

" You'd better muse over your lessons and sums,"
said Marilla, concealing her delight at this development
of the situation.   " If you're going back to school I
hope we'll hear no more of breaking slates over people's
heads and such carryings-on.   Behave yourself and
do just what your teacher tells you."

" I'll try to be a model pupil," agreed Anne dolefully.   " There won't be much fun in it, I expect.
Mr Phillips said Minnie Andrews was a model pupil and
there isn't a spark of imagination or life in her.   She
is just dull and poky and never seems to have a good
time.   But I feel so depressed that perhaps it will
come easy to me now.   I'm going round by the road.
I couldn't bear to go by the Birch Path all alone.   I
should weep bitter tears if I did."

Anne was welcomed back to school with open arms.
Her imagination had been sorely missed in games,

her voice in the singing, and her dramatic ability in the perusal aloud of books at dinner hour. Ruby Gillis smuggled three blue plums over to her during testament reading ; Ella May Macpherson gave her an enormous yellow pansy cut from the covers of a floral catalogue —a species of desk decoration much prized in Avonlea school. Sophia Sloane offered to teach her a perfectly elegant new pattern of knit lace, *so* nice for trimming aprons. Katie Boulter gave her a perfume bottle to keep slate-water in, and Julia Bell copied carefully on a piece of pale pink paper, scalloped on the edges, the following effusion.

To ANNE

When twilight drops her curtain down
And pins it with a star
Remember that you have a friend
Though she may wander far.

" It's so nice to be appreciated," sighed Anne rapturously to Marilla that night.

The girls were not the only scholars who " appreciated " her. When Anne went to her seat after dinner hour—she had been told by Mr Phillips to sit with the model Minnie Andrews—she found on her desk a big, luscious ' strawberry apple.' Anne caught it up all ready to take a bite, when she remembered that the only place in Avonlea where strawberry apples grew was in the old Blythe orchard on the other side of the Lake of Shining Waters. Anne dropped the apple as if it were a red-hot coal and ostentatiously wiped her fingers on her handkerchief. The apple lay untouched on her desk until the next morning, when little Timothy Andrews, who swept the school and kindled the fire, annexed it as one of his perquisites. Charlie Sloane's slate pencil, gorgeously bedizened with striped red and yellow paper, costing two cents where ordinary pencils cost only one, which he sent up to her after dinner hour, met with a more favourable reception. Anne was graciously pleased to accept it and rewarded the donor with a smile which exalted that infatuated youth straightway into the seventh heaven of delight and caused him to make such fearful errors in his dictation that Mr Phillips kept him in after school to rewrite it.

But as

> The Cæsar's pageant shorn of Brutus' bust
> Did but of Rome's best son remind her more,

so the marked absence of any tribute or recognition from Diana Barry, who was sitting with Gertie Pye, embittered Anne's little triumph.

" Diana might just have smiled at me once, I think," she mourned to Marilla that night. But the next morning a note, most fearfully and wonderfully twisted and folded, and a small parcel, were passed across to Anne.

DEAR ANNE [ran the former],

Mother says I'm not to play with you or talk to you even in school. It isn't my fault and don't be cross at me, because I love you as much as ever. I miss you awfully to tell all my secrets to and I don't like Gertie Pye one bit. I made you one of the new bookmarkers out of red tissue paper. They are awfully fashionable now and only three girls in school know how to make them. When you look at it remember

Your true friend,
DIANA BARRY

Anne read the note, kissed the bookmark, and despatched a prompt reply back to the other side of the school.

MY OWN DARLING DIANA,

Of course I am not cross at you because you have to obey your mother. Our spirits can commune. I shall keep your lovely present for ever. Minnie Andrews is a very nice little girl—although she has no imagination—but after having been Diana's busum friend I cannot be Minnie's. Please excuse mistakes because my spelling isn't very good yet, although much improoved.

Yours until death us do part,

ANNE or CORDELIA SHIRLEY

P.S. I shall sleep with your letter under my pillow to-night.

A. or C. S.

Marilla pessimistically expected more trouble since Anne had again begun to go to school. But none developed. Perhaps Anne caught something of the "model" spirit from Minnie Andrews ; at least she got on very well with Mr Phillips thenceforth. She flung herself into her studies heart and soul, determined not to be outdone in any class by Gilbert Blythe. The rivalry between them was soon apparent ; it was entirely good-natured on Gilbert's side ; but it is much to be feared that the same thing cannot be said of Anne, who had certainly an unpraiseworthy tenacity for holding grudges. She was as intense in her hatreds as in her loves. She would not stoop to admit that she meant to rival Gilbert in school work, because that would have been to acknowledge his existence which Anne persistently ignored ; but the rivalry was there and honours fluctuated between them. Now Gilbert was head of the spelling class ; now Anne, with a toss of her long red braids, spelled him down. One morning Gilbert had all his sums done correctly and had his name written on the blackboard on the roll of honour ; the next morning Anne, having wrestled wildly with decimals the entire evening before, would be first. One awful day they were ties and their names were written up together. It was almost as bad as a " take-notice," and Anne's mortification was as evident as Gilbert's satisfaction. When the written examinations at the end of each month were held the suspense was terrible. The first month Gilbert came out three marks ahead. The second Anne beat him by five. But her triumph was marred by the fact that Gilbert congratulated her heartily before the whole school. It would have been ever so much sweeter to her if he had felt the sting of his defeat.

Mr Phillips might not be a very good teacher ; but a pupil so inflexibly determined on learning as Anne was could hardly escape making progress under any kind of a teacher. By the end of the term Anne and Gilbert were both promoted into the fifth class and allowed to begin studying the elements of " the branches "—by which Latin, geometry, French and algebra were meant. In geometry Anne met her Waterloo.

" It's perfectly awful stuff, Marilla," she groaned. " I'm sure I'll never be able to make head or tail of it. There is no scope for imagination in it at all. Mr Phillips says I'm the worst dunce he ever saw at it. And Gil—I mean some of the others are so smart at it. It is extremely mortifying, Marilla. Even Diana gets along better than I do. But I don't mind being beaten by Diana. Even although we meet as strangers now I still love her with an *inextinguishable* love. It makes me very sad at times to think about her. But really, Marilla, one can't stay sad very long in such an interesting world, can one ? "

CHAPTER XVIII

ANNE TO THE RESCUE

ALL things great are wound up with all things little. At first glance it might not seem that the decision of a certain Canadian Premier to include Prince Edward Island in a political tour could have much or anything to do with the fortunes of little Anne Shirley at Green Gables. But it had.

It was in January the Premier came, to address his loyal supporters and such of his non-supporters as chose to be present at the monster mass meeting held in Charlottetown. Most of the Avonlea people were on the Premier's side of politics ; hence, on the night of the meeting nearly all the men and a goodly proportion of the women had gone to town, thirty miles away. Mrs Rachel Lynde had gone too. Mrs Rachel Lynde was a red-hot politician and couldn't have believed that the political rally could be carried through without her, although she was on the opposite side of politics. So she went to town and took her husband—Thomas would be useful in looking after the horse—and Marilla Cuthbert with her. Marilla had a sneaking interest in politics herself, and as she thought it might be her only chance to see a real live Premier, she promptly took it, leaving Anne and Matthew to keep house until her return the following day.

Hence, while Marilla and Mrs Rachel were enjoying themselves hugely at the mass meeting, Anne and Matthew had the cheerful kitchen at Green Gables all to themselves. A bright fire was glowing in the old-fashioned Waterloo stove and blue-white frost crystals were shining on the window-panes. Matthew nodded over a *Farmers' Advocate* on the sofa and Anne at the table studied her lessons with grim determination, despite sundry wistful glances at the clock shelf, where lay a new book that Jane Andrews had lent her that day. Jane had assured her that it was warranted to produce any number of thrills, or words to that effect, and Anne's fingers tingled to reach out for it. But that would mean Gilbert Blythe's triumph on the morrow. Anne turned her back on the clock shelf and tried to imagine it wasn't there.

" Matthew, did you ever study geometry when you went to school ? "

" Well now, no, I didn't," said Matthew, coming out of his doze with a start.

I wish you had," sighed Anne, " because then you'd be able to sympathize with me. You can't sympathize properly if you've never studied it. It is casting a cloud over my whole life. I'm such a dunce at it, Matthew."

" Well now, I dunno," said Matthew soothingly. " I guess you're all right at anything. Mr Phillips told me last week in Blair's store at Carmody that you was the smartest scholar in school and was making rapid progress. ' Rapid progress ' was his very words. There's them as runs down Teddy Phillips and says he ain't much of a teacher ; but I guess he's all right."

Matthew would have thought anyone who praised Anne was " all right."

" I'm sure I'd get on better with geometry if only he wouldn't change the letters," complained Anne. " I learn the proposition off by heart, and then he draws in on the blackboard and puts different letters from what are in the book and I get all mixed up. I don't think a teacher should take such a mean advantage, do you ? We're studying agriculture now and I've found out at last what makes the roads red. It's a great comfort. I wonder how Marilla and Mrs Lynde are enjoying themselves. Mrs Lynde says Canada is going to the dogs the way things are being run at Ottawa, and that it's an awful warning to the electors. She says if women were allowed to vote we would soon see a blessed change. What way do you vote, Matthew ? "

" Conservative," said Matthew promptly. To vote Conservative was part of Matthew's religion.

" Then I'm Conservative too," said Anne decidedly. " I'm glad, because Gil—because some of the boys in school are Grits. I guess Mr Phillips is a Grit too, because Prissy Andrews' father is one, and Ruby Gillis says that when a man is courting he always has to agree with the girl's mother in religion and her father in politics. Is that true, Matthew ? "

" Well now, I dunno," said Matthew.

" Did you ever go courting, Matthew ? "

" Well now, no, I dunno's I ever did," said Matthew, who had certainly never thought of such a thing in his whole existence.

Anne reflected with her chin in her hands.

" It must be rather interesting, don't you think, Matthew ? Ruby Gillis says when she grows up she's going to have ever so many beaus on the string and have them all crazy about her ; but I think that would be too exciting. I'd rather have just one in his right mind. But Ruby Gillis knows a great deal about such matters because she has so many big sisters, and Mrs Lynde says the Gillis girls have gone off like hot cakes. Mr Phillips goes up to see Prissy Andrews nearly every evening. He says it is to help her with her lessons, but Miranda Sloane is studying for Queen's, too, and I should think she needed help a lot more than Prissy because she's ever so much stupider, but he never goes

to help her in the evenings at all.   There are a great
many things in this world that I can't understand very
well, Matthew."

"Well, now, I dunno as I comprehend them all
myself," acknowledged Matthew.

"Well, I suppose I must finish up my lessons.   I
won't allow myself to open that new book Jane lent
me until I'm through.   But it's a terrible temptation,
Matthew.   Even when I turn my back on it I can
see it there just as plain.   Jane said she cried herself
sick over it.   I love a book that makes me cry.   But
I think I'll carry that book into the sitting-room and
lock it in the jam closet and give you the key.   And
you must *not* give it to me, Matthew, until my lessons
are done, not even if I implore you on my bended knees.
It's all very well to say resist temptation, but it's ever
so much easier to resist it if you can't get the key.
And then shall I run down the cellar and get some
russets, Matthew ? . Wouldn't you like some russets ? "

"Well, now, I dunno but what I would," said
Matthew, who never ate russets but knew Anne's
weakness for them.

Just as Anne emerged triumphantly from the cellar
with her plateful of russets came the sound of flying
footsteps on the icy board walk outside and the next
moment the kitchen door was flung open and in rushed
Diana Barry, white-faced and breathless, with a shawl
wrapped hastily around her head.   Anne promptly let
go of her candle and plate in her surprise, and plate,
candle, and apples crashed together down the cellar
ladder and were found at the bottom, embedded in
melted grease, the next day, by Marilla, who gathered
them up and thanked mercy the house hadn't been
set on fire.

"Whatever is the matter, Diana ? " cried Anne.
" Has your mother relented at last ? "

" Oh, Anne, do come quick," implored Diana nervously. " Minnie May is awful sick—she's got croup, Young Mary Joe says—and father and mother are away to town and there's nobody to go for the doctor. Minnie May is awful bad and Young Mary Joe doesn't know what to do—and oh, Anne, I'm so scared ! "

Matthew, without a word, reached out for cap and coat, slipped past Diana and away into the darkness of the yard.

" He's gone to harness the sorrel mare to go to Carmody for the doctor," said Anne, who was hurrying on hood and jacket. " I know it as well as if he'd said so. Matthew and I are such kindred spirits I can read his thoughts without words at all."

" I don't believe he'll find the doctor at Carmody," sobbed Diana. " I know that Doctor Blair went to town and I guess Doctor Spencer would go too, Young Mary Joe never saw anybody with croup and Mrs Lynde is away. Oh, Anne ! "

" Don't cry, Di," said Anne cheerily. " I know exactly what to do for croup. You forget that Mrs Hammond had twins three times. When you look after three pairs of twins you naturally get a lot of experience. They all had croup regularly. Just wait till I get the ipecac bottle—you mayn't have any at your house. Come on now."

The two little girls hastened out hand in hand and hurried through Lovers' Lane and across the crusted field beyond, for the snow was too deep to go by the shorter wood way. Anne, although sincerely sorry for Minnie May, was far from being insensible to the romance of the situation and to the sweetness of once more sharing that romance with a kindred spirit.

The night was clear and frosty, all ebony of shadow and silver of snowy slope ; big stars were shining over the silent fields ; here and there the dark pointed firs stood up with snow powdering their branches and the wind whistling through them. Anne thought it was truly delightful to go skimming through all this mystery and loveliness with your bosom friend who had been so long estranged.

Minnie May, aged three, was really very sick. She lay on the kitchen sofa, feverish and restless, while her hoarse breathing could be heard all over the house. Young Mary Joe, a buxom, broad-faced French girl from the Creek, whom Mrs Barry had engaged to stay with the children during her absence, was helpless and bewildered, quite incapable of thinking what to do, or doing it if she thought of it.

Anne went to work with skill and promptness.

" Minnie May has croup all right ; she's pretty bad, but I've seen them worse. First we must have lots of hot water. I declare, Diana, there isn't more than a cupful in the kettle ! There, I've filled it up, and, Mary Joe, you may put some wood in the stove. I don't want to hurt your feelings, but it seems to me you might have thought of this before if you'd any imagination. Now, I'll undress Minnie May and put her to bed, and you try to find some soft flannel cloths, Diana. I'm going to give her a dose of ipecac first of all."

Minnie May did not take kindly to the ipecac, but Anne had not brought up three pairs of twins for nothing. Down that ipecac went, not only once, but many times during the long, anxious night when the two little girls worked patiently over the suffering Minnie May, and Young Mary Joe, honestly anxious to do all she could, kept on a roaring fire and heated more water than would have been needed for a hospital of croupy babies.

It was three o'clock when Matthew came with the doctor, for he had been obliged to go all the way to Spencervale for one. But the pressing need for assistance was past. Minnie May was much better and was sleeping soundly.

" I was awfully near giving up in despair," explained Anne. " She got worse and worse until she was sicker than ever the Hammond twins were, even the last pair. I actually thought she was going to choke to death. I gave her every drop of ipecac in that bottle, and when the last dose went down I said to myself—not to Diana or Young Mary Joe, because I didn't want to worry them any more than they were worried, but I had to say it to myself just to relieve my feelings— ' This is the last lingering hope and I fear 'tis a vain one.' But in about three minutes she coughed up the phlegm and began to get better right away. You must just imagine my relief, doctor, because I can't express it in words. You know there are some things that cannot be expressed in words."

" Yes, I know," nodded the doctor. He looked at Anne as if he were thinking some things about her that couldn't be expressed in words. Later on, how-ever, he expressed them to Mr and Mrs Barry.

" That little red-headed girl they have over at Cuthbert's is as smart as they make 'em. I tell you she saved that baby's life, for it would have been too late by the time I got here. She seems to have a skill and presence of mind perfectly wonderful in a child of her age. I never saw anything like the eyes of her when she was explaining the case out to me."

Anne had gone home in the wonderful, white-frosted winter morning, heavy-eyed from loss of sleep, but still talking unweariedly to Matthew as they crossed the long white field and walked under the glittering fairy arch of the Lovers' Lane maples.

" Oh, Matthew, isn't it a wonderful morning ? The world looks like something God had just imagined for His own pleasure, doesn't it ? Those trees look as if

I could blow them away with a breath—pouf! I'm so glad I live in a world where there are white frosts, aren't you? And I'm so glad Mrs Hammond had three pairs of twins after all. If she hadn't I mightn't have known what to do for Minnie May. I'm real sorry I was ever cross with Mrs Hammond for having twins. But, oh, Matthew, I'm so sleepy. I can't go to school. I just know I couldn't keep my eyes open and I'd be so stupid. But I hate to stay home for Gil—some of the others will get head of the class, and it's so hard to get up again—although of course the harder it is the more satisfaction you have when you do get up, haven't you?"

"Well, now, I guess you'll manage all right," said Matthew, looking at Anne's white little face and the dark shadows under her eyes. "You just go right to bed and have a good sleep. I'll do all the chores."

Anne accordingly went to bed and slept so long and soundly that it was well on in the white and rosy winter afternoon when she awoke and descended to the kitchen where Marilla, who had arrived home in the meantime, was sitting knitting.

"Oh, did you see the Premier?" exclaimed Anne at once. "What did he look like, Marilla?"

"Well, he never got to be Premier on account of his looks," said Marilla. "Such a nose as that man had! But he can speak. I was proud of being a Conservative. Rachel Lynde, of course, being a Liberal, had no use for him. Your dinner is in the oven, Anne; and you can get yourself some blue-plum preserve out of the pantry. I guess you're hungry. Matthew has been telling me about last night. I must say it was fortunate you knew what to do. I wouldn't have had any idea myself, for I never saw a case of croup. There now, never mind talking till you've had

your dinner. I can tell by the look of you that you're
just full up with speeches, but they'll keep."

Marilla had something to tell Anne, but she did not
tell it just then, for she knew if she did Anne's consequent excitement would lift her clear out of the region
of such material matters as appetite or dinner. Not
until Anne had finished her saucer of blue plums did
Marilla say :

" Mrs Barry was here this afternoon, Anne. She
wanted to see you, but I wouldn't wake you up. She
says you saved Minnie May's life, and she is very sorry
she acted as she did in that affair of the currant wine.
She says she knows now you didn't mean to set Diana
drunk, and she hopes you'll forgive her and be good
friends with Diana again. You're to go over this
evening if you like, for Diana can't stir outside the door
on account of a bad cold she caught last night. Now,
Anne Shirley, for pity's sake don't fly clean up into
the air."

The warning seemed not unnecessary, so uplifted and
aerial was Anne's expression and attitude as she sprang
to her feet, her face irradiated with the flame of her
spirit.

" Oh, Marilla, can I go right now—without washing
my dishes ? I'll wash them when I come back, but I
cannot tie myself down to anything so unromantic as
dish-washing at this thrilling moment."

" Yes, yes, run along," said Marilla indulgently.
" Anne Shirley—are you crazy ? Come back this
instant and put something on you. I might as well
call to the wind. She's gone without a cap or wrap.
Look at her tearing through the orchard with her hair
streaming. It'll be a mercy if she doesn't catch her
death of cold."

Anne came dancing home in the purple winter
twilight across the snowy places. Afar in the south-

west was the great shimmering, pearl-like sparkle of an evening star in a sky that was pale golden and ethereal rose over gleaming white spaces and dark glens of spruce. The tinkles of sleigh-bells among the snowy hills came like elfin chimes through the frosty air, but their music was not sweeter than the song in Anne's heart and on her lips.

" You see before you a perfectly happy person, Marilla," she announced. " I'm perfectly happy—yes, in spite of my red hair. Just at present I have a soul above red hair. Mrs Barry kissed me and cried and said she was so sorry and she could never repay me. I felt fearfully embarrassed, Marilla, but I just said as politely as I could, ' I have no hard feelings for you, Mrs Barry. I assure you once for all that I did not mean to intoxicate Diana and henceforth I shall cover the past with the mantle of oblivion.' That was a pretty dignified way of speaking, wasn't it, Marilla ? I felt that I was heaping coals of fire on Mrs Barry's head. And Diana and I had a lovely afternoon. Diana showed me a new fancy crochet stitch her aunt over at Carmody taught her. Not a soul in Avonlea knows it but us, and we pledged a solemn vow never to reveal it to anyone else. Diana gave me a beautiful card with a wreath of roses on it and a verse of poetry ;

> If you love me as I love you
> Nothing but death can part us two.

And that is true, Marilla. We're going to ask Mr Phillips to let us sit together in school again, and Gertie Pye can go with Minnie Andrews. We had an elegant tea. Mrs Barry had the very best china set out, Marilla, just as if I was real company. I can't tell you what a thrill it gave me. Nobody ever used their very best china on my account before. And we had fruit-cake and pound-cake and dough-nuts and two kinds of preserves, Marilla. And Mrs Barry asked me if I took tea and said, ' Pa, why don't you pass the biscuits to Anne ? ' It must be lovely to be grown up, Marilla, when just being treated as if you were is so nice."

" I don't know about that," said Marilla with a brief sigh.

" Well, anyway, when I am grown up," said Anne decidedly, " I'm always going to talk to little girls as if they were, too, and I'll never laugh when they use big words. I know from sorrowful experience how that hurts one's feelings. After tea Diana and I made taffy. The taffy wasn't very good, I suppose because neither Diana nor I had ever made any before. Diana left me to stir it while she buttered the plates and I forgot and let it burn ; and then when we set it out on the platform to cool the cat walked over one plate and that had to be thrown away. But the making of it was splendid fun. Then when I came home Mrs Barry asked me to come over as often as I could and Diana stood at the window and threw kisses to me all the way down to Lovers' Lane. I assure you, Marilla, that I feel like praying to-night and I'm going to think out a special brand-new prayer in honour of the occasion."

CHAPTER XIX

A CONCERT, A CATASTROPHE, AND A CONFESSION

"MARILLA, can I go over to see Diana just for a minute?" asked Anne, running breathlessly down from the east gable one February evening.

"I don't see what you want to be trapesing about after dark for," said Marilla shortly. "You and Diana walked home from school together and then stood down there in the snow for half an hour more, your tongues going the whole blessed time, clickety-clack. So I don't think you're very badly off to see her again."

"But she wants to see me," pleaded Anne. "She has something very important to tell me."

"How do you know she has?"

"Because she just signalled to me from her window. We have arranged a way to signal with our candles and cardboard. We set the candle on the window-sill and make flashes by passing the cardboard back and forth. So many flashes mean a certain thing. It was my idea, Marilla."

"I'll warrant you it was," said Marilla emphatically. "And the next thing you'll be setting fire to the curtain with your signalling nonsense."

"Oh, we're very careful, Marilla. And it's so interesting. Two flashes mean, 'Are you there?' Three mean 'yes' and four 'no.' Five mean, 'Come over as soon as possible, because I have something important to reveal.' Diana has just signalled five flashes, and I'm really suffering to know what it is."

" Well, you needn't suffer any longer," said Marilla sarcastically. " You can go, but you're to be back here in just ten minutes, remember that."

Anne did remember it and was back in the stipulated time, although probably no mortal will ever know just what it cost her to confine the discussion of Diana's important communication within the limits of ten minutes. But at least she had made good use of them.

" Oh, Marilla, what do you think ? You know tomorrow is Diana's birthday. Well, her mother told her she could ask me to go home with her from school and stay all night with her. And her cousins are coming over from Newbridge in a big pung sleigh to go to the Debating Club concert at the hall to-morrow night. And they are going to take Diana and me to the concert—if you'll let me go, that is. You will, won't you, Marilla ? Oh, I feel so excited."

" You can calm down then, because you're not going. You're better at home in your own bed, and as for that Club concert, it's all nonsense, and little girls should not be allowed to go out to such places at all."

" I'm sure the Debating Club is a most respectable affair," pleaded Anne.

" I'm not saying it isn't. But you're not going to begin gadding about to concerts and staying out all hours of the night. Pretty doings for children. I'm surprised at Mrs Barry's letting Diana go."

" But it's such a very special occasion," mourned Anne, on the verge of tears. " Diana has only one birthday in a year. It isn't as if birthdays were common things, Marilla. Prissy Andrews is going to recite " Curfew Must Not Ring To-night." That is such a good moral piece, Marilla, I'm sure it would do me lots of good to hear it. And the choir are going to sing four lovely pathetic songs that are pretty near as good as hymns. And oh, Marilla, the minister is going to take part ; yes, indeed, he is ; he's going to give an address. That will be just about the same thing as a sermon. Please, mayn't I go, Marilla ? "

" You heard what I said, Anne, didn't you ? Take off your boots now and go to bed. It's past eight."

" There's just one more thing, Marilla," said Anne, with the air of producing the last shot in her locker. " Mrs Barry told Diana that we might sleep in the spare-room bed. Think of the honour of your little Anne being put in the spare-room bed."

" It's an honour you'll have to get along without. Go to bed, Anne, and don't let me hear another word out of you."

When Anne, with tears rolling over her cheeks had gone sorrowfully upstairs, Matthew, who had been apparently sound asleep on the lounge during the whole dialogue, opened his eyes and said decidedly :

" Well, now, Marilla, I think you ought to let Anne go."

" I don't then," retorted Marilla. " Who's bringing this child up, Matthew, you or me ? "

" Well now, you," admitted Matthew.

" Don't interfere then."

" Well now, I ain't interfering. It ain't interfering to have your own opinion. And my opinion is that you ought to let Anne go."

" You'd think I ought to let Anne go to the moon if she took the notion, I've no doubt," was Marilla's amiable rejoinder. " I might have let her spend the night with Diana, if that was all. But I don't approve of this concert plan. She'd go there and catch cold like as not, and have her head filled up with nonsense and excitement. It would unsettle her for a week. I understand that child's disposition and what's good for it better than you, Matthew."

" I think you ought to let Anne go," repeated Matthew firmly. Argument was not his strong point, but holding fast to his opinion certainly was. Marilla gave a gasp of helplessness and took refuge in silence. The next morning, when Anne was washing the breakfast dishes in the pantry, Matthew paused on his way out to the barn to say to Marilla again :

" I think you ought to let Anne go, Marilla."

For a moment Marilla looked things not lawful to be uttered. Then she yielded to the inevitable and said tartly :

" Very well, she can go, since nothing else'll please you."

Anne flew out of the pantry, dripping dish-cloth in hand.

" Oh, Marilla, Marilla, say those blessed words again."

" I guess once is enough to say them. This is Matthew's doings and I wash my hands of it. If you catch pneumonia sleeping in a strange bed or coming out of that hot hall in the middle of the night, don't blame me, blame Matthew. Anne Shirley, you're dripping greasy water all over the floor. I never saw such a careless child."

" Oh, I know I'm a great trial to you, Marilla," said Anne repentantly. " I make so many mistakes. But then just think of all the mistakes I don't make, although I might. I'll get some sand and scrub up the spots before I go to school. Oh, Marilla, my heart was just set on going to that concert. I never was to a concert in my life, and when the other girls talk about them in school I feel so out of it. You didn't know just how I felt about it, but you see Matthew did. Matthew understands me, and it's so nice to be understood, Marilla."

Anne was too excited to do herself justice as to lessons that morning in school. Gilbert Blythe spelled her down in class and left her clear out of sight in mental arithmetic. Anne's consequent humiliation was less than it might have been, however, in view of the concert and the spare-room bed. She and Diana talked so constantly about it all day that with a stricter teacher than Mr Phillips, dire disgrace must inevitably have been their portion.

Anne felt that she could not have borne it if she had not been going to the concert, for nothing else was discussed that day in school. The Avonlea Debating Club, which met fortnightly all winter, had had several smaller free entertainments; but this was to be a big affair, admission ten cents, in aid of the library. The Avonlea young people had been practising for weeks, and all the scholars were especially interested in it by reason of older brothers and sisters who were going to take part. Everybody in school over nine years of age expected to go, except Carrie Sloane, whose father shared Marilla's opinions about small girls going out to night concerts. Carrie Sloane cried into her grammar all the afternoon and felt that life was not worth living.

For Anne the real excitement began with the dismissal of school and increased therefrom in crescendo until it reached to a crash of positive ecstasy in the concert itself. They had a " perfectly elegant tea "; and then came the delicious occupation of dressing in Diana's little room upstairs. Diana did Anne's front hair in the new pompadour style and Anne tied Diana's bows with the especial knack she possessed; and they experimented with at least half a dozen different ways of arranging their back hair. At last they were ready, cheeks scarlet and eyes glowing with excitement.

True, Anne could not help a little pang when she contrasted her plain black tam and shapeless, tight-sleeved, home-made grey cloth coat with Diana's jaunty fur cap and smart little jacket. But she remembered in time that she had an imagination and could use it.

Then Diana's cousins, the Murrays from Newbridge, came; they all crowded into the big pung sleigh, among

straw and furry robes. Anne revelled in the drive to
the hall, slipping along over the satin-smooth roads
with the snow crisping under the runners. There was
a magnificent sunset, and the snowy hills and deep blue
water of the St Lawrence Gulf seemed to rim in the
splendour like a huge bowl of pearl and sapphire
brimmed with wine and fire. Tinkles of sleigh-bells
and distant laughter that seemed like the mirth of
wood elves, came from every quarter.

" Oh, Diana," breathed Anne, squeezing Diana's
mittened hand under the fur robe, " isn't it all like a
beautiful dream ?   Do I really look the same as usual ?
I feel so different that it seems to me it must show in
my looks."

" You look awfully nice," said Diana, who having
just received a compliment from one of her cousins,
felt that she ought to pass it on. " You've got the
loveliest colour."

The programme that night was a series of ' thrills,'
for at least one listener in the audience, and, as Anne
assured Diana, every succeeding thrill was thrillier
than the last. When Prissy Andrews, attired in a new
pink silk waist with a string of pearls about her smooth
white throat and real carnations in her hair—rumour
whispered that the master had sent all the way to town
for them for her—" climbed the slimy ladder, dark
without one ray of light," Anne shivered in luxurious
sympathy ; when the choir sang " Far above the Gentle
Daisies," Anne gazed at the ceiling as if it were frescoed
with angels ; when Sam Sloane proceeded to explain
and illustrate " How Sockery Set a Hen," Anne laughed
until people sitting near her laughed too, more out of
sympathy with her than with amusement at a selection
that was rather threadbare even in Avonlea ; and when
Mr Phillips gave Mark Antony's oration over the dead
body of Caesar in the most heart-stirring tones—looking

at Prissy Andrews at the end of every sentence—Anne felt that she could rise and mutiny on the spot if but one Roman citizen led the way.

Only one number on the programme failed to interest her. When Gilbert Blythe recited " Bingen on the Rhine," Anne picked up Rhoda Murray's library book and read it until he had finished, when she sat rigidly stiff and motionless while Diana clapped her hands until they tingled.

It was eleven when they got home, sated with dissipation, but with the exceeding sweet pleasure of talking it all over still to come. Everybody seemed asleep and the house was dark and silent. Anne and Diana tiptoed into the parlour, a long narrow room out of which the spare room opened. It was pleasantly warm and dimly lighted by the embers of a fire in the grate.

" Let's undress here," said Diana. " It's so nice and warm."

" Hasn't it been a delightful time ? " sighed Anne rapturously. " It must be splendid to get up and recite there. Do you suppose we will ever be asked to do it, Diana ? "

" Yes, of course, some day. They're always wanting the big scholars to recite. Gilbert Blythe does often and he's only two years older than us. Oh, Anne, how could you pretend not to listen to him ? When he came to the line,

There's another, *not* a sister,

he looked right down at you."

" Diana," said Anne with dignity, " you are my bosom friend, but I cannot allow even you to speak to me of that person. Are you ready for bed ? Let's run a race and see who'll get to the bed first."

The suggestion appealed to Diana. The two little white-clad figures flew down the long room, through the spare-room door, and bounded on the bed at the same moment. And then—something—moved beneath them, there was a gasp and a cry—and somebody said in muffled accents :

" Merciful goodness ! "

Anne and Diana were never able to tell just how they got off that bed and out of the room. They only knew that after one frantic rush they found themselves tiptoeing shiveringly upstairs.

" Oh, who was it—*what* was it ? " whispered Anne, her teeth chattering with cold and fright.

" It was Aunt Josephine," said Diana, gasping with laughter. " Oh, Anne, it was Aunt Josephine, however she came to be there. Oh, and I know she will be furious. It's dreadful—it's really dreadful—but did you ever know anything so funny, Anne ? "

" Who is your Aunt Josephine ? "

" She's father's aunt and she lives in Charlottetown. She's awfully old—seventy anyhow—and I don't believe she was *ever* a little girl. We were expecting her out for a visit, but not so soon. She's awfully prim and proper and she'll scold dreadfully about this, I know. Well, we'll have to sleep with Minnie May— and you can't think how she kicks."

Miss Josephine Barry did not appear at the early breakfast the next morning. Mrs Barry smiled kindly at the two little girls.

" Did you have a good time last night ? I tried to stay awake until you came home, for I wanted to tell you Aunt Josephine had come and that you would have to go upstairs after all, but I was so tired I fell asleep. I hope you didn't disturb your aunt, Diana."

Diana preserved a discreet silence, but she and Anne exchanged furtive smiles of guilty amusement across the table. Anne hurried home after breakfast and so remained in blissful ignorance of the disturbance which presently resulted in the Barry household until the

late afternoon, when she went down to Mrs Lynde's on
an errand for Marilla.

" So you and Diana nearly frightened poor old Miss
Barry to death last night ? " said Mrs Lynde severely,
but with a twinkle in her eye. " Mrs Barry was here
a few minutes ago on her way to Carmody. She's
feeling real worried over it. Old Miss Barry was in a
terrible temper when she got up this morning—and
Josephine Barry's temper is no joke, I can tell you that.
She wouldn't speak to Diana at all."

" It wasn't Diana's fault," said Anne contritely.
" It was mine. I suggested racing to see who would
get into bed first."

" I knew it ! " said Mrs Lynde with the exultation
of a correct guesser. " I knew that idea came out of
your head. Well, it's made a nice lot of trouble, that's
what. Old Miss Barry came out to stay for a month,
but she declares she won't stay another day and is
going right back to town to-morrow, Sunday and all
as it is. She'd have gone to-day if they could have
taken her. She had promised to pay for a quarter's
music lessons for Diana, but now she is determined to
do nothing at all for such a tomboy. Oh, I guess they
had a lively time of it there this morning. The Barrys
must feel cut up. Old Miss Barry is rich and they'd
like to keep on the good side of her. Of course, Mrs
Barry didn't say just that to me, but I'm a pretty good
judge of human nature, that's what."

" I'm such an unlucky girl," mourned Anne. " I'm
always getting into scrapes myself and getting my best
friends—people I'd shed my heart's blood for—into
them, too. Can you tell me why it is so, Mrs Lynde ? "

" It's because you're too heedless and impulsive,
child, that's what. You never stop to think—whatever comes into your head to say or do you say or do
it without a moment's reflection."

" Oh, but that's the best of it," protested Anne.
" Something just flashes into your mind, so exciting,
and you must out with it. If you stop to think it
over you spoil it all. Haven't you never felt that
yourself, Mrs Lynde ? "

No, Mrs Lynde had not. She shook her head sagely.
" You must learn to think a little, Anne, that's what.
The proverb you need to go by is ' Look before you
leap '—especially into spare-room beds."

Mrs Lynde laughed comfortably over her mild joke,
but Anne remained pensive. She saw nothing to laugh
at in the situation, which to her eyes appeared very
serious. When she left Mrs Lynde's she took her way
across the crusted fields to Orchard Slope. Diana met
her at the kitchen door.

" Your Aunt Josephine was very cross about it,
wasn't she ? " whispered Anne.

" Yes," answered Diana, stifling a giggle with an
apprehensive glance over her shoulder at the closed
sitting-room door. " She was fairly dancing with
rage, Anne. Oh, how she scolded. She said I was
the worst-behaved girl she ever saw and that my
parents ought to be ashamed of the way they had
brought me up. She says she won't stay and I'm sure
I don't care. But father and mother do."

" Why didn't you tell them it was my fault ? "
demanded Anne.

" It's likely I'd do such a thing, isn't it ? " said
Diana with just scorn. " I'm no tell-tale, Anne Shirley,
and anyhow I was just as much to blame as you."

" Well, I'm going in to tell her myself," said Anne
resolutely.

Diana stared.

" Anne Shirley, you'd never ! why—she'll eat you
alive ! "

" Don't frighten me any more than I am frightened,"

implored Anne. " I'd rather walk up to a cannon's mouth. But I've got to do it, Diana. It was my fault and I've got to confess. I've had practice in confessing fortunately."

" Well, she's in the room," said Diana. " You can go in if you want to. I wouldn't dare. And I don't believe you'll do a bit of good."

With this encouragement Anne bearded the lion in its den—that is to say, walked resolutely up to the sitting-room door and knocked faintly. A sharp " Come in " followed.

Miss Josephine Barry, thin, prim and rigid, was knitting fiercely by the fire, her wrath quite unappeased and her eyes snapping through her gold-rimmed glasses. She wheeled around in her chair, expecting to see Diana, and beheld a white-faced girl whose great eyes were brimmed up with a mixture of desperate courage and shrinking terror.

" Who are you ? " demanded Miss Josephine Barry without ceremony.

" I'm Anne of Green Gables," said the small visitor tremulously, clasping her hands with her characteristic gesture, " and I've come to confess, if you please."

" Confess what ? "

" That it was all my fault about jumping into bed on you last night. I suggested it. Diana would never have thought of such a thing, I am sure. Diana is a very lady-like girl, Miss Barry. So you must see how unjust it is to blame her."

" Oh, I must, hey ? I rather think Diana did her share of the jumping at least. Such carryings-on in a respectable house ! "

" But we were only in fun," persisted Anne. " I think you ought to forgive us, Miss Barry, now that we've apologized. And anyhow, please forgive Diana and let her have her music lessons. Diana's heart is set on her music lessons, Miss Barry, and I know too well what it is to set your heart on a thing and not get it. If you must be cross with anyone, be cross with me. I've been so used in my early days to having people cross at me that I can endure it much better than Diana can."

Much of the snap had gone out of the old lady's eyes by this time and was replaced by a twinkle of amused interest. But she still said severely :

" I don't think it is any excuse for you that you were only in fun. Little girls never indulged in that kind of fun when I was young. You don't know what it is to be awakened out of a sound sleep, after a long and arduous journey, by two great girls coming bounce down on you."

" I don't *know*, but I can *imagine*," said Anne eagerly. " I'm sure it must have been very disturbing. But then, there is our side of it too. Have you any imagination, Miss Barry ? If you have, just put yourself in our place. We didn't know there was anybody in that bed and you nearly scared us to death. It was simply awful the way we felt. And then we couldn't sleep in the spare room after being promised. I suppose you are used to sleeping in spare rooms. But just imagine what you would feel like if you were a little orphan girl who had never had such an honour."

All the snap had gone by this time. Miss Barry actually laughed—a sound which caused Diana waiting in speechless anxiety in the kitchen outside, to give a great gasp of relief.

" I'm afraid my imagination is a little rusty—it's so long since I used it," she said. " I dare say your claim to sympathy is just as strong as mine. It all depends on the way we look at it. Sit down here and tell me about yourself."

" I am very sorry I can't," said Anne firmly. " I

would like to, because you seem like an interesting lady, and you might even be a kindred spirit although you don't look very much like it. But it is my duty to go home to Miss Marilla Cuthbert. Miss Marilla Cuthbert is a very kind lady who has taken me to bring up properly. She is doing her best, but it is very discouraging work. You must not blame her because I jumped on the bed. But before I go I do wish you would tell me if you will forgive Diana and stay just as long as you meant to in Avonlea."

" I think perhaps I will if you will come over and talk to me occasionally," said Miss Barry.

That evening Miss Barry gave Diana a silver bangle bracelet and told the senior members of the household that she had unpacked her valise.

" I've made up my mind to stay simply for the sake of getting better acquainted with that Anne-girl," she said frankly. " She amuses me, and at my time of life an amusing person is a rarity."

Marilla's only comment when she heard the story was " I told you so." This was for Matthew's benefit.

Miss Barry stayed her month out and over. She was a more agreeable guest than usual, for Anne kept her in good humour. They became firm friends.

When Miss Barry went away she said :

" Remember, you Anne-girl, when you come to town you're to visit me and I'll put you in my very sparest spare-room bed to sleep."

" Miss Barry was a kindred spirit, after all," Anne confided to Marilla. " You wouldn't think so to look at her, but she is. You don't find it right out at first, as in Matthew's case, but after awhile you come to see it. Kindred spirits are not so scarce as I used to think. It's splendid to find out there are so many of them in the world."

CHAPTER XX

A GOOD IMAGINATION GONE WRONG

SPRING had come once more to Green Gables—the beautiful, capricious, reluctant Canadian spring, lingering along through April and May in a succession of sweet, fresh, chilly days, with pink sunsets and miracles of resurrection and growth. The maples in Lovers' Lane were red-budded and little curly ferns pushed up around the Dryad's Bubble. Away up in the barrens, behind Mr Silas Sloane's place, the May-flowers blossomed out, pink and white stars of sweetness under their brown leaves. All the schoolgirls and boys had one golden afternoon gathering them, coming home in the clear, echoing twilight with arms and baskets full of flowery spoil.

"I'm so sorry for people who live in lands where there are no Mayflowers," said Anne. "Diana says perhaps they have something better, but there couldn't be anything better than Mayflowers, could there, Marilla? And Diana says if they don't know what they are like they don't miss them. But I think that is the saddest thing of all. I think it would be *tragic*, Marilla, not to know what Mayflowers are like and *not* to miss them. Do you know what I think May-flowers are, Marilla? I think they must be the souls of the flowers that died last summer and this is their heaven. But we had a splendid time to-day, Marilla. We had our lunch down in a big mossy hollow by an old well—such a *romantic* spot. Charlie Sloane dared Arty Gillis to jump over it, and Arty did because he wouldn't take a dare. Nobody would in school. It is very *fashionable* to dare. Mr Phillips gave all the Mayflowers he found to Prissy Andrews and I heard him say ' sweets to the sweet.' He got that out of a book, I know ; but it shows he has some imagination. I was offered some Mayflowers too, but I rejected them with scorn. I can't tell you the person's name because I have vowed never to let it cross my lips. We made wreaths of the Mayflowers and put them on our hats ; and when the time came to go home we marched in procession down the road, two by two, with our bouquets and wreaths, singing ' My Home on the Hill.' Oh, it was so thrilling, Marilla. All Mr Silas Sloane's folks rushed out to see us and everybody we met on the road stopped and stared after us. We made a real sensation."

" Not much wonder ! Such silly doings ! " was Marilla's response.

After the Mayflowers came the violets, and Violet Vale was empurpled with them. Anne walked through it on her way to school with reverent steps and worshipping eyes, as if she trod on holy ground.

" Somehow," she told Diana, " when I'm going through here I don't really care whether Gil—whether anybody gets ahead of me in class or not. But when I'm up in school it's all different and I care as much as ever. There's such a lot of different Annes in me. I sometimes think that is why I'm such a troublesome person. If I was just the one Anne it would be ever so much more comfortable, but then it wouldn't be half so interesting."

One June evening, when the orchards were pink-blossomed again, when the frogs were singing silvery-sweet in the marshes about the head of the Lake of Shining Waters, and the air was full of the savour of clover fields and balsamic fir woods, Anne was sitting by her gable window. She had been studying her lessons, but it had grown too dark to see the book, so she had fallen into wide-eyed reverie, looking out past the boughs of the Snow Queen, once more bestarred with its tufts of blossom.

In all essential respects the little gable chamber was unchanged. The walls were as white, the pincushion as hard, the chairs as stiffly and yellowly upright as ever. Yet the whole character of the room was altered. It was full of a new vital, pulsing personality that seemed to pervade it and to be quite independent of schoolgirl books and dresses and ribbons, and even of the cracked blue jug full of apple blossoms on the table. It was as if all the dreams, sleeping and waking, of its vivid occupant had taken a visible although immaterial form and had tapestried the bare room with splendid filmy tissues of rainbow and moonshine. Presently Marilla came briskly in with some of Anne's freshly ironed school aprons. She hung them over a chair and sat down with a short sigh. She had had one of her headaches that afternoon, and although the pain had gone she felt weak and " tuckered out," as she expressed it. Anne looked at her with eyes limpid with sympathy.

" I do truly wish I could have had the headache in your place, Marilla. I would have endured it joyfully for your sake."

" I guess you did your part in attending to the work and letting me rest," said Marilla. " You seem to have got on fairly well and made fewer mistakes than usual. Of course it wasn't exactly necessary to starch Matthew's handkerchiefs ! And most people when they put a pie in the oven to warm up for dinner take it out and eat it when it gets hot instead of leaving it to be burned to a crisp. But that doesn't seem to be your way evidently."

Headaches always left Marilla somewhat sarcastic.

" Oh, I'm so sorry," said Anne penitently. " I never thought about that pie from the moment I put it in the oven till now, although I felt *instinctively* that there was something missing on the dinner table. I was firmly resolved, when you left me in charge this morning, not to imagine anything, but keep my thoughts on facts. I did pretty well until I put the pie in, and then an irresistible temptation came to me to imagine I was an enchanted princess shut up in a lonely tower with a handsome knight riding to my rescue on a coal-black steed. So that is how I came to forget the pie. I didn't know I starched the handkerchiefs. All the time I was ironing I was trying to think of a name for a new island Diana and I have discovered up the brook. It's the most ravishing spot, Marilla. There are two maple-trees on it and the brook flows right round it. At last it struck me that it would be splendid to call it Victoria Island because we found it on the Queen's birthday. Both Diana and I are very loyal. But I'm very sorry about that pie and the handkerchiefs. I wanted to be extra good to-day because it's an anniversary. Do you remember what happened this day last year, Marilla ? "

" No, I can't think of anything special."

" Oh, Marilla, it was the day I came to Green Gables. I shall never forget it. It was the turning-point in my life. Of course it wouldn't seem so important to you. I've been here for a year and I've been so happy. Of course, I've had my troubles, but one can live down troubles. Are you sorry you kept me, Marilla ? "

" No, I can't say I'm sorry," said Marilla, who sometimes wondered how she could have lived before Anne came to Green Gables, " no, not exactly sorry. If you've finished your lessons, Anne, I want you to run over and ask Mrs Barry if she'll lend me Diana's apron pattern."

" Oh—it's—it's too dark," cried Anne.

" Too dark ? Why, it's only twilight. And goodness knows you've gone over often enough after dark."

" I'll go over early in the morning," said Anne eagerly. " I'll get up at sunrise and go over, Marilla."

" What has got into your head now, Anne Shirley ? I want that pattern to cut out your new apron this evening. Go at once and be smart, too."

" I'll have to go around by the road, then," said Anne, taking up her hat reluctantly.

" Go by the road and waste half an hour ! I'd like to catch you ! "

" I can't go through the Haunted Wood, Marilla," cried Anne desperately.

Marilla stared.

" The Haunted Wood ! Are you crazy ? What under the canopy is the Haunted Wood ? "

" The spruce wood over the brook," said Anne in a whisper.

" Fiddlesticks ! There is no such thing as a haunted wood anywhere. Who has been telling you such stuff ? "

" Nobody," confessed Anne. " Diana and I just imagined the wood was haunted. All the places around here are so—so—*commonplace*. We just got this up for our own amusement. We began it in April. A haunted wood is so very romantic, Marilla. We chose the spruce grove because it's so gloomy. Oh, we have imagined the most harrowing things. There's a white lady walks along the brook just about this time of the night and wrings her hands and utters wailing cries. She appears when there is to be a death in the family. And the ghost of a little murdered child haunts the corner up by Idlewild ; it creeps up behind you and lays its cold fingers on your hand—so. Oh, Marilla, it gives me a shudder to think of it. And there's a headless man stalks up and down the path and skeletons glower at you between the boughs. Oh, Marilla, I wouldn't go through the Haunted Wood after dark now for anything. I'd be sure that white things would reach out from behind the trees and grab me."

" Did ever anyone hear the like ! " ejaculated Marilla, who had listened in dumb amazement. " Anne Shirley, do you mean to tell me you believe all that wicked nonsense of your own imagination ? "

" Not believe *exactly*," faltered Anne. " At least, I don't believe it in daylight. But after dark, Marilla, it's different. That is when ghosts walk."

" There are no such things as ghosts, Anne."

" Oh, but there are, Marilla," cried Anne eagerly. " I know people who have seen them. And they are respectable people. Charlie Sloane says that his grandmother saw his grandfather driving home the cows one night after he'd been buried for a year. You know Charlie Sloane's grandmother wouldn't tell a story for anything. She's a very religious woman. And Mrs Thomas' father was pursued home one night by a lamb of fire with its head cut off hanging by a strip of skin. He said he knew it was the spirit of his brother and that it was a warning he would die within nine days. He didn't, but he died two years after, so you see it was really true. And Ruby Gillis says——"

" Anne Shirley," interrupted Marilla firmly, " I never want to hear you talking in this fashion again. I've had my doubts about that imagination of yours right along, and if this is going to be the outcome of it, I won't countenance any such doings. You'll go right over to Barry's, and you'll go through that spruce grove, just for a lesson and a warning to you. And never let me hear a word out of your head about haunted woods again."

Anne might plead and cry as she liked—and did, for her terror was very real. Her imagination had run away with her and she held the spruce grove in mortal dread after nightfall. But Marilla was inexorable. She marched the shrinking ghostseer down to the spring and ordered her to proceed straightway over the bridge and into the dusky retreats of wailing ladies and headless spectres beyond.

" Oh, Marilla, how can you be so cruel ? " sobbed Anne. " What would you feel like if a white thing did snatch me up and carry me off ? "

" I'll risk it," said Marilla unfeelingly. " You know I always mean what I say. I'll cure you of imagining ghosts into places. March, now."

Anne marched. That is, she stumbled over the bridge and went shuddering up the horrible dim path beyond. Anne never forgot that walk. Bitterly did she repent the licence she had given to her imagination. The goblins of her fancy lurked in every shadow about her, reaching out their cold, fleshless hands to grasp the terrified small girl who had called them into being. A white strip of birch bark blowing up from the hollow over the brown floor of the grove made her heart stand still. The long-drawn wail of two old boughs rubbing against each other brought out the perspiration in beads on her forehead. The swoop of bats in the darkness over her was as the wings of unearthly creatures. When she reached Mr William Bell's field she fled across it as if pursued by an army of white things, and arrived at the Barry kitchen door so out of breath that she could hardly gasp out her request for the apron pattern. Diana was away so that she had no excuse to linger. The dreadful return journey had to be faced. Anne went back over it with shut eyes, preferring to take the risk of dashing her brains out among the boughs to that of seeing a white thing.

When she finally stumbled over the log bridge she drew one long shivering breath of relief.

" Well, so nothing caught you ? " said Marilla unsympathetically.

" Oh, Mar—Marilla," chattered Anne, " I'll b-b-be cont-t-tented with c-c-commonplace places after this."

CHAPTER XXI

A NEW DEPARTURE IN FLAVOURINGS

DEAR me, there is nothing but meetings and partings in this world, as Mrs Lynde says," remarked Anne plaintively, putting her slate and books down on the kitchen table on the last day of June and wiping her red eyes with a very damp handkerchief. "Wasn't it fortunate, Marilla, that I took an extra handkerchief to school to-day? I had a presentiment that it would be needed."

"I never thought you were so fond of Mr Phillips that you'd require two handkerchiefs to dry your tears just because he was going away," said Marilla.

"I don't think I was crying because I was really so very fond of him," reflected Anne. "I just cried because all the others did. It was Ruby Gillis started it. Ruby Gillis has always declared she hated Mr Phillips, but just as soon as he got up to make his farewell speech she burst into tears. Then all the girls began to cry, one after the other. I tried to hold out, Marilla. I tried to remember the time Mr Phillips made me sit with Gil—with a boy; and the time he spelled my name without an *e* on the blackboard; and how he said I was the worst dunce he ever saw at geometry and laughed at my spelling; and all the times he had been so horrid and sarcastic; but somehow I couldn't, Marilla, and I just had to cry too. Jane Andrews has been talking for a month about how glad she'd be when Mr Phillips went away and she declared she'd never shed a tear. Well, she was worse than any of us and had to borrow a handkerchief from her brother—of course the boys didn't cry—because she hadn't brought one of her own, not expecting to need it. Oh, Marilla, it was heartrending. Mr Phillips made such a beautiful farewell speech beginning, ' The time has come for us to part.' It was very affecting. And he had tears in his eyes too, Marilla. Oh, I felt dreadfully sorry and remorseful for all the times I'd talked in school and drawn pictures of him on my slate and made fun of him and Prissy. I can tell you I wished I'd been a model pupil like Minnie Andrews. *She* hadn't anything on her conscience. The girls cried all the way home from school. Carrie Sloane kept saying every few minutes, ' The time has come for us to part,' and that would start us off again whenever we were in any danger of cheering up. I do feel dreadfully sad, Marilla. But one can't feel quite in the depths of despair with two months vacation before them, can they, Marilla ? And besides, we met the new minister and his wife coming from the station. For all I was feeling so bad about Mr Phillips going away I couldn't help taking a little interest in a new minister, could I ? His wife is very pretty. Not exactly regally lovely, of course—it wouldn't do, I suppose, for a minister to have a regally lovely wife, because it might set a bad example. Mrs Lynde says the minister's wife over at Newbridge sets a very bad example because she dresses so fashionably. Our new minister's wife was dressed in blue muslin with lovely puffed sleeves and a hat trimmed with roses. Jane Andrews said she thought puffed sleeves were too worldly for a minister's wife, but I didn't make any such uncharitable remark, Marilla, because I know what it is to long for puffed sleeves. Besides, she's only been a minister's wife for a little while, so one should make allowances, shouldn't they ? They are going to board with Mrs Lynde until the manse is ready."

If Marilla, in going down to Mrs Lynde's that evening, was actuated by any motive save her avowed one of returning the quilting-frames she had borrowed the preceding winter, it was an amiable weakness shared by most of the Avonlea people. Many a thing Mrs Lynde had lent, sometimes never expecting to see it again, came home that night in charge of the borrowers thereof. A new minister, and moreover a minister with a wife, was a lawful object of curiosity in a quiet little country settlement where sensations were few and far between.

Old Mr Bentley, the minister whom Anne had found lacking in imagination, had been pastor of Avonlea for eighteen years. He was a widower when he came, and a widower he remained, despite the fact that gossip regularly married him to this, that or the other one, every year of his sojourn. In the preceding February he had resigned his charge and departed amid the regrets of his people, most of whom had the affection born of long intercourse for their good old minister in spite of his shortcomings as an orator. Since then the Avonlea church had enjoyed a variety of religious dissipation in listening to the many and various candidates and 'supplies' who came Sunday after Sunday to preach on trial. These stood or fell by the judgment of the fathers and mothers in Israel; but a certain small, red-headed girl who sat meekly in the corner of the old Cuthbert pew also had her opinions about them and discussed the same in full with Matthew, Marilla always declining from principle to criticize ministers in any shape or form.

" I don't think Mr Smith would have done, Matthew," was Anne's final summing up. " Mrs Lynde says his delivery was so poor, but I think his worst fault was just like Mr Bentley's—he had no imagination. And Mr Terry had too much ; he let it run away with him just as I did mine in the matter of the Haunted Wood. Besides, Mrs Lynde says his theology wasn't sound. Mr Gresham was a very good man and a very religious man, but he told too many funny stories and made the people laugh in church ; he was undignified, and you must have some dignity about a minister, mustn't you, Matthew ? I thought Mr Marshall was decidedly attractive ; but Mrs Lynde says he isn't married, or even engaged, because she made special inquiries about him, and she says it would never do to have a young unmarried minister in Avonlea, because he might marry in the congregation and that would make trouble. Mrs Lynde is a very far-seeing woman, isn't she, Matthew ? I'm very glad they've called Mr Allan. I liked him because his sermon was interesting and he prayed as if he meant it and not just as if he did it because he was in the habit of it. Mrs Lynde says he isn't perfect, but she says she supposes we couldn't expect a perfect minister for seven hundred and fifty dollars a year, and anyhow his theology is sound because she questioned him thoroughly on all the points of doctrine. And she knows his wife's people and they are most respectable and the women are all good housekeepers. Mrs Lynde says that sound doctrine in the man and good housekeeping in the woman make an ideal combination for a minister's family."

The new minister and his wife were a young, pleasant-faced couple, still in their honeymoon, and full of all good and beautiful enthusiasms for their chosen life-work. Avonlea opened its heart to them from the start. Old and young liked the frank, cheerful young man with his high ideals, and the bright, gentle little lady who assumed the mistress-ship of the manse. With Mrs Allan, Anne fell promptly and whole-heart-edly in love. She had discovered another kindred spirit.

" Mrs Allan is perfectly lovely," she announced one Sunday afternoon. " She's taken our class and she's a splendid teacher. She said right away she didn't think it was fair for the teacher to ask all the questions, and you know, Marilla, that is exactly what I've always thought. She said we could ask her any question we liked, and I asked ever so many. I'm good at asking questions, Marilla."

" I believe you," was Marilla's emphatic comment.

" Nobody else asked any except Ruby Gillis, and she asked if there was to be a Sunday-school picnic this summer. I didn't think that was a very proper question to ask because it hadn't any connection with the lesson—the lesson was about Daniel in the lions' den—but Mrs Allan just smiled and said she thought there would be. Mrs Allan has a lovely smile ; she has such *exquisite* dimples in her cheeks. I wish I had dimples in my cheeks, Marilla. I'm not half so skinny as I was when I came here, but I have no dimples yet. If I had perhaps I could influence people for good. Mrs Allan said we ought always to try to influence other people for good. She talked so nice about everything. I never knew before that religion was such a cheerful thing. I always thought it was kind of melancholy, but Mrs Allan's isn't, and I'd like to be a Christian if I could be one like her. I wouldn't want to be one like Mr Superintendent Bell."

" It's very naughty of you to speak so about Mr Bell," said Marilla severely. " Mr Bell is a real good man."

" Oh, of course he's good," agreed Anne, " but he doesn't seem to get any comfort out of it. If I could be good I'd dance and sing all day because I was glad of it. I suppose Mrs Allan is too old to dance and sing and of course it wouldn't be dignified in a minister's wife. But I can just feel she's glad she's a Christian and that she'd be one even if she could get to heaven without it."

" I suppose we must have Mr and Mrs Allan up to tea some day soon," said Marilla reflectively. " They've been most everywhere but here. Let me see. Next Wednesday would be a good time to have them. But don't say a word to Matthew about it, for if he knew they were coming he'd find some excuse to be away that day. He's got so used to Mr Bentley he didn't mind him, but he's going to find it hard to get acquainted with a new minister, and a new minister's wife will frighten him to death."

" I'll be as secret as the dead," assured Anne. " But oh, Marilla, will you let me make a cake for the occasion ? I'd love to do something for Mrs Allan, and you know I can make a pretty good cake by this time."

" You can make a layer cake," promised Marilla.

Monday and Tuesday great preparations went on at Green Gables. Having the minister and his wife to tea was a serious and important undertaking, and Marilla was determined not to be eclipsed by any of the Avonlea housekeepers. Anne was wild with excitement and delight. She talked it all over with Diana on Tuesday night in the twilight, as they sat on the big red stones by the Dryad's Bubble and made rainbows in the water with little twigs dipped in fir balsam.

" Everything is ready, Diana, except my cake, which I'm to make in the morning, and the baking-powder biscuits which Marilla will make just before tea-time. I assure you, Diana, that Marilla and I have had a busy two days of it. It's such a responsibility having a minister's family to tea. I never went through such an experience before. You should just see our pantry. It's a sight to behold. We're going to have jellied chicken and cold tongue. We're to have two kinds of jelly, red and yellow, and whipped cream and lemon pie, and cherry pie, and three kinds of cookies, and fruit-cake, and Marilla's famous yellow-plum preserves that she keeps especially for ministers, and pound cake and layer cake, and biscuits as aforesaid ; and new bread and old both, in case the minister is dyspeptic and can't eat new. Mrs Lynde says ministers mostly are dyspeptic, but I don't think Mr Allan has been a minister long enough for it to have had a bad effect on him. I just grow cold when I think of my layer cake. Oh, Diana, what if it shouldn't be good ! I dreamed last night that I was chased all round by a fearful goblin with a big layer cake for a head."

" It'll be good, all right," assured Diana, who was a very comfortable sort of friend. " I'm sure that piece of the one you made that we had for lunch in Idlewild two weeks ago was perfectly elegant."

" Yes ; but cakes have such a terrible habit of turning out bad just when you especially want them to be good," sighed Anne, setting a particularly well-balsamed twig afloat. " However, I suppose I shall just have to trust to Providence and be careful to put in the flour. Oh, look, Diana, what a lovely rainbow ! Do you suppose the dryad will come out after we go away and take it for a scarf ? "

" You know there is no such thing as a dryad," said Diana. Diana's mother had found out about the Haunted Wood and had been decidedly angry over it. As a result Diana had abstained from any further imitative flights of imagination and did not think it prudent to cultivate a spirit of belief even in harmless dryads.

" But it's so easy to imagine there is," said Anne. " Every night, before I go to bed, I look out of my window and wonder if the dryad is really sitting here, combing her locks with the spring for a mirror. Some-times I look for her footprints in the dew in the morning. Oh, Diana, don't give up your faith in the dryad ! "

Wednesday morning came. Anne got up at sunrise because she was too excited to sleep. She had caught a severe cold in the head by reason of her dabbling in the spring on the preceding evening ; but nothing short of absolute pneumonia could have quenched her interest in culinary matters that morning. After breakfast she proceeded to make her cake. When she finally shut the oven door upon it she drew a long breath.

" I'm sure I haven't forgotten anything this time, Marilla. But do you think it will rise ? Just suppose perhaps the baking-powder isn't good ? I used it out of the new can. And Mrs Lynde says you can never be sure of getting good baking-powder nowadays when everything is so adulterated. Mrs Lynde says the Government ought to take the matter up, but she says we'll never see the day when a Tory Government will do it. Marilla, what if that cake doesn't rise ? "

" We'll have plenty without it," was Marilla's un-impassioned way of looking at the subject.

The cake did rise, however, and came out of the oven as light and feathery as golden foam. Anne, flushed with delight, clapped it together with layers of ruby jelly, and, in imagination, saw Mrs Allan eating it and possibly asking for another piece!

" You'll be using the best tea-set, of course, Marilla," she said. " Can I fix up the table with ferns and wild roses ? "

" I think that's all nonsense," sniffed Marilla. " In my opinion it's the eatables that matter and not flummery decorations."

" Mrs Barry had *her* table decorated," said Anne, who was not entirely guiltless of the wisdom of the serpent, " and the minister paid her an elegant compliment. He said it was a feast for the eye as well as the palate."

" Well, do as you like," said Marilla, who was quite determined not to be surpassed by Mrs Barry or anybody else. " Only mind you leave enough room for the dishes and the food."

Anne laid herself out to decorate in a manner and after a fashion that should leave Mrs Barry's nowhere. Having abundance of roses and ferns and a very artistic taste of her own, she made that tea-table such a thing of beauty that when the minister and his wife sat down to it they exclaimed in chorus over its loveliness.

" It's Anne's doings," said Marilla, grimly just ; and Anne felt that Mrs Allan's approving smile was almost too much happiness for this world.

Matthew was there, having been inveigled into the party only goodness and Anne knew how. He had been in such a state of shyness and nervousness that Marilla had given him up in despair, but Anne took him in hand so successfully that he now sat at the table in his best clothes and white collar and talked to the minister not uninterestingly. He never said a word to Mrs Allan, but that perhaps was not to be expected.

All went merry as a marriage bell until Anne's layer cake was passed. Mrs Allan, having already been helped to a bewildering variety, declined it. But Marilla, seeing the disappointment on Anne's face, said smilingly :

" Oh, you must take a piece of this, Mrs Allan. Anne made it on purpose for you."

" In that case I must sample it," laughed Mrs Allan, helping herself to a plump triangle, as did also the minister and Marilla.

Mrs Allan took a mouthful of hers and a most peculiar expression crossed her face ; not a word did she say,

however, but steadily ate away at it. Marilla saw the
expression and hastened to taste the cake.

" Anne Shirley ! " she exclaimed, " what on earth
did you put into that cake ? "

" Nothing but what the recipe said, Marilla," cried
Anne with a look of anguish. " Oh, isn't it all right ? "

" All right ! It's simply horrible. Mrs Allan, don't
try to eat it. Anne, taste it yourself. What flavouring
did you use ? "

" Vanilla," said Anne, her face scarlet with mortification after tasting the cake. " Only vanilla. Oh,
Marilla, it must have been the baking-powder. I had
my suspicions of that bak——"

" Baking-powder fiddlesticks ! Go and bring me the
bottle of vanilla you used."

Anne fled to the pantry and returned with a small
bottle partially filled with a brown liquid and labelled
yellowly, " Best Vanilla."

Marilla took it, uncorked it, smelled it.

" Mercy on us, Anne, you've flavoured that cake
with *anodyne liniment*. I broke the liniment bottle
last week and poured what was left into an old empty
vanilla bottle. I suppose it's partly my fault—I
should have warned you—but for pity's sake why
couldn't you have smelled it ? "

Anne dissolved into tears under this double disgrace.

" I couldn't—I had such a cold ! " and with this she
fairly fled to the gable chamber, where she cast herself
on the bed and wept as one who refuses to be comforted.

Presently a light step sounded on the stairs and
somebody entered the room.

" Oh, Marilla," sobbed Anne without looking up,
" I'm disgraced for ever. I shall never be able to live
this down. It will get out—things always do get out
in Avonlea. Diana will ask me how my cake turned
out and I shall have to tell her the truth. I shall always

be pointed at as the girl who flavoured a cake with anodyne liniment. Gil— the boys in school will never get over laughing at it. Oh, Marilla, if you have a spark of Christian pity don't tell me that I must go down and wash the dishes after this. I'll wash them when the minister and his wife are gone, but I cannot ever look Mrs Allan in the face again. Perhaps she'll think I tried to poison her. Mrs Lynde says she knows an orphan girl who tried to poison her benefactor. But the liniment isn't poisonous. It's meant to be taken internally—although not in cakes. Won't you tell Mrs Allan so, Marilla ? "

" Suppose you jump up and tell her so yourself," said a merry voice.

Anne flew up, to find Mrs Allan standing by her bed, surveying her with laughing eyes.

" My dear little girl, you mustn't cry like this," she said, genuinely disturbed by Anne's tragic face. " Why, it's all just a funny mistake that anybody might make."

" Oh, no, it takes me to make such a mistake," said Anne forlornly. " And I wanted to have that cake so nice for you, Mrs Allan."

" Yes, I know, dear. And I assure you I appreciate your kindness and thoughtfulness just as much as if it had turned out all right. Now, you mustn't cry any more, but come down with me and show me your flower garden. Miss Cuthbert tells me you have a little plot all your own. I want to see it, for I'm very much interested in flowers."

Anne permitted herself to be led down and comforted, reflecting that it was really providential that Mrs Allan was a kindred spirit. Nothing more was said about the liniment cake, and when the guests went away Anne found that she had enjoyed the evening more than could have been expected, considering that terrible incident. Nevertheless she sighed deeply.

"Marilla, isn't it nice to think that to-morrow is a new day with no mistakes in it yet?"

"I'll warrant you'll make plenty in it," said Marilla. "I never saw your beat for making mistakes, Anne."

"Yes, and well I know it," admitted Anne mournfully. "But have you ever noticed one encouraging thing about me, Marilla? I never make the same mistake twice."

"I don't know as that's much benefit when you're always making new ones."

"Oh, don't you see, Marilla? There *must* be a limit to the mistakes one person can make, and when I get to the end of them, then I'll be through with them. That's a very comforting thought."

"Well, you'd better go and give that cake to the pigs," said Marilla. "It isn't fit for any human to eat, not even Jerry Buote."

CHAPTER XXII

ANNE IS INVITED OUT TO TEA

AND what are your eyes popping out of your head about now ? " asked Marilla, when Anne had just come in from a run to the post-office. " Have you discovered another kindred spirit ? "

Excitement hung around Anne like a garment, shone in her eyes, kindled in every feature. She had come dancing up the lane, like a wind-blown sprite, through the mellow sunshine and lazy shadows of the August evening.

" No, Marilla, but oh, what do you think ? I am invited to tea at the manse to-morrow afternoon ! Mrs Allan left the letter for me at the post-office. Just look at it, Marilla. ' Miss Anne Shirley, Green Gables.' That is the first time I was ever called ' Miss.' Such a thrill as it gave me ! I shall cherish it for ever among my choicest treasures."

" Mrs Allan told me she meant to have all the members of her Sunday school class to tea in turn," said Marilla, regarding the wonderful event very coolly. " You needn't get in such a fever over it. Do learn to take things calmly, child."

For Anne to take things calmly would have been to change her nature. All " spirit and fire and dew," as she was, the pleasures and pains of life came to her with trebled intensity. Marilla felt this and was vaguely troubled over it, realizing that the ups and downs of existence would probably bear hardly on this impulsive soul and not sufficiently understanding that the equally great capacity for delight might more

than compensate. Therefore Marilla conceived it to
be her duty to drill Anne into a tranquil uniformity
of disposition as impossible and alien to her as to a
dancing sunbeam in one of the brook shallows. She
did not make much headway, as she sorrowfully admitted to herself. The downfall of some dear hope or
plan plunged Anne into "deeps of affliction." The
fulfilment thereof exalted her to dizzy realms of delight.
Marilla had almost begun to despair of ever fashioning
this waif of the world into her model little girl of demure
manners and prim deportment. Neither would she
have believed that she really liked Anne much better
as she was.

Anne went to bed that night speechless with misery
because Matthew had said the wind was round northeast and he feared it would be a rainy day to-morrow.
The rustle of the poplar leaves about the house worried
her, it sounded so like pattering raindrops, and the
dull, far-away roar of the gulf, to which she listened
delightedly at other times, loving its strange, sonorous,
haunting rhythm, now seemed like a prophecy of storm
and disaster to a small maiden who particularly wanted
a fine day. Anne thought that the morning would
never come.

But all things have an end, even nights before the
day on which you are invited to take tea at the manse.
The morning, in spite of Matthew's predictions, was
fine, and Anne's spirits soared to their highest.

"Oh, Marilla, there is something in me to-day that
makes me just love everybody I see," she exclaimed
as she washed the breakfast dishes. "You don't
know how good I feel! Wouldn't it be nice if it
could last? I believe I could be a model child if I were
just invited out to tea every day. But oh, Marilla,
it's a solemn occasion, too. I feel so anxious. What
if I shouldn't behave properly? You know I never

had tea at a manse before, and I'm not sure that I know all the rules of etiquette, although I've been studying the rules given in the Etiquette Department of the *Family Herald* ever since I came here. I'm so afraid I'll do something silly or forget to do something I should do. Would it be good manners to take a second helping of anything if you wanted to *very* much ? "

" The trouble with you, Anne, is that you're thinking too much about yourself. You should just think of Mrs Allan and what would be nicest and most agreeable for her," said Marilla, hitting for once in her life on a very sound and pithy piece of advice. Anne instantly realized this.

" You are right, Marilla. I'll try not to think about myself at all."

Anne evidently got through her visit without any serious breach of ' etiquette,' for she came home through the twilight, under a great, high-sprung sky gloried over with trails of saffron and rosy cloud, in a beatified state of mind, and told Marilla all about it happily, sitting on the big red sandstone slab at the kitchen door with her tired curly head in Marilla's gingham lap.

A cool wind was blowing down over the long harvest fields from the rims of firry western hills and whistling through the poplars. One clear star hung above the orchard and the fireflies were flitting over in Lovers' Lane, in and out among the ferns and rustling boughs. Anne watched them as she talked and somehow felt that wind and stars and fireflies were all tangled up together into something unutterably sweet and enchanting.

" Oh, Marilla, I've had a most *fascinating* time. I feel that I have not lived in vain and I shall always feel like that even if I should never be invited to tea at a

manse again. When I got there Mrs Allan met me at
the door. She was dressed in the sweetest dress of
pale pink organdy, with dozens of frills and elbow
sleeves, and she looked just like a seraph. I really
think I'd like to be a minister's wife when I grow up,
Marilla. A minister mightn't mind my red hair
because he wouldn't be thinking of such worldly things.
But then of course one would have to be naturally
good and I'll never be that, so I suppose there's no use
in thinking about it. Some people are naturally good,
you know, and others are not. I'm one of the others.
Mrs Lynde says I'm full of original sin. No matter
how hard I try to be good I can never make such a
success of it as those who are naturally good. It's
a good deal like geometry, I expect. But don't you
think the trying so hard ought to count for something ?
Mrs Allan is one of the naturally good people. I love
her passionately. You know there are some people,
like Matthew and Mrs Allan, that you can love right
off without any trouble. And there are others, like
Mrs Lynde, that you have to try very hard to love.
You know you *ought* to love them because they know
so much and are such active workers in the church, but
you have to keep reminding yourself of it all the time
or else you forget. There was another little girl at the
manse to tea, from the White Sands Sunday school.
Her name was Lauretta Bradley, and she was a very
nice little girl. Not exactly a kindred spirit, you know,
but still very nice. We had an elegant tea, and I
think I kept all the rules of etiquette pretty well.
After tea Mrs Allan played and sang and she got
Lauretta and me to sing, too. Mrs Allan says I have
a good voice and she says I must sing in the Sunday-
school choir after this. You can't think how I was
thrilled at the mere thought. I've longed so to sing
in the Sunday-school choir, as Diana does, but I feared

it was an honour I could never aspire to. Lauretta had to go home early because there is a big concert in the White Sands hotel to-night and her sister is to recite at it. Lauretta says that the Americans at the hotel give a concert every fortnight in aid of the Charlottetown hospital, and they ask lots of the White Sands people to recite. Lauretta said she expected to be asked herself some day. I just gazed at her in awe. After she had gone Mrs Allan and I had a heart-to-heart talk. I told her everything—about Mrs Thomas and the twins and Katie Maurice and Violetta, and coming to Green Gables and my troubles over geometry. And would you believe it, Marilla? Mrs Allan told me she was a dunce at geometry, too. You don't know how that encouraged me. Mrs Lynde came to the manse just before I left, and what do you think, Marilla? The trustees have hired a new teacher and it's a lady. Her name is Miss Muriel Stacy. Isn't that a romantic name? Mrs Lynde says they've never had a female teacher in Avonlea before and she thinks it is a dangerous innovation. But I think it will be splendid to have a lady teacher, and I really don't see how I'm going to live through the two weeks before school begins, I'm so impatient to see her."

CHAPTER XXIII

ANNE COMES TO GRIEF IN AN AFFAIR OF HONOUR

ANNE had to live through more than two weeks, as it happened. Almost a month having elapsed since the liniment cake episode, it was high time for her to get into fresh trouble of some sort, little mistakes, such as absent-mindedly emptying a pan of skim milk into a basket of yarn balls in the pantry instead of into the pigs' bucket, and walking clean over the edge of the log bridge into the brook while wrapped in imaginative reverie, not really being worth counting.

A week after the tea at the manse, Diana Barry gave a party.

" Small and select," Anne assured Marilla. " Just the girls in our class."

They had a very good time and nothing untoward happened until after tea, when they found themselves in the Barry garden, a little tired of all their games and ripe for any enticing form of mischief which might present itself. This presently took the form of ' daring.'

Daring was the fashionable amusement among the Avonlea small fry just then. It had begun among the boys, but soon spread to the girls, and all the silly things that were done in Avonlea that summer because the doers thereof were ' dared ' to do them would fill a book by themselves.

First of all Carrie Sloane dared Ruby Gillis to climb to a certain point in the huge old willow-tree before the front door : which Ruby Gillis, albeit in mortal dread of the fat green caterpillars with which said tree was infested and with the fear of her mother before her eyes if she should tear her new muslin dress, nimbly did, to the discomforture of the aforesaid Carrie Sloane.

Then Josie Pye dared Jane Andrews to hop on her left leg around the garden without stopping once or putting her right foot to the ground ; which Jane Andrews gamely tried to do, but gave out at the third corner and had to confess herself defeated.

Josie's triumph being rather more pronounced than good taste permitted, Anne Shirley dared her to walk along the top of the board fence which bounded the garden to the east. Now, to ' walk ' board fences requires more skill and steadiness of head and heel than one might suppose who has never tried it. But Josie Pye, if deficient in some qualities that make for popularity, had at least a natural and inborn gift, duly cultivated, for walking board fences. Josie walked the Barry fence with an airy unconcern which seemed to imply that a little thing like that wasn't worth a ' dare.' Reluctant admiration greeted her exploit, for most of the other girls could appreciate it, having suffered many things themselves in their efforts to walk fences. Josie descended from her perch, flushed with victory, and darted a defiant glance at Anne.

Anne tossed her red braids.

" I don't think it's such a very wonderful thing to walk a little, low, board fence," she said. " I knew a girl in Marysville who could walk the ridge-pole of a roof."

" I don't believe it," said Josie flatly. " I don't believe anybody could walk a ridge-pole. *You* couldn't anyhow."

" Couldn't I ? " cried Anne rashly.

" Then I dare you to do it," said Josie defiantly.

" I dare you to climb up there and walk the ridge-pole of Mr Barry's kitchen roof."

Anne turned pale, but there was clearly only one thing to be done. She walked towards the house, where a ladder was leaning against the kitchen roof. All the fifth-class girls said, " Oh ! " partly in excitement, partly in dismay.

" Don't you do it, Anne," entreated Diana. " You'll fall off and be killed. Never mind Josie Pye. It isn't fair to dare anybody to do anything so dangerous."

" I must do it. My honour is at stake," said Anne solemnly. " I shall walk that ridge-pole, Diana, or perish in the attempt. If I am killed you are to have my pearl bead ring."

Anne climbed the ladder amid breathless silence. gained the ridge-pole, balanced herself uprightly on that precarious footing, and started to walk along it, dizzily conscious that she was uncomfortably high up in the world and that walking ridge-poles was not a thing in which your imagination helped you out much. Nevertheless, she managed to take several steps before the catastrophe came. Then she swayed, lost her balance, stumbled, staggered and fell, sliding down over the sun-baked roof and crashing off it through the tangle of Virginia creeper beneath—all before the dismayed circle below could give a simultaneous, terrified shriek.

If Anne had tumbled off the roof on the side up which she ascended, Diana would probably have fallen heir to the pearl bead ring then and there. Fortunately she fell on the other side, where the roof extended down over the porch so nearly to the ground that a fall therefrom was a much less serious thing. Nevertheless, when Diana and the other girls had rushed frantically around the house—except Ruby Gillis, who remained as if rooted to the ground and went into hysterics—they found Anne lying all white and limp among the wreck and ruin of the Virginia creeper.

" Anne, are you killed ? " shrieked Diana, throwing herself on her knees beside her friend. " Oh, Anne, dear Anne, speak just one word to me and tell me if you're killed."

To the immense relief of all the girls, and especially of Josie Pye, who, in spite of lack of imagination, had been seized with horrible visions of a future branded as the girl who was the cause of Anne Shirley's early and tragic death, Anne sat dizzily up and answered uncertainly :

" No, Diana, I am not killed, but I think I am rendered unconscious."

" Where ? " sobbed Carrie Sloane. " Oh, where, Anne ? "

Before Anne could answer Mrs Barry appeared on the scene. At sight of her Anne tried to scramble to her feet, but sank back again with a sharp little cry of pain.

" What's the matter ? Where have you hurt yourself ? " demanded Mrs Barry.

" My ankle," gasped Anne. " Oh, Diana, please find your father and ask him to take me home. I know I can never walk there. And I'm sure I couldn't hop so far on one foot when Jane couldn't even hop around the garden."

Marilla was out in the orchard picking a panful of summer apples when she saw Mr Barry coming over the log bridge and up the slope, with Mrs Barry beside him and a whole procession of little girls trailing after him. In his arms he carried Anne, whose head lay limply against his shoulder.

At that moment Marilla had a revelation. In the sudden stab of fear that pierced to her very heart she realized what Anne had come to mean to her. She would have admitted that she liked Anne—nay, that she was very fond of Anne. But now she knew as she hurried wildly down the slope that Anne was dearer to her than anything on earth.

" Mr Barry, what has happened to her ? " she gasped, more white and shaken than the self-contained, sensible Marilla had been for many years.

Anne herself answered, lifting her head.

" Don't be frightened, Marilla. I was walking the ridge-pole and I fell off. I expect I have sprained my ankle. But, Marilla, I might have broken my neck. Let us look on the bright side of things."

" I might have known you'd go and do something of the sort when I let you go to that party," said Marilla, sharp and shrewish in her very relief. " Bring her in here, Mr Barry, and lay her on the sofa. Mercy me, the child has gone and fainted ! "

It was quite true. Overcome by the pain of her injury, Anne had one more of her wishes granted to her. She had fainted dead away.

Matthew, hastily summoned from the harvest field, was straightway despatched for the doctor, who in due time came, to discover that the injury was more serious than they had supposed. Anne's ankle was broken.

That night, when Marilla went up to the east gable, where a white-faced girl was lying, a plaintive voice greeted her from the bed.

" Aren't you very sorry for me, Marilla ? "

" It was your own fault," said Marilla, twitching down the blind and lighting a lamp.

" And that is just why you should be sorry for me," said Anne, " because the thought that it *is* all my own fault is what makes it so hard. If I could blame it on anybody I would feel so much better. But what would you have done, Marilla, if you had been dared to walk a ridge-pole ? "

" I'd have stayed on good firm ground and let them dare away. Such absurdity ! " said Marilla.

Anne sighed.

" But you have such strength of mind, Marilla. I haven't. I just felt that I couldn't bear Josie Pye's scorn. She would have crowed over me all my life. And I think I have been punished so much that you needn't be very cross with me, Marilla. It's not a bit nice to faint, after all. And the doctor hurt me dreadfully when he was setting my ankle. I won't be able to go around for six or seven weeks and I'll miss the new lady teacher. She won't be new any more by the time I'm able to go to school. And Gil— everybody will get ahead of me in class. Oh, I am an afflicted mortal. But I'll try to bear it all bravely if only you won't be cross with me, Marilla."

" There, there, I'm not cross," said Marilla. " You're an unlucky child, there's no doubt about that ; but, as you say, you'll have the suffering of it. Here, now, try and eat some supper."

" Isn't it fortunate I've got such an imagination ? " said Anne. " It will help me through splendidly, I expect. What do people who haven't any imagination do when they break their bones, do you suppose, Marilla ? "

Anne had good reason to bless her imagination many a time and oft during the tedious seven weeks that followed. But she was not solely dependent on it. She had many visitors and not a day passed without one or more of the schoolgirls dropping in to bring her flowers and books and tell her all the happenings in the juvenile world of Avonlea.

" Everybody has been so good and kind, Marilla," sighed Anne happily, on the day when she could first limp across the floor. " It isn't very pleasant to be laid up ; but there *is* a bright side to it, Marilla. You find out how many friends you have. Why, even Superintendent Bell came to see me, and he's really a very fine man. Not a kindred spirit, of course ; but still I like him and I'm awfully sorry I ever criticized his prayers. I believe now he really does mean them, only he has got into the habit of saying them as if he didn't. He could get over that if he'd take a little trouble. I gave him a good broad hint. I told him how hard I tried to make my own little private prayers interesting. He told me all about the time he broke his ankle when he was a boy. It does seem so strange to think of Superintendent Bell ever being a boy. Even my imagination has its limits for I can't imagine *that*. When I try to imagine him as a boy I see him with grey whiskers and spectacles, just as he looks in Sunday school, only small. Now, it's so easy to imagine Mrs Allan as a little girl. Mrs Allan has been to see me fourteen times. Isn't that something to be proud of, Marilla ? When a minister's wife has so many claims on her time ! She is such a cheerful person to have visit you, too. She never tells you it's your own fault and she hopes you'll be a better girl on account of it. Mrs Lynde always told me that when she came to see me ; and she said it in a kind of way that made me feel she might hope I'd be a better girl, but didn't really believe I would. Even Josie Pye came to see me. I received her as politely as I could, because I think she was sorry she dared me to walk a ridge-pole. If I had been killed she would have had to carry a dark burden of remorse all her life. Diana has been a faithful friend. She's been over every day to cheer my lonely pillow. But oh, I shall be so glad when I can go to school, for I've heard such exciting things about the new teacher. The girls all think she is perfectly sweet. Diana says she has the loveliest fair curly hair and such fascinating eyes. She dresses

beautifully, and her sleeve puffs are bigger than anybody else's in Avonlea. Every other Friday afternoon
she has recitations and everybody has to say a piece
or take part in a dialogue. Oh, it's just glorious to
think of it. Josie Pye says she hates it, but that is
just because Josie has so little imagination. Diana
and Ruby Gillis and Jane Andrews are preparing a
dialogue called ' A Morning Visit,' for next Friday.
And the Friday afternoons they don't have recitations
Miss Stacy takes them all to the woods for a ' field '
day and they study ferns and flowers and birds. And
they have physical culture exercises morning and evening. Mrs Lynde says she never heard of such goings-on
and it all comes of having a lady teacher. But I think
it must be splendid and I believe I shall find that Miss
Stacy is a kindred spirit."

"There's one thing plain to be seen, Anne," said
Marilla, " and that is that your fall off the Barry roof
hasn't injured your tongue at all."

CHAPTER XXIV

MISS STACY AND HER PUPILS GET UP A CONCERT

IT was October again when Anne was ready to go back to school—a glorious October, all red and gold, with mellow mornings when the valleys were filled with delicate mists as if the spirit of autumn had poured them in for the sun to drain—amethyst, pearl, silver, rose, and smoke-blue. The dews were so heavy that the fields glistened like cloth of silver and there were such heaps of rustling leaves in the hollows of many-stemmed woods to run crisply through. The Birch Path was a canopy of yellow and the ferns were sear and brown all along it. There was a tang in the very air that inspired the hearts of small maidens tripping, unlike snails, swiftly and willingly to school ; and it *was* jolly to be back again at the little brown desk beside Diana, with Ruby Gillis nodding across the aisle and Carrie Sloane sending up notes and Julia Bell passing a " chew " of gum down from the back seat. Anne drew a long breath of happiness as she sharpened her pencil and arranged her picture cards in her desk. Life was certainly very interesting.

In the new teacher she found another true and helpful friend. Miss Stacy was a bright, sympathetic young woman with the happy gift of winning and holding the affections of her pupils and bringing out the best that was in them mentally and morally. Anne expanded like a flower under this wholesome influence and carried home to the admiring Matthew and the critical Marilla glowing accounts of school work and aims.

" I love Miss Stacy with my whole heart, Marilla. She is so ladylike and she has such a sweet voice. When she pronounces my name I feel *instinctively* that she's spelling it with an *e*. We had recitations this afternoon. I just wish you could have been there to hear me recite ' Mary Queen of Scots.' I just put my whole soul into it. Ruby Gillis told me coming home that the way I said the line,

Now for my father's arm, she said, my woman's heart farewell,

just made her blood run cold."

" Well now, you might recite it for me some of these days, out in the barn," suggested Matthew.

" Of course I will," said Anne meditatively, " but I won't be able to do it so well, I know. It won't be so exciting as it is when you have a whole schoolful before you hanging breathlessly on your words. I know I won't be able to make your blood run cold."

" Mrs Lynde says it made *her* blood run cold to see the boys climbing to the very tops of those big trees on Bell's hill after crows' nests last Friday," said Marilla. " I wonder at Miss Stacy for encouraging it."

" But we wanted a crow's nest for nature study," explained Anne. " That was on our field afternoon. Field afternoons are splendid, Marilla. And Miss Stacy explains everything so beautifully. We have to write compositions on our field afternoons and I write the best ones."

" It's very vain of you to say so then. You'd better let your teacher say it."

" But she *did* say it, Marilla. And indeed I'm not vain about it. How can I be, when I'm such a dunce at geometry ? Although I'm really beginning to see through it a little, too. Miss Stacy makes it so clear. Still, I'll never be good at it and I assure you it is a humbling reflection. But I love writing compositions. Mostly Miss Stacy lets us choose our own subjects ;

but next week we are to write a composition on some remarkable person. It's hard to choose among so many remarkable people who have lived. Mustn't it be splendid to be remarkable and have compositions written about you after you're dead ? Oh, I would dearly love to be remarkable. I think when I grow up I'll be a trained nurse and go with the Red Crosses to the field of battle as a messenger of mercy. That is, if I don't go out as a foreign missionary. That would be very romantic, but one would have to be very good to be a missionary, and that would be a stumbling-block. We have physical culture exercises every day, too. They make you graceful and promote digestion."

" Promote fiddlesticks ! " said Marilla, who honestly thought it was all nonsense.

But all the field afternoons and recitation Fridays and physical culture contortions paled before a project which Miss Stacy brought forward in November. This was that the scholars of Avonlea school should get up a concert and hold it in the hall on Christmas night, for the laudable purpose of helping to pay for a school-house flag. The pupils one and all taking graciously to this plan, the preparations for a programme were begun at once. And of all the excited performers-elect none was so excited as Anne Shirley, who threw herself into the undertaking heart and soul hampered as she was by Marilla's disapproval. Marilla thought it all rank foolishness.

" It's just filling your heads up with nonsense and taking time that ought to be put on your lessons," she grumbled. " I don't approve of children's getting up concerts and racing about to practices. It makes them vain and forward and fond of gadding."

" But think of the worthy object," pleaded Anne. " A flag will cultivate a spirit of patriotism, Marilla."

" Fudge ! There's precious little patriotism in the

thoughts of any of you. All you want is a good time."

" Well, when you can combine patriotism and fun, isn't it all right ? Of course it's real nice to be getting up a concert. We're going to have six choruses and Diana is to sing a solo. I'm in two dialogues—*The Society for the Suppression of Gossip* and *The Fairy Queen*. The boys are going to have a dialogue, too. And I'm to have two recitations, Marilla. I just tremble when I think of it, but it's a nice thrilly kind of tremble. And we're to have a tableau at the last— *Faith, Hope, and Charity*. Diana and Ruby and I are to be in it, all draped in white with flowing hair. I'm to be Hope, with my hands clasped—so—and my eyes uplifted. I'm going to practise my recitations in the garret. Don't be alarmed if you hear me groaning. I have to groan heartrendingly in one of them, and it's really hard to get up a good artistic groan, Marilla. Josie Pye is sulky because she didn't get the part she wanted in the dialogue. She wanted to be the fairy queen. That would have been ridiculous, for who ever heard of a fairy queen as fat as Josie ? Fairy queens must be slender. Jane Andrews is to be the queen and I am to be one of her maids of honour. Josie says she thinks a red-haired fairy is just as ridiculous as a fat one, but I do not let myself mind what Josie says. I'm to have a wreath of white roses on my hair and Ruby Gillis is going to lend me her slippers because I haven't any of my own. It's necessary for fairies to have slippers, you know. You couldn't imagine a fairy wearing boots, could you ? Especially with copper toes ? We are going to decorate the hall with creeping spruce and fir mottoes with pink tissue-paper roses in them. And we are all to march in two by two after the audience is seated, while Emma White plays a march on the organ. Oh, Marilla, I know you are not so enthusiastic about it as I am, but don't you hope your little Anne will distinguish herself ? "

" All I hope is that you'll behave yourself. I'll be heartily glad when all this fuss is over and you'll be able to settle down. You are simply good for nothing just now with your head stuffed full of dialogues and groans and tableaus. As for your tongue, it's a marvel it's not clean worn out."

Anne sighed and betook herself to the back yard, over which a young new moon was shining through the leafless poplar boughs from an apple-green western sky, and where Matthew was splitting wood. Anne perched herself on a block and talked the concert over with him, sure of an appreciative and sympathetic listener in this instance at least.

" Well now, I reckon it's going to be a pretty good concert. And I expect you'll do your part fine," he said, smiling down into her eager, vivacious little face. Anne smiled back at him. Those two were the best of friends and Matthew thanked his stars many a time and oft that he had nothing to do with bringing her up. That was Marilla's exclusive duty ; if it had been his he would have been worried over frequent conflicts between inclination and said duty. As it was, he was free to " spoil Anne "—Marilla's phrasing—as much as he liked. But it was not such a bad arrangement after all ; a little ' appreciation ' sometimes does quite as much good as all the conscientious ' bringing up ' in the world.

CHAPTER XXV

MATTHEW INSISTS ON PUFFED SLEEVES

MATTHEW was having a bad ten minutes of it. He had come into the kitchen, in the twilight of a cold, grey December evening, and had sat down in the wood-box corner to take off his heavy boots, unconscious of the fact that Anne and a bevy of her schoolmates were having a practice of *The Fairy Queen* in the sitting-room. Presently they came trooping through the hall and out into the kitchen, laughing and chattering gaily. They did not see Matthew, who shrank bashfully back into the shadows beyond the wood-box with a boot in one hand and a bootjack in the other, and he watched them shyly for the aforesaid ten minutes as they put on caps and jackets and talked about the dialogue and the concert. Anne stood among them, bright-eyed and animated as they ; but Matthew suddenly became conscious that there was something about her different from her mates. And what worried Matthew was that the difference impressed him as being something that should not exist. Anne had a brighter face, and bigger, starrier eyes, and more delicate features than the others ; even shy, unobservant Matthew had learned to take note of these things ; but the difference that disturbed him did not consist in any of these respects. Then in what did it consist ?

Matthew was haunted by this question long after the girls had gone, arm in arm, down the long, hard-frozen lane and Anne had betaken herself to her books. He could not refer it to Marilla, who, he felt, would be quite sure to sniff scornfully and remark that the only difference she saw between Anne and the other girls was that they sometimes kept their tongues quiet while Anne never did. This, Matthew felt, would be no great help.

He had recourse to his pipe that evening to help him study it out, much to Marilla's disgust. After two hours of smoking and hard reflection Matthew arrived at the solution of his problem. Anne was not dressed like the other girls !

The more Matthew thought about the matter the more he was convinced that Anne never had been dressed like the other girls—never since she had come to Green Gables. Marilla kept her clothed in plain, dark dresses, all made after the same unvarying pattern. If Matthew knew there was such a thing as fashion in dress it is as much as he did ; but he was quite sure that Anne's sleeves did not look at all like the sleeves the other girls wore. He recalled the cluster of little girls he had seen around her that evening—all gay in waists of red and blue and pink and white—and he wondered why Marilla always kept her so plainly and soberly gowned.

Of course, it must be all right. Marilla knew best and Marilla was bringing her up. Probably some wise inscrutable motive was to be served thereby. But surely it would do no harm to let the child have one pretty dress—something like Diana Barry always wore. Matthew decided that he would give her one ; that surely could not be objected to as an unwarranted putting in of his oar. Christmas was only a fortnight off. A nice new dress would be the very thing for a present. Matthew, with a sigh of satisfaction, put away his pipe and went to bed, while Marilla opened all the doors and aired the house.

The very next evening Matthew betook himself to

Carmody to buy the dress, determined to get the worst over and have done with it. It would be, he felt assured, no trifling ordeal. There were some things Matthew could buy and prove himself no mean bargainer ; but he knew he would be at the mercy of shopkeepers when it came to buying a girl's dress.

After much cogitation Matthew resolved to go to Samuel Lawson's store instead of William Blair's. To be sure, the Cuthberts always had gone to William Blair's ; it was almost as much a matter of conscience with them as to attend the Presbyterian church and vote Conservative. But William Blair's two daughters frequently waited on customers there and Matthew held them in absolute dread. He could contrive to deal with them when he knew exactly what he wanted and could point it out ; but in such a matter as this, requiring explanation and consultation, Matthew felt that he must be sure of a man behind the counter. So he would go to Lawson's, where Samuel or his son would wait on him.

Alas ! Matthew did not know that Samuel, in the recent expansion of his business, had set up a lady clerk also ; she was a niece of his wife's and a very dashing young person indeed, with a huge, drooping pompadour, big, rolling brown eyes, and a most extensive and bewildering smile. She was dressed with exceeding smartness and wore several bangle bracelets that glittered and rattled and tinkled with every movement of her hands. Matthew was covered with confusion at finding her there at all ; and those bangles completely wrecked his wits at one fell swoop.

" What can I do for you this evening, Mr Cuthbert ? " Miss Lucilla Harris inquired, briskly and ingratiatingly, tapping the counter with both hands.

" Have you any—any—any—well now, say any garden rakes ? " stammered Matthew.

Miss Harris looked somewhat surprised, as well she might, to hear a man inquiring for garden rakes in the middle of December.

" I believe we have one or two left over," she said, " but they're up-stairs in the lumber-room. I'll go and see."

During her absence Matthew collected his scattered senses for another effort.

When Miss Harris returned with the rake and cheerfully inquired : " Anything else to-night, Mr Cuthbert ? " Matthew took his courage in both hands and replied : " Well now, since you suggest it, I might as well—take—that is—look at—buy some—some hayseed."

Miss Harris had heard Matthew Cuthbert called odd. She now concluded that he was entirely crazy.

" We only keep hayseed in the spring," she explained loftily. " We've none on hand just now."

" Oh, certainly—certainly—just as you say," stammered unhappy Matthew, seizing the rake and making for the door. At the threshold he recollected that he had not paid for it and he turned miserably back. While Miss Harris was counting out his change he rallied his powers for a final desperate attempt.

" Well now—if it isn't too much trouble—I might as well—that is—I'd like to look at—at—some sugar."

" White or brown ? " queried Miss Harris patiently.

" Oh—well now—brown," said Matthew feebly.

" There's a barrel of it over there," said Miss Harris, shaking her bangles at it. " It's the only kind we have."

" I'll—I'll take twenty pounds of it," said Matthew, with beads of perspiration standing on his forehead.

Matthew had driven half-way home before he was his own man again. It had been a gruesome experience, but it served him right, he thought, for committing the

heresy of going to a strange store. When he reached
home he hid the rake in the tool-house, but the sugar
he carried in to Marilla.

" Brown sugar ! " exclaimed Marilla. " Whatever
possessed you to get so much ? You know I never use
it except for the hired man's porridge or black fruit-
cake. Jerry's gone and I've made my cake long ago.
It's not good sugar, either—it's coarse and dark—
William Blair doesn't usually keep sugar like that."

" I—I thought it might come in handy sometime,"
said Matthew, making good his escape.

When Matthew came to think the matter over he
decided that a woman was required to cope with the
situation. Marilla was out of the question. Matthew
felt sure she would throw cold water on his project
at once. Remained only Mrs Lynde ; for of no other
woman in Avonlea would Matthew have dared to ask
advice. To Mrs Lynde he went accordingly, and that
good lady promptly took the matter out of the harassed
man's hands.

" Pick out a dress for you to give Anne ? To be
sure I will. I'm going to Carmody to-morrow and I'll
attend to it. Have you something particular in mind ?
No ? Well, I'll just go by my own judgment then.
I believe a nice rich brown would just suit Anne, and
William Blair has some new gloria in that's real pretty.
Perhaps you'd like me to make it up for her, too, seeing
that if Marilla was to make it Anne would probably
get wind of it before the time and spoil the surprise ?
Well, I'll do it. No, it isn't a mite of trouble. I like
sewing. I'll make it to fit my niece, Jenny Gillis, for
she and Anne are as like as two peas as far as figure
goes."

" Well now, I'm much obliged," said Matthew, " and
—and—I dunno—but I'd like—I think they make the
sleeves different nowadays to what they used to be.

If it wouldn't be asking too much I—I'd like them
made in the new way."

" Puffs ? Of course. You needn't worry a speck
more about it, Matthew. I'll make it up in the very
latest fashion," said Mrs Lynde. To herself she added
when Matthew had gone :

" It'll be a real satisfaction to see that poor child
wearing something decent for once. The way Marilla
dresses her is positively ridiculous, that's what, and I've
ached to tell her so plainly a dozen times. I've held
my tongue though, for I can see Marilla doesn't want
advice and she thinks she knows more about bringing
children up than I do for all she's an old maid. But
that's always the way. Folks that has brought up
children know that there's no hard and fast method
in the world that'll suit every child. But them as
never have think it's all as plain and easy as Rule of
Three—just set your three terms down so-fashion, and
the sum'll work out correct. But flesh and blood
don't come under the head of arithmetic and that's
where Marilla Cuthbert makes her mistake. I suppose
she's trying to cultivate a spirit of humility in Anne by
dressing her as she does ; but it's more likely to cultivate envy and discontent. I'm sure the child must feel
the difference between her clothes and the other girls'.
But to think of Matthew taking notice of it ! That
man is waking up after being asleep for over sixty
years."

Marilla knew all the following fortnight that Matthew
had something on his mind, but what it was she could
not guess, until Christmas Eve, when Mrs Lynde
brought up the new dress. Marilla behaved pretty
well on the whole, although it is very likely she dis-
trusted Mrs Lynde's diplomatic explanation that she
had made the dress because Matthew was afraid Anne
would find out about it too soon if Marilla made it.

" So this is what Matthew has been looking so mysterious over and grinning about to himself for two weeks, is it ? " she said a little stiffly but tolerantly. " I knew he was up to some foolishness. Well, I must say I don't think Anne needed any more dresses. I made her three good, warm, serviceable ones this fall, and anything more is sheer extravagance. There's enough material in those sleeves alone to make a waist, I declare there is. You'll just pamper Anne's vanity, Matthew, and she's as vain as a peacock now. Well, I hope she'll be satisfied at last, for I know she's been hankering after those silly sleeves ever since they came in, although she never said a word after the first. The puffs have been getting bigger and more ridiculous right along ; they're as big as balloons now. Next year anybody who wears them will have to go through a door sideways."

Christmas morning broke on a beautiful white world. It had been a very mild December and people had looked forward to a green Christmas ; but just enough snow fell softly in the night to transfigure Avonlea. Anne peeped out from her frosted gable window with delighted eyes. The firs in the Haunted Wood were all feathery and wonderful ; the birches and wild cherry-trees were outlined in pearl ; the ploughed fields were stretches of snowy dimples ; and there was a crisp tang in the air that was glorious. Anne ran downstairs singing until her voice re-echoed through Green Gables.

" Merry Christmas, Marilla ! Merry Christmas, Matthew ! Isn't it a lovely Christmas ? I'm so glad it's white. Any other kind of Christmas doesn't seem real, does it ? I don't like green Christmases. They're *not* green—they're just nasty faded browns and greys. What makes people call them green ? Why—why— Matthew, is that for me ? Oh, Matthew ! "

Matthew had sheepishly unfolded the dress from its

paper swathings and held it out with a deprecatory
glance at Marilla, who feigned to be contemptuously
filling the teapot, but nevertheless watched the scene
out of the corner of her eye with a rather interested air.

Anne took the dress and looked at it in reverent
silence. Oh, how pretty it was—a lovely soft brown
gloria with all the gloss of silk ; a skirt with dainty
frills and shirrings ; a waist elaborately pin-tucked in
the most fashionable way, with a little ruffle of filmy
lace at the neck. But the sleeves—they were the
crowning glory ! Long elbow cuffs and above them
two beautiful puffs divided by rows of shirring and
bows of brown silk ribbon.

" That's a Christmas present for you, Anne," said
Matthew shyly. " Why,—why—Anne, don't you like
it ? Well now—well now."

For Anne's eyes had suddenly filled with tears.

" *Like* it ! Oh, Matthew ! " Anne laid the dress
over a chair and clasped her hands. " Matthew, it's
perfectly exquisite. Oh, I can never thank you enough.
Look at those sleeves ! Oh, it seems to me this must
be a happy dream."

" Well, well, let us have breakfast," interrupted
Marilla. " I must say, Anne, I don't think you needed
the dress ; but since Matthew has got it for you, see
that you take good care of it. There's a hair ribbon
Mrs Lynde left for you. It's brown, to match the
dress. Come now, sit in."

" I don't see how I'm going to eat breakfast," said
Anne rapturously. " Breakfast seems so commonplace
at such an exciting moment. I'd rather feast my eyes
on that dress. I'm so glad that puffed sleeves are still
fashionable. It did seem to me that I'd never get
over it if they went out before I had a dress with them.
I'd never have felt quite satisfied, you see. It was
lovely of Mrs Lynde to give me the ribbon, too. I feel

that I ought to be a very good girl indeed. It's at times like this I'm sorry I'm not a model little girl ; and I always resolve that I will be in future. But somehow it's hard to carry out your resolutions when irresistible temptations come. Still, I really will make an extra effort after this."

When the commonplace breakfast was over Diana appeared, crossing the white log bridge in the hollow, a gay little figure in her crimson ulster. Anne flew down the slope to meet her.

" Merry Christmas, Diana ! And oh, it's a wonderful Christmas. I've something splendid to show you. Matthew has given me the loveliest dress, with *such* sleeves. I couldn't even imagine any nicer."

" I've got something more for you," said Diana breathlessly. " Here—this box. Aunt Josephine sent us out a big box with ever so many things in it—and this is for you. I'd have brought it over last night, but it didn't come until after dark, and I never feel very comfortable coming through the Haunted Wood in the dark now."

Anne opened the box and peeped in. First a card with " For the Anne-girl and Merry Christmas," written on it ; and then, a pair of the daintiest little kid slippers, with beaded toes and satin bows and glistening buckles.

" Oh," said Anne, " Diana, this is too much. I must be dreaming."

" *I* call it providential," said Diana. " You won't have to borrow Ruby's slippers now, and that's a blessing, for they're two sizes too big for you, and it would be awful to hear a fairy shuffling. Josie Pye would be delighted. Mind you, Rob Wright went home with Gertie Pye from the practice night before last. Did you ever hear anything equal to that ? "

All the Avonlea scholars were in a fever of excitement that day, for the hall had to be decorated and a last grand rehearsal held.

The concert came off in the evening and was a pronounced success. The little hall was crowded ; all the performers did excellently well, but Anne was the bright particular star of the occasion, as even envy, in the shape of Josie Pye, dared not deny.

" Oh, hasn't it been a brilliant evening ? " sighed Anne, when it was all over and she and Diana were walking home together under a dark, starry sky.

" Everything went off very well," said Diana practically. " I guess we must have made as much as ten dollars. Mind you, Mr Allan is going to send an account of it to the Charlottetown papers."

" Oh, Diana, will we really see our names in print ? It makes me thrill to think of it. Your solo was perfectly elegant, Diana. I felt prouder than you did when it was encored. I just said to myself, ' It is my dear bosom friend who is so honoured.' "

" Well, your recitations just brought down the house, Anne. That sad one was simply splendid."

" Oh, I was so nervous, Diana. When Mr Allan called out my name I really cannot tell how I ever got up on that platform. I felt as if a million eyes were looking at me and through me, and for one dreadful moment I was sure I couldn't begin at all. Then I thought of my lovely puffed sleeves and took courage. I knew that I must live up to those sleeves, Diana. So I started in, and my voice seemed to be coming from ever so far away. I just felt like a parrot. It's providential that I practised those recitations so often up in the garret, or I'd never have been able to get through. Did I groan alright ? "

" Yes, indeed, you groaned lovely," assured Diana.

" I saw old Mrs Sloane wiping away tears when I sat down. It was splendid to think I had touched somebody's heart. It's so romantic to take part in a concert, isn't it? Oh, it's been a very memorable occasion indeed."

"Wasn't the boys' dialogue fine?" said Diana. "Gilbert Blythe was just splendid. Anne, I do thing it's awful mean the way you treat Gil. Wait till I tell you. When you ran off the platform after the fairy dialogue one of your roses fell out of your hair. I saw Gil pick it up and put it in his breast-pocket. There now. You're so romantic that I'm sure you ought to be pleased at that."

"It's nothing to me what that person does," said Anne loftily. "I simply never waste a thought on him, Diana."

That night Marilla and Matthew, who had been out to a concert for the first time in twenty years, sat for awhile by the kitchen fire after Anne had gone to bed.

"Well now, I guess our Anne did as well as any of them," said Matthew proudly.

"Yes, she did," admitted Marilla. "She's a bright child, Matthew. And she looked real nice, too. I've been kind of opposed to this concert scheme, but I suppose there's no real harm in it after all. Anyhow, I was proud of Anne to-night, although I'm not going to tell her so."

"Well now, I was proud of her and I did tell her so 'fore she went up-stairs," said Matthew. "We must see what we can do for her some of these days, Marilla. I guess she'll need something more than Avonlea school by and by."

"There's time enough to think of that," said Marilla. "She's only thirteen in March. Though to-night it struck me she was growing quite a big girl. Mrs Lynde made that dress a mite too long, and it makes Anne look so tall. She's quick to learn and I guess the best thing we can do for her will be to send her to Queen's after a spell.   But nothing need be said about that for a year or two yet."

" Well now, it'll do no harm to be thinking it over off and on," said Matthew.   " Things like that are all the better for lots of thinking over."

CHAPTER XXVI

THE STORY CLUB IS FORMED

JUNIOR Avonlea found it hard to settle down to humdrum existence again. To Anne in particular things seemed fearfully flat, stale, and unprofitable after the goblet of excitement she had been sipping for weeks. Could she go back to the former quiet pleasures of those far-away days before the concert? At first, as she told Diana, she did not really think she could.

" I'm positively certain, Diana, that life can never be quite the same again as it was in those olden days," she said mournfully, as if referring to a period of at least fifty years back. " Perhaps after awhile I'll get used to it, but I'm afraid concerts spoil people for everyday life. I suppose that is why Marilla disapproves of them. Marilla is such a sensible woman. It must be a great deal better to be sensible ; but still, I don't believe I'd really want to be a sensible person, because they are so unromantic. Mrs Lynde says there is no danger of my ever being one, but you can never tell. I feel just now that I may grow up to be sensible yet. But perhaps that is only because I'm tired. I simply couldn't sleep last night for ever so long. I just lay awake and imagined the concert over and over again. That's one splendid thing about such affairs—it's so lovely to look back to them."

Eventually, however, Avonlea school slipped back into its old groove and took up its old interests. To be sure, the concert left traces. Ruby Gillis and Emma White, who had quarrelled over a point of

precedence in their platform seats, no longer sat at
the same desk, and a promising friendship of three
years was broken up. Josie Pye and Julia Bell did
not ' speak ' for three months, because Josie Pye had
told Bessie Wright that Julia Bell's bow when she got
up to recite made her think of a chicken jerking its
head, and Bessie told Julia. None of the Sloanes
would have any dealings with the Bells, because the
Bells had declared that the Sloanes had too much to
do in the programme, and the Sloanes had retorted
that the Bells were not capable of doing the little they
had to do properly. Finally, Charlie Sloane fought
Moody Spurgeon MacPherson, because Moody Spurgeon had said that Anne Shirley put on airs about her
recitations, and Moody Spurgeon was ' licked '; consequently Moody Spurgeon's sister, Ella May, would
not ' speak ' to Anne Shirley all the rest of the winter.
With the exception of these trifling frictions, work in
Miss Stacy's little kingdom went on with regularity
and smoothness.

The winter weeks slipped by. It was an unusually
mild winter, with so little snow that Anne and Diana
could go to school nearly every day by way of the
Birch Path. On Anne's birthday they were tripping
lightly down it, keeping eyes and ears alert amid all
their chatter, for Miss Stacy had told them that
they must soon write a composition on ' A Winter's
Walk in the Woods,' and it behoved them to be
observant.

" Just think, Diana, I'm thirteen years old to-day,"
remarked Anne in an awed voice. " I can scarcely
realize that I'm in my teens. When I woke this
morning it seemed to me that everything must be
different. You've been thirteen for a month, so I
suppose it doesn't seem such a novelty to you as it
does to me. It makes life seem so much more inter-

esting. In two more years I'll be really grown up. It's a great comfort to think that I'll be able to use big words then without being laughed at."

" Ruby Gillis says she means to have a beau as soon as she's fifteen," said Diana.

" Ruby Gillis thinks of nothing but beaus," said Anne disdainfully. " She's actually delighted when any one writes her name up in a take-notice for all she pretends to be so mad. But I'm afraid that is an uncharitable speech. Mrs Allan says we should never make uncharitable speeches ; but they do slip out so often before you think, don't they ? I simply can't talk about Josie Pye without making an uncharitable speech, so I never mention her at all. You may have noticed that. I'm trying to be as much like Mrs Allan as I possibly can, for I think she's perfect. Mr Allan thinks so too. Mrs Lynde says he just worships the ground she treads on and she doesn't really think it right for a minister to set his affections so much on a mortal being. But then, Diana, even ministers are human and have their besetting sins just like everybody else. I had such an interesting talk with Mrs Allan about besetting sins last Sunday afternoon. There are just a few things it's proper to talk about on Sundays and that is one of them. My besetting sin is imagining too much and forgetting my duties. I'm striving very hard to overcome it and now that I'm really thirteen perhaps I'll get on better."

" In four more years we'll be able to put our hair up," said Diana. " Alice Bell is only sixteen and she is wearing hers up, but I think that's ridiculous. I shall wait until I'm seventeen.

" If I had Alice Bell's crooked nose," said Anne decidedly, " I wouldn't—but there ! I won't say what I was going to because it was extremely uncharitable. Besides, I was comparing it with my own nose and

that's vanity. I'm afraid I think too much about my
nose ever since I heard that compliment about it long
ago. It really is a great comfort to me. Oh, Diana,
look, there's a rabbit. That's something to remember
for our woods composition. I really think the woods
are just as lovely in winter as in summer. They're so
white and still, as if they were asleep and dreaming
pretty dreams."

" I won't mind writing that composition when its
time comes," sighed Diana. " I can manage to write
about the woods, but the one we're to hand in Monday
is terrible. The idea of Miss Stacy telling us to write
a story out of our own heads ! "

" Why, it's as easy as wink," said Anne.

" It's easy for you because you have an imagination," retorted Diana, " but what would you do if you
had been born without one ? I suppose you have your
composition all done ? "

Anne nodded, trying hard not to look virtuously
complacent and failing miserably.

" I wrote it last Monday evening. It's called ' The
Jealous Rival ; or, In Death not Divided.' I read it
to Marilla and she said it was stuff and nonsense.
Then I read it to Matthew and he said it was fine.
That is the kind of critic I like. It's a sad, sweet
story. I just cried like a child while I was writing
it. It's about two beautiful maidens called Cordelia
Montmorency and Geraldine Seymour who lived in
the same village and were devotedly attached to each
other. Cordelia was a real brunette with a coronet
of midnight hair and duskly flashing eyes. Geraldine
was a queenly blonde with hair like spun gold and
velvety purple eyes."

" I never saw anybody with purple eyes," said
Diana dubiously.

" Neither did I. I just imagined them. I wanted

something out of the common. Geraldine had an alabaster brow, too. I've found out what an alabaster brow is. That is one of the advantages of being thirteen. You know so much more than you did when you were only twelve."

" Well, what became of Cordelia and Geraldine ? " asked Diana, who was beginning to feel rather interested in their fate.

" They grew in beauty side by side until they were sixteen. Then Bertram DeVere came to their native village and fell in love with the fair Geraldine. He saved her life when her horse ran away with her in a carriage, and she fainted in his arms and he carried her home three miles ; because, you understand, the carriage was all smashed up. I found it rather hard to imagine the proposal because I had no experience to go by. I asked Ruby Gillis if she knew anything about how men proposed because I thought she'd likely be an authority on the subject, having so many sisters married. Ruby told me she was hid in the hall pantry when Malcolm Andrews proposed to her sister Susan. She said Malcolm told Susan that his dad had given him the farm in his own name and then said, ' What do you say, darling pet, if we get hitched this fall ? ' And Susan said, ' Yes—no— I don't know—let me see'—and there they were, engaged as quick as that. But I didn't think that sort of a proposal was a very romantic one, so in the end I had to imagine it out as well as I could. I made it very flowery and poetical and Bertram went on his knees, although Ruby Gillis says it isn't done nowadays. Geraldine accepted him in a speech a page long. I can tell you I took a lot of trouble with that speech. I rewrote it five times and I look upon it as my masterpiece. Bertram gave her a diamond ring and a ruby necklace and told her they would go to Europe for a wedding tour, for he was immensely wealthy. But then, alas, shadows began to darken over their path. Cordelia was secretly in love with Bertram herself and when Geraldine told her about the engagement she was simply furious, especially when she saw the necklace and the diamond ring. All her affection for Geraldine turned to bitter hate and she vowed that she should never marry Bertram. But she pretended to be Geraldine's friend the same as ever. One evening they were standing on the bridge over a rushing turbulent stream and Cordelia, thinking they were alone, pushed Geraldine over the brink with a wild, mocking, ' Ha, ha, ha.' But Bertram saw it all and he at once plunged into the current, exclaiming, ' I will save thee, my peerless Geraldine.' But alas, he had forgotten he couldn't swim, and they were both drowned, clasped in each other's arms. Their bodies were washed ashore soon afterwards. They were buried in the one grave and their funeral was most imposing, Diana. It's so much more romantic to end a story up with a funeral than a wedding. As for Cordelia, she went insane with remorse and was shut up in a lunatic asylum. I thought that was a poetical retribution for her crime."

" How perfectly lovely ! " sighed Diana, who belonged to Matthew's school of critics. " I don't see how you can make up such thrilling things out of your own head, Anne. I wish my imagination was as good as yours."

" It would be if you'd only cultivate it," said Anne cheeringly. " I've just thought of a plan, Diana. Let you and I have a story club all our own and write stories for practice. I'll help you along until you can do them by yourself. You ought to cultivate your imagination, you know. Miss Stacy says so. Only we must take the right way. I told her about the Haunted

Wood, but she said we went the wrong way about it in that."

This was how the story club came into existence. It was limited to Diana and Anne at first, but soon it was extended to include Jane Andrews and Ruby Gillis and one or two others who felt that their imaginations needed cultivating. No boys were allowed in it—although Ruby Gillis opined that their admission would make it more exciting—and each member had to produce one story a week.

" It's extremely interesting," Anne told Marilla. " Each girl has to read her story out loud and then we talk it over. We are going to keep them all sacredly and have them to read to our descendants. We each write under a *nom de plume*. Mine is Rosamond Montmorency. All the girls do pretty well. Ruby Gillis is rather sentimental. She puts too much love-making into her stories and you know too much is worse than too little. Jane never puts any because she says it makes her feel so silly, when she has to read it out aloud. Jane's stories are extremely sensible. Then Diana puts too many murders into hers. She says most of the time she doesn't know what to do with the people so she kills them off to get rid of them. I mostly always have to tell them what to write about, but that isn't hard for I've millions of ideas."

" I think this story-writing business is the foolishest yet," scoffed Marilla. " You'll get a pack of nonsense into your heads and waste time that should be put on your lessons. Reading stories is bad enough but writing them is worse."

" But we're so careful to put a moral into them all, Marilla," explained Anne. " I insist upon that. All the good people are rewarded and all the bad ones are suitably punished. I'm sure that must have a wholesome effect. The moral is the great thing. Mr

Allan says so. I read one of my stories to him and
Mrs Allan and they both agreed that the moral was
excellent. Only they laughed in the wrong places.
I like it better when people cry. Jane and Ruby
almost always cry when I come to the pathetic parts.
Diana wrote her Aunt Josephine about our club and
her Aunt Josephine wrote back that we were to send
her some of our stories. So we copied out four of
our very best and sent them. Miss Josephine Barry
wrote back that she had never read anything so amusing in her life. That kind of puzzled us because the
stories were all very pathetic and almost everybody
died. But I'm glad Miss Barry liked them. It shows
our club is doing some good in the world. Mrs Allan
says that ought to be our object in everything. I do
really try to make it my object but I forget so often
when I'm having fun. I hope I shall be a little like
Mrs Allan when I grow up. Do you think there is any
prospect of it, Marilla ? "

" I shouldn't say there was a great deal," was
Marilla's encouraging answer. " I'm sure Mrs Allan
was never such a silly, forgetful little girl as you are."

" No ; but she wasn't always so good as she is now
either," said Anne seriously. " She told me so herself—that is, she said she was a dreadful mischief
when she was a girl and was always getting into scrapes.
I felt so encouraged when I heard that. Is it very
wicked of me, Marilla, to feel encouraged when I hear
that other people have been bad and mischievous ?
Mrs. Lynde says it is. Mrs Lynde says she always
feels shocked when she hears of any one ever having
been naughty, no matter how small they were. Mrs
Lynde says she once heard a minister confess that
when he was a boy he stole a strawberry tart out of
his aunt's pantry and she never had any respect for
that minister again. Now, I wouldn't have felt that

way. I'd have thought that it was real noble of him to confess it, and I'd have thought what an encouraging thing it would be for small boys nowadays who do naughty things and are sorry for them to know that perhaps they may grow up to be ministers in spite of it. That's how I'd feel, Marilla."

"The way I feel at present, Anne," said Marilla, "is that it's high time you had those dishes washed. You've taken half an hour longer than you should with all your chattering. Learn to work first and talk afterwards."

CHAPTER XXVII

VANITY AND VEXATION OF SPIRIT

MARILLA, walking home one late April evening from an Aid meeting, realized that the winter was over and gone with the thrill of delight that spring never fails to bring to the oldest and saddest as well as to the youngest and merriest. Marilla was not given to subjective analysis of her thoughts and feelings. She probably imagined that she was thinking about the Aids and their missionary box and the new carpet for the vestry-room, but under these reflections was a harmonious consciousness of red fields smoking into pale-purply mists in the declining sun, of long, sharp-pointed fir shadows falling over the meadow beyond the brook, of still, crimson-budded maples around a mirror-like wood-pool, of a wakening in the world and a stir of hidden pulses under the grey sod. The spring was abroad in the land and Marilla's sober, middle-aged step was lighter and swifter because of its deep, primal gladness.

Her eyes dwelt affectionately on Green Gables, peering through its network of trees and reflecting the sunlight back from its windows in several little coruscations of glory. Marilla, as she picked her steps along the damp lane, thought that it was really a satisfaction to know that she was going home to a briskly snapping wood fire and a table nicely spread for tea, instead of to the cold comfort of old Aid meeting evenings before Anne had come to Green Gables.

Consequently, when Marilla entered her kitchen and found the fire black out, with no sign of Anne anywhere she felt justly disappointed and irritated. She had told Anne to be sure and have tea ready at five o'clock, but now she must hurry to take off her second-best dress and prepare the meal herself against Matthew's return from ploughing.

" I'll settle Miss Anne when she comes home," said Marilla grimly, as she shaved up kindlings with a carving knife and more vim than was strictly necessary. Matthew had come in and was waiting patiently for his tea in his corner. " She's gadding off somewhere with Diana, writing stories or practising dialogues or some such tomfoolery, and never thinking once about the time or her duties. She's just got to be pulled up short and sudden on this sort of thing. I don't care if Mrs Allan does say she's the brightest and sweetest child she ever knew. She may be bright and sweet enough, but her head is full of nonsense and there's never any knowing what shape it'll break out in next. Just as soon as she grows out of one freak she takes up with another. But there ! Here I am saying the very thing I was so riled with Rachel Lynde for saying at the Aid to-day. I was real glad when Mrs Allan spoke up for Anne, for if she hadn't I know I'd have said something too sharp to Rachel before everybody. Anne's got plenty of faults, goodness knows, and far be it from me to deny it. But I'm bringing her up and not Rachel Lynde, who'd pick faults in the Angel Gabriel himself if he lived in Avonlea. Just the same, Anne has no business to leave the house like this when I told her she was to stay home this afternoon and look after things. I must say, with all her faults, I never found her disobedient or untrustworthy before and I'm real sorry to find her so now."

" Well now, I dunno," said Matthew, who, being patient and wise and, above all, hungry, had deemed it best to let Marilla talk her wrath out unhindered, having learned by experience that she got through with whatever work was on hand much quicker if not delayed by untimely argument. " Perhaps you're judging her too hasty, Marilla. Don't call her untrustworthy until you're sure she has disobeyed you. Mebbe it can all be explained—Anne's a great hand at explaining."

" She's not here when I told her to stay," retorted Marilla. " I reckon she'll find it hard to explain *that* to my satisfaction. Of course I knew you'd take her part, Matthew. But I'm bringing her up, not you."

It was dark when supper was ready, and still no sign of Anne, coming hurriedly over the log bridge or up Lovers' Lane, breathless and repentant with a sense of neglected duties. Marilla washed and put away the dishes grimly. Then, wanting a candle to light her down cellar, she went up to the east gable for the one that generally stood on Anne's table. Lighting it, she turned around to see Anne herself lying on the bed, face downward among the pillows.

" Mercy on us," said astonished Marilla, " have you been asleep, Anne ? "

" No," was the muffled reply.

" Are you sick then ? " demanded Marilla anxiously, going over to the bed.

Anne cowered deeper into her pillows as if desirous of hiding herself for ever from mortal eyes.

" No. But please, Marilla, go away and don't look at me. I'm in the depths of despair and I don't care who gets head in class or writes the best composition or sings in the Sunday-school choir any more. Little things like that are of no importance now because I don't suppose I'll ever be able to go anywhere again. My career is closed. Please, Marilla, go away and don't look at me."

" Did anyone ever hear the like ? " the mystified

Marilla wanted to know. " Anne Shirley, whatever
is the matter with you ? What have you done ? Get
right up this minute and tell me. This minute, I say.
There now, what is it ? "

Anne had slid to the floor in despairing obedience.

" Look at my hair, Marilla," she whispered.

Accordingly, Marilla lifted her candle and looked
scrutinizingly at Anne's hair, flowing in heavy masses
down her back. It certainly had a very strange appearance.

" Anne Shirley, what have you done to your hair ?
Why, it's *green !* "

Green it might be called, if it were any earthly
colour—a queer, dull, bronzy green, with streaks here
and there of the original red to heighten the ghastly
effect. Never in all her life had Marilla seen anything
so grotesque as Anne's hair at that moment.

" Yes, it's green," moaned Anne. " I thought
nothing could be as bad as red hair. But now I know
it's ten times worse to have green hair. Oh, Marilla,
you little know how utterly wretched I am."

" I little know how you got into this fix but I mean
to find out," said Marilla. " Come right down to the
kitchen—it's too cold up here—and tell me just what
you've done. I've been expecting something queer for
some time. You haven't got into any scrape for over
two months, and I was sure another one was due.
Now, then, what did you do to your hair ? "

" I dyed it."

" Dyed it ! Dyed your hair ! Anne Shirley, didn't
you know it was a wicked thing to do ? "

" Yes, I knew it was a little wicked," admitted
Anne. " But I thought it was worth while to be a
little wicked to get rid of red hair. I counted the
cost, Marilla. Besides, I meant to be extra good in
other ways to make up for it."

" Well," said Marilla sarcastically, " if I'd decided it was worth while to dye my hair I'd have dyed it a decent colour at least. I wouldn't have dyed it green."

" But I didn't mean to dye it green, Marilla," protested Anne dejectedly. " If I was wicked I meant to be wicked to some purpose. He said it would turn my hair a beautiful raven black—he positively assured me that it would. How could I doubt his word, Marilla ? I know what it feels like to have your word doubted. And Mrs Allan says we should never suspect any one of not telling us the truth unless we have proof that they're not. I have proof now—green hair is proof enough for anybody. But I hadn't then and I believed every word he said *implicitly*."

" Who said ? Who are you talking about ? "

" The pedlar that was here this afternoon. I bought the dye from him."

" Anne Shirley, how often have I told you never to let one of those Italians in the house ! I don't believe in encouraging them to come around at all."

" Oh, I didn't let him in the house. I remembered what you told me, and I went out, carefully shut the door, and looked at his things on the step. Besides, he wasn't an Italian—he was a German Jew. He had a big box full of very interesting things and he told me he was working hard to make enough money to bring his wife and children out from Germany. He spoke so feelingly about them that it touched my heart. I wanted to buy something from him to help him in such a worthy object. Then all at once I saw the bottle of hair dye. The pedlar said it was warranted to dye any hair a beautiful raven black and wouldn't wash off. In a trice I saw myself with beautiful raven black hair and the temptation was irresistible. But the price of the bottle was seventy-five cents and I had only fifty cents left out of my chicken money. I think the pedlar had a very kind heart, for he said that, seeing it was me, he'd sell it for fifty cents and that was just giving it away. So I bought it, and as soon as he had gone I came up here and applied it with an old hair-brush as the directions said. I used up the whole bottle, and oh, Marilla, when I saw the dreadful colour it turned my hair I repented of being wicked, I can tell you. And I've been repenting ever since."

" Well, I hope you'll repent to good purpose," said Marilla severely, " and that you've got your eyes opened to where your vanity has led you, Anne. Goodness knows what's to be done. I suppose the first thing is to give your hair a good washing and see if that will do any good."

Accordingly, Anne washed her hair, scrubbing it vigorously with soap and water, but for all the difference it made she might as well have been scouring its original red. The pedlar had certainly spoken the truth when he declared that the dye wouldn't wash off, however his veracity might be impeached in other respects.

" Oh, Marilla, what shall I do ? " questioned Anne in tears. " I can never live this down. People have pretty well forgotten my other mistakes—the liniment cake and setting Diana drunk and flying into a temper with Mrs Lynde. But they'll never forget this. They will think I am not respectable. Oh, Marilla, ' what a tangled web we weave when first we practise to deceive.' That is poetry, but it is true. And oh, how Josie Pye will laugh ! Marilla, I *cannot* face Josie Pye. I am the unhappiest girl in Prince Edward Island."

Anne's unhappiness continued for a week. During that time she went nowhere and shampooed her hair every day. Diana alone of outsiders knew the fatal secret, but she promised solemnly never to tell, and it may be stated here and now that she kept her word. At the end of the week Marilla said decidedly :

" It's no use, Anne. That is fast dye if ever there was any. Your hair must be cut off ; there is no other way. You can't go out with it looking like that."

Anne's lips quivered, but she realized the bitter truth of Marilla's remarks. With a dismal sigh she went for the scissors.

" Please cut it off at once, Marilla, and have it over. Oh, I feel that my heart is broken. This is such an unromantic affliction. The girls in books lose their hair in fevers or sell it to get money for some good deed, and I'm sure I wouldn't mind losing my hair in some such fashion half so much. But there is nothing comforting in having your hair cut off because you've dyed it a dreadful colour, is there ? I'm going to weep all the time you're cutting it off, if it wont interfere. It seems such a tragic thing."

Anne wept then, but later on, when she went upstairs and looked in the glass, she was calm with despair. Marilla had done her work thoroughly and it had been necessary to shingle the hair as closely as possible. The result was not becoming, to state the case as mildly as may be. Anne promptly turned her glass to the wall.

" I'll never, never look at myself again until my hair grows," she exclaimed passionately.

Then she suddenly righted the glass.

" Yes, I will, too. I'd do penance for being wicked that way. I'll look at myself every time I come to my room and see how ugly I am. And I won't try to imagine it away, either. I never thought I was vain about my hair, of all things, but now I know I was, in spite of its being red, because it was so long and thick and curly. I expect something will happen to my nose next."

Anne's clipped head made a sensation in school on the following Monday, but to her relief nobody guessed the real reason for it, not even Josie Pye, who, however, did not fail to inform Anne that she looked like a perfect scarecrow.

" I didn't say anything when Josie said that to me," Anne confided that evening to Marilla, who was lying on the sofa after one of her headaches, " because I thought it was part of my punishment and I ought to bear it patiently. It's hard to be told you look like a scarecrow and I wanted to say something back. But I didn't. I just swept her one scornful look and then I forgave her. It makes you feel very virtuous when you forgive people, doesn't it ? I mean to devote all my energies to being good after this and I shall never try to be beautiful again. Of course it's better to be good. I know it is, but it's sometimes so hard to believe a thing even when you know it. I do really want to be good, Marilla, like you and Mrs Allan and Miss Stacy, and grow up to be a credit to you. Diana says when my hair begins to grow to tie a black velvet ribbon around my head with a bow at one side. She says she thinks it will be very becoming. I will call it a snood—that sounds so romantic. But am I talking too much Marilla ? Does it hurt your head ? "

" My head is better now. It was terrible bad this afternoon, though. These headaches of mine are getting worse and worse. I'll have to see a doctor about them. As for your chatter, I don't know that I mind it—I've got so used to it."

Which was Marilla's way of saying that she liked to hear it.

CHAPTER XXVIII

AN UNFORTUNATE LILY MAID

"OF course you must be Elaine, Anne," said Diana. "I could never have the courage to float down there."

"Nor I," said Ruby Gillis with a shiver. "I don't mind floating down when there's two or three of us in the flat and we can sit up. It's fun then. But to lie down and pretend I was dead—I just couldn't. I'd die really of fright."

"Of course it would be romantic," conceded Jane Andrews. "But I know I couldn't keep still. I'd be popping up every minute or so to see where I was and if I wasn't drifting too far out. And you know, Anne, that would spoil the effect."

"But it's so ridiculous to have a red-headed Elaine," mourned Anne. "I'm not afraid to float down and I'd *love* to be Elaine. But it's ridiculous just the same. Ruby ought to be Elaine because she is so fair and has such lovely long golden hair—Elaine had 'all her bright hair streaming down,' you know. And Elaine was the lily maid. Now, a red-haired person cannot be a lily maid."

"Your complexion is just as fair as Ruby's said Diana earnestly, "and your hair is ever so much darker than it used to be before you cut it."

"Oh, do you really think so?" exclaimed Anne, flushing sensitively with delight. "I've sometimes thought it was myself—but I never dared to ask any one for fear she would tell me it wasn't. Do you think it could be called auburn now, Diana?"

" Yes, and I think it is real pretty," said Diana, looking admiringly at the short, silky curls that clustered over Anne's head and were held in place by a very jaunty black velvet ribbon and bow.

They were standing on the bank of the pond, below Orchard Slope, where a little headland fringed with birches ran out from the bank ; at its tip was a small wooden platform built out into the water for the convenience of fishermen and duck hunters. Ruby and Jane were spending the midsummer afternoon with Diana, and Anne had come over to play with them.

Anne and Diana had spent most of their playtime that summer on and about the pond. Idlewild was a thing of the past, Mr Bell having ruthlessly cut down the little circle of trees in his back pasture in the spring. Anne had sat among the stumps and wept, not without an eye to the romance of it ; but she was speedily consoled, for, after all, as she and Diana said, big girls of thirteen, going on fourteen, were too old for such childish amusements as play-houses, and there were more fascinating sports to be found about the pond. It was splendid to fish for trout over the bridge and the two girls learned to row themselves about in the little flat-bottomed dory Mr Barry kept for duck shooting.

It was Anne's idea that they dramatize Elaine. They had studied Tennyson's poem in school the preceding winter, the Superintendent of Education having prescribed it in the English course for the Prince Edward Island Schools. They had analysed and parsed it and torn it to pieces in general until it was a wonder there was any meaning at all left in it for them, but at least the fair lily maid and Lancelot and Guinevere and King Arthur had become very real people to them, and Anne was devoured by secret regret that she had not been born in Camelot. Those days, she said, were so much more romantic than the present.

Anne's plan was hailed with enthusiasm. The girls had discovered that if the flat were pushed off from the landing-place it would drift down with the current under the bridge and finally strand itself on another headland lower down which ran out at a curve in the pond. They had often gone down like this and nothing could be more convenient for playing Elaine.

" Well, I'll be Elaine," said Anne, yielding reluctantly, for, although she would have been delighted to play the principal character, yet her artistic sense demanded fitness for it and this, she felt, her limitations made impossible. " Ruby, you must be King Arthur and Jane will be Guinevere and Diana must be Lancelot. But first you must be the brothers and the father. We can't have the old dumb servitor because there isn't room for two in the flat when one is lying down. We must pall the barge all its length in blackest samite. That old black shawl of your mother's will be just the thing, Diana."

The black shawl having been procured, Anne spread it over the flat and then lay down on the bottom, with closed eyes and hands folded over her breast.

" Oh, she does look really dead," whispered Ruby Gillis nervously, watching the still, white little face under the flickering shadows of the birches. " It makes me feel frightened, girls. Do you suppose it's really right to act like this ? Mrs Lynde says that all play-acting is abominably wicked."

" Ruby, you shouldn't talk about Mrs Lynde," said Anne severely. " It spoils the effect because this is hundreds of years before Mrs Lynde was born. Jane, you arrange this. It's silly for Elaine to be talking when she's dead."

Jane rose to the occasion. Cloth of gold for cover-

let there was none, but an old piano scarf of yellow
Japanese *crêpe* was an excellent substitute. A white
lily was not obtainable just then, but the effect of a
tall blue iris placed in one of Anne's folded hands was
all that could be desired.

" Now, she's all ready," said Jane. " We must
kiss her quiet brows and, Diana, you say, ' Sister,
farewell for ever,' and Ruby, you say, ' Farewell,
sweet sister,' both of you as sorrowfully as you possibly
can. Anne, for goodness sake smile a little. You
know Elaine ' lay as though she smiled.' That's better.
Now push the flat off."

The flat was accordingly pushed off, scraping roughly
over an old embedded stake in the process. Diana
and Jane and Ruby only waited long enough to see
it caught in the current and headed for the bridge
before scampering up through the woods, across the
road, and down to the lower headland where, as
Lancelot and Guinevere and the King, they were to
be in readiness to receive the lily maid.

For a few minutes Anne, drifting slowly down,
enjoyed the romance of her situation to the full. Then
something happened not at all romantic. The flat
began to leak. In a very few moments it was necessary
for Elaine to scramble to her feet, pick up her cloth
of gold coverlet and pall of blackest samite and gaze
blankly at a big crack in the bottom of her barge
through which the water was literally pouring. That
sharp stake at the landing had torn off the strip of
batting nailed on the flat. Anne did not know this,
but it did not take her long to realize that she was in a
dangerous plight. At this rate the flat would fill and
sink long before it could drift to the lower headland.
Where were the oars ? Left behind at the landing !

Anne gave one gasping little scream which nobody
ever heard ; she was white to the lips, but she did not

lose her self-possession. There was one chance—just one.

" I was horribly frightened," she told Mrs Allan the next day, " and it seemed like years while the flat was drifting down to the bridge and the water rising in it every moment. I prayed, Mrs Allan, most earnestly, but I didn't shut my eyes to pray, for I knew the only way God could save me was to let the flat float close enough to one of the bridge piles for me to climb up on it. You know the piles are just old tree trunks and there are lots of knots and old branch stubs on them. It was proper to pray, but I had to do my part by watching out and right well I knew it. I just said, ' Dear God, please take the flat close to a pile and I'll do the rest,' over and over again. Under such circumstances you don't think much about making a flowery prayer. But mine was answered, for the flat bumped right into a pile for a minute and I flung the scarf and the shawl over my shoulder and scrambled up on a big providential stub. And there I was, Mrs Allan, clinging to that slippery old pile with no way of getting up or down. It was a very unromantic position, but I didn't think about that at the time. You don't think much about romance when you have just escaped from a watery grave. I said a grateful prayer at once and then I gave all my attention to holding on tight, for I knew I should probably have to depend on human aid to get back to dry land."

The flat drifted under the bridge and then promptly sank in midstream. Ruby, Jane, and Diana, already awaiting it on the lower headland, saw it disappear before their very eyes and had not a doubt but that Anne had gone down with it. For a moment they stood still, white as sheets, frozen with horror at the tragedy ; then, shrieking at the tops of their voices, they started on a frantic run up through the woods, never pausing as they crossed the main road to glance the way of the bridge. Anne, clinging desperately to her precarious foothold, saw their flying forms and heard their shrieks. Help would soon come, but meanwhile her position was a very uncomfortable one.

The minutes passed by, each seeming an hour to the unfortunate lily maid. Why didn't somebody come ? Where had the girls gone ? Suppose they had fainted, one and all ! Suppose nobody ever came ! Suppose she grew so tired and cramped that she could hold on no longer ! Anne looked at the wicked green depths below her, wavering with long, oily shadows, and shivered. Her imagination began to suggest all manner of gruesome possibilities to her.

Then, just as she thought she really could not endure the ache in her arms and wrists another moment, Gilbert Blythe came rowing under the bridge in Harmon Andrew's dory !

Gilbert glanced up and, much to his amazement, beheld a little white scornful face looking down upon him with big, frightened but also scornful grey eyes.

" Anne Shirley ! How on earth did you get there ? " he exclaimed.

Without waiting for an answer he pulled close to the pile and extended his hand. There was no help for it ; Anne, clinging to Gilbert Blythe's hand, scrambled down into the dory, where she sat, drabbled and furious, in the stern with her arms full of dripping shawl and wet *crêpe*. It was certainly extremely difficult to be dignified under the circumstances !

" What has happened, Anne ? " asked Gilbert, taking up his oars.

" We were playing Elaine," explained Anne frigidly, without even looking at her rescuer, " and I had to drift down to Camelot in the barge—I mean the flat.

The flat began to leak and I climbed out on the pile. The girls went for help. Will you be kind enough to row me to the landing ? "

Gilbert obligingly rowed to the landing and Anne, disdaining assistance, sprang nimbly on shore.

" I'm very much obliged to you," she said haughtily as she turned away. But Gilbert had also sprung from the boat and now laid a detaining hand on her arm.

" Anne," he said hurriedly, " look here. Can't we be good friends ? I'm awfully sorry I made fun of your hair that time. I didn't mean to vex you and I only meant it for a joke. Besides, it's so long ago. I think your hair is awfully pretty now—honest I do. Let's be friends."

For a moment Anne hesitated. She had an odd, newly awakened consciousness under all her outraged dignity that the half-shy, half-eager expression in Gilbert's hazel eyes was something that was very good to see. Her heart gave a quick, queer little beat. But the bitterness of her old grievance promptly stiffened up her wavering determination. That scene of two years before flashed back into her recollection as vividly as if it had taken place yesterday. Gilbert had called her " carrots " and had brought about her disgrace before the whole school. Her resentment, which to other and older people might be as laughable as its cause, was in no whit allayed and softened by time seemingly. She hated Gilbert Blythe ! She would never forgive him !

" No," she said coldly, " I shall never be friends with you, Gilbert Blythe ; and I don't want to be ! "

" All right ! " Gilbert sprang into his skiff with an angry colour in his cheeks. " I'll never ask you to be friends again, Anne Shirley. And I don't care either ! "

He pulled away with swift defiant strokes, and

Anne went up the steep, ferny little path under the maples. She held her head very high, but she was conscious of an odd feeling of regret. She almost wished she had answered Gilbert differently. Of course, he had insulted her terribly, but still—— ! Altogether, Anne rather thought it would be a relief to sit down and have a good cry. She was really quite unstrung, for the reaction from her fright and cramped clinging was making itself felt.

Half-way up the path she met Jane and Diana rushing back to the pond in a state narrowly removed from positive frenzy. They had found nobody at Orchard Slope, both Mr and Mrs Barry being away. Here Ruby Gillis had succumbed to hysterics, and was left to recover from them as best she might, while Jane and Diana flew through the Haunted Wood and across the brook to Green Gables. There they had found nobody either, for Marilla had gone to Carmody and Matthew was making hay in the back field.

" Oh, Anne," gasped Diana, fairly falling on the former's neck and weeping with relief and delight, " Oh, Anne—we thought—you were—drowned—and we felt like murderers—because we had made—you be—Elaine. And Ruby is in hysterics—oh, Anne, how did you escape ? "

" I climbed up on one of the piles," explained Anne wearily, " and Gilbert Blythe came along in Mr Andrews' dory and brought me to land."

" Oh, Anne, how splendid of him ! Why, it's so romantic ! " said Jane, finding breath enough for utterance at last. " Of course you'll speak to him after this."

" Of course I won't," flashed Anne with a momentary return of her old spirit. " And I don't want ever to hear the word romantic again, Jane Andrews. I'm awfully sorry you were so frightened, girls. It is all my fault. I feel sure I was born under an unlucky star. Everything I do gets me or my dearest friends into a scrape. We've gone and lost your father's flat, Diana, and I have a presentiment that we'll not be allowed to row on the pond any more."

Anne's presentiment proved more trustworthy than presentiments are apt to do. Great was the consternation in the Barry and Cuthbert households when the events of the afternoon became known.

" Will you *ever* have any sense, Anne ? " groaned Marilla.

" Oh, yes, I think I will, Marilla," returned Anne optimistically. A good cry, indulged in the grateful solitude of the east gable, had soothed her nerves and restored her to her wonted cheerfulness. " I think my prospects of becoming sensible are brighter now than ever."

" I don't see how," said Marilla.

" Well," explained Anne, " I've learned a new and valuable lesson to-day. Ever since I came to Green Gables I've been making mistakes, and each mistake has helped to cure me of some great shortcoming. The affair of the amethyst brooch cured me of meddling with things that didn't belong to me. The Haunted Wood mistake cured me of letting my imagination run away with me. The liniment cake mistake cured me of carelessness in cooking. Dyeing my hair cured me of vanity. I never think about my hair and nose now—at least, very seldom. And to-day's mistake is going to cure me of being too romantic. I have come to the conclusion that it is no use trying to be romantic in Avonlea. It was probably easy enough in towered Camelot hundreds of years ago, but romance is not appreciated now. I feel quite sure that you will soon see a great improvement in me in this respect, Marilla."

" I'm sure I hope so," said Marilla sceptically.

But Matthew, who had been sitting mutely in his corner, laid a hand on Anne's shoulder when Marilla had gone out.

" Don't give up all your romance, Anne," he whispered shyly, " a little of it is a good thing—not too much, of course—but keep a little of it, Anne, keep a little of it."

CHAPTER XXIX

AN EPOCH IN ANNE'S LIFE

ANNE was bringing the cows home from the back pasture by way of Lovers' Lane. It was a September evening and all the gaps and clearings in the woods were brimmed up with ruby sunset light. Here and there the lane was splashed with it, but for the most part it was already quite shadowy beneath the maples, and the spaces under the firs were filled with a clear violet dusk like airy wine. The winds were out in their tops, and there is no sweeter music on earth than that which the wind makes in the fir-trees at evening.

The cows swung placidly down the lane, and Anne followed them dreamily, repeating aloud the battle canto from *Marmion*—which had also been part of their English course the preceding winter and which Miss Stacy had made them learn off by heart—and exulting in its rushing lines and the clash of spears in its imagery. When she came to the lines :

> The stubborn spearsmen still made good
> Their dark impenetrable wood,

she stopped in ecstasy to shut her eyes that she might the better fancy herself one of that heroic ring. When she opened them again it was to behold Diana coming through the gate that led into the Barry field and looking so important that Anne instantly divined there was news to be told. But betray too eager curiosity she would not.

" Isn't this evening just like a purple dream, Diana ?

It makes me so glad to be alive. In the mornings I always think the mornings are best ; but when evening comes I think it's lovelier still."

" It's a very fine evening," said Diana, " but oh, I have such news, Anne. Guess. You can have three guesses."

" Charlotte Gillis is going to be married in the church after all and Mrs Allan wants us to decorate it," cried Anne.

" No. Charlotte's beau won't agree to that, because nobody ever has been married in the church yet, and he thinks it would seem too much like a funeral. It's too mean, because it would be such fun. Guess again."

" Jane's mother is going to let her have a birthday party ? "

Diana shook her head, her black eyes dancing with merriment.

" I can't think what it can be," said Anne in despair, " unless it's that Moody Spurgeon MacPherson saw you home from prayer-meeting last night. Did he ? "

" I should think not," exclaimed Diana indignantly. " I wouldn't be likely to boast of it if he did, the horrid creature ! I knew you couldn't guess it. Mother had a letter from Aunt Josephine to-day, and Aunt Josephine wants you and me to go to town next Tuesday and stop with her for the Exhibition. There ! "

" Oh, Diana," whispered Anne, finding it necessary to lean up against a maple-tree for support, " do you really mean it ? But I'm afraid Marilla won't let me go. She will say that she can't encourage gadding about. That was what she said last week when Jane invited me to go with them in their double-seated buggy to the American concert at the White Sands Hotel. I wanted to go, but Marilla said I'd be better at home learning my lessons and so would Jane. I was bitterly disappointed, Diana. I felt so heart-broken that I wouldn't say my prayers when I went to bed. But I repented of that and got up in the middle of the night and said them."

" I'll tell you," said Diana, " we'll get mother to ask Marilla. She'll be more likely to let you go then ; and if she does we'll have the time of our lives, Anne. I've never been to an Exhibition, and it's so aggravating to hear the other girls talking about their trips. Jane and Ruby have been twice, and they're going this year again."

" I'm not going to think about it at all until I know whether I can go or not," said Anne resolutely. " If I did and then was disappointed, it would be more than I could bear. But in case I do go I'm very glad my new coat will be ready by that time. Marilla didn't think I needed a new coat. She said my old one would do very well for another winter and that I ought to be satisfied with having a new dress. The dress is very pretty, Diana—navy blue and made so fashionably. Marilla always makes my dresses fashionably now, because she says she doesn't intend to have Matthew going to Mrs Lynde to make them. I'm so glad. It is ever so much easier to be good if your clothes are fashionable. At least, it is easier for me. I suppose it doesn't make such a difference to naturally good people. But Matthew said I must have a new coat, so Marilla bought a lovely piece of blue broadcloth, and it's being made by a real dress-maker over at Carmody. It's to be done Saturday night, and I'm trying not to imagine myself walking up the church aisle on Sunday in my new suit and cap, because I'm afraid it isn't right to imagine such things. But it just slips into my mind in spite of me. My cap is so pretty. Matthew bought it for me the day we were over at Carmody. It is one of those little blue velvet ones that are all the rage, with gold cord and tassels. Your new hat is elegant, Diana, and so becoming. When I saw you come into church last Sunday my heart swelled with pride to think you were my dearest friend. Do you suppose it's wrong for us to think so much about our clothes? Marilla says it is very sinful. But it *is* such an interesting subject, isn't it ? "

Marilla agreed to let Anne go to town, and it was arranged that Mr Barry should take the girls in on the following Tuesday. As Charlottetown was thirty miles away and Mr Barry wished to go and return the same day, it was necessary to make a very early start. But Anne counted it all joy, and was up before sunrise on Tuesday morning. A glance from her window assured her that the day would be fine, for the eastern sky behind the firs of the Haunted Wood was all silvery and cloudless. Through the gap in the trees a light was shining in the western gable of Orchard Slope, a token that Diana was also up.

Anne was dressed by the time Matthew had the fire on, and had the breakfast ready when Marilla came down, but for her own part was much too excited to eat. After breakfast the jaunty new cap and jacket were donned, and Anne hastened over the brook and up through the firs to Orchard Slope. Mr Barry and Diana were waiting for her, and they were soon on the road.

It was a long drive, but Anne and Diana enjoyed every minute of it. It was delightful to rattle along over the moist roads in the early red sunlight that was creeping across the shorn harvest fields. The air was fresh and crisp, and little smoke-blue mists curled through the valleys and floated off from the hills. Sometimes the road went through woods where maples were beginning to hang out scarlet banners ; sometimes it crossed rivers on bridges that made Anne's flesh cringe with the old, half-delightful fear ; sometimes it wound along a harbour shore and passed by a little cluster of weather-grey fishing huts ; again it mounted to hills whence a far sweep of curving upland or misty blue sky could be seen ; but wherever it went there was much of interest to discuss. It was almost noon when they reached town and found their way to Beechwood. It was quite a fine old mansion, set back from the street in a seclusion of green elms and branching beeches. Miss Barry met them at the door with a twinkle in her sharp black eyes.

" So, you've come to see me at last, you Anne-girl," she said. " Mercy, child, how you have grown ! You're taller than I am, I declare. And you're ever so much better-looking than you used to be, too. But I dare say you know that without being told."

" Indeed I didn't," said Anne radiantly. " I know I'm not so freckled as I used to be, so I've much to be thankful for, but I really hadn't dared to hope there was any other improvement. I'm so glad you think there is, Miss Barry."

Miss Barry's house was furnished with " great magnificence," as Anne told Marilla afterwards. The two little country girls were rather abashed by the splendour of the parlour where Miss Barry left them when she went to see about dinner.

" Isn't it just like a palace ? " whispered Diana. " I never was in Aunt Josephine's house before, and I'd no idea it was so grand. I just wish Julia Bell could see this—she puts on such airs about her mother's parlour."

" Velvet carpet," sighed Anne luxuriously, " *and* silk curtains ! I've dreamed of such things, Diana. But do you know I don't believe I feel very comfortable with them after all. There are so many things in this room and all so splendid that there is no scope for imagination. That is one consolation when you are poor—there are so many more things you can imagine about."

Their sojourn in town was something that Anne and Diana dated from for years. From first to last it was crowded with delights.

On Wednesday Miss Barry took them to the Exhibition grounds and kept them there all day.

" It was splendid," Anne related to Marilla later on. " I never imagined anything so interesting. I don't really know which department was the most interesting. I think I liked the horses and the flowers and the fancy work best. Josie Pye took first prize for knitted lace. I was real glad she did. And I was glad that I felt glad, for it shows I'm improving, don't you think, Marilla, when I can rejoice in Josie's success ? Mr Harmon Andrews took second prize for Gravenstein apples and Mr Bell took first prize for a pig. Diana said she thought it was ridiculous for a Sunday-school superintendent to take a prize in pigs, but I don't see why. Do you ? She said she would always think of it after this when he was praying so solemnly. Clara Louise MacPherson took a prize for painting, and Mrs Lynde got first prize for home-made butter and cheese. So Avonlea was pretty well represented, wasn't it ? Mrs Lynde was there that day, and I never knew how much I really liked her until I saw her familiar face among all those strangers. There were thousands of people there, Marilla. It made me feel dreadfully insignificant. And Miss Barry took us up to the grand stand to see the horse-races. Mrs Lynde wouldn't go ; she said horse-racing was an abomination, and she being a church-member, thought it her bounden duty to set a good example by staying away.

But there were so many there I don't believe Mrs Lynde's absence would ever be noticed. I don't think, though, that I ought to go very often to horse-races, because they *are* awfully fascinating. Diana got so excited that she offered to bet me ten cents that the red horse would win. I didn't believe he would, but I refused to bet, because I wanted to tell Mrs Allan all about everything, and I felt sure it wouldn't do to tell her that. It's always wrong to do anything you can't tell the minister's wife. It's as good as an extra conscience to have a minister's wife for your friend. And I was very glad I didn't bet, because the red horse *did* win, and I would have lost ten cents. So you see that virtue was its own reward. We saw a man go up in a balloon. I'd love to go up in a balloon, Marilla; it would be simply thrilling; and we saw a man selling fortunes. You paid him ten cents and a little bird picked out your fortune for you. Miss Barry gave Diana and me ten cents each to have our fortunes told. Mine was that I would marry a dark-complected man who was very wealthy, and I would go across water to live. I looked carefully at all the dark men I saw after that, but I didn't care much for any of them, and anyhow I suppose it's too early to be looking out for him yet. Oh, it was a never-to-be-forgotten day, Marilla. I was so tired I couldn't sleep at night. Miss Barry put us in the spare room, according to promise. It was an elegant room, Marilla, but somehow sleeping in a spare room isn't what I used to think it was. That's the worst of growing up, and I'm beginning to realize it. The things you wanted so much when you were a child don't seem half so wonderful to you when you get them."

Thursday the girls had a drive in the park, and in the evening Miss Barry took them to a concert in the Academy of Music, where a noted prima donna was to sing. To Anne the evening was a glittering vision of delight.

" Oh, Marilla, it was beyond description. I was so excited I couldn't even talk, so you may know what it was like. I just sat in enraptured silence. Madame Selitsky· was perfectly beautiful, and wore white satin and diamonds. But when she began to sing I never thought about anything else. Oh, I can't tell you how I felt. But it seemed to me that it could never be hard to be good any more. I felt like I do when I look up to the stars. Tears came into my eyes, but, oh, they were such happy tears. I was so sorry when it was all over, and I told Miss Barry I didn't see how I was ever to return to common life again. She said she thought if we went over to the restaurant across the street and had an ice-cream it might help me. That sounded so prosaic ; but to my surprise I found it true. The ice-cream was delicious, Marilla, and it was so lovely and dissipated to be sitting there eating it at eleven o'clock at night. Diana said she believed she was born for city life. Miss Barry asked me what my opinion was, but I said I would have to think it over very seriously before I could tell her what I really thought. So I thought it over after I went to bed. That is the best time to think things out. And I came to the conclusion, Marilla, that I wasn't born for city life and that I was glad of it. It's nice to be eating ice-cream at brilliant restaurants at eleven o'clock at night once in awhile ; but as a regular thing I'd rather be in the east gable at eleven, sound asleep, but kind of knowing even in my sleep that the stars were shining outside and that the wind was blowing in the firs across the brook. I told Miss Barry so at breakfast the next morning and she laughed. Miss Barry generally laughed at anything I said, even when I said the most solemn things.

I don't think I liked it, Marilla, because I wasn't trying to be funny. But she is a most hospitable lady and treated us royally."

Friday brought going-home time, and Mr Barry drove in for the girls.

" Well, I hope you've enjoyed yourselves," said Miss Barry, as she bade them good-bye.

" Indeed we have," said Diana.

" And you, Anne-girl ? "

" I've enjoyed every minute of the time," said Anne, throwing her arms impulsively about the old woman's neck and kissing her wrinkled cheek. Diana would never have dared to do such a thing, and felt rather aghast at Anne's freedom. But Miss Barry was pleased, and she stood on her veranda and watched the buggy out of sight. Then she went back into her big house with a sigh. It seemed very lonely, lacking those fresh young lives. Miss Barry was a rather selfish old lady, if the truth must be told, and had never cared much for anybody but herself. She valued people only as they were of service to her or amused her. Anne had amused her, and consequently stood high in the old lady's good graces. But Miss Barry found herself thinking less about Anne's quaint speeches than of her fresh enthusiasms, her transparent emotions, her little winning ways, and the sweetness of her eyes and lips.

" I thought Marilla Cuthbert was an old fool when I heard she'd adopted a girl out of an orphan asylum," she said to herself, " but I guess she didn't make much of a mistake after all. If I'd a child like Anne in the house all the time I'd be a better and happier woman."

Anne and Diana found the drive home as pleasant as the drive in—pleasanter, indeed, since there was the delightful consciousness of home waiting at the end of it. It was sunset when they passed through

White Sands and turned into the shore road. Beyond, the Avonlea hills came out darkly against the saffron sky. Behind them the moon was rising out of the sea that grew all radiant and transfigured in her light. Every little cove along the curving road was a marvel of dancing ripples. The waves broke with a soft swish on the rocks below them, and the tang of the sea was in the strong, fresh air.

" Oh, but it's good to be alive and to be going home," breathed Anne.

When she crossed the log bridge over the brook the kitchen light of Green Gables winked her a friendly welcome back, and through the open door shone the hearth fire, sending out its warm red glow athwart the chilly autumn night. Anne ran blithely up the hill and into the kitchen, where a hot supper was waiting on the table.

" So you've got back ? " said Marilla, folding up her knitting.

" Yes, and, oh, it's so good to be back," said Anne joyously. " I could kiss everything, even to the clock. Marilla, a broiled chicken ! You don't mean to say you cooked that for me ! "

" Yes, I did," said Marilla. " I thought you'd be hungry after such a drive and need something real appetizing. Hurry and take off your things, and we'll have supper as soon as Matthew comes in. I'm glad you've got back, I must say. It's been fearful lonesome here without you, and I never put in four longer days."

After supper Anne sat before the fire between Matthew and Marilla, and gave them a full account of her visit.

" I've had a splendid time," she concluded happily, " and I feel that it marks an epoch in my life. But the best of it all was the coming home."

CHAPTER XXX

THE QUEEN'S CLASS IS ORGANIZED

MARILLA laid her knitting on her lap and leaned back in her chair. Her eyes were tired, and she thought vaguely that she must see about having her glasses changed the next time she went to town, for her eyes had grown tired very often of late.

It was nearly dark, for the dull November twilight had fallen around Green Gables, and the only light in the kitchen came from the dancing red flames in the stove.

Anne was curled up Turk-fashion on the hearth-rug, gazing into that joyous glow where the sunshine of a hundred summers was being distilled from the maple cord-wood. She had been reading, but her book had slipped to the floor, and now she was dreaming, with a smile on her parted lips. Glittering castles in Spain were shaping themselves out of the mists and rainbows of her lively fancy ; adventures wonderful and enthralling were happening to her in cloudland —adventures that always turned out triumphantly and never involved her in scrapes like those of actual life.

Marilla looked at her with a tenderness that would never have been suffered to reveal itself in any clearer light than that soft mingling of fireshine and shadow. The lesson of a love that should display itself easily in spoken word and open look was one Marilla could never learn. But she had learned to love this slim, grey-eyed girl with an affection all the deeper and stronger from its very undemonstrativeness. Her love made her afraid of being unduly indulgent, indeed. She had an uneasy feeling that it was rather sinful to set one's heart so intensely on any human creature as she had set hers on Anne, and perhaps she performed a sort of unconscious penance for this by being stricter and more critical than if the girl had been less dear to her. Certainly Anne herself had no idea how Marilla loved her. She sometimes thought wistfully that Marilla was very hard to please and distinctly lacking in sympathy and understanding. But she always checked the thought reproachfully, remembering what she owed to Marilla.

" Anne," said Marilla abruptly, " Miss Stacy was here this afternoon when you were out with Diana."

Anne came back from her other world with a start and a sigh.

" Was she ? Oh, I'm so sorry I wasn't in. Why didn't you call me, Marilla ? Diana and I were only over in the Haunted Wood. It's lovely in the woods now. All the little wood things—the ferns and the satin leaves and the crackerberries—have gone to sleep, just as if somebody had tucked them away until spring under a blanket of leaves. I think it was a little grey fairy with a rainbow scarf that came tiptoeing along the last moonlight night and did it. Diana wouldn't say much about that, though. Diana has never forgotten the scolding her mother gave her about imagining ghosts into the Haunted Wood. It had a very bad effect on Diana's imagination. It blighted it. Mrs Lynde says Myrtle Bell is a blighted being. I asked Ruby Gillis why Myrtle was blighted, and Ruby said she guessed it was because her young man had gone back on her. Ruby Gillis thinks of nothing but young men, and the older she gets the worse she is. Young men are all very well in their place, but it doesn't do to drag them into everything, does it ? Diana and I are thinking seriously of promising each other that we will never marry, but be nice old maids and live together for ever. Diana hasn't quite made up her mind though, because she thinks perhaps it would be nobler to marry some wild, dashing, wicked young man and reform him. Diana and I talk a great deal about serious subjects now, you know. We feel that we are so much older than we used to be that it isn't becoming to talk of childish matters. It's such a solemn thing to be almost fourteen, Marilla. Miss Stacy took all us girls who are in our teens down to the brook last Wednesday, and talked to us about it. She said we couldn't be too careful what habits we formed and what ideals we acquired in our teens, because by the time we were twenty our characters would be developed and the foundation laid for our whole future life. And she said if the foundation was shaky we could never build anything really worth while on it. Diana and I talked the matter over coming home from school. We felt extremely solemn, Marilla. And we decided that we would try to be very careful indeed and form respectable habits and learn all we could and be as sensible as possible, so that by the time we were twenty our characters would be properly developed. It's perfectly appalling to think of being twenty, Marilla. It sounds so fearfully old and grown up. But why was Miss Stacy here this afternoon ? "

" That is what I want to tell you, Anne, if you'll ever give me a chance to get a word in edgewise. She was talking about you."

" About me ? " Anne looked rather scared. Then she flushed and exclaimed :

" Oh, I know what she was saying. I meant to tell you, Marilla, honestly I did, but I forgot. Miss Stacy caught me reading *Ben Hur* in school yester-

day afternoon when I should have been studying my
Canadian history. Jane Andrews lent it to me. I
was reading it at dinner-hour, and I had just got to
the chariot-race when school went in. I was simply
wild to know how it turned out—although I felt
sure *Ben Hur* must win, because it wouldn't be poetical
justice if he didn't—so I spread the history open on
my desk-lid and then tucked *Ben Hur* between the
desk and my knee. It just looked as if I were studying
Canadian history, you know, while all the while I was
revelling in *Ben Hur*. I was so interested in it that I
never noticed Miss Stacy coming down the aisle until
all at once I just looked up and there she was looking
down at me, so reproachful like. I can't tell you how
ashamed I felt, Marilla, especially when I heard Josie
Pye giggling. Miss Stacy took *Ben Hur* away, but
she never said a word then. She kept me in at recess
and talked to me. She said I had done very wrong
in two respects. First, I was wasting the time I
ought to have put on my studies ; and secondly I
was deceiving my teacher in trying to make it appear
I was reading a history when it was a story-book
instead. I had never realized until that moment,
Marilla, that what I was doing was deceitful. I was
shocked. I cried bitterly, and asked Miss Stacy to
forgive me and I'd never do such a thing again ; and
I offered to do penance by never so much as looking
at *Ben Hur* for a whole week, not even to see how
the chariot-race turned out. But Miss Stacy said she
wouldn't require that, and she forgave me freely. So
I think it wasn't very kind of her to come up here to
you about it after all."

" Miss Stacy never mentioned such a thing to me,
Anne, and it's only your guilty conscience that's the
matter with you. You have no business to be taking
story-books to school. You read too many novels

anyhow. When I was a girl I wasn't so much as allowed to look at a novel."

" Oh, how can you call *Ben Hur* a novel when it's really such a religious book ? " protested Anne. " Of course it's a little too exciting to be proper reading for Sunday, and I only read it on week-days. And I never read *any* book now unless either Miss Stacy or Mrs Allan thinks it is a proper book for a girl thirteen and three-quarters to read. Miss Stacy made me promise that. She found me reading a book one day called, *The Lurid Mystery of the Haunted Hall*. It was one Ruby Gillis had lent me, and, oh, Marilla, it was so fascinating and creepy. It just curdled the blood in my veins. But Miss Stacy said it was a very silly, unwholesome book, and she asked me not to read any more of it or any like it. I didn't mind promising not to read any more like it, but it was *agonizing* to give back that book without knowing how it turned out. But my love for Miss Stacy stood the test and I did. It's really wonderful, Marilla, what you can do when you're truly anxious to please a certain person."

" Well, I guess I'll light the lamp and get to work," said Marilla. " I see plainly that you don't want to hear what Miss Stacy had to say. You're more interested in the sound of your own tongue than in anything else."

" Oh, indeed, Marilla, I do want to hear it," cried Anne contritely. " I won't say another word—not one. I know I talk too much, but I am really trying to overcome it, and although I say far too much, yet if you only knew how many things I want to say and don't, you'd give me some credit for it. Please tell me, Marilla."

" Well, Miss Stacy wants to organize a class among her advanced students who mean to study for the entrance examination into Queen's. She intends to give them extra lessons for an hour after school. And she came to ask Matthew and me if we would like to have you join it. What do you think about it yourself, Anne ? Would you like to go to Queen's and pass for a teacher ? "

" Oh, Marilla ! " Anne straightened to her knees and clasped her hands. " It's been the dream of my life—that is, for the last six months, ever since Ruby and Jane began to talk of studying for the entrance. But I didn't say anything about it, because I supposed it would be perfectly useless. I'd love to be a teacher. But won't it be dreadfully expensive ? Mr Andrews says it cost him one hundred and fifty dollars to put Prissy through, and Prissy wasn't a dunce in geometry."

" I guess you needn't worry about that part of it. When Matthew and I took you to bring up we resolved we would do the best we could for you and give you a good education. I believe in a girl being fitted to earn her own living whether she ever has to or not. You'll always have a home at Green Gables as long as Matthew and I are here, but nobody knows what is going to happen in this uncertain world, and it's just as well to be prepared. So you can join the Queen's class if you like, Anne."

" Oh, Marilla, thank you." Anne flung her arms about Marilla's waist and looked up earnestly into her face. " I'm extremely grateful to you and Matthew. And I'll study as hard as I can and do my very best to be a credit to you. I warn you not to expect much in geometry, but I think I can hold my own in anything else if I work hard."

" I dare say you'll get along well enough. Miss Stacy says you are bright and diligent." Not for worlds would Marilla have told Anne just what Miss

Stacy had said about her ; that would have been to
pamper vanity. " You needn't rush to any extreme of
killing yourself over your books. There is no hurry.
You won't be ready to try the entrance for a year
and a half yet. But it's well to begin in time and be
thoroughly grounded, Miss Stacy says."

" I shall take more interest than ever in my studies
now," said Anne blissfully, " because I have a purpose
in life. Mr Allan says everybody should have a purpose in life and pursue it faithfully. Only he says we
must first make sure that it is a worthy purpose. I
would call it a worthy purpose to want to be a teacher
like Miss Stacy, wouldn't you, Marilla ? I think it's
a very noble profession."

The Queen's class was organized in due time. Gilbert
Blythe, Anne Shirley, Ruby Gillis, Jane Andrews,
Josie Pye, Charlie Sloane, and Moody Spurgeon Mac-
Pherson joined it. Diana Barry did not, as her parents
did not intend to send her to Queen's. This seemed
nothing short of a calamity to Anne. Never, since the
night on which Minnie May had had the croup, had
she and Diana been separated in anything. On the
evening when the Queen's class first remained in
school for the extra lessons and Anne saw Diana go
slowly out with the others, to walk home alone through
the Birch Path and Violet Vale, it was all the former
could do to keep her seat and refrain from rushing
impulsively after her chum. A lump came into her
throat, and she hastily retired behind the pages of her
uplifted Latin grammar to hide the tears in her eyes.
Not for worlds would Anne have had Gilbert Blythe
or Josie Pye see those tears.

" But, oh, Marilla, I really felt that I had tasted the
bitterness of death, as Mr Allan said in his sermon
last Sunday, when I saw Diana go out alone," she said
mournfully that night. " I thought how splendid it

would have been if Diana had only been going to study for the Entrance, too. But we can't have things perfect in this imperfect world, as Mrs Lynde says. Mrs Lynde isn't exactly a comforting person sometimes, but there's no doubt she says a great many very true things. And I think the Queen's class is going to be extremely interesting. Jane and Ruby are just going to study to be teachers. That is the height of their ambition. Ruby says she will only teach for two years after she gets through, and then she intends to be married. Jane says she will devote her whole life to teaching, and never, never marry, because you are paid a salary for teaching, but a husband won't pay you anything, and growls if you ask for a share in the egg and butter money. I expect Jane speaks from mournful experience, for Mrs Lynde says that her father is a perfect old crank, and meaner than second skimmings. Josie Pye says she is just going to college for education's sake, because she won't have to earn her own living ; she says of course it is different with orphans who are living on charity—*they* have to hustle. Moody Spurgeon is going to be a minister. Mrs Lynde says he couldn't be anything else with a name like that to live up to. I hope it isn't wicked of me, Marilla, but really the thought of Moody Spurgeon being a minister makes me laugh. He's such a funny-looking boy with that big fat face, and his little blue eyes, and his ears sticking out like flaps. But perhaps he will be more intellectual-looking when he grows up. Charlie Sloane says he's going to go into politics and be a member of Parliament, but Mrs Lynde says he'll never succeed at that, because the Sloanes are all honest people, and it's only rascals that get on in politics nowadays."

" What is Gilbert Blythe going to be ? " queried Marilla, seeing that Anne was opening her Cæsar.

" I don't happen to know what Gilbert Blythe's ambition in life is—if he has any," said Anne scornfully.

There was open rivalry between Gilbert and Anne now. Previously the rivalry had been rather one-sided, but there was no longer any doubt that Gilbert was as determined to be first in class as Anne was. He was a foeman worthy of her steel. The other members of the class tacitly acknowledged their superiority, and never dreamed of trying to compete with them.

Since the day by the pond when she had refused to listen to his plea for forgiveness, Gilbert, save for the aforesaid determined rivalry, had evinced no recognition whatever of the existence of Anne Shirley. He talked and jested with the other girls, exchanged books and puzzles with them, discussed lessons and plans, sometimes walked home with one or the other of them from prayer-meeting or Debating Club. But Anne Shirley he simply ignored, and Anne found out that it is not pleasant to be ignored. It was in vain that she told herself with a toss of her head that she did not care. Deep down in her wayward, feminine little heart she knew that she did care, and that if she had that chance of the Lake of Shining Waters again she would answer very differently. All at once, as it seemed, and to her secret dismay, she found that the old resentment she had cherished against him was gone—gone just when she most needed its sustaining power. It was in vain that she recalled every incident and emotion of that memorable occasion and tried to feel the old satisfying anger. That day by the pond had witnessed its last spasmodic flicker. Anne realized that she had forgiven and forgotten without knowing it. But it was too late.

And at least neither Gilbert nor anybody else, not even Diana, should ever suspect how sorry she was and how much she wished she hadn't been so proud and horrid! She determined to " shroud her feelings in deepest oblivion," and it may be stated here and now that she did it, so successfully that Gilbert, who possibly was not quite so indifferent as he seemed, could not console himself with any belief that Anne felt his retaliatory scorn. The only poor comfort he had was that she snubbed Charlie Sloane, unmercifully, continually and undeservedly.

Otherwise the winter passed away in a round of pleasant duties and studies. For Anne the days slipped by like golden beads on the necklace of the year. She was happy, eager, interested ; there were lessons to be learned and honours to be won ; delightful books to read ; new pieces to be practised for the Sunday-school choir ; pleasant Saturday afternoons at the manse with Mrs Allan ; and then, almost before Anne realized it, spring had come again to Green Gables and all the world was abloom once more.

Studies palled just a wee bit then ; the Queen's class, left behind in school while the others scattered to green lanes and leafy wood-cuts and meadow by-ways, looked wistfully out of the windows and discovered that Latin verbs and French exercises had somehow lost the tang and zest they had possessed in the crisp winter months. Even Anne and Gilbert lagged and grew indifferent. Teacher and taught were alike glad when the term was ended and the glad vacation days stretched rosily before them.

" But you've done good work this past year," Miss Stacy told them on the last evening, " and you deserve a good, jolly vacation. Have the best time you can in the out-of-door world and lay in a good stock of health and vitality and ambition to carry you through next year. It will be the tug of war, you know—the last year before the Entrance."

" Are you going to be back next year, Miss Stacy ? " asked Josie Pye.

Josie Pye never scrupled to ask questions ; in this instance the rest of the class felt grateful to her ; none of them would have dared to ask it of Miss Stacy, but all wanted to, for there had been alarming rumours running at large through the school for some time that Miss Stacy was not coming back the next year —that she had been offered a position in the graded school of her own home district and meant to accept. The Queen's class listened in breathless suspense for her answer.

" Yes, I think I will," said Miss Stacy. " I thought of taking another school, but I have decided to come back to Avonlea. To tell the truth, I've grown so interested in my pupils here that I found I couldn't leave them. So I'll stay and see you through."

" Hurrah ! " said Moody Spurgeon. Moody Spurgeon had never been so carried away by his feelings before, and he blushed uncomfortably every time he thought about it for a week.

" Oh, I'm so glad," said Anne with shining eyes. " Dear Miss Stacy, it would be perfectly dreadful if you didn't come back. I don't believe I could have the heart to go on with my studies at all if another teacher came here."

When Anne got home that night she stacked all her text-books away in an old trunk in the attic, locked it, and threw the key into the blanket box.

" I'm not even going to look at a school book in vacation," she told Marilla. " I've studied as hard all the term as I possibly could and I've pored over that geometry until I know every proposition in the first book off by heart, even when the letters *are* changed. I just feel tired of everything sensible and I'm going to let my imagination run riot for the summer. Oh, you needn't be alarmed, Marilla. I'll only let it run riot within reasonable limits. But I want to have a real good, jolly time this summer, for maybe it's the last summer I'll be a little girl. Mrs Lynde says that if I keep stretching out next year as I've done this I'll have to put on longer skirts. She says I'm all running to legs and eyes. And when I put on longer skirts I shall feel that I have to live up to them and be very dignified. It won't even do to believe in fairies then, I'm afraid ; so I'm going to believe in them with all my whole heart this summer. I think we're going to have a very gay vacation. Ruby Gillis is going to have a birthday party soon and there's the Sunday-school picnic and the missionary concert next month. And Mr Barry says that some evening he'll take Diana and me over to the White Sands Hotel and have dinner there. They have dinner there in the evening, you know. Jane Andrews was over once last summer and she says it was a dazzling sight to see the electric lights and the flowers and all the lady guests in such beautiful dresses. Jane says it was her first glimpse into high life and she'll never forget it to her dying day."

Mrs Lynde came up the next afternoon to find out why Marilla had not been at the Aid meeting on Thursday. When Marilla was not at Aid meeting people knew there was something wrong at Green Gables.

" Matthew had a bad spell with his heart on Thursday," Marilla explained, " and I didn't feel like leaving him. Oh, yes, he's all right again now, but he takes them spells oftener than he used to and I'm anxious about him. The doctor says he must be careful to avoid excitement. That's easy enough, for Matthew doesn't go about looking for excitement by any means and never did, but he's not to do any very heavy work either and you might as well tell Matthew not to breathe as not to work. Come and lay off your things, Rachel. You'll stay to tea ? "

" Well, seeing you're so pressing, perhaps I might as well stay," said Mrs Rachel, who had not the slightest intention of doing anything else.

Mrs Rachel and Marilla sat comfortably in the parlour while Anne got the tea and made hot biscuits that were light and white enough to defy even Mrs Rachel's criticism.

" I must say Anne has turned out a real smart girl," admitted Mrs Rachel, as Marilla accompanied her to the end of the lane at sunset. " She must be a great help to you."

" She is," said Marilla, " and she's real steady and reliable now. I used to be afraid she'd never get over her feather-brained ways, but she has and I wouldn't be afraid to trust her in anything now."

" I never would have thought she'd have turned out so well that first day I was here three years ago," said Mrs Rachel. " Lawful heart, shall I ever forget that tantrum of hers ! When I went home that night I says to Thomas, says I, ' Mark my words, Thomas, Marilla Cuthbert'll live to rue the step she's took. But I was mistaken and I'm real glad of it. I ain't one of those kind of people, Marilla, as can never be brought to own up that they've made a mistake. No, that never was my way, thank goodness. I did make a mistake in judging Anne, but it weren't no wonder, for an odder, unexpecteder witch of a child there never was in this world, that's what. There was no ciphering her out by the rules that worked with other children. It's nothing short of wonderful how she's improved these three years, but especially in looks. She's a real pretty girl got to be, though I can't say I'm overly partial to that pale, big-eyed style myself. I like more snap and colour, like Diana Barry has or Ruby Gillis. Ruby Gillis' looks are real showy. But somehow—I don't know how it is but when Anne and them are together, though she ain't half as handsome, she makes them look kind of common and overdone—something like them white June lilies she calls narcissus alongside of the big, red peonies, that's what."

CHAPTER XXXI

WHERE THE BROOK AND RIVER MEET

ANNE had her "good" summer and enjoyed it whole-heartedly. She and Diana fairly lived out of doors, revelling in all the delights that Lovers' Lane and the Dryad's Bubble and Willowmere and Victoria Island afforded. Marilla offered no objections to Anne's gipsyings. The Spencervale doctor who had come the night Minnie May had the croup met Anne at the house of a patient one afternoon early in vacation, looked her over sharply, screwed up his mouth, shook his head, and sent a message to Marilla Cuthbert by another person. It was :

" Keep that red-headed girl of yours in the open air all summer and don't let her read books until she gets more spring into her step."

This message frightened Marilla wholesomely. She read Anne's death warrant by consumption in it unless it was scrupulously obeyed. As a result, Anne had the golden summer of her life as far as freedom and frolic went. She walked, rowed, berried and dreamed to her heart's content ; and when September came she was bright-eyed and alert, with a step that would have satisfied the Spencervale doctor and a heart full of ambition and zest once more.

" I feel just like studying with might and main," she declared as she brought her books down from the attic. " Oh, you good old friends, I'm glad to see your honest faces once more—yes, even you, geometry. I've had a perfectly beautiful summer, Marilla, and now I'm rejoicing as a strong man to run a race, as Mr Allan said last Sunday. Doesn't Mr Allan preach magnificent sermons ? Mrs Lynde says he is improving every day and the first thing we know some city church will gobble him up and then we'll be left and have to turn to and break in another green preacher. But I don't see the use of meeting trouble half-way, do you, Marilla ? I think it would be better just to enjoy Mr Allan while we have him. If I were a man I think I'd be a minister. They can have such an influence for good, if their theology is sound ; and it must be thrilling to preach splendid sermons and stir your hearers' hearts. Why can't women be ministers, Marilla ? I asked Mrs Lynde that and she was shocked and said it would be a scandalous thing. She said there might be female ministers in the States and she believed there was, but thank goodness we hadn't got to that stage in Canada yet and she hoped we never would. But I don't see why. I think women would make splendid ministers. When there is a social to be got up or a church tea or anything else to raise money the women have to turn to and do the work. I'm sure Mrs Lynde can pray every bit as well as Superintendent Bell and I've no doubt she could preach too with a little practice."

" Yes, I believe she could," said Marilla drily. " She does plenty of unofficial preaching as it is. Nobody has much of a chance to go wrong in Avonlea with Rachel to oversee them."

" Marilla," said Anne in a burst of confidence, " I want to tell you something and ask you what you think about it. It has worried me terribly—on Sunday afternoons, that is, when I think specially about such matters. I do really want to be good ; and when I'm with you or Mrs Allan or Miss Stacy I want it more than ever and I want to do just what would please

you and what you would approve of. But mostly
when I'm with Mrs Lynde I feel desperately wicked
and as if I wanted to go and do the very thing she
tells me I oughtn't to do. I feel irresistibly tempted
to do it. Now, what do you think is the reason I
feel like that ? Do you think it's because I'm really
bad and unregenerate ? "

Marilla looked dubious for a moment. Then she
laughed.

" If you are I guess I am too, Anne, for Rachel
often has that very effect on me. I sometimes think
she'd have more of an influence for good, as you say
yourself, if she didn't keep nagging people to do right.
There should have been a special commandment
against nagging. But there, I shouldn't talk so.
Rachel is a good Christian woman and she means
well. There isn't a kinder soul in Avonlea and she
never shirks her share of work."

" I'm very glad you feel the same," said Anne
decidedly. " It's so encouraging. I sha'n't worry so
much over that after this. But I dare say there'll be
other things to worry me. They keep coming up new
all the time—things to perplex you, you know. You
settle one question and there's another right after.
There are so many things to be thought over and
decided when you're beginning to grow up. It keeps
me busy all the time thinking them over and deciding
what is right. It's a serious thing to grow up, isn't
it, Marilla ? But when I have such good friends as
you and Matthew and Mrs Allan and Miss Stacy
I ought to grow up successfully, and I'm sure it will
be my own fault if I don't. I feel it's a great responsibility because I have only the one chance. If
I don't grow up right I can't go back and begin over
again. I've grown two inches this summer, Marilla.
Mr Gillis measured me at Ruby's party. I'm so glad

you made my new dresses longer. That dark green one is so pretty and it was sweet of you to put on the flounce. Of course I know it wasn't really necessary, but flounces are so stylish this fall and Josie Pye has flounces on all her dresses. I know I'll be able to study better because of mine. I shall have such a comfortable feeling deep down in my mind about that flounce."

" It's worth something to have that," admitted Marilla.

Miss Stacy came back to Avonlea school and found all her pupils eager for work once more. Especially did the Queen's class gird up their loins for the fray, for at the end of the coming year, dimly shadowing their pathway already, loomed up that fateful thing known as " the Entrance," at the thought of which one and all felt their hearts sink into their very shoes. Suppose they did not pass ! That thought was doomed to haunt Anne through the waking hours of that winter, Sunday afternoons inclusive, to the almost entire exclusion of moral and theological problems. When Anne had bad dreams she found herself staring miserably at pass lists of the Entrance exams, where Gilbert Blythe's name was blazoned at the top and in which hers did not appear at all.

But it was a jolly, busy, happy swift-flying winter. School work was as interesting, class rivalry as absorbing, as of yore. New worlds of thought, feeling, and ambition, fresh, fascinating fields of unexplored knowledge seemed to be opening out before Anne's eager eyes.

Hills peeped o'er hill and Alps on Alps arose.

Much of all this was due to Miss Stacy's tactful, careful, broad-minded guidance. She led her class to think and explore and discover for themselves and encouraged straying from the old beaten paths to a degree that quite shocked Mrs Lynde and the school trustees, who viewed all innovations on established methods rather dubiously.

Apart from her studies Anne expanded socially, for Marilla, mindful of the Spencervale doctor's dictum, no longer vetoed occasional outings. The Debating Club flourished and gave several concerts ; there were one or two parties almost verging on grown-up affairs ; there were sleigh drives and skating frolics galore.

Between times Anne grew, shooting up so rapidly that Marilla was astonished one day, when they were standing side by side, to find the girl was taller than herself.

" Why, Anne, how you've grown ! " she said, almost unbelievingly. A sigh followed on the words. Marilla felt a queer regret over Anne's inches. The child she had learned to love had vanished somehow and here was this tall, serious-eyed girl of fifteen, with the thoughtful brows and the proudly poised little head, in her place. Marilla loved the girl as much as she had loved the child, but she was conscious of a queer sorrowful sense of loss. And that night when Anne had gone to prayer-meeting with Diana, Marilla sat alone in the wintry twilight and indulged in the weakness of a cry. Matthew, coming in with a lantern, caught her at it and gazed at her in such consternation that Marilla had to laugh through her tears.

" I was thinking about Anne," she explained. " She's got to be such a big girl—and she'll probably be away from us next winter. I'll miss her terrible."

" She'll be able to come home often," comforted Matthew, to whom Anne was as yet and always would be the little, eager girl he had brought home from Bright River on that June evening four years before. " The branch railroad will be built to Carmody by that time."

" It won't be the same thing as having her here all the time," sighed Marilla gloomily, determined to enjoy her luxury of grief uncomforted. " But there—men can't understand these things ! "

There were other changes in Anne no less real than the physical change. For one thing, she became much quieter. Perhaps she thought all the more and dreamed as much as ever, but she certainly talked less. Marilla noticed and commented on this also.

" You don't chatter half as much as you used to, Anne, nor use half as many big words. What has come over you ? "

Anne coloured and laughed a little, as she dropped her book and looked dreamily out of the window, where big fat red buds were bursting out on the creeper in response to the lure of the spring sunshine.

" I don't know—I don't want to talk as much," she said, denting her chin thoughtfully with her forefinger. " It's nicer to think dear, pretty thoughts and keep them in one's heart, like treasures. I don't like to have them laughed at or wondered over. And somehow I don't want to use big words any more. It's almost a pity, isn't it, now that I'm really growing big enough to say them if I did want to. It's fun to be almost grown up in some ways, but it's not the kind of fun I expected, Marilla. There's so much to learn and do and think that there isn't time for big words. Besides, Miss Stacy says the short ones are much stronger and better. She makes us write all our essays as simply as possible. It was hard at first. I was so used to crowding in all the fine big words I could think of—and I thought of any number of them. But I've got used to it now and I see it's so much better."

" What has become of your story club ? I haven't heard you speak of it for a long time."

" The story club isn't in existence any longer. We hadn't time for it—and anyhow I think we had got tired of it. It was silly to be writing about love and murder and elopements and mysteries. Miss Stacy sometimes has us write a story for training in composition, but she won't let us write anything but what might happen in Avonlea in our own lives, and she criticizes it very sharply and makes us criticize our own too. I never thought my compositions had so many faults until I began to look for them myself. I felt so ashamed I wanted to give up altogether, but Miss Stacy said I could learn to write well if I only trained myself to be my own severest critic. And so I am trying to."

" You've only two more months before the Entrance," said Marilla. " Do you think you'll be able to get through ? "

Anne shivered.

" I don't know. Sometimes I think I'll be all right —and then I get horribly afraid. We've studied hard and Miss Stacy has drilled us thoroughly, but we mayn't get through for all that. We've each got a stumbling-block. Mine is geometry of course, and Jane's is Latin and Ruby's and Charlie's is algebra and Josie's is arithmetic. Moody Spurgeon says he feels it in his bones that he is going to fail in English history. Miss Stacy is going to give us examinations in June just as hard as we'll have at the Entrance and mark us just as strictly, so we'll have some idea. I wish it was all over, Marilla. It haunts me. Sometimes I wake up in the night and wonder what I'll do if I don't pass."

" Why, go to school next year and try again," said Marilla unconcernedly.

" Oh, I don't believe I'd have the heart for it. It would be such a disgrace to fail, especially if Gil— if the others passed. And I get so nervous in an ex-

amination that I'm likely to make a mess of it.   I
wish I had nerves like Jane Andrews.   Nothing rattles
her."

Anne sighed and, dragging her eyes from the witch-
eries of the spring world, the beckoning day of breeze
and blue, and the green things upspringing in the
garden, buried herself resolutely in her book.   There
would be other springs, but if she did not succeed in
passing the Entrance Anne felt convinced that she
would never recover sufficiently to enjoy them.

CHAPTER XXXII

THE PASS LIST IS OUT

WITH the end of June came the close of the term and the close of Miss Stacy's rule in Avonlea school. Anne and Diana walked home that evening feeling very sober indeed. Red eyes and damp handkerchiefs bore convincing testimony to the fact that Miss Stacy's farewell words must have been quite as touching as Mr Phillips' had been under similar circumstances three years before. Diana looked back at the school-house from the foot of the spruce hill and sighed deeply.

" It does seem as if it was the end of everything, doesn't it ? " she said dismally.

" You oughtn't to feel half as badly as I do," said Anne, hunting vainly for a dry spot on her handkerchief. " You'll be back again next winter, but I suppose I've left the dear old school for ever—if I have good luck, that is."

" It won't be a bit the same. Miss Stacy won't be there, nor you nor Jane nor Ruby probably. I shall have to sit all alone, for I couldn't bear to have another deskmate after you. Oh, we have had jolly times, haven't we, Anne ? It's dreadful to think they're all over."

Two big tears rolled down by Diana's nose.

" If you would stop crying I could," said Anne imploringly. " Just as soon as I put away my hanky I see you brimming up and that starts me off again. As Mrs Lynde says, ' If you can't be cheerful, be as cheerful as you can.' After all, I dare say I'll be back next year. This is one of the times I *know* I'm not going to pass. They're getting alarmingly frequent."

" Why, you came out splendidly in the exams Miss Stacy gave."

" Yes, but those exams didn't make me nervous. When I think of the real thing you can't imagine what a horrid cold fluttery feeling comes round my heart. And then my number is thirteen and Josie Pye says it's so unlucky. I am *not* superstitious and I know it can make no difference. But still I wish it wasn't thirteen."

" I do wish I were going in with you," said Diana. " Wouldn't we have a perfectly elegant time ? But I suppose you'll have to cram in the evenings."

" No ; Miss Stacy has made us promise not to open a book at all. She says it would only tire and confuse us and we are to go out walking and not think about the exams at all and go to bed early. It's good advice, but I expect it will be hard to follow ; good advice is apt to be, I think. Prissy Andrews told me that she sat up half the night every night of her Entrance week and crammed for dear life ; and I had determined to sit up *at least* as long as she did. It was so kind of your Aunt Josephine to ask me to stay at Beechwood while I'm in town."

" You'll write to me while you're in, won't you ? "

" I'll write Tuesday night and tell you how the first day goes," promised Anne.

" I'll be haunting the post office on Wednesday," vowed Diana.

Anne went to town the following Monday and on Wednesday Diana haunted the post office, as agreed, and got her letter.

DEAREST DIANA [wrote Anne],

Here it is Tuesday night and I'm writing this in the library at Beechwood. Last night I was horribly lonesome all alone in my room and wished so much you were with me. I couldn't cram because I'd promised Miss Stacy not to, but it was as hard to keep from opening my history as it used to be to keep from reading a story before my lessons were learned.

This morning Miss Stacy came for me and we went to the Academy, calling for Jane and Ruby and Josie on our way. Ruby asked me to feel her hands and they were as cold as ice. Josie said I looked as if I hadn't slept a wink and she didn't believe I was strong enough to stand the grind of the teacher's course even if I did get through. There are times and seasons even yet when I don't feel that I've made any great headway in learning to like Josie Pye !

When we reached the Academy there were scores of students there from all over the Island. The first person we saw was Moody Spurgeon sitting on the steps and muttering away to himself. Jane asked him what on earth he was doing and he said he was repeating the multiplication table over and over to steady his nerves and for pity's sake not to interrupt him, because if he stopped for a moment he got frightened and forgot everything he ever knew, but the multiplication table kept all his facts firmly in their proper place !

When we were assigned to our rooms Miss Stacy had to leave us. Jane and I sat together and Jane was so composed that I envied her. No need of the multiplication table for good, steady, sensible Jane ! I wondered if I looked as I felt and if they could hear my heart thumping clear across the room. Then a man came in and began distributing the English examination sheets. My hands grew cold then and my head fairly whirled around as I picked it up. Just one awful moment,— Diana, I felt exactly as I did four years ago when I asked Marilla if I might stay at Green Gables—and then everything cleared up in my mind and my heart began beating again—I forgot to say that it had stopped altogether !—for I knew I could do something with *that* paper anyhow.

At noon we went home for dinner and then back again

for history in the afternoon. The history was a pretty hard paper and I got dreadfully mixed up in the dates. Still, I think I did fairly well to-day. But oh, Diana, to-morrow the geometry exam comes off and when I think of it it takes every bit of determination I possess to keep from opening my Euclid. If I thought the multiplication table would help me any I would recite it from now till to-morrow morning.

I went down to see the other girls this evening. On my way I met Moody Spurgeon wandering distractedly around. He said he knew he had failed in history and he was born to be a disappointment to his parents and he was going home on the morning train ; and it would be easier to be a carpenter than a minister, anyhow. I cheered him up and persuaded him to stay to the end because it would be unfair to Miss Stacy if he didn't. Sometimes I have wished I was born a boy, but when I see Moody Spurgeon I'm always glad I'm a girl and not his sister.

Ruby was in hysterics when I reached their boarding-house ; she had just discovered a fearful mistake she had made in her English paper. When she recovered we went up-town and had an ice-cream. How we wished you had been with us.

Oh, Diana, if only the geometry examination were over ! But there, as Mrs Lynde would say, the sun will go on rising and setting whether I fail in geometry or not. That is true but not especially comforting. I think I'd rather it *didn't* go on if I failed !

Yours devotedly,
ANNE

The geometry examination and all the others were over in due time and Anne arrived home on Friday evening, rather tired but with an air of chastened triumph about her. Diana was over at Green Gables when she arrived and they met as if they had been parted for years.

" You old darling, it's perfectly splendid to see you

back again. It seems like an age since you went to town and oh, Anne, how did you get along ? "

" Pretty well, I think, in everything but the geometry. I don't know whether I passed in it or not and I have a creepy, crawly presentiment that I didn't. Oh, how good it is to be back ! Green Gables is the dearest, loveliest spot in the world."

" How did the others do ? "

" The girls say they know they didn't pass, but I think they did pretty well. Josie says the geometry was so easy a child of ten could do it ! Moody Spurgeon still thinks he failed in history and Charlie says he failed in algebra. But we don't really know anything about it and won't until the pass list is out. That won't be for a fortnight. Fancy living a fortnight in such suspense ! I wish I could go to sleep and never wake up until it is over."

Diana knew it would be useless to ask how Gilbert Blythe had fared, so she merely said :

" Oh, you'll pass all right. Don't worry."

" I'd rather not pass at all than not come out pretty well up on the list," flashed Anne, by which she meant —and Diana knew she meant—that success would be incomplete and bitter if she did not come out ahead of Gilbert Blythe.

With this end in view Anne had strained every nerve during the examinations. So had Gilbert. They had met and passed each other on the street a dozen times without any sign of recognition and every time Anne had held her head a little higher and wished a little more earnestly that she had made friends with Gilbert when he asked her, and vowed a little more determinedly to surpass him in the examination. She knew that all Avonlea junior was wondering which would come out first ; she even knew that Jimmy Glover and Ned Wright had a bet on the question and that

Josie Pye had said there was no doubt in the world that Gilbert would be first ; and she felt that her humiliation would be unbearable if she failed.

But she had another and nobler motive for wishing to do well. She wanted to " pass high " for the sake of Matthew and Marilla—especially Matthew. Matthew had declared to her his conviction that she " would beat the whole Island." That, Anne felt, was something it would be foolish to hope for even in the wildest dreams. But she did hope fervently that she would be among the first ten at least, so that she might see Matthew's kindly brown eyes gleam with pride in her achievement. That, she felt, would be a sweet reward indeed for all her hard work and patient grubbing among unimaginative equations and conjugations.

At the end of the fortnight Anne took to " haunting " the post office also, in the distracted company of Jane, Ruby, and Josie, opening the Charlottetown dailies with shaking hands and cold, sinkaway feelings as bad as any experienced during the Entrance week. Charlie and Gilbert were not above doing this too, but Moody Spurgeon stayed resolutely away.

" I haven't got the grit to go there and look at a paper in cold blood," he told Anne. " I'm just going to wait until somebody comes and tells me suddenly whether I've passed or not."

When three weeks had gone by without the pass list appearing Anne began to feel that she really couldn't stand the strain much longer. Her appetite failed and her interest in Avonlea doings languished. Mrs Lynde wanted to know what else you could expect with a Tory superintendent of education at the head of affairs, and Matthew, noting Anne's paleness and indifference and the lagging steps that bore her home from the post office every afternoon, began seriously to wonder if he hadn't better vote Grit at the next election.

But one evening the news came. Anne was sitting at her open window, for the time forgetful of the woes of examinations and the cares of the world, as she drank in the beauty of the summer dusk, sweet-scented with flower-breaths from the garden below and sibilant and rustling from the stir of poplars. The eastern sky above the firs was flushed faintly pink from the reflection of the west, and Anne was wondering dreamily if the spirit of colour looked like that, when she saw Diana come flying down through the firs, over the log bridge, and up the slope, with a fluttering newspaper in her hand.

Anne sprang to her feet, knowing at once what that paper contained. The pass list was out! Her head whirled and her heart beat until it hurt her. She could not move a step. It seemed an hour to her before Diana came rushing along the hall and burst into the room without even knocking, so great was her excitement.

" Anne, you've passed," she cried, " passed the *very first*—you and Gilbert both—you're ties—but your name is first. Oh, I'm so proud ! "

Diana flung the paper on the table and herself on Anne's bed, utterly breathless and incapable of further speech. Anne lighted the lamp, oversetting the match-safe and using up half a dozen matches before her shaking hands could accomplish the task. Then she snatched up the paper. Yes, she had passed—there was her name at the very top of a list of two hundred ! That moment was worth living for.

" You did just splendidly, Anne," puffed Diana, recovering sufficiently to sit up and speak, for Anne, starry-eyed and rapt, had not uttered a word. " Father brought the paper home from Bright River not ten minutes ago—it came out on the afternoon train, you know, and won't be here till to-morrow by mail—and when I saw the pass list I just rushed over like a wild thing. You've all passed, every one of you, Moody Spurgeon and all, although he's conditioned in history. Jane and Ruby did pretty well—they're half-way up—and so did Charlie. Josie just scraped through with three marks to spare, but you'll see she'll put on as many airs as if she'd led. Won't Miss Stacy be delighted? Oh, Anne, what does it feel like to see your name at the head of a pass list like that? If it were me I know I'd go crazy with joy. I am pretty near crazy as it is, but you're as calm and cool as a spring evening."

" I'm just dazzled inside," said Anne. " I want to say a hundred things, and I can't find words to say them in. I never dreamed of this—yes, I did, too, just once ! I let myself think *once,* ' What if I should come out first ? ' quakingly, you know, for it seemed so vain and presumptuous to think I could lead the Island. Excuse me a minute, Diana. I must run right out to the field to tell Matthew. Then we'll go up the road and tell the good news to the others."

They hurried to the hayfield below the barn where Matthew was coiling hay, and, as luck would have it, Mrs Lynde was talking to Marilla at the lane fence.

" Oh, Matthew," exclaimed Anne, " I've passed and I'm first—or one of the first ! I'm not vain, but I'm thankful."

" Well now, I always said it," said Matthew, gazing at the pass list delightedly. " I knew you could beat them all easy."

" You've done pretty well, I must say, Anne," said Marilla, trying to hide her extreme pride in Anne from Mrs Rachel's critical eye. But that good soul said heartily :

"I just guess she has done well, and far be it from me to be backward in saying it. You're a credit to your friends, Anne, that's what, and we're all proud of you."

That night Anne, who had wound up a delightful evening by a serious little talk with Mrs Allan at the manse, knelt sweetly by her open window in a great sheen of moonshine and murmured a prayer of gratitude and aspiration that came straight from her heart. There was in it thankfulness for the past and reverent petition for the future; and when she slept on her white pillow her dreams were as fair and bright and beautiful as maidenhood might desire.

CHAPTER XXXIII

THE HOTEL CONCERT

PUT on your white organdy, by all means, Anne," advised Diana decidedly.

They were together in the east gable chamber ; outside it was only twilight—a lovely yellowish-green twilight with a clear blue cloudless sky. A big round moon, slowly deepening from her pallid lustre into burnished silver, hung over the Haunted Wood ; the air was full of sweet summer sounds—sleepy birds twittering, freakish breezes, far-away voices and laughter. But in Anne's room the blind was drawn and the lamp lighted, for an important toilet was being made.

The east gable was a very different place from what it had been on that night four years before, when Anne had felt its bareness penetrate to the marrow of her spirit with its inhospitable chill. Changes had crept in, Marilla conniving at them resignedly, until it was as sweet and dainty a nest as a young girl could desire.

The velvet carpet with the pink roses and the pink silk curtains of Anne's early visions had certainly never materialized ; but her dreams had kept pace with her growth, and it is not probable she lamented them. The floor was covered with a pretty matting, and the curtains that softened the high window and fluttered in the vagrant breezes were of pale green art muslin. The walls, hung not with gold and silver brocade tapestry, but with a dainty apple-blossom paper, were adorned with a few good pictures given Anne by Mrs Allan. Miss Stacy's photograph occupied the place of honour, and Anne made a sentimental point of keeping fresh flowers on the bracket under it. To-night a spike of white lilies faintly perfumed the room like the dream of a fragrance. There was no " mahogany furniture," but there was a white-painted bookcase filled with books, a cushioned wicker rocker, a toilet-table befrilled with white muslin, a quaint, gilt-framed mirror with chubby pink cupids and purple grapes painted over its arched top, that used to hang in the spare room, and a low white bed.

Anne was dressing for a concert at the White Sands Hotel. The guests had got it up in aid of the Charlotte-town hospital, and had hunted out all the available amateur talent in the surrounding districts to help it along. Bertha Sampson and Pearl Clay of the White Sands Baptist choir had been asked to sing a duet ; Milton Clark of Newbridge was to give a violin solo ; Winnie Adella Blair of Carmody was to sing a Scotch ballad ; and Laura Spencer of Spencervale and Anne Shirley of Avonlea were to recite.

As Anne would have said at one time, it was " an epoch in her life," and she was deliciously athrill with the excitement of it. Matthew was in the seventh heaven of gratified pride over the honour conferred on his Anne, and Marilla was not far behind, although she would have died rather than admit it, and said she didn't think it was very proper for a lot of young folks to be gadding over to the hotel without any responsible person with them.

Anne and Diana were to drive over with Jane Andrews and her brother Billy in their double-seated buggy ; and several other Avonlea girls and boys were going, too. There was a party of visitors expected out from town, and after the concert a supper was to be given to the performers.

" Do you really think the organdy will be best ? " queried Anne anxiously. " I don't think it's as pretty as my blue-flowered muslin—and it certainly isn't so fashionable."

" But it suits you ever so much better," said Diana. " It's so soft and frilly and clinging. The muslin is stiff, and makes you look too dressed up. But the organdy seems as if it grew on you."

Anne sighed and yielded. Diana was beginning to have a reputation for notable taste in dressing, and her advice on such subjects was much sought after. She was looking very pretty herself on this particular night in a dress of the lovely wild-rose pink, from which Anne was for ever debarred ; but she was not to take any part in the concert, so her appearance was of minor importance. All her pains were bestowed upon Anne, who, she vowed, must, for the credit of Avonlea, be dressed and combed and adorned to the queen's taste.

" Pull out that frill a little more—so ; here, let me tie your sash ; now for your slippers. I'm going to braid your hair in two thick braids, and tie them half-way up with big white bows—no, don't pull out a single curl over your forehead—just have the soft part. There is no way you do your hair suits you so well, Anne, and Mrs Allan says you look like a Madonna when you part it so. I shall fasten this little white house-rose just behind your ear. There was just one on my bush, and I saved it, for you."

" Shall I put my pearl beads on ? " asked Anne. " Matthew brought me a string from town last week, and I know he'd like to see them on me."

Diana pursed up her lips, put her black head on one side critically, and finally pronounced in favour of the beads, which were thereupon tied around Anne's slim milk-white throat.

" There's something so stylish about you, Anne," said Diana, with unenvious admiration. " You hold your head with such an air. I suppose it's your figure.

I am just a dumpling. I've always been afraid of it, and now I know it is so. Well, I suppose I shall just have to resign myself to it."

" But you have such dimples," said Anne, smiling affectionately into the pretty, vivacious face so near her own. " Lovely dimples, like little dents in cream. I have given up all hope of dimples. My dimple-dream will never come true ; but so many of my dreams have that I mustn't complain. Am I all ready now ? "

" All ready," assured Diana, as Marilla appeared in the doorway, a gaunt figure with greyer hair than of yore and no fewer angles, but with a much softer face. " Come right in and look at our elocutionist, Marilla ; Doesn't she look lovely ? "

Marilla emitted a sound between a sniff and a grunt.

" She looks neat and proper. I like that way of fixing her hair. But I expect she'll ruin that dress driving over there in the dust and dew with it, and it looks most too thin for these damp nights. Organdy's the most unserviceable stuff in the world anyhow, and I told Matthew so when he got it. But there is no use in saying anything to Matthew nowadays. Time was when he would take my advice, but now he just buys things for Anne regardless, and the clerks at Carmody know they can palm anything off on him. Just let them tell him a thing is pretty and fashionable, and Matthew plunks his money down for it. Mind you keep your skirt clear of the wheel, Anne, and put your warm jacket on."

Then Marilla stalked downstairs, thinking proudly how sweet Anne looked, with that

One moonbeam from the forehead to the crown

and regretting that she could not go to the concert herself to hear her girl recite.

" I wonder if it *is* too damp for my dress," said Anne anxiously.

" Not a bit of it," said Diana, pulling up the window blind. " It's a perfect night, and there won't be any dew. Look at the moonlight."

" I'm so glad my window looks east into the sunrising," said Anne, going over to Diana. " It's so splendid to see the morning coming up over those long hills and glowing through those sharp fir tops. It's new every morning, and I feel as if I washed my very soul in that bath of earliest sunshine. Oh, Diana, I love this little room so dearly. I don't know how I'll get along without it when I go to town next month."

" Don't speak of your going away to-night," begged Diana. " I don't want to think of it, it makes me so miserable, and I do want to have a good time this evening. What are you going to recite, Anne ? And are you nervous ? "

" Not a bit. I've recited so often in public I don't mind at all now. I've decided to give ' The Maiden's Vow.' It's so pathetic. Laura Spencer is going to give a comic recitation, but I'd rather make people cry than laugh."

" What will you recite if they encore you ? "

" They won't dream of encoring me," scoffed Anne, who was not without her own secret hopes that they would, and already visioned herself telling Matthew all about it at the next morning's breakfast-table. " There are Billy and Jane now—I hear the wheels. Come on."

Billy Andrews insisted that Anne should ride on the front seat with him, so she unwillingly climbed up. She would have much preferred to sit back with the girls, where she could have laughed and chattered to her heart's content. There was not much of either laughter or chatter in Billy. He was a big, fat, stolid youth of twenty, with a round, expressionless face, and a painful lack of conversational gifts. But he admired Anne immensely, and was puffed up with pride over the prospect of driving to White Sands with that slim, upright figure beside him.

Anne, by dint of talking over her shoulder to the girls and occasionally passing a sop of civility to Billy—who grinned and chuckled and never could think of any reply until it was too late—contrived to enjoy the drive in spite of all. It was a night for enjoyment. The road was full of buggies, all bound for the hotel, and laughter, silver-clear, echoed and re-echoed along it. When they reached the hotel it was a blaze of light from top to bottom. They were met by the ladies of the concert committee, one of whom took Anne off to the performers' dressing-room, which was filled with the members of a Charlottetown Symphony Club, among whom Anne felt suddenly shy and frightened and countrified. Her dress, which, in the east gable, had seemed so dainty and pretty, now seemed simple and plain—too simple and plain, she thought, among all the silks and laces that glistened and rustled around her. What were her pearl beads compared to the diamonds of the big, handsome lady near her? And how poor her one wee white rose must look beside all the hot-house flowers the others wore! Anne laid her hat and jacket away, and shrank miserably into a corner. She wished herself back in the white room at Green Gables.

It was still worse on the platform of the big concert hall of the hotel, where she presently found herself. The electric lights dazzled her eyes, the perfume and hum bewildered her. She wished she were sitting down in the audience with Diana and Jane, who seemed to be having a splendid time away at the back. She was wedged in between a stout lady in pink silk and a tall, scornful-looking girl in a white lace dress. The stout lady occasionally turned her head squarely round and surveyed Anne through her eyeglasses until Anne, acutely sensitive of being so scrutinized, felt that she must scream aloud ; and the white-lace girl kept talking audibly to her next neighbour about the " country bumpkins " and " rustic belles " in the audience, languidly anticipating " such fun " from the displays of local talent on the programme. Anne believed that she would hate that white-lace girl to the end of life.

Unfortunately for Anne, a professional elocutionist was staying at the hotel and had consented to recite. She was a lithe, dark-eyed woman in a wonderful gown of shimmering grey stuff like woven moonbeams, with gems on her neck and in her dark hair. She had a marvellously flexible voice and wonderful power of expression ; the audience went wild over her selection. Anne, forgetting all about herself and her troubles for the time, listened with rapt and shining eyes ; but when the recitation ended she suddenly put her hands over her face. She could never get up and recite after that—never. Had she ever thought she could recite ? Oh, if she were only back at Green Gables !

At this unpropitious moment her name was called. Somehow, Anne—who did not notice the rather guilty little start of surprise the white-lace girl gave, and would not have understood the subtle compliment implied therein if she had—got on her feet, and moved dizzily out to the front. She was so pale that Diana and Jane, down in the audience, clasped each other's hands in nervous sympathy.

Anne was the victim of an overwhelming attack of stage fright. Often as she had recited in public, she had never before faced such an audience as this, and the sight of it paralysed her energies completely. Everything was so strange, so brilliant, so bewildering—the rows of ladies in evening dress, the critical faces, the whole atmosphere of wealth and culture about her. Very different this from the plain benches at the Debating Club, filled with the homely, sympathetic faces of friends and neighbours. These people, she thought, would be merciless critics. Perhaps, like the white-lace girl, they anticipated amusement from her " rustic " efforts. She felt hopelessly, helplessly ashamed and miserable. Her knees trembled, her heart fluttered, a horrible faintness came over her ; not a word could she utter, and the next moment she would have fled from the platform despite the humiliation which, she felt, must ever after be her portion if she did so.

But suddenly, as her dilated, frightened eyes gazed out over the audience, she saw Gilbert Blythe away at the back of the room, bending forward with a smile on his face—a smile which seemed to Anne at once triumphant and taunting. In reality it was nothing of the kind. Gilbert was merely smiling with appreciation of the whole affair in general, and of the effect produced by Anne's slender white form and spiritual face against a background of palms in particular. Josie Pye, whom he had driven over, sat beside him, and her face certainly was both triumphant and taunting. But Anne did not see Josie, and would not have cared if she had. She drew a long breath and flung her head up proudly, courage and determination tingling over her like an electric shock. She *would not* fail before Gilbert Blythe—he should never be able to laugh at her, never, never ! Her fright and nervousness vanished ; and she began her recitation, her clear, sweet voice reaching to the farthest corner of the room without a tremor or a break. Self-possession was fully restored to her, and in the reaction from that horrible moment of powerlessness she recited as she had never done before. When she finished there were bursts of honest applause. Anne, stepping back to her seat, blushing with shyness and delight, found her hand vigorously clasped and shaken by the stout lady in pink silk.

" My dear, you did splendidly," she puffed. " I've been crying like a baby, actually I have. There, they're encoring you—they're bound to have you back ! "

" Oh, I can't go," said Anne confusedly. " But yet—I must, or Matthew will be disappointed. He said they would encore me."

" Then don't disappoint Matthew," said the pink lady, laughing.

Smiling, blushing, limpid-eyed, Anne tripped back and gave a quaint, funny little selection that captivated her audience still further. The rest of the evening was quite a little triumph for her.

When the concert was over, the stout, pink lady —who was the wife of an American millionaire—took her under her wing, and introduced her to everybody ; and everybody was very nice to her. The professional elocutionist, Mrs Evans, came and chatted with her, telling her that she had a charming voice and " interpreted " her selections beautifully. Even the white-lace girl paid her a languid little compliment. They had supper in the big, beautifully decorated dining-room ; Diana and Jane were invited to partake of this, also, since they had come with Anne, but Billy was nowhere to be found, having decamped in mortal fear of some such invitation. He was in waiting for them, with the team, however, when it was all over, and the three girls came merrily out into the calm, white moonshine radiance.   Anne breathed deeply, and looked into the clear sky beyond the dark boughs of the firs.

Oh, it was good to be out again in the purity and silence of the night ! How great and still and wonderful everything was, with the murmur of the sea sounding through it and the darkling cliffs beyond like grim giants guarding enchanted coasts.

" Hasn't it been a perfectly splendid time ? " sighed Jane, as they drove away.   " I just wish I was a rich American and could spend my summer at a hotel and wear jewels and low-necked dresses and have ice-cream and chicken salad every blessed day. I'm sure it would be ever so much more fun than teaching school. Anne, your recitation was simply great, although I thought at first you were never going to begin. I think it was better than Mrs. Evans'."

" Oh, no, don't say things like that, Jane," said Anne quickly, " because it sounds silly. It couldn't be better than Mrs Evans', you know, for she is a professional, and I'm only a schoolgirl, with a little knack of reciting. I'm quite satisfied if the people just liked mine pretty well."

" I've a compliment for you, Anne," said Diana. " At least I think it must be a compliment because of the tone he said it in. Part of it was anyhow. There was an American sitting behind Jane and me —such a romantic-looking man, with coal-black hair and eyes. Josie Pye says he is a distinguished artist, and that her mother's cousin in Boston is married to a man that used to go to school with him. Well, we heard him say—didn't we, Jane ?—' Who is that girl on the platform with the splendid Titian hair ? She has a face I should like to paint.' There now, Anne. But what does Titian hair mean ? "

" Being interpreted it means plain red, I guess,"
laughed Anne. " Titian was a very famous artist who
liked to paint red-haired women."

" *Did* you see all the diamonds those ladies wore ? "
sighed Jane. " They were simply dazzling. Wouldn't
you just love to be rich, girls ? "

" We *are* rich," said Anne stanchly. " Why, we
have sixteen years to our credit, and we're happy as
queens, and we've all got imaginations, more or less.
Look at that sea, girls—all silver and shallow and
vision of things not seen. We couldn't enjoy its
loveliness any more if we had millions of dollars and
ropes of diamonds. You wouldn't change into any
of those women if you could. Would you want to be
that white-lace girl and wear a sour look all your
life, as if you'd been born turning up your nose at
the world ? Or the pink lady, kind and nice as she
is, so stout and short that you'd really no figure at
all ? Or even Mrs Evans, with that sad, sad look in
her eyes ? She must have been dreadfully unhappy
sometime to have such a look. You *know* you wouldn't,
Jane Andrews ! "

" I *don't* know—exactly," said Jane unconvinced.
" I think diamonds would comfort a person for a
good deal."

" Well, I don't want to be anyone but myself,
even if I go uncomforted by diamonds all my life,"
declared Anne. " I'm quite content to be Anne of
Green Gables, with my string of pearl beads. I know
Matthew gave me as much love with them as ever went
with Madame the Pink Lady's jewels."

CHAPTER XXXIV

A QUEEN'S GIRL

THE next three weeks were busy ones at Green Gables, for Anne was getting ready to go to Queen's, and there was much sewing to be done, and many things to be talked over and arranged. Anne's outfit was ample and pretty, for Matthew saw to that, and Marilla for once made no objections whatever to anything he purchased or suggested. More— one evening she went up to the east gable with her arms full of a delicate pale green material.

"Anne, here's something for a nice light dress for you. I don't suppose you really need it ; you've plenty of pretty waists ; but I thought maybe you'd like something real dressy to wear if you were asked out anywhere of an evening in town, to a party or anything like that. I hear that Jane and Ruby and Josie have got 'evening dresses,' as they call them, and I don't mean you shall be behind them. I got Mrs Allan to help me pick it in town last week, and we'll get Emily Gillis to make it for you. Emily has got taste, and her fits aren't to be equalled."

"Oh, Marilla, it's just lovely," said Anne. "Thank you so much. I don't believe you ought to be so kind to me—it's making it harder every day for me to go away."

The green dress was made up with as many tucks and frills and shirrings as Emily's taste permitted. Anne put it on one evening for Matthew's and Marilla's benefit, and recited "The Maiden's Vow" for them in the kitchen. As Marilla watched the bright, animated face and graceful motions her thoughts went back to the evening Anne had arrived at Green Gables, and memory recalled a vivid picture of the odd, frightened child in her preposterous yellowish-brown wincey dress, the heartbreak looking out of her tearful eyes. Something in the memory brought tears to Marilla's own eyes.

" I declare, my recitation has made you cry, Marilla," said Anne gaily, stooping over Marilla's chair to drop a butterfly kiss on that lady's cheek. " Now, I call that a positive triumph."

" No, I wasn't crying over your piece," said Marilla, who would have scorned to be betrayed into such weakness by any " poetry stuff." " I just couldn't help thinking of the little girl you used to be, Anne. And I was wishing you could have stayed a little girl, even with all your queer ways. You're grown up now and you're going away ; and you look so tall and stylish and so—so—different altogether in that dress—as if you didn't belong in Avonlea at all—and I just got lonesome thinking it all over."

" Marilla ! " Anne sat down on Marilla's gingham lap, took Marilla's lined face between her hands, and looked gravely and tenderly into Marilla's eyes. " I'm not a bit changed—not really. I'm only just pruned down and branched out. The real *me*—back here— is just the same. It won't make a bit of difference where I go or how much I change outwardly ; at heart I shall always be your little Anne, who will love you and Matthew and dear Green Gables more and better every day of her life."

Anne laid her fresh young cheek against Marilla's faded one, and reached out a hand to pat Matthew's shoulder. Marilla would have given much just then to have possessed Anne's power of putting her feelings into words ; but nature and habit had willed it otherwise, and she could only put her arms close about her girl and hold her tenderly to her heart, wishing that she need never let her go.

Matthew, with a suspicious moisture in his eyes, got up and went out of doors. Under the stars of the blue summer night he walked agitatedly across the yard to the gate under the poplars.

" Well, now, I guess she ain't been much spoiled," he muttered, proudly. " I guess my putting in my oar occasional never did much harm after all. She's smart and pretty, and loving, too, which is better than all the rest. She's been a blessing to us, and there never was a luckier mistake than what Mrs Spencer made—if it *was* luck. I don't belive it was any such thing. It was Providence, because the Almighty saw we needed her, I reckon."

The day finally came when Anne must go to town. She and Matthew drove in one fine September morning, after a tearful parting with Diana and an untearful, practical one—on Marilla's side at least— with Marilla. But when Anne had gone Diana dried her tears and went to a beach picnic at White Sands with some of her Carmody cousins, where she contrived to enjoy herself tolerably well ; while Marilla plunged fiercely into unnecessary work and kept at it all day long with the bitterest kind of a heartache —the ache that burns and gnaws and cannot wash itself away in ready tears. But that night, when Marilla went to bed, acutely and miserably conscious that the little gable room at the end of the hall was untenanted by any vivid young life and unstirred by any soft breathing, she buried her face in her pillow, and wept for her girl in a passion of sobs that appalled her when she grew calm enough to reflect how very wickedit must be to ' take on ' so about a sinful fellow creature.

Anne and the rest of the Avonlea scholars reached town just in time to hurry off to the Academy. That first day passed pleasantly enough in a whirl of excitement, meeting all the new students, learning to know the professors by sight and being assorted and organized into classes. Anne intended taking up the Second Year work, being advised to do so by Miss Stacy ; Gilbert Blythe elected to do the same. This meant getting a First Class teacher's licence in one year instead of two, if they were successful ; but it also meant much more and harder work. Jane, Ruby, Josie, Charlie, and Moody Spurgeon, not being troubled with the stirrings of ambition, were content to take up the Second Class work. Anne was conscious of a pang of loneliness when she found herself in a room with fifty other students, not one of whom she knew, except the tall, brown-haired boy across the room ; and knowing him in the fashion she did, did not help her much, as she reflected pessimistically. Yet she was undeniably glad that they were in the same class ; the old rivalry could still be carried on, and Anne would hardly have known what to do if it had been lacking.

" I wouldn't feel comfortable without it," she thought. " Gilbert looks awfully determined. I suppose he's making up his mind, here and now, to win the medal. What a splendid chin he has ! I never noticed it before. I do wish Jane and Ruby had gone in for First Class, too. I suppose I won't feel so much like a cat in a strange garret when I get acquainted, though. I wonder which of the girls here are going to be my friends. It's really an interesting speculation. Of course I promised Diana that no Queen's girl, no matter how much I liked her, should ever be as dear to me as she is ; but I've lots of second-best affections to bestow. I like the look of that girl with the brown eyes and the crimson waist. She looks vivid and red-rosy ; then there's that pale, fair one gazing out of the window. She has lovely hair, and looks as if she knew a thing or two about dreams. I'd like to know them both—know them well—well enough to walk with my arm about their waists, and call them nicknames. But just now I don't know them and they don't know me, and probably don't want to know me particularly. Oh, it's lonesome ! "

It was lonesomer still when Anne found herself alone in her hall bedroom that night at twilight. She was not to board with the other girls, who all had relatives in town to take pity on them. Miss Josephine Barry would have liked to board her, but Beechwood was so far from the Academy that it was out of the question ; so Miss Barry hunted up a boarding-house, assuring Matthew and Marilla that it was the very place for Anne.

" The lady who keeps it is a reduced gentlewoman," explained Miss Barry. " Her husband was a British officer, and she is very careful what sort of boarders she takes. Anne will not meet with any objectionable persons under her roof. The table is good, and the house is near the Academy, in a quiet neighbourhood."

All this might be quite true, and, indeed, proved to be so, but it did not materially help Anne in the first agony of homesickness that seized upon her. She looked dismally about her narrow little room, with its dull-papered, pictureless walls, its small iron bedstead and empty bookcase ; and a horrible choke came into her throat as she thought of her own white room at Green Gables, where she would have the pleasant consciousness of a great; green, still outdoors, of sweet peas growing in the garden, and moonlight falling on the orchard, of the brook below the slope and the spruce boughs tossing in the night wind beyond it, of a vast starry sky, and the light from Diana's window shining out through the gap in the trees. Here there was nothing of this; Anne knew that outside of her window was a hard street, with a network of telephone wires shutting out the sky, the tramp of alien feet, and a thousand lights gleaming on stranger faces. She knew that she was going to cry, and fought against it.

" I *won't* cry. It's silly—and weak—there's the third tear splashing down by my nose. There are more coming! I must think of something funny to stop them. But there's nothing funny except what is connected with Avonlea, and that only makes things worse—four—five—I'm going home next Friday, but that seems a hundred years away. Oh, Matthew is nearly home by now—and Marilla is at the gate, looking down the lane for him—six—seven—eight—oh, there's no use in counting them! They're coming in a flood presently. I can't cheer up—I don't *want* to cheer up. It's nicer to be miserable! "

The flood of tears would have come, no doubt, had not Josie Pye appeared at that moment. In the joy of seeing a familiar face Anne forgot that there had never been much love lost between her and Josie. As a part of Avonlea life even a Pye was welcome.

" I'm so glad you came up," Anne said sincerely.

" You've been crying," remarked Josie, with aggravating pity. " I suppose you're homesick—some people have so little self-control in that respect. I've no intention of being homesick, I can tell you. Town's too jolly after that poky old Avonlea. I wonder how I ever existed there so long. You shouldn't cry, Anne ; it isn't becoming, for your nose and eyes get red, and then you seem *all* red. I'd a perfectly scrumptious time in the Academy to-day. Our French professor is simply a duck. His moustache would give you kerwollops of the heart. Have you anything eatable around, Anne? I'm literally starving. Ah, I guessed likely Marilla'd load you up with cake. That's why I called round. Otherwise I'd have gone to the park to hear the band play with Frank Stockley. He boards same place as I do, and he's a sport. He noticed you in class to-day, and asked me who the red-headed girl was. I told him you were an orphan that the Cuthberts had adopted, and nobody knew very much about what you'd been before that."

Anne was wondering if, after all, solitude and tears were not more satisfactory than Josie Pye's companion-ship when Jane and Ruby appeared, each with an inch of Queen's colour ribbon—purple and scarlet—pinned proudly to her coat. As Josie was not ' speaking ' to Jane just then she had to subside into comparative harmlessness.

" Well," said Jane with a sigh, " I feel as if I'd lived many moons since the morning. I ought to be home studying my Virgil—that horrid old professor gave us twenty lines to start in on to-morrow. But I simply couldn't settle down to study to-night. Anne, methinks I see the traces of tears. If you've been crying *do* own up. It will restore my self-respect, for I was shedding tears freely before Ruby came along. I don't mind being a goose so much if somebody else is goosey, too. Cake? You'll give me a teeny piece, won't you? Thank you. It has the real Avonlea flavour."

Ruby, perceiving the Queen's calendar lying on the table, wanted to know if Anne meant to try for the gold medal.

Anne blushed and admitted she was thinking of it.

" Oh, that reminds me," said Josie, " Queen's is to get one of the Avery scholarships after all. The word

came to-day. Frank Stockley told me—his uncle is
one of the board of governors, you know. It will be
announced in the Academy to-morrow."

An Avery scholarship! Anne felt her heart beat
more quickly, and the horizons of her ambition shifted
and broadened as if by magic. Before Josie had told
the news Anne's highest pinnacle of aspiration had
been a teacher's provincial licence, Class First, at the
end of the year, and perhaps the medal! But now in
one moment Anne saw herself winning the Avery
scholarship, taking an Arts course at Redmond College,
and graduating in a gown and mortar-board, all before
the echo of Josie's words had died away. For the
Avery scholarship was in English, and Anne felt that
here her foot was on her native heath.

A wealthy manufacturer of New Brunswick had
died and left part of his fortune to endow a large
number of scholarships to be distributed among the
various high schools and academies of the Maritime
Provinces, according to their respective standings.
There had been much doubt whether one would be
allotted to Queen's, but the matter was settled at last,
and at the end of the year the graduate who made the
highest mark in English and English Literature would
win the scholarship—two hundred and fifty dollars
a year for four years at Redmond College. No wonder
that Anne went to bed that night with tingling cheeks!

" I'll win that scholarship if hard work can do it,"
she resolved. " Wouldn't Matthew be proud if I got
to be a B.A. ? Oh, it's delightful to have ambitions.
I'm so glad I have such a lot. And there never seems
to be any end to them—that's the best of it. Just
as soon as you attain to one ambition you see another
one glittering higher up still. It does make life so
interesting."

CHAPTER XXXV

THE WINTER AT QUEEN'S

ANNE'S homesickness wore off, greatly helped in the wearing by her week-end visits home. As long as the open weather lasted the Avonlea students went out to Carmody on the new branch railway every Friday night. Diana and several other Avonlea young folks were generally on hand to meet them and they all walked over to Avonlea in a merry party. Anne thought those Friday evening gipsyings over the autumnal hills in the crisp golden air, with the homelights of Avonlea twinkling beyond, were the best and dearest hours in the whole week.

Gilbert Blythe nearly always walked with Ruby Gillis and carried her satchel for her. Ruby was a very handsome young lady, now thinking herself quite as grown up as she really was ; she wore her skirts as long as her mother would let her and did her hair up in town, though she had to take it down when she went home. She had large, bright blue eyes, a brilliant complexion, and a plump showy figure. She laughed a great deal, was cheerful and good-tempered, and enjoyed the pleasant things of life frankly.

" But I shouldn't think she was the sort of girl Gilbert would like," whispered Jane to Anne. Anne did not think so either, but she would not have said so for the Avery scholarship. She could not help thinking, too, that it would be very pleasant to have such a friend as Gilbert to jest and chatter with and exchange ideas about books and studies and ambitions. Gilbert had ambitions, she knew, and Ruby Gillis did not seem the sort of person with whom such could be profitably discussed.

There was no silly sentiment in Anne's ideas concerning Gilbert. Boys were to her, when she thought about them at all, merely possible good comrades. If she and Gilbert had been friends she would not have cared how many other friends he had nor with whom he walked. She had a genius for friendship; girl friends she had in plenty; but she had a vague consciousness that masculine friendship might also be a good thing to round out one's conceptions of companionship and furnish broader standpoints of judgment and comparison. Not that Anne could have put her feelings on the matter into just such clear definition. But she thought that if Gilbert had ever walked home with her from the train, over the crisp fields and along the ferny byways, they might have had many and merry and interesting conversations about the new world that was opening around them and their hopes and ambitions therein. Gilbert was a clever young fellow, with his own thoughts about things and a determination to get the best out of life and put the best into it. Ruby Gillis told Jane Andrews that she didn't understand half the things Gilbert Blythe said; he talked just like Anne Shirley did when she had a thoughtful fit on and for her part she didn't think it any fun to be bothering about books and that sort of thing when you didn't have to. Frank Stockley had lots more dash and go, but then he wasn't half as good-looking as Gilbert, and she really couldn't decide which she liked best !

In the Academy Anne gradually drew a little circle of friends about her, thoughtful, imaginative, ambitious students like herself. With the " rose-red " girl, Stella Maynard, and the " dream girl," Priscilla Grant, she soon became intimate, finding the latter pale spiritual-looking maiden to be full to the brim of mischief and pranks and fun, while the vivid, black-eyed Stella had a heartful of wistful dreams and fancies, as aerial and rainbow-like as Anne's own.

After the Christmas holidays the Avonlea students gave up going home on Fridays and settled down to hard work. By this time all the Queen's scholars had gravitated into their own places in the ranks and the various classes had assumed distinct and settled shadings of individuality. Certain facts had become generally accepted. It was admitted that the medal contestants had practically narrowed down to three —Gilbert Blythe, Anne Shirley, and Lewis Wilson; the Avery scholarship was more doubtful, any one of a certain six being a possible winner. The bronze medal for mathematics was considered as good as won by a fat, funny little up-country boy with a bumpy forehead and a patched coat.

Ruby Gillis was the handsomest girl of the year at the Academy; in the Second Year classes Stella Maynard carried off the palm for beauty, with a small but critical minority in favour of Anne Shirley. Ethel Marr was admitted by all competent judges to have the most stylish modes of hair-dressing, and Jane Andrews—plain, plodding, conscientious Jane—carried off the honours in the domestic science course. Even Josie Pye attained a certain pre-eminence as the sharpest-tongued young lady in attendance at Queen's. So it may be fairly stated that Miss Stacy's old pupils held their own in the wider arena of the academical course.

Anne worked hard and steadily. Her rivalry with Gilbert was as intense as it had ever been in Avonlea school, although it was not known in the class at large, but somehow the bitterness had gone out of it. Anne no longer wished to win for the sake of defeating Gilbert ; rather, for the proud consciousness of a well-won victory over a worthy foeman. It would be worth while to win, but she no longer thought life would be insupportable if she did not.

In spite of lessons the students found opportunities for pleasant times. Anne spent many of her spare hours at Beechwood and generally ate her Sunday dinners there and went to church with Miss Barry. The latter was, as she admitted, growing old, but her black eyes were not dim nor the vigour of her tongue in the least abated. But she never sharpened the latter on Anne, who continued to be a prime favourite with the critical old lady.

" That Anne-girl improves all the time," she said. " I get tired of other girls—there is such a provoking and eternal sameness about them. Anne has as many shades as a rainbow and every shade is the prettiest while it lasts. I don't know that she is as amusing as she was when she was a child, but she makes me love her and I like people who make me love them. It saves me so much trouble in making myself love them."

Then, almost before anybody realized it, spring had come ; out in Avonlea the Mayflowers were peeping pinkly out on the sere barrens where snow-wreaths lingered ; and the " mist of green " was on the woods and in the valleys. But in Charlottetown harassed Queen's students thought and talked only of examinations.

" It doesn't seem possible that the term is nearly over," said Anne. " Why, last fall it seemed so long to look forward to—a whole winter of studies and classes. And here we are, with the exams looming up next week. Girls, sometimes I feel as if those exams meant everything, but when I look at the big buds swelling on those chestnut-trees and the misty blue air at the end of the streets they don't seem half so important."

Jane and Ruby and Josie, who had dropped in, did not take this view of it. To them the coming examinations were constantly very important indeed—far more important than chestnut buds or May-time hazes. It was all very well for Anne, who was sure of passing at least, to have her moments of belittling them, but when your whole future depended on them—as the girls truly thought theirs did—you could not regard them philosophically.

" I've lost seven pounds in the last two weeks," sighed Jane. " It's no use to say don't worry. I *will* worry. Worrying helps you some—it seems as if you were doing something when you're worrying. It would be dreadful if I failed to get my licence after going to Queen's all winter and spending so much money."

" *I* don't care," said Josie Pye. " If I don't pass this year I'm coming back next. My father can afford to send me. Anne, Frank Stockley says that Professor Tremaine said Gilbert Blythe was sure to get the medal and that Emily Clay would likely win the Avery scholarship."

" That may make me feel badly to-morrow, Josie," laughed Anne, " but just now I honestly feel that as long as I know the violets are coming out all purple down in the hollow below Green Gables and that little ferns are poking their heads up in Lovers' Lane, it's not a great deal of difference whether I win the Avery or not. I've done my best and I begin to understand what is meant by the ' joy of the strife.' Next to trying and winning, the best thing is trying and failing. Girls, don't talk about exams ! Look at that arch of pale green sky over those houses and picture to yourselves what it must look like over the purply-dark beech-woods back of Avonlea."

"What are you going to wear for commencement, Jane?" asked Ruby practically.

Jane and Josie both answered at once and the chatter drifted into a side eddy of fashions. But Anne, with her elbows on the window sill, her soft cheek laid against her clasped hands, and her eyes filled with visions, looked out unheedingly across city roof and spire to that glorious dome of sunset sky and wove her dreams of a possible future from the golden tissue of youth's own optimism. All the Beyond was hers with its possibilities lurking rosily in the oncoming years—each year a rose of promise to be woven into an immortal chaplet.

CHAPTER XXXVI

THE GLORY AND THE DREAM

ON the morning when the final results of all the examinations were to be posted on the bulletin board at Queen's, Anne and Jane walked down the street together. Jane was smiling and happy; examinations were over and she was comfortably sure she had made a pass at least; further considerations troubled Jane not at all; she had no soaring ambitions and consequently was not affected with the unrest attendant thereon. For we pay a price for everything we get or take in this world; and although ambitions are well worth having, they are not to be cheaply won, but exact their dues of work and self-denial, anxiety and discouragement. Anne was pale and quiet; in ten more minutes she would know who had won the medal and who the Avery. Beyond those ten minutes there did not seem, just then, to be anything worth being called Time.

"Of course you'll win one of them anyhow," said Jane, who couldn't understand how the faculty could be so unfair as to order it otherwise.

"I have no hope of the Avery," said Anne. "Everybody says Emily Clay will win it. And I'm not going to march up to that bulletin board and look at it before everybody. I haven't the moral courage I'm going straight to the girls' dressing-room. You must read the announcements and then come and tell me, Jane. And I implore you in the name of our old friendship to do it as quickly as possible. If I have failed just say so, without trying to break it gently;

and whatever you do *don't* sympathize with me. Promise me this, Jane."

Jane promised solemnly ; but, as it happened, there was no necessity for such a promise. When they went up the entrance steps of Queen's they found the hall full of boys who were carrying Gilbert Blythe around on their shoulders and yelling at the tops of their voices, " Hurrah for Blythe, Medallist ! "

For a moment Anne felt one sickening pang of defeat and disappointment. So she had failed and Gilbert had won ! Well, Matthew would be sorry—he had been so sure she would win.

And then !

Somebody called out :

" Three cheers for Miss Shirley, winner of the Avery ! "

" Oh, Anne," gasped Jane, as they fled to the girls' dressing-room amid hearty cheers. " Oh, Anne, I'm so proud ! Isn't it splendid ? "

And then the girls were around them and Anne was the centre of a laughing, congratulating group. Her shoulders were thumped and her hands shaken vigorously. She was pushed and pulled and hugged and among it all she managed to whisper to Jane :

" Oh, won't Matthew and Marilla be pleased ! I must write the news home right away."

Commencement was the next important happening. The exercises were held in the big assembly hall of the Academy. Addresses were given, essays read, songs sung, the public award of diplomas, prizes and medals made.

Matthew and Marilla were there, with eyes and ears for only one student on the platform—a tall girl in pale green, with faintly flushed cheeks and starry eyes, who read the best essay and was pointed out and whispered about as the Avery winner.

" Reckon you're glad we kept her, Marilla ? " whispered Matthew, speaking for the first time since he had entered the hall, when Anne had finished her essay.

" It's not the first time I've been glad," retorted Marilla. " You do like to rub things in, Matthew Cuthbert."

Miss Barry, who was sitting behind them, leaned forward and poked Marilla in the back with her parasol.

" Aren't you proud of that Anne-girl ? I am," she said.

Anne went home to Avonlea with Matthew and Marilla that evening. She had not been home since April and she felt that she could not wait another day. The apple-blossoms were out and the world was fresh and young. Diana was at Green Gables to meet her. In her own white room, where Marilla had set a flowering house-rose on the window sill, Anne looked about her and drew a long breath of happiness.

" Oh, Diana, it's so good to be back again. It's so good to see those pointed firs coming out against the pink sky—and that white orchard and the old Snow Queen. Isn't the breath of the mint delicious ? And that tea-rose—why, it's a song and a hope and a prayer all in one. And it's *good* to see you again, Diana ! "

" I thought you liked that Stella Maynard better than me," said Diana reproachfully. " Josie Pye told me you did. Josie said you were *infatuated* with her."

Anne laughed and pelted Diana with the faded " June lilies " of her bouquet.

" Stella Maynard is the dearest girl in the world except one and you are that one, Diana," she said. " I love you more than ever—and I've so many things to tell you. But just now I feel as if it were joy enough to sit here and look at you. I'm tired, I think—tired of being studious and ambitious. I mean to spend at least two hours to-morrow lying out in the orchard grass, thinking of absolutely nothing."

" You've done splendidly, Anne. I suppose you won't be teaching now that you've won the Avery ? "

" No. I'm going to Redmond in September. Doesn't it seem wonderful ? I'll have a brand-new stock of ambition laid in by that time after three glorious, golden months of vacation. Jane and Ruby are going to teach. Isn't it splendid to think we all got through even to Moody Spurgeon and Josie Pye ? "

" The Newbridge trustees have offered Jane their school already," said Diana. " Gilbert Blythe is going to teach, too. He has to. His father can't afford to send him to college next year, after all, so he means to earn his own way through. I expect he'll get the school here if Miss Ames decides to leave."

Anne felt a queer little sensation of dismayed surprise. She had not known this ; she had expected that Gilbert would be going to Redmond also. What would she do without their inspiring rivalry ? Would not work, even at a co-educational college with a real degree in prospect, be rather flat without her friend the enemy ?

The next morning at breakfast it suddenly struck Anne that Matthew was not looking well. Surely he was much greyer than he had been a year before.

" Marilla," she said hesitatingly when he had gone out, " is Matthew quite well ? "

" No, he isn't," said Marilla in a troubled tone. " He's had some real bad spells with his heart this spring and he won't spare himself a mite. I've been real worried about him, but he's some better this while back and we've got a good hired man, so I'm hoping he'll kind of rest and pick up. Maybe he will now you're home. You always cheer him up."

Anne leaned across the table and took Marilla's face in her hands.

" You are not looking as well yourself as I'd like to see you, Marilla. You look tired. I'm afraid you've been working too hard. You must take a rest, now that I'm home. I'm just going to take this one day off to visit all the dear old spots and hunt up my old dreams, and then it will be your turn to be lazy while I do the work."

Marilla smiled affectionately at her girl.

" It's not the work—it's my head. I've a pain so often now—behind my eyes. Doctor Spencer's been fussing with glasses, but they don't do me any good. There is a distinguished oculist coming to the Island the last of June and the doctor says I must see him. I guess I'll have to. I can't read or sew with any comfort now. Well, Anne, you've done real well at Queen's I must say. To take First Class Licence in one year and win the Avery scholarship—well, well, Mrs Lynde says pride goes before a fall and she doesn't believe in the higher education of women at all ; she says it unfits them for woman's true sphere. I don't believe a word of it. Speaking of Rachel reminds me —did you hear anything about the Abbey Bank lately, Anne ? "

" I heard that it was shaky," answered Anne. " Why ? "

" That is what Rachel said. She was up here one day last week and said there was some talk about it. Matthew felt real worried. All we have saved is in that bank—every penny. I wanted Matthew to put it in the Savings Bank in the first place, but old Mr Abbey was a great friend of father's and he'd always banked with him. Matthew said any bank with him at the head of it was good enough for anybody."

" I think he has only been its nominal head for

many years," said Anne. "He is a very old man; his nephews are really at the head of the institution."

"Well, when Rachel told us that, I wanted Matthew to draw our money right out and he said he'd think of it. But Mr Russell told him yesterday that the bank was all right."

Anne had her good day in the companionship of the outdoor world. She never forgot that day; it was so bright and golden and fair, so free from shadow and so lavish of blossom. Anne spent some of its rich hours in the orchard; she went to the Dryad's Bubble and Willowmere and Violet Vale; she called at the manse and had a satisfying talk with Mrs Allan; and finally in the evening she went with Matthew for the cows, through Lovers' Lane to the back pasture. The woods were all gloried through with sunset and the warm splendour of it streamed down through the hill gaps in the west. Matthew walked slowly with bent head; Anne, tall and erect, suited her springing step to his.

"You've been working too hard to-day, Matthew," she said reproachfully. "Why won't you take things easier?"

"Well now, I can't seem to," said Matthew, as he opened the yard gate to let the cows through. "It's only that I'm getting old, Anne, and keep forgetting it. Well, well, I've always worked pretty hard and I'd rather drop in harness."

"If I had been the boy you sent for," said Anne wistfully, "I'd be able to help you so much now and spare you in a hundred ways. I could find it in my heart to wish I had been, just for that."

"Well now, I'd rather have you than a dozen boys, Anne," said Matthew patting her hand. "Just mind you that—rather than a dozen boys. Well now, I guess it wasn't a boy that took the Avery scholarship, was it ? It was a girl—my girl—my girl that I'm proud of."

He smiled his shy smile at her as he went into the yard. Anne took the memory of it with her when she went to her room that night and sat for a long while at her open window, thinking of the past and dreaming of the future. Outside the Snow Queen was mistily white in the moonshine ; the frogs were singing in the marsh beyond Orchard Slope. Anne always remembered the silvery, peaceful beauty and fragrant calm of that night. It was the last night before sorrow touched her life ; and no life is ever quite the same again when once that cold, sanctifying touch has been laid upon it.

CHAPTER XXXVII

THE REAPER WHOSE NAME IS DEATH

"MATTHEW—Matthew—what is the matter? Matthew, are you sick?"

It was Marilla who spoke, alarm in every jerky word. Anne came through the hall, her hands full of white narcissus,—it was long before Anne could love the sight or odour of white narcissus again,— in time to hear her and to see Matthew standing in the porch doorway, a folded paper in his hand, and his face strangely drawn and grey. Anne dropped her flowers and sprang across the kitchen to him at the same moment as Marilla. They were both too late; before they could reach him Matthew had fallen across the threshold.

"He's fainted," gasped Marilla. "Anne, run for Martin—quick, quick! He's at the barn."

Martin, the hired man, who had just driven home from the post office, started at once for the doctor, calling at Orchard Slope on his way to send Mr and Mrs Barry over. Mrs Lynde, who was there on an errand, came too. They found Anne and Marilla distractedly trying to restore Matthew to consciousness.

Mrs Lynde pushed them gently aside, tried his pulse, and then laid her ear over his heart. She looked at their anxious faces sorrowfully and the tears came into her eyes.

"Oh, Marilla," she said gravely. "I don't think— we can do anything for him."

"Mrs Lynde, you don't think—you can't think

Matthew is—is—" Anne could not say the dreadful word ; she turned sick and pallid.

" Child, yes, I'm afraid of it. Look at his face. When you've seen that look as often as I have you'll know what it means."

Anne looked at the still face and there beheld the seal of the Great Presence.

When the doctor came he said that death had been instantaneous and probably painless, caused in all likelihood by some sudden shock. The secret of the shock was discovered to be in the paper Matthew had held and which Martin had brought from the office that morning. It contained an account of the failure of the Abbey Bank.

The news spread quickly through Avonlea, and all day friends and neighbours thronged Green Gables and came and went on errands of kindness for the dead and living. For the first time shy, quiet Matthew Cuthbert was a person of central importance ; the white majesty of death had fallen on him and set him apart as one crowned.

When the calm night came softly down over Green Gables the old house was hushed and tranquil. In the parlour lay Matthew Cuthbert in his coffin, his long grey hair framing his placid face on which there was a little kindly smile as if he but slept, dreaming pleasant dreams. There were flowers about him— sweet old-fashioned flowers which his mother had planted in the homestead garden in her bridal days and for which Matthew had always had a secret, wordless love. Anne had gathered them and brought them to him, her anguished, tearless eyes burning in her white face. It was the last thing she could do for him.

The Barrys and Mrs Lynde stayed with them that night. Diana, going to the east gable, where Anne was standing at her window, said gently :

" Anne dear, would you like to have me sleep with you to-night ? "

" Thank you, Diana." Anne looked earnestly into her friend's face. " I think you won't misunderstand me when I say that I want to be alone. I'm not afraid. I haven't been alone one minute since it happened—and I want to be. I want to be quite silent and quiet and try to realize it. I *can't* realize it. Half the time it seems to me that Matthew can't be dead ; and the other half it seems as if he must have been dead for a long time and I've had this horrible dull ache ever since."

Diana did not quite understand. Marilla's impassioned grief, breaking all the bounds of natural reserve and lifelong habit in its stormy rush, she could comprehend better than Anne's tearless agony. But she went away kindly, leaving Anne alone to keep her first vigil with sorrow.

Anne hoped that tears would come in solitude. It seemed to her a terrible thing that she could not shed a tear for Matthew, whom she had loved so much and who had been so kind to her, Matthew, who had walked with her last evening at sunset and was now lying in the dim room below with that awful peace on his brow. But no tears came at first, even when she knelt by her window in the darkness and prayed, looking up to the stars beyond the hills—no tears, only the same horrible dull ache of misery that kept on aching until she fell asleep, worn out with the day's pain and excitement.

In the night she awakened, with the stillness and the darkness about her, and the recollection of the day came over her like a wave of sorrow. She could see Matthew's face smiling at her as he had smiled when they parted at the gate that last evening—she could hear his voice saying, " My girl—my girl that I'm proud of." Then the tears came and Anne wept her heart out. Marilla heard her and crept in to comfort her.

" There—there—don't cry so, dearie. It can't bring him back. It—it—isn't right to cry so. I knew that to-day, but I couldn't help it then. He'd always been such a good, kind brother to me—but God knows best."

" Oh, just let me cry, Marilla," sobbed Anne. " The tears don't hurt me like that ache did. Stay here for a little while with me and keep your arm round me— so. I couldn't have Diana stay, she's good and kind and sweet—but it's not her sorrow—she's outside of it and she couldn't come close enough to my heart to help me. It's our sorrow—yours and mine. Oh, Marilla, what will we do without him ? "

" We've got each other, Anne. I don't know what I'd do if you weren't here—if you'd never come. Oh, Anne, I know I've been kind of strict and harsh with you maybe—but you mustn't think I didn't love you as well as Matthew did, for all that. I want to tell you now when I can. It's never been easy for me to say things out of my heart, but at times like this it's easier. I love you as dear as if you were my own flesh and blood and you've been my joy and comfort ever since you came to Green Gables."

Two days afterwards they carried Matthew Cuthbert over his homestead threshold and away from the fields he had tilled and the orchards he had loved and the trees he had planted ; and then Avonlea settled back to its usual placidity and even at Green Gables affairs slipped into their old groove and work was done and duties fulfilled with regularity as before, although always with the aching sense of " loss in all familiar things." Anne, new to grief, thought it almost sad that it could be so—that they *could* go on in the old way without Matthew. She felt something like shame and remorse when she discovered that the sunrises behind the firs and the pale pink buds opening in the garden gave her the old inrush of gladness when she saw them—that Diana's visits were pleasant to her and that Diana's merry words and ways moved her to laughter and smiles—that, in brief, the beautiful world of blossom and love and friendship had lost none of its power to please her fancy and thrill her heart, that life still called to her with many insistent voices.

" It seems like disloyalty to Matthew, somehow, to find pleasure in these things now that he has gone," she said wistfully to Mrs Allan one evening when they were together in the manse garden. " I miss him so much—all the time—and yet, Mrs Allan, the world and life seem very beautiful and interesting to me for all. To-day Diana said something funny and I found myself laughing. I thought when it happened I could never laugh again. And it somehow seems as if I oughtn't to."

" When Matthew was here he liked to hear you laugh and he liked to know that you found pleasure in the pleasant things around you," said Mrs Allan gently. " He is just away now ; and he likes to know it just the same. I am sure we should not shut our hearts against the healing influences that nature offers us. But I understand your feeling. I think we all experience the same thing. We resent the thought that anything can please us when some one we love is no longer here to share the pleasure with us, and we almost feel as if we were unfaithful to our sorrow when we find our interest in life returning to us."

" I was down to the graveyard to plant a rosebush on Matthew's grave this afternoon," said Anne dreamily. " I took a slip of the little white Scotch rose-bush his mother brought out from Scotland long ago; Matthew always liked those roses the best—they were so small and sweet on their thorny stems. It made me feel glad that I could plant it by his grave —as if I were doing something that must please him in taking it there to be near him. I hope he has roses like them in heaven. Perhaps the souls of all those little white roses that he has loved so many summers were all there to meet him. I must go home now. Marilla is all alone and she gets lonely at twilight."

" She will be lonelier still, I fear, when you go away again to college," said Mrs Allan.

Anne did not reply; she said good night and went slowly back to Green Gables. Marilla was sitting on the front door-steps and Anne sat down beside her. The door was open behind them, held back by a big pink conch-shell with hints of sea sunsets in its smooth inner convolutions.

Anne gathered some sprays of pale yellow honey-suckle and put them in her hair. She liked the delicious hint of fragrance, as of some aerial benediction, above her every time she moved.

" Doctor Spencer was here while you were away," Marilla said. " He says that the specialist will be in town to-morrow and he insists that I must go in and have my eyes examined. I suppose I'd better go and have it over. I'll be more than thankful if the man can give me the right kind of glasses to suit my eyes. You won't mind staying here alone while I'm away, will you ? Martin will have to drive me in and there's ironing and baking to do."

" I shall be all right. Diana will come over for company for me. I shall attend to the ironing and baking beautifully—you needn't fear that I'll starch the handkerchiefs or flavour the cake with liniment."

Marilla laughed.

" What a girl you were for making mistakes in them days, Anne. You were always getting into scrapes. I did use to think you were possessed. Do you mind the time you dyed your hair ? "

" Yes, indeed. I shall never forget it," smiled Anne, touching the heavy braid of hair that was wound about her shapely head. " I laugh a little now sometimes when I think what a worry my hair used to be to me—but I don't laugh *much*, because it was a very real trouble then. I did suffer terribly over my hair and my freckles. My freckles are really gone ; and people are nice enough to tell me my hair is auburn now—all but Josie Pye. She informed me yesterday that she really thought it was redder than ever, or at least my black dress made it look redder, and she asked me if people who had red hair ever got used to having it. Marilla, I've almost decided to give up trying to like Josie Pye. I've made what I would once have called a heroic effort to like her, but Josie Pye won't *be* liked."

" Josie is a Pye," said Marilla sharply, " so she can't help being disagreeable. I suppose people of that kind serve some useful purpose in society, but I must say I don't know what it is any more than I know the use of thistles. Is Josie going to teach ? "

" No, she is going back to Queen's next year. So are Moody Spurgeon and Charlie Sloane. Jane and Ruby are going to teach and they have both got schools—Jane at Newbridge and Ruby at some place up west."

" Gilbert Blythe is going to teach too, isn't he ? "

" Yes "—briefly.

" What a nice-looking young fellow he is," said Marilla absently. " I saw him in church last Sunday and he seemed so tall and manly. He looks a lot like his father did at the same age. John Blythe was a nice boy. We used to be real good friends, he and I. People called him my beau."

Anne looked up with swift interest.

" Oh Marilla—and what happened ?—why didn't you——"

" We had a quarrel. I wouldn't forgive him when he asked me to. I meant to, after awhile—but I was sulky and angry and I wanted to punish him first. He never came back—the Blythes were all mighty independent. But I always felt—rather sorry. I've always kind of wished I'd forgiven him when I had the chance."

" So you've had a bit of romance in your life, too," said Anne softly.

" Yes, I suppose you might call it that. You wouldn't think so to look at me, would you ? But you never can tell about people from their outsides. Everybody has forgot about me and John. I'd forgotten myself. But it all came back to me when I saw Gilbert last Sunday."

CHAPTER XXXVIII

THE BEND IN THE ROAD

MARILLA went to town the next day and returned in the evening. Anne had gone over to Orchard Slope with Diana and came back to find Marilla in the kitchen, sitting by the table with her head leaning on her hand. Something in her dejected attitude struck a chill to Anne's heart. She had never seen Marilla sit limply inert like that.

" Are you very tired, Marilla ? "

" Yes—no—I don't know," said Marilla wearily, looking up. " I suppose I am tired but I haven't thought about it. It's not that."

" Did you see the oculist ? What did he say ? " asked Anne anxiously.

" Yes, I saw him. He examined my eyes. He says that if I give up all reading and sewing entirely and any kind of work that strains the eyes, and if I'm careful not to cry, and if I wear the glasses he's given me he thinks my eyes may not get any worse and my headaches will be cured. But if I don't he says I'll certainly be stone blind in six months. Blind ! Anne, just think of it ! "

For a minute Anne, after her first quick exclamation of dismay, was silent. It seemed to her that she could *not* speak. Then she said bravely, but with a catch in her voice :

" Marilla, *don't* think of it. You know he has given you hope. If you are careful you won't lose your sight altogether ; and if his glasses cure your headaches it will be a great thing."

" I don't call it much hope," said Marilla bitterly.
" What am I to live for if I can't read or sew or do
anything like that ? I might as well be blind—or
dead. And as for crying, I can't help that when I
get lonesome. But there, it's no good talking about it.
If you'll get me a cup of tea I'll be thankful. I'm
about done out. Don't say anything about this to
anyone for a spell yet, anyway. I can't bear that
folks should come here to question and sympathize
and talk about it."

When Marilla had eaten her lunch Anne persuaded
her to go to bed. Then Anne went herself to the east
gable and sat down by her window in the darkness
alone with her tears and her heaviness of heart. How
sadly things had changed since she had sat there the
night after coming home ! Then she had been full of
hope and joy and the future had looked rosy with
promise. Anne felt as if she had lived years since
then, but before she went to bed there was a smile on
her lips and peace in her heart. She had looked her
duty courageously in the face and found it a friend—
as duty ever is when we meet it frankly.

One afternoon a few days later Marilla came slowly
in from the yard where she had been talking to a
caller—a man whom Anne knew by sight as John
Sadler from Carmody. Anne wondered what he could
have been saying to bring that look to Marilla's face.

" What did Mr. Sadler want, Marilla ? "

Marilla sat down by the window and looked at
Anne. There were tears in her eyes in defiance of the
oculist's prohibition and her voice broke as she said :

" He heard that I was going to sell Green Gables
and he wants to buy it."

" Buy it ! Buy Green Gables ? " Anne wondered
if she had heard aright. " Oh, Marilla, you don't mean
to sell Green Gables ! "

" Anne, I don't know what else is to be done. I've thought it all over. If my eyes were strong I could stay here and make out to look after things and manage, with a good hired man. But as it is I can't. I may lose my sight altogether ; and anyway I'll not be fit to run things. Oh, I never thought I'd live to see the day when I'd have to sell my home. But things would only go behind worse and worse all the time, till nobody would want to buy it. Every cent of our money went in that bank ; and there's some notes Matthew gave last fall to pay. Mrs Lynde advises me to sell the farm and board somewhere— with her I suppose. It won't bring much—it's small and the buildings are old. But it'll be enough for me to live on I reckon. I'm thankful you're provided for with that scholarship, Anne. I'm sorry you won't have a home to come to in your vacations, that's all, but I suppose you'll manage somehow."

Marilla broke down and wept bitterly.

" You mustn't sell Green Gables," said Anne resolutely.

" Oh, Anne, I wish I didn't have to. But you can see for yourself. I can't stay here alone. I'd go crazy with trouble and loneliness. And my sight would go —I know it would."

" You won't have to stay here alone, Marilla. I'll be with you. I'm not going to Redmond."

" Not going to Redmond ! " Marilla lifted her worn face from her hands and looked at Anne. " Why, what do you mean ? "

" Just what I say. I'm not going to take the scholarship. I decided so the night after you came home from town. You surely don't think I could leave you alone in your trouble, Marilla, after all you've done for me. I've been thinking and planning. Let me tell you my plans. Mr Barry wants to rent the farm for next year. So you won't have any bother over that. And I'm going to teach. I've applied for the school here—but I don't expect to get it for I understand the trustees have promised it to Gilbert Blythe. But I can have the Carmody School—Mr Blair told me so last night at the store. Of course that won't be quite as nice or convenient as if I had the Avonlea school. But I can board home and drive myself over to Carmody and back, in the warm weather at least. And even in winter I can come home on Fridays. We'll keep a horse for that. Oh, I have it all planned out, Marilla. And I'll read to you and keep you cheered up. You sha'n't be dull or lonesome. And we'll be real cosy and happy here together, you and I."

Marilla had listened like a woman in a dream.

" Oh, Anne, I could get on real well if you were here, I know. But I can't let you sacrifice yourself so for me. It would be terrible."

" Nonsense!" Anne laughed merrily. "There is no sacrifice. Nothing could be worse than giving up Green Gables—nothing could hurt me more. We must keep the dear old place. My mind is quite made up, Marilla. I'm *not* going to Redmond ; and I *am* going to stay here and teach. Don't you worry about me a bit."

" But your ambitions—and——"

" I'm just as ambitious as ever. Only, I've changed the object of my ambitions. I'm going to be a good teacher—and I'm going to save your eyesight. Besides, I mean to study at home here and take a little college course all by myself. Oh, I've dozens of plans, Marilla. I've been thinking them out for a week. I shall give life here my best, and I believe it will give its best to me in return. When I left Queen's my future seemed to stretch out before me like a straight road. I thought I could see along it for many a mile-stone. Now there is a bend in it. I don't know what lies around the bend, but I'm going to believe that the best does. It has a fascination of its own, that bend, Marilla. I wonder how the road beyond it goes—what there is of green glory and soft, check-ered light and shadows—what new landscapes—what new beauties—what curves and hills and valleys far-ther on."

" I don't feel as if I ought to let you give it up," said Marilla, referring to the scholarship.

" But you can't prevent me. I'm sixteen and a half, ' obstinate as a mule,' as Mrs Lynde once told me," laughed Anne. " Oh, Marilla, don't you go pitying me. I don't like to be pitied, and there is no need for it. I'm heart glad over the very thought of stay-ing at dear Green Gables. Nobody could love it as you and I do—so we must keep it."

" You blessed girl ! " said Marilla, yielding. " I feel as if you'd given me new life. I guess I ought to stick out and make you go to college—but I know I can't, so I ain't going to try. I'll make it up to you though, Anne."

When it became noised abroad in Avonlea that Anne Shirley had given up the idea of going to college and intended to stay home and teach there was a good deal of discussion over it. Most of the good folks, not knowing about Marilla's eyes, thought she was foolish. Mrs Allan did not. She told Anne so in approving words that brought tears of pleasure to the girl's eyes. Neither did good Mrs Lynde. She came up one evening and found Anne and Marilla sitting at the front door in the warm, scented summer dusk. They liked to sit there when the twilight came down and the white moths flew about in the garden and the odour of mint filled the dewy air.

Mrs Rachel deposited her substantial person upon the stone bench by the door, behind which grew a row of tall pink and yellow hollyhocks, with a long breath of mingled weariness and relief.

" I declare I'm glad to sit down. I've been on my feet all day, and two hundred pounds is a good bit for two feet to carry round. It's a great blessing not to be fat, Marilla. I hope you appreciate it. Well, Anne, I hear you've given up your notion of going to college. I was real glad to hear it. You've got as much education now as a woman can be comfortable with. I don't believe in girls going to college with the men and cramming their heads full of Latin and Greek and all that nonsense."

" But I'm going to study Latin and Greek just the same, Mrs Lynde," said Anne laughing. " I'm going to take my Arts course right here at Green Gables, and study everything that I would at college."

Mrs Lynde lifted her hands in holy horror.

" Anne Shirley, you'll kill yourself."

" Not a bit of it. I shall thrive on it. Oh, I'm not going to overdo things. As ' Josiah Allen's wife ' says, I shall be ' mejum.' But I'll have lots of spare time in the long winter evenings, and I've no vocation for fancy work. I'm going to teach over at Carmody, you know."

" I don't know it. I guess you're going to teach right here in Avonlea. The trustees have decided to give you the school."

" Mrs Lynde ! " cried Anne, springing to her feet in her surprise. " Why, I thought they had promised it to Gilbert Blythe ! "

" So they did. But as soon as Gilbert heard that you had applied for it he went to them—they had a business meeting at the school last night, you know —and told them that he withdrew his application, and suggested that they accept yours. He said he was going to teach at White Sands. Of course he gave up the school just to oblige you, because he knew how much you wanted to stay with Marilla, and I must say I think it was real kind and thoughtful in him, that's what. Real self-sacrificing, too, for he'll have his board to pay at White Sands, and everybody knows he's got to earn his own way through college. So the trustees decided to take you. I was tickled to death when Thomas came home and told me."

" I don't feel that I ought to take it," murmured Anne. " I mean—I don't think I ought to let Gilbert make such a sacrifice for—for me."

" I guess you can't prevent him now. He's signed papers with the White Sands trustees. So it wouldn't do him any good now if you were to refuse. Of course you'll take the school. You'll get along all right, now that there are no Pyes going. Josie was the last of them, and a good thing she was, that's what. There's been some Pye or other going to Avonlea school for the last twenty years, and I guess their mission in life was to keep school-teachers reminded that earth isn't their home. Bless my heart! What does all that winking and blinking at the Barry gable mean ? "

" Diana is signalling for me to go over," laughed Anne. " You know we keep up the old custom. Excuse me while I run over and see what she wants."

Anne ran down the clover slope like a deer, and disappeared in the firry shadows of the Haunted Wood. Mrs Lynde looked after her indulgently.

" There's a good deal of the child about her yet in some ways."

" There's a good deal more of the woman about her in others," retorted Marilla, with a momentary return of her old crispness.

But crispness was no longer Marilla's distinguishing characteristic. As Mrs Lynde told her Thomas that night.

"Marilla Cuthbert has got *mellow*. That's what."

Anne went to the little Avonlea graveyard the next evening to put fresh flowers on Matthew's grave and water the Scotch rose-bush. She lingered there until dusk, liking the peace and calm of the little place, with its poplars whose rustle was like low, friendly speech, and its whispering grasses growing at will among the graves. When she finally left it and walked down the long hill that sloped to the Lake of Shining Waters it was past sunset and all Avonlea lay before her in a dreamlike afterlight—" a haunt of ancient peace." There was a freshness in the air as of a wind that had blown over honey-sweet fields of clover. Home lights twinkled out here and there among the homestead trees. Beyond lay the sea, misty and purple, with its haunting, unceasing murmur. The west was a glory of soft mingled hues, and the pond reflected them all in still softer shadings. The beauty of it all thrilled Anne's heart, and she gratefully opened the gates of her soul to it.

" Dear old world," she murmured, " you are very lovely, and I am glad to be alive in you."

Half-way down the hill a tall lad came whistling out of a gate before the Blythe homestead. It was Gilbert, and the whistle died on his lips as he recognized Anne. He lifted his cap courteously, but he would have passed on in silence, if Anne had not stopped and held out her hand.

" Gilbert," she said, with scarlet cheeks, " I want to thank you for giving up the school for me. It was very good of you—and I want you to know that I appreciate it."

Gilbert took the offered hand eagerly.

" It wasn't particularly good of me at all, Anne. I was pleased to be able to do you some small service. Are we going to be friends after this ? Have you really forgiven me my old fault ? "

Anne laughed and tried unsuccessfully to withdraw her hand.

" I forgave you that day by the pond landing, although I didn't know it. What a stubborn little goose I was. I've been—I may as well make a complete confession—I've been sorry ever since."

" We are going to be the best of friends," said Gilbert, jubilantly. " We were born to be good friends, Anne. You've thwarted destiny long enough. I know we can help each other in many ways. You are going to keep up your studies, aren't you ? So am I. Come, I'm going to walk home with you."

Marilla looked curiously at Anne when the latter entered the kitchen.

" Who was that came up the lane with you, Anne ? "

" Gilbert Blythe," answered Anne, vexed to find herself blushing. " I met him on Barry's hill."

" I didn't think you and Gilbert Blythe were such good friends that you'd stand for half an hour at the gate talking to him," said Marilla, with a dry smile.

" We haven't been—we've been good enemies. But we have decided that it will be much more sensible to be good friends in future. Were we really there half an hour ? It seemed just a few minutes. But, you see, we have five years' lost conversations to catch up with, Marilla."

Anne sat long at her window that night companioned by a glad content. The wind purred softly in the cherry boughs, and the mint breaths came up to her. The stars twinkled over the pointed firs in the hollow and Diana's light gleamed through the old gap.

Anne's horizons had closed in since the night she

had sat there after coming home from Queen's; but if the path set before her feet was to be narrow she knew that flowers of quiet happiness would bloom along it.   The joys of sincere work and worthy aspiration and congenial friendship were to be hers; nothing could rob her of her birthright of fancy or her ideal world of dreams.   And there was always the bend in the road!

" ' God's in his heaven, all's right with the world,' " whispered Anne softly

ANNE
of Avonlea

LUCY MAUD MONTGOMERY

NIMBUS
PUBLISHING LTD.
— NIMBUS.CA —

to
my former teacher,
HATTIE GORDON SMITH
in grateful remembrance of her
sympathy and encouragement

I

An Irate Neighbor

A tall, slim girl, "half-past sixteen," with serious gray eyes and hair which her friends called auburn, had sat down on the broad red sandstone doorstep of a Prince Edward Island farmhouse one ripe afternoon in August, firmly resolved to construe so many lines of Virgil.

But an August afternoon, with blue hazes scarfing the harvest slopes, little winds whispering elfishly in the poplars, and a dancing splendor of red poppies outflaming against the dark coppice of young firs in a corner of the cherry orchard, was fitter for dreams than dead languages. The Virgil soon slipped unheeded to the ground, and Anne, her chin propped on her clasped hands, and her eyes on the splendid mass of fluffy clouds that were heaping up just over Mr. J. A. Harrison's house like a great white mountain, was far away in a delicious world where a certain schoolteacher was doing a wonderful work, shaping the destinies of future statesmen, and inspiring youthful minds and hearts with high and lofty ambitions.

To be sure, if you came down to harsh facts . . . which, it must be confessed, Anne seldom did until she had to . . . it did not seem likely that there was much promising material for celebrities in Avonlea school; but you could never tell what might happen if a teacher used her influence for good. Anne had certain rosetinted ideals of what a teacher might accomplish if she only went the right way about it; and she was in the midst of a delightful scene, forty years hence, with a famous personage . . . just exactly what he was to be famous for was left in convenient haziness, but Anne thought it would be rather nice to have him a college president or a Canadian premier . . . bowing low over her wrinkled hand and assuring her that it was she who had first kindled his ambition, and that all his success in life was due to the lessons she had instilled so long ago in Avonlea school. This pleasant vision was shattered by a most unpleasant interruption.

A demure little Jersey cow came scuttling down the lane and five seconds later Mr. Harrison arrived . . . if "arrived" be not too mild a term to describe the manner of his irruption into the yard.

He bounced over the fence without waiting to open the gate, and angrily confronted astonished Anne, who had risen to her feet and stood looking at him in some bewilderment. Mr. Harrison was their new righthand neighbor and she had never met him before, although she had seen him once or twice.

In early April, before Anne had come home from Queen's, Mr. Robert Bell, whose farm adjoined the Cuthbert place on the west, had sold out and moved to Charlottetown. His farm had been bought by a certain Mr. J. A. Harrison, whose name, and the fact that he was a New Brunswick man, were all that was known about him. But before he had been a month in Avonlea he had won the reputation of being an odd person . . . "a crank," Mrs. Rachel Lynde said. Mrs. Rachel was an outspoken lady, as those of you who may have already made her acquaintance will remember. Mr. Harrison was certainly different from other people . . . and that is the essential characteristic of a crank, as everybody knows.

In the first place he kept house for himself and had publicly stated that he wanted no fools of women around his diggings. Feminine Avonlea took its revenge by the gruesome tales it related about his house-

keeping and cooking. He had hired little John Henry
Carter of White Sands and John Henry started the
stories. For one thing, there was never any stated time
for meals in the Harrison establishment. Mr. Harrison
"got a bite" when he felt hungry, and if John Henry
were around at the time, he came in for a share, but if
he were not, he had to wait until Mr. Harrison's next
hungry spell. John Henry mournfully averred that he
would have starved to death if it wasn't that he got
home on Sundays and got a good filling up, and that
his mother always gave him a basket of "grub" to take
back with him on Monday mornings.

As for washing dishes, Mr. Harrison never made
any pretence of doing it unless a rainy Sunday came.
Then he went to work and washed them all at once in
the rainwater hogshead, and left them to drain dry.

Again, Mr. Harrison was "close." When he was
asked to subscribe to the Rev. Mr. Allan's salary he
said he'd wait and see how many dollars' worth of
good he got out of his preaching first . . . *he* didn't
believe in buying a pig in a poke. And when Mrs.
Lynde went to ask for a contribution to missions . . .
and incidentally to see the inside of the house . . . he
told her there were more heathens among the old
woman gossips in Avonlea than anywhere else he knew
of, and he'd cheerfully contribute to a mission for
Christianizing them if she'd undertake it. Mrs. Rachel
got herself away and said it was a mercy poor Mrs.
Robert Bell was safe in her grave, for it would have
broken her heart to see the state of her house in
which she used to take so much pride.

"Why, she scrubbed the kitchen floor every
second day," Mrs. Lynde told Marilla Cuthbert
indignantly, "and if you could see it now! I had to
hold up my skirts as I walked across it."

Finally, Mr. Harrison kept a parrot called Ginger.
Nobody in Avonlea had ever kept a parrot before;
consequently that proceeding was considered barely
respectable. And such a parrot! If you took John Henry
Carter's word for it, never was such an unholy bird. It

swore terribly. Mrs. Carter would have taken John
Henry away at once if she had been sure she could
get another place for him. Besides, Ginger had bitten a
piece right out of the back of John Henry's neck one
day when he had stooped down too near the cage.
Mrs. Carter showed everybody the mark when the
luckless John Henry went home on Sundays.

All these things flashed through Anne's mind as
Mr. Harrison stood, quite speechless with wrath
apparently, before her. In his most amiable mood Mr.
Harrison could not have been considered a handsome
man; he was short and fat and bald; and now, with his
round face purple with rage and his prominent blue
eyes almost sticking out of his head, Anne thought he
was really the ugliest person she had ever seen.

All at once Mr. Harrison found his voice.

"I'm not going to put up with this," he spluttered,
"not a day longer, do you hear, miss. Bless my soul,
this is the third time, miss . . . the third time!
Patience has ceased to be a virtue, miss. I warned your
aunt the last time not to let it occur again . . . and
she's let it . . . she's done it . . . what does she
mean by it, that is what I want to know. That is what
I'm here about, miss."

"Will you explain what the trouble is?" asked
Anne, in her most dignified manner. She had been
practicing it considerably of late to have it in good
working order when school began; but it had no
apparent effect on the irate J. A. Harrison.

"Trouble, is it? Bless my soul, trouble enough, I
should think. The trouble is, miss, that I found that
Jersey cow of your aunt's in my oats again, not half an
hour ago. The third time, mark you. I found her in last
Tuesday and I found her in yesterday. I came here and
told your aunt not to let it occur again. She *has* let it
occur again. Where's your aunt, miss? I just want to
see her for a minute and give her a piece of my mind
. . . a piece of J. A. Harrison's mind, miss."

"If you mean Miss Marilla Cuthbert, she is *not*
my aunt, and she has gone down to East Grafton to

see a distant relative of hers who is very ill," said
Anne, with due increase of dignity at every word. "I
am very sorry that my cow should have broken into
your oats . . . she *is* my cow and not Miss Cuthbert's
. . . Matthew gave her to me three years ago when
she was a little calf and he bought her from Mr. Bell."

"Sorry, miss! Sorry isn't going to help matters any.
You'd better go and look at the havoc that animal has
made in my oats . . . trampled them from center to
circumference, miss."

"I am very sorry," repeated Anne firmly, "but
perhaps if you kept your fences in better repair Dolly
might not have broken in. It is your part of the line
fence that separates your oatfield from our pasture and
I noticed the other day that it was not in very good
condition."

"My fence is all right," snapped Mr. Harrison,
angrier than ever at this carrying of the war into the
enemy's country. "The jail fence couldn't keep a
demon of a cow like that out. And I can tell you, you
redheaded snippet, that if the cow is yours, as you say,
you'd be better employed in watching her out of other
people's grain than in sitting round reading yellow-
covered novels," . . . with a scathing glance at the
innocent tan-colored Virgil by Anne's feet.

Something at that moment was red besides Anne's
hair . . . which had always been a tender point with
her.

"I'd rather have red hair than none at all, except a
little fringe round my ears," she flashed.

The shot told, for Mr. Harrison was really very
sensitive about his bald head. His anger choked him
up again and he could only glare speechlessly at Anne,
who recovered her temper and followed up her
advantage.

"I can make allowance for you, Mr. Harrison,
because I have an imagination. I can easily imagine
how very trying it must be to find a cow in your oats
and I shall not cherish any hard feelings against you
for the things you've said. I promise you that Dolly

shall never break into your oats again. I give you my word of honor on *that* point."

"Well, mind you she doesn't," muttered Mr. Harrison in a somewhat subdued tone; but he stamped off angrily enough and Anne heard him growling to himself until he was out of earshot.

Grievously disturbed in mind, Anne marched across the yard and shut the naughty Jersey up in the milking pen.

"She can't possibly get out of that unless she tears the fence down," she reflected. "She looks pretty quiet now. I daresay she has sickened herself on those oats. I wish I'd sold her to Mr. Shearer when he wanted her last week, but I thought it was just as well to wait until we had the auction of the stock and let them all go together. I believe it is true about Mr. Harrison being a crank. Certainly there's nothing of the kindred spirit about *him.*"

Anne had always a weather eye open for kindred spirits.

Marilla Cuthbert was driving into the yard as Anne returned from the house, and the latter flew to get tea ready. They discussed the matter at the tea table.

"I'll be glad when the auction is over," said Marilla. "It is too much responsibility having so much stock about the place and nobody but that unreliable Martin to look after them. He has never come back yet and he promised that he would certainly be back last night if I'd give him the day off to go to his aunt's funeral. I don't know how many aunts he has got, I am sure. That's the fourth that's died since he hired here a year ago. I'll be more than thankful when the crop is in and Mr. Barry takes over the farm. We'll have to keep Dolly shut up in the pen till Martin comes, for she must be put in the back pasture and the fences there have to be fixed. I declare, it is a world of trouble, as Rachel says. Here's poor Mary Keith dying and what is to become of those two children of hers is more than I know. She has a brother in British Columbia and she has written to him about them, but she hasn't heard from him yet."

"What are the children like? How old are they?"

"Six past . . . they're twins."

"Oh, I've always been especially interested in twins ever since Mrs. Hammond had so many," said Anne eagerly. "Are they pretty?"

"Goodness, you couldn't tell . . . they were too dirty. Davy had been out making mud pies and Dora went out to call him in. Davy pushed her headfirst into the biggest pie and then, because she cried, he got into it himself and wallowed in it to show her it was nothing to cry about. Mary said Dora was really a very good child but that Davy was full of mischief. He has never had any bringing up you might say. His father died when he was a baby and Mary has been sick almost ever since."

"I'm always sorry for children that have had no bringing up," said Anne soberly. "You know I hadn't any till you took me in hand. I hope their uncle will look after them. Just what relation is Mrs. Keith to you?"

"Mary? None in the world. It was her husband . . . he was our third cousin. There's Mrs. Lynde coming through the yard. I thought she'd be up to hear about Mary."

"Don't tell her about Mr. Harrison and the cow," implored Anne.

Marilla promised; but the promise was quite unnecessary, for Mrs. Lynde was no sooner fairly seated than she said,

"I saw Mr. Harrison chasing your Jersey out of his oats today when I was coming home from Carmody. I thought he looked pretty mad. Did he make much of a rumpus?"

Anne and Marilla furtively exchanged amused smiles. Few things in Avonlea ever escaped Mrs. Lynde. It was only that morning Anne had said,

"If you went to your own room at midnight, locked the door, pulled down the blind, and *sneezed*,

Mrs. Lynde would ask you the next day how your cold was!"

"I believe he did," admitted Marilla. "I was away. He gave Anne a piece of his mind."

"I think he is a very disagreeable man," said Anne, with a resentful toss of her ruddy head.

"You never said a truer word," said Mrs. Rachel solemnly. "I knew there'd be trouble when Robert Bell sold his place to a New Brunswick man, that's what. I don't know what Avonlea is coming to, with so many strange people rushing into it. It'll soon not be safe to go to sleep in our beds."

"Why, what other strangers are coming in?" asked Marilla.

"Haven't you heard? Well, there's a family of Donnells, for one thing. They've rented Peter Sloane's old house. Peter has hired the man to run his mill. They belong down east and nobody knows anything about them. Then that shiftless Timothy Cotton family are going to move up from White Sands and they'll simply be a burden on the public. He is in consumption . . . when he isn't stealing . . . and his wife is a slack-twisted creature that can't turn her hand to a thing. She washes her dishes *sitting down*. Mrs. George Pye has taken her husband's orphan nephew, Anthony Pye. He'll be going to school to you, Anne, so you may expect trouble, that's what. And you'll have another strange pupil, too. Paul Irving is coming from the States to live with his grandmother. You remember his father, Marilla . . . Stephen Irving, him that jilted Lavendar Lewis over at Grafton?"

"I don't think he jilted her. There was a quarrel . . . I suppose there was blame on both sides."

"Well, anyway, he didn't marry her, and she's been as queer as possible ever since, they say . . . living all by herself in that little stone house she calls Echo Lodge. Stephen went off to the States and went into business with his uncle and married a Yankee. He's never been home since, though his mother has been up to see him once or twice. His wife died two years ago and he's sending the boy home to his mother for a spell. He's ten years old and I don't know if he'll be a very desirable pupil. You can never tell about those Yankees."

Mrs. Lynde looked upon all people who had the misfortune to be born or brought up elsewhere than in Prince Edward Island with a decided can-any-good-thing-come-out-of-Nazareth air. They *might* be good people, of course; but you were on the safe side in doubting it. She had a special prejudice against "Yankees." Her husband had been cheated out of ten dollars by an employer for whom he had once worked in Boston and neither angels nor principalities nor powers could have convinced Mrs. Rachel that the whole United States was not responsible for it.

"Avonlea school won't be the worse for a little new blood," said Marilla drily, "and if this boy is anything like his father he'll be all right. Steve Irving was the nicest boy that was ever raised in these parts, though some people did call him proud. I should think Mrs. Irving would be very glad to have the child. She has been very lonesome since her husband died."

"Oh, the boy may be well enough, but he'll be different from Avonlea children," said Mrs. Rachel, as if that clinched the matter. Mrs. Rachel's opinions concerning any person, place, or thing, were always warranted to wear. "What's this I hear about your going to start up a Village Improvement Society, Anne?"

"I was just talking it over with some of the girls and boys at the last Debating Club," said Anne, flushing. "They thought it would be rather nice . . . and so do Mr. and Mrs. Allan. Lots of villages have them now."

"Well, you'll get into no end of hot water if you do. Better leave it alone, Anne, that's what. People don't like being improved."

"Oh, we are not going to try to improve the *people*. It is Avonlea itself. There are lots of things which might be done to make it prettier. For instance, if we could coax Mr. Levi Boulter to pull down that dreadful old house on his upper farm wouldn't that be an improvement?"

"It certainly would," admitted Mrs. Rachel. "That old ruin has been an eyesore to the settlement for years. But if you Improvers can coax Levi Boulter to do anything for the public that he isn't to be paid for doing, may I be there to see and hear the process, that's what. I don't want to discourage you, Anne, for there may be something in your idea, though I suppose you did get it out of some rubbishy Yankee magazine; but you'll have your hands full with your school and I advise you as a friend not to bother with your improvements, that's what. But there, I know you'll go ahead with it if you've set your mind on it. You were always one to carry a thing through somehow."

Something about the firm outlines of Anne's lips told that Mrs. Rachel was not far astray in this estimate. Anne's heart was bent on forming the Improvement Society. Gilbert Blythe, who was to teach in White Sands but would always be home from Friday night to Monday morning, was enthusiastic about it; and most of the other young folks were willing to go in for anything that meant occasional meetings and consequently some "fun." As for what the "improvements" were to be, nobody had any very clear idea except Anne and Gilbert. They had talked them over and planned them out until an ideal Avonlea existed in their minds, if nowhere else.

Mrs. Rachel had still another item of news.

"They've given the Carmody school to a Priscilla Grant. Didn't you go to Queen's with a girl of that name, Anne?"

"Yes, indeed. Priscilla to teach at Carmody! How perfectly lovely!" exclaimed Anne, her gray eyes lighting up until they looked like evening stars, causing Mrs. Lynde to wonder anew if she would ever get it settled to her satisfaction whether Anne Shirley were really a pretty girl or not.

II

Selling in Haste and Repenting at Leisure

Anne drove over to Carmody on a shopping expedition the next afternoon and took Diana Barry with her. Diana was, of course, a pledged member of the Improvement Society, and the two girls talked about little else all the way to Carmody and back.

"The very first thing we ought to do when we get started is to have that hall painted," said Diana, as they drove past the Avonlea hall, a rather shabby building set down in a wooded hollow, with spruce trees hooding it about on all sides. "It's a disgraceful looking place and we must attend to it even before we try to get Mr. Levi Boulter to pull his house down. Father says we'll never succeed in doing *that* . . . Levi Boulter is too mean to spend the time it would take."

"Perhaps he'll let the boys take it down if they promise to haul the boards and split them up for him for kindling wood," said Anne hopefully. "We must do our best and be content to go slowly at first. We can't expect to improve everything all at once. We'll have to educate public sentiment first, of course."

Diana wasn't exactly sure what educating public sentiment meant; but it sounded fine and she felt rather proud that she was going to belong to a society with such an aim in view.

"I thought of something last night that we could do, Anne. You know that three-cornered piece of

ground where the roads from Carmody and Newbridge
and White Sands meet? It's all grown over with young
spruce; but wouldn't it be nice to have them all
cleared out, and just leave the two or three birch trees
that are on it?"

"Splendid," agreed Anne gaily. "And have a rustic
seat put under the birches. And when spring comes
we'll have a flower-bed made in the middle of it and
plant geraniums."

"Yes; only we'll have to devise some way of
getting old Mrs. Hiram Sloane to keep her cow off the
road, or she'll eat our geraniums up," laughed Diana.
"I begin to see what you mean by educating public
sentiment, Anne. There's the old Boulter house now.
Did you ever see such a rookery? And perched right
close to the road too. An old house with its windows
gone always makes me think of something dead with
its eyes picked out."

"I think an old, deserted house is such a sad
sight," said Anne dreamily. "It always seems to me to
be thinking about its past and mourning for its old-
time joys. Marilla says that a large family was raised in
that old house long ago, and that it was a real pretty
place, with a lovely garden and roses climbing all over
it. It was full of little children and laughter and songs;
and now it is empty, and nothing ever wanders
through it but the wind. How lonely and sorrowful it
must feel! Perhaps they all come back on moonlit
nights . . . the ghosts of the little children of long ago
and the roses and the songs . . . and for a little while
the old house can dream it is young and joyous again."

Diana shook her head.

"I never imagine things like that about places
now, Anne. Don't you remember how cross mother
and Marilla were when we imagined ghosts into the
Haunted Wood? To this day I can't go through that
bush comfortably after dark; and if I began imagining
such things about the old Boulter house I'd be
frightened to pass it too. Besides, those children aren't
dead. They're all grown up and doing well . . . and

one of them is a butcher. And flowers and songs couldn't have ghosts anyhow."

Anne smothered a little sigh. She loved Diana dearly and they had always been good comrades. But she had long ago learned that when she wandered into the realm of fancy she must go alone. The way to it was by an enchanted path where not even her dearest might follow her.

A thunder-shower came up while the girls were at Carmody; it did not last long, however, and the drive home, through lanes where the raindrops sparkled on the boughs and little leafy valleys where the drenched ferns gave out spicy odors, was delightful. But just as they turned into the Cuthbert lane Anne saw something that spoiled the beauty of the landscape for her.

Before them on the right extended Mr. Harrison's broad, gray-green field of late oats, wet and luxuriant; and there, standing squarely in the middle of it, up to her sleek sides in the lush growth, and blinking at them calmly over the intervening tassels, was a Jersey cow!

Anne dropped the reins and stood up with a tightening of the lips that boded no good to the predatory quadruped. Not a word said she, but she climbed nimbly down over the wheels, and whisked across the fence before Diana understood what had happened.

"Anne, come back," shrieked the latter, as soon as she found her voice. "You'll ruin your dress in that wet grain . . . ruin it. She doesn't hear me! Well, she'll never get that cow out by herself. I must go and help her, of course."

Anne was charging through the grain like a mad thing. Diana hopped briskly down, tied the horse securely to a post, turned the skirt of her pretty gingham dress over her shoulders, mounted the fence, and started in pursuit of her frantic friend. She could run faster than Anne, who was hampered by her clinging and drenched skirt, and soon overtook her.

Behind them they left a trail that would break Mr. Harrison's heart when he should see it.

"Anne, for mercy's sake, stop," panted poor Diana. "I'm right out of breath and you are wet to the skin."

"I must . . . get . . . that cow . . . out . . . before . . . Mr. Harrison . . . sees her," gasped Anne. "I don't . . . care . . . if I'm . . . drowned . . . if we . . . can . . . only . . . do that."

But the Jersey cow appeared to see no good reason for being hustled out of her luscious browsing ground. No sooner had the two breathless girls got near her than she turned and bolted squarely for the opposite corner of the field.

"Head her off," screamed Anne. "Run, Diana, run."

Diana did run. Anne tried to, and the wicked Jersey went around the field as if she were possessed. Privately, Diana thought she was. It was fully ten minutes before they headed her off and drove her through the corner gap into the Cuthbert lane.

There is no denying that Anne was in anything but an angelic temper at that precise moment. Nor did it soothe her in the least to behold a buggy halted just outside the lane, wherein sat Mr. Shearer of Carmody and his son, both of whom wore a broad smile.

"I guess you'd better have sold me that cow when I wanted to buy her last week, Anne," chuckled Mr. Shearer.

"I'll sell her to you now, if you want her," said her flushed and disheveled owner. "You may have her this very minute."

"Done. I'll give you twenty for her as I offered before, and Jim here can drive her right over to Carmody. She'll go to town with the rest of the shipment this evening. Mr. Reed of Brighton wants a Jersey cow."

Five minutes later Jim Shearer and the Jersey cow were marching up the road, and impulsive Anne was driving along the Green Gables lane with her twenty dollars.

"What will Marilla say?" asked Diana.

"Oh, she won't care. Dolly was my own cow and it isn't likely she'd bring more than twenty dollars at the auction. But oh dear, if Mr. Harrison sees that grain he will know she has been in again, and after my giving him my word of honor that I'd never let it happen! Well, it has taught me a lesson not to give my word of honor about cows. A cow that could jump over or break through our milk-pen fence couldn't be truated anywhere."

Marilla had gone down to Mrs. Lynde's, and when she returned knew all about Dolly's sale and transfer, for Mrs. Lynde had seen most of the transaction from her window and guessed the rest.

"I suppose it's just as well she's gone, though you *do* do things in a dreadful headlong fashion, Anne. I don't see how she got out of the pen, though. She must have broken some of the boards off."

"I didn't think of looking," said Anne, "but I'll go and see now. Martin has never come back yet. Perhaps some more of his aunts have died. I think it's something like Mr. Peter Sloane and the octogenarians. The other evening Mrs. Sloane was reading a newspaper and she said to Mr. Sloane, 'I see here that another octogenarian has just died. What *is* an octogenarian, Peter?' And Mr. Sloane said he didn't know, but they must be very sickly creatures, for you never heard tell of them but they were dying. That's the way with Martin's aunts."

"Martin's just like all the rest of those French," said Marilla in disgust. "You can't depend on them for a day."

Marilla was looking over Anne's Carmody purchases when she heard a shrill shriek in the barnyard. A minute later Anne dashed into the kitchen, wringing her hands.

"Anne Shirley, what's the matter now?"

"Oh, Marilla, whatever shall I do? This is terrible. And it's all my fault. Oh, will I *ever* learn to stop and reflect a little before doing reckless things? Mrs. Lynde always told me I would do something dreadful some day, and now I've done it!"

"Anne, you are the most exasperating girl! *What* is it you've done?"

"Sold Mr. Harrison's Jersey cow . . . the one he bought from Mr. Bell . . . to Mr. Shearer! Dolly is out in the milking pen this very minute."

"Anne Shirley, are you dreaming?"

"I only wish I were. There's no dream about it, though it's very like a nightmare. And Mr. Harrison's cow is in Charlottetown by this time. Oh, Marilla, I thought I'd finished getting into scrapes, and here I am in the very worst one I ever was in in my life. What can I do?"

"Do? There's nothing to do, child, except go and see Mr. Harrison about it. We can offer him our Jersey in exchange if he doesn't want to take the money. She is just as good as his."

"I'm sure he'll be awfully cross and disagreeable about it, though," moaned Anne.

"I daresay he will. He seems to be an irritable sort of a man. I'll go and explain to him if you like."

"No, indeed, I'm not as mean as that," exclaimed Anne. "This is all my fault and I'm certainly not going to let you take my punishment. I'll go myself and I'll go at once. The sooner it's over the better, for it will be terribly humiliating."

Poor Anne got her hat and her twenty dollars and was passing out when she happened to glance through the open pantry door. On the table reposed a nut cake which she had baked that morning . . . a particularly toothsome concoction iced with pink icing and adorned with walnuts. Anne had intended it for Friday evening, when the youth of Avonlea were to meet at Green Gables to organize the Improvement Society. But what were they compared to the justly offended Mr. Harrison? Anne thought that cake ought to soften the heart of any man, especially one who had to do his own cooking, and she promptly popped it into a box. She would take it to Mr. Harrison as a peace offering.

"That is, if he gives me a chance to say anything at all," she thought ruefully, as she climbed the lane fence and started on a short cut across the fields, golden in the light of the dreamy August evening. "I know now just how people feel who are being led to execution."

III

Mr. Harrison at Home

Mr. Harrison's house was an old-fashioned, low-eaved, whitewashed structure, set against a thick spruce grove.

Mr. Harrison himself was sitting on his vine-shaded veranda, in his shirt sleeves, enjoying his evening pipe. When he realized who was coming up the path he sprang suddenly to his feet, bolted into the house, and shut the door. This was merely the uncomfortable result of his surprise, mingled with a good deal of shame over his outburst of temper the day before. But it nearly swept the remnant of her courage from Anne's heart.

"If he's so cross now what will he be when he hears what I've done," she reflected miserably, as she rapped at the door.

But Mr. Harrison opened it, smiling sheepishly, and invited her to enter in a tone quite mild and friendly, if somewhat nervous. He had laid aside his pipe and donned his coat; he offered Anne a very dusty chair very politely, and her reception would have passed off pleasantly enough if it had not been for that telltale of a parrot who was peering through the bars of his cage with wicked golden eyes. No sooner had Anne seated herself than Ginger exclaimed,

"Bless my soul, what's that redheaded snippet coming here for?"

It would be hard to say whose face was the redder, Mr. Harrison's or Anne's.

"Don't you mind that parrot," said Mr. Harrison, casting a furious glance at Ginger. "He's . . . he's always talking nonsense. I got him from my brother who was a sailor. Sailors don't always use the choicest language, and parrots are very imitative birds."

"So I should think," said poor Anne, the remembrance of her errand quelling her resentment. She couldn't afford to snub Mr. Harrison under the circumstances, that was certain. When you had just sold a man's Jersey cow offhand, without his knowledge or consent, you must not mind if his parrot repeated uncomplimentary things. Nevertheless, the "redheaded snippet" was not quite so meek as she might otherwise have been.

"I've come to confess something to you, Mr. Harrison," she said resolutely. "It's . . . it's about . . . that Jersey cow."

"Bless my soul," exclaimed Mr. Harrison nervously, "has she gone and broken into my oats again? Well, never mind . . . never mind if she has. It's no difference . . . none at all. I . . . I was too hasty yesterday, that's a fact. Never mind if she has."

"Oh, if it were only that," sighed Anne. "But it's ten times worse. I don't . . ."

"Bless my soul, do you mean to say she's got into my wheat?"

"No . . . no . . . not the wheat. But . . ."

"Then it's the cabbages! She's broken into my cabbages that I was raising for Exhibition, hey?"

"It's *not* the cabbages, Mr. Harrison. I'll tell you everything . . . that is what I came for—but please don't interrupt me. It makes me so nervous. Just let me tell my story and don't say anything till I get through—and then no doubt you'll say plenty," Anne concluded, but in thought only.

"I won't say another word," said Mr. Harrison, and he didn't. But Ginger was not bound by any contract of silence and kept ejaculating, "Redheaded snippet" at intervals until Anne felt quite wild.

"I shut my Jersey cow up in our pen yesterday. This morning I went to Carmody and when I came back I saw a Jersey cow in your oats. Diana and I chased her out and you can't imagine what a hard time we had. I was so dreadfully wet and tired and vexed— and Mr. Shearer came by that very minute and offered to buy the cow. I sold her to him on the spot for twenty dollars. It was wrong of me. I should have waited and consulted Marilla, of course. But I'm dreadfully given to doing things without thinking— everybody who knows me will tell you that. Mr. Shearer took the cow right away to ship her on the afternoon train."

"Redheaded snippet," quoted Ginger in a tone of profound contempt.

At this point Mr. Harrison arose and, with an expression that would have struck terror into any bird but a parrot, carried Ginger's cage into an adjoining room and shut the door. Ginger shrieked, swore, and otherwise conducted himself in keeping with his reputation, but finding himself left alone, relapsed into sulky silence.

"Excuse me and go on," said Mr. Harrison, sitting down again. "My brother the sailor never taught that bird any manners."

"I went home and after tea I went out to the milking pen. Mr. Harrison," . . . Anne leaned forward, clasping her hands with her old childish gesture, while her big gray eyes gazed imploringly into Mr. Harrison's embarrassed face . . . "I found my cow still shut up in the pen. It was *your* cow I had sold to Mr. Shearer."

"Bless my soul," exclaimed Mr. Harrison, in blank amazement at this unlooked-for conclusion. "What a *very* extraordinary thing!"

"Oh, it isn't in the least extraordinary that I should be getting myself and other people into scrapes," said Anne mournfully. "I'm noted for that.

You might suppose I'd have grown out of it by this time . . . I'll be seventeen next March . . . but it seems that I haven't. Mr. Harrison, is it too much to hope that you'll forgive me? I'm afraid it's too late to get your cow back, but here is the money for her . . . or you can have mine in exchange if you'd rather. She's a very good cow. And I can't express how sorry I am for it all."

"Tut, tut," said Mr. Harrison briskly, "don't say another word about it, miss. It's of no consequence . . . no consequence whatever. Accidents will happen. I'm too hasty myself sometimes, miss . . . far too hasty. But I can't help speaking out just what I think and folks must take me as they find me. If that cow had been in my cabbages now . . . but never mind, she wasn't, so it's all right. I think I'd rather have your cow in exchange, since you want to be rid of her."

"Oh, thank you, Mr. Harrison. I'm so glad you are not vexed. I was afraid you would be."

"And I suppose you were scared to death to come here and tell me, after the fuss I made yesterday, hey? But you mustn't mind me, I'm a terrible outspoken old fellow, that's all . . . awful apt to tell the truth, no matter if it is a bit plain."

"So is Mrs. Lynde," said Anne, before she could prevent herself.

"Who? Mrs. Lynde? Don't you tell me I'm like that old gossip," said Mr. Harrison irritably. "I'm not . . . not a bit. What have you got in that box?"

"A cake," said Anne archly. In her relief at Mr. Harrison's unexpected amiability her spirits soared upward feather-light. "I brought it over for you . . . I thought perhaps you didn't have cake very often."

"I don't, that's a fact, and I'm mighty fond of it, too. I'm much obliged to you. It looks good on top. I hope it's good all the way through."

"It is," said Anne, gaily confident. "I have made cakes in my time that were *not*, as Mrs. Allan could tell you, but this one is all right. I made it for the

Improvement Society, but I can make another for them."

"Well, I'll tell you what, miss, you must help me eat it. I'll put the kettle on and we'll have a cup of tea. How will that do?"

"Will you let me make the tea?" said Anne dubiously.

Mr. Harrison chuckled.

"I see you haven't much confidence in my ability to make tea. You're wrong . . . I can brew up as good a jorum of tea as you ever drank. But go ahead yourself. Fortunately it rained last Sunday, so there's plenty clean dishes."

Anne hopped briskly up and went to work. She washed the teapot in several waters before she put the tea to steep. Then she swept the stove and set the table, bringing the dishes out of the pantry. The state of that pantry horrified Anne, but she wisely said nothing. Mr. Harrison told her where to find the bread and butter and a can of peaches. Anne adorned the table with a bouquet from the garden and shut her eyes to the stains on the tablecloth. Soon the tea was ready and Anne found herself sitting opposite Mr. Harrison at his own table, pouring his tea for him, and chatting freely to him about her school and friends and plans. She could hardly believe the evidence of her senses.

Mr. Harrison had brought Ginger back, averring that the poor bird would be lonesome; and Anne, feeling that she could forgive everybody and everything, offered him a walnut. But Ginger's feelings had been grievously hurt and he rejected all overtures of friendship. He sat moodily on his perch and ruffled his feathers up until he looked like a mere ball of green and gold.

"Why do you call him Ginger?" asked Anne, who liked appropriate names and thought Ginger accorded not at all with such gorgeous plumage.

"My brother the sailor named him. Maybe it had some reference to his temper. I think a lot of that bird though . . . you'd be surprised if you knew how much. He has his faults of course. That bird has cost me a good deal one way and another. Some people object to his swearing habits but he can't be broken of them. I've tried . . . other people have tried. Some folks have prejudices against parrots. Silly, ain't it? I like them myself. Ginger's a lot of company to me. Nothing would induce me to give that bird up . . . nothing in the world, miss."

Mr. Harrison flung the last sentence at Anne as explosively as if he suspected her of some latent design of persuading him to give Ginger up. Anne, however, was beginning to like the queer, fussy, fidgety little man, and before the meal was over they were quite good friends. Mr. Harrison found out about the Improvement Society and was disposed to approve of it.

"That's right. Go ahead. There's lots of room for improvement in this settlement . . . and in the people too."

"Oh, I don't know," flashed Anne. To herself, or to her particular cronies, she might admit that there were some small imperfections, easily removable, in Avonlea and its inhabitants. But to hear a practical outsider like Mr. Harrison saying it was an entirely different thing. "I think Avonlea is a lovely place; and the people in it are very nice, too."

"I guess you've got a spice of temper," commented Mr. Harrison, surveying the flushed cheeks and indignant eyes opposite him. "It goes with hair like yours, I reckon. Avonlea is a pretty decent place or I wouldn't have located here; but I suppose even you will admit that it has *some* faults?"

"I like it all the better for them," said loyal Anne. "I don't like places or people either that haven't any faults. I think a truly perfect person would be very uninteresting. Mrs. Milton White says she never met a perfect person, but she's heard enough about one . . . her husband's first wife. Don't you think it must be very uncomfortable to be married to a man whose first wife was perfect?"

"It would be more uncomfortable to be married to the perfect wife," declared Mr. Harrison, with a sudden and inexplicable warmth.

When tea was over Anne insisted on washing the dishes, although Mr. Harrison assured her that there were enough in the house to do for weeks yet. She would dearly have loved to sweep the floor also, but no broom was visible and she did not like to ask where it was for fear there wasn't one at all.

"You might run across and talk to me once in a while," suggested Mr. Harrison when she was leaving. "'Tisn't far and folks ought to be neighborly. I'm kind of interested in that society of yours. Seems to me there'll be some fun in it. Who are you going to tackle first?"

"We are not going to meddle with *people* . . . it is only *places* we mean to improve," said Anne, in a dignified tone. She rather suspected that Mr. Harrison was making fun of the project.

When she had gone Mr. Harrison watched her from the window . . . a lithe, girlish shape, tripping lightheartedly across the fields in the sunset afterglow.

"I'm a crusty, lonesome, crabbed old chap," he said aloud, "but there's something about that little girl makes me feel young again . . . and it's such a pleasant sensation I'd like to have it repeated once in a while."

"Redheaded snippet," croaked Ginger mockingly.

Mr. Harrison shook his fist at the parrot.

"You ornery bird," he muttered, "I almost wish I'd wrung your neck when my brother the sailor brought you home. Will you never be done getting me into trouble?"

Anne ran home blithely and recounted her adventures to Marilla, who had been not a little alarmed by her long absence and was on the point of starting out to look for her.

"It's a pretty good world, after all, isn't it,

Marilla?" concluded Anne happily. "Mrs. Lynde was complaining the other day that it wasn't much of a world. She said whenever you looked forward to anything pleasant you were sure to be more or less disappointed . . . that nothing ever came up to your expectations. Well, perhaps that is true. But there is a good side to it too. The bad things don't always come up to your expectations either . . . they nearly always turn out ever so much better than you think. I looked forward to a dreadfully unpleasant experience when I went over to Mr. Harrison's tonight; and instead he was quite kind and I had almost a nice time. I think we're going to be real good friends if we make plenty of allowances for each other, and everything has turned out for the best. But all the same, Marilla, I shall certainly never again sell a cow before making sure to whom she belongs. And I do *not* like parrots!"

IV

Different Opinions

One evening at sunset, Jane Andrews, Gilbert Blythe, and Anne Shirley were lingering by a fence in the shadow of gently swaying spruce boughs, where a wood cut known as the Birch Path joined the main road. Jane had been up to spend the afternoon with Anne, who walked part of the way home with her; at the fence they met Gilbert, and all three were now talking about the fateful morrow; for that morrow was the first of September and the schools would open. Jane would go to Newbridge and Gilbert to White Sands.

"You both have the advantage of me," sighed Anne. "You're going to teach children who don't know you, but I have to teach my own old schoolmates, and Mrs. Lynde says she's afraid they won't respect me as they would a stranger unless I'm very cross from the first. But I don't believe a teacher should be cross. Oh, it seems to me such a responsibility!"

"I guess we'll get on all right," said Jane comfortably. Jane was not troubled by any aspirations to be an influence for good. She meant to earn her salary fairly, please the trustees, and get her name on the School Inspector's roll of honor. Further ambitions Jane had none. "The main thing will be to keep order and a teacher has to be a little cross to do that. If my pupils won't do as I tell them I shall punish them."

"How?"

"Give them a good whipping, of course."

"Oh, Jane, you wouldn't," cried Anne, shocked. "Jane, you *couldn't!*"

"Indeed, I could and would, if they deserved it," said Jane decidedly.

"I could *never* whip a child," said Anne with equal decision. "I don't believe in it *at all.* Miss Stacy never whipped any of us and she had perfect order; and Mr. Phillips was always whipping and he had no order at all. No, if I can't get along without whipping I shall not try to teach school. There are better ways of managing. I shall try to win my pupils' affections and then they will *want* to do what I tell them."

"But suppose they don't?" said practical Jane.

"I wouldn't whip them anyhow. I'm sure it wouldn't do any good. Oh, don't whip your pupils, Jane dear, no matter what they do."

"What do you think about it, Gilbert?" demanded Jane. "Don't you think there are some children who really need a whipping now and then?"

"Don't you think it's a cruel, barbarous thing to whip a child . . . *any* child?" exclaimed Anne, her face flushing with earnestness.

"Well," said Gilbert slowly, torn between his real convictions and his wish to measure up to Anne's ideal, "there's something to be said on both sides. I don't believe in whipping children *much.* I think, as you say, Anne, that there are better ways of managing as a rule, and that corporal punishment should be a last resort. But on the other hand, as Jane says, I believe there is an occasional child who can't be influenced in any other way and who, in short, needs a whipping and would be improved by it. Corporal punishment as a last resort is to be my rule."

Gilbert, having tried to please both sides, succeeded, as is usual and eminently right, in pleasing neither. Jane tossed her head.

"I'll whip my pupils when they're naughty. It's the shortest and easiest way of convincing them."

Anne gave Gilbert a disappointed glance.

"I shall never whip a child," she repeated firmly. "I feel sure it isn't either right or necessary."

"Suppose a boy sauced you back when you told him to do something?" said Jane.

"I'd keep him in after school and talk kindly and firmly to him," said Anne. "There is some good in every person if you can find it. It is a teacher's duty to find and develop it. That is what our School Management professor at Queen's told us, you know. Do you suppose you could find any good in a child by whipping him? It's far more important to influence the children aright than it is even to teach them the three R's, Professor Rennie says."

"But the Inspector examines them in the three R's, mind you, and he won't give you a good report if they don't come up to his standard," protested Jane.

"I'd rather have my pupils love me and look back to me in after years as a real helper than be on the roll of honor," asserted Anne decidedly.

"Wouldn't you punish children at all, when they misbehaved?" asked Gilbert.

"Oh, yes, I suppose I shall have to, although I know I'll hate to do it. But you can keep them in at recess or stand them on the floor or give them lines to write."

"I suppose you won't punish the girls by making them sit with the boys?" said Jane slyly.

Gilbert and Anne looked at each other and smiled rather foolishly. Once upon a time, Anne had been made to sit with Gilbert for punishment and sad and bitter had been the consequences thereof.

"Well, time will tell which is the best way," said Jane philosophically as they parted.

Anne went back to Green Gables by way of the Birch Path, shadowy, rustling, fern-scented, through Violet Vale and past Willowmere, where dark and light kissed each other under the firs, and down through Lover's Lane . . . spots she and Diana had so named long ago. She walked slowly, enjoying the sweetness of wood and field and the starry summer twilight, and thinking soberly about the new duties she was to take up on the morrow. When she reached the yard at Green Gables Mrs. Lynde's loud, decided tones floated out through the open kitchen window.

"Mrs. Lynde has come up to give me good advice about tomorrow," thought Anne with a grimace, "but I don't believe I'll go in. Her advice is much like pepper, I think . . . excellent in small quantities but rather scorching in her doses. I'll run over and have a chat with Mr. Harrison instead."

This was not the first time Anne had run over and chatted with Mr. Harrison since the notable affair of the Jersey cow. She had been there several evenings and Mr. Harrison and she were very good friends, although there were times and seasons when Anne found the outspokenness on which he prided himself rather trying. Ginger still continued to regard her with suspicion, and never failed to greet her sarcastically as "redheaded snippet." Mr. Harrison had tried vainly to break him of the habit by jumping excitedly up whenever he saw Anne coming and exclaiming,

"Bless my soul, here's that pretty little girl again," or something equally flattering. But Ginger saw through the scheme and scorned it. Anne was never to know how many compliments Mr. Harrison paid her behind her back. He certainly never paid her any to her face.

"Well, I suppose you've been back in the woods laying in a supply of switches for tomorrow?" was his greeting as Anne came up the veranda steps.

"No, indeed," said Anne indignantly. She was an excellent target for teasing because she always took things so seriously. "I shall never have a switch in my school, Mr. Harrison. Of course, I shall have to have a pointer, but I shall use it for pointing *only*."

"So you mean to strap them instead? Well, I don't know but you're right. A switch stings more at the time but the strap smarts longer, that's a fact."

"I shall not use anything of the sort. I'm not going to whip my pupils."

"Bless my soul," exclaimed Mr. Harrison in genuine astonishment, "how do you lay out to keep order then?"

"I shall govern by affection, Mr. Harrison."

"It won't do," said Mr. Harrison, "won't do at all, Anne. 'Spare the rod and spoil the child.' When I went to school the master whipped me regular every day because he said if I wasn't in mischief just then I was plotting it."

"Methods have changed since your schooldays, Mr. Harrison."

"But human nature hasn't. Mark my words, you'll never manage the young fry unless you keep a rod in pickle for them. The thing is impossible."

"Well, I'm going to try my way first," said Anne, who had a fairly strong will of her own and was apt to cling very tenaciously to her theories.

"You're pretty stubborn, I reckon," was Mr. Harrison's way of putting it. "Well, well, we'll see. Some day when you get riled up . . . and people with hair like yours are desperate apt to get riled . . . you'll forget all your pretty little notions and give some of them a whaling. You're too young to be teaching anyhow . . . far too young and childish."

Altogether, Anne went to bed that night in a rather pessimistic mood. She slept poorly and was so pale and tragic at breakfast next morning that Marilla was alarmed and insisted on making her take a cup of scorching ginger tea. Anne sipped it patiently, although she could not imagine what good ginger tea would do. Had it been some magic brew, potent to confer age and experience, Anne would have swallowed a quart of it without flinching.

"Marilla, what if I fail!"

"You'll hardly fail completely in one day and there's plenty more days coming," said Marilla. "The trouble with you, Anne, is that you'll expect to teach those children everything and reform all their faults right off, and if you can't you'll think you've failed."

V

A Full-fledged Schoolma'am

When Anne reached the school that morning . . .
for the first time in her life she had traversed the
Birch Path deaf and blind to its beauties . . . all was
quiet and still. The preceding teacher had trained the
children to be in their places at her arrival, and when
Anne entered the schoolroom she was confronted by
prim rows of "shining morning faces" and bright,
inquisitive eyes. She hung up her hat and faced her
pupils, hoping that she did not look as frightened and
foolish as she felt and that they would not perceive
how she was trembling.

She had sat up until nearly twelve the preceding
night composing a speech she meant to make to her
pupils upon opening the school. She had revised and
improved it painstakingly, and then she had learned it
off by heart. It was a very good speech and had some
very fine ideas in it, especially about mutual help and
earnest striving after knowledge. The only trouble was
that she could not now remember a word of it.

After what seemed to her a year . . . about ten
seconds in reality . . . she said faintly,

"Take your Testaments, please," and sank
breathlessly into her chair under cover of the rustle
and clatter of desk lids that followed. While the
children read their verses Anne marshalled her shaky
wits into order and looked over the array of little
pilgrims to the Grown-up Land.

Most of them were, of course, quite well known to her. Her own classmates had passed out in the preceding year but the rest had all gone to school with her, excepting the primer class and ten newcomers to Avonlea. Anne secretly felt more interest in these ten than in those whose possibilities were already fairly well mapped out to her. To be sure, they might be just as commonplace as the rest; but on the other hand there *might* be a genius among them. It was a thrilling idea.

Sitting by himself at a corner desk was Anthony Pye. He had a dark, sullen little face, and was staring at Anne with a hostile expression in his black eyes. Anne instantly made up her mind that she would win that boy's affection and discomfit the Pyes utterly.

In the other corner another strange boy was sitting with Arty Sloane . . . a jolly looking little chap, with a snub nose, freckled face, and big, light blue eyes, fringed with whitish lashes . . . probably the Donnell boy; and if resemblance went for anything, his sister was sitting across the aisle with Mary Bell. Anne wondered what sort of a mother the child had, to send her to school dressed as she was. She wore a faded pink silk dress, trimmed with a great deal of cotton lace, soiled white kid slippers, and silk stockings. Her sandy hair was tortured into innumerable kinky and unnatural curls, surmounted by a flamboyant bow of pink ribbon bigger than her head. Judging from her expression she was very well satisfied with herself.

A pale little thing, with smooth ripples of fine, silky, fawn-colored hair flowing over her shoulders, must, Anne thought, be Annetta Bell, whose parents had formerly lived in the Newbridge school district, but, by reason of hauling their house fifty yards north of its old site were now in Avonlea. Three pallid little girls crowded into one seat were certainly Cottons; and there was no doubt that the small beauty with the long brown curls and hazel eyes, who was casting coquettish looks at Jack Gillis over the edge of her Testament, was Prillie Rogerson, whose father had recently married a second wife and brought Prillie home from her grandmother's in Grafton. A tall, awkward girl in a back seat, who seemed to have too many feet and hands, Anne could not place at all, but later on discovered that her name was Barbara Shaw and that she had come to live with an Avonlea aunt. She was also to find that if Barbara ever managed to walk down the aisle without falling over her own or somebody else's feet the Avonlea scholars wrote the unusual fact up on the porch wall to commemorate it.

But when Anne's eyes met those of the boy at the front desk facing her own, a queer little thrill went over her, as if she had found her genius. She knew this must be Paul Irving and that Mrs. Rachel Lynde had been right for once when she prophesied that he would be unlike the Avonlea children. More than that, Anne realized that he was unlike other children anywhere, and that there was a soul subtly akin to her own gazing at her out of the very dark blue eyes that were watching her so intently.

She knew Paul was ten but he looked no more than eight. He had the most beautiful little face she had ever seen in a child . . . features of exquisite delicacy and refinement, framed in a halo of chestnut curls. His mouth was delicious, being full without pouting, the crimson lips just softly touching and curving into finely finished little corners that narrowly escaped being dimpled. He had a sober, grave, meditative expression, as if his spirit was much older than his body; but when Anne smiled softly at him it vanished in a sudden answering smile, which seemed an illumination of his whole being, as if some lamp had suddenly kindled into flame inside of him, irradiating him from top to toe. Best of all, it was involuntary, born of no external effort or motive, but simply the outflashing of a hidden personality, rare and fine and sweet. With that quick interchange of smiles Anne and Paul were fast friends forever before a word had passed between them.

The day went by like a dream. Anne could never clearly recall it afterwards. It almost seemed as if it were not she who was teaching but somebody else. She heard classes and worked sums and set copies mechanically. The children behaved quite well; only two cases of discipline occurred. Morley Andrews was caught driving a pair of trained crickets in the aisle. Anne stood Morley on the platform for an hour and . . . which Morley felt much more keenly . . . confiscated his crickets. She put them in a box and on the way from school set them free in Violet Vale; but Morley believed, then and ever afterwards, that she took them home and kept them for her own private amusement.

The other culprit was Anthony Pye, who poured the last drops of water from his slate bottle down the back of Aurelia Clay's neck. Anne kept Anthony in at recess and talked to him about what was expected of gentlemen, admonishing him that they never poured water down ladies' necks. She wanted all her boys to be gentlemen, she said. Her little lecture was quite kind and touching; but unfortunately Anthony remained absolutely untouched. He listened to her in silence, with the same sullen expression, and whistled scornfully as he went out. Anne sighed; and then cheered herself up by remembering that winning a Pye's affections, like the building of Rome, wasn't the work of a day. In fact, it was doubtful whether some of the Pyes had any affections to win; but Anne hoped better things of Anthony, who looked as if he might be a rather nice boy if one ever got behind his sullenness.

When school was dismissed and the children had gone Anne dropped wearily into her chair. Her head ached and she felt woefully discouraged. There was no real reason for discouragement, since nothing very dreadful had occurred; but Anne was very tired and inclined to believe that she would never learn to like teaching. And how terrible it would be to be doing something you didn't like every day for . . . well, say forty years. Anne was of two minds whether to have her cry out then and there, or wait till she was safely in her own white room at home. Before she could decide there was a click of heels and a silken swish on the porch floor, and Anne found herself confronted by a lady whose appearance made her recall a recent criticism of Mr. Harrison's on an overdressed female he had seen in a Charlottetown store. "She looked like a head-on collision between a fashion plate and a nightmare."

The newcomer was gorgeously arrayed in a pale blue summer silk, puffed, frilled, and shirred wherever puff, frill, or shirring could possibly be placed. Her head was surmounted by a huge white chiffon hat, bedecked with three long but rather stringy ostrich feathers. A veil of pink chiffon, lavishly sprinkled with huge black dots, hung like a flounce from the hat brim to her shoulders and floated off in two airy streamers behind her. She wore all the jewelry that could be crowded on one small woman, and a very strong odor of perfume attended her.

"I am Mrs. Donnell . . . Mrs. H. B. Donnell," announced this vision, "and I have come in to see you about something Clarice Almira told me when she came home to dinner today. It annoyed me *excessively.*"

"I'm sorry," faltered Anne, vainly trying to recollect any incident of the morning connected with the Donnell children.

"Clarice Almira told me that you pronounced our name *Don*nell. Now, Miss Shirley, the correct pronunciation of our name is Don*nell* . . . accent on the last syllable. I *hope* you'll remember this in future."

"I'll try to," gasped Anne, choking back a wild desire to laugh. "I know by experience that it's very unpleasant to have one's name *spelled* wrong and I suppose it must be even worse to have it pronounced wrong."

"Certainly it is. And Clarice Almira also informed me that you call my son Jacob."

"He told me his name was Jacob," protested Anne.

"I might have expected that," said Mrs. H. B. Don*nell*, in a tone which implied that gratitude in children was not to be looked for in this degenerate age. "That boy has such plebeian tastes, Miss Shirley. When he was born I wanted to call him St. Clair . . . it sounds *so* aristocratic, doesn't it? But his father insisted he should be called Jacob after his uncle. I yielded, because Uncle Jacob was a rich old bachelor. And what do you think, Miss Shirley? When our innocent boy was five years old Uncle Jacob actually went and got married and now he has three boys of his own. Did you ever hear of such ingratitude? The moment the invitation to the wedding . . . for he had the impertinence to send us an invitation, Miss Shirley . . . came to the house I said, 'No more Jacobs for me, thank you.' From that day I called my son St. Clair and St. Clair I am determined he shall be called. His father obstinately continues to call him Jacob, and the boy himself has a perfectly unaccountable preference for the vulgar name. But St. Clair he is and St. Clair he shall remain. You will kindly remember this, Miss Shirley, will you not? *Thank* you. I told Clarice Almira that I was sure it was only a misunderstanding and that a word would set it right. Don*nell* . . . accent on last syllable . . . and St. Clair . . . on *no* account Jacob. You'll remember? *Thank* you."

When Mrs. H. B. Don*nell* had skimmed away Anne locked the school door and went home. At the foot of the hill she found Paul Irving by the Birch Path. He held out to her a cluster of the dainty little wild orchids which Avonlea children called "rice lillies."

"Please, teacher, I found these in Mr. Wright's field," he said shyly, "and I came back to give them to you because I thought you were the kind of lady that would like them, and because . . ." he lifted his big, beautiful eyes . . . "I like you, teacher."

"You darling," said Anne, taking the fragrant spikes. As if Paul's words had been a spell of magic, discouragement and weariness passed from her spirit, and hope upwelled in her heart like a dancing fountain. She went through the Birch Path light-footedly, attended by the sweetness of her orchids as by a benediction.

"Well, how did you get along?" Marilla wanted to know.

"Ask me that a month later and I may be able to tell you. I can't now . . . I don't know myself . . . I'm too near it. My thoughts feel as if they had been all stirred up until they were thick and muddy. The only thing I feel really sure of having accomplished today is that I taught Cliffie Wright that A is A. He never knew it before. Isn't it something to have started a soul along a path that may end in Shakespeare and Paradise Lost?"

Mrs. Lynde came up later on with more encouragement. That good lady had waylaid the schoolchildren at her gate and demanded of them how they liked their new teacher.

"And every one of them said they liked you splendid, Anne, except Anthony Pye. I must admit he didn't. He said you 'weren't any good, just like all girl teachers.' There's the Pye leaven for you. But never mind."

"I'm not going to mind," said Anne quietly, "and I'm going to make Anthony Pye like me yet. Patience and kindness will surely win him."

"Well, you can never tell about a Pye," said Mrs. Rachel cautiously. "They go by contraries, like dreams, often as not. As for that Donnell woman, she'll get no Donnelling from me, I can assure you. The name is Donnell and always has been. The woman is crazy, that's what. She has a pug dog she calls Queenie and it has its meals at the table along with the family, eating off a china plate. I'd be afraid of a judgment if I was her. Thomas says Donnell himself is a sensible, hard-working man, but he hadn't much gumption when he picked out a wife, that's what."

VI

All Sorts and Conditions of Men . . . and Women

A September day on Prince Edward Island hills; a crisp wind blowing up over the sand dunes from the sea; a long red road, winding through fields and woods, now looping itself about a corner of thick set spruces, now threading a plantation of young maples with great feathery sheets of ferns beneath them, now dipping down into a hollow where a brook flashed out of the woods and into them again, now basking in open sunshine between ribbons of goldenrod and smoke-blue asters; air athrill with the pipings of myriads of crickets, those glad little pensioners of the summer hills; a plump brown pony ambling along the road; two girls behind him, full to the lips with the simple, priceless joy of youth and life.

"Oh, this is a day left over from Eden, isn't it, Diana?" . . . and Anne sighed for sheer happiness. "The air has magic in it. Look at the purple in the cup of that harvest valley, Diana. And oh, do smell the dying fir! It's coming up from that little sunny hollow where Mr. Eben Wright has been cutting fence poles. Bliss is it on such a day to be alive; but to smell dying fir is very heaven. That's two thirds Wordsworth and one third Anne Shirley. It doesn't seem possible that there should be dying fir in heaven, does it? And yet it doesn't seem to me that heaven would be quite perfect if you couldn't get a whiff of dead fir as you went through its woods. Perhaps we'll have the odor there without the death. Yes, I think that will be the way. That delicious aroma must be the souls of the firs . . . and of course it will be just souls in heaven."

"Trees haven't souls," said practical Diana, "but the smell of dead fir is certainly lovely. I'm going to make a cushion and fill it with fir needles. You'd better make one too, Anne."

"I think I shall . . . and use it for my naps. I'd be certain to dream I was a dryad or a wood-nymph then. But just this minute I'm well content to be Anne Shirley, Avonlea schoolma'am, driving over a road like this on such a sweet, friendly day."

"It's a lovely day but we have anything but a lovely task before us," sighed Diana. "Why on earth did you offer to canvass this road, Anne? Almost all the cranks in Avonlea live along it, and we'll probably be treated as if we were begging for ourselves. It's the very worst road of all."

"That is why I chose it. Of course Gilbert and Fred would have taken this road if we had asked them. But you see, Diana, I feel myself responsible for the A. V. I. S., since I was the first to suggest it, and it seems to me that I ought to do the most disagreeable things. I'm sorry on your account; but you needn't say a word at the cranky places. I'll do all the talking . . . Mrs. Lynde would say I was well able to. Mrs. Lynde doesn't know whether to approve of our enterprise or not. She inclines to, when she remembers that Mr. and Mrs. Allan are in favor of it; but the fact that village improvement societies first originated in the States is a count against it. So she is halting between two opinions and only success will justify us in Mrs. Lynde's eyes. Priscilla is going to write a paper for our next Improvement meeting, and I expect it will be good, for her aunt is such a clever writer and no doubt it runs in the family. I shall never forget the thrill it gave me when I found out that Mrs. Charlotte E. Morgan was Priscilla's aunt. It seemed so wonderful that I was a friend of the girl whose aunt wrote 'Edgewood Days' and 'The Rosebud Garden.' "

"Where does Mrs. Morgan live?"

"In Toronto. And Priscilla says she is coming to the Island for a visit next summer, and if it is possible Priscilla is going to arrange to have us meet her. That seems almost too good to be true—but it's something pleasant to imagine after you go to bed."

The Avonlea Village Improvement Society was an organized fact. Gilbert Blythe was president, Fred Wright vice-president, Anne Shirley secretary, and Diana Barry treasurer. The "Improvers," as they were promptly christened, were to meet once a fortnight at the homes of the members. It was admitted that they could not expect to affect many improvements so late in the season; but they meant to plan the next summer's campaign, collect and discuss ideas, write and read papers, and, as Anne said, educate public sentiment generally.

There was some disapproval, of course, and . . . which the Improvers felt much more keenly . . . a good deal of ridicule. Mr. Elisha Wright was reported to have said that a more appropriate name for the organization would be Courting Club. Mrs. Hiram Sloane declared she had heard the Improvers meant to plough up all the roadsides and set them out with geraniums. Mr. Levi Boulter warned his neighbors that the Improvers would insist that everybody pull down his house and rebuild it after plans approved by the society. Mr. James Spencer sent them word that he wished they would kindly shovel down the church hill. Eben Wright told Anne that he wished the Improvers could induce old Josiah Sloane to keep his whiskers trimmed. Mr. Lawrence Bell said he would whitewash his barns if nothing else would please them but he would *not* hang lace curtains in his cowstable windows. Mr. Major Spencer asked Clifton Sloane, an Improver who drove the milk to the Carmody cheese factory, if it was true that everybody would have to have his milk-stand hand-painted next summer and keep an embroidered centerpiece on it.

In spite of . . . or perhaps, human nature being

what it is, because of . . . this, the Society went gamely to work at the only improvement they could hope to bring about that fall. At the second meeting, in the Barry parlor, Oliver Sloane moved that they start a subscription to re-shingle and paint the hall; Julia Bell seconded it, with an uneasy feeling that she was doing something not exactly ladylike. Gilbert put the motion, it was carried unanimously, and Anne gravely recorded it in her minutes. The next thing was to appoint a committee, and Gertie Pye, determined not to let Julia Bell carry off all the laurels, boldly moved that Miss Jane Andrews be chairman of said committee. This motion being also duly seconded and carried, Jane returned the compliment by appointing Gertie on the committee, along with Gilbert, Anne, Diana, and Fred Wright. The committee chose their routes in private conclave. Anne and Diana were told off for the Newbridge road, Gilbert and Fred for the White Sands road, and Jane and Gertie for the Carmody road.

"Because," explained Gilbert to Anne, as they walked home together through the Haunted Wood, "the Pyes all live along that road and they won't give a cent unless one of themselves canvasses them."

The next Saturday Anne and Diana started out. They drove to the end of the road and canvassed homeward, calling first on the "Andrews girls."

"If Catherine is alone we may get something," said Diana, "but if Eliza is there we won't."

Eliza was there . . . very much so . . . and looked even grimmer than usual. Miss Eliza was one of those people who give you the impression that life is indeed a vale of tears, and that a smile, never to speak of a laugh, is a waste of nervous energy truly reprehensible. The Andrews girls had been "girls" for fifty odd years and seemed likely to remain girls to the end of their earthly pilgrimage. Catherine, it was said, had not entirely given up hope, but Eliza, who was born a pessimist, had never had any. They lived in a little brown house built in a sunny corner scooped out of Mark Andrews' beech woods. Eliza complained that it was terrible hot in summer, but Catherine was wont to say it was lovely and warm in winter.

Eliza was sewing patchwork, not because it was needed but simply as a protest against the frivolous lace Catherine was crocheting. Eliza listened with a frown and Catherine with a smile, as the girls explained their errand. To be sure, whenever Catherine caught Eliza's eye she discarded the smile in guilty confusion; but it crept back the next moment.

"If I had money to waste," said Eliza grimly, "I'd burn it up and have the fun of seeing a blaze maybe; but I wouldn't give it to that hall, not a cent. It's no benefit to the settlement . . . just a place for young folks to meet and carry on when they's better be home in their beds."

"Oh, Eliza, young folks must have some amusement," protested Catherine.

"I don't see the necessity. We didn't gad about to halls and places when we were young, Catherine Andrews. This world is getting worse every day."

"I think it's getting better," said Catherine firmly.

"You think!" Miss Eliza's voice expressed the utmost contempt. "It doesn't signify what you think, Catherine Andrews. Facts is facts."

"Well, I always like to look on the bright side, Eliza."

"There isn't any bright side."

"Oh, indeed there is," cried Anne, who couldn't endure such heresy in silence. "Why, there are ever so many bright sides, Miss Andrews. It's really a beautiful world."

"You won't have such a high opinion of it when you've lived as long in it as I have," retorted Miss Eliza sourly, "and you won't be so enthusiastic about improving it either. How is your mother, Diana? Dear me, but she has failed of late. She looks terrible run down. And how long is it before Marilla expects to be stone blind, Anne?"

"The doctor thinks her eyes will not get any worse if she is very careful," faltered Anne.

Eliza shook her head.

"Doctors always talk like that just to keep people cheered up. I wouldn't have much hope if I was her. It's best to be prepared for the worst."

"But oughtn't we to be prepared for the best too?" pleaded Anne. "It's just as likely to happen as the worst."

"Not in my experience, and I've fifty-seven years to set against your sixteen," retorted Eliza. "Going, are you? Well, I hope this new society of yours will be able to keep Avonlea from running any further down hill but I haven't much hope of it."

Anne and Diana got themselves thankfully out, and drove away as fast as the fat pony could go. As they rounded the curve below the beech wood a plump figure came speeding over Mr. Andrews' pasture, waving to them excitedly. It was Catherine Andrews and she was so out of breath that she could hardly speak, but she thrust a couple of quarters into Anne's hand.

"That's my contribution to painting the hall," she gasped. "I'd like to give you a dollar but I don't dare take more from my egg money for Eliza would find it out if I did. I'm real interested in your society and I believe you're going to do a lot of good. I'm an optimist. I *have* to be, living with Eliza. I must hurry back before she misses me . . . she thinks I'm feeding the hens. I hope you'll have good luck canvassing, and don't be cast down over what Eliza said. The world *is* getting better . . . it certainly is."

The next house was Daniel Blair's.

"Now, it all depends on whether his wife is home or not," said Diana, as they jolted along a deep-rutted lane. "If she is we won't get a cent. Everybody says Dan Blair doesn't dare have his hair cut without asking her permission; and it's certain she's very close, to state it moderately. She says she has to be just before she's generous. But Mrs. Lynde says she's so much 'before' that generosity never catches up with her at all."

Anne related their experience at the Blair place to Marilla that evening.

"We tied the horse and then rapped at the kitchen door. Nobody came but the door was open and we could hear somebody in the pantry, going on dreadfully. We couldn't make out the words but Diana says she knows they were swearing by the sound of them. I can't believe that of Mr. Blair, for he is always so quiet and meek; but at least he had great provocation, for Marilla, when that poor man came to the door, red as a beet, with perspiration streaming down his face, he had on one of his wife's big gingham aprons. 'I can't get this durned thing off,' he said, 'for the strings are tied in a hard knot and I can't bust 'em, so you'll have to excuse me, ladies.' We begged him not to mention it and went in and sat down. Mr. Blair sat down too; he twisted the apron around to his back and rolled it up, but he did look so ashamed and worried that I felt sorry for him, and Diana said she feared we had called at an inconvenient time. 'Oh, not at all,' said Mr. Blair, trying to smile . . . you know he is always very polite . . . 'I'm a little busy . . . getting ready to bake a cake as it were. My wife got a telegram today that her sister from Montreal is coming tonight and she's gone to the train to meet her and left orders for me to make a cake for tea. She writ out the recipe and told me what to do but I've clean forgot half the directions already. And it says, "flavor according to taste." What does that mean? How can you tell? And what if my taste doesn't happen to be other people's taste? Would a tablespoon of vanilla be enough for a small layer cake?'

"I felt sorrier than ever for the poor man. He didn't seem to be in his proper sphere at all. I had heard of henpecked husbands and now I felt that I saw one. It was on my lips to say, 'Mr. Blair, if you'll give us a subscription for the hall I'll mix up your cake for you.' But I suddenly thought it wouldn't be neighborly to drive too sharp a bargain with a fellow creature in distress. So I offered to mix the cake for

him without any conditions at all. He just jumped at
my offer. He said he'd been used to making his own
bread before he was married but he feared cake was
beyond him, and yet he hated to disappoint his wife.
He got me another apron, and Diana beat the eggs
and I mixed the cake. Mr. Blair ran about and got us
the materials. He had forgotten all about his apron and
when he ran it streamed out behind him and Diana
said she thought she would die to see it. He said he
could bake the cake all right . . . he was used to that
. . . and then he asked for our list and he put down
four dollars. So you see we were rewarded. But even if
he hadn't given a cent I'd always feel that we had
done a truly Christian act in helping him."

Theodore White's was the next stopping place.
Neither Anne nor Diana had ever been there before,
and they had only a very slight acquaintance with Mrs.
Theodore, who was not given to hospitality. Should
they go to the back or front door? While they held a
whispered consultation Mrs. Theodore appeared at the
front door with an armful of newspapers. Deliberately
she laid them down one by one on the porch floor and
the porch steps, and then down the path to the very
feet of her mystified callers.

"Will you please wipe your feet carefully on the
grass and then walk on these papers?" she said
anxiously. "I've just swept the house all over and I
can't have any more dust tracked in. The path's been
real muddy since the rain yesterday."

"Don't you dare laugh," warned Anne in a
whisper, as they marched along the newspapers. "And
I implore you, Diana, not to look at me, no matter
what she says, or I shall not be able to keep a sober
face."

The papers extended across the hall and into a
prim, fleckless parlor. Anne and Diana sat down
gingerly on the nearest chairs and explained their
errand. Mrs. White heard them politely, interrupting
only twice, once to chase out an adventurous fly, and
once to pick up a tiny wisp of grass that had fallen on

the carpet from Anne's dress. Anne felt wretchedly guilty; but Mrs. White subscribed two dollars and paid the money down . . . "to prevent us from having to go back for it," Diana said when they got away. Mrs. White had the newspapers gathered up before they had their horse untied and as they drove out of the yard they saw her busily wielding a broom in the hall.

"I've always heard that Mrs. Theodore White was the neatest woman alive and I'll believe it after this," said Diana, giving way to her suppressed laughter as soon as it was safe.

"I am glad she has no children," said Anne solemnly. "It would be dreadful beyond words for them if she had."

At the Spencers' Mrs. Isabella Spencer made them miserable by saying something ill-natured about everyone in Avonlea. Mr. Thomas Boulter refused to give anything because the hall, when it had been built, twenty years before, hadn't been built on the site he recommended. Mrs. Esther Bell, who was the picture of health, took half an hour to detail all her aches and pains, and sadly put down fifty cents because she wouldn't be there that time next year to do it . . . no, she would be in her grave.

Their worst reception, however, was at Simon Fletcher's. When they drove into the yard they saw two faces peering at them through the porch window. But although they rapped and waited patiently and persistently nobody came to the door. Two decidedly ruffled and indignant girls drove away from Simon Fletcher's. Even Anne admitted that she was beginning to feel discouraged. But the tide turned after that. Several Sloane homesteads came next, where they got liberal subscriptions, and from that to the end they fared well, with only an occasional snub. Their last place of call was at Robert Dickson's by the pond bridge. They stayed to tea here, although they were nearly home, rather than risk offending Mrs. Dickson, who had the reputation of being a very "touchy" woman.

While they were there old Mrs. James White called in.

"I've just been down to Lorenzo's," she announced. "He's the proudest man in Avonlea this minute. What do you think? There's a brand new boy there . . . and after seven girls that's quite an event, I can tell you."

Anne pricked up her ears, and when they drove away she said,

"I'm going straight to Lorenzo White's."

"But he lives on the White Sands road and it's quite a distance out of our way," protested Diana. "Gilbert and Fred will canvass him."

"They are not going around until next Saturday and it will be too late by then," said Anne firmly. "The novelty will be worn off. Lorenzo White is dreadfully mean but he will subscribe to *anything* just now. We mustn't let such a golden opportunity slip, Diana."

The result justified Anne's foresight. Mr. White met them in the yard, beaming like the sun upon an Easter day. When Anne asked for a subscription he agreed enthusiastically.

"Certain, certain. Just put me down for a dollar more than the highest subscription you've got."

"That will be five dollars . . . Mr. Daniel Blair put down four," said Anne, half afraid. But Lorenzo did not flinch.

"Five it is . . . and here's the money on the spot. Now, I want you to come into the house. There's something in there worth seeing . . . something very few people have seen as yet. Just come in and pass *your* opinion."

"What will we say if the baby isn't pretty?" whispered Diana in trepidation as they followed the excited Lorenzo into the house.

"Oh, there will certainly be something else nice to say about it," said Anne easily. "There always is about a baby."

The baby *was* pretty, however, and Mr. White felt that he got his five dollars' worth out of the girls' honest delight over the plump little newcomer. But that was the first, last, and only time that Lorenzo White ever subscribed to anything.

Anne, tired as she was, made one more effort for the public weal that night, slipping over the fields to interview Mr. Harrison, who was as usual smoking his pipe on the veranda with Ginger beside him. Strictly speaking he was on the Carmody road; but Jane and Gertie, who were not acquainted with him save by doubtful report, had nervously begged Anne to canvass him.

Mr. Harrison, however, flatly refused to subscribe a cent, and all Anne's wiles were in vain.

"But I thought you approved of our society, Mr. Harrison," she mourned.

"So I do . . . so I do . . . but my approval doesn't go as deep as my pocket, Anne."

"A few more experiences such as I have had today would make me as much of a pessimist as Miss Eliza Andrews," Anne told her reflection in the east gable mirror at bedtime.

VII

The Pointing of Duty

Anne leaned back in her chair one mild October evening and sighed. She was sitting at a table covered with text books and exercises, but the closely written sheets of paper before her had no apparent connection with studies or school work.

"What is the matter?" asked Gilbert, who had arrived at the open kitchen door just in time to hear the sigh.

Anne colored, and thrust her writing out of sight under some school compositions.

"Nothing very dreadful. I was just trying to write out some of my thoughts, as Professor Hamilton advised me, but I couldn't get them to please me. They seem so stiff and foolish directly they're written down on white paper with black ink. Fancies are like shadows . . . you can't cage them, they're such wayward, dancing things. But perhaps I'll learn the secret some day if I keep on trying. I haven't a great many spare moments, you know. By the time I finish correcting school exercises and compositions, I don't always feel like writing any of my own."

"You are getting on splendidly in school, Anne. All the children like you," said Gilbert, sitting down on the stone step.

"No, not all. Anthony Pye doesn't and *won't* like me. What is worse, he doesn't respect me . . . no, he doesn't. He simply holds me in contempt and I don't mind confessing to you that it worries me miserably. It isn't that he is so very bad . . . he is only rather mischievous, but no worse than some of the others. He seldom disobeys me; but he obeys with a scornful air of toleration as if it wasn't worthwhile disputing the point or he would . . . and it has a bad effect on the others. I've tried every way to win him but I'm beginning to fear I never shall. I want to, for he's rather a cute little lad, if he *is* a Pye, and I could like him if he'd let me."

"Probably it's merely the effect of what he hears at home."

"Not altogether. Anthony is an independent little chap and makes up his own mind about things. He has always gone to men before and he says girl teachers are no good. Well, we'll see what patience and kindness will do. I like overcoming difficulties and teaching is really very interesting work. Paul Irving makes up for all that is lacking in the others. That child is a perfect darling, Gilbert, and a genius into the bargain. I'm persuaded the world will hear of him some day," concluded Anne in a tone of conviction.

"I like teaching, too," said Gilbert. "It's good training, for one thing. Why, Anne, I've learned more in the weeks I've been teaching the young ideas of White Sands than I learned in all the years I went to school myself. We all seem to be getting on pretty well. The Newbridge people like Jane, I hear; and I think White Sands is tolerably satisfied with your humble servant . . . all except Mr. Andrew Spencer. I met Mrs. Peter Blewett on my way home last night and she told me she thought it her duty to inform me that Mr. Spencer didn't approve of my methods."

"Have you ever noticed," asked Anne reflectively, "that when people say it is their duty to tell you a certain thing you may prepare for something disagreeable? Why is it that they never seem to think it a duty to tell you the pleasant things they hear about you? Mrs. H. B. Don*nell* called at the school again yesterday and told me she thought it *her* duty to inform me that Mrs. Harmon Andrews didn't approve of my reading fairy tales to the children, and that Mr. Rogerson thought Prillie wasn't coming on fast enough in arithmetic. If Prillie would spend less time making eyes at the boys over her slate she might do better. I feel quite sure that Jack Gillis works her class sums for her, though I've never been able to catch him red-handed."

"Have you succeeded in reconciling Mrs. Donnel's hopeful son to his saintly name?"

"Yes," laughed Anne, "but it was really a difficult task. At first, when I called him 'St. Clair' he would not take the least notice until I'd spoken two or three times; and then, when the other boys nudged him, he would look up with such an aggrieved air, as if I'd called him John or Charlie and he couldn't be expected to know I meant him. So I kept him in after school one night and talked kindly to him. I told him his mother wished me to call him St. Clair and I couldn't go against her wishes. He saw it when it was all explained out . . . he's really a very reasonable little fellow . . . and he said I could call him St. Clair but that he'd 'lick the stuffing' out of any of the boys that tried it. Of course, I had to rebuke him again for using such shocking language. Since then I call him St. Clair and the boys call him Jake and all goes smoothly. He informs me that he means to be a carpenter, but Mrs. Donnell says I am to make a college professor out of him."

The mention of college gave a new direction to Gilbert's thoughts, and they talked for a time of their plans and wishes . . . gravely, earnestly, hopefully, as youth love to talk, while the future is yet an untrodden path full of wonderful possibilities.

Gilbert had finally made up his mind that he was going to be a doctor.

"It's a splendid profession," he said enthusiastically. "A fellow has to fight something all through life . . . didn't somebody once define man as a fighting animal? . . . and I want to fight disease and pain and ignorance . . . which are all members one of another. I want to do my share of honest, real work in the world, Anne . . . add a little to the sum of human knowledge that all the good men have been accumulating since it began. The folks who lived before me have done so much for me that I want to show my gratitude by doing something for the folks who will live after me. It seems to me that is the only way a fellow can get square with his obligations to the race."

"I'd like to add some beauty to life," said Anne dreamily. "I don't exactly want to make people *know* more . . . though I know that *is* the noblest ambition . . . but I'd love to make them have a pleasanter time because of me . . . to have some little joy or happy thought that would never have existed if I hadn't been born."

"I think you're fulfilling that ambition every day," said Gilbert admiringly.

And he was right. Anne was one of the children of light by birthright. After she had passed through a life with a smile or a word thrown across it like a gleam of sunshine the owner of that life saw it, for the time being at least, as hopeful and lovely and of good report.

Finally Gilbert rose regretfully.

"Well, I must run up to MacPhersons'. Moody Spurgeon came home from Queen's today for Sunday and he was to bring me out a book Professor Boyd is lending me."

"And I must get Marilla's tea. She went to see Mrs. Keith this evening and she will soon be back."

Anne had tea ready when Marilla came home; the fire was crackling cheerily, a vase of frost-bleached ferns and ruby-red maple leaves adorned the table, and delectable odors of ham and toast pervaded the air. But Marilla sank into her chair with a deep sigh.

"Are your eyes troubling you? Does your head ache?" queried Anne anxiously.

"No. I'm only tired . . . and worried. It's about

Mary and those children . . . Mary is worse . . . she can't last much longer. And as for the twins, *I* don't know what is to become of them."

"Hasn't their uncle been heard from?"

"Yes, Mary had a letter from him. He's working in a lumber camp and 'shacking it,' whatever that means. Anyway, he says he can't possibly take the children till the spring. He expects to be married then and will have a home to take them to; but he says she must get some of the neighbors to keep them for the winter. She says she can't bear to ask any of them. Mary never got on any too well with the East Grafton people and that's a fact. And the long and short of it is, Anne, that I'm sure Mary wants me to take those children . . . she didn't say so but she *looked* it."

"Oh!" Anne clasped her hands, all athrill with excitement. "And of course you will, Marilla, won't you?"

"I haven't made up my mind," said Marilla rather tartly. "I don't rush into things in your headlong way, Anne. Third cousinship is a pretty slim claim. And it will be a fearful responsibility to have two children of six years to look after . . . twins, at that."

Marilla had an idea that twins were just twice as bad as single children.

"Twins are very interesting . . . at least one pair of them," said Anne. "It's only when there are two or three pairs that it gets monotonous. And I think it would be real nice for you to have something to amuse you when I'm away in school."

"I don't reckon there'd be much amusement in it . . . more worry and bother than anything else, I should say. It wouldn't be so risky if they were even as old as you were when I took you. I wouldn't mind Dora so much . . . she seems good and quiet. But that Davy is a limb."

Anne was fond of children and her heart yearned over the Keith twins. The remembrance of her own neglected childhood was very vivid with her still. She knew that Marilla's only vulnerable point was her stern devotion to what she believed to be her duty, and Anne skillfully marshalled her arguments along this line.

"If Davy is naughty it's all the more reason why he should have good training, isn't it, Marilla? If we don't take them we don't know who will, nor what kind of influences may surround them. Suppose Mrs. Keith's next door neighbors, the Sprotts, were to take them. Mrs. Lynde says Henry Sprott is the most profane man that ever lived and you can't believe a word his children say. Wouldn't it be dreadful to have the twins learn anything like that? Or suppose they went to the Wiggins'. Mrs. Lynde says that Mr. Wiggins sells everything off the place that can be sold and brings his family up on skim milk. You wouldn't like your relations to be starved, even if they were only third cousins, would you? It seems to me, Marilla, that it is our duty to take them."

"I suppose it is," assented Marilla gloomily. "I daresay I'll tell Mary I'll take them. You needn't look so delighted, Anne. It will mean a good deal of extra work for you. I can't sew a stitch on account of my eyes, so you'll have to see to the making and mending of their clothes. And you don't like sewing."

"I hate it," said Anne calmly, "but if you are willing to take those children from a sense of duty surely I can do their sewing from a sense of duty. It does people good to have to do things they don't like . . . in moderation."

VIII

Marilla Adopts Twins

Mrs. Rachel Lynde was sitting at her kitchen window, knitting a quilt, just as she had been sitting one evening several years previously when Matthew Cuthbert had driven down over the hill with what Mrs. Rachel called "his imported orphan." But that had been in springtime; and this was late autumn, and all the woods were leafless and the fields sere and brown. The sun was just setting with a great deal of purple and golden pomp behind the dark woods west of Avonlea when a buggy drawn by a comfortable brown nag came down the hill. Mrs. Rachel peered at it eagerly.

"There's Marilla getting home from the funeral," she said to her husband, who was lying on the kitchen lounge. Thomas Lynde lay more on the lounge nowadays than he had been used to do, but Mrs. Rachel, who was so sharp at noticing anything beyond her own household, had not as yet noticed this. "And she's got the twins with her . . . yes, there's Davy leaning over the dashboard grabbing at the pony's tail and Marilla jerking him back. Dora's sitting up on the seat as prim as you please. She always looks as if she'd just been starched and ironed. Well, poor Marilla is going to have her hands full this winter and no mistake. Still, I don't see that she could do anything less than take them, under the circumstances, and she'll have Anne to help her. Anne's tickled to death over the whole business, and she has a real knacky way with children, I must say. Dear me, it doesn't seem a day since poor Matthew brought Anne herself home and everybody laughed at the idea of Marilla bringing up a child. And now she has adopted twins. You're never safe from being surprised till you're dead."

The fat pony jogged over the bridge in Lynde's Hollow and along the Green Gables lane. Marilla's face was rather grim. It was ten miles from East Grafton and Davy Keith seemed to be possessed with a passion for perpetual motion. It was beyond Marilla's power to make him sit still and she had been in an agony the whole way lest he fall over the back of the wagon and break his neck, or tumble over the dashboard under the pony's heels. In despair she finally threatened to whip him soundly when she got him home. Whereupon Davy climbed into her lap, regardless of the reins, flung his chubby arms about her neck and gave her a bear-like hug.

"I don't believe you mean it," he said, smacking her wrinkled cheek affectionately. "You don't *look* like a lady who'd whip a little boy just 'cause he couldn't keep still. Didn't you find it awful hard to keep still when you was only 's old as me?"

"No, I always kept still when I was told," said Marilla, trying to speak sternly, albeit she felt her heart waxing soft within her under Davy's impulsive caresses.

"Well, I s'pose that was 'cause you was a girl," said Davy, squirming back to his place after another hug. "You *was* a girl once, I s'pose, though it's awful funny to think of it. Dora can sit still . . . but there ain't much fun in it *I* don't think. Seems to me it must be slow to be a girl. Here, Dora, let me liven you up a bit."

Davy's method of "livening up" was to grasp Dora's curls in his fingers and give them a tug. Dora shrieked and then cried.

"How can you be such a naughty boy and your

poor mother just laid in her grave this very day?" demanded Marilla despairingly.

"But she was glad to die," said Davy confidentially. "I know, 'cause she told me so. She was awful tired of being sick. We'd a long talk the night before she died. She told me you was going to take me and Dora for the winter and I was to be a good boy. I'm going to be good, but can't you be good running round just as well as sitting still? And she said I was always to be kind to Dora and stand up for her, and I'm going to."

"Do you call pulling her hair being kind to her?"

"Well, I ain't going to let anybody else pull it," said Davy, doubling up his fists and frowning. "They'd just better try it. I didn't hurt her much . . . she just cried 'cause she's a girl. I'm glad I'm a boy but I'm sorry I'm a twin. When Jimmy Sprott's sister conterdicks him he just says, 'I'm oldern you, so of course I know better,' and that settles *her*. But I can't tell Dora that, and she just goes on thinking diffrunt from me. You might let me drive the gee-gee for a spell, since I'm a man."

Altogether, Marilla was a thankful woman when she drove into her own yard, where the wind of the autumn night was dancing with the brown leaves. Anne was at the gate to meet them and lift the twins out. Dora submitted calmly to be kissed, but Davy responded to Anne's welcome with one of his hearty hugs and the cheerful announcement, "I'm Mr. Davy Keith."

At the supper table Dora behaved like a little lady, but Davy's manners left much to be desired.

"I'm so hungry I ain't got time to eat p'litely," he said when Marilla reproved him. "Dora ain't half as hungry as I am. Look at all the ex'cise I took on the road here. That cake's awful nice and plummy. We haven't had any cake at home for ever'n ever so long, 'cause mother was too sick to make it and Mrs. Sprott said it was as much as she could do to bake our bread for us. And Mrs. Wiggins never puts any plums in *her* cakes. Catch her! Can I have another piece?"

Marilla would have refused but Anne cut a generous second slice. However, she reminded Davy that he ought to say "Thank you" for it. Davy merely grinned at her and took a huge bite. When he had finished the slice he said,

"If you'll give me *another* piece I'll say thank you for *it.*"

"No, you have had plenty of cake," said Marilla in a tone which Anne knew and Davy was to learn to be final.

Davy winked at Anne, and then, leaning over the table, snatched Dora's first piece of cake, from which she had just taken one dainty little bite, out of her very fingers and, opening his mouth to the fullest extent, crammed the whole slice in. Dora's lip trembled and Marilla was speechless with horror. Anne promptly exclaimed, with her best "schoolma'am" air,

"Oh, Davy, gentlemen don't do things like that."

"I know they don't," said Davy, as soon as he could speak, "but I ain't a gemplum."

"But don't you want to be?" said shocked Anne.

"Course I do. But you can't be a gemplum till you grow up."

"Oh, indeed you can," Anne hastened to say, thinking she saw a chance to sow good seed betimes. "You can begin to be a gentleman when you are a little boy. And gentlemen *never* snatch things from ladies. . . . or forget to say thank you . . . or pull anybody's hair."

"They don't have much fun, that's a fact," said Davy frankly. "I guess I'll wait till I'm grown up to be one."

Marilla, with a resigned air, had cut another piece of cake for Dora. She did not feel able to cope with Davy just then. It had been a hard day for her, what with the funeral and the long drive. At that moment she looked forward to the future with a pessimism that would have done credit to Eliza Andrews herself.

The twins were not noticeably alike, although both were fair. Dora had long sleek curls that never got out of order. Davy had a crop of fuzzy little yellow ringlets all over his round head. Dora's hazel eyes were gentle and mild; Davy's were as roguish and dancing as an elf's. Dora's nose was straight, Davy's was a positive snub; Dora had a "prunes and prisms" mouth, Davy's was all smiles; and besides, he had a dimple in one cheek and none in the other, which gave him a dear, comical, lopsided look when he laughed. Mirth and mischief lurked in every corner of his little face.

"They'd better go to bed," said Marilla, who thought it was the easiest way to dispose of them. "Dora will sleep with me and you can put Davy in the west gable. You're not afraid to sleep alone, are you, Davy?"

"No; but I ain't going to bed for ever so long yet," said Davy comfortably.

"Oh, yes, you are." That was all the much-tried Marilla said, but something in her tone squelched even Davy. He trotted obediently upstairs with Anne.

"When I'm grown up the very first thing I'm going to do is stay up *all* night just to see what it would be like," he told her confidentially.

In after years Marilla never thought of that first week of the twins' sojourn at Green Gables without a shiver. Not that it really was so much worse than the weeks that followed it; but it seemed so by reason of its novelty. There was seldom a waking minute of any day when Davy was not in mischief or devising it; but his first notable exploit occurred two days after his arrival, on Sunday morning . . . a fine, warm day, as hazy and mild as September. Anne dressed him for church while Marilla attended to Dora. Davy at first objected strongly to having his face washed.

"Marilla washed it yesterday . . . and Mrs. Wiggins scoured me with hard soap the day of the funeral. That's enough for one week. I don't see the good of being so awful clean. It's lots more comfable being dirty."

"Paul Irving washes his face every day of his own accord," said Anne astutely.

Davy had been an inmate of Green Gables for little over forty-eight hours; but he already worshipped Anne and hated Paul Irving, whom he had heard Anne praising enthusiastically the day after his arrival. If Paul Irving washed his face every day, that settled it. He, Davy Keith, would do it too, if it killed him. The same consideration induced him to submit meekly to the other details of his toilet, and he was really a handsome little lad when all was done. Anne felt an almost maternal pride in him as she led him into the old Cuthbert pew.

Davy behaved quite well at first, being occupied in casting covert glances at all the small boys within view and wondering which was Paul Irving. The first two hymns and the Scripture reading passed off uneventfully. Mr. Allan was praying when the sensation came.

Lauretta White was sitting in front of Davy, her head slightly bent and her fair hair hanging in two long braids, between which a tempting expanse of white neck showed, encased in a loose lace frill. Lauretta was a fat, placid-looking child of eight, who had conducted herself irreproachably in church from the very first day her mother carried her there, an infant of six months.

Davy thrust his hand into his pocket and produced . . . a caterpillar, a furry, squirming caterpillar. Marilla saw and clutched at him but she was too late. Davy dropped the caterpillar down Lauretta's neck.

Right into the middle of Mr. Allan's prayer burst a series of piercing shrieks. The minister stopped appalled and opened his eyes. Every head in the congregation flew up. Lauretta White was dancing up and down in her pew, clutching frantically at the back of her dress.

"Ow . . . mommer . . . mommer . . . ow . . . take it off . . . ow . . . get it out . . . ow . . . that bad boy put it down my neck . . . ow . . . mommer . . . it's going further down. . . . ow . . . ow . . . ow. . . ."

Mrs. White rose and with a set face carried the hysterical, writhing Lauretta out of church. Her shrieks died away in the distance and Mr. Allan proceeded with the service. But everybody felt that it was a failure that day. For the first time in her life Marilla took no notice of the text and Anne sat with scarlet cheeks of mortification.

When they got home Marilla put Davy to bed and made him stay there for the rest of the day. She would not give him any dinner but allowed him a plain tea of bread and milk. Anne carried it to him and sat sorrowfully by him while he ate it with an unrepentant relish. But Anne's mournful eyes troubled him.

"I s'pose," he said reflectively, "that Paul Irving wouldn't have dropped a caterpillar down a girl's neck in church, would he?"

"Indeed he wouldn't," said Anne sadly.

"Well, I'm kind of sorry I did it, then," conceded Davy. "But it was such a jolly big caterpillar . . . I picked him up on the church steps just as we went in. It seemed a pity to waste him. And say, wasn't it fun to hear that girl yell?"

Tuesday afternoon the Aid Society met at Green Gables. Anne hurried home from school, for she knew that Marilla would need all the assistance she could give. Dora, neat and proper, in her nicely starched white dress and black sash, was sitting with the members of the Aid in the parlor, speaking demurely when spoken to, keeping silence when not, and in every way comporting herself as a model child. Davy, blissfully dirty, was making mud pies in the barnyard.

"I told him he might," said Marilla wearily. "I thought it would keep him out of worse mischief. He can only get dirty at that. We'll have our teas over before we call him to his. Dora can have hers with us, but I would never dare to let Davy sit down at the table with all the Aids here."

When Anne went to call the Aids to tea she found that Dora was not in the parlor. Mrs. Jasper Bell said Davy had come to the front door and called her out. A hasty consultation with Marilla in the pantry resulted in a decision to let both children have their teas together later on.

Tea was half over when the dining room was invaded by a forlorn figure. Marilla and Anne stared in dismay, the Aids in amazement. Could that be Dora . . . that sobbing nondescript in a drenched, dripping dress and hair from which the water was streaming on Marilla's new coin-spot rug?

"Dora, what has happened to you?" cried Anne, with a guilty glance at Mrs. Jasper Bell, whose family was said to be the only one in the world in which accidents never occurred.

"Davy made me walk the pigpen fence," wailed Dora. "I didn't want to but he called me a fraid-cat. And I fell off into the pigpen and my dress got all dirty and the pig runned right over me. My dress was just awful but Davy said if I'd stand under the pump he'd wash it clean, and I did and he pumped water all over me but my dress ain't a bit cleaner and my pretty sash and shoes is all spoiled."

Anne did the honors of the table alone for the rest of the meal while Marilla went upstairs and redressed Dora in her old clothes. Davy was caught and sent to bed without any supper. Anne went to his room at twilight and talked to him seriously . . . a method in which she had great faith, not altogether unjustified by results. She told him she felt very badly over his conduct.

"I feel sorry now myself," admitted Davy, "but the trouble is I never feel sorry for doing things till after I've did them. Dora wouldn't help me make pies 'cause she was afraid of messing her clo'es and that made me hopping mad. I s'pose Paul Irving wouldn't have made *his* sister walk a pigpen fence if he knew she'd fall in?"

"No, he would never dream of such a thing. Paul is a perfect little gentleman."

Davy screwed his eyes tight shut and seemed to meditate on this for a time. Then he crawled up and put his arms about Anne's neck, snuggling his flushed little face down on her shoulder.

"Anne, don't you like me a little bit, even if I ain't a good boy like Paul?"

"Indeed I do," said Anne sincerely. Somehow, it was impossible to help liking Davy. "But I'd like you better still if you weren't so naughty."

"I . . . did something else today," went on Davy in a muffled voice. "I'm sorry now but I'm awful scared to tell you. You won't be very cross, will you? And you won't tell Marilla, will you?"

"I don't know, Davy. Perhaps I ought to tell her. But I think I can promise you I won't if you promise me that you will never do it again, whatever it is."

"No, I never will. Anyhow, it's not likely I'd find any more of them this year. I found this one on the cellar steps."

"Davy, what is it you've done?"

"I put a toad in Marilla's bed. You can go and take it out if you like. But say, Anne, wouldn't it be fun to leave it there?"

"Davy Keith!" Anne sprang from Davy's clinging arms and flew across the hall to Marilla's room. The bed was slightly rumpled. She threw back the blankets in nervous haste and there in very truth was the toad, blinking at her from under a pillow.

"How can I carry that awful thing out?" moaned Anne with a shudder. The fire shovel suggested itself to her and she crept down to get it while Marilla was busy in the pantry. Anne had her own troubles carrying that toad downstairs, for it hopped off the shovel three times and once she thought she had lost it in the hall. When she finally deposited it in the cherry orchard she drew a long breath of relief.

"If Marilla knew she'd never feel safe getting into bed again in her life. I'm so glad that little sinner repented in time. There's Diana signaling to me from her window. I'm glad . . . I really feel the need of some diversion, for what with Anthony Pye in school and Davy Keith at home my nerves have had about all they can endure for one day."

IX

A Question of Color

"That old nuisance of a Rachel Lynde was here again today, pestering me for a subscription towards buying a carpet for the vestry room," said Mr. Harrison wrathfully. "I detest that woman more than anybody I know. She can put a whole sermon, text, comment, and application, into six words, and throw it at you like a brick."

Anne, who was perched on the edge of the veranda, enjoying the charm of a mild west wind blowing across a newly ploughed field on a gray November twilight and piping a quaint little melody among the twisted firs below the garden, turned her dreamy face over her shoulder.

"The trouble is, you and Mrs. Lynde don't understand one another," she explained. "That is always what is wrong when people don't like each other. I didn't like Mrs. Lynde at first either; but as soon as I came to understand her I learned to."

"Mrs. Lynde may be an acquired taste with some folks; but I didn't keep on eating bananas because I was told I'd learn to like them if I did," growled Mr. Harrison. "And as for understanding her, I understand that she is a confirmed busybody and I told her so."

"Oh, that must have hurt her feelings very much," said Anne reproachfully. "How could you say such a thing? *I* said some dreadful things to Mrs. Lynde long ago but it was when I had lost my temper. I couldn't say them *deliberately*."

"It was the truth and I believe in telling the truth to everybody."

"But you don't tell the whole truth," objected Anne. "You only tell the disagreeable part of the truth. Now, you've told me a dozen times that my hair was red, but you've never once told me that I had a nice nose."

"I daresay you know it without any telling," chuckled Mr. Harrison.

"I know I have red hair too . . . although it's *much* darker than it used to be . . . so there's no need of telling me that either."

"Well, well, I'll try and not mention it again since you're so sensitive. You must excuse me, Anne. I've got a habit of being outspoken and folks mustn't mind it."

"But they can't help minding it. And I don't think it's any help that it's your habit. What would you think of a person who went about sticking pins and needles into people and saying, 'Excuse me, you mustn't mind it . . . it's just a habit I've got.' You'd think he was crazy, wouldn't you? And as for Mrs. Lynde being a busybody, perhaps she is. But did you tell her she had a very kind heart and always helped the poor, and never said a word when Timothy Cotton stole a crock of butter out of her dairy and told his wife he'd bought it from her? Mrs. Cotton cast it up to her the next time they met that it tasted of turnips and Mrs. Lynde just said she was sorry it had turned out so poorly."

"I suppose she has some good qualities," conceded Mr. Harrison grudgingly. "Most folks have. I have some myself, though you might never suspect it. But anyhow I ain't going to give anything to that carpet. Folks are everlasting begging for money here, it seems to me. How's your project of painting the hall coming on?"

"Splendidly. We had a meeting of the A.V.I.S. last Friday night and found that we had plenty of money subscribed to paint the hall and shingle the roof too. *Most* people gave very liberally, Mr. Harrison."

Anne was a sweet-souled lass, but she could instill some venom into innocent italics when occasion required.

"What color are you going to have it?"

"We have decided on a very pretty green. The roof will be dark red, of course. Mr. Roger Pye is going to get the paint in town today."

"Who's got the job?"

"Mr. Joshua Pye of Carmody. He has nearly finished the shingling. We had to give him the contract, for every one of the Pyes . . . and there are four families, you know . . . said they wouldn't give a cent unless Joshua got it. They had subscribed twelve dollars between them and we thought that was too much to lose, although some people think we shouldn't have given in to the Pyes. Mrs. Lynde says they try to run everything."

"The main question is will this Joshua do his work well. If he does I don't see that it matters whether his name is Pye or Pudding."

"He has the reputation of being a good workman, though they say he's a very peculiar man. He hardly ever talks."

"He's peculiar enough all right then," said Mr. Harrison drily. "Or at least, folks here will call him so. I never was much of a talker till I came to Avonlea and then I had to begin in self-defense or Mrs. Lynde would have said I was dumb and started a subscription to have me taught sign language. You're not going yet, Anne?"

"I must. I have some sewing to do for Dora this evening. Besides, Davy is probably breaking Marilla's heart with some new mischief by this time. This morning the first thing he said was, 'Where does the dark go, Anne? I want to know.' I told him it went around to the other side of the world but after breakfast he declared it didn't . . . that it went down the well. Marilla says she caught him hanging over the well-box four times today, trying to reach down to the dark."

"He's a limb," declared Mr. Harrison. "He came over here yesterday and pulled six feathers out of Ginger's tail before I could get in from the barn. The poor bird has been moping ever since. Those children must be a sight of trouble to you folks."

"Everything that's worth having is some trouble," said Anne, secretly resolving to forgive Davy's next offence, whatever it might be, since he had avenged her on Ginger.

Mr. Roger Pye brought the hall paint home that night and Mr. Joshua Pye, a surly, taciturn man, began painting the next day. He was not disturbed in his task. The hall was situated on what was called "the lower road." In late autumn this road was always muddy and wet, and people going to Carmody traveled by the longer "upper" road. The hall was so closely surrounded by fir woods that it was invisible unless you were near it. Mr. Joshua Pye painted away in the solitude and independence that were so dear to his unsociable heart.

Friday afternoon he finished his job and went home to Carmody. Soon after his departure Mrs. Rachel Lynde drove by, having braved the mud of the lower road out of curiosity to see what the hall looked like in its new coat of paint. When she rounded the spruce curve she saw.

The sight affected Mrs. Lynde oddly. She dropped the reins, held up her hands, and said "Gracious Providence!" She stared as if she could not believe her eyes. Then she laughed almost hysterically.

"There must be some mistake . . . there *must*. I knew those Pyes would make a mess of things."

Mrs. Lynde drove home, meeting several people on the road and stopping to tell them about the hall. The news flew like wildfire. Gilbert Blythe, poring over a text book at home, heard it from his father's hired boy at sunset, and rushed breathlessly to Green Gables, joined on the way by Fred Wright. They found

Diana Barry, Jane Andrews, and Anne Shirley, despair personified, at the yard gate of Green Gables, under the big leafless willows.

"It isn't true surely, Anne?" exclaimed Gilbert.

"It *is* true," answered Anne, looking like the muse of tragedy. "Mrs. Lynde called on her way from Carmody to tell me. Oh, it is simply dreadful! *What* is the use of trying to improve anything?"

"What is dreadful?" asked Oliver Sloane, arriving at this moment with a bandbox he had brought from town for Marilla.

"Haven't you heard?" said Jane wrathfully. "Well, its simply this . . . Joshua Pye *has gone and painted the hall blue instead of green* . . . a deep, brilliant blue, the shade they use for painting carts and wheelbarrows. And Mrs. Lynde says it is the most hideous color for a building, especially when combined with a red roof, that she ever saw or imagined. You could simply have knocked me down with a feather when I heard it. It's heartbreaking, after all the trouble we've had."

"How on earth could such a mistake have happened?" wailed Diana.

The blame of this unmerciful disaster was eventually narrowed down to the Pyes. The Improvers had decided to use Morton-Harris paints and the Morton-Harris paint cans were numbered according to a color card. A purchaser chose his shade on the card and ordered by the accompanying number. Number 147 was the shade of green desired and when Mr. Roger Pye sent word to the Improvers by his son, John Andrew, that he was going to town and would get their paint for them, the Improvers told John Andrew to tell his father to get 147. John Andrew always averred that he did so, but Mr. Roger Pye as stanchly declared that John Andrew told him 157; and there the matter stands to this day.

That night there was blank dismay in every Avonlea house where an Improver lived. The gloom at

Green Gables was so intense that it quenched even Davy. Anne wept and would not be comforted.

"I *must* cry, even if I am almost seventeen, Marilla," she sobbed. "It's so mortifying. And it sounds the death knell of our society. We'll simply be laughed out of existence."

In life, as in dreams, however, things often go by contraries. The Avonlea people did not laugh; they were too angry. *Their* money had gone to paint the hall and consequently *they* felt themselves bitterly aggrieved by the mistake. Public indignation centered on the Pyes. Roger Pye and John Andrew had bungled the matter between them; and as for Joshua Pye, he must be a born fool not to suspect there was something wrong when he opened the cans and saw the color of the paint. Joshua Pye, when thus animadverted upon, retorted that the Avonlea taste in colors was no business of his, whatever his private opinion of it might be; he had been hired to paint the hall, not to talk about it; and he meant to have his money for it.

The Improvers paid him his money in bitterness of spirit, after consulting Mr. Peter Sloane, who was a magistrate.

"You'll have to pay it," Peter told him. "You can't hold him responsible for the mistake, since he claims he was never told what the color was supposed to be but just given the cans and told to go ahead. But it's a burning shame and that hall certainly does look awful."

The luckless Improvers expected that Avonlea would be more prejudiced than ever against them; but instead, public sympathy veered around in their favor. People thought the eager, enthusiastic little band who had worked so hard for their object had been badly used. Mrs. Lynde told them to keep on and show the Pyes that there really were people in the world who could do things without making a muddle of them. Mr. Major Spencer sent them word that he would clean out all the stumps along the road front of his farm and seed it down with grass at his own expense; and Mrs.

Hiram Sloane called at the school one day and beckoned Anne mysteriously out into the porch to tell her that if the "Sassiety" wanted to make a geranium bed at the crossroads in the spring they needn't be afraid of her cow, for she would see that the marauding animal was kept within safe bounds. Even Mr. Harrison chuckled, if he chuckled at all, in private, and was all sympathy outwardly.

"Never mind, Anne. Most paints fade uglier every year but that blue is as ugly as it can be to begin with, so it's bound to fade prettier. And the roof is shingled and painted all right. Folks will be able to sit in the hall after this without being leaked on. You've accomplished so much anyhow."

"But Avonlea's blue hall will be a byword in all the neighboring settlements from this time out," said Anne bitterly.

And it must be confessed that it was.

X

Davy in Search of a Sensation

Anne, walking home from school through the Birch Path one November afternoon, felt convinced afresh that life was a very wonderful thing. The day had been a good day; all had gone well in her little kingdom. St. Clair Donnell had *not* fought any of the other boys over the question of his name; Prillie Rogerson's face had been so puffed up from the effects of toothache that she did not once try to coquette with the boys in her vicinity. Barbara Shaw had met with only *one* accident . . . spilling a dipper of water over the floor . . . and Anthony Pye had not been in school at all.

"What a nice month this November has been!" said Anne, who had never quite got over her childish habit of talking to herself. "November is usually such a disagreeable month . . . as if the year had suddenly found out that she was growing old and could do nothing but weep and fret over it. This year is growing old gracefully . . . just like a stately old lady who knows she can be charming even with gray hair and wrinkles. We've had lovely days and delicious twilights. This last fortnight has been so peaceful, and even Davy has been almost well-behaved. I really think he is improving a great deal. How quiet the woods are today . . . not a murmur except that soft wind purring in the treetops! It sounds like surf on a faraway shore.

How dear the woods are! You beautiful trees! I love every one of you as a friend."

Anne paused to throw her arm about a slim young birch and kiss its cream-white trunk. Diana, rounding a curve in the path, saw her and laughed.

"Anne Shirley, you're only pretending to be grown up. I believe when you're alone you're as much a little girl as you ever were."

"Well, one can't get over the habit of being a little girl all at once," said Anne gaily. "You see, I was little for fourteen years and I've only been grown-uppish for scarcely three. I'm sure I shall always feel like a child in the woods. These walks home from school are almost the only time I have for dreaming . . . except the half hour or so before I go to sleep. I'm so busy with teaching and studying and helping Marilla with the twins that I haven't another moment for imagining things. You don't know what splendid adventures I have for a little while after I go to bed in the east gable every night. I always imagine I'm something very brilliant and triumphant and splendid . . . a great prima donna or a Red Cross nurse or a queen. Last night I was a queen. It's really splendid to imagine you are a queen. You have all the fun of it without any of the inconveniences and you can stop being a queen whenever you want to, which you couldn't in real life. But here in the woods I like best to imagine quite different things . . . I'm a dryad living in an old pine, or a little brown wood-elf hiding under a crinkled leaf. That white birch you caught me kissing is a sister of mine. The only difference is, she's a tree and I'm a girl, but that's no real difference. Where are you going, Diana?"

"Down to the Dicksons. I promised to help Alberta cut out her new dress. Can't you walk down in the evening, Anne, and come home with me?"

"I might . . . since Fred Wright is away in town," said Anne with a rather too innocent face.

Diana blushed, tossed her head, and walked on. She did not look offended, however.

Anne fully intended to go down to the Dicksons' that evening, but she did not. When she arrived at Green Gables she found a state of affairs which banished every other thought from her mind. Marilla met her in the yard . . . a wild-eyed Marilla.

"Anne, Dora is lost!"

"Dora! Lost!" Anne looked at Davy, who was swinging on the yard gate, and detected merriment in his eyes. "Davy, do you know where she is?"

"No, I don't," said Davy stoutly. "I haven't seen her since dinner time, cross my heart."

"I've been away ever since one o'clock," said Marilla. "Thomas Lynde took sick all of a sudden and Rachel sent up for me to go at once. When I left here Dora was playing with her doll in the kitchen and Davy was making mud pies behind the barn. I only got home half an hour ago . . . and no Dora to be seen. Davy declares he never saw her since I left."

"Neither I did," avowed Davy solemnly.

"She must be somewhere around," said Anne. "She would never wander far away alone . . . you know how timid she is. Perhaps she has fallen asleep in one of the rooms."

Marilla shook her head.

"I've hunted the whole house through. But she may be in some of the buildings."

A thorough search followed. Every corner of house, yard, and outbuildings was ransacked by those two distracted people. Anne roved the orchards and the Haunted Wood, calling Dora's name. Marilla took a candle and explored the cellar. Davy accompanied each of them in turn, and was fertile in thinking of places where Dora could possibly be. Finally they met again in the yard.

"It's a most mysterious thing," groaned Marilla.

"Where can she be?" said Anne miserably.

"Maybe she's tumbled into the well," suggested Davy cheerfully.

Anne and Marilla looked fearfully into each other's eyes. The thought had been with them both through their entire search but neither had dared to put it it into words.

"She . . . she might have," whispered Marilla.

Anne, feeling faint and sick, went to the well-box and peered over. The bucket sat on the shelf inside. Far down below was a tiny glimmer of still water. The Cuthbert well was the deepest in Avonlea. If Dora . . . but Anne could not face the idea. She shuddered and turned away.

"Run across for Mr. Harrison," said Marilla, wringing her hands.

"Mr. Harrison and John Henry are both away . . . they went to town today. I'll go for Mr. Barry."

Mr. Barry came back with Anne, carrying a coil of rope to which was attached a claw-like instrument that had been the business end of a grubbing fork. Marilla and Anne stood by, cold and shaken with horror and dread, while Mr. Barry dragged the well, and Davy, astride the gate, watched the group with a face indicative of huge enjoyment.

Finally Mr. Barry shook his head, with a relieved air.

"She can't be down there. It's a mighty curious thing where she could have got to, though. Look here, young man, are you sure you've no idea where your sister is?"

"I've told you a dozen times that I haven't," said Davy, with an injured air. "Maybe a tramp come and stole her."

"Nonsense," said Marilla sharply, relieved from her horrible fear of the well. "Anne, do you suppose she could have strayed over to Mr. Harrison's? She has always been talking about his parrot ever since that time you took her over."

"I can't believe Dora would venture so far alone but I'll go over and see," said Anne.

Nobody was looking at Davy just then or it would have been seen that a very decided change came over his face. He quietly slipped off the gate and ran, as fast as his fat legs could carry him, to the barn.

Anne hastened across the fields to the Harrison establishment in no very hopeful frame of mind. The house was locked, the window shades were down, and there was no sign of anything living about the place. She stood on the veranda and called Dora loudly.

Ginger, in the kitchen behind her, shrieked and swore with sudden fierceness; but between his outbursts Anne heard a plaintive cry from the little building in the yard which served Mr. Harrison as a toolhouse. Anne flew to the door, unhasped it, and caught up a small mortal with a tearstained face who was sitting forlornly on an upturned nail keg.

"Oh, Dora, Dora, what a fright you have given us! How came you to be here?"

"Davy and I come over to see Ginger," sobbed Dora, "but we couldn't see him after all, only Davy made him swear by kicking the door. And then Davy brought me here and run out and shut the door; and I couldn't get out. I cried and cried, I was so frightened, and oh, I'm so hungry and cold; and I thought you'd never come, Anne."

"Davy?" But Anne could say no more. She carried Dora home with a heavy heart. Her joy at finding the child safe and sound was drowned out in the pain caused by Davy's behavior. The freak of shutting Dora up might easily have been pardoned. But Davy had told falsehoods . . . downright cold-blooded falsehoods about it. That was the ugly fact and Anne could not shut her eyes to it. She could have sat down and cried with sheer disappointment. She had grown to love Davy dearly . . . how dearly she had not known until this minute . . . and it hurt her unbearably to discover that he was guilty of deliberate falsehood.

Marilla listened to Anne's tale in a silence that boded no good Davy-ward; Mr. Barry laughed and advised that Davy be summarily dealt with. When he had gone home Anne soothed and warmed the sobbing, shivering Dora, got her her supper and put her to bed. Then she returned to the kitchen, just as Marilla came grimly in, leading, or rather pulling, the

reluctant, cobwebby Davy, whom she had just found
hidden away in the darkest corner of the stable.

She jerked him to the mat on the middle of the
floor and then went and sat down by the east window.
Anne was sitting limply by the west window. Between
them stood the culprit. His back was toward Marilla
and it was a meek, subdued, frightened back; but his
face was toward Anne and although it was a little
shamefaced there was a gleam of comradeship in
Davy's eyes, as if he knew he had done wrong and
was going to be punished for it, but could count on a
laugh over it all with Anne later on.

But no half hidden smile answered him in Anne's
gray eyes, as there might have done had it been only a
question of mischief. There was something else . . .
something ugly and repulsive.

"How could you behave so, Davy?" she asked
sorrowfully.

Davy squirmed uncomfortably.

"I just did it for fun. Things have been so awful
quiet here for so long that I thought it would be fun
to give you folks a big scare. It was, too."

In spite of fear and a little remorse Davy grinned
over the recollection.

"But you told a falsehood about it, Davy," said
Anne, more sorrowfully than ever.

Davy looked puzzled.

"What's a falsehood? Do you mean a whopper?"

"I mean a story that was not true."

"Course I did," said Davy frankly. "If I hadn't you
wouldn't have been scared. I *had* to tell it."

Anne was feeling the reaction from her fright and
exertions. Davy's impenitent attitude gave the finishing
touch. Two big tears brimmed up in her eyes.

"Oh, Davy, how could you?" she said, with a
quiver in her voice. "Don't you know how wrong it
was?"

Davy was aghast. Anne crying . . . he had made
Anne cry! A flood of real remorse rolled like a wave
over his warm little heart and engulfed it. He rushed

to Anne, hurled himself into her lap, flung his arms around her neck, and burst into tears.

"I didn't know it was wrong to tell whoppers," he sobbed. "How did you expect me to know it was wrong? All Mr. Sprott's children told them *regular* every day, and cross their hearts too. I s'pose Paul Irving never tells whoppers and here I've been trying awful hard to be as good as him, but now I s'pose you'll never love me again. But I think you might have told me it was wrong. I'm awful sorry I've made you cry, Anne, and I'll never tell a whopper again."

Davy buried his face in Anne's shoulder and cried stormily. Anne, in a sudden glad flash of understanding, held him tight and looked over his curly thatch at Marilla.

"He didn't know it was wrong to tell falsehoods, Marilla. I think we must forgive him for that part of it this time if he will promise never to say what isn't true again."

"I never will, now that I know it's bad," asseverated Davy between sobs. "If you ever catch me telling a whopper again you can . . ." Davy groped mentally for a suitable penance . . . "you can skin me alive, Anne."

"Don't say 'whopper,' Davy . . . say 'falsehood,'" said the schoolma'am.

"Why?" queried Davy, settling comfortably down and looking up with a tearstained, investigating face. "Why ain't whopper as good as falsehood? I want to know. It's just as big a word."

"It's slang; and it's wrong for little boys to use slang."

"There's an awful lot of things it's wrong to do," said Davy with a sigh. "I never s'posed there was so many. I'm sorry it's wrong to tell whop . . . falsehoods, 'cause it's awful handy, but since it is I'm never going to tell any more. What are you going to do to me for telling them this time? I want to know." Anne looked beseechingly at Marilla.

"I don't want to be too hard on the child," said

Marilla. "I daresay nobody ever did tell him it was
wrong to tell lies, and those Sprott children were no fit
companions for him. Poor Mary was too sick to train
him properly and I presume you couldn't expect a six-
year-old child to know things like that by instinct. I
suppose we'll just have to assume he doesn't know
anything right and begin at the beginning. But he'll
have to be punished for shutting Dora up, and I can't
think of any way except to send him to bed without
his supper and we've done that so often. Can't you
suggest something else, Anne? I should think you
ought to be able to, with that imagination you're
always talking of."

"But punishments are so horrid and I like to
imagine only pleasant things," said Anne, cuddling
Davy. "There are so many unpleasant things in the
world already that there is no use in imagining any
more."

In the end Davy was sent to bed, as usual, there
to remain until noon next day. He evidently did some
thinking, for when Anne went up to her room a little
later she heard him calling her name softly. Going in,
she found him sitting up in bed, with his elbows on
his knees and his chin propped on his hands.

"Anne," he said solemnly, "is it wrong for
everybody to tell whop . . . falsehoods? I want to
know."

"Yes, indeed."

"Is it wrong for a grown-up person?"

"Yes."

"Then," said Davy decidedly, "Marilla is bad, for
she tells them. And she's worse'n me, for I didn't
know it was wrong but she does."

"Davy Keith, Marilla never told a story in her
life," said Anne indignantly.

"She did so. She told me last Tuesday that
something dreadful would happen to me if I didn't say
my prayers every night. And I haven't said them for
over a week, just to see what *would* happen . . . and
nothing has," concluded Davy in an aggrieved tone.

Anne choked back a mad desire to laugh with the conviction that it would be fatal, and then earnestly set about saving Marilla's reputation.

"Why, Davy Keith," she said solemnly, "something dreadful *has* happened to you this very day."

Davy looked sceptical.

"I s'pose you mean being sent to bed without any supper," he said scornfully, "but *that* isn't dreadful. Course, I don't like it, but I've been sent to bed so much since I come here that I'm getting used to it. And you don't save anything by making me go without supper either, for I always eat twice as much for breakfast."

"I don't mean your being sent to bed. I mean the fact that you told a falsehood today. And, Davy," . . . Anne leaned over the footboard of the bed and shook her finger impressively at the culprit . . . "for a boy to tell what isn't true is almost the worst thing that *could* happen to him . . . almost the very worst. So you see Marilla told you the truth."

"But I thought the something bad would be exciting," protested Davy in an injured tone.

"Marilla isn't to blame for what you thought. Bad things aren't always exciting. They're very often just nasty and stupid."

"It was awful funny to see Marilla and you looking down the well, though," said Davy, hugging his knees.

Anne kept a sober face until she got downstairs and then she collapsed on the sitting room lounge and laughed until her sides ached.

"I wish you'd tell me the joke," said Marilla, a little grimly. "I haven't seen much to laugh at today."

"You'll laugh when you hear this," assured Anne. And Marilla did laugh, which showed how much her education had advanced since the adoption of Anne. But she sighed immediately afterwards.

"I suppose I shouldn't have told him that, although I heard a minister say it to a child once. But he did aggravate me so. It was that night you were at the Carmody concert and I was putting him to bed. He said he didn't see the good of praying until he got big enough to be of some importance to God. Anne, I do not know what we are going to do with that child. I never saw him beat. I'm feeling clean discouraged."

"Oh, don't say that, Marilla. Remember how bad I was when I came here."

"Anne, you never were bad . . . *never*. I see that now, when I've learned what real badness is. You were always getting into terrible scrapes, I'll admit, but your motive was always good. Davy is just bad from sheer love of it."

"Oh, no, I don't think it is real badness with him either," pleaded Anne. "It's just mischief. And it is rather quiet for him here, you know. He has no other boys to play with and his mind has to have something to occupy it. Dora is so prim and proper she is no good for a boy's playmate. I really think it would be better to let them go to school, Marilla."

"No," said Marilla resolutely, "my father always said that no child should be cooped up in the four walls of a school until it was seven years old, and Mr. Allan says the same thing. The twins can have a few lessons at home but go to school they shan't till they're seven."

"Well, we must try to reform Davy at home then," said Anne cheerfully. "With all his faults he's really a dear little chap. I can't help loving him. Marilla, it may be a dreadful thing to say, but honestly, I like Davy better than Dora, for all she's so good."

"I don't know but that I do, myself," confessed Marilla, "and it isn't fair, for Dora isn't a bit of trouble. There couldn't be a better child and you'd hardly know she was in the house."

"Dora is too good," said Anne. "She'd behave just as well if there wasn't a soul to tell her what to do. She was born already brought up, so she doesn't need us; and I think," concluded Anne, hitting on a very vital truth, "that we always love best the people who need us. Davy needs us badly."

"He certainly needs something," agreed Marilla. "Rachel Lynde would say it was a good spanking."

XI

Facts and Fancies

"Teaching is really very interesting work," wrote Anne to a Queen's Academy chum. "Jane says she thinks it is monotonous but I don't find it so. Something funny is almost sure to happen every day, and the children say such amusing things. Jane says she punishes her pupils when they make funny speeches, which is probably why she finds teaching monotonous. This afternoon little Jimmy Andrews was trying to spell 'speckled' and couldn't manage it. 'Well,' he said finally, 'I can't spell it but I know what it means.'

" 'What?' I asked.

" 'St. Clair Donnell's face, miss.'

"St. Clair is certainly very much freckled, although I try to prevent the others from commenting on it . . . for I was freckled once and well do I remember it. But I don't think St. Clair minds. It was because Jimmy called him 'St. Clair' that St. Clair pounded him on the way home from school. I heard of the pounding, but not officially, so I don't think I'll take any notice of it.

"Yesterday I was trying to teach Lottie Wright to do addition. I said, 'If you had three candies in one hand and two in the other, how many would you have altogether?' 'A mouthful,' said Lottie. And in the nature study class, when I asked them to give me a good reason why toads shouldn't be killed, Benjie Sloane gravely answered, 'Because it would rain the next day.'

"It's so hard not to laugh, Stella. I have to save up all my amusement until I get home, and Marilla says it makes her nervous to hear wild shrieks of mirth proceeding from the east gable without any apparent cause. She says a man in Grafton went insane once and that was how it began.

"Did you know that Thomas à Becket was canonized as a *snake?* Rose Bell says he was . . . also that William Tyndale *wrote* the New Testament. Claude White says a 'glacier' is a man who puts in window frames!

"I think the most difficult thing in teaching, as well as the most interesting, is to get the children to tell you their real thoughts about things. One stormy day last week I gathered them around me at dinner hour and tried to get them to talk to me just as if I were one of themselves. I asked them to tell me the things they most wanted. Some of the answers were commonplace enough . . . dolls, ponies, and skates. Others were decidedly original. Hester Boulter wanted 'to wear her Sunday dress every day and eat in the sitting room.' Hannah Bell wanted 'to be good without having to take any trouble about it.' Marjory White, aged ten, wanted to be a *widow.* Questioned why, she gravely said that if you weren't married people called you an old maid, and if you were your husband bossed you; but if you were a widow there'd be no danger of either. The most remarkable wish was Sally Bell's. She wanted a 'honeymoon.' I asked her if she knew what it was and she said she thought it was an extra nice kind of bicycle because her cousin in Montreal went on a honeymoon when he was married and he had always had the very latest in bicycles!

"Another day I asked them all to tell me the naughtiest thing they had ever done. I couldn't get the older ones to do so, but the third class answered quite freely. Eliza Bell had 'set fire to her aunt's carded rolls.' Asked if she meant to do it she said, 'not altogether.' She just tried a little end to see how it would burn and the whole bundle blazed up in a jiffy. Emerson Gillis had spent ten cents for candy when he should have put it in his missionary box. Annetta Bell's worst crime was 'eating some blueberries that grew in the graveyard.' Willie White had 'slid down the sheephouse roof a lot of times with his Sunday trousers on.' 'But I was punished for it 'cause I had to wear patched pants to Sunday School all summer, and when you're punished for a thing you don't have to repent of it,' declared Willie.

"I wish you could see some of their compositions . . . so much do I wish it that I'll send you copies of some written recently. Last week I told the fourth class I wanted them to write me letters about anything they pleased, adding by way of suggestion that they might tell me of some place they had visited or some interesting thing or person they had seen. They were to write the letters on real note paper, seal them in an envelope, and address them to me, all without any assistance from other people. Last Friday morning I found a pile of letters on my desk and that evening I realized afresh that teaching has its pleasures as well as its pains. Those compositions would atone for much. Here is Ned Clay's, address, spelling, and grammar as originally penned.

" 'Miss teacher ShiRley
　　" 'Green gabels.
　　　　" 'p. e. Island can

　　　　" 'birds

" 'Dear teacher I think I will write you a composition about birds. birds is very useful animals. my cat catches birds. His name is William but pa calls him tom, he is oll striped and he got one of his ears froz of last winter. only for that he would be a good-looking cat. My unkle has adopted a cat. it come to his house one day and woudent go away and unkle says it has forgot more than most people ever knowed. he lets it sleep on his rocking chare and my aunt says he thinks more of it than he does of his children, that is not right. we ought to be kind to cats and give them new milk but we ought not to be better to them than to our children. this is oll I can think of so no more at present from

"'edward blake ClaY.'

"St. Clair Donnell's is, as usual, short and to the point. St. Clair never wastes words. I do not think he chose his subject or added the postscript out of malice aforethought. It is just that he has not a great deal of tact or imagination.

"'Dear Miss Shirley
"'You told us to describe something strange we have seen. I will describe the Avonlea Hall. It has two doors, an inside one and an outside one. It has six windows and a chimney. It has two ends and two sides. It is painted blue. That is what makes it strange. It is built on the lower Carmody road. It is the third most important building in Avonlea. The others are the church and the blacksmith shop. They hold debating clubs and lectures in it and concerts.

"'Your truly,
"'Jacob Donnell.

"'P.S. The hall is a very bright blue.'

"Annetta Bell's letter was quite long, which surprised me, for writing essays is not Annetta's forte, and hers are generally as brief as St. Clair's. Annetta is a quiet little puss and a model of good behavior, but there isn't a shadow of orginality in her. Here is her letter;—

"'Dearest teacher,
"'I think I will write you a letter to tell you how much I love you. I love you with my whole heart and soul and mind . . . with all there is of me to love . . . and I want to serve you for ever. It would be my high-

est privilege. That is why I try so hard to be good in school and learn my lessuns.

" 'You are so beautiful, my teacher. Your voice is like music and your eyes are like pansies when the dew is on them. You are like a tall stately queen. Your hair is like rippling gold. Anthony Pye says it is red, but you needn't pay any attention to Anthony.

" 'I have only known you for a few months but I cannot realize that there was ever a time when I did not know you . . . when you had not come into my life to bless and hallow it. I will always look back to this year as the most wonderful in my life because it brought you to me. Besides, it's the year we moved to Avonlea from newbridge. My love for you has made my life very rich and it has kept me from much of harm and evil. I owe this all to you, my sweetest teacher.

" 'I shall never forget how sweet you looked the last time I saw you in that black dress with flowers in your hair. I shall see you like that for ever, even when we are both old and gray. You will always be young and fair to me, dearest teacher. I am thinking of you all the time . . . in the morning and at the noontide and at the twilight. I love you when you laugh and when you sigh . . . even when you look disdainful. I never saw you look cross though Anthony Pye says you always look so but I don't wonder you look cross at him for he deserves it. I love you in every dress . . . you seem more adorable in each new dress than the last.

" 'Dearest teacher, good night. The sun has set and the stars are shining . . . stars that are as bright and beautiful as your eyes. I kiss your hands and face, my sweet. May God watch over you and protect you from all harm.

" 'Your afecksionate pupil
                              " 'Annetta Bell.'

"This extraordinary letter puzzled me not a little. I knew Annetta couldn't have composed it any more than she could fly. When I went to school the next day I took her for a walk down to the brook at recess and asked her to tell me the truth about the letter. Annetta cried and 'fessed up freely. She said she had never written a letter and she didn't know how to, or what to say, but there was a bundle of love letters in her mother's top bureau drawer which had been written to her by an old 'beau.'

"'It wasn't father,' sobbed Annetta, 'it was someone who was studying for a minister, and so he could write lovely letters, but ma didn't marry him after all. She said she couldn't make out what he was driving at half the time. But I thought the letters were sweet and that I'd just copy things out of them here and there to write you. I put "teacher" where he put "lady" and I put in something of my own when I could think of it and I changed some words. I put "dress" in place of "mood." I didn't know just what a "mood" was but I s'posed it was something to wear. I didn't s'pose you'd know the difference. I don't see how you found out it wasn't all mine. You must be awful clever, teacher.'

"I told Annetta it was very wrong to copy another person's letter and pass it off as her own. But I'm afraid that all Annetta repented of was being found out.

"'And I *do* love you, teacher,' she sobbed. 'It was all true, even if the minister wrote it first. I do love you with all my heart.'

"It's very difficult to scold anybody properly under such circumstances.

"Here is Barbara Shaw's letter. I can't reproduce the blots of the original.

"'Dear teacher,
"'You said we might write about a visit. I never visited but once. It was at my Aunt Mary's last winter. My Aunt Mary is a very particular woman and a great housekeeper. The first night I was there we were at tea. I knocked over a jug and broke it. Aunt Mary said she had had that jug ever since she was married and nobody had ever broken it before. When we got up I stepped on her dress and all the gathers tore out of the skirt. The next morning when I got up I hit the pitcher against the basin and cracked them both and I upset a cup of tea on the tablecloth at breakfast. When I was

helping Aunt Mary with the dinner dishes I dropped a
china plate and it smashed. That evening I fell downstairs and sprained my ankle and had to stay in bed for
a week. I heard Aunt Mary tell Uncle Joseph it was a
mercy or I'd have broken everything in the house.
When I got better it was time to go home. I don't like
visiting very much. I like going to school better, especially since I came to Avonlea.

> " 'Yours respectfully,
> " 'Barbara Shaw.'

"Willie White's began,

" 'Respected Miss,
　" 'I want to tell you about my Very Brave Aunt.
She lives in Ontario and one day she went out to the
barn and saw a dog in the yard. The dog had no business there so she got a stick and whacked him hard and
drove him into the barn and shut him up. Pretty soon a
man came looking for an imaginary lion' (Query;—Did
Willie mean a menagerie lion?) 'that had run away from
a circus. And it turned out that the dog was a lion and
my Very Brave Aunt had drüv him into the barn with a
stick. It is a wonder she was not et up but she was
very brave. Emerson Gillis says if she thought it was a
dog she wasn't any braver than if it really was a dog.
But Emerson is jealous because he hasn't got a Brave
Aunt himself, nothing but uncles.'

"I have kept the best for the last. You laugh at me
because I think Paul is a genius but I am sure his letter will convince you that he is a very uncommon
child. Paul lives away down near the shore with his
grandmother and he has no playmates . . . no *real*
playmates. You remember our School Management professor told us that we must not have 'favorites' among
our pupils, but I can't help loving Paul Irving the best
of all mine. I don't think it does any harm, though, for
everybody loves Paul, even Mrs. Lynde, who says she
could never have believed she'd get so fond of a Yankee. The other boys in school like him too. There is

nothing weak or girlish about him in spite of his dreams and fancies. He is very manly and can hold his own in all games. He fought St. Clair Donnell recently because St. Clair said the Union Jack was away ahead of the Stars and Stripes as a flag. The result was a drawn battle and a mutual agreement to respect each other's patriotism henceforth. St. Clair says he can hit the *hardest* but Paul can hit the *oftenest*.

"Paul's Letter.

" 'My dear teacher,

" 'You told us we might write you about some interesting people we knew. I think the most interesting people I know are my rock people and I mean to tell you about them. I have never told anybody about them except grandma and father but I would like to have you know about them because you understand things. There are a great many people who do *not* understand things so there is no use in telling them.

" 'My rock people live at the shore. I used to visit them almost every evening before the winter came. Now I can't go till spring, but they will be there, for people like that never change . . . that is the splendid thing about them. Nora was the first one of them I got acquainted with and so I think I love her the best. She lives in Andrews' Cove and she has black hair and black eyes, and she knows all about the mermaids and the water kelpies. You ought to hear the stories she can tell. Then there are the Twin Sailors. They don't live anywhere, they sail all the time, but they often come ashore to talk to me. They are a pair of jolly tars and they have seen everything in the world . . . and more than what is in the world. Do you know what happened to the youngest Twin Sailor once? He was sailing and he sailed right into a moonglade. A moonglade is the track the full moon makes on the water when it is rising from the sea, you know, teacher. Well, the youngest Twin Sailor sailed along the moonglade till he came right up to the moon, and there was a little golden door in the moon and he opened it and sailed right through. He had some wonderful adventures in the moon but it would make this letter too long to tell them.

" 'Then there is the Golden Lady of the cave. One day I found a big cave down on the shore and I went away in and after a while I found the Golden Lady. She has golden hair right down to her feet and her dress is all glittering and glistening like gold that is alive. And she has a golden harp and plays on it all day long . . . you can hear the music any time along shore if you listen carefully but most people would think it was only the wind among the rocks. I've never told Nora about the Golden Lady. I was afraid it might hurt her feelings. It even hurt her feelings if I talked too long with the Twin Sailors.

" 'I always met the Twin Sailors at the Striped Rocks. The youngest Twin Sailor is very good-tempered but the oldest Twin Sailor can look dreadfully fierce at times. I have my suspicions about that oldest Twin. I believe he'd be a pirate if he dared. There's really something very mysterious about him. He swore once and I told him if he ever did it again he needn't come ashore to talk to me because I'd promised grandmother I'd never associate with anybody that swore. He was pretty well scared, I can tell you, and he said if I would forgive him he would take me to the sunset. So the next evening when I was sitting on the Striped Rocks the oldest Twin came sailing over the sea in an enchanted boat and I got in her. The boat was all pearly and rainbowy, like the inside of the mussel shells, and her sail was like moonshine. Well, we sailed right across to the sunset. Think of that, teacher, I've been in the sunset. And what do you suppose it is? The sunset is a land all flowers, like a great garden, and the clouds are beds of flowers. We sailed into a great harbor, all the color of gold, and I stepped right out of the boat on a big meadow all covered with buttercups as big as roses. I stayed there for ever so long. It seemed nearly a year but the Oldest Twin says it was only a few minutes. You see, in the sunset land the time is ever so much longer than it is here.

" 'Your loving pupil,
" 'Paul Irving.

" 'P.S. Of course, this letter isn't really true, teacher.   P.I.' "

XII

A Jonah Day

It really began the night before with a restless, wakeful vigil of grumbling toothache. When Anne arose in the dull, bitter winter morning she felt that life was flat, stale, and unprofitable.

She went to school in no angelic mood. Her cheek was swollen and her face ached. The schoolroom was cold and smoky, for the fire refused to burn and the children were huddled about it in shivering groups. Anne sent them to their seats with a sharper tone than she had ever used before. Anthony Pye strutted to his with his usual impertinent swagger and she saw him whisper something to his seat-mate and then glance at her with a grin.

Never, so it seemed to Anne, had there been so many squeaky pencils as there were that morning; and when Barbara Shaw came up to the desk with a sum she tripped over the coal scuttle with disastrous results. The coal rolled to every part of the room, her slate was broken into fragments, and when she picked herself up, her face, stained with coat dust, sent the boys into roars of laughter.

Anne turned from the second reader class which she was hearing.

"Really, Barbara," she said icily, "if you cannot move without falling over something you'd better remain in your seat. It is positively disgraceful for a girl of your age to be so awkward."

Poor Barbara stumbled back to her desk, her tears combining with the coal dust to produce an effect truly grotesque. Never before had her beloved, sympathetic teacher spoken to her in such a tone or fashion, and Barbara was heartbroken. Anne herself felt a prick of conscience but it only served to increase her mental irritation, and the second reader class remember that lesson yet, as well as the unmerciful infliction of arithmetic that followed. Just as Anne was snapping the sums out St. Clair Donnell arrived breathlessly.

"You are half an hour late, St. Clair," Anne reminded him frigidly. "Why is this?"

"Please, miss, I had to help ma make a pudding for dinner 'cause we're expecting company and Clarice Almira's sick," was St. Clair's answer, given in a perfectly respectful voice but nevertheless provocative of great mirth among his mates.

"Take your seat and work out the six problems on page eighty-four of your arithmetic for punishment," said Anne. St. Clair looked rather amazed at her tone but he went meekly to his desk and took out his slate. Then he stealthily passed a small parcel to Joe Sloane across the aisle. Anne caught him in the act and jumped to a fatal conclusion about that parcel.

Old Mrs. Hiram Sloane had lately taken to making and selling "nut cakes" by way of adding to her scanty income. The cakes were specially tempting to small boys and for several weeks Anne had had not a little trouble in regard to them. On their way to school the boys would invest their spare cash at Mrs. Hiram's, bring the cakes along with them to school, and, if possible, eat them and treat their mates during school hours. Anne had warned them that if they brought any more cakes to school they would be confiscated; and yet here was St. Clair Donnell coolly passing a parcel of them, wrapped up in the blue and white striped paper Mrs. Hiram used, under her very eyes.

"Joseph," said Anne quietly, "bring that parcel here."

Joe, startled and abashed, obeyed. He was a fat

urchin who always blushed and stuttered when he was frightened. Never did anybody look more guilty than poor Joe at that moment.

"Throw it into the fire," said Anne.

Joe looked very blank.

"P . . . p . . . p . . . lease, m . . . m . . . miss," he began.

"Do as I tell you, Joseph, without any words about it."

"B . . . b . . . but m . . . m . . . miss . . . th . . . th . . . they're . . ." gasped Joe in desperation.

"Joseph, are you going to obey me or are you *not?*" said Anne.

A bolder and more self-possessed lad than Joe Sloane would have been overawed by her tone and the dangerous flash of her eyes. This was a new Anne whom none of her pupils had ever seen before. Joe, with an agonized glance at St. Clair, went to the stove, opened the big, square front door, and threw the blue and white parcel in, before St. Clair, who had sprung to his feet, could utter a word. Then he dodged back just in time.

For a few moments the terrified occupants of Avonlea school did not know whether it was an earthquake or a volcanic explosion that had occurred. The innocent looking parcel which Anne had rashly supposed to contain Mrs. Hiram's nut cakes really held an assortment of firecrackers and pinwheels for which Warren Sloane had sent to town by St. Clair Donnell's father the day before, intending to have a birthday celebration that evening. The crackers went off in a thunderclap of noise and the pinwheels bursting out of the door spun madly around the room, hissing and spluttering. Anne dropped into her chair white with dismay and all the girls climbed shrieking upon their desks. Joe Sloane stood as one transfixed in the midst of the commotion and St. Clair, helpless with laughter, rocked to and fro in the aisle. Prillie Rogerson fainted and Annetta Bell went into hysterics.

It seemed a long time, although it was really only

a few minutes, before the last pinwheel subsided. Anne, recovering herself, sprang to open doors and windows and let out the gas and smoke which filled the room. Then she helped the girls carry the unconscious Prillie into the porch, where Barbara Shaw, in an agony of desire to be useful, poured a pailful of half frozen water over Prillie's face and shoulders before anyone could stop her.

It was a full hour before quiet was restored . . . but it was a quiet that might be felt. Everybody realized that even the explosion had not cleared the teacher's mental atmosphere. Nobody, except Anthony Pye, dared whisper a word. Ned Clay accidentally squeaked his pencil while working a sum, caught Anne's eye and wished the floor would open and swallow him up. The geography class were whisked through a continent with a speed that made them dizzy. The grammar class were parsed and analyzed within an inch of their lives. Chester Sloane, spelling "odoriferous" with two f's, was made to feel that he could never live down the disgrace of it, either in this world or that which is to come.

Anne knew that she had made herself ridiculous and that the incident would be laughed over that night at a score of tea-tables, but the knowledge only angered her further. In a calmer mood she could have carried off the situation with a laugh but now that was impossible; so she ignored it in icy disdain.

When Anne returned to the school after dinner all the children were as usual in their seats and every face was bent studiously over a desk except Anthony Pye's. He peered across his book at Anne, his black eyes sparkling with curiosity and mockery. Anne twitched open the drawer of her desk in search of chalk and under her very hand a lively mouse sprang out of the drawer, scampered over the desk, and leaped to the floor.

Anne screamed and sprang back, as if it had been a snake, and Anthony Pye laughed aloud.

Then   a   silence   fell . . . a   very   creepy,

uncomfortable silence. Annetta Bell was of two minds whether to go into hysterics again or not, especially as she didn't know just where the mouse had gone. But she decided not to. Who could take any comfort out of hysterics with a teacher so white-faced and so blazing-eyed standing before one?

"Who put that mouse in my desk?" said Anne. Her voice was quite low but it made a shiver go up and down Paul Irving's spine. Joe Sloane caught her eye, felt responsible from the crown of his head to the sole of his feet, but stuttered out wildly,

"N . . . n . . . not m . . . m . . . me t . . . t . . . teacher, n . . . n . . . not m . . . m . . . me."

Anne paid no attention to the wretched Joseph. She looked at Anthony Pye, and Anthony Pye looked back, unabashed and unashamed.

"Anthony, was it you?"

"Yes, it was," said Anthony insolently.

Anne took her pointer from her desk. It was a long, heavy hardwood pointer.

"Come here, Anthony."

It was far from being the most severe punishment Anthony Pye had ever undergone. Anne, even the stormy-souled Anne she was at that moment, could not have punished any child cruelly. But the pointer nipped keenly and finally Anthony's bravado failed him; he winced and the tears came to his eyes.

Anne, conscience-stricken, dropped the pointer and told Anthony to go to his seat. She sat down at her desk feeling ashamed, repentant, and bitterly mortified. Her quick anger was gone and she would have given much to have been able to seek relief in tears. So all her boasts had come to this . . . she had actually whipped one of her pupils. How Jane would triumph! And how Mr. Harrison would chuckle! But worse than this, bitterest thought of all, she had lost her last chance of winning Anthony Pye. Never would he like her now.

Anne, by what somebody has called "a Herculaneum effort," kept back her tears until she got home that night. Then she shut herself in the east gable room and wept all her shame and remorse and disappointment into her pillows . . . wept so long that Marilla grew alarmed, invaded the room, and insisted on knowing what the trouble was.

"The trouble is, I've got things the matter with my conscience," sobbed Anne. "Oh, this has been such a Jonah day, Marilla. I'm so ashamed of myself. I lost my temper and whipped Anthony Pye."

"I'm glad to hear it," said Marilla with decision. "It's what you should have done long ago."

"Oh, no, no, Marilla. And I don't see how I can ever look those children in the face again. I feel that I have humiliated myself to the very dust. You don't know how cross and hateful and horrid I was. I can't forget the expression in Paul Irving's eyes . . . he looked so surprised and disappointed. Oh, Marilla, I *have* tried so hard to be patient and to win Anthony's liking . . . and now it has all gone for nothing."

Marilla passed her hard work-worn hand over the girl's glossy, tumbled hair with a wonderful tenderness. When Anne's sobs grew quieter she said, very gently for her,

"You take things too much to heart, Anne. We all make mistakes . . . but people forget them. And Jonah days come to everybody. As for Anthony Pye, why need you care if he does dislike you? He is the only one."

"I can't help it. I want everybody to love me and it hurts me so when anybody doesn't. And Anthony never will now. Oh, I just made an idiot of myself today, Marilla. I'll tell you the whole story."

Marilla listened to the whole story, and if she smiled at certain parts of it Anne never knew. When the tale was ended she said briskly.

"Well, never mind. This day's done and there's a new one coming tomorrow, with no mistakes in it yet, as you used to say yourself. Just come downstairs and have your supper. You'll see if a good cup of tea and those plum puffs I made today won't hearten you up."

"Plum puffs won't minister to a mind diseased," said Anne disconsolately; but Marilla thought it a good sign that she had recovered sufficiently to adapt a quotation.

The cheerful supper table, with the twins' bright faces, and Marilla's matchless plum puffs . . . of which Davy ate four . . . did "hearten her up" considerably after all. She had a good sleep that night and awakened in the morning to find herself and the world transformed. It had snowed softly and thickly all through the hours of darkness and the beautiful whiteness, glittering in the frosty sunshine, looked like a mantle of charity cast over all the mistakes and humiliations of the past.

> *"Every morn is a fresh beginning,*
> *Every morn is the world made new,"*

sang Anne, as she dressed.

Owing to the snow she had to go around by the road to school and she thought it was certainly an impish coincidence that Anthony Pye should come ploughing along just as she left the Green Gables lane. She felt as guilty as if their positions were reversed; but to her unspeakable astonishment Anthony not only lifted his cap . . . which he had never done before . . . but said easily,

"Kind of bad walking, ain't it? Can I take those books for you, teacher?"

Anne surrendered her books and wondered if she could possibly be awake. Anthony walked on in silence to the school, but when Anne took her books she smiled down at him . . . not the stereotyped "kind" smile she had so persistently assumed for his benefit but a sudden outflashing of good comradeship. Anthony smiled . . . no, if the truth must be told, Anthony *grinned* back. A grin is not generally supposed to be a respectful thing; yet Anne suddenly felt that if she had not yet won Anthony's liking she had, somehow or other, won his respect.

Mrs. Rachel Lynde came up the next Saturday and confirmed this.

"Well, Anne, I guess you've won over Anthony Pye, that's what. He says he believes you are some good after all, even if you are a girl. Says that whipping you gave him was 'just as good as a man's.'"

"I never expected to win him by whipping him, though," said Anne, a little mournfully, feeling that her ideals had played her false somewhere. "It doesn't seem right. I'm *sure* my theory of kindness *can't* be wrong."

"No, but the Pyes are an exception to every known rule, that's what," declared Mrs. Rachel with conviction.

Mr. Harrison said "Thought you'd come to it," when he heard it, and Jane rubbed it in rather unmercifully.

XIII

A Golden Picnic

Anne, on her way to Orchard Slope, met Diana, bound for Green Gables, just where the mossy old log bridge spanned the brook below the Haunted Wood, and they sat down by the margin of the Dryad's Bubble, where tiny ferns were unrolling like curly-headed green pixy folk wakening up from a nap.

"I was just on my way over to invite you to help me celebrate my birthday on Saturday," said Anne.

"Your birthday? But your birthday was in March!"

"That wasn't my fault," laughed Anne. "If my parents had consulted me it would never have happened then. I should have chosen to be born in spring, of course. It must be delightful to come into the world with the mayflowers and violets. You would always feel that you were their foster sister. But since I didn't, the next best thing is to celebrate my birthday in the spring. Priscilla is coming over Saturday and Jane will be home. We'll all four start off to the woods and spend a golden day making the acquaintance of the spring. We none of us really know her yet, but we'll meet her back there as we never can anywhere else. I want to explore all those fields and lonely places anyhow. I have a conviction that there are scores of beautiful nooks there that have never really been *seen* although they may have been *looked* at. We'll make friends with wind and sky and sun, and bring home the spring in our hearts."

"It *sounds* awfully nice," said Diana, with some inward distrust of Anne's magic of words. "But won't it be very damp in some places yet?"

"Oh, we'll wear rubbers," was Anne's concession to practicalities. "And I want you to come over early Saturday morning and help me prepare lunch. I'm going to have the daintiest things possible . . . things that will match the spring, you understand . . . little jelly tarts and lady fingers, and drop cookies frosted with pink and yellow icing, and buttercup cake. And we must have sandwiches too, though they're *not* very poetical."

Saturday proved an ideal day for a picnic . . . a day of breeze and blue, warm, sunny, with a little rollicking wind blowing across meadow and orchard. Over every sunlit upland and field was a delicate, flower-starred green.

Mr. Harrison, harrowing at the back of his farm and feeling some of the spring witch-work even in his sober, middle-aged blood, saw four girls, basket laden, tripping across the end of his field where it joined a fringing woodland of birch and fir. Their blithe voices and laughter echoed down to him.

"It's so easy to be happy on a day like this, isn't it?" Anne was saying, with true Anneish philosophy. "Let's try to make this a really golden day, girls, a day to which we can always look back with delight. We're to seek for beauty and refuse to see anything else. 'Begone, dull care!' Jane, you are thinking of something that went wrong in school yesterday."

"How do you know?" gasped Jane, amazed.

"Oh, I know the expression . . . I've felt it often enough on my own face. But put it out of your mind, there's a dear. It will keep till Monday . . . or if it doesn't so much the better. Oh, girls, girls, see that patch of violets! There's something for memory's picture gallery. When I'm eighty years old . . . if I ever am . . . I shall shut my eyes and see those violets just as I see them now. That's the first good gift our day has given us."

"If a kiss could be seen I think it would look like a violet," said Priscilla.

Anne glowed.

"I'm so glad you *spoke* that thought, Priscilla, instead of just thinking it and keeping it to yourself. This world would be a much more interesting place . . . although it *is* very interesting anyhow . . . if people spoke out their real thoughts."

"It would be too hot to hold some folks," quoted Jane sagely.

"I suppose it might be, but that would be their own faults for thinking nasty things. Anyhow, we can tell all our thoughts today because we are going to have nothing but beautiful thoughts. Everybody can say just what comes into her head. *That* is conversation. Here's a little path I never saw before. Let's explore it."

The path was a winding one, so narrow that the girls walked in single file and even then the fir boughs brushed their faces. Under the firs were velvety cushions of moss, and further on, where the trees were smaller and fewer, the ground was rich in a variety of green growing things.

"What a lot of elephant's ears," exclaimed Diana. "I'm going to pick a big bunch, they're so pretty."

"How did such graceful feathery things ever come to have such a dreadful name?" asked Priscilla.

"Because the person who first named them either had no imagination at all or else far too much," said Anne. "Oh, girls, look at that!"

"That" was a shallow woodland pool in the center of a little open glade where the path ended. Later on in the season it would be dried up and its place filled with a rank growth of ferns; but now it was a glimmering placid sheet, round as a saucer and clear as crystal. A ring of slender young birches encircled it and little ferns fringed its margin.

"*How* sweet!" said Jane.

"Let us dance around it like wood-nymphs," cried Anne, dropping her basket and extending her hands.

But the dance was not a success for the ground was boggy and Jane's rubbers came off.

"You can't be a wood-nymph if you have to wear rubbers," was her decision.

"Well, we must name this place before we leave it," said Anne, yielding to the indisputable logic of facts. "Everybody suggest a name and we'll draw lots, Diana?"

"Birch Pool," suggested Diana promptly.

"Crystal Lake," said Jane.

Anne, standing behind them, implored Priscilla with her eyes not to perpetrate another such name and Priscilla rose to the occasion with "Glimmer-glass." Anne's selection was "The Fairies' Mirror."

The names were written on strips of birch bark with a pencil Schoolma'am Jane produced from her pocket, and placed in Anne's hat. Then Priscilla shut her eyes and drew one. "Crystal Lake," read Jane triumphantly. Crystal Lake it was, and if Anne thought that chance had played the pool a shabby trick she did not say so.

Pushing through the undergrowth beyond, the girls came out to the young green seclusion of Mr. Silas Sloane's back pasture. Across it they found the entrance to a lane striking up through the woods and voted to explore it also. It rewarded their quest with a succession of pretty surprises. First, skirting Mr. Sloane's pasture, came an archway of wild cherry trees all in bloom. The girls swung their hats on their arms and wreathed their hair with the creamy, fluffy blossoms. Then the lane turned at right angles and plunged into a spruce wood so thick and dark that they walked in a gloom as of twilight, with not a glimpse of sky or sunlight to be seen.

"This is where the bad wood elves dwell," whispered Anne. "They are impish and malicious but they can't harm us, because they are not allowed to do evil in the spring. There was one peeping at us around that old twisted fir; and didn't you see a group of them on that big freckly toadstool we just passed? The good fairies always dwell in the sunshiny places."

"I wish there really were fairies," said Jane. "Wouldn't it be nice to have three wishes granted you . . . or even only one? What would you wish for, girls, if you could have a wish granted? I'd wish to be rich and beautiful and clever."

"I'd wish to be tall and slender," said Diana.

"I would wish to be famous," said Priscilla.

Anne thought of her hair and then dismissed the thought as unworthy.

"I'd wish it might be spring all the time and in everybody's heart and all our lives," she said.

"But that," said Priscilla, "would be just wishing this world were like heaven."

"Only like a part of heaven. In the other parts there would be summer and autumn . . . yes, and a bit of winter, too. I think I want glittering snowy fields and white frosts in heaven sometimes. Don't you, Jane?"

"I . . . I don't know," said Jane uncomfortably. Jane was a good girl, a member of the church, who tried conscientiously to live up to her profession and believed everything she had been taught. But she never thought about heaven any more than she could help, for all that.

"Minnie May asked me the other day if we would wear our best dresses every day in heaven," laughed Diana.

"And didn't you tell her we would?" asked Anne.

"Mercy, no! I told her we wouldn't be thinking of dresses at all there."

"Oh, I think we will . . . a *little,*" said Anne earnestly. "There'll be plenty of time in all eternity for it without neglecting more important things. I believe we'll all wear beautiful dresses . . . or I suppose *raiment* would be a more suitable way of speaking. I shall want to wear pink for a few centuries at first . . . it would take me that long to get tired of it, I feel sure. I do love pink so and I can never wear it in *this* world."

Past the spruces the lane dipped down into a sunny little open where a log bridge spanned a brook; and then came the glory of a sunlit beechwood where the air was like transparent golden wine, and the leaves fresh and green, and the wood floor a mosaic of tremulous sunshine. Then more wild cherries, and a little valley of lissome firs, and then a hill so steep that the girls lost their breath climbing it; but when they reached the top and came out into the open the prettiest surprise of all awaited them.

Beyond were the "back fields" of the farms that ran out to the upper Carmody road. Just before them, hemmed in by beeches and firs but open to the south, was a little corner and in it a garden . . . or what had once been a garden. A tumbledown stone dyke, overgrown with mosses and grass, surrounded it. Along the eastern side ran a row of garden cherry trees, white as a snowdrift. There were traces of old paths still and a double line of rosebushes through the middle; but all the rest of the space was a sheet of yellow and white narcissi, in their airiest, most lavish, wind-swayed bloom above the lush green grasses.

"Oh, how perfectly lovely!" three of the girls cried. Anne only gazed in eloquent silence.

"How in the world does it happen that there ever was a garden back here?" said Priscilla in amazement.

"It must be Hester Gray's garden," said Diana. "I've heard mother speak of it but I never saw it before, and I wouldn't have supposed that it could be in existence still. You've heard the story, Anne?"

"No, but the name seems familiar to me."

"Oh, you've seen it in the graveyard. She is buried down there in the poplar corner. You know the little brown stone with the opening gates carved on it and "Sacred to the memory of Hester Gray, aged twenty-two.' Jordan Gray is buried right beside her but there's no stone to him. It's a wonder Marilla never told you about it, Anne. To be sure, it happened thirty years ago and everybody has forgotten."

"Well, if there's a story we must have it," said Anne. "Let's sit right down here among the narcissi and Diana will tell it. Why, girls, there are hundreds of them . . . they've spread over everything. It looks as if the garden were carpeted with moonshine and sunshine combined. This is a discovery worth making. To think that I've lived within a mile of this place for six years and have never seen it before! Now, Diana."

"Long ago," began Diana, "this farm belonged to old Mr. David Gray. He didn't live on it . . . he lived where Silas Sloane lives now. He had one son, Jordan, and he went up to Boston one winter to work and while he was there he fell in love with a girl named Hester Murray. She was working in a store and she hated it. She'd been brought up in the country and she always wanted to get back. When Jordan asked her to marry him she said she would if he'd take her away to some quiet spot where she'd see nothing but fields and trees. So he brought her to Avonlea. Mrs. Lynde said he was taking a fearful risk in marrying a Yankee, and it's certain that Hester was very delicate and a very poor housekeeper; but mother says she was very pretty and sweet and Jordan just worshipped the ground she walked on. Well, Mr. Gray gave Jordan this farm and he built a little house back here and Jordan and Hester lived in it for four years. She never went out much and hardly anybody went to see her except mother and Mrs. Lynde. Jordan made her this garden and she was crazy about it and spent most of her time in it. She wasn't much of a housekeeper but she had a knack with flowers. And then she got sick. Mother says she thinks she was in consumption before she ever came here. She never really laid up but just grew weaker and weaker all the time. Jordan wouldn't have anybody to wait on her. He did it all himself and mother says he was as tender and gentle as a woman.

Every day he'd wrap her in a shawl and carry her out to the garden and she'd lie there on a bench quite happy. They say she used to make Jordan kneel down by her every night and morning and pray with her that she might die out in the garden when the time came. And her prayer was answered. One day Jordan carried her out to the bench and then he picked all the roses that were out and heaped them over her; and she just smiled up at him . . . and closed her eyes . . . and that," concluded Diana softly, "was the end."

"Oh, what a dear story," sighed Anne, wiping away her tears.

"What became of Jordan?" asked Priscilla.

"He sold the farm after Hester died and went back to Boston. Mr. Jabez Sloane bought the farm and hauled the little house out to the road. Jordan died about ten years after and he was brought home and buried beside Hester."

"I can't understand how she could have wanted to live back here, away from everything," said Jane.

"Oh, I can easily understand *that*," said Anne thoughtfully. "I wouldn't want it myself for a steady thing, because, although I love the fields and woods, I love people too. But I can understand it in Hester. She was tired to death of the noise of the big city and the crowds of people always coming and going and caring nothing for her. She just wanted to escape from it all to some still, green, friendly place where she could rest. And she got just what she wanted, which is something very few people do, I believe. She had four beautiful years before she died . . . four years of perfect happiness, so I think she was to be envied more than pitied. And then to shut your eyes and fall asleep among roses, with the one you loved best on earth smiling down at you . . . oh, I think it was beautiful!"

"She set out those cherry trees over there," said Diana. "She told mother she'd never live to eat their fruit, but she wanted to think that something she had planted would go on living and helping to make the world beautiful after she was dead."

"I'm so glad we came this way," said Anne, the shining-eyed. "This is my adopted birthday, you know, and this garden and its story is the birthday gift it has given me. Did your mother ever tell you what Hester Gray looked like, Diana?"

"No . . . only just that she was pretty."

"I'm rather glad of that, because I can imagine what she looked like, without being hampered by facts. I think she was very slight and small, with softly curling dark hair and big, sweet, timid brown eyes, and a little wistful, pale face."

The girls left their baskets in Hester's garden and spent the rest of the afternoon rambling in the woods and fields surrounding it, discovering many pretty nooks and lanes. When they got hungry they had lunch in the prettiest spot of all . . . on the steep bank of a gurgling brook where white birches shot up out of long feathery grasses. The girls sat down by the roots and did full justice to Anne's dainties, even the unpoetical sandwiches being greatly appreciated by hearty, unspoiled appetites sharpened by all the fresh air and exercise they had enjoyed. Anne had brought glasses and lemonade for her guests, but for her own part drank cold brook water from a cup fashioned out of birch bark. The cup leaked, and the water tasted of earth, as brook water is apt to do in spring; but Anne thought it more appropriate to the occasion than lemonade.

"Look, do you see that poem?" she said suddenly, pointing.

"Where?" Jane and Diana stared, as if expecting to see Runic rhymes on the birch trees.

"There . . . down in the brook . . . that old green, mossy log with the water flowing over it in those smooth ripples that look as if they'd been combed, and that single shaft of sunshine falling right athwart it, far down into the pool. Oh, it's the most beautiful poem I ever saw."

"I should rather call it a picture," said Jane. "A poem is lines and verses."

"Oh dear me, no." Anne shook her head with its fluffy wild cherry coronal positively. "The lines and verses are only the outward garments of the poem and are no more really it than your ruffles and flounces are *you*, Jane. The real poem is the soul within them . . . and that beautiful bit is the soul of an unwritten poem. It is not every day one sees a soul . . . even of a poem."

"I wonder what a soul . . . a person's soul . . . would look like," said Priscilla dreamily.

"Like that, I should think," answered Anne, pointing to a radiance of sifted sunlight streaming through a birch tree. "Only with shape and features of course. I like to fancy souls as being made of light. And some are all shot through with rosy stains and quivers . . . and some have a soft glitter like moonlight on the sea . . . and some are pale and transparent like mist at dawn."

"I read somewhere once that souls were like flowers," said Priscilla.

"Then your soul is a golden narcissus," said Anne, "and Diana's is like a red, red rose. Jane's is an apple blossom, pink and wholesome and sweet."

"And your own is a white violet, with purple streaks in its heart," finished Priscilla.

Jane whispered to Diana that she really could not understand what they were talking about. Could she?

The girls went home by the light of a calm golden sunset, their baskets filled with narcissus blossoms from Hester's garden, some of which Anne carried to the cemetery next day and laid upon Hester's grave. Minstrel robins were whistling in the firs and the frogs were singing in the marshes. All the basins among the hills were brimmed with topaz and emerald light.

"Well, we have had a lovely time after all," said Diana, as if she had hardly expected to have it when she set out.

"It has been a truly golden day," said Priscilla.

"I'm really awfully fond of the woods myself," said Jane.

Anne said nothing. She was looking afar into the western sky and thinking of little Hester Gray.

XIV

A Danger Averted

Anne, walking home from the post office one Friday evening, was joined by Mrs. Lynde, who was as usual cumbered with all the cares of church and state.

"I've just been down to Timothy Cotton's to see if I could get Alice Louise to help me for a few days," she said. "I had her last week, for, though she's too slow to stop quick, she's better than nobody. But she's sick and can't come. Timothy's sitting there, too, coughing and complaining. He's been dying for ten years and he'll go on dying for ten years more. That kind can't even die and have done with it . . . they can't stick to anything, even to being sick, long enough to finish it. They're a terrible shiftless family and what is to become of them I don't know, but perhaps Providence does."

Mrs. Lynde sighed as if she rather doubted the extent of Providential knowledge on the subject.

"Marilla was in about her eyes again Tuesday, wasn't she? What did the specialist think of them?" she continued.

"He was much pleased," said Anne brightly. "He says there is a great improvement in them and he thinks the danger of her losing her sight completely is past. But he says she'll never be able to read much or do any fine hand-work again. How are your preparations for your bazaar coming on?"

The Ladies' Aid Society was preparing for a fair

and supper, and Mrs. Lynde was the head and front of the enterprise.

"Pretty well . . . and that reminds me. Mrs. Allan thinks it would be nice to fix up a booth like an old-time kitchen and serve a supper of baked beans, doughnuts, pie, and so on. We're collecting old-fashioned fixings everywhere. Mrs. Simon Fletcher is going to lend us her mother's braided rugs and Mrs. Levi Boulter some old chairs and Aunt Mary Shaw will lend us her cupboard with the glass doors. I suppose Marilla will let us have her brass candlesticks? And we want all the old dishes we can get. Mrs. Allan is specially set on having a real blue willow ware platter if we can find one. But nobody seems to have one. Do you know where we could get one?"

"Miss Josephine Barry has one. I'll write and ask her if she'll lend it for the occasion," said Anne.

"Well, I wish you would. I guess we'll have the supper in about a fortnight's time. Uncle Abe Andrews is prophesying rain and storms for about that time; and that's a pretty sure sign we'll have fine weather."

The said "Uncle Abe," it may be mentioned, was at least like other prophets in that he had small honor in his own country. He was, in fact, considered in the light of a standing joke, for few of his weather predictions were ever fulfilled. Mr. Elisha Wright, who labored under the impression that he was a local wit, used to say that nobody in Avonlea ever thought of looking in the Charlottetown dailies for weather probabilities. No; they just asked Uncle Abe what it was going to be tomorrow and expected the opposite. Nothing daunted, Uncle Abe kept on prophesying.

"We want to have the fair over before the election comes off," continued Mrs. Lynde, "for the candidates will be sure to come and spend lots of money. The Tories are bribing right and left, so they might as well be given a chance to spend their money honestly for once."

Anne was a red-hot Conservative, out of loyalty to

Matthew's memory, but she said nothing. She knew better than to get Mrs. Lynde started on politics.

She had a letter for Marilla, postmarked from a town in British Columbia.

"It's probably from the children's uncle," she said excitedly, when she got home. "Oh, Marilla, I wonder what he says about them."

"The best plan might be to open it and see," said Marilla curtly. A close observer might have thought that she was excited also, but she would rather have died than show it.

Anne tore open the letter and glanced over the somewhat untidy and poorly written contents.

"He says he can't take the children this spring . . . he's been sick most of the winter and his wedding is put off. He wants to know if we can keep them till the fall and he'll try and take them then. We will, of course, won't we, Marilla?"

"I don't see that there is anything else for us to do," said Marilla rather grimly, although she felt a secret relief. "Anyhow they're not so much trouble as they were . . . or else we've got used to them. Davy has improved a great deal."

"His *manners* are certainly much better," said Anne cautiously, as if she were not prepared to say as much for his morals.

Anne had come home from school the previous evening, to find Marilla away at an Aid meeting, Dora asleep on the kitchen sofa, and Davy in the sitting room closet, blissfully absorbing the contents of a jar of Marilla's famous yellow plum preserves . . . "company jam," Davy called it . . . which he had been forbidden to touch. He looked very guilty when Anne pounced on him and whisked him out of the closet.

"Davy Keith, don't you know that it is very wrong of you to be eating that jam, when you were told never to meddle with anything in *that* closet?"

"Yes, I knew it was wrong," admitted Davy uncomfortably, "but plum jam is awful nice, Anne. I just peeped in and it looked so good I thought I'd take just a weeny taste. I stuck my finger in . . ." Anne groaned . . . "and licked it clean. And it was so much gooder than I'd ever thought that I got a spoon and just *sailed in.*"

Anne gave him such a serious lecture on the sin of stealing plum jam that Davy became conscience stricken and promised with repentant kisses never to do it again.

"Anyhow, there'll be plenty of jam in heaven, that's one comfort," he said complacently.

Anne nipped a smile in the bud.

"Perhaps there will . . . if we want it," she said, "But what makes you think so?"

"Why, it's in the catechism," said Davy.

"Oh, no, there is nothing like *that* in the catechism, Davy."

"But I tell you there is," persisted Davy. "It was in that question Marilla taught me last Sunday. 'Why should we love God?' It says, 'Because He makes preserves, and redeems us.' Preserves is just a holy way of saying jam."

"I must get a drink of water," said Anne hastily. When she came back it cost her some time and trouble to explain to Davy that a certain comma in the said catechism question made a great deal of difference in the meaning.

"Well, I thought it was too good to be true," he said at last, with a sigh of disappointed conviction. "And besides, I didn't see when He'd find time to make jam if it's one endless Sabbath day, as the hymn says. I don't believe I want to go to heaven. Won't there ever be any Saturdays in heaven, Anne?"

"Yes, Saturdays, and every other kind of beautiful days. And every day in heaven will be more beautiful than the one before it, Davy," assured Anne, who was rather glad that Marilla was not by to be shocked. Marilla, it is needless to say, was bringing the twins up in the good old ways of theology and discouraged all fanciful speculations thereupon. Davy and Dora were taught a hymn, a catechism question, and two Bible verses every Sunday. Dora learned meekly and recited like a little machine, with perhaps as much understanding or interest as if she were one. Davy, on the contrary, had a lively curiosity, and frequently asked questions which made Marilla tremble for his fate.

"Chester Sloane says we'll do nothing all the time in heaven but walk around in white dresses and play on harps; and he says he hopes he won't have to go till he's an old man, 'cause maybe he'll like it better then. And he thinks it will be horrid to wear dresses and I think so too. Why can't men angels wear trousers, Anne? Chester Sloane is interested in those things, 'cause they're going to make a minister of him. He's *got* to be a minister 'cause his grandmother left the money to send him to college and he can't have it unless he is a minister. She thought a minister was such a 'spectable thing to have in a family. Chester says he doesn't mind much . . . though he'd rather be a blacksmith . . . but he's bound to have all the fun he can before he begins to be a minister, 'cause he doesn't expect to have much afterwards. *I* ain't going to be a minister. I'm going to be a storekeeper, like Mr. Blair, and keep heaps of candy and bananas. But I'd rather like going to your kind of a heaven if they'd let me play a mouth organ instead of a harp. Do you s'pose they would?"

"Yes, I think they would if you wanted it," was all Anne could trust herself to say.

The A. V. I. S. met at Mr. Harmon Andrews' that evening and a full attendance had been requested, since important business was to be discussed. The A. V. I. S. was in a flourishing condition, and had already accomplished wonders. Early in the spring Mr. Major Spencer had redeemed his promise and had stumped, graded, and seeded down all the road front of his farm. A dozen other men, some prompted by a determination not to let a Spencer get ahead of them, others goaded into action by Improvers in their own households, had followed his example. The result was that there were long strips of smooth velvet turf where once had been unsightly undergrowth or brush. The farm fronts that had not been done looked so badly by contrast that their owners were secretly shamed into resolving to see what they could do another spring. The triangle of ground at the cross roads had also been cleared and seeded down, and Anne's bed of geraniums, unharmed by any marauding cow, was already set out in the center.

Altogether, the Improvers thought that they were getting on beautifully, even if Mr. Levi Boulter, tactfully approached by a carefully selected committee in regard to the old house on his upper farm, did bluntly tell them that he wasn't going to have it meddled with.

At this especial meeting they intended to draw up a petition to the school trustees, humbly praying that a fence be put around the school grounds; and a plan was also to be discussed for planting a few ornamental trees by the church, if the funds of the society would permit of it . . . for, as Anne said, there was no use in starting another subscription as long as the hall remained blue. The members were assembled in the Andrews' parlor and Jane was already on her feet to move the appointment of a committee which should find out and report on the price of said trees, when Gertie Pye swept in, pompadoured and frilled within an inch of her life. Gertie had a habit of being late . . . "to make her entrance more effective," spiteful people said. Gertie's entrance in this instance was certainly effective, for she paused dramatically on the middle of the floor, threw up her hands, rolled her eyes, and exclaimed,

"I've just heard something perfectly awful. What *do* you think? Mr. Judson Parker *is going to rent all the road fence of his farm to a patent medicine company to paint advertisements on.*"

For once in her life Gertie Pye made all the sensation she desired. If she had thrown a bomb among the complacent Improvers she could hardly have made more.

"It *can't* be true," said Anne blankly.

"That's just what *I* said when I heard it first, don't you know," said Gertie, who was enjoying herself hugely. "*I* said it couldn't be true . . . that Judson Parker wouldn't have the *heart* to do it, don't you know. But father met him this afternoon and asked him about it and he said it *was* true. Just fancy! His farm is side-on to the Newbridge road and how perfectly awful it will look to see advertisements of pills and plasters all along it, don't you know?"

The Improvers *did* know, all too well. Even the least imaginative among them could picture the grotesque effect of half a mile of board fence adorned with such advertisements. All thought of church and school grounds vanished before this new danger. Parliamentary rules and regulations were forgotten, and Anne, in despair, gave up trying to keep minutes at all. Everybody talked at once and fearful was the hubbub.

"Oh, let us keep calm," implored Anne, who was the most excited of them all, "and try to think of some way of preventing him."

"I don't know how you're going to prevent him," exclaimed Jane bitterly. "Everybody knows what Judson Parker is. He'd do *anything* for money. He hasn't a *spark* of public spirit or *any* sense of the beautiful."

The prospect looked rather unpromising. Judson Parker and his sister were the only Parkers in Avonlea, so that no leverage could be exerted by family connections. Martha Parker was a lady of all too certain age who disapproved of young people in general and the Improvers in particular. Judson was a jovial, smooth-spoken man, so uniformly good-natured and bland that it was surprising how few friends he had. Perhaps he had got the better in too many business transactions . . . which seldom makes for popularity. He was reputed to be very "sharp" and it was the general opinion that he "hadn't much principle."

"If Judson Parker has a chance to 'turn an honest penny,' as he says himself, he'll never lose it," declared Fred Wright.

"Is there *nobody* who has any influence over him?" asked Anne despairingly.

"He goes to see Louisa Spencer at White Sands," suggested Carrie Sloane. "Perhaps she could coax him not to rent his fences."

"Not she," said Gilbert emphatically. "I know Louisa Spencer well. She doesn't 'believe' in Village Improvement Societies, but she *does* believe in dollars and cents. She'd be more likely to urge Judson on than to dissuade him."

"The only thing to do is to appoint a committee to wait on him and protest," said Julia Bell, "and you must send girls, for he'd hardly be civil to boys . . . but *I* won't go, so nobody need nominate me."

"Better send Anne alone," said Oliver Sloane. "She can talk Judson over if anybody can."

Anne protested. She was willing to go and do the talking; but she must have others with her "for moral support." Diana and Jane were therefore appointed to support her morally and the Improvers broke up, buzzing like angry bees with indignation. Anne was so worried that she didn't sleep until nearly morning, and then she dreamed that the trustees had put a fence around the school and painted "Try Purple Pills" all over it.

The committee waited on Judson Parker the next afternoon. Anne pleaded eloquently against his nefarious design and Jane and Diana supported her morally and valiantly. Judson was sleek, suave, flattering; paid them several compliments of the delicacy of sunflowers; felt real bad to refuse such charming young ladies . . . but business was business; couldn't afford to let sentiment stand in the way these hard times.

"But I'll tell what I *will* do," he said, with a

twinkle in his light, full eyes. "I'll tell the agent he must use only handsome, tasty colors . . . red and yellow and so on. I'll tell him he mustn't paint the ads. *blue* on any account."

The vanquished committee retired, thinking things not lawful to be uttered.

"We have done all we can do and must simply trust the rest to Providence," said Jane, with an unconscious imitation of Mrs. Lynde's tone and manner.

"I wonder if Mr. Allan could do anything," reflected Diana.

Anne shook her head.

"No, it's no use to worry Mr. Allan, especially now when the baby's so sick. Judson would slip away from him as smoothly as from us, although he *has* taken to going to church quite regularly just now. That is simply because Louisa Spencer's father is an elder and very particular about such things."

"Judson Parker is the only man in Avonlea who would dream of renting his fences," said Jane indignantly. "Even Levi Boulter or Lorenzo White would never stoop to that, tightfisted as they are. They would have too much respect for public opinion."

Public opinion was certainly down on Judson Parker when the facts became known, but that did not help matters much. Judson chuckled to himself and defied it, and the Improvers were trying to reconcile themselves to the prospect of seeing the prettiest part of the Newbridge road defaced by advertisements, when Anne rose quietly at the president's call for reports of committees on the occasion of the next meeting of the Society, and announced that Mr. Judson Parker had instructed her to inform the Society that he was *not* going to rent his fences to the Patent Medicine Company.

Jane and Diana stared as if they found it hard to believe their ears. Parliamentary etiquette, which was generally very strictly enforced in the A. V. I. S., forbade them giving instant vent to their curiosity, but after the Society adjourned Anne was besieged for explanations. Anne had no explanation to give. Judson Parker had overtaken her on the road the preceding evening and told her that he had decided to humor the A. V. I. S. in its peculiar prejudice against patent medicine advertisements. That was all Anne would say, then or ever afterwards, and it was the simple truth; but when Jane Andrews, on her way home, confided to Oliver Sloane her firm belief that there was more behind Judson Parker's mysterious change of heart than Anne Shirley had revealed, she spoke the truth also.

Anne had been down to old Mrs. Irving's on the shore road the preceding evening and had come home by a short cut which led her first over the low-lying shore fields, and then through the beech wood below Robert Dickson's, by a little footpath that ran out to the main road just above the Lake of Shining Waters . . . known to unimaginative people as Barry's pond.

Two men were sitting in their buggies, reined off to the side of the road, just at the entrance of the path. One was Judson Parker; the other was Jerry Corcoran, a Newbridge man against whom, as Mrs. Lynde would have told you in eloquent italics, nothing shady had ever been *proved.* He was an agent for agricultural implements and a prominent personage in matters political. He had a finger . . . some people said *all* his fingers . . . in every political pie that was cooked; and as Canada was on the eve of a general election Jerry Corcoran had been a busy man for many weeks, canvassing the county in the interests of his party's candidate. Just as Anne emerged from under the overhanging beech boughs she heard Corcoran say,

"If you'll vote for Amesbury, Parker . . . well, I've a note for that pair of harrows you've got in the spring. I suppose you wouldn't object to having it back, eh?"

"We . . . ll, since you put it in that way," drawled Judson with a grin, "I reckon I might as well do it. A man must look out for his own interests in these hard times."

Both saw Anne at this moment and conversation abruptly ceased. Anne bowed frostily and walked on, with her chin slightly more tilted than usual. Soon Judson Parker overtook her.

"Have a lift, Anne?" he inquired genially.

"Thank you, no," said Anne politely, but with a fine, needle-like disdain in her voice that pierced even Judson Parker's none too sensitive consciousness. His face reddened and he twitched his reins angrily; but the next second prudential considerations checked him. He looked uneasily at Anne, as she walked steadily on, glancing neither to the right nor to the left. Had she heard Corcoran's unmistakable offer and his own too plain acceptance of it? Confound Corcoran! If he couldn't put his meaning into less dangerous phrases he'd get into trouble some of these long-come-shorts. And confound redheaded school-ma'ams with a habit of popping out of beechwoods where they had no business to be. If Anne had heard, Judson Parker, measuring her corn in his own half bushel, as the country saying went, and cheating himself thereby, as such people generally do, believed that she would tell it far and wide. Now, Judson Parker, as has been seen, was not overly regardful of public opinion; but to be known as having accepted a bribe would be a nasty thing; and if it ever reached Isaac Spencer's ears farewell forever to all hope of winning Louisa Jane with her comfortable prospects as the heiress of a well-to-do farmer. Judson Parker knew that Mr. Spencer looked somewhat askance at him as it was; he could not afford to take any risks.

"Ahem . . . Anne, I've been wanting to see you about that little matter we were discussing the other day. I've decided not to let my fences to that company after all. A society with an aim like yours ought to be encouraged."

Anne thawed out the merest trifle.

"Thank you," she said.

"And . . . and . . . you needn't mention that little conversation of mine with Jerry."

"I have no intention of mentioning it in any case," said Anne icily, for she would have seen every fence in Avonlea painted with advertisements before she would have stooped to bargain with a man who would sell his vote.

"Just so . . . just so," agreed Judson, imagining that they understood each other beautifully. "I didn't suppose you would. Of course, I was only stringing Jerry . . . he thinks he's so all-fired cute and smart. I've no intention of voting for Amesbury. I'm going to vote for Grant as I've always done . . . you'll see that when the election comes off. I just led Jerry on to see if he would commit himself. And it's all right about the fence . . . you can tell the Improvers that."

"It takes all sorts of people to make a world, as I've often heard, but I think there are some who could be spared," Anne told her reflection in the east gable mirror that night. "I wouldn't have mentioned the disgraceful thing to a soul anyhow, so my conscience is clear on *that* score. I really don't know who or what is to be thanked for this. *I* did nothing to bring it about, and it's hard to believe that Providence ever works by means of the kind of politics men like Judson Parker and Jerry Corcoran have."

XV

The Beginning of Vacation

Anne locked the schoolhouse door on a still, yellow evening, when the winds were purring in the spruces around the playground, and the shadows were long and lazy by the edge of the woods. She dropped the key into her pocket with a sigh of satisfaction. The school year was ended, she had been reëngaged for the next, with many expressions of satisfaction . . . only Mr. Harmon Andrews told her she ought to use the strap oftener . . . and two delightful months of a well-earned vacation beckoned her invitingly. Anne felt at peace with the world and herself as she walked down the hill with her basket of flowers in her hand. Since the earliest mayflowers Anne had never missed her weekly pilgrimage to Matthew's grave. Everybody else in Avonlea, except Marilla, had already forgotten quiet, shy, unimportant Matthew Cuthbert; but his memory was still green in Anne's heart and always would be. She could never forget the kind old man who had been the first to give her the love and sympathy her starved childhood had craved.

At the foot of the hill a boy was sitting on the fence in the shadow of the spruces . . . a boy with big, dreamy eyes and a beautiful, sensitive face. He swung down and joined Anne, smiling; but there were traces of tears on his cheeks.

"I thought I'd wait for you, teacher, because I knew you were going to the graveyard," he said,

slipping his hand into hers. "I'm going there, too . . .
I'm taking this bouquet of geraniums to put on
Grandpa Irving's grave for grandma. And look, teacher,
I'm going to put this bunch of white roses beside
Grandpa's grave in memory of my little mother . . .
because I can't go to her grave to put it there. But
don't you think she'll know all about it, just the
same?"

"Yes, I am sure she will, Paul."

"You see, teacher, it's just three years today since
my little mother died. It's such a long, long time but it
hurts just as much as ever . . . and I miss her just as
much as ever. Sometimes it seems to me that I just
can't bear it, it hurts so."

Paul's voice quivered and his lip trembled. He
looked down at his roses, hoping that his teacher
would not notice the tears in his eyes.

"And yet," said Anne, very softly, "you wouldn't
want it to stop hurting . . . you wouldn't want to
forget your little mother even if you could."

"No, indeed, I wouldn't . . . that's just the way I
feel. You're so good at understanding, teacher. Nobody
else understands so well . . . not even grandma,
although she's so good to me. Father understood pretty
well, but still I couldn't talk much to him about
mother, because it made him feel so bad. When he
put his hand over his face I always knew it was time
to stop. Poor father, he must be dreadfully lonesome
without me; but you see he has nobody but a
housekeeper now and he thinks housekeepers are no
good to bring up little boys, especially when he has to
be away from home so much on business.
Grandmothers are better, next to mothers. Someday,
when I'm brought up, I'll go back to father and we're
never going to be parted again."

Paul had talked so much to Anne about his
mother and father that she felt as if she had known
them. She thought his mother must have been very
like what he was himself, in temperament and
disposition; and she had an idea that Stephen Irving

was a rather reserved man with a deep and tender nature which he kept hidden scrupulously from the world.

"Father's not very easy to get acquainted with," Paul had said once. "I never got really acquainted with him until after my little mother died. But he's splendid when you do get to know him. I love him the best in all the world, and Grandma Irving next, and then you, teacher. I'd love you next to father if it wasn't my *duty* to love Grandma Irving best, because she's doing so much for me. *You* know, teacher. I wish she would leave the lamp in my room till I go to sleep, though. She takes it right out as soon as she tucks me up because she says I mustn't be a coward. I'm *not* scared, but I'd *rather* have the light. My little mother used always to sit beside me and hold my hand till I went to sleep. I expect she spoiled me. Mothers do sometimes, you know."

No, Anne did not know this, although she might imagine it. She thought sadly of *her* "little mother," the mother who had thought her so "perfectly beautiful" and who had died so long ago and was buried beside her boyish husband in that unvisited grave far away. Anne could not remember her mother and for this reason she almost envied Paul.

"My birthday is next week," said Paul, as they walked up the long red hill, basking in the June sunshine, "and father wrote me that he is sending me something that he thinks I'll like better than anything else he could send. I believe it has come already, for Grandma is keeping the bookcase drawer locked and that is something new. And when I asked her why, she just looked mysterious and said little boys mustn't be too curious. It's very exciting to have a birthday, isn't it? I'll be eleven. You'd never think it to look at me, would you? Grandma says I'm very small for my age and that it's all because I don't eat enough porridge. I do my very best, but Grandma gives such *generous* platefuls . . . there's nothing mean about Grandma, I can tell you. Ever since you and I had that talk about praying going home from Sunday School that day, teacher . . . when you said we ought to pray about all our difficulties . . . I've prayed every night that God would give me enough grace to enable me to eat every bit of my porridge in the mornings. But I've never been able to do it yet, and whether it's because I have too little grace or too much porridge I really can't decide. Grandma says father was brought up on porridge, and it certainly did work well in his case, for you ought to see the shoulders he has. But sometimes," concluded Paul with a sigh and a meditative air, "I really think porridge will be the death of me."

Anne permitted herself a smile, since Paul was not looking at her. All Avonlea knew that old Mrs. Irving was bringing her grandson up in accordance with the good, old-fashioned methods of diet and morals.

"Let us hope not, dear," she said cheerfully. "How are your rock people coming on? Does the oldest Twin still continue to behave himself?"

"He *has* to," said Paul emphatically. "He knows I won't associate with him if he doesn't. He *is* really full of wickedness, *I* think."

"And has Nora found out about the Golden Lady yet?"

"No; but I think she suspects. I'm almost sure she watched me the last time I went to the cave. I don't mind if she finds out . . . it is only for *her* sake I don't want her to . . . so that her feelings won't be hurt. But if she is *determined* to have her feelings hurt it can't be helped."

"If I were to go to the shore some night with you do you think I could see your rock people too?"

Paul shook his head gravely.

"No, I don't think you could see *my* rock people. I'm the only person who can see them. But you could see rock people of your own. You're one of the kind that can. We're both that kind. *You* know, teacher," he added, squeezing her hand chummily. "Isn't it spendid to be that kind, teacher?"

"Spendid," Anne agreed, gray shining eyes looking down into blue shining ones. Anne and Paul both knew

> *How fair the realm*
> *Imagination opens to the view,"*

and both knew the way to that happy land. There the rose of joy bloomed immortal by dale and stream; clouds never darkened the sunny sky; sweet bells never jangled out of tune; and kindred spirits abounded. The knowledge of that land's geography . . . "east o' the sun, west o' the moon" . . . is priceless lore, not to be bought in any market place. It must be the gift of the good fairies at birth and the years can never deface it or take it away. It is better to possess it, living in a garret, than to be the inhabitant of palaces without it.

The Avonlea graveyard was as yet the grass-grown solitude it had always been. To be sure, the Improvers had an eye on it, and Priscilla Grant had read a paper on cemeteries before the last meeting of the Society. At some future time the Improvers meant to have the lichened, wayward old board fence replaced by a neat wire railing, the grass mown and the leaning monuments straightened up.

Anne put on Matthew's grave the flowers she had brought for it, and then went over to the little poplar shaded corner where Hester Gray slept. Ever since the day of the spring picnic Anne had put flowers on Hester's grave when she visited Matthew's. The evening before she had made a pilgrimage back to the little deserted garden in the woods and brought therefrom some of Hester's own white roses.

"I thought you would like them better than any others, dear," she said softly.

Anne was still sitting there when a shadow fell over the grass and she looked up to see Mrs. Allan. They walked home together.

Mrs. Allan's face was not the face of the girl-bride

whom the minister had brought to Avonlea five years before. It had lost some of its bloom and youthful curves, and there were fine, patient lines about eyes and mouth. A tiny grave in that very cemetery accounted for some of them; and some new ones had come during the recent illness, now happily over, of her little son. But Mrs. Allan's dimples were as sweet and sudden as ever, her eyes as clear and bright and true; and what her face lacked of girlish beauty was now more than atoned for in added tenderness and strength.

"I suppose you are looking forward to your vacation, Anne?" she said, as they left the graveyard.

Anne nodded.

"Yes. . . . I could roll the word as a sweet morsel under my tongue. I think the summer is going to be lovely. For one thing, Mrs. Morgan is coming to the Island in July and Priscilla is going to bring her up. I feel one of my old 'thrills' at the mere thought."

"I hope you'll have a good time, Anne. You've worked very hard this past year and you have succeeded."

"Oh, I don't know. I've come so far short in so many things. I haven't done what I meant to do when I began to teach last fall. . . . I haven't lived up to my ideals."

"None of us ever do," said Mrs. Allan with a sigh. "But then, Anne, you know what Lowell says, 'Not failure but low aim is crime.' We must have ideals and try to live up to them, even if we never quite succeed. Life would be a sorry business without them. With them it's grand and great. Hold fast to your ideals, Anne."

"I shall try. But I have let go most of my theories," said Anne, laughing a little. "I had the most beautiful set of theories you ever knew when I started out as a schoolma'am, but every one of them has failed me at some pinch or another."

"Even the theory on corporal punishment," teased Mrs. Allan.

But Anne flushed.

"I shall never forgive myself for whipping Anthony."

"Nonsense, dear, he deserved it. And it agreed with him. You have had no trouble with him since and he has come to think there's nobody like you. Your kindness won his love after the idea that a 'girl was no good' was rooted out of his stubborn mind."

"He may have deserved it, but that is not the point. If I had calmly and deliberately decided to whip him because I thought it a just punishment for him I would not feel over it as I do. But the truth is, Mrs. Allan, that I just flew into a temper and whipped him because of that. I wasn't thinking whether it was just or unjust . . . even if he hadn't deserved it I'd have done it just the same. That is what humiliates me."

"Well, we all make mistakes, dear, so just put it behind you. We should regret our mistakes and learn from them, but never carry them forward into the future with us. There goes Gilbert Blythe on his wheel . . . home for his vacation too, I suppose. How are you and he getting on with your studies?"

"Pretty well. We plan to finish the Virgil tonight . . . there are only twenty lines to do. Then we are not going to study any more until September."

"Do you think you will ever get to college?"

"Oh, I don't know." Anne looked dreamily afar to the opal-tinted horizon. "Marilla's eyes will never be much better than they are now, although we are so thankful to think that they will not get worse. And then there are the twins . . . somehow I don't believe their uncle will ever really send for them. Perhaps college may be around the bend in the road, but I haven't got to the bend yet and I don't think much about it lest I might grow discontented."

"Well, I should like to see you go to college, Anne; but if you never do, don't be discontented about it. We make our own lives wherever we are, after all . . . college can only help us to do it more easily. They are broad or narrow according to what we put

into them, not what we get out. Life is rich and full
here . . . everywhere . . . if we can only learn how
to open our whole hearts to its richness and fulness."

"I think I understand what you mean," said Anne
thoughtfully, "and I know I have so much to feel
thankful for . . . oh, so much . . . my work, and Paul
Irving, and the dear twins, and all my friends. Do you
know, Mrs. Allan, I'm so thankful for friendship. It
beautifies life so much."

"True friendship is a very helpful thing indeed,"
said Mrs. Allan, "and we should have a very high ideal
of it, and never sully it by any failure in truth and
sincerity. I fear the name of friendship is often de-
graded to a kind of intimacy that has nothing of real
friendship in it."

"Yes . . . like Gertie Pye's and Julia Bell's. They
are very intimate and go everywhere together; but
Gertie is always saying nasty things of Julia behind her
back and everybody thinks she is jealous of her because she is always so pleased when anybody criticizes
Julia. I think it is desecration to call *that* friendship. If
we have friends we should look only for the best in
them and give them the best that is in us, don't you
think? Then friendship would be the most beautiful
thing in the world."

"Friendship *is* very beautiful," smiled Mrs. Allan,
"but some day . . . "

Then she paused abruptly. In the delicate,
whitebrowed face beside her, with its candid eyes and
mobile features, there was still far more of the child
than of the woman. Anne's heart so far harbored only
dreams of friendship and ambition, and Mrs. Allan did
not wish to brush the bloom from her sweet uncon-
sciousness. So she left her sentence for the future
years to finish.

XVI

The Substance of Things Hoped For

"Anne," said Davy appealingly, scrambling up on the shiny, leather-covered sofa in the Green Gables kitchen, where Anne sat, reading a letter, "Anne, I'm *awful* hungry. You've no idea."

"I'll get you a piece of bread and butter in a minute," said Anne absently. Her letter evidently contained some exciting news, for her cheeks were as pink as the roses on the big bush outside, and her eyes were as starry as only Anne's eyes could be.

"But I ain't bread and butter hungry," said Davy in a disgusted tone. "I'm plum cake hungry."

"Oh," laughed Anne, laying down her letter and putting her arm about Davy to give him a squeeze, "that's a kind of hunger that can be endured very comfortably, Davy-boy. You know it's one of Marilla's rules that you can't have anything but bread and butter between meals."

"Well, gimme a piece then . . . please."

Davy had been at last taught to say "please," but he generally tacked it on as an afterthought. He looked with approval at the generous slice Anne presently brought to him. "You always put such a nice lot of butter on it, Anne. Marilla spreads it pretty thin. It slips down a lot easier when there's plenty of butter."

The slice "slipped down" with tolerable ease, judging from its rapid disappearance. Davy slid head first off the sofa, turned a double somersault on the rug, and then sat up and announced decidedly,

"Anne, I've made up my mind about heaven. I don't want to go there."

"Why not?" asked Anne gravely.

"'Cause heaven is in Simon Fletcher's garret, and I don't like Simon Fletcher."

"Heaven in . . . Simon Fletcher's garret!" gasped Anne, too amazed even to laugh. "Davy Keith, whatever put such an extraordinary idea into your head?"

"Milty Boulter says that's where it is. It was last Sunday in Sunday School. The lesson was about Elijah and Elisha, and I up and asked Miss Rogerson where heaven was. Miss Rogerson looked awful offended. She was cross anyhow, because when she'd asked us what Elijah left Elisha when he went to heaven Milty Boulter said, 'His old clo'es,' and us fellows all laughed before we thought. I wish you could think first and do things afterwards, 'cause then you wouldn't do them. But Milty didn't mean to be disrespeckful. He just couldn't think of the name of the thing. Miss Rogerson said heaven was where God was and I wasn't to ask questions like that. Milty nudged me and said in a whisper, 'Heaven's in Uncle Simon's garret and I'll esplain about it on the road home.' So when we was coming home he esplained. Milty's a great hand at esplaining things. Even if he don't know anything about a thing he'll make up a lot of stuff and so you get it esplained all the same. His mother is Mrs. Simon's sister and he went with her to the funeral when his cousin, Jane Ellen, died. The minister said she'd gone to heaven, though Milty says she was lying right before them in the coffin. But he s'posed they carried the coffin up to the garret afterwards. Well, when Milty and his mother went upstairs after it was all over to get her bonnet he asked her where heaven was that Jane Ellen had gone to, and she pointed right to the ceiling and said, 'Up there.' Milty knew there wasn't anything but the garret over the ceiling, so that's how *he* found out. And he's been awful scared to go to his Uncle Simon's ever since."

Anne took Davy on her knee and did her best to straighten out this theological tangle also. She was much better fitted for the task than Marilla, for she remembered her own childhood and had an instinctive understanding of the curious ideas that seven-year-olds sometimes get about matters that are, of course, very plain and simple to grown up people. She had just succeeded in convincing Davy that heaven was *not* in Simon Fletcher's garret when Marilla came in from the garden, where she and Dora had been picking peas. Dora was an industrious little soul and never happier than when "helping" in various small tasks suited to her chubby fingers. She fed chickens, picked up chips, wiped dishes, and ran errands galore. She was neat, faithful and observant; she never had to be told how to do a thing twice and never forgot any of her little duties. Davy, on the other hand, was rather heedless and forgetful; but he had the born knack of winning love, and even yet Anne and Marilla liked him the better.

While Dora proudly shelled the peas and Davy made boats of the pods, with masts of matches and sails of paper, Anne told Marilla about the wonderful contents of her letter.

"Oh, Marilla, what do you think? I've had a letter from Priscilla and she says that Mrs. Morgan is on the Island, and that if it is fine Thursday they are going to drive up to Avonlea and will reach here about twelve. They will spend the afternoon with us and go to the hotel at White Sands in the evening, because some of Mrs. Morgan's American friends are staying there. Oh, Marilla, isn't it wonderful? I can hardly believe I'm not dreaming."

"I daresay Mrs. Morgan is a lot like other people," said Marilla drily, although she did feel a trifle excited herself. Mrs. Morgan was a famous woman and a visit from her was no commonplace occurrence. "They'll be here to dinner, then?"

"Yes; and oh, Marilla, may I cook every bit of the dinner myself? I want to feel that I can do something for the author of 'The Rosebud Garden,' if it is only to cook a dinner for her. You won't mind, will you?"

"Goodness, I'm not so fond of stewing over a hot fire in July that it would vex me very much to have someone else do it. You're quite welcome to the job."

"Oh, thank you," said Anne, as if Marilla had just conferred a tremendous favor, "I'll make out the menu this very night."

"You'd better not try to put on too much style," warned Marilla, a little alarmed by the high-flown sound of "menu." "You'll likely come to grief if you do."

"Oh, I'm not going to put on any 'style,' if you mean trying to do or have things we don't usually have on festal occasions," assured Anne. "That would be affectation, and, although I know I haven't as much sense and steadiness as a girl of seventeen and a schoolteacher ought to have, I'm not so silly as *that*. But I want to have everything as nice and dainty as possible. Davy-boy, don't leave those peapods on the back stairs . . . someone might slip on them. I'll have a light soup to begin with . . . you know I can make lovely cream-of-onion soup . . . and then a couple of roast fowls. I'll have the two white roosters. I have a real affection for those roosters and they've been pets ever since the gray hen hatched out just the two of them . . . little balls of yellow down. But I know they would have to be sacrificed sometime, and surely there couldn't be a worthier occasion than this. But oh, Marilla, *I* cannot kill them . . . not even for Mrs. Morgan's sake. I'll have to ask John Henry Carter to come over and do it for me."

"I'll do it," volunteered Davy, "if Marilla'll hold them by the legs, 'cause I guess it'd take both my hands to manage the axe. It's awful jolly fun to see them hopping about after their heads are cut off."

"Then I'll have peas and beans and creamed potatoes and a lettuce salad, for vegetables," resumed

Anne, "and for dessert, lemon pie with whipped cream, and coffee and cheese and lady fingers. I'll make the pies and lady fingers tomorrow and do up my white muslin dress. And I must tell Diana tonight, for she'll want to do up hers. Mrs. Morgan's heroines are nearly always dressed in white muslin, and Diana and I have always resolved that that was what we would wear if we ever met her. It will be such a delicate compliment, don't you think? Davy, dear, you mustn't poke peapods into the cracks of the floor. I must ask Mr. and Mrs. Allan and Miss Stacy to dinner, too, for they're all very anxious to meet Mrs. Morgan. It's so fortunate she's coming while Miss Stacy is here. Davy dear, don't sail the peapods in the water bucket . . . go out to the trough. Oh, I do hope it will be fine Thursday, and I think it will, for Uncle Abe said last night when he called at Mr. Harrison's, that it was going to rain most of this week."

"That's a good sign," agreed Marilla.

Anne ran across to Orchard Slope that evening to tell the news to Diana, who was also very much excited over it, and they discussed the matter in the hammock swung under the big willow in the Barry garden.

"Oh, Anne, mayn't I help you cook the dinner?" implored Diana. "You know I can make splendid lettuce salad."

"Indeed you may," said Anne unselfishly. "And I shall want you to help me decorate too. I mean to have the parlor simply a *bower* of blossoms . . . and the dining table is to be adorned with wild roses. Oh, I do hope everything will go smoothly. Mrs. Morgan's heroines *never* get into scrapes or are taken at a disadvantage, and they are always so self-possessed and such good housekeepers. They seem to be *born* good housekeepers. You remember that *Gertrude* in 'Edgewood Days' kept house for her father when she was only eight years old. When I was eight years old I hardly knew how to do a thing except bring up children. Mrs. Morgan must be an authority on girls when she has written so much about them, and I do want her to have a good opinion of us. I've imagined it all out a dozen different ways . . . what she'll look like, and what she'll say, and what I'll say. And I'm so anxious about my nose. There are seven freckles on it, as you can see. They came at the A. V. I. S. picnic, when I went around in the sun without my hat. I suppose it's ungrateful of me to worry over them, when I should be thankful they're not spread all over my face as they once were; but I do wish they hadn't come . . . all Mrs. Morgan's heroines have such perfect complexions. I can't recall a freckled one among them."

"Yours are not very noticeable," comforted Diana. "Try a little lemon juice on them tonight."

The next day Anne made her pies and lady fingers, did up her muslin dress, and swept and dusted every room in the house . . . a quite unnecessary proceeding, for Green Gables was, as usual, in the apple pie order dear to Marilla's heart. But Anne felt that a fleck of dust would be a desecration in a house that was to be honored by a visit from Charlotte E. Morgan. She even cleaned out the "catch-all" closet under the stairs, although there was not the remotest possibility of Mrs. Morgan's seeing its interior.

"But I want to *feel* that it is in perfect order, even if she isn't to see it," Anne told Marilla. "You know, in her book 'Golden Keys,' she makes her two heroines *Alice* and *Louisa* take for their motto that verse of Longfellow's,

> " '*In the elder days of art*
> *Builders wrought with greatest care*
> *Each minute and unseen part,*
> *For the gods see everywhere,* '

and so they always kept their cellar stairs scrubbed and never forgot to sweep under the beds. I should have a guilty conscience if I thought this closet was in disorder when Mrs. Morgan was in the house. Ever since we read 'Golden Keys,' last April, Diana and I have taken that verse for our motto too."

That night John Henry Carter and Davy between them contrived to execute the two white roosters, and Anne dressed them, the usually distasteful task quite glorified in her eyes by the destination of the plump birds.

"I don't like picking fowls," she told Marilla, "but isn't it fortunate we don't have to put our souls into what our hands may be doing? I've been picking chickens with my hands but in imagination I've been roaming the Milky Way."

"I thought you'd scattered more feathers over the floor than usual," remarked Marilla.

Then Anne put Davy to bed and made him promise that he would behave perfectly the next day.

"If I'm as good as good can be all day tomorrow will you let me be just as bad as I like all the next day?" asked Davy.

"I couldn't do that," said Anne discreetly, "but I'll take you and Dora for a row in the flat right to the bottom of the pond, and we'll go ashore on the sandhills and have a picnic."

"It's a bargain," said Davy. "I'll be good, you bet. I meant to go over to Mr. Harrison's and fire peas from my new popgun at Ginger but another day'll do as well. I espect it will be just like Sunday, but a picnic at the shore'll make up for *that*."

XVII

A Chapter of Accidents

Anne woke three times in the night and made pilgrimages to her window to make sure that Uncle Abe's prediction was not coming true. Finally the morning dawned pearly and lustrous in a sky full of silver sheen and radiance, and the wonderful day had arrived.

Diana appeared soon after breakfast, with a basket of flowers over one arm and *her* muslin dress over the other . . . for it would not do to don it until all the dinner preparations were completed. Meanwhile she wore her afternoon pink print and a lawn apron fearfully and wonderfully ruffled and frilled; and very neat and pretty and rosy she was.

"You look simply sweet," said Anne admiringly.

Diana sighed.

"But I've had to let out every one of my dresses *again*. I weigh four pounds more than I did in July. Anne, *where* will this end? Mrs. Morgan's heroines are all tall and slender."

"Well, let's forget our troubles and think of our mercies," said Anne gaily. "Mrs. Allan says that whenever we think of anything that is a trial to us we should also think of something nice that we can set over against it. If you are slightly too plump you've got the dearest dimples; and if I have a freckled nose the *shape* of it is all right. Do you think the lemon juice did any good?"

"Yes, I really think it did," said Diana critically; and, much elated, Anne led the way to the garden, which was full of airy shadows and wavering golden lights.

"We'll decorate the parlor first. We have plenty of time, for Priscilla said they'd be here about twelve or half past at the latest, so we'll have dinner at one."

There may have been two happier and more excited girls somewhere in Canada or the United States at that moment, but I doubt it. Every snip of the scissors, as rose and peony and bluebell fell, seemed to chirp, "Mrs. Morgan is coming today." Anne wondered how Mr. Harrison *could* go on placidly mowing hay in the field across the lane, just as if nothing were going to happen.

The parlor at Green Gables was a rather severe and gloomy apartment, with rigid horsehair furniture, stiff lace curtains, and white antimacassars that were always laid at a perfectly correct angle, except at such times as they clung to unfortunate people's buttons. Even Anne had never been able to infuse much grace into it, for Marilla would not permit any alterations. But it is wonderful what flowers can accomplish if you give them a fair chance; when Anne and Diana finished with the room you would not have recognized it.

A great blue bowlful of snowballs overflowed on the polished table. The shining black mantelpiece was heaped with roses and ferns. Every shelf of the whatnot held a sheaf of bluebells; the dark corners on either side of the grate were lighted up with jars full of glowing crimson peonies, and the grate itself was aflame with yellow poppies. All this splendor and color, mingled with the sunshine falling through the honeysuckle vines at the windows in a leafy riot of dancing shadows over walls and floor, made of the usually dismal little room the veritable "bower" of Anne's imagination, and even extorted a tribute of admiration from Marilla, who came in to criticize and remained to praise.

"Now, we must set the table," said Anne, in the tone of a priestess about to perform some sacred rite in honor of a divinity. "We'll have a big vaseful of wild roses in the center and one single rose in front of everybody's plate—and a special bouquet of rosebuds only by Mrs. Morgan's—an allusion to 'The Rosebud Garden' you know."

The table was set in the sitting room, with Marilla's finest linen and the best china, glass, and silver. You may be perfectly certain that every article placed on it was polished or scoured to the highest possible perfection of gloss and glitter.

Then the girls tripped out to the kitchen, which was filled with appetizing odors emanating from the oven, where the chickens were already sizzling splendidly. Anne prepared the potatoes and Diana got the peas and beans ready. Then, while Diana shut herself into the pantry to compound the lettuce salad, Anne, whose cheeks were already beginning to glow crimson, as much with excitement as from the heat of the fire, prepared the bread sauce for the chickens, minced her onions for the soup, and finally whipped the cream for her lemon pies.

And what about Davy all this time? Was he redeeming his promise to be good? He was, indeed. To be sure, he insisted on remaining in the kitchen, for his curiosity wanted to see all that went on. But as he sat quietly in a corner, busily engaged in untying the knots in a piece of herring net he had brought home from his last trip to the shore, nobody objected to this.

At half past eleven the lettuce salad was made, the golden circles of the pies were heaped with whipped cream, and everything was sizzling and bubbling that ought to sizzle and bubble.

"We'd better go and dress now," said Anne, "for they may be here by twelve. We must have dinner at sharp one, for the soup must be served as soon as it's done."

Serious indeed were the toilet rites presently performed in the east gable. Anne peered anxiously at her nose and rejoiced to see that its freckles were not at all prominent, thanks either to the lemon juice or to the unusual flush on her cheeks. When they were ready they looked quite as sweet and trim and girlish as ever did any of "Mrs. Morgan's heroines."

"I do hope I'll be able to say something once in a while, and not sit like a mute," said Diana anxiously. "All Mrs. Morgan's heroines converse so beautifully. But I'm afraid I'll be tongue-tied and stupid. And I'll be sure to say 'I seen.' I haven't often said it since Miss Stacy taught here; but in moments of excitement it's sure to pop out. Anne, if I were to say 'I seen' before Mrs. Morgan I'd die of mortification. And it would be almost as bad to have nothing to say."

"I'm nervous about a good many things," said Anne, "but I don't think there is much fear that I won't be able to *talk.*"

And, to do her justice, there wasn't.

Anne shrouded her muslin glories in a big apron and went down to concoct her soup. Marilla had dressed herself and the twins, and looked more excited than she had ever been known to look before. At half past twelve the Allans and Miss Stacy came. Everything was going well but Anne was beginning to feel nervous. It was surely time for Priscilla and Mrs. Morgan to arrive. She made frequent trips to the gate and looked as anxiously down the lane as ever her namesake in the Bluebeard story peered from the tower casement.

"Suppose they don't come at all?" she said piteously.

"Don't suppose it. It would be too mean," said Diana, who, however, was beginning to have uncomfortable misgivings on the subject.

"Anne," said Marilla, coming out from the parlor, "Miss Stacy wants to see Miss Barry's willowware platter."

Anne hastened to the sitting room closet to get the platter. She had, in accordance with her promise to Mrs. Lynde, written to Miss Barry of Charlottetown, asking for the loan of it. Miss Barry was an old friend of Anne's, and she promptly sent the platter out, with a letter exhorting Anne to be very careful of it, for she had paid twenty dollars for it. The platter had served its purpose at the Aid bazaar and had then been returned to the Green Gables closet, for Anne would not trust anybody but herself to take it back to town.

She carried the platter carefully to the front door where her guests were enjoying the cool breeze that blew up from the brook. It was examined and admired; then, just as Anne had taken it back into her own hands, a terrific crash and clatter sounded from the kitchen pantry. Marilla, Diana, and Anne fled out, the latter pausing only long enough to set the precious platter hastily down on the second step of the stairs.

When they reached the pantry a truly harrowing spectacle met their eyes . . . a guilty-looking small boy scrambling down from the table, with his clean print blouse liberally plastered with yellow filling, and on the table the shattered remnants of what had been two brave, becreamed lemon pies.

Davy had finished ravelling out his herring net and had wound the twine into a ball. Then he had gone into the pantry to put it up on the shelf above the table, where he already kept a score or so of similar balls, which, so far as could be discovered, served no useful purpose save to yield the joy of possession. Davy had to climb on the table and reach over to the shelf at a dangerous angle . . . something he had been forbidden by Marilla to do, as he had come to grief once before in the experiment. The result in this instance was disastrous. Davy slipped and came sprawling squarely down on the lemon pies. His clean blouse was ruined for that time and the pies for all time. It is, however, an ill wind that blows nobody good, and the pig was eventually the gainer by Davy's mischance.

"Davy Keith," said Marilla, shaking him by the shoulder, "didn't I forbid you to climb up on that table again? Didn't I?"

"I forgot," whimpered Davy. "You've told me not to do such an awful lot of things that I can't remember them all."

"Well, you march upstairs and stay there till after dinner. Perhaps you'll get them sorted out in your memory by that time. No, Anne, never you mind interceding for him. I'm not punishing him because he spoiled your pies . . . that was an accident. I'm punishing him for his disobedience. Go, Davy, I say."

"Ain't I to have any dinner?" wailed Davy.

"You can come down after dinner is over and have yours in the kitchen."

"Oh, all right," said Davy, somewhat comforted. "I know Anne'll save some nice bones for me, won't you, Anne? 'Cause you know I didn't mean to fall on the pies. Say, Anne, since they *are* spoiled can't I take some of the pieces upstairs with me?"

"No, no lemon pie for you, Master Davy," said Marilla, pushing him toward the hall.

"What shall we do for dessert?" asked Anne, looking regretfully at the wreck and ruin.

"Get out a crock of strawberry preserves," said Marilla consolingly. "There's plenty of whipped cream left in the bowl for it."

One o'clock came . . . but no Priscilla or Mrs. Morgan. Anne was in an agony. Everything was done to a turn and the soup was just what soup should be, but couldn't be depended on to remain so for any length of time.

"I don't believe they're coming after all," said Marilla crossly.

Anne and Diana sought comfort in each other's eyes.

At half past one Marilla again emerged from the parlor.

"Girls, we *must* have dinner. Everybody is hungry and it's no use waiting any longer. Priscilla and Mrs. Morgan are not coming, that's plain, and nothing is being improved by waiting."

Anne and Diana set about lifting the dinner, with all the zest gone out of the performance.

"I don't believe I'll be able to eat a mouthful," said Diana dolefully.

"Nor I. But I hope everything will be nice for Miss Stacy's and Mr. and Mrs. Allan's sakes," said Anne listlessly.

When Diana dished the peas she tasted them and a very peculiar expression crossed her face.

"Anne, did *you* put sugar in these peas?"

"Yes," said Anne, mashing the potatoes with the air of one expected to do her duty. "I put a spoonful of sugar in. We always do. Don't you like it?"

"But *I* put a spoonful in too, when I set them on the stove," said Diana.

Anne dropped her masher and tasted the peas also. Then she made a grimace.

"How awful! I never dreamed you had put sugar in, because I knew your mother never does. I happened to think of it, for a wonder . . . I'm always forgetting it . . . so I popped a spoonful in."

"It's a case of too many cooks, I guess," said Marilla, who had listened to this dialogue with a rather guilty expression. "I didn't think you'd remember about the sugar, Anne, for I'm perfectly certain you never did before . . . so *I* put in a spoonful."

The guests in the parlor heard peal after peal of laughter from the kitchen, but they never knew what the fun was about. There were no green peas on the dinner table that day, however.

"Well," said Anne, sobering down again with a sigh of recollection, "we have the salad anyhow and I don't think anything has happened to the beans. Let's carry the things in and get it over."

It cannot be said that that dinner was a notable success socially. The Allans and Miss Stacy exerted themselves to save the situation and Marilla's customary placidity was not noticeably ruffled. But Anne and Diana, between their disappointment and the reaction from their excitement of the forenoon, could neither talk nor eat. Anne tried heroically to bear her part in the conversation for the sake of her guests; but all the sparkle had been quenched in her for the time being, and, in spite of her love for the Allans and Miss Stacy, she couldn't help thinking how nice it would be when everybody had gone home and she could bury her weariness and disappointment in the pillows of the east gable.

There is an old proverb that really seems at times to be inspired . . . "it never rains but it pours." The measure of that day's tribulations was not yet full. Just as Mr. Allan had finished returning thanks there arose a strange, ominous sound on the stairs, as of some hard, heavy object bounding from step to step, finishing up with a grand smash at the bottom. Everybody ran out into the hall. Anne gave a shriek of dismay.

At the bottom of the stairs lay a big pink conch shell amid the fragments of what had been Miss Barry's platter; and at the top of the stairs knelt a terrified Davy, gazing down with wide-open eyes at the havoc.

"Davy," said Marilla ominously, "did you throw that conch down *on purpose?*"

"No, I never did," whimpered Davy. "I was just kneeling here, quiet as quiet, to watch you folks through the bannisters, and my foot struck that old thing and pushed it off . . . and I'm awful hungry . . . and I do wish you'd lick a fellow and have done with it, instead of always sending him upstairs to miss all the fun."

"Don't blame Davy," said Anne, gathering up the fragments with trembling fingers. "It was my fault. I set that platter there and forgot all about it. I am properly punished for my carelessness; but oh, what will Miss Barry say?"

"Well, you know she only bought it, so it isn't the same as if it was an heirloom," said Diana, trying to console.

The guests went away soon after, feeling that it

was the most tactful thing to do, and Anne and Diana
washed the dishes, talking less than they had ever
been known to do before. Then Diana went home with
a headache and Anne went with another to the east
gable, where she stayed until Marilla came home from
the post office at sunset, with a letter from Priscilla,
written the day before. Mrs. Morgan had sprained her
ankle so severely that she could not leave her room.

"And oh, Anne dear," wrote Priscilla, "I'm so
sorry, but I'm afraid we won't get up to Green Gables
at all now, for by the time Aunty's ankle is well she
will have to go back to Toronto. She has to be there
by a certain date."

"Well," sighed Anne, laying the letter down on the
red sandstone step of the back porch, where she was
sitting, while the twilight rained down out of a dappled
sky, "I always thought it was too good to be true that
Mrs. Morgan should really come. But there . . . that
speech sounds as pessimistic as Miss Eliza Andrews
and I'm ashamed of making it. After all, it was *not* too
good to be true . . . things just as good and far better
are coming true for me all the time. And I suppose
the events of today have a funny side too. Perhaps
when Diana and I are old and gray we shall be able to
laugh over them. But I feel that I can't expect to do it
before then, for it has truly been a bitter
disappointment."

"You'll probably have a good many more and
worse disappointments than that before you get
through life," said Marilla, who honestly thought she
was making a comforting speech. "It seems to me,
Anne, that you are never going to outgrow your
fashion of setting your heart so on things and then
crashing down into despair because you don't get
them."

"I know I'm too much inclined that way," agreed
Anne ruefully. "When I think something nice is going
to happen I seem to fly right up on the wings of
anticipation; and then the first thing I realize I drop
down to earth with a thud. But really, Marilla, the

flying part *is* glorious as long as it lasts . . . it's like soaring through a sunset. I think it almost pays for the thud."

"Well, maybe it does," admitted Marilla. "I'd rather walk calmly along and do without both flying and thud. But everybody has her own way of living . . . I used to think there was only one right way . . . but since I've had you and the twins to bring up I don't feel so sure of it. What are you going to do about Miss Barry's platter?"

"Pay her back the twenty dollars she paid for it, I suppose. I'm so thankful it wasn't a cherished heirloom because then no money could replace it."

"Maybe you could find one like it somewhere and buy it for her."

"I'm afraid not. Platters as old as that are very scarce. Mrs. Lynde couldn't find one anywhere for the supper. I only wish I could, for of course Miss Barry would just as soon have one platter as another, if both were equally old and genuine. Marilla, look at that big star over Mr. Harrison's maple grove, with all that holy hush of silvery sky about it. It gives me a feeling that is like a prayer. After all, when one can see stars and skies like that, little disappointments and accidents can't matter so much, can they?"

"Where's Davy?" said Marilla, with an indifferent glance at the star.

"In bed. I've promised to take him and Dora to the shore for a picnic tomorrow. Of course, the original agreement was that he must be good. But he *tried* to be good . . . and I hadn't the heart to disappoint him."

"You'll drown yourself or the twins, rowing about the pond in that flat," grumbled Marilla. "I've lived here for sixty years and I've never been on the pond yet."

"Well, it's never too late to mend," said Anne roguishly. "Suppose you come with us tomorrow. We'll shut Green Gables up and spend the whole day at the shore, daffing the world aside."

"No, thank you," said Marilla, with indignant emphasis. "I'd be a nice sight, wouldn't I, rowing down the pond in a flat? I think I hear Rachel pronouncing on it. There's Mr. Harrison driving away somewhere. Do you suppose there is any truth in the gossip that Mr. Harrison is going to see Isabella Andrews?"

"No, I'm sure there isn't. He just called there one evening on business with Mr. Harmon Andrews and Mrs. Lynde saw him and said she knew he was courting because he had a white collar on. I don't believe Mr. Harrison will ever marry. He seems to have a prejudice against marriage."

"Well, you can never tell about those old bachelors. And if he had a white collar on I'd agree with Rachel that it looks suspicious, for I'm sure he never was seen with one before."

"I think he only put it on because he wanted to conclude a business deal with Harmon Andrews," said Anne. "I've heard him say that's the only time a man needs to be particular about his appearance, because if he looks prosperous the party of the second part won't be so likely to try to cheat him. I really feel sorry for Mr. Harrison; I don't believe he feels satisfied with his life. It must be very lonely to have no one to care about except a parrot, don't you think? But I notice Mr. Harrison doesn't like to be pitied. Nobody does, I imagine."

"There's Gilbert coming up the lane," said Marilla. "If he wants you to go for a row on the pond mind you put on your coat and rubbers. There's a heavy dew tonight."

XVIII

An Adventure on the Tory Road

"Anne," said Davy, sitting up in bed and propping his chin on his hands, "Anne, where is sleep? People go to sleep every night, and of course I know it's the place where I do the things I dream, but I want to know *where* it is and how I get there and back without knowing anything about it . . . and in my nighty too. Where is it?"

Anne was kneeling at the west gable window watching the sunset sky that was like a great flower with petals of crocus and a heart of fiery yellow. She turned her head at Davy's question and answered dreamily,

> " *'Over the mountains of the moon,*
> *Down the valley of the shadow.'* "

Paul Irving would have known the meaning of this, or made a meaning out of it for himself, if he didn't; but practical Davy, who, as Anne often despairingly remarked, hadn't a particle of imagination, was only puzzled and disgusted.

"Anne, I believe you're just talking nonsense."

"Of course I was, dear boy. Don't you know that it is only very foolish folk who talk sense all the time?"

"Well, I think you might give a sensible answer when I ask a sensible question," said Davy in an injured tone.

"Oh, you are too little to understand," said Anne. But she felt rather ashamed of saying it; for had she not, in keen remembrance of many similar snubs administered in her own early years, solemnly vowed that she would never tell any child it was too little to understand? Yet here she was doing it . . . so wide sometimes is the gulf between theory and practice.

"Well, I'm doing my best to grow," said Davy, "but it's a thing you can't hurry much. If Marilla wasn't so stingy with her jam I believe I'd grow a lot faster."

"Marilla is not stingy, Davy," said Anne severely. "It is very ungrateful of you to say such a thing."

"There's another word that means the same thing and sounds a lot better, but I don't just remember it," said Davy, frowning intently. "I heard Marilla say she was it, herself, the other day."

"If you mean *economical*, it's a *very* different thing from being stingy. It is an excellent trait in a person if she is economical. If Marilla had been stingy she wouldn't have taken you and Dora when your mother died. Would you have liked to live with Mrs. Wiggins?"

"You just bet I wouldn't!" Davy was emphatic on that point. "Nor I don't want to go out to Uncle Richard neither. I'd far rather live here, even if Marilla is that long-tailed word when it comes to jam, 'cause *you're* here, Anne. Say, Anne, won't you tell me a story 'fore I go to sleep? I don't want a fairy story. They're all right for girls, I s'pose, but I want something exciting . . . lots of killing and shooting in it, and a house on fire, and in'trusting things like that."

Fortunately for Anne, Marilla called out at this moment from her room.

"Anne, Diana's signaling at a great rate. You'd better see what she wants."

Anne ran to the east gable and saw flashes of light coming through the twilight from Diana's window in groups of five, which meant, according to their old childish code, "Come over at once for I have something important to reveal." Anne threw her white shawl over her head and hastened through the Haunted Wood and across Mr. Bell's pasture corner to Orchard Slope.

"I've good news for you, Anne," said Diana. "Mother and I have just got home from Carmody, and I saw Mary Sentner from Spencervale in Mr. Blair's store. She says the old Copp girls on the Tory Road have a willow-ware platter and she thinks it's exactly like the one we had at the supper. She says they'll likely sell it, for Martha Copp has never been known to keep anything she *could* sell; but if they won't there's a platter at Wesley Keyson's at Spencervale and she knows they'd sell it, but she isn't sure it's just the same kind as Aunt Josephine's."

"I'll go right over to Spencervale after it tomorrow," said Anne resolutely, "and you must come with me. It will be such a weight off my mind, for I have to go to town day after tomorrow and how can I face your Aunt Josephine without a willow-ware platter? It would be even worse than the time I had to confess about jumping on the spare room bed."

Both girls laughed over the old memory . . . concerning which, if any of my readers are ignorant and curious, I must refer them to Anne's earlier history.

The next afternoon the girls fared forth on their platter hunting expedition. It was ten miles to Spencervale and the day was not especially pleasant for traveling. It was very warm and windless, and the dust on the road was such as might have been expected after six weeks of dry weather.

"Oh, I do wish it would rain soon," sighed Anne. "Everything is so parched up. The poor fields just seem pitiful to me and the trees seem to be stretching out their hands pleading for rain. As for my garden, it hurts me every time I go into it. I suppose I shouldn't complain about a garden when the farmers' crops are suffering so. Mr. Harrison says his pastures are so scorched up that his poor cows can hardly get a bite to eat and he feels guilty of cruelty to animals every time he meets their eyes."

After a wearisome drive the girls reached Spencervale and turned down the "Tory" Road . . . a green, solitary highway where the strips of grass between the wheel tracks bore evidence to lack of travel. Along most of its extent it was lined with thick-set young spruces crowding down to the roadway, with here and there a break where the back field of a Spencervale farm came out to the fence or an expanse of stumps was aflame with fireweed and goldenrod.

"Why is it called the Tory Road?" asked Anne.

"Mr. Allan says it is on the principle of calling a place a grove because there are no trees in it," said Diana, "for nobody lives along the road except the Copp girls and old Martin Bovyer at the further end, who is a Liberal. The Tory government ran the road through when they were in power just to show they were doing something."

Diana's father was a Liberal, for which reason she and Anne never discussed politics. Green Gables folk had always been Conservatives.

Finally the girls came to the old Copp homestead . . . a place of such exceeding external neatness that even Green Gables would have suffered by contrast. The house was a very old-fashioned one, situated on a slope, which fact had necessitated the building of a stone basement under one end. The house and outbuildings were all whitewashed to a condition of blinding perfection and not a weed was visible in the prim kitchen garden surrounded by its white paling.

"The shades are all down," said Diana ruefully. "I believe that nobody is home."

This proved to be the case. The girls looked at each other in perplexity.

"I don't know what to do," said Anne. "If I were sure the platter was the right kind I would not mind waiting until they came home. But if it isn't it may be too late to go to Wesley Keyson's afterward."

Diana looked at a certain little square window over the basement.

"That is the pantry window, I feel sure," she said, "because this house is just like Uncle Charles' at Newbridge, and that is their pantry window. The shade isn't down, so if we climbed up on the roof of that little house we could look into the pantry and might be able to see the platter. Do you think it would be any harm?"

"No, I don't think so," decided Anne, after due reflection, "since our motive is not idle curiosity."

This important point of ethics being settled, Anne prepared to mount the aforesaid "little house," a construction of lathes, with a peaked roof, which had in times past served as a habitation for ducks. The Copp girls had given up keeping ducks . . . "because they were such untidy birds" . . . and the house had not been in use for some years, save as an abode of correction for setting hens. Although scrupulously whitewashed it had become somewhat shaky, and Anne felt rather dubious as she scrambled up from the vantage point of a keg placed on a box.

"I'm afraid it won't bear my weight," she said as she gingerly stepped on the roof.

"Lean on the window sill," advised Diana, and Anne accordingly leaned. Much to her delight, she saw, as she peered through the pane, a willow-ware platter, exactly such as she was in quest of, on the shelf in front of the window. So much she saw before the catastrophe came. In her joy Anne forgot the precarious nature of her footing, incautiously ceased to lean on the window sill, gave an impulsive little hop of pleasure . . . and the next moment she had crashed through the roof up to her armpits, and there she hung, quite unable to extricate herself. Diana dashed into the duck house and, seizing her unfortunate friend by the waist, tried to draw her down.

"Ow . . . don't," shrieked poor Anne. "There are some long splinters sticking into me. See if you can put something under my feet . . . then perhaps I can draw myself up."

Diana hastily dragged in the previously mentioned keg and Anne found that it was just sufficiently high to furnish a secure resting place for her feet. But she could not release herself.

"Could I pull you out if I crawled up?" suggested Diana.

Anne shook her head hopelessly.

"No . . . the splinters hurt too badly. If you can find an axe you might chop me out, though. Oh dear, I do really begin to believe that I *was* born under an ill-omened star."

Diana searched faithfully but no axe was to be found.

"I'll have to go for help," she said, returning to the prisoner.

"No, indeed, you won't," said Anne vehemently. "If you do the story of this will get out everywhere and I shall be ashamed to show my face. No, we must just wait until the Copp girls come home and bind them to secrecy. They'll know where the axe is and get me out. I'm not uncomfortable as long as I keep perfectly still . . . not uncomfortable in *body* I mean. I wonder what the Copp girls value this house at. I shall have to pay for the damage I've done, but I wouldn't mind that if I were only sure they would understand my motive in peeping in at their pantry window. My sole comfort is that the platter is just the kind I want and if Miss Copp will only sell it to me I shall be resigned to what has happened."

"What if the Copp girls don't come home until after night . . . or till tomorrow?" suggested Diana.

"If they're not back by sunset you'll have to go for other assistance, I suppose," said Anne reluctantly, "but you mustn't go until you really have to. Oh dear, this is a dreadful predicament. I wouldn't mind my misfortunes so much if they were romantic, as Mrs. Morgan's heroines' always are, but they are always just simply ridiculous. Fancy what the Copp girls will think when they drive into their yard and see a girl's head and shoulders sticking out of the roof of one of their outhouses. Listen . . . is that a wagon? No, Diana, I believe it is thunder."

Thunder it was undoubtedly, and Diana, having made a hasty pilgrimage around the house, returned to announce that a very black cloud was rising rapidly in the northwest.

"I believe we're going to have a heavy thunder-shower," she exclaimed in dismay. "Oh, Anne, what will we do?"

"We must prepare for it," said Anne tranquilly. A thunderstorm seemed a trifle in comparison with what had already happened. "You'd better drive the horse and buggy into that open shed. Fortunately my parasol is in the buggy. Here . . . take my hat with you. Marilla told me I was a goose to put on my best hat to come to the Tory Road and she was right, as she always is."

Diana untied the pony and drove into the shed, just as the first heavy drops of rain fell. There she sat and watched the resulting downpour, which was so thick and heavy that she could hardly see Anne through it, holding the parasol bravely over her bare head. There was not a great deal of thunder, but for the best part of an hour the rain came merrily down. Occasionally Anne slanted back her parasol and waved an encouraging hand to her friend; but conversation at that distance and under the circumstances was quite out of the question. Finally the rain ceased, the sun came out, and Diana ventured across the puddles of the yard.

"Did you get very wet?" she asked anxiously.

"Oh, no," returned Anne cheerfully. "My head and shoulders are quite dry and my skirt is only a lit-tle damp where the rain beat through the lathes. Don't pity me, Diana, for I haven't minded it at all. I kept thinking how much good the rain will do and how glad my garden must be for it, and imagining what the flowers and buds would think when the drops began to fall. I imagined out a most interesting dialogue between the asters and the sweet peas and the wild canaries in the lilac bush and the guardian spirit of the garden. When I go home I mean to write it down. I wish I had a pencil and paper to do it now, because I daresay I'll forget the best parts before I reach home."

Diana the faithful had a pencil and discovered a sheet of wrapping paper in the box of the buggy. Anne folded up her dripping parasol, put on her hat, spread the wrapping paper on a shingle Diana handed up, and wrote out her garden idyl under conditions that could hardly be considered as favorable to literature. Nevertheless, the result was quite pretty, and Diana was "enraptured" when Anne read it to her.

"Oh, Anne, it's sweet . . . just sweet. *Do* send it to the *Canadian Woman.*"

Anne shook her head.

"Oh, no, it wouldn't be suitable at all. There is no *plot* in it, you see. It's just a string of fancies. I like writing such things, but of course nothing of the sort would ever do for publication, for editors insist on plots, so Priscilla says. Oh, there's Miss Sarah Copp now. *Please,* Diana, go and explain."

Miss Sarah Copp was a small person, garbed in shabby black, with a hat chosen less for vain adornment than for qualities that would wear well. She looked as amazed as might be expected on seeing the curious tableau in her yard, but when she heard Diana's explanation she was all sympathy. She hurriedly unlocked the back door, produced the axe, and with a few skillful blows set Anne free. The latter, somewhat tired and stiff, ducked down into the interior of her prison and thankfully emerged into liberty once more.

"Miss Copp," she said earnestly, "I assure you I looked into your pantry window *only* to discover if you had a willow-ware platter. I didn't see anything else—I didn't *look* for anything else."

"Bless you, that's all right," said Miss Sarah amiably. "You needn't worry—there's no harm done. Thank goodness, we Copps keep our pantries presentable at all times and don't care who sees into them. As for that old duckhouse, I'm glad it's smashed, for maybe now Martha will agree to having it taken down. She never would before for fear it might come in handy sometime and I've had to whitewash it every spring. But you might as well argue with a post as with Martha. She went to town today—I drove her to the station. And you want to buy my platter. Well, what will you give for it?"

"Twenty dollars," said Anne, who was never meant to match business wits with a Copp, or she would not have offered her price at the start.

"Well, I'll see," said Miss Sarah cautiously. "That platter is mine fortunately, or I'd never dare to sell it when Martha wasn't here. As it is, I daresay she'll raise a fuss. Martha's the boss of this establishment I can tell you. I'm getting awful tired of living under another woman's thumb. But come in, come in. You must be real tired and hungry. I'll do the best I can for you in the way of tea but I warn you not to expect anything but bread and butter and some cowcumbers. Martha locked up all the cake and cheese and preserves afore she went. She always does, because she says I'm too extravagant with them if company comes."

The girls were hungry enough to do justice to any fare, and they enjoyed Miss Sarah's excellent bread and butter and "cowcumbers" thoroughly. When the meal was over Miss Sarah said,

"I don't know as I mind selling the platter. But it's worth twenty-five dollars. It's a very old platter."

Diana gave Anne's foot a gentle kick under the table, meaning, "Don't agree—she'll let it go for twenty if you hold out." But Anne was not minded to take any chances in regard to that precious platter. She promptly agreed to give twenty-five and Miss Sarah looked as if she felt sorry she hadn't asked for thirty.

"Well, I guess you may have it. I want all the money I can scare up just now. The fact is—" Miss Sarah threw up her head importantly, with a proud flush on her thin cheeks—"I'm going to be married—

to Luther Wallace. He wanted me twenty years ago. I liked him real well but he was poor then and father packed him off. I s'pose I shouldn't have let him go so meek but I was timid and frightened of father. Besides, I didn't know men were so skurse."

When the girls were safely away, Diana driving and Anne holding the coveted platter carefully on her lap, the green, rain-freshened solitudes of the Tory Road were enlivened by ripples of girlish laughter.

"I'll amuse your Aunt Josephine with the 'strange eventful history' of this afternoon when I go to town tomorrow. We've had a rather trying time but it's over now. I've got the platter, and that rain has laid the dust beautifully. So 'all's well that ends well.'"

"We're not home yet," said Diana rather pessimistically, "and there's no telling what may happen before we are. You're such a girl to have adventures, Anne."

"Having adventures comes natural to some people," said Anne serenely. "You just have a gift for them or you haven't."

XIX

Just a Happy Day

"After all," Anne had said to Marilla once, "I believe the nicest and sweetest days are not those on which anything very splendid or wonderful or exciting happens but just those that bring simple little pleasures, following one another softly, like pearls slipping off a string."

Life at Green Gables was full of just such days, for Anne's adventures and misadventures, like those of other people, did not all happen at once, but were sprinkled over the year, with long stretches of harmless, happy days between, filled with work and dreams and laughter and lessons. Such a day came late in August. In the forenoon Anne and Diana rowed the delighted twins down the pond to the sandshore to pick "sweet grass" and paddle in the surf, over which the wind was harping an old lyric learned when the world was young.

In the afternoon Anne walked down to the old Irving place to see Paul. She found him stretched out on the grassy bank beside the thick fir grove that sheltered the house on the north, absorbed in a book of fairy tales. He sprang up radiantly at sight of her.

"Oh, I'm so glad you've come, teacher," he said eagerly, "because Grandma's away. You'll stay and have tea with me, won't you? It's so lonesome to have tea all by oneself. *You* know, teacher. I've had serious thoughts of asking Young Mary Joe to sit down and eat her tea with me, but I expect Grandma wouldn't approve. She says the French have to be kept in their place. And anyhow, it's difficult to talk with Young Mary Joe. She just laughs and says, 'Well, yous do beat all de kids I ever knowed.' That isn't my idea of conversation."

"Of course I'll stay to tea," said Anne gaily. "I was dying to be asked. My mouth has been watering for some more of your grandma's delicious shortbread ever since I had tea here before."

Paul looked very sober.

"If it depended on me, teacher," he said, standing before Anne with his hands in his pockets and his beautiful little face shadowed with sudden care, "you should have shortbread with a right good will. But it depends on Mary Joe. I heard Grandma tell her before she left that she wasn't to give me any shortcake because it was too rich for little boys' stomachs. But maybe Mary Joe will cut some for you if I promise I won't eat any. Let us hope for the best."

"Yes, let us," agreed Anne, whom this cheerful philosophy suited exactly, "and if Mary Joe proves hard-hearted and won't give me any shortbread it doesn't matter in the least, so you are not to worry over that."

"You're sure you won't mind if she doesn't?" said Paul anxiously.

"Perfectly sure, dear heart."

"Then I won't worry," said Paul, with a long breath of relief, "especially as I really think Mary Joe will listen to reason. She's not a naturally unreasonable person, but she has learned by experience that it doesn't do to disobey Grandma's orders. Grandma is an excellent woman but people must do as she tells them. She was very much pleased with me this morning because I managed at last to eat all my plateful of porridge. It was a great effort but I succeeded. Grandma says she thinks she'll make a man of me yet. But, teacher, I want to ask you a very important question. You will answer it truthfully, won't you?"

"I'll try," promised Anne.

"Do you think I'm wrong in my upper story?" asked Paul, as if his very existence depended on her reply.

"Goodness, no, Paul," exclaimed Anne in amazement. "Certainly you're not. What put such an idea into your head?"

"Mary Joe . . . but she didn't know I heard her. Mrs. Peter Sloane's hired girl, Veronica, came to see Mary Joe last evening and I heard them talking in the kitchen as I was going through the hall. I heard Mary Joe say, 'Dat Paul, he is de queeres' leetle boy. He talks dat queer. I tink dere's someting wrong in his upper story.' I couldn't sleep last night for ever so long, thinking of it, and wondering if Mary Joe was right. I couldn't bear to ask Grandma about it somehow, but I made up my mind I'd ask you. I'm so glad you think I'm all right in my upper story."

"Of course you are. Mary Joe is a silly, ignorant girl, and you are never to worry about anything she says," said Anne indignantly, secretly resolving to give Mrs. Irving a discreet hint as to the advisability of restraining Mary Joe's tongue.

"Well, that's a weight off my mind," said Paul. "I'm perfectly happy now, teacher, thanks to you. It wouldn't be nice to have something wrong in your upper story, would it, teacher? I suppose the reason Mary Joe imagines I have is because I tell her what I think about things sometimes."

"It *is* a rather dangerous practice," admitted Anne, out of the depths of her own experience.

"Well, by and by I'll tell you the thoughts I told Mary Joe and you can see for yourself if there's anything queer in them," said Paul, "but I'll wait till it begins to get dark. That is the time I ache to tell people things, and when nobody else is handy I just *have* to tell Mary Joe. But after this I won't, if it makes her imagine I'm wrong in my upper story. I'll just ache and bear it."

"And if the ache gets too bad you can come up to

Green Gables and tell me your thoughts," suggested Anne, with all the gravity that endeared her to children, who so dearly love to be taken seriously.

"Yes, I will. But I hope Davy won't be there when I go because he makes faces at me. I don't mind *very* much because he is such a little boy and I am quite a big one, but still it is not pleasant to have faces made at you. And Davy makes such terrible ones. Sometimes I am frightened he will never get his face straightened out again. He makes them at me in church when I ought to be thinking of sacred things. Dora likes me though, and I like her, but not so well as I did before she told Minnie May Barry that she meant to marry me when I grew up. I may marry somebody when I grow up but I'm far too young to be thinking of it yet, don't you think, teacher?"

"Rather young," agreed teacher.

"Speaking of marrying, reminds me of another thing that has been troubling me of late," continued Paul. "Mrs. Lynde was down here one day last week having tea with Grandma, and Grandma made me show her my little mother's picture . . . the one father sent me for my birthday present. I didn't exactly want to show it to Mrs. Lynde. Mrs. Lynde is a good, kind woman, but she isn't the sort of person you want to show your mother's picture to. *You* know, teacher. But of course I obeyed Grandma. Mrs. Lynde said she was very pretty but kind of actressy looking, and must have been an awful lot younger than father. Then she said, 'Some of these days your pa will be marrying again likely. How will you like to have a new ma, Master Paul?' Well, the idea almost took my breath away, teacher, but I wasn't going to let Mrs. Lynde see *that*. I just looked her straight in the face . . . like this . . . and I said, 'Mrs. Lynde, father made a pretty good job of picking out my first mother and I could trust him to pick out just as good a one the second time.' And I *can* trust him, teacher. But still, I hope, if he ever does give me a new mother, he'll ask my opinion about her before it's too late. There's Mary Joe coming to call us to tea. I'll go and consult with her about the shortbread."

As a result of the "consultation," Mary Joe cut the shortbread and added a dish of preserves to the bill of fare. Anne poured the tea and she and Paul had a very merry meal in the dim old sitting room whose windows were open to the gulf breezes, and they talked so much "nonsense" that Mary Joe was quite scandalized and told Veronica the next evening that "de school mees" was as queer as Paul. After tea Paul took Anne up to his room to show her his mother's picture, which had been the mysterious birthday present kept by Mrs. Irving in the bookcase. Paul's little low-ceilinged room was a soft whirl of ruddy light from the sun that was setting over the sea and swinging shadows from the fir trees that grew close to the square, deep-set window. From out this soft glow and glamor shone a sweet, girlish face, with tender mother eyes, that was hanging on the wall at the foot of the bed.

"That's my little mother," said Paul with loving pride. "I got Grandma to hang it there where I'd see it as soon as I opened my eyes in the morning. I never mind not having the light when I go to bed now, because it just seems as if my little mother was right here with me. Father knew just what I would like for a birthday present, although he never asked me. Isn't it wonderful how much fathers *do* know?"

"Your mother was very lovely, Paul, and you look a little like her. But her eyes and hair are darker than yours."

"My eyes are the same color as father's," said Paul, flying about the room to heap all available cushions on the window seat, "but father's hair is gray. He has lots of it, but it is gray. You see, father is nearly fifty. That's ripe old age, isn't it? But it's only *outside* he's old. *Inside* he's just as young as anybody. Now, teacher, please sit here; and I'll sit at your feet. May I lay my head against your knee? That's the way my little mother and I used to sit. Oh, this is real splendid, I think."

"Now, I want to hear those thoughts which Mary Joe pronounces so queer," said Anne, patting the mop of curls at her side. Paul never needed any coaxing to tell his thoughts . . . at least, to congenial souls.

"I thought them out in the fir grove one night," he said dreamily. "Of course I didn't *believe* them but I *thought* them. *You* know, teacher. And then I wanted to tell them to somebody and there was nobody but Mary Joe. Mary Joe was in the pantry setting bread and I sat down on the bench beside her and I said, 'Mary Joe, do you know what I think? I think the evening star is a lighthouse on the land where the fairies dwell.' And Mary Joe said, 'Well, yous are de queer one. Dare ain't no such ting as fairies.' I was very much provoked. Of course, I knew there are no fairies; but that needn't prevent my thinking there is. *You* know, teacher. But I tried again quite patiently. I said, 'Well then, Mary Joe, do you know what I think? I think an angel walks over the world after the sun sets . . . a great, tall, white angel, with silvery folded wings . . . and sings the flowers and birds to sleep. Children can hear him if they know how to listen.' Then Mary Joe held up her hands all over flour and said, 'Well, yous are de queer leetle boy. Yous make me feel scare.' And she really did looked scared. I went out then and whispered the rest of my thoughts to the garden. There was a little birch tree in the garden and it died. Grandma says the salt spray killed it; but I think the dryad belonging to it was a foolish dryad who wandered away to see the world and got lost. And the little tree was so lonely it died of a broken heart."

"And when the poor, foolish little dryad gets tired of the world and comes back to her tree *her* heart will break," said Anne.

"Yes; but if dryads are foolish they must take the consequences, just as if they were real people," said Paul gravely. "Do you know what I think about the new moon, teacher? I think it is a little golden boat full of dreams."

"And when it tips on a cloud some of them spill out and fall into your sleep."

"Exactly, teacher. Oh, you *do* know. And I think the violets are little snips of the sky that fell down when the angels cut out holes for the stars to shine through. And the buttercups are made out of old sunshine; and I think the sweet peas will be butterflies when they go to heaven. Now, teacher, do you see anything so very queer about those thoughts?"

"No, laddie dear, they are not queer at all; they are strange and beautiful thoughts for a little boy to think, and so people who couldn't think anything of the sort themselves, if they tried for a hundred years, think them queer. But keep on thinking them, Paul . . . some day you are going to be a poet, I believe."

When Anne reached home she found a very different type of boyhood waiting to be put to bed. Davy was sulky; and when Anne had undressed him he bounced into bed and buried his face in the pillow.

"Davy, you have forgotten to say your prayers," said Anne rebukingly.

"No, I didn't forget," said Davy defiantly, "but I ain't going to say my prayers any more. I'm going to give up trying to be good, 'cause no matter how good I am you'd like Paul Irving better. So I might as well be bad and have the fun of it."

"I don't like Paul Irving *better*," said Anne seriously. "I like you just as well, only in a different way."

"But I want you to like me the same way," pouted Davy.

"You can't like different people the same way. You don't like Dora and me the same way, do you?"

Davy sat up and reflected.

"No . . . o . . . o," he admitted at last, "I like Dora because she's my sister but I like you because you're *you*."

"And I like Paul because he is Paul and Davy because he is Davy," said Anne gaily.

"Well, I kind of wish I'd said my prayers then," said Davy, convinced by this logic. "But it's too much bother getting out now to say them. I'll say them twice over in the morning, Anne. Won't that do as well?"

No, Anne was positive it would not do as well. So Davy scrambled out and knelt down at her knee. When he had finished his devotions he leaned back on his little, bare, brown heels and looked up at her.

"Anne, I'm gooder than I used to be."

"Yes, indeed you are, Davy," said Anne, who never hesitated to give credit where credit was due.

"I *know* I'm gooder," said Davy confidently, "and I'll tell you how I know it. Today Marilla give me two pieces of bread and jam, one for me and one for Dora. One was a good deal bigger than the other and Marilla didn't say which was mine. But I give the biggest piece to Dora. That was good of me, wasn't it?"

"Very good, and very manly, Davy."

"Of course," admitted Davy, "Dora wasn't very hungry and she only et half her slice and then she give the rest to me. But I didn't know she was going to do that when I give it to her, so I *was* good, Anne."

In the twilight Anne sauntered down to the Dryad's Bubble and saw Gilbert Blythe coming down through the dusky Haunted Wood. She had a sudden realization that Gilbert was a schoolboy no longer. And how manly he looked—the tall, frank-faced fellow, with the clear, straightforward eyes and the broad shoulders. Anne thought Gilbert was a very handsome lad, even though he didn't look at all like her ideal man. She and Diana had long ago decided what kind of a man they admired and their tastes seemed exactly similar. He must be very tall and distinguished looking, with melancholy, inscrutable eyes, and a melting, sympathetic voice. There was nothing either melancholy or inscrutable in Gilbert's physiognomy, but of course that didn't matter in friendship!

Gilbert stretched himself out on the ferns beside

the Bubble and looked approvingly at Anne. If Gilbert had been asked to describe his ideal woman the description would have answered point for point to Anne, even to those seven tiny freckles whose obnoxious presence still continued to vex her soul. Gilbert was as yet little more than a boy; but a boy has his dreams as have others, and in Gilbert's future there was always a girl with big, limpid gray eyes, and a face as fine and delicate as a flower. He had made up his mind, also, that his future must be worthy of its goddess. Even in quiet Avonlea there were temptations to be met and faced. White Sands youth were a rather "fast" set, and Gilbert was popular wherever he went. But he meant to keep himself worthy of Anne's friendship and perhaps some distant day her love; and he watched over word and thought and deed as jealously as if her clear eyes were to pass in judgment on it. She held over him the unconscious influence that every girl, whose ideals are high and pure, wields over her friends; an influence which would endure as long as she was faithful to those ideals and which she would as certainly lose if she were ever false to them. In Gilbert's eyes Anne's greatest charm was the fact that she never stooped to the petty practices of so many of the Avonlea girls—the small jealousies, the little deceits and rivalries, the palpable bids for favor. Anne held herself apart from all this, not consciously or of design, but simply because anything of the sort was utterly foreign to her transparent, impulsive nature, crystal clear in its motives and aspirations.

But Gilbert did not attempt to put his thoughts into words, for he had already too good reason to know that Anne would mercilessly and frostily nip all attempts at sentiment in the bud—or laugh at him, which was ten times worse.

"You look like a real dryad under that birch tree," he said teasingly.

"I love birch trees," said Anne, laying her cheek against the creamy satin of the slim bole, with one of the pretty, caressing gestures that came so natural to her.

"Then you'll be glad to hear that Mr. Major Spencer has decided to set out a row of white birches all along the road front of his farm, by way of encouraging the A. V. I. S.," said Gilbert. "He was talking to me about it today. Major Spencer is the most progressive and public-spirited man in Avonlea. And Mr. William Bell is going to set out a spruce hedge along his road front and up his lane. Our Society is getting on splendidly, Anne. It is past the experimental stage and is an accepted fact. The older folks are beginning to take an interest in it and the White Sands people are talking of starting one too. Even Elisha Wright has come around since that day the Americans from the hotel had the picnic at the shore. They praised our roadsides so highly and said they were so much prettier than in any other part of the Island. And when, in due time, the other farmers follow Mr. Spencer's good example and plant ornamental trees and hedges along their road fronts Avonlea will be the prettiest settlement in the province."

"The Aids are talking of taking up the graveyard," said Anne, "and I hope they will, because there will have to be a subscription for that, and it would be no use for the Society to try it after the hall affair. But the Aids would never have stirred in the matter if the Society hadn't put it into their thoughts unofficially. Those trees we planted on the church grounds are flourishing, and the trustees have promised me that they will fence in the school grounds next year. If they do I'll have an arbor day and every scholar shall plant a tree; and we'll have a garden in the corner by the road."

"We've succeeded in almost all our plans so far, except in getting the old Boulter house removed," said Gilbert, "and I've given *that* up in despair. Levi won't have it taken down just to vex us. There's a contrary streak in all the Boulters and it's strongly developed in him."

"Julia Bell wants to send another committee to him, but I think the better way will just be to leave him severely alone," said Anne sagely.

"And trust to Providence, as Mrs. Lynde says," smiled Gilbert. "Certainly, no more committees. They only aggravate him. Julia Bell thinks you can do anything, if you only have a committee to attempt it. Next spring, Anne, we must start an agitation for nice lawns and grounds. We'll sow good seed betimes this winter. I've a treatise here on lawns and lawn-making and I'm going to prepare a paper on the subject soon. Well, I suppose our vacation is almost over. School opens Monday. Has Ruby Gillis got the Carmody school?"

"Yes; Priscilla wrote that she had taken her own home school, so the Carmody trustees gave it to Ruby. I'm sorry Priscilla is not coming back, but since she can't I'm glad Ruby has got the school. She will be home for Saturdays and it will seem like old times, to have her and Jane and Diana and myself all together again."

Marilla, just home from Mrs. Lynde's, was sitting on the back porch step when Anne returned to the house.

"Rachel and I have decided to have our cruise to town tomorrow," she said. "Mr. Lynde is feeling better this week and Rachel wants to go before he has another sick spell."

"I intend to get up extra early tomorrow morning, for I've ever so much to do," said Anne virtuously. "For one thing, I'm going to shift the feathers from my old bedtick to the new one. I ought to have done it long ago but I've just kept putting it off . . . it's such a detestable task. It's a very bad habit to put off disagreeable things, and I never mean to again, or else I can't comfortably tell my pupils not to do it. That would be inconsistent. Then I want to make a cake for Mr. Harrison and finish my paper on gardens for the

A. V. I. S., and write Stella, and wash and starch my muslin dress, and make Dora's new apron."

"You won't get half done," said Marilla pessimistically. "I never yet planned to do a lot of things but something happened to prevent me."

XX

The Way It Often Happens

Anne rose betimes the next morning and blithely greeted the fresh day, when the banners of the sunrise were shaken triumphantly across the pearly skies. Green Gables lay in a pool of sunshine, flecked with the dancing shadows of poplar and willow. Beyond the lane was Mr. Harrison's wheatfield, a great, wind-rippled expanse of pale gold. The world was so beautiful that Anne spent ten blissful minutes hanging idly over the garden gate drinking the loveliness in.

After breakfast Marilla made ready for her journey. Dora was to go with her, having been long promised this treat.

"Now, Davy, you try to be a good boy and don't bother Anne," she straitly charged him. "If you are good I'll bring you a striped candy cane from town."

For alas, Marilla had stooped to the evil habit of bribing people to be good!

"I won't be bad on purpose, but s'posen I'm bad zacksidentally?" Davy wanted to know.

"You'll have to guard against accidents," admonished Marilla. "Anne, if Mr. Shearer comes today get a nice roast and some steak. If he doesn't you'll have to kill a fowl for dinner tomorrow."

Anne nodded.

"I'm not going to bother cooking any dinner for just Davy and myself today," she said. "That cold ham bone will do for noon lunch and I'll have some steak fried for you when you come home at night."

"I'm going to help Mr. Harrison haul dulse this morning," announced Davy. "He asked me to, and I guess he'll ask me to dinner too. Mr. Harrison is an awful kind man. He's a real sociable man. I hope I'll be like him when I grow up. I mean *behave* like him . . . I don't want to *look* like him. But I guess there's no danger, for Mrs. Lynde says I'm a very handsome child. Do you s'pose it'll last, Anne? I want to know."

"I daresay it will," said Anne gravely. "You *are* a handsome boy, Davy," . . . Marilla looked volumes of disapproval . . . "but you must live up to it and be just as nice and gentlemanly as you look to be."

"And you told Minnie May Barry the other day, when you found her crying 'cause some one said she was ugly, that if she was nice and kind and loving people wouldn't mind her looks," said Davy discontentedly. "Seems to me you can't get out of being good in this world for some reason or 'nother. You just *have* to behave."

"Don't you want to be good?" asked Marilla, who had learned a great deal but had not yet learned the futility of asking such questions.

"Yes, I want to be good but not *too* good," said Davy cautiously. "You don't have to be very good to be a Sunday School superintendent. Mr. Bell's that, and he's a real bad man."

"Indeed he's not," said Marilla indignantly.

"He is . . . he says he is himself," asseverated Davy. "He said it when he prayed in Sunday School last Sunday. He said he was a vile worm and a miserable sinner and guilty of the blackest 'niquity. What did he do that was so bad, Marilla? Did he kill anybody? Or steal the collection cents? I want to know."

Fortunately Mrs. Lynde came driving up the lane at this moment and Marilla made off, feeling that she had escaped from the snare of the fowler, and wishing devoutly that Mr. Bell were not quite so highly figurative in his public petitions, especially in the hearing of small boys who were always "wanting to know."

Anne, left alone in her glory, worked with a will. The floor was swept, the beds made, the hens fed, the muslin dress washed and hung out on the line. Then Anne prepared for the transfer of feathers. She mounted to the garret and donned the first old dress that came to hand . . . a navy blue cashmere she had worn at fourteen. It was decidedly on the short side and as "skimpy" as the notable wincey Anne had worn upon the occasion of her debut at Green Gables; but at least it would not be materially injured by down and feathers. Anne completed her toilet by tying a big red and white spotted handkerchief that had belonged to Matthew over her head, and, thus accoutred, betook herself to the kitchen chamber, whither Marilla, before her departure, had helped her carry the feather bed.

A cracked mirror hung by the chamber window and in an unlucky moment Anne looked into it. There were those seven freckles on her nose, more rampant than ever, or so it seemed in the glare of light from the unshaded window.

"Oh, I forgot to rub that lotion on last night," she thought. "I'd better run down to the pantry and do it now."

Anne had already suffered many things trying to remove those freckles. On one occasion the entire skin had peeled off her nose but the freckles remained. A few days previously she had found a recipe for a freckle lotion in a magazine and, as the ingredients were within her reach, she straightway compounded it, much to the disgust of Marilla, who thought that if Providence had placed freckles on your nose it was your bounden duty to leave them there.

Anne scurried down to the pantry, which, always dim from the big willow growing close to the window, was now almost dark by reason of the shade drawn to exclude flies. Anne caught the bottle containing the lotion from the shelf and copiously annointed her nose therewith by means of a little sponge sacred to the purpose. This important duty done, she returned to her work. Any one who has ever shifted feathers from one tick to another will not need to be told that when Anne finished she was a sight to behold. Her dress was white with down and fluff, and her front hair, escaping from under the handkerchief, was adorned with a veritable halo of feathers. At this auspicious moment a knock sounded at the kitchen door.

"That must be Mr. Shearer," thought Anne. "I'm in a dreadful mess but I'll have to run down as I am, for he's always in a hurry."

Down flew Anne to the kitchen door. If ever a charitable floor did open to swallow up a miserable, befeathered damsel the Green Gables porch floor should promptly have engulfed Anne at that moment. On the doorstep were standing Priscilla Grant, golden and fair in silk attire, a short, stout, gray-haired lady in a tweed suit, and another lady, tall, stately, wonderfully gowned, with a beautiful, highbred face and large, black-lashed violet eyes, whom Anne "instinctively felt," as she would have said in her earlier days, to be Mrs. Charlotte E. Morgan.

In the dismay of the moment one thought stood out from the confusion of Anne's mind and she grasped at it as at the proverbial straw. All Mrs. Morgan's heroines were noted for "rising to the occasion." No matter what their troubles were, they invariably rose to the occasion and showed their superiority over all ills of time, space, and quantity. Anne therefore felt it was *her* duty to rise to the occasion and she did it, so perfectly that Priscilla afterward declared she never admired Anne Shirley more than at that moment. No matter what her outraged feelings were she did not show them. She greeted Priscilla and was introduced to her companions as calmly and composedly as if she had been arrayed in purple and fine linen. To be sure, it was somewhat of a shock to find that the lady she had instinctively felt to be Mrs. Morgan was not Mrs. Morgan at all, but an unknown Mrs. Pendexter, while the stout little gray-haired woman was Mrs. Morgan; but in the greater shock the lesser lost its power. Anne ushered her guests to the spare room and thence into the parlor, where she left them while she hastened out to help Priscilla unharness her horse.

"It's dreadful to come upon you so unexpectedly as this," apologized Priscilla, "but I did not know till last night that we were coming. Aunt Charlotte is going away Monday and she had promised to spend today with a friend in town. But last night her friend telephoned to her not to come because they were quarantined for scarlet fever. So I suggested we come here instead, for I knew you were longing to see her. We called at the White Sands Hotel and brought Mrs. Pendexter with us. She is a friend of aunt's and lives in New York and her husband is a millionaire. We can't stay very long, for Mrs. Pendexter has to be back at the hotel by five o'clock."

Several times while they were putting away the horse Ann caught Priscilla looking at her in a furtive, puzzled way.

"She needn't stare at me so," Ann thought a little resentfully. "If she doesn't *know* what it is to change a feather bed she might *imagine* it."

When Priscilla had gone to the parlor, and before Anne could escape upstairs, Diana walked into the kitchen. Anne caught her astonished friend by the arm.

"Diana Barry, who do you suppose is in that parlor at this very moment? Mrs. Charlotte E. Morgan . . . and a New York millionaire's wife . . . and here I am like *this* . . . and *not a thing in the house for dinner but a cold ham bone,* Diana!"

By this time Anne had become aware that Diana was staring at her in precisely the same bewildered fashion as Priscilla had done. It was really too much.

"Oh, Diana, don't look at me so," she implored. "*You,* at least, must know that the neatest person in the world couldn't empty feathers from one tick into another and remain neat in the process."

"It . . . it . . . isn't the feathers," hesitated Diana. "It's . . . it's . . . your nose, Anne."

"My nose? Oh, Diana, surely nothing has gone wrong with it!"

Anne rushed to the little looking glass over the sink. One glance revealed the fatal truth. Her nose was a brilliant scarlet!

Anne sat down on the sofa, her dauntless spirit subdued at last.

"What is the matter with it?" asked Diana, curiosity overcoming delicacy.

"I thought I was rubbing my freckle lotion on it, but I must have used that red dye Marilla has for marking the pattern on her rugs," was the despairing response. "What shall I do?"

"Wash it off," said Diana practically.

"Perhaps it won't wash off. First I dye my hair; then I dye my nose. Marilla cut my hair off when I dyed it but that remedy would hardly be practicable in this case. Well, this is another punishment for vanity and I suppose I deserve it . . . though there's not much comfort in *that*. It is really almost enough to make one believe in ill-luck, though Mrs. Lynde says there is no such thing, because everything is foreordained."

Fortunately the dye washed off easily and Anne, somewhat consoled, betook herself to the east gable while Diana ran home. Presently Anne came down again, clothed and in her right mind. The muslin dress she had fondly hoped to wear was bobbing merrily about on the line outside, so she was forced to content herself with her black lawn. She had the fire on and the tea steeping when Diana returned; the latter wore *her* muslin, at least, and carried a covered platter in her hand.

"Mother sent you this," she said, lifting the cover and displaying a nicely carved and jointed chicken to Anne's grateful eyes.

The chicken was supplemented by light new bread, excellent butter and cheese, Marilla's fruit cake and a dish of preserved plums, floating in their golden syrup as in congealed summer sunshine. There was a big bowlful of pink-and-white asters also, by way of decoration; yet the spread seemed very meager beside the elaborate one formerly prepared for Mrs. Morgan.

Anne's hungry guests, however, did not seem to think anything was lacking and they ate the simple viands with apparent enjoyment. But after the first few moments Anne thought no more of what was or was not on her bill of fare. Mrs. Morgan's appearance might be somewhat disappointing, as even her loyal worshippers had been forced to admit to each other; but she proved to be a delightful conversationalist. She had traveled extensively and was an excellent storyteller. She had seen much of men and women, and crystalized her experiences into witty little sentences and epigrams which made her hearers feel as if they were listening to one of the people in clever books. But under all her sparkle there was a strongly felt undercurrent of true, womanly sympathy and kindheartedness which won affection as easily as her brilliancy won admiration. Nor did she monopolize the conversation. She could draw others out as skillfully and fully as she could talk herself, and Anne and Diana found themselves chattering freely to her. Mrs. Pendexter said little; she merely smiled with her lovely eyes and lips, and ate chicken and fruit cake and preserves with such exquisite grace that she conveyed the impression of dining on ambrosia and honeydew. But then, as Anne said to Diana later on, anybody so divinely beautiful as Mrs. Pendexter didn't need to talk; it was enough for her just to *look*.

After dinner they all had a walk through Lover's Lane and Violet Vale and the Birch Path, then back through the Haunted Wood to the Dryad's Bubble, where they sat down and talked for a delightful last half hour. Mrs. Morgan wanted to know how the Haunted Wood came by its name, and laughed until she cried when she heard the story and Anne's dramatic account of a certain memorable walk through it at the witching hour of twilight.

"It has indeed been a feast of reason and flow of soul, hasn't it?" said Anne, when her guests had gone and she and Diana were alone again. "I don't know which I enjoyed more . . . listening to Mrs. Morgan or gazing at Mrs. Pendexter. I believe we had a nicer time than if we'd known they were coming and been cumbered with much serving. You must stay to tea with me, Diana, and we'll talk it all over."

"Priscilla says Mrs. Pendexter's husband's sister is married to an English earl; and yet she took a second helping of the plum preserves," said Diana, as if the two facts were somehow incompatible.

"I daresay even the English earl himself wouldn't have turned up his aristocratic nose at Marilla's plum preserves," said Anne proudly.

Anne did not mention the misfortune which had befallen *her* nose when she related the day's history to Marilla that evening. But she took the bottle of freckle lotion and emptied it out of the window.

"I shall never try any beautifying messes again," she said, darkly resolute. "They may do for careful, deliberate people; but for anyone so hopelessly given over to making mistakes as I seem to be it's tempting fate to meddle with them."

XXI

Sweet Miss Lavendar

School opened and Anne returned to her work, with fewer theories but considerably more experience. She had several new pupils, six- and seven-year-olds just venturing, round-eyed, into a world of wonder. Among them were Davy and Dora. Davy sat with Milty Boulter, who had been going to school for a year and was therefore quite a man of the world. Dora had made a compact at Sunday School the previous Sunday to sit with Lily Sloane; but Lily Sloane not coming the first day, she was temporarily assigned to Mirabel Cotton, who was ten years old and therefore, in Dora's eyes, one of the "big girls."

"I think school is great fun," Davy told Marilla when he got home that night. "You said I'd find it hard to sit still and I did . . . you mostly do tell the truth, I notice . . . but you can wriggle your legs about under the desk and that helps a lot. It's splendid to have so many boys to play with. I sit with Milty Boulter and he's fine. He's longer than me but I'm wider. It's nicer to sit in the back seats but you can't sit there till your legs grow long enough to touch the floor. Milty drawed a picture of Anne on his slate and it was awful ugly and I told him if he made pictures of Anne like that I'd lick him at recess. I thought first I'd draw one of him and put horns and a tail on it, but I was afraid it would hurt his feelings, and Anne says you should never hurt anyone's feelings. It seems it's dreadful to have your feelings hurt. It's better to knock a boy down than hurt his feelings if you *must* do something. Milty said he wasn't scared of me but he'd just as soon call it somebody else to 'blige me, so he rubbed out Anne's name and printed Barbara Shaw's under it. Milty doesn't like Barbara 'cause she calls him a sweet little boy and once she patted him on his head."

Dora said primly that she liked school; but she was very quiet, even for her; and when at twilight Marilla bade her go upstairs to bed she hesitated and began to cry.

"I'm . . . I'm frightened," she sobbed. "I . . . I don't want to go upstairs alone in the dark."

"What notion have you got into your head now?" demanded Marilla. "I'm sure you've gone to bed alone all summer and never been frightened before."

Dora still continued to cry, so Anne picked her up, cuddled her sympathetically, and whispered,

"Tell Anne all about it, sweetheart. What are you frightened of?"

"Of . . . of Mirabel Cotton's uncle," sobbed Dora. "Mirabel Cotton told me all about her family today in school. Nearly everybody in her family has died . . . all her grandfathers and grandmothers and ever so many uncles and aunts. They have a habit of dying, Mirabel says. Mirabel's awful proud of having so many dead relations, and she told me what they all died of, and what they said, and how they looked in their coffins. And Mirabel says one of her uncles was seen walking around the house after he was buried. Her mother saw him. I don't mind the rest so much but I can't help thinking about that uncle."

Anne went upstairs with Dora and sat by her until she fell asleep. The next day Mirabel Cotton was kept in at recess and "gently but firmly" given to understand that when you were so unfortunate as to possess an uncle who persisted in walking about houses after he had been decently interred it was not in good taste to talk about that eccentric gentleman to your deskmate of tender years. Mirabel thought this very harsh. The Cottons had not much to boast of. How was she to keep up her prestige among her schoolmates if she were forbidden to make capital out of the family ghost?

September slipped by into a gold and crimson graciousness of October. One Friday evening Diana came over.

"I'd a letter from Ella Kimball today, Anne, and she wants us to go over to tea tomorrow afternoon to meet her cousin, Irene Trent, from town. But we can't get one of our horses to go, for they'll all be in use tomorrow, and your pony is lame . . . so I suppose we can't go."

"Why can't we walk?" suggested Anne. "If we go straight back through the woods we'll strike the West Grafton road not far from the Kimball place. I was through that way last winter and I know the road. It's no more than four miles and we won't have to walk home, for Oliver Kimball will be sure to drive us. He'll be only too glad of the excuse, for he goes to see Carrie Sloane and they say his father will hardly ever let him have a horse."

It was accordingly arranged that they should walk, and the following afternoon they set out, going by way of Lover's Lane to the back of the Cuthbert farm, where they found a road leading into the heart of acres of glimmering beech and maple woods, which were all in a wondrous glow of flame and gold, lying in a great purple stillness and peace.

"It's as if the year were kneeling to pray in a vast cathedral full of mellow stained light, isn't it?" said Anne dreamily. "It doesn't seem right to hurry through it, does it? It seems irreverent, like running in a church."

"We *must* hurry though," said Diana, glancing at her watch. "We've left ourselves little enough time as it is."

"Well, I'll walk fast but don't ask me to talk," said Anne, quickening her pace. "I just want to drink the day's loveliness in . . . I feel as if she were holding it out to my lips like a cup of airy wine and I'll take a sip at every step."

Perhaps it was because she was so absorbed in "drinking it in" that Anne took the left turning when they came to a fork in the road. She should have taken the right, but ever afterward she counted it the most fortunate mistake of her life. They came out finally to a lonely, grassy road, with nothing in sight along it but ranks of spruce saplings.

"Why, where are we?" exclaimed Diana in bewilderment. "This isn't the West Grafton road."

"No, it's the base line road in Middle Grafton," said Anne, rather shamefacedly. "I must have taken the wrong turning at the fork. I don't know where we are exactly, but we must be all of three miles from Kimballs' still."

"Then we can't get there by five, for it's half past four now," said Diana, with a despairing look at her watch. "We'll arrive after they have had their tea, and they'll have all the bother of getting ours over again."

"We'd better turn back and go home," suggested Anne humbly. But Diana, after consideration, vetoed this.

"No, we may as well go and spend the evening, since we have come this far."

A few yards further on the girls came to a place where the road forked again.

"Which of these do we take?" asked Diana dubiously.

Anne shook her head.

"I don't know and we can't afford to make any more mistakes. Here is a gate and a lane leading right into the wood. There must be a house at the other side. Let us go down and inquire."

"What a romantic old lane this is," said Diana, as they walked along its twists and turns. It ran under patriarchal old firs whose branches met above, creating a perpetual gloom in which nothing except moss could grow. On either hand were brown wood floors, crossed here and there by fallen lances of sunlight. All was very still and remote, as if the world and the cares of the world were far away.

"I feel as if we were walking through an enchanted forest," said Anne in a hushed tone. "Do you suppose we'll ever find our way back to the real world again, Diana? We shall presently come to a palace with a spellbound princess in it, I think."

Around the next turn they came in sight, not indeed of a palace, but of a little house almost as surprising as a palace would have been in this province of conventional wooden farmhouses, all as much alike in general characteristics as if they had grown from the same seed. Anne stopped short in rapture and Diana exclaimed,

"Oh, I know where we are now. That is the little stone house where Miss Lavendar Lewis lives . . . Echo Lodge, she calls it, I think. I've often heard of it but I've never seen it before. Isn't it a romantic spot?"

"It's the sweetest, prettiest place I ever saw or imagined," said Anne delightedly. "It looks like a bit out of a story book or a dream."

The house was a low-eaved structure built of undressed blocks of red Island sandstone, with a little peaked roof out of which peered two dormer windows, with quaint wooden hoods over them, and two great chimneys. The whole house was covered with a luxuriant growth of ivy, finding easy foothold on the rough stonework and turned by autumn frosts to most beautiful bronze and wine-red tints.

Before the house was an oblong garden into which the lane gate where the girls were standing opened. The house bounded it on one side; on the three others it was enclosed by an old stone dyke, so overgrown with moss and grass and ferns that it looked like a high, green bank. On the right and left the tall, dark spruces spread their palm-like branches over it; but below it was a little meadow, green with clover aftermath, sloping down to the blue loop of the Grafton River. No other house or clearing was in sight

. . . nothing but hills and valleys covered with feathery young firs.

"I wonder what sort of a person Miss Lewis is," speculated Diana as they opened the gate into the garden. "They say she is very peculiar."

"She'll be interesting then," said Anne decidedly. "Peculiar people are always that at least, whatever else they are or are not. Didn't I tell you we would come to an enchanted palace? I knew the elves hadn't woven magic over that lane for nothing."

"But Miss Lavendar Lewis is hardly a spellbound princess," laughed Diana. "She's an old maid . . . she's forty-five and quite gray, I've heard."

"Oh, that's only part of the spell," asserted Anne confidently. "At heart she's young and beautiful still . . . and if we only knew how to unloose the spell she would step forth radiant and fair again. But we don't know how . . . it's always and only the prince who knows that . . . and Miss Lavendar's prince hasn't come yet. Perhaps some fatal mischance has befallen him . . . though *that's* against the law of all fairy tales."

"I'm afraid he came long ago and went away again," said Diana. "They say she used to be engaged to Stephen Irving . . . Paul's father . . . when they were young. But they quarreled and parted."

"Hush," warned Anne. "The door is open."

The girls paused in the porch under the tendrils of ivy and knocked at the open door. There was a patter of steps inside and a rather odd little personage presented herself . . . a girl of about fourteen, with a freckled face, a snub nose, a mouth so wide that it did really seem as if it stretched "from ear to ear," and two long braids of fair hair tied with two enormous bows of blue ribbon.

"Is Miss Lewis at home?" asked Diana.

"Yes, ma'am. Come in, ma'am . . . this way, ma'am . . . and sit down, ma'am. I'll tell Miss Lavendar you're here, ma'am. She's upstairs, ma'am."

With this the small handmaiden whisked out of

sight and the girls, left alone, looked about them with delighted eyes. The interior of this wonderful little house was quite as interesting as its exterior.

The room had a low ceiling and two square, small-paned windows, curtained with muslin frills. All the furnishings were old-fashioned, but so well and daintily kept that the effect was delicious. But it must be candidly admitted that the most attractive feature, to two healthy girls who had just tramped four miles through autumn air, was a table, set out with pale blue china and laden with delicacies, while little golden-hued ferns scattered over the cloth gave it what Anne would have termed "a festal air."

"Miss Lavendar must be expecting company to tea," she whispered. "There are six places set. But what a funny little girl she has. She looked like a messenger from pixy land. I suppose she could have told us the road, but I was curious to see Miss Lavendar. S . . . s . . . sh, she's coming."

And with that Miss Lavendar Lewis was standing in the doorway. The girls were so surprised that they forgot good manners and simply stared. They had unconsciously been expecting to see the usual type of elderly spinster as known to their experience . . . a rather angular personage, with prim gray hair and spectacles. Nothing more unlike Miss Lavendar could possibly be imagined.

She was a little lady with snow-white hair beautifully wavy and thick, and carefully arranged in becoming puffs and coils. Beneath it was an almost girlish face, pink cheeked and sweet lipped, with big soft brown eyes and dimples . . . actually dimples. She wore a very dainty gown of cream muslin with pale-hued roses on it . . . a gown which would have seemed ridiculously juvenile on most women of her age, but which suited Miss Lavendar so perfectly that you never thought about it at all.

"Charlotta the Fourth says that you wished to see me," she said, in a voice that matched her appearance. "We wanted to ask the right road to West

Grafton," said Diana. "We are invited to tea at Mr. Kimball's, but we took the wrong path coming through the woods and came out to the base line instead of the West Grafton road. Do we take the right or left turning at your gate?"

"The left," said Miss Lavendar, with a hesitating glance at her tea table. Then she exclaimed, as if in a sudden little burst of resolution,

"But oh, won't you stay and have tea with me? Please, do. Mr. Kimball's will have tea over before you get there. And Charlotta the Fourth and I will be so glad to have you."

Diana looked mute inquiry at Anne.

"We'd like to stay," said Anne promptly, for she had made up her mind that she wanted to know more of this surprising Miss Lavendar, "if it won't inconvenience you. But you are expecting other guests, aren't you?"

Miss Lavendar looked at her tea table again, and blushed.

"I know you'll think me dreadfully foolish," she said. "I *am* foolish . . . and I'm ashamed of it when I'm found out, but never unless I *am* found out. I'm not expecting anybody . . . I was just pretending I was. You see, I was so lonely. I love company . . . that is, the right kind of company . . . but so few people ever come here because it is so far out of the way. Charlotta the Fourth was lonely too. So I just pretended I was going to have a tea party. I cooked for it . . . and decorated the table for it . . . and set it with my mother's wedding china . . . and I dressed up for it."

Diana secretly thought Miss Lavendar quite as peculiar as report had pictured her. The idea of a woman of forty-five playing at having a tea party, just as if she were a little girl! But Anne of the shining eyes exclaimed joyfully,

"Oh, do *you* imagine things too?"

That "too" revealed a kindred spirit to Miss Lavendar.

"Yes, I do," she confessed, boldly. "Of course it's silly in anybody as old as I am. But what is the use of being an independent old maid if you can't be silly when you want to, and when it doesn't hurt anybody? A person must have some compensations. I don't believe I could live at times if I didn't pretend things. I'm not often caught at it though, and Charlotta the Fourth never tells. But I'm glad to be caught today, for you have really come and I have tea all ready for you. Will you go up to the spare room and take off your hats? It's the white door at the head of the stairs. I must run out to the kitchen and see that Charlotta the Fourth isn't letting the tea boil. Charlotta the Fourth is a very good girl but she *will* let the tea boil."

Miss Lavendar tripped off to the kitchen on hospitable thoughts intent and the girls found their way up to the spare room, an apartment as white as its door, lighted by the ivy-hung dormer window and looking, as Anne said, like the place where happy dreams grew.

"This is quite an adventure, isn't it?" said Diana. "And isn't Miss Lavendar sweet, if she *is* a little odd? She doesn't look a bit like an old maid."

"She looks just as music sounds, I think," answered Anne.

When they went down Miss Lavendar was carrying in the teapot, and behind her, looking vastly pleased, was Charlotta the Fourth, with a plate of hot biscuits.

"Now, you must tell me your names," said Miss Lavendar. "I'm so glad you are young girls. I love young girls. It's so easy to pretend I'm a girl myself when I'm with them. I do hate" . . . with a little grimace . . . "to believe I'm old. Now, who are you . . . just for convenience' sake? Diana Barry? And Anne Shirley? May I pretend that I've known you for a hundred years and call you Anne and Diana right away?"

"You may," the girls said both together.

"Then just let's sit comfily down and eat

everything," said Miss Lavendar happily. "Charlotta, you sit at the foot and help the chicken. It is so fortunate that I made the sponge cake and doughnuts. Of course, it was foolish to do it for imaginary guests. . . . I know Charlotta the Fourth thought so, didn't you, Charlotta? But you see how well it has turned out. Of course they wouldn't have been wasted, for Charlotta the Fourth and I could have eaten them through time. But sponge cake is not a thing that improves with time."

That was a merry and memorable meal; and when it was over they all went out to the garden, lying in the glamor of sunset.

"I do think you have the loveliest place here," said Diana, looking round her admiringly.

"Why do you call it Echo Lodge?" asked Anne.

"Charlotta," said Miss Lavendar, "go into the house and bring out the little tin horn that is hanging over the clock shelf."

Charlotta the Fourth skipped off and returned with the horn.

"Blow it, Charlotta," commanded Miss Lavendar.

Charlotta accordingly blew, a rather raucous, strident blast. There was a moment's stillness . . . and then from the woods over the river came a multitude of fairy echoes, sweet, elusive, silvery, as if all the "horns of elfland" were blowing against the sunset. Anne and Diana exclaimed in delight.

"Now laugh, Charlotta . . . laugh loudly."

Charlotta, who would probably have obeyed if Miss Lavendar had told her to stand on her head, climbed upon the stone bench and laughed loud and heartily. Back came the echoes, as if a host of pixy people were mimicking her laughter in the purple woodlands and along the fir-fringed points.

"People always admire my echoes very much," said Miss Lavendar, as if the echoes were her personal property. "I love them myself. They are very good company . . . with a little pretending. On calm evenings Charlotta the Fourth and I often sit out here and amuse ourselves with them. Charlotta, take back the horn and hang it carefully in its place."

"Why do you call her Charlotta the Fourth?" asked Diana, who was bursting with curiosity on this point.

"Just to keep her from getting mixed up with the other Charlottas in my thoughts," said Miss Lavendar seriously. "They all look so much alike there's no telling them apart. Her name isn't really Charlotta at all. It is . . . let me see . . . what is it? I *think* it's Leonora . . . yes, it *is* Leonora. You see, it is this way. When mother died ten years ago I couldn't stay here alone . . . and I couldn't afford to pay the wages of a grown-up girl. So I got little Charlotta Bowman to come and stay with me for board and clothes. Her name really was Charlotta . . . she was Charlotte the First. She was just thirteen. She stayed with me till she was sixteen and then she went away to Boston, because she could do better there. Her sister came to stay with me then. Her name was Julietta . . . Mrs. Bowman had a weakness for fancy names I think . . . but she looked so like Charlotta that I kept calling her that all the time . . . and she didn't mind. So I just gave up trying to remember her right name. She was Charlotta the Second, and when she went away Evelina came and she was Charlotta the Third. Now I have Charlotta the Fourth; but when she is sixteen . . . she's fourteen now . . . she will want to go to Boston too, and what I shall do then I really do not know. Charlotta the Fourth is the last of the Bowman girls, and the best. The other Charlottas always let see that they thought it silly of me to pretend things but Charlotta the Fourth never does, no matter what she may really think. I don't care what people think about me if they don't let me see it."

"Well," said Diana looking regretfully at the setting sun. "I suppose we must go if we want to get to Mr. Kimball's before dark. We've had a lovely time, Miss Lewis."

"Won't you come again to see me?" pleaded Miss Lavendar.

Tall Anne put her arm about the little lady.

"Indeed we shall," she promised. "Now that we have discovered you we'll wear out our welcome coming to see you. Yes, we must go . . . 'we must tear ourselves away,' as Paul Irving says every time he comes to Green Gables."

"Paul Irving?" There was a subtle change in Miss Lavendar's voice. "Who is he? I didn't think there was anybody of that name in Avonlea."

Anne felt vexed at her own heedlessness. She had forgotten about Miss Lavendar's old romance when Paul's name slipped out.

"He is a little pupil of mine," she explained slowly. "He came from Boston last year to live with his grandmother, Mrs. Irving of the shore road."

"Is he Stephen Irving's son?" Miss Lavendar asked, bending over her namesake border so that her face was hidden.

"Yes."

"I'm going to give you girls a bunch of lavender apiece," said Miss Lavendar brightly, as if she had not heard the answer to her question. "It's very sweet, don't you think? Mother always loved it. She planted these borders long ago. Father named me Lavendar because he was so fond of it. The very first time he saw mother was when he visited her home in East Grafton with her brother. He fell in love with her at first sight; and they put him in the spare room bed to sleep and the sheets were scented with lavender and he lay awake all night and thought of her. He always loved the scent of lavender after that . . . and that was why he gave me the name. Don't forget to come back soon, girls dear. We'll be looking for you, Charlotta the Fourth and I."

She opened the gate under the firs for them to pass through. She looked suddenly old and tired; the glow and radiance had faded from her face; her parting smile was as sweet with ineradicable youth as ever, but when the girls looked back from the first curve in the lane they saw her sitting on the old stone bench under the silver poplar in the middle of the garden with her head leaning wearily on her hand.

"She does look lonely," said Diana softly. "We must come often to see her."

"I think her parents gave her the only right and fitting name that could possibly be given her," said Anne. "If they had been so blind as to name her Elizabeth or Nellie or Muriel she must have been called Lavendar just the same, I think. It's so suggestive of sweetness and old-fashioned graces and 'silk attire.' Now, my name just smacks of bread and butter, patchwork and chores."

"Oh, I don't think so," said Diana. "Anne seems to me real stately and like a queen. But I'd like Kerrenhappuch if it happened to be your name. I think people make their names nice or ugly just by what they are themselves. I can't bear Josie or Gertie for names now but before I knew the Pye girls I thought them real pretty."

"That's a lovely idea, Diana," said Anne enthusiastically. "Living so that you beautify your name, even if it wasn't beautiful to begin with . . . making it stand in people's thoughts for something so lovely and pleasant that they never think of it by itself. Thank you, Diana."

XXII

Odds and Ends

"So you had tea at the stone house with Lavendar Lewis?" said Marilla at the breakfast table next morning. "What is she like now? It's over fifteen years since I saw her last . . . it was one Sunday in Grafton church. I suppose she has changed a great deal. Davy Keith, when you want something you can't reach, ask to have it passed and don't spread yourself over the table in that fashion. Did you ever see Paul Irving doing that when he was here to meals?"

"But Paul's arms are longer'n mine," grumbled Davy. "They've had eleven years to grow and mine've only had seven. 'Sides, I *did* ask, but you and Anne was so busy talking you didn't pay any 'tention. 'Sides, Paul's never been here to any meal escept tea, and it's easier to be p'lite at tea than at breakfast. You ain't half as hungry. It's an awful long while between supper and breakfast. Now, Anne, that spoonful ain't any bigger than it was last year and *I'm* ever so much bigger."

"Of course, I don't know what Miss Lavendar used to look like but I don't fancy somehow that she has changed a great deal," said Anne, after she had helped Davy to maple syrup, giving him two spoonfuls to pacify him. "Her hair is snow-white but her face is fresh and almost girlish, and she has the sweetest brown eyes . . . such a pretty shade of wood-brown with little golden glints in them . . . and her voice makes you think of white satin and tinkling water and fairy bells all mixed up together."

"She was reckoned a great beauty when she was a girl," said Marilla. "I never knew her very well but I liked her as far as I did know her. Some folks thought her peculiar even then. *Davy*, if ever I catch you at such a trick again you'll be made to wait for your meals til everyone else is done, like the French."

Most conversations between Anne and Marilla in the presence of the twins, were punctuated by these rebukes Davy-ward. In this instance, Davy, sad to relate, not being able to scoop up the last drops of his syrup with his spoon, had solved the difficulty by lifting his plate in both hands and applying his small pink tongue to it. Anne looked at him with such horrified eyes that the little sinner turned red and said, half shamefacedly, half defiantly,

"There ain't any wasted that way."

"People who are different from other people are always called peculiar," said Anne. "And Miss Lavendar is certainly different, though it's hard to say just where the difference comes in. Perhaps it is because she is one of those people who never grow old."

"One might as well grow old when all your generation do," said Marilla, rather reckless of her pronouns. "If you don't, you don't fit in anywhere. Far as I can learn Lavendar Lewis has just dropped out of everything. She's lived in that out of the way place until everybody has forgotten her. That stone house is one of the oldest on the Island. Old Mr. Lewis built it eighty years ago when he came out from England. Davy, stop joggling Dora's elbow. Oh, I saw you! You needn't try to look innocent. What does make you behave so this morning?"

"Maybe I got out of the wrong side of the bed," suggested Davy. "Milty Boulter says if you do that things are bound to go wrong with you all day. His grandmother told him. But which *is* the right side?

And what are you to do when your bed's against the wall? I want to know."

"I've always wondered what went wrong between Stephen Irving and Lavendar Lewis," continued Marilla, ignoring Davy. "They were certainly engaged twenty-five years ago and then all at once it was broken off. I don't know what the trouble was but it must have been something terrible, for he went away to the States and never come home since."

"Perhaps it was nothing very dreadful after all. I think the little things in life often make more trouble than the big things," said Anne, with one of those flashes of insight which experience could not have bettered. "Marilla, please don't say anything about my being at Miss Lavendar's to Mrs. Lynde. She'd be sure to ask a hundred questions and somehow I wouldn't like it . . . nor Miss Lavendar either if she knew, I feel sure."

"I daresay Rachel would be curious," admitted Marilla, "though she hasn't as much time as she used to have for looking after other people's affairs. She's tied home now on account of Thomas; and she's feeling pretty downhearted, for I think she's beginning to lose hope of his ever getting better. Rachel will be left pretty lonely if anything happens to him, with all her children settled out west, except Eliza in town; and she doesn't like her husband."

Marilla's pronouns slandered Eliza, who was very fond of her husband.

"Rachel says if he'd only brace up and exert his will power he'd get better. But what is the use of asking a jellyfish to sit up straight?" continued Marilla. "Thomas Lynde never had any will power to exert. His mother ruled him till he married and then Rachel carried it on. It's a wonder he dared to get sick without asking her permission. But there, I shouldn't talk so. Rachel has been a good wife to him. He'd never have amounted to anything without her, that's certain. He was born to be ruled; and it's well he fell into the hands of a clever, capable manager like

Rachel. He didn't mind her way. It saved him the bother of ever making up his own mind about anything. Davy, do stop squirming like an eel."

"I've nothing else to do," protested Davy. "I can't eat any more, and it's no fun watching you and Anne eat."

"Well, you and Dora go out and give the hens their wheat," said Marilla. "And don't you try to pull any more feathers out of the white rooster's tail either."

"I wanted some feathers for an Injun headdress," said Davy sulkily. "Milty Boulter has a dandy one, made out of the feathers his mother give him when she killed their old white gobbler. You might let me have some. That rooster's got ever so many more'n he wants."

"You may have the old feather duster in the garret," said Anne, "and I'll dye them green and red and yellow for you."

"You do spoil that boy dreadfully," said Marilla, when Davy, with a radiant face, had followed prim Dora out. Marilla's education had made great strides in the past six years; but she had not yet been able to rid herself of the idea that it was very bad for a child to have too many of its wishes indulged.

"All the boys of his class have Indian headdresses, and Davy wants one too," said Anne. "*I* know how it feels . . . I'll never forget how I used to long for puffed sleeves when all the other girls had them. And Davy isn't being spoiled. He is improving every day. Think what a difference there is in him since he came here a year ago."

"He certainly doesn't get into as much mischief since he began to go to school," acknowledged Marilla. "I suppose he works off the tendency with the other boys. But it's a wonder to me we haven't heard from Richard Keith before this. Never a word since last May."

"I'll be afraid to hear from him," sighed Anne, beginning to clear away the dishes. "If a letter should come I'd dread opening it, for fear it would tell us to send the twins to him."

A month later a letter did come. But it was not from Richard Keith. A friend of his wrote to say that Richard Keith had died of consumption a fortnight previously. The writer of the letter was the executor of his will and by that will the sum of two thousand dollars was left to Miss Marilla Cuthbert in trust for David and Dora Keith until they came of age or married. In the meantime the interest was to be used for their maintenance.

"It seems dreadful to be glad of anything in connection with a death," said Anne soberly. "I'm sorry for poor Mr. Keith; but I *am* glad that we can keep the twins."

"It's a very good thing about the money," said Marilla practically. "I wanted to keep them but I really didn't see how I could afford to do it, especially when they grew older. The rent of the farm doesn't do any more than keep the house and I was bound that not a cent of your money should be spent on them. You do far too much for them as it is. Dora didn't need that new hat you bought her any more than a cat needs two tails. But now the way is made clear and they are provided for."

Davy and Dora were delighted when they heard that they were to live at Green Gables "for good." The death of an uncle whom they had never seen could not weigh a moment in the balance against that. But Dora had one misgiving.

"Was Uncle Richard buried?" she whispered to Anne.

"Yes, dear, of course."

"He . . . he . . . isn't like Mirabel Cotton's uncle, is he?" in a still more agitated whisper. "He won't walk about houses after being buried, will he, Anne?"

XXIII

Miss Lavendar's Romance

"I think I'll take a walk through to Echo Lodge this evening," said Anne, one Friday afternoon in December.

"It looks like snow," said Marilla dubiously.

"I'll be there before the snow comes and I mean to stay all night. Diana can't go because she has company, and I'm sure Miss Lavendar will be looking for me tonight. It's a whole fortnight since I was there."

Anne had paid many a visit to Echo Lodge since that October day. Sometimes she and Diana drove around by the road; sometimes they walked through the woods. When Diana could not go Anne went alone. Between her and Miss Lavendar had sprung up one of those fervent, helpful friendships possible only between a woman who has kept the freshness of youth in her heart and soul, and a girl whose imagination and intuition supplied the place of experience. Anne had at last discovered a real "kindred spirit," while into the little lady's lonely, sequestered life of dreams Anne and Diana came with the wholesome joy and exhilaration of the outer existence, which Miss Lavendar, "the world forgetting, by the world forgot," had long ceased to share; they brought an atmosphere of youth and reality to the little stone house. Charlotta the Fourth always greeted them with her very widest smile . . . and Charlotta's smiles *were* fearfully wide

. . . loving them for the sake of her adored mistress as well as for their own. Never had there been such "high jinks" held in the little stone house as were held there that beautiful, late-lingering autumn, when November seemed October over again, and even December aped the sunshine and hazes of summer.

But on this particular day it seemed as if December had remembered that it was time for winter and had turned suddenly dull and brooding, with a windless hush predictive of coming snow. Nevertheless, Anne keenly enjoyed her walk through the great gray maze of the beechlands; though alone she never found it lonely; her imagination peopled her path with merry companions, and with these she carried on a gay, pretended conversation that was wittier and more fascinating than conversations are apt to be in real life, where people sometimes fail most lamentably to talk up to the requirements. In a "make believe" assembly of choice spirits everybody says just the thing you want her to say and so gives you the chance to say just what *you* want to say. Attended by this invisible company, Anne traversed the woods and arrived at the fir lane just as broad, feathery flakes began to flutter down softly.

At the first bend she came upon Miss Lavendar, standing under a big, broad-branching fir. She wore a gown of warm, rich red, and her head and shoulders were wrapped in a silvery gray silk shawl.

"You look like the queen of the fir wood fairies," called Anne merrily.

"I thought you would come tonight, Anne," said Miss Lavendar, running forward. "And I'm doubly glad, for Charlotta the Fourth is away. Her mother is sick and she had to go home for the night. I should have been very lonely if you hadn't come . . . even the dreams and the echoes wouldn't have been enough company. Oh, Anne, how pretty you are," she added suddenly, looking up at the tall, slim girl with the soft rose-flush of walking on her face. "How pretty and how young! It's so delightful to be seventeen, isn't it? I do envy you," concluded Miss Lavendar candidly.

"But you are only seventeen at heart," smiled Anne.

"No, I'm old . . . or rather middle-aged, which is far worse," sighed Miss Lavendar. "Sometimes I can pretend I'm not, but at other times I realize it. And I can't reconcile myself to it as most women seem to. I'm just as rebellious as I was when I discovered my first gray hair. Now, Anne, don't look as if you were trying to understand. Seventeen *can't* understand. I'm going to pretend right away that I am seventeen too, and I can do it, now that you're here. You always bring youth in your hand like a gift. We're going to have a jolly evening. Tea first . . . what do you want for tea? We'll have whatever you like. Do think of something nice and indigestible."

There were sounds of riot and mirth in the little stone house that night. What with cooking and feasting and making candy and laughing and "pretending," it is quite true that Miss Lavendar and Anne comported themselves in a fashion entirely unsuited to the dignity of a spinster of forty-five and a sedate schoolma'am. Then, when they were tired, they sat down on the rug before the grate in the parlor, lighted only by the soft fireshine and perfumed deliciously by Miss Lavendar's open rose-jar on the mantel. The wind had risen and was sighing and wailing around the eaves and the snow was thudding softly against the windows, as if a hundred storm sprites were tapping for entrance.

"I'm so glad you're here, Anne," said Miss Lavendar, nibbling at her candy. "If you weren't I should be blue . . . very blue . . . almost navy blue. Dreams and make-believes are all very well in the daytime and the sunshine, but when dark and storm come they fail to satisfy. One wants real things then. But you don't know this . . . seventeen never knows it. At seventeen dreams *do* satisfy because you think the realities are waiting for you further on. When I was seventeen, Anne, I didn't think forty-five would find me a white-haired little old maid with nothing but dreams to fill my life."

"But you aren't an old maid," said Anne, smiling into Miss Lavendar's wistful wood-brown eyes. "Old maids are *born* . . . they don't *become*."

"Some are born old maids, some achieve old maidenhood, and some have old maidenhood thrust upon them," parodied Miss Lavendar whimsically.

"You are one of those who have achieved it then," laughed Anne, "and you've done it so beautifully that if every old maid were like you they would come into the fashion, I think."

"I always like to do things as well as possible," said Miss Lavendar meditatively, "and since an old maid I had to be I was determined to be a very nice one. People say I'm odd; but it's just because I follow my own way of being an old maid and refuse to copy the traditional pattern. Anne, did anyone ever tell you anything about Stephen Irving and me?"

"Yes," said Anne candidly, "I've heard that you and he were engaged once."

"So we were . . . twenty-five years ago . . . a lifetime ago. And we were to have been married the next spring. I had my wedding dress made, although nobody but mother and Stephen ever knew *that*. We'd been engaged in a way almost all our lives, you might say. When Stephen was a little boy his mother would bring him here when she came to see my mother; and the second time he ever came . . . he was nine and I was six . . . he told me out in the garden that he had pretty well made up his mind to marry me when he grew up. I remember that I said 'Thank you'; and when he was gone I told mother very gravely that there was a great weight off my mind, because I wasn't frightened any more about having to be an old maid. How poor mother laughed!"

"And what went wrong?" asked Anne breathlessly.

"We had just a stupid, silly, commonplace quarrel. So commonplace that, if you'll believe me, I don't even remember just how it began. I hardly know who was the more to blame for it. Stephen did really begin it, but I suppose I provoked him by some foolishness of mine. He had a rival or two, you see. I was vain and coquettish and liked to tease him a little. He was a very high-strung, sensitive fellow. Well, we parted in a temper on both sides. But I thought it would all come right; and it would have if Stephen hadn't come back too soon. Anne, my dear, I'm sorry to say" . . . Miss Lavendar dropped her voice as if she were about to confess a predilection for murdering people, "that I am a dreadfully sulky person. Oh, you needn't smile, . . . it's only too true. I *do* sulk; and Stephen came back before I had finished sulking. I wouldn't listen to him and I wouldn't forgive him; and so he went away for good. He was too proud to come again. And then I sulked because he didn't come. I might have sent for him perhaps, but I couldn't humble myself to do that. I was just as proud as he was . . . pride and sulkiness make a very bad combination, Anne. But I could never care for anybody else and I didn't want to. I knew I would rather be an old maid for a thousand years than marry anybody who wasn't Stephen Irving. Well, it all seems like a dream now, of course. How sympathetic you look, Anne . . . as sympathetic as only seventeen can look. But don't overdo it. I'm really a very happy, contented little person in spite of my broken heart. My heart did break, if ever a heart did, when I realized that Stephen Irving was not coming back. But, Anne, a broken heart in real life isn't half as dreadful as it is in books. It's a good deal like a bad tooth . . . though you won't think *that* a very romantic simile. It takes spells of aching and gives you a sleepless night now and then, but between times it lets you enjoy life and dreams and echoes and peanut candy as if there were nothing the matter with it. And now you're looking disappointed. You don't think I'm half as interesting a person as you did five minutes ago when you believed I was always the prey of a tragic memory bravely hidden beneath external smiles. That's the worst . . . or the best . . . of real life, Anne. It *won't* let you be

miserable. It keeps on trying to make you comfortable
. . . and   succeeding . . . even   when   you're
determined to be unhappy and romantic. Isn't this
candy scrumptious? I've eaten far more than is good
for me already but I'm going to keep recklessly on."

After a little silence Miss Lavendar said abruptly,
"It gave me a shock to hear about Stephen's son
that first day you were here, Anne. I've never been
able to mention him to you since, but I've wanted to
know all about him. What sort of a boy is he?"

"He is the dearest, sweetest child I ever knew,
Miss Lavendar . . . and he pretends things too, just as
you and I do."

"I'd like to see him," said Miss Lavendar softly, as
if talking to herself. "I wonder if he looks anything like
the little dream-boy who lives here with me . . . *my*
little dream-boy."

"If you would like to see Paul I'll bring him
through with me sometime," said Anne.

"I *would* like it . . . but not too soon. I want to
get used to the thought. There might be more pain
than pleasure in it . . . if he looked too much like
Stephen . . . or if he didn't look enough like him. In
a month's time you may bring him."

Accordingly, a month later Anne and Paul walked
through the woods to the stone house, and met Miss
Lavendar in the lane. She had not been expecting
them just then and she turned very pale.

"So this is Stephen's boy," she said in a low tone,
taking Paul's hand and looking at him as he stood,
beautiful and boyish, in his smart little fur coat and
cap. "He . . . he is very like his father."

"Everybody says I'm a chip off the old block,"
remarked Paul, quite at his ease.

Anne, who had been watching the little scene,
drew a relieved breath. She saw that Miss Lavendar
and Paul had "taken" to each other, and that there
would be no constraint or stiffness. Miss Lavendar was
a very sensible person, in spite of her dreams and
romance, and after that first little betrayal she tucked

her feelings out of sight and entertained Paul as brightly and naturally as if he were anybody's son who had come to see her. They all had a jolly afternoon together and such a feast of fat things by way of supper as would have made old Mrs. Irving hold up her hands in horror, believing that Paul's digestion would be ruined for ever.

"Come again, laddie," said Miss Lavendar, shaking hands with him at parting.

"You may kiss me if you like," said Paul gravely.

Miss Lavendar stooped and kissed him.

"How did you know I wanted to?" she whispered.

"Because you looked at me just as my little mother used to do when she wanted to kiss me. As a rule, I don't like to be kissed. Boys don't. *You* know, Miss Lewis. But I think I rather like to have you kiss me. And of course I'll come to see you again. I think I'd like to have you for a particular friend of mine, if you don't object."

"I . . . I don't think I shall object," said Miss Lavendar. She turned and went in very quickly; but a moment later she was waving a gay and smiling good-bye to them from the window.

"I like Miss Lavendar," announced Paul, as they walked through the beech woods. "I like the way she looked at me, and I like her stone house, and I like Charlotta the Fourth. I wish Grandma Irving had a Charlotta the Fourth instead of Mary Joe. I feel sure Charlotta the Fourth wouldn't think I was wrong in my upper story when I told her what I think about things. Wasn't that a splendid tea we had, teacher? Grandma says a boy shouldn't be thinking about what he gets to eat, but he can't help it sometimes when he is real hungry. *You* know, teacher. I don't think Miss Lavendar would make a boy eat porridge for breakfast if he didn't like it. She'd get things for him he did like. But of course" . . . Paul was nothing if not fair-minded . . . "that mightn't be very good for him. It's very nice for a change though, teacher. *You* know."

XXIV

A Prophet in His Own Country

One May day Avonlea folks were mildly excited over some "Avonlea Notes," signed "Observer," which appeared in the Charlottetown *Daily Enterprise*. Gossip ascribed the authorship thereof to Charlie Sloane, partly because the said Charlie had indulged in similar literary flights in times past, and partly because one of the notes seemed to embody a sneer at Gilbert Blythe. Avonlea juvenile society persisted in regarding Gilbert Blythe and Charlie Sloane as rivals in the good graces of a certain damsel with gray eyes and an imagination.

Gossip, as usual, was wrong. Gilbert Blythe, aided and abetted by Anne, had written the notes, putting in the one about himself as a blind. Only two of the notes have any bearing on this history.

"Rumor has it that there will be a wedding in our village ere the daisies are in bloom. A new and highly respected citizen will lead to the hymeneal altar one of our most popular ladies."

"Uncle Abe, our well-known weather prophet, predicts a violent storm of thunder and lightning for the evening of the twenty-third of May, beginning at seven o'clock sharp. The area of the storm will extend over the greater part of the Province. People traveling that evening will do well to take umbrellas and mackintoshes with them."

"Uncle Abe really has predicted a storm for sometime this spring," said Gilbert, "but do you suppose Mr. Harrison really does go to see Isabella Andrews?"

"No," said Anne, laughing, "I'm sure he only goes to play checkers with Mr. Harmon Andrews, but Mrs. Lynde says she knows Isabella Andrews must be going to get married, she's in such good spirits this spring."

Poor old Uncle Abe felt rather indignant over the notes. He suspected that "Observer" was making fun of him. He angrily denied having assigned any particular date for his storm but nobody believed him.

Life in Avonlea continued on the smooth and even tenor of its way. The "planting" was put in; the Improvers celebrated an Arbor Day. Each Improver set out, or caused to be set out, five ornamental trees. As the society now numbered forty members, this meant a total of two hundred young trees. Early oats greened over the red fields; apple orchards flung great blossoming arms about the farmhouses and the Snow Queen adorned itself as a bride for her husband. Anne liked to sleep with her window open and let the cherry fragrance blow over her face all night. She thought it very poetical. Marilla thought she was risking her life.

"Thanksgiving should be celebrated in the spring," said Anne one evening to Marilla, as they sat on the front door steps and listened to the silver-sweet chorus of the frogs. "I think it would be ever so much better than having it in November when everything is dead or asleep. Then you have to remember to be thankful; but in May one simply can't help being thankful . . . that they are alive, if for nothing else. I feel exactly as Eve must have felt in the garden of Eden before the trouble began. *Is* that grass in the hollow green or golden? It seems to me, Marilla, that a pearl of a day like this, when the blossoms are out and the winds don't know where to blow from next for sheer crazy delight must be pretty near as good as heaven."

Marilla looked scandalized and glanced apprehensively around to make sure the twins were not within earshot. They came around the corner of the house just then.

"Ain't it an awful nice-smelling evening?" asked Davy, sniffing delightedly as he swung a hoe in his grimy hands. He had been working in his garden. That spring Marilla, by way of turning Davy's passion for reveling in mud and clay into useful channels, had given him and Dora a small plot of ground for a garden. Both had eagerly gone to work in a characteristic fashion. Dora planted, weeded, and watered carefully, systematically, and dispassionately. As a result, her plot was already green with prim, orderly little rows of vegetables and annuals. Davy, however, worked with more zeal than discretion; he dug and hoed and raked and watered and transplanted so energetically that his seeds had no chance for their lives.

"How is your garden coming on, Davy-boy?" asked Anne.

"Kind of slow," said Davy with a sigh. "I don't know why the things don't grow better. Milty Boulter says I must have planted them in the dark of the moon and that's the whole trouble. He says you must never sow seeds or kill pork or cut your hair or do any 'portant thing in the wrong time of the moon. Is that true, Ann? I want to know."

"Maybe if you didn't pull your plants up by the roots every other day to see how they're getting on 'at the other end,' they'd do better," said Marilla sarcastically.

"I only pulled six of them up," protested Davy. "I wanted to see if there was grubs at the roots. Milty Boulter said if it wasn't the moon's fault it must be grubs. But I only found one grub. He was a great big juicy curly grub. I put him on a stone and got another stone and smashed him flat. He made a jolly sqush I tell you. I was sorry there wasn't more of them. Dora's garden was planted same time's mine and her things are growing all right. It *can't* be the moon," Davy concluded in a reflective tone.

"Marilla, look at that apple tree," said Anne.
"Why, the thing is human. It is reaching out long arms
to pick its own pink skirts daintily up and provoke us
to admiration."

"Those Yellow Duchess trees always bear well,"
said Marilla complacently. "That tree'll be loaded this
year. I'm real glad . . . they're great for pies."

But neither Marilla nor Anne nor anybody else
was fated to make pies out of Yellow Duchess apples
that year.

The twenty-third of May came . . . an
unseasonably warm day, as none realized more keenly
than Anne and her little beehive of pupils, sweltering
over fractions and syntax in the Avonlea schoolroom. A
hot breeze blew all the forenoon; but after noon hour
it died away into a heavy stillness. At half past three
Anne heard a low rumble of thunder. She promptly
dismissed school at once, so that the children might
get home before the storm came.

As they went out to the playground Anne
perceived a certain shadow and gloom over the world
in spite of the fact that the sun was still shining
brightly. Annetta Bell caught her hand nervously.

"Oh, teacher, look at that awful cloud!"

Anne looked and gave an exclamation of dismay.
In the northwest a mass of cloud, such as she had
never in all her life beheld before, was rapidly rolling
up. It was dead black, save where its curled and
fringed edges showed a ghastly, livid white. There was
something about it indescribably menacing as it
gloomed up in the clear blue sky; now and again a
bolt of lightning shot across it, followed by a savage
growl. It hung so low that it almost seemed to be
touching the tops of the wooded hills.

Mr. Harmon Andrews came clattering up the hill
in his truck wagon, urging his team of grays to their
utmost speed. He pulled them to a halt opposite the
school.

"Guess Uncle Abe's hit it for once in his life,
Anne," he shouted. "His storm's coming a leetle ahead

of time. Did ye ever see the like of that cloud? Here, all you young ones, that are going my way, pile in, and those that ain't scoot for the post office if ye've more'n a quarter of a mile to go, and stay there till the shower's over."

Anne caught Davy and Dora by the hands and flew down the hill, along the Birch Path, and past Violet Vale and Willowmere, as fast as the twins' fat legs could go. They reached Green Gables not a moment too soon and were joined at the door by Marilla, who had been hustling her ducks and chickens under shelter. As they dashed into the kitchen the light seemed to vanish, as if blown out by some mighty breath; the awful cloud rolled over the sun and a darkness as of late twilight fell across the world. At the same moment, with a crash of thunder and a blinding glare of lightning, the hail swooped down and blotted the landscape out in one white fury.

Through all the clamor of the storm came the thud of torn branches striking the house and the sharp crack of breaking glass. In three minutes every pane in the west and north windows was broken and the hail poured in through the apertures, covering the floor with stones, the smallest of which was as big as a hen's egg. For three quarters of an hour the storm raged unabated and no one who underwent it ever forgot it. Marilla, for once in her life shaken out of her composure by sheer terror, knelt by her rocking chair in a corner of the kitchen, gasping and sobbing between the deafening thunder peals. Anne, white as paper, had dragged the sofa away from the window and sat on it with a twin on either side. Davy at the first crash had howled, "Anne, Anne, is it the Judgment Day? Anne, Anne, I never *meant* to be naughty," and then had buried his face in Anne's lap and kept it there, his little body quivering. Dora, somewhat pale but quite composed, sat with her hand clasped in Anne's, quiet and motionless. It is doubtful if an earthquake would have disturbed Dora.

Then, almost as suddenly as it began, the storm

ceased. The hail stopped, the thunder rolled and muttered away to the eastward, and the sun burst out merry and radiant over a world so changed that it seemed an absurd thing to think that a scant three quarters of an hour could have effected such a transformation.

Marilla rose from her knees, weak and trembling, and dropped on her rocker. Her face was haggard and she looked ten years older.

"Have we all come out of that alive?" she asked solemnly.

"You bet we have," piped Davy cheerfully, quite his own man again. "I wasn't a bit scared either . . . only just at the first. It come on a fellow so sudden. I made up my mind quick as a wink that I wouldn't fight Teddy Sloane Monday as I'd promised; but now maybe I will. Say, Dora, was you scared?"

"Yes, I was a little scared," said Dora primly, "but I held tight to Anne's hand and said my prayers over and over again."

"Well, I'd have said my prayers too if I'd have thought of it," said Davy; "but," he added triumphantly, "you see I came through just as safe as you for all I didn't say them."

Anne got Marilla a glassful of her potent currant wine . . . *how* potent it was Anne, in her earlier days, had had all too good reason to know . . . and then they went to the door to look out on the strange scene.

Far and wide was a white carpet, knee deep, of hailstones; drifts of them were heaped up under the eaves and on the steps. When, three or four days later, those hailstones melted, the havoc they had wrought was plainly seen, for every green growing thing in field or garden was cut off. Not only was every blossom stripped from the apple trees but great boughs and branches were wrenched away. And out of the two hundred trees set out by the Improvers by far the greater number were snapped off or torn to shreds.

"Can it possibly be the same world it was an hour

ago?" asked Anne, dazedly. "It *must* have taken longer than that to play such havoc."

"The like of this has never been known in Prince Edward Island," said Marilla, "never. I remember when I was a girl there was a bad storm, but it was nothing to this. We'll hear of terrible destruction, you may be sure."

"I do hope none of the children were caught out in it," murmured Anne anxiously. As it was discovered later, none of the children had been, since all those who had any distance to go had taken Mr. Andrews' excellent advice and sought refuge at the post office.

"There comes John Henry Carter," said Marilla.

John Henry came wading through the hailstones with a rather scared grin.

"Oh, ain't this awful, Miss Cuthbert? Mr. Harrison sent me over to see if yous had come out all right."

"We're none of us killed," said Marilla grimly, "and none of the buildings was struck. I hope you got off equally well."

"Yas'm. Not quite so well, ma'am. We was struck. The lightning knocked over the kitchen chimbly and come down the flue and knocked over Ginger's cage and tore a hole in the floor and went into the sullar. Yas'm."

"Was Ginger hurt?" queried Anne.

"Yas'm. He was hurt pretty bad. He was killed." Later on Anne went over to comfort Mr. Harrison. She found him sitting by the table, stroking Ginger's gay dead body with a trembling hand.

"Poor Ginger won't call you any more names, Anne," he said mournfully.

Anne could never have imagined herself crying on Ginger's account, but the tears came into her eyes.

"He was all the company I had, Anne . . . and now he's dead. Well, well, I'm an old fool to care so much. I'll let on I don't care. I know you're going to say something sympathetic as soon as I stop talking . . . but don't. If you did I'd cry like a baby. Hasn't this been a terrible storm? I guess folks won't laugh at

Uncle Abe's predictions again. Seems as if all the storms that he's been prophesying all his life that never happened came all at once. Beats all how he struck the very day though, don't it? Look at the mess we have here. I must hustle round and get some boards to patch up that hole in the floor."

Avonlea folks did nothing the next day but visit each other and compare damages. The roads were impassable for wheels by reason of the hailstones, so they walked or rode on horseback. The mail came late with ill tidings from all over the province. Houses had been struck, people killed and injured; the whole telephone and telegraph system had been disorganized, and any number of young stock exposed in the fields had perished.

Uncle Abe waded out to the blacksmith's forge early in the morning and spent the whole day there. It was Uncle Abe's hour of triumph and he enjoyed it to the full. It would be doing Uncle Abe an injustice to say that he was glad the storm had happened; but since it had to be he was very glad he had predicted it . . . to the very day, too. Uncle Abe forgot that he had ever denied setting the day. As for the trifling discrepancy in the hour, that was nothing.

Gilbert arrived at Green Gables in the evening and found Marilla and Anne busily engaged in nailing strips of oilcloth over the broken windows.

"Goodness only knows when we'll get glass for them," said Marilla. "Mr. Barry went over to Carmody this afternoon but not a pane could he get for love or money. Lawson and Blair were cleaned out by the Carmody people by ten o'clock. Was the storm bad at White Sands, Gilbert?"

"I should say so. I was caught in the school with all the children and I thought some of them would go mad with fright. Three of them fainted, and two girls took hysterics, and Tommy Blewett did nothing but shriek at the top of his voice the whole time."

"I only squealed once," said Davy proudly. "My garden was all smashed flat," he continued mournfully, "but so was Dora's," he added in a tone which indicated that there was yet balm in Gilead.

Anne came running down from the west gable.

"Oh, Gilbert, have you heard the news? Mr. Levi Boulter's old house was struck and burned to the ground. It seems to me that I'm dreadfully wicked to feel glad over *that*, when so much damage has been done. Mr. Boulter says he believes the A. V. I. S. magicked up that storm on purpose."

"Well, one thing is certain," said Gilbert, laughing, " 'Observer' has made Uncle Abe's reputation as a weather prophet. 'Uncle Abe's storm' will go down in local history. It is a most extraordinary coincidence that it should have come on the very day we selected. I actually have a half guilty feeling, as if I really had 'magicked' it up. We may as well rejoice over the old house being removed, for there's not much to rejoice over where our young trees are concerned. Not ten of them have escaped."

"Ah well, we'll just have to plant them over again next spring," said Anne philosophically. "That is one good thing about this world . . . there are always sure to be more springs."

XXV

An Avonlea Scandal

One blithe June morning, a fortnight after Uncle Abe's storm, Anne came slowly through the Green Gables yard from the garden, carrying in her hands two blighted stalks of white narcissus.

"Look, Marilla," she said sorrowfully, holding up the flowers before the eyes of a grim lady, with her hair coifed in a green gingham apron, who was going into the house with a plucked chicken, "these are the only buds the storm spared . . . and even they are imperfect. I'm so sorry . . . I wanted some for Matthew's grave. He was always so fond of June lilies."

"I kind of miss them myself," admitted Marilla, "though it doesn't seem right to lament over them when so many worse things have happened . . . all the crops destroyed as well as the fruit."

"But people have sown their oats over again," said Anne comfortingly, "and Mr. Harrison says he thinks if we have a good summer they will come out all right though late. And my annuals are all coming up again . . . but oh, nothing can replace the June lilies. Poor little Hester Gray will have none either. I went all the way back to her garden last night but there wasn't one. I'm sure she'll miss them."

"I don't think it's right for you to say such things, Anne, I really don't," said Marilla severely. "Hester

Gray has been dead for thirty years and her spirit is in heaven . . . I hope."

"Yes, but I believe she loves and remembers her garden here still," said Anne. "I'm sure no matter how long I'd lived in heaven I'd like to look down and see somebody putting flowers on my grave. If I had had a garden here like Hester Gray's it would take me more than thirty years, even in heaven, to forget being homesick for it by spells."

"Well, don't let the twins hear you talking like that," was Marilla's feeble protest, as she carried her chicken into the house.

Anne pinned her narcissi on her hair and went to the lane gate, where she stood for awhile sunning herself in the June brightness before going in to attend to her Saturday morning duties. The world was growing lovely again; old Mother Nature was doing her best to remove the traces of the storm, and, though she was not to succeed fully for many a moon, she was really accomplishing wonders.

"I wish I could just be idle all day today," Anne told a bluebird, who was singing and swinging on a willow bough, "but a schoolma'am, who is also helping to bring up twins, can't indulge in laziness, birdie. How sweet you are singing, little bird. You are just putting the feelings of my heart into song ever so much better than I could myself. Why, who is coming?"

An express wagon was jolting up the lane, with two people on the front seat and a big trunk behind. When it drew near Anne recognized the driver as the son of the station agent at Bright River; but his companion was a stranger . . . a scrap of a woman who sprang nimbly down at the gate almost before the horse came to a standstill. She was a very pretty little person, evidently nearer fifty than forty, but with rosy cheeks, sparkling black eyes, and shining black hair, surmounted by a wonderful beflowered and beplumed bonnet. In spite of having driven eight miles over a dusty road she was as neat as if she had just stepped out of the proverbial bandbox.

"Is this where Mr. James A. Harrison lives?" she inquired briskly.

"No, Mr. Harrison lives over there," said Anne, quite lost in astonishment.

"Well, I *did* think this place seemed too tidy . . . *much* too tidy for James A. to be living here, unless he has greatly changed since I knew him," chirped the little lady. "Is it true that James A. is going to be married to some woman living in this settlement?"

"No, oh no," cried Anne, flushing so guiltily that the stranger looked curiously at her, as if she half suspected her of matrimonial designs on Mr. Harrison.

"But I saw it in an Island paper," persisted the Fair Unknown. "A friend sent a marked copy to me . . . friends are always so ready to do such things. James A.'s name was written in over 'new citizen.'"

"Oh, that note was only meant as a joke," gasped Anne. "Mr. Harrison has no intention of marrying *anybody*. I assure you he hasn't."

"I'm very glad to hear it," said the rosy lady, climbing nimbly back to her seat in the wagon, "because he happens to be married already. *I* am his wife. Oh, you may well look surprised. I suppose he has been masquerading as a bachelor and breaking hearts right and left. Well, well, James A.," nodding vigorously over the fields at the long white house, "your fun is over. I am here . . . though I wouldn't haven't bothered coming if I hadn't thought you were up to some mischief. I suppose," turning to Anne, "that parrot of his is as profane as ever?"

"His parrot . . . is dead . . . I *think*," gasped poor Anne, who couldn't have felt sure of her own name at that precise moment.

"Dead! Everything will be all right then," cried the rosy lady jubilantly. "I can manage James A. if that bird is out of the way."

With which cryptic utterance she went joyfully on

her way and Anne flew to the kitchen door to meet Marilla.

"Anne, who was that woman?"

"Marilla," said Anne solemnly, but with dancing eyes, "do I look as if I were crazy?"

"Not more so than usual," said Marilla, with no thought of being sarcastic.

"Well then, do you think I am awake?"

"Anne, what nonsense has got into you? Who was that woman, I say?"

"Marilla, if I'm not crazy and not asleep she can't be such stuff as dreams are made of . . . she must be real. Anyway, I'm sure I couldn't have imagined such a bonnet. She says she is Mr. Harrison's wife, Marilla."

Marilla stared in her turn.

"His wife! Anne Shirley! Then what has he been passing himself off as an unmarried man for?"

"I don't suppose he did, really," said Anne, trying to be just. "He never said he wasn't married. People simply took it for granted. Oh Marilla, what will Mrs. Lynde say to this?"

They found out what Mrs. Lynde had to say when she came up that evening. Mrs. Lynde wasn't surprised! Mrs. Lynde had always expected something of the sort! Mrs. Lynde had always known there was *something* about Mr. Harrison!

"To think of his deserting his wife!" she said indignantly. "It's like something you'd read of in the States, but who would expect such a thing to happen right here in Avonlea?"

"But we don't know that he deserted her," protested Anne, determined to believe her friend innocent till he was proved guilty. "We don't know the rights of it at all."

"Well, we soon will. I'm going straight over there," said Mrs. Lynde, who had never learned that there was such a word as delicacy in the dictionary. "I'm not supposed to know anything about her arrival, and Mr. Harrison was to bring some medicine for Thomas from Carmody today, so that will be a good excuse. I'll find out the whole story and come in and tell you on my way back."

Mrs. Lynde rushed in where Anne had feared to tread. Nothing would have induced the latter to go over to the Harrison place; but she had her natural and proper share of curiosity and she felt secretly glad that Mrs. Lynde was going to solve the mystery. She and Marilla waited expectantly for that good lady's return, but waited in vain. Mrs. Lynde did not revisit Green Gables that night. Davy, arriving home at nine o'clock from the Boulter place, explained why.

"I met Mrs. Lynde and some strange woman in the Hollow," he said, "and gracious, how they were talking both at once! Mrs. Lynde said to tell you she was sorry it was too late to call tonight. Anne, I'm awful hungry. We had tea at Milty's at four and I think Mrs. Boulter is real mean. She didn't give us any preserves or cake . . . and even the bread was skurce."

"Davy, when you go visiting you must never criticize anything you are given to eat," said Anne solemnly. "It is very bad manners."

"All right . . . I'll only think it," said Davy cheerfully. "Do give a fellow some supper, Anne."

Anne looked at Marilla, who followed her into the pantry and shut the door cautiously.

"You can give him some jam on his bread, Anne. I know what tea at Levi Boulter's is apt to be."

Davy took his slice of bread and jam with a sigh.

"It's a kind of disappointing world after all," he remarked. "Milty has a cat that takes fits . . . she's took a fit regular every day for three weeks. Milty says it's awful fun to watch her. I went down today on purpose to see her have one but the mean old thing wouldn't take a fit and just kept healthy as healthy, though Milty and me hung round all the afternoon and waited. But never mind" . . . Davy brightened up as the insidious comfort of the plum jam stole into his soul . . . "maybe I'll see her in one sometime yet. It doesn't seem likely she'd stop having them all at once when she's been so in the habit of it, does it? This jam is awful nice."

Davy had no sorrows that plum jam could not cure.

Sunday proved so rainy that there was no stirring abroad; but by Monday everybody had heard some version of the Harrison story. The school buzzed with it and Davy came home, full of information.

"Marilla, Mr. Harrison has a new wife . . . well, not ezackly new, but they've stopped being married for quite a spell, Milty says. I always s'posed people had to keep on being married once they'd begun, but Milty says no, there's ways of stopping if you can't agree. Milty says one way is just to start off and leave your wife, and that's what Mr. Harrison did. Milty says Mr. Harrison left his wife because she throwed things at him . . . *hard* things . . . and Arty Sloane says it was because she wouldn't let him smoke, and Ned Clay says it was 'cause she never let up scolding him. I wouldn't leavy *my* wife for anything like that. I'd just put my foot down and say, 'Mrs. Davy, you've just got to do what'll please *me* 'cause I'm a *man.*' That'd settle her pretty quick I guess. But Annetta Clay says *she* left *him* because he wouldn't scrape his boots at the door and she doesn't blame her. I'm going right over to Mr. Harrison's this minute to see what she's like."

Davy soon returned, somewhat cast down.

"Mrs. Harrison was away . . . she's gone to Carmody with Mrs. Rachel Lynde to get new paper for the parlor. And Mr. Harrison said to tell Anne to go over and see him 'cause he wants to have a talk with her. And say, the floor is scrubbed, and Mr. Harrison is shaved, though there wasn't any preaching yesterday."

The Harrison kitchen wore a very unfamiliar look to Anne. The floor was indeed scrubbed to a wonderful pitch of purity and so was every article of furniture in the room; the stove was polished until she could see her face in it; the walls were whitewashed and the window panes sparkled in the sunlight. By the table

sat Mr. Harrison in his working clothes, which on
Friday had been noted for sundry rents and tatters but
which were now neatly patched and brushed. He was
sprucely shaved and what little hair he had was
carefully trimmed.

"Sit down, Anne, sit down," said Mr. Harrison, in
a tone but two degrees removed from that which
Avonlea people used at funerals. "Emily's gone over to
Carmody with Rachel Lynde . . . she's struck up a
lifelong friendship already with Rachel Lynde. Beats all
how contrary women are. Well, Anne, my easy times
are over . . . all over. It's neatness and tidiness for
me for the rest of my natural life, I suppose."

Mr. Harrison did his best to speak dolefully, but
an irrepressible twinkle in his eye betrayed him.

"Mr. Harrison, you are glad your wife is come
back," cried Anne, shaking her finger at him. "You
needn't pretend you're not, because I can see it
plainly."

Mr. Harrison relaxed into a sheepish smile.

"Well . . . well . . . I'm getting used to it," he
conceded. "I can't say I was sorry to see Emily. A
man really needs some protection in a community like
this, where he can't play a game of checkers with a
neighbor without being accused of wanting to marry
that neighbor's sister and having it put in the paper."

"Nobody would have supposed you went to see
Isabella Andrews if you hadn't pretended to be
unmarried," said Anne severely.

"I didn't pretend I was. If anybody'd have asked
me if I was married I'd have said I was. But they just
took it for granted. I wasn't anxious to talk about the
matter . . . I was feeling too sore over it. It would
have been nuts for Mrs. Rachel Lynde if she had
known my wife had left me, wouldn't it now?"

"But some people say that you left her."

"She started it, Anne, she started it. I'm going to
tell you the whole story, for I don't want you to think
worse of me than I deserve . . . nor of Emily neither.
But let's go out on the veranda. Everything is so

fearful neat in here that it kind of makes me homesick.
I suppose I'll get used to it after awhile but it eases
me up to look at the yard. Emily hasn't had time to
tidy *it* up yet."

As soon as they were comfortably seated on the
veranda Mr. Harrison began his tale of woe.

"I lived in Scottsford, New Brunswick, before I
came here, Anne. My sister kept house for me and she
suited me fine; she was just reasonably tidy and she let
me alone and spoiled me . . . so Emily says. But
three years ago she died. Before she died she worried
a lot about what was to become of me and finally she
got me to promise I'd get married. She advised me to
take Emily Scott because Emily had money of her own
and was a pattern housekeeper. I said, says I, 'Emily
Scott wouldn't look at me.' 'You ask her and see,' says
my sister; and just to ease her mind I promised her I
would . . . and I did. And Emily said she'd have me.
Never was so surprised in my life, Anne . . . a smart
pretty little woman like her and an old fellow like me.
I tell you I thought at first I was in luck. Well, we
were married and took a little wedding trip up to St.
John for a fortnight and then we went home. We got
home at ten o'clock at night, and I give you my word,
Anne, that in half an hour that woman was at work
housecleaning. Oh, I know you're thinking my house
needed it . . . you've got a very expressive face, Anne;
your thoughts just come out on it like print . . . but it
didn't, not that bad. It had got pretty mixed up while I
was keeping bachelor's hall, I admit, but I'd got a
woman to come in and clean it up before I was
married and there'd been considerable painting and
fixing done. I tell you if you took Emily into a brand
new white marble palace she'd be into the scrubbing
as soon as she could get an old dress on. Well, she
cleaned house till one o'clock that night and at four
she was up and at it again. And she kept on that way
. . . far's I could see she never stopped. It was scour
and sweep and dust everlasting, except on Sundays,

and then she was just longing for Monday to begin again. But it was her way of amusing herself and I could have reconciled myself to it if she'd left me alone. But that she wouldn't do. She'd set out to make me over but she hadn't caught me young enough. I wasn't allowed to come into the house unless I changed my boots for slippers at the door. I darsn't smoke a pipe for my life unless I went to the barn. And I didn't use good enough grammar. Emily'd been a schoolteacher in her early life and she'd never got over it. Then she hated to see me eating with my knife. Well, there it was, pick and nag everlasting. But I s'pose, Anne, to be fair, *I* was cantankerous too. I didn't try to improve as I might have done . . . I just got cranky and disagreeable when she found fault. I told her one day she hadn't complained of my grammar when I proposed to her. It wasn't an overly tactful thing to say. A woman would forgive a man for beating her sooner than for hinting she was too much pleased to get him. Well, we bickered along like that and it wasn't exactly pleasant, but we might have got used to each other after a spell if it hadn't been for Ginger. Ginger was the rock we split on at last. Emily didn't like parrots and she couldn't stand Ginger's profane habits of speech. I was attached to the bird for my brother the sailor's sake. My brother the sailor was a pet of mine when we were little tads and he'd sent Ginger to me when he was dying. I didn't see any sense in getting worked up over his swearing. There's nothing I hate worse'n profanity in a human being, but in a parrot, that's just repeating what it's heard with no more understanding of it than I'd have of Chinese, allowances might be made. But Emily couldn't see it that way. Women ain't logical. She tried to break Ginger of swearing but she hadn't any better success than she had in trying to make me stop saying 'I seen' and 'them things.' Seemed as if the more she tried the worse Ginger got, same as me.

"Well, things went on like this, both of us getting

raspier, till the *climax* came. Emily invited our minister and his wife to tea, and another minister and *his* wife that was visiting them. I'd promised to put Ginger away in some safe place where nobody would hear him . . . Emily wouldn't touch his cage with a ten-foot pole . . . and I meant to do it, for I didn't want the ministers to hear anything unpleasant in my house. But it slipped my mind . . . Emily was worrying me so much about clean collars and grammar that it wasn't any wonder . . . and I never thought of that poor parrot till we sat down to tea. Just as minister number one was in the very middle of saying grace, Ginger, who was on the veranda outside the dining room window, lifted up *his* voice. The gobbler had come into view in the yard and the sight of a gobbler always had an unwholesome effect on Ginger. He surpassed himself that time. You can smile, Anne, and I don't deny I've chuckled some over it since myself, but at the time I felt almost as much mortified as Emily. I went out and carried Ginger to the barn. I can't say I enjoyed that meal. I knew by the look of Emily that there was trouble brewing for Ginger and James A. When the folks went away I started for the cow pasture and on the way I did some thinking. I felt sorry for Emily and kind of fancied I hadn't been so thoughtful of her as I might; and besides, I wondered if the ministers would think that Ginger had learned his vocabulary from *me*. The long and short of it was, I decided that Ginger would have to be mercifully disposed of and when I'd druv the cows home I went in to tell Emily so. But there was no Emily and there *was* a letter on the table . . . just according to the rule in story books. Emily writ that I'd have to choose between her and Ginger; she'd gone back to her own house and there she would stay till I went and told her I'd got rid of that parrot.

"I was all riled up, Anne, and I said she might stay till doomsday if she waited for that; and I stuck to it. I packed up her belongings and sent them after her.

It made an awful lot of talk . . . Scottsford was pretty
near as bad as Avonlea for gossip . . . and everybody
sympathized with Emily. It kept me all cross and
cantankerous and I saw I'd have to get out or I'd
never have any peace. I concluded I'd come to the
Island. I'd been here when I was a boy and I liked it;
but Emily had always said she wouldn't live in a place
where folks were scared to walk out after dark for fear
they'd fall off the edge. So, just to be contrary, I
moved over here. And that's all there is to it. I hadn't
ever heard a word from or about Emily till I come
home from the back field Saturday and found her
scrubbing the floor but with the first decent dinner I'd
had since she left me all ready on the table. She told
me to eat it first and then we'd talk . . . by which I
concluded that Emily had learned some lessons about
getting along with a man. So she's here and she's
going to stay . . . seeing that Ginger's dead and the
Island's some bigger than she thought. There's Mrs.
Lynde and her now. No, don't go, Anne. Stay and get
acquainted with Emily. She took quite a notion to you
Saturday . . . wanted to know who that handsome
redhaired girl was at the next house."

Mrs. Harrison welcomed Anne radiantly and
insisted on her staying to tea.

"James A. has been telling me all about you and
how kind you've been, making cakes and things for
him," she said. "I want to get acquainted with all my
new neighbors just as soon as possible. Mrs. Lynde is
a lovely woman, isn't she? So friendly."

When Anne went home in the sweet June dusk,
Mrs. Harrison went with her across the fields where
the fireflies were lighting their starry lamps.

"I suppose," said Mrs. Harrison confidentially,
"that James A. has told you our story?"

"Yes."

"Then I needn't tell it, for James A. is a just man
and he would tell the truth. The blame was far from
being all on his side. I can see that now. I wasn't back

in my own house an hour before I wished I hadn't been so hasty but I wouldn't give in. I see now that I expected too much of a man. And I was real foolish to mind his bad grammar. It doesn't matter if a man does use bad grammar so long as he is a good provider and doesn't go poking round the pantry to see how much sugar you've used in a week. I feel that James A. and I are going to be real happy now. I wish I knew who 'Observer' is, so that I could thank him. I owe him a real debt of gratitude."

Anne kept her own counsel and Mrs. Harrison never knew that her gratitude found its way to its object. Anne felt rather bewildered over the far-reaching consequences of those foolish "notes." They had reconciled a man to his wife and made the reputation of a prophet.

Mrs. Lynde was in the Green Gables kitchen. She had been telling the whole story to Marilla.

"Well, and how do you like Mrs. Harrison?" she asked Anne.

"Very much. I think she's a real nice little woman."

"That's exactly what she is," said Mrs. Rachel with emphasis, "and as I've just been sayin' to Marilla, I think we ought all to overlook Mr. Harrison's peculiarities for her sake and try to make her feel at home here, that's what. Well, I must get back. Thomas'll be wearying for me. I get out a little since Eliza came and he's seemed a lot better these past few days, but I never like to be long away from him. I hear Gilbert Blythe has resigned from White Sands. He'll be off to college in the fall, I suppose."

Mrs. Rachel looked sharply at Anne, but Anne was bending over a sleepy Davy nodding on the sofa and nothing was to be read in her face. She carried Davy away, her oval girlish cheek pressed against his curly yellow head. As they went up the stairs Davy flung a tired arm about Anne's neck and gave her a warm hug and a sticky kiss.

"You're awful nice, Anne. Milty Boulter wrote on his slate today and showed it to Jennie Sloane,

" *'Roses red and vi'lets blue,
    Sugar's sweet, and so are you,'*

and that 'spresses my feelings for you ezackly, Anne."

XXVI

Around the Bend

Thomas Lynde faded out of life as quietly and unobtrusively as he had lived it. His wife was a tender, patient, unwearied nurse. Sometimes Rachel had been a little hard on her Thomas in health, when his slowness or meekness had provoked her; but when he became ill no voice could be lower, no hand more gently skillful, no vigil more uncomplaining.

"You've been a good wife to me, Rachel," he once said simply, when she was sitting by him in the dusk, holding his thin, blanched old hand in her work-hardened one. "A good wife. I'm sorry I ain't leaving you better off; but the children will look after you. They're all smart, capable children, just like their mother. A good mother . . . a good woman. . . ."

He had fallen asleep then; and the next morning, just as the white dawn was creeping up over the pointed firs in the hollow, Marilla went softly into the east gable and wakened Anne.

"Anne, Thomas Lynde is gone . . . their hired boy just brought the word. I'm going right down to Rachel."

On the day after Thomas Lynde's funeral Marilla went about Green Gables with a strangely preoccupied air. Occasionally she looked at Anne, seemed on the point of saying something, then shook her head and buttoned up her mouth. After tea she went down to see Mrs. Rachel; and when she returned she went to the east gable, where Anne was correcting school exercises.

"How is Mrs. Lynde tonight?" asked the latter.

"She's feeling calmer and more composed," answered Marilla, sitting down on Anne's bed . . . a proceeding which betokened some unusual mental excitement, for in Marilla's code of household ethics to sit on a bed after it was made up was an unpardonable offense. "But she's very lonely. Eliza had to go home today . . . her son isn't well and she felt she couldn't stay any longer."

"When I've finished these exercises I'll run down and chat awhile with Mrs. Lynde," said Anne. "I had intended to study some Latin composition tonight but it can wait."

"I suppose Gilbert Blythe is going to college in the fall," said Marilla jerkily. "How would you like to go too, Anne?"

Anne looked up in astonishment.

"I would like it, of course, Marilla. But it isn't possible."

"I guess it can be made possible. I've always felt that you should go. I've never felt easy to think you were giving it all up on my account."

"But, Marilla, I've never been sorry for a moment that I stayed home. I've been so happy . . . Oh, these past two years have just been delightful."

"Oh yes, I know you've been contented enough. But that isn't the question exactly. You ought to go on with your education. You've saved enough to put you through one year at Redmond and the money the stock brought in will do for another year . . . and there's scholarships and things you might win."

"Yes, but I can't go, Marilla. Your eyes are better, of course; but I can't leave you alone with the twins. They need so much looking after."

"I won't be alone with them. That's what I want to discuss with you. I had a long talk with Rachel tonight. Anne, she's feeling dreadful bad over a good many things. She's not left very well off. It seems they mortgaged the farm eight years ago to give the youngest boy a start when he went west; and they've never been able to pay much more than the interest since. And then of course Thomas' illness has cost a good deal, one way and another. The farm will have to be sold and Rachel thinks there'll be hardly anything left after the bills are settled. She says she'll have to go and live with Eliza and it's breaking her heart to think of leaving Avonlea. A woman of her age doesn't make new friends and interests easy. And, Anne, as she talked about it the thought came to me that I would ask her to come and live with me, but I thought I ought to talk it over with you first before I said anything to her. If I had Rachel living with me you could go to college. How do you feel about it?"

"I feel . . . as if . . . somebody . . . had handed me . . . the moon . . . and I didn't know . . . exactly . . . what to do . . . with it," said Anne dazedly. "But as for asking Mrs. Lynde to come here, that is for you to decide, Marilla. Do you think . . . are you sure . . . you would like it? Mrs. Lynde is a good woman and a kind neighbor, but . . . but . . ."

"But she's got her faults, you mean to say? Well, she has, of course; but I think I'd rather put up with far worse faults than see Rachel go away from Avonlea. I'd miss her terrible. She's the only close friend I've got here and I'd be lost without her. We've been neighbors for forty-five years and we've never had a quarrel . . . though we came rather near it that time you flew at Mrs. Rachel for calling you homely and redhaired. Do you remember, Anne?"

"I should think I do," said Anne ruefully. "People don't forget things like that. How I hated poor Mrs. Rachel at that moment!"

"And then that 'apology' you made her. Well, you were a handful, in all conscience, Anne. I did feel so puzzled and bewildered how to manage you. Matthew understood you better."

"Matthew understood everything," said Anne softly, as she always spoke of him.

"Well, I think it could be managed so that Rachel and I wouldn't clash at all. It's always seemed to me that the reason two women can't get along in one house is that they try to share the same kitchen and get in each other's way. Now, if Rachel came here, she could have the north gable for her bedroom and the spare room for a kitchen as well as not, for we don't really need a spare room at all. She could put her stove there and what furniture she wanted to keep, and be real comfortable and independent. She'll have enough to live on of course . . . her children'll see to that . . . so all I'd be giving her would be house room. Yes, Anne, far as I'm concerned I'd like it."

"Then ask her," said Anne promptly. "I'd be very sorry myself to see Mrs. Rachel go away."

"And if she comes," continued Marilla, "you can go to college as well as not. She'll be company for me and she'll do for the twins what I can't do, so there's no reason in the world why you shouldn't go."

Anne had a long meditation at her window that night. Joy and regret struggled together in her heart. She had come at last . . . suddenly and unexpectedly . . . to the bend in the road; and college *was* around it, with a hundred rainbow hopes and visions; but Anne realized as well that when she rounded that curve she must leave many sweet things behind . . . all the little simple duties and interests which had grown so dear to her in the last two years and which she had glorified into beauty and delight by the enthusiasm she had put into them. She must give up her school . . . and she loved every one of her pupils, even the stupid and naughty ones. The mere thought of Paul Irving made her wonder if Redmond were such a name to conjure with after all.

"I've put out a lot of little roots these two years," Anne told the moon, "and when I'm pulled up they're going to hurt a great deal. But it's best to go, I think, and, as Marilla says, there's no good reason why I shouldn't. I must get out all my ambitions and dust them."

Anne sent in her resignation the next day; and Mrs. Rachel, after a heart to heart talk with Marilla, gratefully accepted the offer of a home at Green Gables. She elected to remain in her own house for the summer, however; the farm was not to be sold until the fall and there were many arrangements to be made.

"I certainly never thought of living as far off the road as Green Gables," sighed Mrs. Rachel to herself. "But really, Green Gables doesn't seem as out of the world as it used to do . . . Anne has lots of company and the twins make it real lively. And anyhow, I'd rather live at the bottom of a well than leave Avonlea."

These two decisions being noised abroad speedily ousted the arrival of Mrs. Harrison in popular gossip. Sage heads were shaken over Marilla Cuthbert's rash step in asking Mrs. Rachel to live with her. People opined that they wouldn't get on together. They were both "too fond of their own way," and many doleful predictions were made, none of which disturbed the parties in question at all. They had come to a clear and distinct understanding of the respective duties and rights of their new arrangements and meant to abide by them.

"I won't meddle with you nor you with me," Mrs. Rachel had said decidedly, "and as for the twins, I'll be glad to do all I can for them; but I won't undertake to answer Davy's questions, that's what. I'm not an encyclopedia, neither am I a Philadelphia lawyer. You'll miss Anne for that."

"Sometimes Anne's answers were about as queer as Davy's questions," said Marilla drily. "The twins will miss her and no mistake; but her future can't be sacrificed to Davy's thirst for information. When he asks questions I can't answer I'll just tell him children should be seen and not heard. That was how *I* was brought up, and I don't know but what it was just as good a way as all these new-fangled notions for training children."

"Well, Anne's methods seem to have worked fairly

well with Davy," said Mrs. Lynde smilingly. "He is a reformed character, that's what."

"He isn't a bad little soul," conceded Marilla. "I never expected to get as fond of those children as I have. Davy gets round you somehow . . . and Dora is a lovely child, although she is . . . kind of . . . well, kind of . . ."

"Monotonous? Exactly," supplied Mrs. Rachel. "Like a book where every page is the same, that's what. Dora will make a good, reliable woman but she'll never set the pond on fire. Well, that sort of folks are comfortable to have round, even if they're not as interesting as the other kind."

Gilbert Blythe was probably the only person to whom the news of Anne's resignation brought unmixed pleasure. Her pupils looked upon it as a sheer catastrophe. Annetta Bell had hysterics when she went home. Anthony Pye fought two pitched and unprovoked battles with other boys by way of relieving his feelings. Barbara Shaw cried all night. Paul Irving defiantly told his grandmother that she needn't expect him to eat any porridge for a week.

"I can't do it, Grandma," he said. "I don't really know if I can eat *anything*. I feel as if there was a dreadful lump in my throat. I'd have cried coming home from school if Jake Donnell hadn't been watching me. I believe I will cry after I go to bed. It wouldn't show on my eyes tomorrow, would it? And it would be such a relief. But anyway, I can't eat porridge. I'm going to need all my strength of mind to bear up against this, Grandma, and I won't have any left to grapple with porridge. Oh Grandma, I don't know what I'll do when my beautiful teacher goes away. Milty Boulter says he bets Jane Andrews will get the school. I suppose Miss Andrews is very nice. But I know she won't understand things like Miss Shirley."

Diana also took a very pessimistic view of affairs.

"It will be horribly lonesome here next winter," she mourned, one twilight when the moonlight was raining "airy silver" through the cherry boughs and filling the east gable with a soft, dream-like radiance in which the two girls sat and talked, Anne on her low rocker by the window, Diana sitting Turk-fashion on the bed. "You and Gilbert will be gone . . . and the Allans too. They are going to call Mr. Allan to Charlottetown and of course he'll accept. It's too mean. We'll be vacant all winter, I suppose, and have to listen to a long string of candidates . . . and half of them won't be any good."

"I hope they won't call Mr. Baxter from East Grafton here, anyhow," said Anne decidedly. "He wants the call but he does preach such gloomy sermons. Mr. Bell says he's a minister of the old school, but Mrs. Lynde says there's nothing whatever the matter with him but indigestion. His wife isn't a very good cook, it seems, and Mrs. Lynde says that when a man has to eat sour bread two weeks out of three his theology is bound to get a kink in it somewhere. Mrs. Allan feels very badly about going away. She says everybody has been so kind to her since she came here as a bride that she feels as if she were leaving lifelong friends. And then, there's the baby's grave, you know. She says she doesn't see how she can go away and leave that . . . it was such a little mite of a thing and only three months old, and she says she is afraid it will miss its mother, although she knows better and wouldn't say so to Mr. Allan for anything. She says she has slipped through the birch grove back of the manse nearly every night to the graveyard and sung a little lullaby to it. She told me all about it last evening when I was up putting some of those early wild roses on Matthew's grave. I promised her that as long as I was in Avonlea I would put flowers on the baby's grave and when I was away I felt sure that . . ."

"That I would do it," supplied Diana heartily. "Of course I will. And I'll put them on Matthew's grave too, for your sake, Anne."

"Oh, thank you. I meant to ask you to if you would. And on little Hester Gray's too? Please don't forget hers. Do you know, I've thought and dreamed so much about little Hester Gray that she has become strangely real to me. I think of her, back there in her little garden in that cool, still, green corner; and I have a fancy that if I could steal back there some spring evening, just at the magic time 'twixt light and dark, and tiptoe so softly up the beech hill that my footsteps could not frighten her, I would find the garden just as it used to be, all sweet with June lilies and early roses, with the tiny house beyond it all hung with vines; and little Hester Gray would be there, with her soft eyes, and the wind ruffling her dark hair, wandering about, putting her fingertips under the chins of the lilies and whispering secrets with the roses; and I would go forward, oh, so softly, and hold out my hands and say to her, 'Little Hester Gray, won't you let me be your playmate, for I love the roses too?' And we would sit down on the old bench and talk a little and dream a little, or just be beautifully silent together. And then the moon would rise and I would look around me . . . and there would be no Hester Gray and no little vine-hung house, and no roses . . . only an old waste garden starred with June lilies amid the grasses, and the wind sighing, oh, so sorrowfully in the cherry trees. And I would not know whether it had been real or if I had just imagined it all."

Diana crawled up and got her back against the headboard of the bed. When your companion of twilight hour said such spooky things it was just as well not to be able to fancy there was anything behind you.

"I'm afraid the Improvement Society will go down when you and Gilbert are both gone," she remarked dolefully.

"Not a bit of fear of it," said Anne briskly, coming back from dreamland to the affairs of practical life. "It is too firmly established for that, especially since the older people are becoming so enthusiastic about it. Look what they are doing this summer for their lawns and lanes. Besides, I'll be watching for hints at

Redmond and I'll write a paper for it next winter and
send it over. Don't take such a gloomy view of things,
Diana. And don't grudge me my little hour of gladness
and jubilation now. Later on, when I have to go away,
I'll feel anything but glad."

"It's all right for you to be glad . . . you're going
to college and you'll have a jolly time and make heaps
of lovely new friends."

"I hope I shall make new friends," said Anne
thoughtfully. "The possibilities of making new friends
help to make life very fascinating. But no matter how
many new friends I make they'll never be as dear to
me as the old ones . . . especially a certain girl with
black eyes and dimples. Can you guess who she is,
Diana?"

"But there'll be so many clever girls at Redmond,"
sighed Diana, "and I'm only a stupid little country girl
who says 'I seen' sometimes . . . though I really know
better when I stop to think. Well, of course these past
two years have really been too pleasant to last. I know
somebody who is glad you are going to Redmond
anyhow. Anne, I'm going to ask you a question . . . a
serious question. Don't be vexed and do answer
seriously. Do you care anything for Gilbert?"

"Ever so much as a friend and not a bit in the
way you mean," said Anne calmly and decidedly; she
also thought she was speaking sincerely.

Diana sighed. She wished, somehow, that Anne
had answered differently.

"Don't you mean *ever* to be married, Anne?"

"Perhaps . . . some day . . . when I meet the
right one," said Anne, smiling dreamily up at the
moonlight.

"But how can you be sure when you do meet the
right one?" persisted Diana.

"Oh, I should know him . . . *something* would
tell me. You know what my ideal is, Diana."

"But people's ideals change sometimes."

"Mine won't. And I *couldn't* care for any man who
didn't fulfill it."

"What if you never meet him?"

"Then I shall die an old maid," was the cheerful response. "I daresay it isn't the hardest death by any means."

"Oh, I suppose the dying would be easy enough; it's the living an old maid I shouldn't like," said Diana, with no intention of being humorous. "Although I wouldn't mind being an old maid *very* much if I could be one like Miss Lavendar. But I never could be. When I'm forty-five I'll be horribly fat. And while there might be some romance about a thin old maid there couldn't possibly be any about a fat one. Oh, mind you, Nelson Atkins proposed to Ruby Gillis three weeks ago. Ruby told me all about it. She says she never had any intention of taking him, because any one who married him will have to go in with the old folks; but Ruby says that he made such a perfectly beautiful and romantic proposal that it simply swept her off her feet. But she didn't want to do anything rash so she asked for a week to consider; and two days later she was at a meeting of the Sewing Circle at his mother's and there was a book called 'The Complete Guide To Etiquette,' lying on the parlor table. Ruby said she simply couldn't describe her feelings when in a section of it headed, 'The Deportment of Courtship And Marriage,' she found the very proposal Nelson had made, word for word. She went home and wrote him a perfectly scathing refusal; and she says his father and mother have taken turns watching him ever since for fear he'll drown himself in the river; but Ruby says they needn't be afraid; for in the Deportment of Courtship and Marriage it told how a rejected lover should behave and there's nothing about drowning in *that*. And she says Wilbur Blair is literally pining away for her but she's perfectly helpless in the matter."

Anne made an impatient movement.

"I hate to say it . . . it seems so disloyal . . . but, well, I don't like Ruby Gillis now. I liked her when we went to school and Queen's together . . . though not so well as you and Jane of course. But this

last year at Carmody she seems so different . . . so
. . . so."

"I know," nodded Diana. "It's the Gillis coming
out in her . . . she can't help it. Mrs. Lynde says that
if ever a Gillis girl thought about anything but the
boys she never showed it in her walk and
conversation. She talks about nothing but boys and
what compliments they pay her, and how crazy they all
are about her at Carmody. And the strange thing is,
they *are*, too . . ." Diana admitted this somewhat
resentfully. "Last night when I saw her in Mr. Blair's
store she whispered to me that she'd just made a new
'mash.' I wouldn't ask her who it was, because I knew
she was dying to *be* asked. Well, it's what Ruby always
wanted, I suppose. You remember even when she was
little she always said she meant to have dozens of
beaus when she grew up and have the very gayest
time she could before she settled down. She's so
different from Jane, isn't she? Jane is such a nice,
sensible, lady-like girl."

"Dear old Jane is a jewel," agreed Anne, "but,"
she added, leaning forward to bestow a tender pat on
the plump, dimpled little hand hanging over her
pillow, "there's nobody like my own Diana after all.
Do you remember that evening we first met, Diana,
and 'swore' eternal friendship in your garden? We've
kept that 'oath,' I think . . . we've never had a
quarrel nor even a coolness. I shall never forget the
thrill that went over me the day you told me you
loved me. I had had such a lonely, starved heart all
through my childhood. I'm just beginning to realize
how starved and lonely it really was. Nobody cared
anything for me or wanted to be bothered with me. I
should have been miserable if it hadn't been for that
strange little dream-life of mine, wherein I imagined
all the friends and love I craved. But when I came to
Green Gables everything was changed. And then I met
you. You don't know what your friendship meant to
me. I want to thank you here and now, dear, for the
warm and true affection you've always given me."

"And always, always will," sobbed Diana. "I shall *never* love anybody . . . any *girl* . . . half as well as I love you. And if I ever do marry and have a little girl of my own I'm going to name her *Anne*."

XXVII

An Afternoon at the Stone House

"Where are you going, all dressed up, Anne?" Davy wanted to know. "You look bully in that dress."

Anne had come down to dinner in a new dress of pale green muslin . . . the first color she had worn since Matthew's death. It became her perfectly, bringing out all the delicate, flower-like tints of her face and the gloss and burnish of her hair.

"Davy, how many times have I told you that you mustn't use that word," she rebuked. "I'm going to Echo Lodge."

"Take me with you," entreated Davy.

"I would if I were driving. But I'm going to walk and it's too far for your eight-year-old legs. Besides, Paul is going with me and I fear you don't enjoy yourself in his company."

"Oh, I like Paul lots better'n I did," said Davy, beginning to make fearful inroads into his pudding. "Since I've got pretty good myself I don't mind his being gooder so much. If I can keep on I'll catch up with him some day, both in legs and goodness. 'Sides, Paul's real nice to us second primer boys in school. He won't let the other big boys meddle with us and he shows us lots of games."

"How came Paul to fall into the brook at noon hour yesterday?" asked Anne. "I met him on the playground, such a dripping figure that I sent him promptly home for dry clothes without waiting to find out what had happened."

"Well, it was partly a zacksident," explained Davy. "He stuck his head in on purpose but the rest of him fell in zacksidentally. We was all down at the brook and Prillie Rogerson got mad at Paul about something . . . she's awful mean and horrid anyway, if she *is* pretty . . . and said that his grandmother put his hair up in curl rags every night. Paul wouldn't have minded what she said, I guess, but Gracie Andrews laughed, and Paul got awful red, 'cause Gracie's his girl, you know. He's *clean gone* on her . . . brings her flowers and carries her books as far as the shore road. He got as red as a beet and said his grandmother didn't do any such thing and his hair was born curly. And then he laid down on the bank and stuck his head right into the spring to show them. Oh, it wasn't the spring we drink out of . . ." seeing a horrified look on Marilla's face . . . "it was the little one lower down. But the bank's awful slippy and Paul went right in. I tell you he made a bully splash. Oh, Anne, Anne, I didn't mean to say that . . . it just slipped out before I thought. He made a *splendid* splash. But he looked so funny when he crawled out, all wet and muddy. The girls laughed more'n ever, but Gracie didn't laugh. She looked sorry. Gracie's a nice girl but she's got a snub nose. When I get big enough to have a girl I won't have one with a snub nose . . . I'll pick one with a pretty nose like yours, Anne."

"A boy who makes such a mess of syrup all over his face when he is eating his pudding will never get a girl to look at him," said Marilla severely.

"But I'll wash my face before I go courting," protested Davy, trying to improve matters by rubbing the back of his hand over the smears. "And I'll wash behind my ears too, without being told. I remembered to this morning, Marilla. I don't forget half as often as I did. But . . ." and Davy sighed . . . "there's so many corners about a fellow that it's awful hard to remember them all. Well, if I can't go to Miss

Lavendar's I'll go over and see Mrs. Harrison. Mrs. Harrison's an awful nice woman, I tell you. She keeps a jar of cookies in her pantry a-purpose for little boys, and she always gives me the scrapings out of a pan she's mixed up a plum cake in. A good many plums stick to the sides, you see. Mr. Harrison was always a nice man, but he's twice as nice since he got married over again. I guess getting married makes folks nicer. Why don't *you* get married, Marilla? I want to know."

Marilla's state of single blessedness had never been a sore point with her, so she answered amiably, with an exchange of significant looks with Anne, that she supposed it was because nobody would have her.

"But maybe you never asked anybody to have you," protested Davy.

"Oh, Davy," said Dora primly, shocked into speaking without being spoken to, "it's the *men* that have to do the asking."

"I don't know why they have to do it *always*," grumbled Davy. "Seems to me everything's put on the men in this world. Can I have some more pudding, Marilla?"

"You've had as much as was good for you," said Marilla; but she gave him a moderate second helping.

"I wish people could live on pudding. Why can't they, Marilla? I want to know."

"Because they'd soon get tired of it."

"I'd like to try that for myself," said skeptical Davy. "But I guess it's better to have pudding only on fish and company days than none at all. They never have any at Milty Boulter's. Milty says when company comes his mother gives them cheese and cuts it herself . . . one little bit apiece and one over for manners."

"If Milty Boulter talks like that about his mother at least you needn't repeat it," said Marilla severely.

"Bless my soul," . . . Davy had picked this expression up from Mr. Harrison and used it with great gusto . . . "Milty meant it as a compelment. He's awful proud of his mother 'cause folks say she could scratch a living on a rock."

"I . . . I suppose them pesky hens are in my pansy bed again," said Marilla, rising and going out hurriedly.

The slandered hens were nowhere near the pansy bed and Marilla did not even glance at it. Instead, she sat down on the cellar hatch and laughed until she was ashamed of herself.

When Anne and Paul reached the stone house that afternoon they found Miss Lavendar and Charlotta the Fourth in the garden, weeding, raking, clipping, and trimming as if for dear life. Miss Lavendar herself, all gay and sweet in the frills and laces she loved, dropped her shears and ran joyously to meet her guests, while Charlotta the Fourth grinned cheerfully.

"Welcome, Anne. I thought you'd come today. You belong to the afternoon so it brought you. Things that belong together are sure to come together. What a lot of trouble that would save some people if they only knew it. But they don't . . . and so they waste beautiful energy moving heaven and earth to bring things together that *don't* belong. And you, Paul . . . why, you've grown! You're half a head taller than when you were here before."

"Yes, I've begun to grow like pigweed in the night, as Mrs. Lynde says," said Paul, in frank delight over the fact. "Grandma says it's the porridge taking effect at last. Perhaps it is. Goodness knows . . ." Paul sighed deeply . . . "I've eaten enough to make anyone grow. I do hope, now that I've begun, I'll keep on till I'm as tall as father. He is six feet, you know, Miss Lavendar."

Yes, Miss Lavendar did know; the flush on her pretty cheeks deepened a little; she took Paul's hand on one side and Anne's on the other and walked to the house in silence.

"Is it a good day for the echoes, Miss Lavendar?" queried Paul anxiously. The day of his first visit had been too windy for echoes and Paul had been much disappointed.

"Yes, just the best kind of a day," answered Miss

Lavendar, rousing herself from her reverie. "But first we are all going in to have something to eat. I know you two folks didn't walk all the way back here through those beechwoods without getting hungry, and Charlotta the Fourth and I can eat any hour of the day . . . we have such obliging appetites. So we'll just make a raid on the pantry. Fortunately it's lovely and full. I had a presentiment that I was going to have company today and Charlotta the Fourth and I prepared."

"I think you are one of the people who always have nice things in their pantry," declared Paul. "Grandma's like that too. But she doesn't approve of snacks between meals. I wonder," he added meditatively, "if I *ought* to eat them away from home when I know she doesn't approve."

"Oh, I don't think she would disapprove after you have had a long walk. That makes a difference," said Miss Lavendar, exchanging amused glances with Anne over Paul's brown curls. "I suppose that snacks *are* extremely unwholesome. That is why we have them so often at Echo Lodge. We . . . Charlotta the Fourth and I . . . live in defiance of every known law of diet. We eat all sorts of indigestible things whenever we happen to think of it, by day or night; and we flourish like green bay trees. We are always intending to reform. When we read any article in a paper warning us against something we like we cut it out and pin it up on the kitchen wall so that we'll remember it. But we never can somehow . . . until after we've gone and eaten that very thing. Nothing has ever killed us yet; but Charlotta the Fourth has been known to have bad dreams after we had eaten doughnuts and mince pie and fruit cake before we went to bed."

"Grandma let's me have a glass of milk and a slice of bread and butter before I go to bed; and on Sunday nights she puts jam on the bread," said Paul. "So I'm always glad when it's Sunday night . . . for more reasons than one. Sunday is a very long day on the shore road. Grandma says it's all too short for her and that father never found Sundays tiresome when he was a little boy. It wouldn't seem so long if I could talk to my rock people but I never do that because Grandma doesn't approve of it on Sundays. I think a good deal; but I'm afraid my thoughts are worldly. Grandma says we should never think anything but religious thoughts on Sundays. But teacher here said once that every really beautiful thought was religious, no matter what it was about, or what day we thought it on. But I feel sure Grandma thinks that sermons and Sunday School lessons are the only things you can think truly religious thoughts about. And when it comes to a difference of opinion between Grandma and teacher I don't know what to do. In my heart" . . . Paul laid his hand on his breast and raised very serious blue eyes to Miss Lavendar's immediately sympathetic face . . . "I agree with teacher. But then, you see, Grandma has brought father up *her* way and made a brilliant success of him; and teacher has never brought anybody up yet, though she's helping with Davy and Dora. But you can't tell how they'll turn out till they *are* grown up. So sometimes I feel as if it might be safer to go by Grandma's opinions."

"I think it would," agreed Anne solemnly. "Anyway, I daresay that if your Grandma and I both got down to what we really do mean, under our different ways of expressing it, we'd find out we both meant the same thing. You'd better go by her way of expressing it, since it's been the result of experience. We'll have to wait until we see how the twins do turn out before we can be sure that my way is equally good."

After lunch they went back to the garden, where Paul made the acquaintance of the echoes, to his wonder and delight, while Anne and Miss Lavendar sat on the stone bench under the poplar and talked.

"So you are going away in the fall?" said Miss Lavendar wistfully. "I ought to be glad for your sake, Anne . . . but I'm horribly, selfishly sorry. I shall miss you so much. Oh, sometimes I think it is of no use to make friends. They only go out of your life after awhile and leave a hurt that is worse than the emptiness before they came."

"That sounds like something Miss Eliza Andrews might say but never Miss Lavendar," said Anne. "*Nothing* is worse than emptiness . . . and I'm not going out of your life. There are such things as letters and vacations. Dearest, I'm afraid you're looking a little pale and tired."

"Oh . . . hoo . . . hoo . . . hoo," went Paul on the dyke, where he had been making noises diligently . . . not all of them melodious in the making, but all coming back transmuted into the very gold and silver of sound by the fairy alchemists over the river. Miss Lavendar made an impatient movement with her pretty hands.

"I'm just tired of everything . . . even of the echoes. There is nothing in my life but echoes . . . echoes of lost hopes and dreams and joys. They're beautiful and mocking. Oh Anne, it's horrid of me to talk like this when I have company. It's just that I'm getting old and it doesn't agree with me. I know I'll be fearfully cranky by the time I'm sixty. But perhaps all I need is a course of blue pills."

At this moment Charlotta the Fourth, who had disappeared after lunch, returned, and announced that the northeast corner of Mr. John Kimball's pasture was red with early strawberries, and wouldn't Miss Shirley like to go and pick some.

"Early strawberries for tea!" exclaimed Miss Lavendar. "Oh, I'm not so old as I thought . . . and I don't need a single blue pill! Girls, when you come back with your strawberries we'll have tea out here under the silver poplar. I'll have it all ready for you with home-grown cream."

Anne and Charlotta the Fourth accordingly betook themselves back to Mr. Kimball's pasture, a green remote place where the air was as soft as velvet and fragrant as a bed of violets and golden as amber.

"Oh, isn't it sweet and fresh back here?" breathed

Anne. "I just feel as if I were drinking in the sunshine."

"Yes, ma'am, so do I. That's just exactly how I feel too, ma'am," agreed Charlotta the Fourth, who would have said precisely the same thing if Anne had remarked that she felt like a pelican of the wilderness. Always after Anne had visited Echo Lodge Charlotta the Fourth mounted to her little room over the kitchen and tried before her looking glass to speak and look and move like Anne. Charlotta could never flatter herself that she quite succeeded; but practice makes perfect, as Charlotta had learned at school, and she fondly hoped that in time she might catch the trick of that dainty uplift of chin, that quick, starry outflashing of eyes, that fashion of walking as if you were a bough swaying in the wind. It seemed so easy when you watched Anne. Charlotta the Fourth admired Anne wholeheartedly. It was not that she thought her so very handsome. Diana Barry's beauty of crimson cheek and black curls was much more to Charlotta the Fourth's taste than Anne's moonshine charm of luminous gray eyes and the pale, everchanging roses of her cheeks.

"But I'd rather look like you than be pretty," she told Anne sincerely.

Anne laughed, sipped the honey from the tribute, and cast away the sting. She was used to taking her compliments mixed. Public opinion never agreed on Anne's looks. People who had heard her called handsome met her and were disappointed. People who had heard her called plain saw her and wondered where other people's eyes were. Anne herself would never believe that she had any claim to beauty. When she looked in the glass all she saw was a little pale face with seven freckles on the nose thereof. Her mirror never revealed to her the elusive, ever-varying play of feeling that came and went over her features like a rosy illuminating flame, or the charm of dream and laughter alternating in her big eyes.

While Anne was not beautiful in any strictly

defined sense of the word she possessed a certain evasive charm and distinction of appearance that left beholders with a pleasurable sense of satisfaction in that softly rounded girlhood of hers, with all its strongly felt potentialities. Those who knew Anne best felt, without realizing that they felt it, that her greatest attraction was the aura of possibility surrounding her . . . the power of future development that was in her. She seemed to walk in an atmosphere of things about to happen.

As they picked, Charlotta the Fourth confided to Anne her fears regarding Miss Lavendar. The warm-hearted little handmaiden was honestly worried over her adored mistress' condition.

"Miss Lavendar isn't well, Miss Shirley, ma'am. I'm sure she isn't, though she never complains. She hasn't seemed like herself this long while, ma'am . . . not since that day you and Paul were here together before. I feel sure she caught cold that night, ma'am. After you and him had gone she went out and walked in the garden for long after dark with nothing but a little shawl on her. There was a lot of snow on the walks and I feel sure she got a chill, ma'am. Ever since then I've noticed her acting tired and lonesome like. She don't seem to take an interest in anything, ma'am. She never pretends company's coming, nor fixes up for it, nor nothing, ma'am. It's only when you come she seems to chirk up a bit. And the worst sign of all, Miss Shirley, ma'am . . ." Charlotta the Fourth lowered her voice as if she were about to tell some exceedingly weird and awful symptom indeed . . . "is that she never gets cross now when I breaks things. Why, Miss Shirley, ma'am, yesterday I bruk her green and yaller bowl that's always stood on the bookcase. Her grandmother brought it out from England and Miss Lavendar was awful choice of it. I was dusting it just as careful, Miss Shirley, ma'am, and it slipped out, so fashion, afore I could grab holt of it, and bruk into about forty millyun pieces. I tell you I was sorry and scared. I thought Miss Lavendar would scold me awful, ma'am; and I'd ruther she had than take it the way she did. She just come in and hardly looked at it and said, 'It's no matter, Charlotta. Take up the pieces and throw them away.' Just like that, Miss Shirley, ma'am . . . 'take up the pieces and throw them away,' as if it wasn't her grandmother's bowl from England. Oh, she isn't well and I feel awful bad about it. She's got nobody to look after her but me."

Charlotta the Fourth's eyes brimmed up with tears. Anne patted the little brown paw holding the cracked pink cup sympathetically.

"I think Miss Lavendar needs a change, Charlotta. She stays here alone too much. Can't we induce her to go away for a little trip?"

Charlotta shook her head, with its rampant bows, disconsolately.

"I don't think so, Miss Shirley, ma'am. Miss Lavendar hates visiting. She's only got three relations she ever visits and she says she just goes to see them as a family duty. Last time when she come home she said she wasn't going to visit for family duty no more. 'I've come home in love with loneliness, Charlotta,' she says to me, 'and I never want to stray from my own vine and fig tree again. My relations try so hard to make an old lady of me and it has a bad effect on me.' Just like that, Miss Shirley, ma'am. 'It has a very bad effect on me.' So I don't think it would do any good to coax her to go visiting."

"We must see what can be done," said Anne decidedly, as she put the last possible berry in her pink cup. "Just as soon as I have my vacation I'll come through and spend a whole week with you. We'll have a picnic every day and pretend all sorts of interesting things, and see if we can't cheer Miss Lavendar up."

"That will be the very thing, Miss Shirley, ma'am," exclaimed Charlotta the Fourth in rapture. She was glad for Miss Lavendar's sake and for her own too. With a whole week in which to study Anne constantly she would surely be able to learn how to move and behave like her.

When the girls got back to Echo Lodge they found that Miss Lavendar and Paul had carried the little square table out of the kitchen to the garden and had everything ready for tea. Nothing ever tasted so delicious as those strawberries and cream, eaten under a great blue sky all curdled over with fluffy little white clouds, and in the long shadows of the wood with its lispings and its murmurings. After tea Anne helped Charlotta wash the dishes in the kitchen, while Miss Lavendar sat on the stone bench with Paul and heard all about his rock people. She was a good listener, this sweet Miss Lavendar, but just at the last it struck Paul that she had suddenly lost interest in the Twin Sailors.

"Miss Lavendar, why do you look at me like that?" he asked gravely.

"How do I look, Paul?"

"Just as if you were looking through me at somebody I put you in mind of," said Paul, who had such occasional flashes of uncanny insight that it wasn't quite safe to have secrets when he was about.

"You do put me in mind of somebody I knew long ago," said Miss Lavendar dreamily.

"When you were young?"

"Yes, when I was young. Do I seem very old to you, Paul?"

"Do you know, I can't make up my mind about that," said Paul confidentially. "Your hair looks old . . . I never knew a young person with white hair. But your eyes are as young as my beautiful teacher's when you laugh. I tell you what, Miss Lavendar" . . . Paul's voice and face were as solemn as a judge's . . . "I think you would make a splendid mother. You have just the right look in your eyes . . . the look my little mother always had. I think it's a pity you haven't any boys of your own."

"I have a little dream boy, Paul."

"Oh, have you really? How old is he?"

"About your age I think. He ought to be older because I dreamed him long before you were born. But I'll never let him get any older than eleven or twelve; because if I did some day he might grow up altogether and then I'd lose him."

"I know," nodded Paul. "That's the beauty of dream people . . . they stay any age you want them. You and my beautiful teacher and me myself are the only folks in the world that I know of that have dream people. Isn't it funny and nice we should all know each other? But I guess that kind of people always find each other out. Grandma never has dream people and Mary Joe thinks I'm wrong in the upper story because I have them. But I think it's splendid to have them. *You* know, Miss Lavendar. Tell me all about your little dream boy."

"He has blue eyes and curly hair. He steals in and wakens me with a kiss every morning. Then all day he plays here in the garden . . . and I play with him. Such games as we have. We run races and talk with the echoes; and I tell him stories. And when twilight comes . . ."

"*I* know," interrupted Paul eagerly. "He comes and sits beside you . . . *so* . . . because of course at twelve he'd be too big to climb into your lap . . . and lays his head on your shoulder . . . *so* . . . and you put your arms about him and hold him tight, tight, and rest your cheek on his head . . . yes, that's the very way. Oh, you *do* know, Miss Lavendar."

Anne found the two of them there when she came out of the stone house, and something in Miss Lavendar's face made her hate to disturb them.

"I'm afraid we must go, Paul, if we want to get home before dark. Miss Lavendar, I'm going to invite myself to Echo Lodge for a whole week pretty soon."

"If you come for a week I'll keep you for two," threatened Miss Lavendar.

XXVIII

The Prince Comes Back to the Enchanted Palace

The last day of school came and went. A triumphant "semi-annual examination" was held and Anne's pupils acquitted themselves splendidly. At the close they gave her an address and a writing desk. All the girls and ladies present cried, and some of the boys had it cast up to them later on that they cried too, although they always denied it.

Mrs. Harmon Andrews, Mrs. Peter Sloane, and Mrs. William Bell walked home together and talked things over.

"I do think it is such a pity Anne is leaving when the children seem so much attached to her," sighed Mrs. Peter Sloane, who had a habit of sighing over everything and even finished off her jokes that way. "To be sure," she added hastily, "we all know we'll have a good teacher next year too."

"Jane will do her duty, I've no doubt," said Mrs. Andrews rather stiffly. "I don't suppose she'll tell the children quite so many fairy tales or spend so much time roaming about the woods with them. But she has her name on the Inspector's Roll of Honor and the Newbridge people are in a terrible state over her leaving."

"I'm real glad Anne is going to college," said Mrs. Bell. "She has always wanted it and it will be a splendid thing for her."

"Well, I don't know." Mrs. Andrews was

determined not to agree fully with anybody that day. "I don't see that Anne needs any more education. She'll probably be marrying Gilbert Blythe, if his infatuation for her lasts till he gets through college, and what good will Latin and Greek do her then? If they taught you at college how to manage a man there might be some sense in her going."

Mrs. Harmon Andrews, so Avonlea gossip whispered, had never learned how to manage her "man," and as a result the Andrews household was not exactly a model of domestic happiness.

"I see that the Charlottetown call to Mr. Allan is up before the Presbytery," said Mrs. Bell. "That means we'll be losing him soon, I suppose."

"They're not going before September," said Mrs. Sloane. "It will be a great loss to the community . . . though I always did think that Mrs. Allan dressed rather too gay for a minister's wife. But we are none of us perfect. Did you notice how neat and snug Mr. Harrison looked today? I never saw such a changed man. He goes to church every Sunday and has subscribed to the salary."

"Hasn't that Paul Irving grown to be a big boy?" said Mrs. Andrews. "He was such a mite for his age when he came here. I declare I hardly knew him today. He's getting to look a lot like his father."

"He's a very smart boy," said Mrs. Bell.

"He's smart enough, but" . . . Mrs. Andrews lowered her voice . . . "I believe he tells queer stories. Gracie came home from school one day last week with the greatest rigmarole he had told her about people who lived down at the shore . . . stories there couldn't be a word of truth in, you know. I told Gracie not to believe them, and she said Paul didn't intend her to. But if he didn't what did he tell them to her for?"

"Anne says Paul is a genius," said Mrs. Sloane.

"He may be. You never know what to expect of them Americans," said Mrs. Andrews. Mrs. Andrews' only acquaintance with the word "genius" was derived from the colloquial fashion of calling any eccentric individual "a queer genius." She probably thought, with Mary Joe, that it meant a person with something wrong in his upper story.

Back in the schoolroom Anne was sitting alone at her desk, as she had sat on the first day of school two years before, her face leaning on her hand, her dewy eyes looking wistfully out of the window to the Lake of Shining Waters. Her heart was so wrung over the parting with her pupils that for the moment college had lost all its charm. She still felt the clasp of Annetta Bell's arms about her neck and heard the childish wail, "I'll *never* love any teacher as much as you, Miss Shirley, never, never."

For two years she had worked earnestly and faithfully, making many mistakes and learning from them. She had had her reward. She had taught her scholars something, but she felt that they had taught her much more . . . lessons of tenderness, self-control, innocent wisdom, lore of childish hearts. Perhaps she had not succeeded in "inspiring" any wonderful ambitions in her pupils, but she had taught them, more by her own sweet personality than by all her careful precepts, that it was good and necessary in the years that were before them to live their lives finely and graciously, holding fast to truth and courtesy and kindness, keeping aloof from all that savored of falsehood and meanness and vulgarity. They were, perhaps, all unconscious of having learned such lessons; but they would remember and practice them long after they had forgotten the capital of Afghanistan and the dates of the Wars of the Roses.

"Another chapter in my life is closed," said Anne aloud, as she locked her desk. She really felt very sad over it; but the romance in the idea of that "closed chapter" did comfort her a little.

Anne spent a fortnight at Echo Lodge early in her vacation and everybody concerned had a good time.

She took Miss Lavendar on a shopping expedition to town and persuaded her to buy a new organdy dress; then came the excitement of cutting and making it together, while the happy Charlotta the Fourth basted and swept up clippings. Miss Lavender had complained that she could not feel much interest in anything; but the sparkle came back to her eyes over her pretty dress.

"What a foolish, frivolous person I must be," she sighed. "I'm wholesomely ashamed to think that a new dress . . . even if it is a forget-me-not organdy . . . should exhilarate me so, when a good conscience and an extra contribution to Foreign Missions couldn't do it."

Midway in her visit Anne went home to Green Gables for a day to mend the twins' stockings and settle up Davy's accumulated store of questions. In the evening she went down to the shore road to see Paul Irving. As she passed by the low, square window of the Irving sitting room she caught a glimpse of Paul on somebody's lap; but the next moment he came flying through the hall.

"Oh, Miss Shirley," he cried excitedly, "you can't think what has happened! Something so splendid. Father is here . . . just think of that! Father is here! Come right in. Father, this is my beautiful teacher. *You* know, father."

Stephen Irving came forward to meet Anne with a smile. He was a tall, handsome man of middle age, with iron-gray hair, deep-set, dark blue eyes, and a strong, sad face, splendidly modeled about chin and brow. Just the face for a hero of romance, Anne thought with a thrill of intense satisfaction. It was so disappointing to meet someone who ought to be a hero and find him bald or stooped, or otherwise lacking in manly beauty. Anne would have thought it dreadful if the object of Miss Lavender's romance had not looked the part.

"So this is my little son's 'beautiful teacher,' of whom I have heard so much," said Mr. Irving with a hearty handshake. "Paul's letters have been so full of you, Miss Shirley, that I feel as if I were pretty well acquainted with you already. I want to thank you for what you have done for Paul. I think that your influence has been just what he needed. Mother is one of the best and dearest of women; but her robust, matter-of-fact Scotch common sense could not always understand a temperament like my laddie's. What was lacking in her you have supplied. Between you, I think Paul's training in these two past years has been as nearly ideal as a motherless boy's could be."

Everybody likes to be appreciated. Under Mr. Irving's praise Anne's face "burst flower-like into rosy bloom," and the busy, weary man of the world, looking at her, thought he had never seen a fairer, sweeter slip of girlhood than this little "down east" schoolteacher with her red hair and wonderful eyes.

Paul sat between them blissfully happy.

"I never dreamed father was coming," he said radiantly. "Even Grandma didn't know it. It was a great surprise. As a general thing . . ." Paul shook his brown curls gravely . . . "I don't like to be surprised. You lose all the fun of expecting things when you're surprised. But in a case like this it is all right. Father came last night after I had gone to bed. And after Grandma and Mary Joe had stopped being surprised he and Grandma came upstairs to look at me, not meaning to wake me up till morning. But I woke right up and saw father. I tell you I just sprang at him."

"With a hug like a bear's," said Mr. Irving, putting his arm around Paul's shoulder smilingly. "I hardly knew my boy, he had grown so big and brown and sturdy."

"I don't know which was the most pleased to see father, Grandma or I," continued Paul. "Grandma's been in kitchen all day making the things father likes to eat. She wouldn't trust them to Mary Joe, she says. That's *her* way of showing gladness. *I* like best just to sit and talk to father. But I'm going to leave you for a little while now if you'll excuse me. I must get the cows for Mary Joe. That is one of my daily duties."

When Paul had scampered away to do his "daily

duty" Mr. Irving talked to Anne of various matters. But Anne felt that he was thinking of something else underneath all the time. Presently it came to the surface.

"In Paul's last letter he spoke of going with you to visit an old . . . friend of mine . . . Miss Lewis at the stone house in Grafton. Do you know her well?"

"Yes, indeed, she is a *very* dear friend of mine," was Anne's demure reply, which gave no hint of the sudden thrill that tingled over her from head to foot at Mr. Irving's question. Anne "felt instinctively" that romance was peeping at her around a corner.

Mr. Irving rose and went to the window, looking out on a great, golden, billowing sea where a wild wind was harping. For a few moments there was silence in the little, dark-walled room. Then he turned and looked down into Anne's sympathetic face with a smile, half-whimsical, half-tender.

"I wonder how much you know," he said.

"I know all about it," replied Anne promptly. "You see," she explained hastily, "Miss Lavendar and I are very intimate. She wouldn't tell things of such a sacred nature to everybody. We are kindred spirits."

"Yes, I believe you are. Well, I am going to ask a favor of you. I would like to go and see Miss Lavendar if she will let me. Will you ask her if I may come?"

Would she not? Oh, indeed she would! Yes, this was romance, the very, the real thing, with all the charm of rhyme and story and dream. It was a little belated, perhaps, like a rose blooming in October which should have bloomed in June; but none the less a rose, all sweetness and fragrance, with the gleam of gold in its heart. Never did Anne's feet bear her on a more willing errand than on that walk through the beechwoods to Grafton the next morning. She found Miss Lavendar in the garden. Anne was fearfully excited. Her hands grew cold and her voice trembled.

"Miss Lavendar, I have something to tell you . . . something very important. Can you guess what it is?"

Anne never supposed that Miss Lavendar *could*

guess; but Miss Lavendar's face grew very pale and Miss Lavendar said in a quiet, still voice, from which all the color and sparkle that Miss Lavendar's voice usually suggested had faded,

"Stephen Irving is home?"

"How did you know? Who told you?" cried Anne disappointedly, vexed that her great revelation had been anticipated.

"Nobody. I knew that must be it, just from the way you spoke."

"He wants to come and see you," said Anne. "May I send him word that he may?"

"Yes, of course," fluttered Miss Lavendar. "There is no reason why he shouldn't. He is only coming as any old friend might."

Anne had her own opinion about that as she hastened into the house to write a note at Miss Lavendar's desk.

"Oh, it's delightful to be living in a storybook," she thought gaily. "It will come out all right of course . . . it must . . . and Paul will have a mother after his own heart and everybody will be happy. But Mr. Irving will take Miss Lavendar away . . . and dear knows what will happen to the little stone house . . . and so there are two sides to it, as there seems to be to everything in this world."

The important note was written and Anne herself carried it to the Grafton post office, where she waylaid the mail carrier and asked him to leave it at the Avonlea office.

"It's so very important," Anne assured him anxiously. The mail carrier was a rather grumpy old personage who did not at all look the part of a messenger of Cupid; and Anne was none too certain that his memory was to be trusted. But he said he would do his best to remember and she had to be contented with that.

Charlotta the Fourth felt that some mystery pervaded the stone house that afternoon . . . a mystery from which she was excluded. Miss Lavendar roamed about the garden in a distracted fashion. Anne, too, seemed possessed by a demon of unrest, and walked to and fro and went up and down. Charlotta the Fourth endured it till patience ceased to be a virtue; then she confronted Anne on the occasion of that romantic young person's third aimless peregrination through the kitchen.

"Please, Miss Shirley, ma'am," said Charlotta the Fourth, with an indignant toss of her very blue bows, "it's plain to be seen you and Miss Lavendar have got a secret and I think, begging your pardon if I'm too forward, Miss Shirley, ma'am, that it's real mean not to tell me when we've all been such chums."

"Oh, Charlotta dear, I'd have told you all about it if it were my secret . . . but it's Miss Lavendar's, you see. However, I'll tell you this much . . . and if nothing comes of it you must never breathe a word about it to a living soul. You see, Prince Charming is coming tonight. He came long ago, but in a foolish moment went away and wandered afar and forgot the secret of the magic pathway to the enchanted castle, where the princess was weeping her faithful heart out for him. But at last he remembered it again and the princess is waiting still . . . because nobody but her own dear prince could carry her off."

"Oh, Miss Shirley, ma'am, what is that in prose?" gasped the mystified Charlotta.

Anne laughed.

"In prose, an old friend of Miss Lavendar's is coming to see her tonight."

"Do you mean an old beau of hers?" demanded the literal Charlotta.

"That is probably what I do mean . . . in prose," answered Anne gravely. "It is Paul's father . . . Stephen Irving. And goodness knows what will come of it, but let us hope for the best, Charlotta."

"I hope that he'll marry Miss Lavendar," was Charlotta's unequivocal response. "Some women's intended from the start to be old maids, and I'm afraid I'm one of them, Miss Shirley, ma'am, because I've awful little patience with the men. But Miss Lavendar never was. And I've been awful worried, thinking what on earth she'd do when I got so big I'd *have* to go to Boston. There ain't any more girls in our family and dear knows what she'd do if she got some stranger that might laugh at her pretendings and leave things lying round out of their place and not be willing to be called Charlotta the Fifth. She might get someone who wouldn't be as unlucky as me in breaking dishes but she'd never get anyone who'd love her better."

And the faithful little handmaiden dashed to the oven door with a sniff.

They went through the form of having tea as usual that night at Echo Lodge; but nobody really ate anything. After tea Miss Lavendar went to her room and put on her new forget-me-not organdy, while Anne did her hair for her. Both were dreadfully excited; but Miss Lavendar pretended to be very calm and indifferent.

"I must really mend that rent in the curtain tomorrow," she said anxiously, inspecting it as if it were the only thing of any importance just then. "Those curtains have not worn as well as they should, considering the price I paid. Dear me, Charlotta has forgotten to dust the stair railing *again*. I really *must* speak to her about it."

Anne was sitting on the porch steps when Stephen Irving came down the lane and across the garden.

"This is the one place where time stands still," he said, looking around him with delighted eyes. "There is nothing changed about this house or garden since I was here twenty-five years ago. It makes me feel young again."

"You know time always does stand still in an enchanted palace," said Anne seriously. "It is only when the prince comes that things begin to happen."

Mr. Irving smiled a little sadly into her uplifted face, all astar with its youth and promise.

"Sometimes the prince comes too late," he said.

He did not ask Anne to translate her remark into prose. Like all kindred spirits he "understood."

"Oh, no, not if he is the real prince coming to the true princess," said Anne, shaking her red head decidedly, as she opened the parlor door. When he had gone in she shut it tightly behind him and turned to confront Charlotta the Fourth, who was in the hall, all "nods and becks and wreathed smiles."

"Oh, Miss Shirley, ma'am," she breathed, "I peeked from the kitchen window . . . and he's awful handsome . . . and just the right age for Miss Lavendar. And oh, Miss Shirley, ma'am, do you think it would be much harm to listen at the door?"

"It would be dreadful, Charlotta," said Anne firmly, "so just you come away with me out of the reach of temptation."

"I can't do anything, and it's awful to hang round just waiting," sighed Charlotta. "What if he don't propose after all, Miss Shirley, ma'am? You can never be sure of them men. My oldest sister, Charlotta the First, thought she was engaged to one once. But it turned out *he* had a different opinion and she says she'll never trust one of them again. And I heard of another case where a man thought he wanted one girl awful bad when it was really her sister he wanted all the time. When a man don't know his own mind, Miss Shirley, ma'am, how's a poor woman going to be sure of it?"

"We'll go to the kitchen and clean the silver spoons," said Anne. "That's a task which won't require much thinking fortunately . . . for I *couldn't* think tonight. And it will pass the time."

It passed an hour. Then, just as Anne laid down the last shining spoon, they heard the front door shut. Both sought comfort fearfully in each other's eyes.

"Oh, Miss Shirley, ma'am," gasped Charlotta, "if he's going away this early there's nothing into it and never will be."

They flew to the window. Mr. Irving had no intention of going away. He and Miss Lavendar were strolling slowly down the middle path to the stone bench.

"Oh, Miss Shirley, ma'am, he's got his arm around her waist," whispered Charlotta the Fourth delightedly. "He *must* have proposed to her or she'd never allow it."

Anne caught Charlotta the Fourth by her own plump waist and danced her around the kitchen until they were both out of breath.

"Oh, Charlotta," she cried gaily, "I'm neither a prophetess nor the daughter of a prophetess but I'm going to make a prediction. There'll be a wedding in this old stone house before the maple leaves are red. Do you want that translated into prose, Charlotta?"

"No, I can understand that," said Charlotta. "A wedding ain't poetry. Why, Miss Shirley, ma'am, you're crying! What for?"

"Oh, because it's all so beautiful . . . and story bookish . . . and romantic . . . and sad," said Anne, winking the tears out of her eyes. "It's all perfectly lovely . . . but there's a little sadness mixed up in it too, somehow."

"Oh, of course there's a resk in marrying anybody," conceded Charlotta the Fourth, "but, when all's said and done, Miss Shirley, ma'am, there's many a worse thing than a husband."

XXIX

Poetry and Prose

For the next month Anne lived in what, for Avonlea, might be called a whirl of excitement. The preparation of her own modest outfit for Redmond was of secondary importance. Miss Lavendar was getting ready to be married and the stone house was the scene of endless consultations and plannings and discussions, with Charlotta the Fourth hovering on the outskirts of things in agitated delight and wonder. Then the dressmaker came, and there was the rapture and wretchedness of choosing fashions and being fitted. Anne and Diana spent half their time at Echo Lodge and there were nights when Anne could not sleep for wondering whether she had done right in advising Miss Lavendar to select brown rather than navy blue for her traveling dress, and to have her gray silk made princess.

Everybody concerned in Miss Lavendar's story was very happy. Paul Irving rushed to Green Gables to talk the news over with Anne as soon as his father had told him.

"I knew I could trust father to pick me out a nice little second mother," he said proudly. "It's a fine thing to have a father you can depend on, teacher. I just love Miss Lavendar. Grandma is pleased, too. She says she's real glad father didn't pick out an American for his second wife, because, although it turned out all right the first time, such a thing wouldn't be likely to happen twice. Mrs. Lynde says she thoroughly approves of the match and thinks its likely Miss Lavendar will give up her queer notions and be like other people, now that she's going to be married. But I hope she won't give her queer notions up, teacher, because I like them. And I don't want her to be like other people. There are too many other people around as it is. *You* know, teacher."

Charlotta the Fourth was another radiant person.

"Oh, Miss Shirley, ma'am, it has all turned out so beautiful. When Mr. Irving and Miss Lavendar come back from their tower I'm to go up to Boston and live with them . . . and me only fifteen, and the other girls never went till they were sixteen. Ain't Mr. Irving splendid? He just worships the ground she treads on and it makes me feel so queer sometimes to see the look in his eyes when he's watching her. It beggars description, Miss Shirley, ma'am. I'm awful thankful they're so fond of each other. It's the best way, when all's said and done, though some folks can get along without it. I've got an aunt who has been married three times and she says she married the first time for love and the last two times for strictly business, and was happy with all three except at the times of the funerals. But I think she took a resk, Miss Shirley, ma'am."

"Oh, it's all so romantic," breathed Anne to Marilla that night. "If I hadn't taken the wrong path that day we went to Mr. Kimball's I'd never have known Miss Lavendar; and if I hadn't met her I'd never have taken Paul there . . . and he'd never have written to his father about visiting Miss Lavendar just as Mr. Irving was starting for San Francisco. Mr. Irving says whenever he got that letter he made up his mind to send his partner to San Francisco and come here instead. He hadn't heard anything of Miss Lavendar for fifteen years. Somebody had told him then that she was to be married and he thought she was and never asked anybody anything about her. And now everything has come right. And I had a hand in bringing it about. Perhaps, as Mrs. Lynde says, everything is foreordained and it was bound to happen anyway. But even so, it's nice to think one was an instrument used by predestination. Yes indeed, it's very romantic."

"I can't see that it's so terribly romantic at all," said Marilla rather crisply. Marilla thought Anne was too worked up about it and had plenty to do with getting ready for college without "traipsing" to Echo Lodge two days out of three helping Miss Lavendar. "In the first place two young fools quarrel and turn sulky; then Steve Irving goes to the States and after a spell gets married up there and is perfectly happy from all accounts. Then his wife dies and after a decent interval he thinks he'll come home and see if his first fancy'll have him. Meanwhile, she's been living single, probably because nobody nice enough came along to want her, and they meet and agree to be married after all. Now, where is the romance in all that?"

"Oh, there isn't any, when you put it that way," gasped Anne, rather as if somebody had thrown cold water over her. "I suppose that's how it looks in prose. But it's very different if you look at it through poetry . . . and *I* think it's nicer . . ." Anne recovered herself and her eyes shone and her cheeks flushed . . . "to look at it through poetry."

Marilla glanced at the radiant young face and refrained from further sarcastic comments. Perhaps some realization came to her that after all it was better to have, like Anne, "the vision and the faculty divine" . . . that gift which the world cannot bestow or take away, of looking at life through some transfiguring . . . or revealing? . . . medium, whereby everything seemed apparelled in celestial light, wearing a glory and a freshness not visible to those who, like herself and Charlotta the Fourth, looked at things only through prose.

"When's the wedding to be?" she asked after a pause.

"The last Wednesday in August. They are to be

married in the garden under the honeysuckle trellis
. . . the very spot where Mr. Irving proposed to her
twenty-five years ago. Marilla, that *is* romantic, even in
prose. There's to be nobody there except Mrs. Irving
and Paul and Gilbert and Diana and I, and Miss
Lavendar's cousins. And they will leave on the six
o'clock train for a trip to the Pacific coast. When they
come back in the fall Paul and Charlotta the Fourth
are to go up to Boston to live with them. But Echo
Lodge is to be left just as it is . . . only of course
they'll sell the hens and cow, and board up the
windows . . . and every summer they're coming down
to live in it. I'm so glad. It would have hurt me
dreadfully next winter at Redmond to think of that
dear stone house all stripped and deserted, with empty
rooms . . . or far worse still, with other people living
in it. But I can think of it now, just as I've always
seen it, waiting happily for the summer to bring life
and laughter back to it again."

There was more romance in the world than that
which had fallen to the share of the middle-aged lovers
of the stone house. Anne stumbled suddenly on it one
evening when she went over to Orchard Slope by the
wood cut and came out into the Barry garden. Diana
Barry and Fred Wright were standing together under
the big willow. Diana was leaning against the gray
trunk, her lashes cast down on very crimson cheeks.
One hand was held by Fred, who stood with his face
bent toward her, stammering something in low earnest
tones. There were no other people in the world except
their two selves at that magic moment; so neither of
them saw Anne, who, after one dazed glance of
comprehension, turned and sped noiselessly back
through the spruce wood, never stopping till she
gained her own gable room, where she sat breathlessly
down by her window and tried to collect her scattered
wits.

"Diana and Fred are in love with each other," she
gasped. "Oh, it does seem so . . . so . . . so
hopelessly grown up."

Anne, of late, had not been without her suspicions that Diana was proving false to the melancholy Byronic hero of her early dreams. But as "things seen are mightier than things heard," or suspected, the realization that it was actually so came to her with almost the shock of perfect surprise. This was succeeded by a queer, little lonely feeling . . . as if, somehow, Diana had gone forward into a new world, shutting a gate behind her, leaving Anne on the outside.

"Things are changing so fast it almost frightens me," Anne thought, a little sadly. "And I'm afraid that this can't help making some difference between Diana and me. I'm sure I can't tell her all my secrets after this . . . she might tell Fred. And what *can* she see in Fred? He's very nice and jolly . . . but he's just Fred Wright."

It is always a very puzzling question . . . what can somebody see in somebody else? But how fortunate after all that it is so, for if everybody saw alike . . . well, in that case, as the old Indian said, "Everybody would want my squaw." It was plain that Diana *did* see something in Fred Wright, however Anne's eyes might be holden. Diana came to Green Gables the next evening, a pensive, shy young lady, and told Anne the whole story in the dusky seclusion of the east gable. Both girls cried and kissed and laughed.

"I'm so happy," said Diana, "but it does seem ridiculous to think of me being engaged."

"What is it really like to be engaged?" asked Anne curiously.

"Well, that all depends on who you're engaged to," answered Diana, with that maddening air of superior wisdom always assumed by those who are engaged over those who are not. "It's perfectly lovely to be engaged to Fred . . . but I think it would be simply horrid to be engaged to anyone else."

"There's not much comfort for the rest of us in

that, seeing that there is only one Fred," laughed
Anne.

"Oh, Anne, you don't understand," said Diana in
vexation. "I didn't mean *that* . . . it's so hard to
explain. Never mind, you'll understand sometime, when
your own turn comes."

"Bless you, dearest of Dianas, I understand now.
What is an imagination for if not to enable you to
peep at life through other people's eyes?"

"You must be my bridesmaid, you know, Anne.
Promise me that . . . wherever you may be when I'm
married."

"I'll come from the ends of the earth if
necessary," promised Anne solemnly.

"Of course, it won't be for ever so long yet," said
Diana, blushing. "Three years at the very least . . .
for I'm only eighteen and mother says no daughter of
hers shall be married before she's twenty-one. Besides,
Fred's father is going to buy the Abraham Fletcher
farm for him and he says he's got to have it two thirds
paid for before he'll give it to him in his own name.
But three years isn't any too much time to get ready
for housekeeping, for I haven't a speck of fancy work
made yet. But I'm going to begin crocheting doilies
tomorrow. Myra Gillis had thirty-seven doilies when
she was married and I'm determined I shall have as
many as she had."

"I suppose it would be perfectly impossible to
keep house with only thirty-six doilies," conceded
Anne, with a solemn face but dancing eyes.

Diana looked hurt.

"I didn't think you'd make fun of me, Anne," she
said reproachfully.

"Dearest, I wasn't making fun of you," cried Anne
repentantly. "I was only teasing you a bit. I think
you'll make the sweetest little housekeeper in the
world. And I think it's perfectly lovely of you to be
planning already for your home o'dreams."

Anne had no sooner uttered the phrase, "home o'
dreams," than it captivated her fancy and she

immediately began the erection of one of her own. It was, of course, tenanted by an ideal master, dark, proud, and melancholy; but oddly enough, Gilbert Blythe persisted in hanging about too, helping her arrange pictures, lay out gardens, and accomplish sundry other tasks which a proud and melancholy hero evidently considered beneath his dignity. Anne tried to banish Gilbert's image from her castle in Spain but, somehow, he went on being there, so Anne, being in a hurry, gave up the attempt and pursued her aerial architecture with such success that her "home o' dreams" was built and furnished before Diana spoke again.

"I suppose, Anne, you must think it's funny I should like Fred so well when he's so different from the kind of man I've always said I would marry . . . the tall, slender kind? But somehow I wouldn't want Fred to be tall and slender . . . because, don't you see, he wouldn't be Fred then. Of course," added Diana rather dolefully, "we will be a dreadfully pudgy couple. But after all that's better than one of us being short and fat and the other tall and lean, like Morgan Sloane and his wife. Mrs. Lynde says it always makes her think of the long and short of it when she sees them together."

"Well," said Anne to herself that night, as she brushed her hair before her gilt framed mirror, "I am glad Diana is so happy and satisfied. But when my turn comes . . . if it ever does . . . I do hope there'll be something a little more thrilling about it. But then Diana thought so too, once. I've heard her say time and again she'd never get engaged any poky commonplace way . . . he'd *have* to do something splendid to win her. But she has changed. Perhaps I'll change too. But I won't . . . I'm determined I won't. Oh, I think these engagements are dreadfully unsettling things when they happen to your intimate friends."

XXX

A Wedding at the Stone House

The last week in August came. Miss Lavendar was
to be married in it. Two weeks later Anne and Gilbert
would leave for Redmond College. In a week's time
Mrs. Rachel Lynde would move to Green Gables and
set up her lares and penates in the erstwhile spare
room, which was already prepared for her coming. She
had sold all her superfluous household plenishings by
auction and was at present reveling in the congenial
occupation of helping the Allans pack up. Mr. Allan
was to preach his farewell sermon the next Sunday.
The old order was changing rapidly to give place to
the new, as Anne felt with a little sadness threading all
her excitement and happiness.

"Changes ain't totally pleasant but they're
excellent things," said Mr. Harrison philosophically.
"Two years is about long enough for things to stay
exactly the same. If they stayed put any longer they
might grow mossy."

Mr. Harrison was smoking on his veranda. His
wife had self-sacrificingly told him that he might
smoke in the house if he took care to sit by an open
window. Mr. Harrison rewarded this concession by
going outdoors altogether to smoke in fine weather,
and so mutual goodwill reigned.

Anne had come over to ask Mrs. Harrison for
some of her yellow dahlias. She and Diana were going
through to Echo Lodge that evening to help Miss

Lavendar and Charlotta the Fourth with their final preparations for the morrow's bridal. Miss Lavendar herself never had dahlias; she did not like them and they would not have suited the fine retirement of her old-fashioned garden. But flowers of any kind were rather scarce in Avonlea and the neighboring districts that summer, thanks to Uncle Abe's storm; and Anne and Diana thought that a certain old cream-colored stone jug, usually kept sacred to doughnuts, brimmed over with yellow dahlias, would be just the thing to set in a dim angle of the stone house stairs, against the dark background of red hall paper.

"I s'pose you'll be starting off for college in a fortnight's time?" continued Mr. Harrison. "Well, we're going to miss you an awful lot, Emily and me. To be sure, Mrs. Lynde'll be over there in your place. There ain't nobody but a substitute can be found for them."

The irony of Mr. Harrison's tone is quite untransferable to paper. In spite of his wife's intimacy with Mrs. Lynde, the best that could be said of the relationship between her and Mr. Harrison, even under the new regime, was that they preserved an armed neutrality.

"Yes, I'm going," said Anne. "I'm very glad with my head . . . and very sorry with my heart."

"I s'pose you'll be scooping up all the honors that are lying round loose at Redmond."

"I may try for one or two of them," confessed Anne, "but I don't care so much for things like that as I did two years ago. What I want to get out of my college course is some knowledge of the best way of living life and doing the most and best with it. I want to learn to understand and help other people and myself."

Mr. Harrison nodded.

"That's the idea exactly. That's what college ought to be for, instead of for turning out a lot of B.A.'s, so chock full of book-learning and vanity that there ain't room for anything else. You're all right. College won't be able to do you much harm, I reckon."

Diana and Anne drove over to Echo Lodge after tea, taking with them all the flowery spoil that several predatory expeditions in their own and their neighbors' gardens had yielded. They found the stone house agog with excitement. Charlotta the Fourth was flying around with such vim and briskness that her blue bows seemed really to possess the power of being everywhere at once. Like the helmet of Navarre, Charlotta's blue bows waved ever in the thickest of the fray.

"Praise be to goodness you've come," she said devoutly, "for there's heaps of things to do . . . and the frosting on that cake *won't* harden . . . and there's all the silver to be rubbed up yet . . . and the horsehair trunk to be packed . . . and the roosters for the chicken salad are running out there beyant the henhouse yet, *crowing,* Miss Shirley, ma'am. And Miss Lavendar ain't to be trusted to do a thing. I was thankful when Mr. Irving came a few minutes ago and took her off for a walk in the woods. Courting's all right in its place, Miss Shirley, ma'am, but if you try to mix it up with cooking and scouring everything's spoiled. That's *my* opinion, Miss Shirley, ma'am."

Anne and Diana worked so heartily that by ten o'clock even Charlotta the Fourth was satisfied. She braided her hair in innumerable plaits and took her weary little bones off to bed.

"But I'm sure I shan't sleep a blessed wink, Miss Shirley, ma'am, for fear that something'll go wrong at the last minute . . . the cream won't whip . . . or Mr. Irving'll have a stroke and not be able to come."

"He isn't in the habit of having strokes, is he?" asked Diana, the dimpled corners of her mouth twitching. To Diana, Charlotta the Fourth was, if not exactly a thing of beauty, certainly a joy forever.

"They're not things that go by habit," said Charlotta the Fourth with dignity. "They just *happen* . . . and there you are. *Anybody* can have a stroke. You don't have to learn how. Mr. Irving looks a lot like an uncle of mine that had one once just as he was sitting down to dinner one day. But maybe everything'll go all right. In this world you've just got to hope for the best and prepare for the worst and take whatever God sends."

"The only thing I'm worried about is that it won't be fine tomorrow," said Diana. "Uncle Abe predicted rain for the middle of the week, and ever since the big storm I can't help believing there's a good deal in what Uncle Abe says."

Anne, who knew better than Diana just how much Uncle Abe had to do with the storm, was not much disturbed by this. She slept the sleep of the just and weary, and was roused at an unearthly hour by Charlotta the Fourth.

"Oh, Miss Shirley, ma'am, it's awful to call you so early," came wailing through the keyhole, "but there's so much to do yet . . . and oh, Miss Shirley, ma'am, I'm skeered it's going to rain and I wish you'd get up and tell me you think it ain't."

Anne flew to the window, hoping against hope that Charlotta the Fourth was saying this merely by way of rousing her effectually. But alas, the morning did look unpropitious. Below the window Miss Lavender's garden, which should have been a glory of pale virgin sunshine, lay dim and windless; and the sky over the firs was dark with moody clouds.

"Isn't it too mean!" said Diana.

"We must hope for the best," said Anne determinedly. "If it only doesn't actually rain, a cool, pearly gray day like this would really be nicer than hot sunshine."

"But it will rain," mourned Charlotta, creeping into the room, a figure of fun, with her many braids wound about her head, the ends, tied up with white thread, sticking out in all directions. "It'll hold off till the last minute and then pour cats and dogs. And all the folks will get sopping . . . and track mud all over the house . . . and they won't be able to be married under the honeysuckle . . . and it's awful unlucky for no sun to shine on a bride, say what you will, Miss Shirley, ma'am. I *knew* things were going too well to last."

Charlotta the Fourth seemed certainly to have borrowed a leaf out of Miss Eliza Andrews' book.

It did not rain, though it kept on looking as if it meant to. By noon the rooms were decorated, the table beautifully laid; and upstairs was waiting a bride, "adorned for her husband."

"You do look sweet," said Anne rapturously.

"Lovely," echoed Diana.

"Everything's ready, Miss Shirley, ma'am, and nothing dreadful has happened *yet*," was Charlotta's cheerful statement as she betook herself to her little back room to dress. Out came all the braids; the resultant rampant crinkliness was plaited into two tails and tied, not with two bows alone, but with four, of brand-new ribbon, brightly blue. The two upper bows rather gave the impression of overgrown wings sprouting from Charlotta's neck, somewhat after the fashion of Raphael's cherubs. But Charlotta the Fourth thought them very beautiful, and after she had rustled into a white dress, so stiffly starched that it could stand alone, she surveyed herself in her glass with great satisfaction . . . a satisfaction which lasted until she went out in the hall and caught a glimpse through the spare room door of a tall girl in some softly clinging gown, pinning white, star-like flowers on the smooth ripples of her ruddy hair.

"Oh, I'll *never* be able to look like Miss Shirley," thought poor Charlotta despairingly. "You just have to be born so, I guess . . . don't seem's if any amount of practice could give you that *air*."

By one o'clock the guests had come, including Mr. and Mrs. Allan, for Mr. Allan was to perform the ceremony in the absence of the Grafton minister on his vacation. There was no formality about the marriage. Miss Lavendar came down the stairs to meet her bridegroom at the foot, and as he took her hand she lifted her big brown eyes to his with a look that made Charlotta the Fourth, who intercepted it, feel queerer than ever. They went out to the honeysuckle arbor, where Mr. Allan was awaiting them. The guests grouped themselves as they pleased. Anne and Diana stood by the old stone bench, with Charlotta the Fourth between them, desperately clutching their hands in her cold, tremulous little paws.

Mr. Allan opened his blue book and the ceremony proceeded. Just as Miss Lavendar and Stephen Irving were pronounced man and wife a very beautiful and symbolic thing happened. The sun suddenly burst through the gray and poured a flood of radiance on the happy bride. Instantly the garden was alive with dancing shadows and flickering lights.

"What a lovely omen," thought Anne, as she ran to kiss the bride. Then the three girls left the rest of the guests laughing around the bridal pair while they flew into the house to see that all was in readiness for the feast.

"Thanks be to goodness, it's over, Miss Shirley, ma'am," breathed Charlotta the Fourth, "and they're married safe and sound, no matter what happens now. The bags of rice are in the pantry, ma'am, and the old shoes are behind the door, and the cream for whipping is on the sullar steps."

At half past two Mr. and Mrs. Irving left, and everybody went to Bright River to see them off on the afternoon train. As Miss Lavendar . . . I beg her pardon, Mrs. Irving . . . stepped from the door of her old home Gilbert and the girls threw the rice and Charlotta the Fourth hurled an old shoe with such excellent aim that she struck Mr. Allan squarely on the head. But it was reserved for Paul to give the prettiest send-off. He popped out of the porch ringing furiously a huge old brass dinner bell which had adorned the dining room mantel. Paul's only motive was to make a joyful noise; but as the clangor died away, from point and curve and hill across the river came the chime of "fairy wedding bells," ringing clearly, sweetly, faintly and more faint, as if Miss Lavendar's beloved echoes were bidding her greeting and farewell. And so, amid this benediction of sweet sounds, Miss Lavender drove away from the old life of dreams and make-believes to a fuller life of realities in the busy world beyond.

Two hours later Anne and Charlotta the Fourth came down the lane again. Gilbert had gone to West Grafton on an errand and Diana had to keep an engagement at home. Anne and Charlotta had come back to put things in order and lock up the little stone house. The garden was a pool of late golden sunshine, with butterflies hovering and bees booming; but the little house had already that indefinable air of desolation which always follows a festivity.

"Oh dear me, don't it look lonesome?" sniffed Charlotta the Fourth, who had been crying all the way home from the station. "A wedding ain't much cheerfuller than a funeral after all, when it's all over, Miss Shirley, ma'am."

A busy evening followed. The decorations had to be removed, the dishes washed, the uneaten delicacies packed into a basket for the delectation of Charlotta the Fourth's young brothers at home. Anne would not rest until everything was in apple-pie order; after Charlotta had gone home with her plunder Anne went over the still rooms, feeling like one who trod alone some banquet hall deserted, and closed the blinds. Then she locked the door and sat down under the silver poplar to wait for Gilbert, feeling very tired but still unweariedly thinking "long, long thoughts."

"What are you thinking of, Anne?" asked Gilbert, coming down the walk. He had left his horse and buggy out at the road.

"Of Miss Lavender and Mr. Irving," answered Anne dreamily. "Isn't it beautiful to think how everything has turned out . . . how they have come together again after all the years of separation and misunderstanding?"

"Yes, it's beautiful," said Gilbert, looking steadily down into Anne's uplifted face, "but wouldn't it have been more beautiful still, Anne, if there had been *no* separation or misunderstanding . . . if they had come hand in hand all the way through life, with no memories behind them but those which belonged to each other?"

For a moment Anne's heart fluttered queerly and for the first time her eyes faltered under Gilbert's gaze and a rosy flush stained the paleness of her face. It was as if a veil that had hung before her inner consciousness had been lifted, giving to her view a revelation of unsuspected feelings and realities. Perhaps, after all, romance did not come into one's life with pomp and blare, like a gay knight riding down; perhaps it crept to one's side like an old friend through quiet ways; perhaps it revealed itself in seeming prose, until some sudden shaft of illumination flung athwart its pages betrayed the rhythm and the music; perhaps . . . perhaps . . . love unfolded naturally out of a beautiful friendship, as a golden-hearted rose slipping from its green sheath.

Then the veil dropped again; but the Anne who walked up the dark lane was not quite the same Anne who had driven gaily down it the evening before. The page of girlhood had been turned, as by an unseen finger, and the page of womanhood was before her with all its charm and mystery, its pain and gladness.

Gilbert wisely said nothing more; but in his silence he read the history of the next four years in the light of Anne's remembered blush. Four years of earnest, happy work . . . and then the guerdon of a useful knowledge gained and a sweet heart won.

Behind them in the garden the little stone house brooded among the shadows. It was lonely but not forsaken. It had not yet done with dreams and laughter and the joy of life; there were to be future summers for the little stone house; meanwhile, it could wait. And over the river in purple durance the echoes bided their time.